THE RAGGED TROUSERED

PHILANTHROPISTS

The Ragged Trousered Philanthropists

◆

ROBERT TRESSELL

with a Foreword by
TONY BENN

and with an Introduction by
LIONEL KELLY

WORDSWORTH CLASSICS

For my husband
ANTHONY JOHN RANSON
with love from your wife, the publisher.
Eternally grateful for your unconditional love.

Readers who are interested in other titles from
Wordsworth Editions are invited to visit our website at
www.wordsworth-editions.com

For our latest list and a full mail-order service, contact
Bibliophile Books, 5 Datapoint, South Crescent, London E16 4TL
TEL: +44 (0)20 7474 2474 FAX: +44 (0)20 7474 8589
ORDERS: orders@bibliophilebooks.com
WEBSITE: www.bibliophilebooks.com

This edition first published in 2012 by
Wordsworth Editions Limited
8B East Street, Ware, Hertfordshire SG12 9HJ

ISBN 978 1 84022 682 9

Text © Lawrence & Wishart 1955
Foreword © Tony Benn 2012
Introduction © Lionel Kelly 2012

Wordsworth® is a registered trade mark of
Wordsworth Editions Limited

Wordsworth Editions
is the company founded in 1987 by
MICHAEL TRAYLER

Typeset in Great Britain by Antony Gray
Printed and bound by Clays Ltd, St Ives plc

CONTENTS

FOREWORD   7

GENERAL INTRODUCTION   9

INTRODUCTION   9

NOTE ON THE TEXT   27

SELECT BIBLIOGRAPHY   28

THE RAGGED TROUSERED PHILANTHROPISTS

PREFACE   33

1 *An Imperial Banquet. A Philosophical Discussion.*
   The Mysterious Stranger. Britons Never shall be Slaves.   35
2 *Nimrod: A Mighty Hunter Before the Lord*   52
3 *The Financiers*   68
4 *The Placard*   85
5 *The Clock Case*   89
6 *It is not My Crime*   95
7 *The Exterminating Machines*   112
8 *The Cap on the Stairs*   123
9 *Who is to Pay?*   129
10 *The Long Hill*   132
11 *Hands and Brains*   138
12 *The Letting of the Room*   143
13 *Penal Servitude and Death*   145
14 *Three Children. The Wages of Intelligence*   152
15 *The Undeserving Persons and the Upper and*
   Nether Millstones   157
16 *True Freedom*   175
17 *The Rev. John Starr*   183
18 *The Lodger*   195
19 *The Filling of the Tank*   200
20 *The Forty Thieves. The Battle: Brigands versus Bandits* 212

21 *The Reign of Terror. The Great MoneyTrick.*   220
22 *The Phrenologist*   235
23 *The 'Open Air'*   245
24 *Ruth*   254
25 *The Oblong*   269
26 *The Slaughter*   301
27 *The March of the Imperialists*   307
28 *The Week before Christmas*   311
29 *The Pandora*   319
30 *The Brigands Hold a Council of War*   327
31 *The Deserter*   332
32 *The Veteran*   333
33 *The Soldier's Children*   335
34 *The Beginning of the End*   341
35 *Facing the 'Problem'*   353
36 *The O. B. S.*   358
37 *A Brilliant Epigram*   363
38 *The Brigands' Cave*   372
39 *The Brigands at Work*   376
40 *Vive la System!*   383
41 *The Easter Offering. The Beano Meeting.*   392
42 *June*   401
43 *The Good Old Summer-Time*   408
44 *The Beano*   452
45 *The Great Oration*   481
46 *The 'Sixty-Five'*   524
47 *The Ghouls*   532
48 *The Wise Men of the East*   547
49 *The Undesired*   571
50 *Sundered*   574
51 *The Widow's Son*   581
52 *'It's a Far, Far Better Thing That I do,*
        Than I have ever Done'   587
53 *Barrington Finds a Situation*   592
54 *The End*   597
APPENDIX: *Mugsborough*   607
NOTES   611

FOREWORD

Published in 1914, three years after the death of its author Robert Tressell, *The Raggered Trousered Philanthropists* was a novel which explored the plight of working men trying to make sense of capitalist society in the early twentieth century. The hero of the book, Frank Owen, identifies their role as people whose task it is to make their employers wealthy, a task which therefore makes them – the workers – philanthropists.

The discussions in the novel all took place in a town, Mugsborough (really Hastings, where Tressell lived), where a group of workers was engaged on renovating a house.

Despite Frank's arguments, his companions seemed to remain convinced that they were part of a settled system which they had no capacity – even if they had the desire – to change, and it was in the discussions they had on the subject that some of the basic problems of social and political change which confronted the working class emerged most clearly.

Frank became frustrated with his colleagues over the very issues all socialists face as they argue their case with those who seem to be at once contented and dissatisfied with their role in the world.

At the time the book was published, the Labour Party had only just been founded and no serious political alternative was available to the general public. This led to despair and cynicism on the part of those who might have benefited from new policies and this paralysed the political process.

Thinking about the developments in the last century that led to the winning of the Welfare State, the NHS and many other public services, it is obvious to anybody reading this book today that that pessimism and cynicism slowed down the processes of reform because the element of hope that made them possible later was wholly lacking.

The book is not about such reforms alone but about the far more fundamental need to replace the entire capitalist system with a new and more radical socialist society, and its relevance is particularly acute in the current era of cuts and austerity. But those who support this thesis are up against that same deep pessimism among those who would benefit from such a change.

The recent events in Tunisia and Egypt, Libya and Syria have shown that the key ingredients in all major progressive change are the confidence of those demanding it that it can be done, and the willingness of enough people to make the effort necessary to bring it about.

I have given this book to many, many people in the course of my life and all the recipients have been as inspired by it as I have been. Every generation has to fight the same battles again and again, and every time it is the confidence of the campaigners that determines the speed of their success.

The campaign against the poll tax in the fourteenth century was led by such people, and their example inspired those of us who fought against Mrs Thatcher's version in the 1990s. Similarly, it was the Chartists of the mid nineteenth century who inspired the suffragettes fifty years later, and the courage of the Tolpuddle Martyrs which strengthens the morale of those who are now fighting the cuts.

TONY BENN
March 2012

GENERAL INTRODUCTION

Wordsworth Classics are inexpensive editions designed to appeal to the general reader and students. We commission teachers and specialists to write wide-ranging, jargon-free introductions and in some cases to provide notes that will assist the understanding of our readers rather than interpret the stories for them. In the same spirit, because the pleasures of reading are inseparable from the surprises, secrets and revelations that all narratives contain, we strongly advise you to enjoy this book before turning to the Introduction.

General Adviser: KEITH CARABINE
Rutherford College, University of Kent at Canterbury

INTRODUCTION

TRESSELL AND HIS NOVEL

Robert Noonan (Tressell) was born in Dublin in 1870, the illegitimate son of Samuel Croker and Mary Noonan. Croker was an inspector in the Royal Irish Constabulary and later a magistrate of the city, and was already a married man with a family when he set up home with Mary Noonan, with whom he then had three children. They appear to have had a middle-class upbringing consistent with Croker's status, and this goes some way to explain Robert Noonan's literary and linguistic skills, beyond the range of the men he would commonly work with in his adult years. On Croker's death, Robert's mother married, but he disliked her new husband, left the family home and thereafter took his mother's surname of Noonan. In 1890 he emigrated to South Africa and found work as a signwriter, though where and when he first learned those skills is difficult to say because documentary evidence about his early years is scant. He married Elizabeth Hartel in Cape Town in 1891, and they had a daughter, Kathleen. The marriage was unhappy, and his wife eventually left him for another man, an experience of marital betrayal echoed in his novel. In 1895 Noonan moved to Johannesburg with Kathleen where they remained for the next six years during which time he became known as a skilled signwriter with radical political views. He left South Africa for England in 1901, with Kathleen, and settled in Hastings in the house of his sister, probably motivated by concern for his daughter at a time when he was already ill with tuberculosis from which he died in 1911. The name of Tressell he used as an author derives from the trestle tables used by house painters and signwriters in their work.

The manuscript of his novel was left in Kathleen's care and it is something of a miracle that the novel ever made it to publication. This came about when Kathleen mentioned its existence to Jessie Pope, a visitor to the house in London where Kathleen was then a servant. Pope, a writer of verses for children, read the manuscript and thought well enough of it to interest her publisher, Grant Richards. He thought it much too long but arranged for Pope to edit it for publication and issued it in an abridged form in 1914, with a second edition, further abridged, in 1918. These abridged versions gave a truncated rendering of the novel's political polemic, but despite these cuts its reputation flourished in the working classes and among political activists for social change across the social spectrum. The first unabridged edition did not appear until 1955, when it was produced by the left-wing publishers Lawrence and Wishart, an outcome brought about by the labours of Fred C. Ball, a Hastings man in the same trade as Noonan. He traced the manuscript through Grant Richards's connections in the years after the end of the Second World War, organised a fund to buy it, and set about restoring the manuscript to something like its original condition, a heroic feat in the circumstances. Ball went on to write two biographies of Noonan, *Tressell of Mugsborough* (1951) and *One of the Damned: The Life and Times of Robert Tressell* (1973). The novel has been continuously in print since the time of its first publication in 1914, but all editions after the 'restored' text of 1955 follow that edition.

The Ragged Trousered Philanthropists set in Edwardian England is a novel driven by arguments against capitalism and the need for a socialist politics on behalf of the working classes. In his Preface, Tressell describes his work as 'not a treatise or essay, but a novel. My main object was to write a readable story full of human interest and based on the happenings of everyday life, the subject of Socialism being treated incidentally' (p. 33–4). The latter part of this claim is somewhat tongue-in-cheek, because the arguments for socialism are inseparable from his presentation of the workers and their families throughout, and the case he makes is beyond challenge. Epic in scale, it presents the experiences of a group of working-class men, their fragile opportunities for work, the quality of work they are required to do against the grain of their particular skills, and the consequences for them when there is no work. Its central topics are therefore work, poverty and wealth in the community of Mugsborough, charity in the private and public domain, religious conformity and atheism, and the need for a socialist politics in an age of rampant capitalism. It is built up in a series of chapters of greatly differing lengths, from three pages to forty pages or more, with indicative chapter headings perhaps intended as an aid for the working-class readership Tressell must have hoped for. Many of these chapter headings are deliberately ironic in tone. Its great virtue is in the depiction of workers in the workplace and their individual characters in a sequence of scenes where they are seen as units of labour yet clearly individuated as distinct personalities. The realism of the workplace and domestic scenes are in contrast to the satiric energy of Tressell's exposure of the strategies by which the ruling classes exercise control. The title turns the conventional meaning of 'philanthropy' on its head, for these men – philanthropists because they enrich their employers through their labours – are rewarded for their work in the meanest possible terms by businessmen who remorselessly cheat them, in keeping with the capitalist economy of the times.

NAMES

In his creation of characters Tressell uses names as indicative of the people and situations they apply to. While the names of some of the workers we meet in the first chapter are tonally neutral such as Sawkins, Old Linden, Easton and Harlow, the central character Frank Owen is named in homage to Robert Owen, the nineteenth-century foundational figure in the history of socialism in Britain. Owen's first name 'Frank' bears the overtones of one who is honest and speaks the truth as he sees it. He is a man without guile in a communal scene where guile is the operative mode for self-advancement. It is Owen who principally makes the case for socialism to his sceptical workmates, and in this he is aided by Barrington, the young man who normally sits silently among the men during their meal breaks but who eventually speaks about 'the plan or system upon which the Co-operative Commonwealth of the future will be organised' in Chapter 45, 'The Great Oration'. While the women in this novel are rather muted figures, bound in by poverty and forced to work for derisory rewards, two of them are named after iconic women in the Bible, Mary (Linden) and Ruth (Easton), mothers whose names are part of the language of scripture in the novel's repeated use of quotations from the Bible, especially in Christ's injunction as reported in the Gospels – 'Suffer the little children to come unto me . . . ' here related to the depiction of the children in this community, within the family and in the workplace.

What is invoked here is a New Testament ethic in contrast to the self-serving religiosity of the town employers and functionaries of the Church. On the other hand the names of some of the workers, such as Crass and Slyme, are deliberately pejorative, as is Tressell's satiric naming of the employers such as Sweater, Grinder and the others, who also run the town council as a private profit-making enterprise. To some extent this satiric vocabulary is common to the idiom of working-class men, used conspiratorially behind the backs of those they work for, as in Bundy's list of the other businessmen who competed for the renovation of the house they are working on: 'There was six other firms after this job . . . Pushem and Sloggem, Bluffum and Doemdown, Dodger and Scampit, Snatcham and Graball, Smeeriton and Leavit, Makehaste and Sloggitt, and Gord only knows 'ow many more' (p. 182). We might see this naming as naively parodic, natural to the uncultivated speaker, Bundy, but it is part of Tressell's animus against the system. They are renovating a house called 'The Cave', a pointedly unusual house name but made appropriate through association with its purchaser Sweater, several times mayor of the town, and a leading figure on the town council, a body otherwise referred to as the 'Forty Thieves', a borrowing from the tale of Ali Baba. The firm the men are working for as the novel opens, 'Rushton', implies that the job is to be rushed, and the supervisor whose job it is to turn up unexpectedly in the hope of catching men working too slowly or taking an unofficial break, is Hunter, otherwise derisively known as Misery and Nimrod, after the biblical figure known as a 'mighty hunter'. This satiric naming extends to the other institutions of the community, such as the newspapers the *Daily Obscurer*, the *Chloroform* and the *Daily Ananais*, and the naming of the Member of Parliament for Mugsborough, Sir Graball D'Englander.

WORK

The opening chapters give us a view of the material circumstances of men at work remarkable in its intimacy, unmatched in British novels of working-class life, other than perhaps in Mrs Gaskell's *Mary Barton* and *North and South*. In Dickens's *Hard Times*, for example, though the economic plight of the labour force is central to his subject, the actuality of that life in the workplace is barely attended to in the kind of significant detail we get in Tressell's novel, informed as it is by his comprehensive practical knowledge of that working world. Here we get an authoritative portrait of the men united in their contempt for the botched work they are compelled to do, yet divided by those who, through desperate self-interest, connive with their employers. They are also divided by their understanding of the political and economic conditions that determine their circumstances. These chapters are supremely well done especially in the way they give voice to a body of people who did not commonly speak for themselves in novels before this time. The idiosyncratic language of these working-class men is by turns jocular, cynical, abrasive, occasionally obscene, and yet stoical in the face of their circumstances. Consider this sequence in the first chapter where they talk about the shortage of work and blame various causes such as foreign workers in England, machinery displacing men, women going out to work, over-population and so on. From this the conversation turns to marriage, sex and drink. Slyme says that early marriage is one of the problems and, ' "no man oughtn't to be allowed to get married unless he's in a position to keep a family" '. Harlow, with a wink to the others, turns this into a question of sexual needs – ' "what's a man to do during the years he's savin' up?" ' Slyme replies, ' "Well, he must conquer hisself," ' which a man can do if he has ' "the Grace of God" ' in him" '. ' "Chuck it, fer Christ's sake!" said Harlow in a tone of disgust. "We've only just 'ad our dinner!" ' Joe Philpot suddenly calls out, ' "And wot about drink?" ' ' " 'Ear, 'ear," cried Harlow. "That's the bleedin' talk. I wouldn't mind 'avin 'arf a pint now, if somebody else will pay for it" ' (pp. 48). The authenticity of their language here comes from the drama of their vernacular speech attuned to their individual personalities. Slyme's argument that belief in God will aid a man's sexual continence will be shown to be a shallow hypocrisy on his part as we read on. Throughout the novel the sense of communality among them is expressed in the way they pick up on and join in the singing of music-hall and popular songs, and hymns, as occasions arise. By contrast the speech of the Forty Thieves, though well suited to Tressell's satiric purposes, is of a different order from the compelling realism of his representation of the workers, perhaps because the villainy of Sweater, Rushton and the others is so bare-faced as to be barely credible. However, in his Appendix on 'Mugsborough', where he clearly means the town of Hastings, he writes of the town corporation and its dealings with the gas and electricity companies, and the way profits are accrued and paid out in inflated salaries to company members while the rising costs of supply are imposed without restraint on the town citizens. The effect of this is to authenticate the fictional world of the Forty Thieves in a specific place and time.

In this world of working-class men, distinctions normally operate between those who have served their time as apprentices and journey-men in order to become masters of their trade and the less skilled labourers working under the supervision of a skilled tradesman at a lower rate of pay. However, Hunter will happily dismiss a skilled man if he can find another man to do the same job at a lower hourly rate, as in the case of Old Linden, who is dismissed for smoking his pipe at work, with consequences that lead him inexorably to the workhouse and the grave. And there is the case of Bert White, the young teenage boy taken on as an apprentice painter who receives no real training from Rushton and is used to mix paints and to fetch and carry materials between Rushton's premises and the work sites. His impoverished widowed mother has of course to pay for the boy's indentures. However, Owen takes a kindly interest in Bert and 'had taught him lots of things and had promised to do some patterns of graining for him so that he might practise copying them at home in the evenings' and insists on Bert helping him in the painting of the decorative ceiling in The Cave.

The ease with which Hunter can hire and fire workers reflects a world of work where men lacked the protection that came with the emergence of trade unions in Britain during the nineteenth century. Owen and his companions are trapped in a non-unionised working environment directly under the control of their employers and agents such as Hunter, who determine wages and how work is to be done. Hired as individuals, they have no collective voice and must operate in a system where the employer's profit is the only imperative. Here it is worth dwelling on the issue of the painted ceiling that Sweater wants for the drawing-room of The Cave, a work he doesn't believe Rushton can get done satisfactorily. Frank Owen's skills as a signwriter are called on by Rushton who knows that there is 'no likelihood of his scamping it for the sake of getting it done quickly' but wants to make sure Owen will not charge too much for this special job, for 'Any profit that it was possible to make out of the work, Rushton meant to secure for himself' (p. 141). Owen agrees to make designs for the ceiling in his own time at home in the evenings on the understanding that if they are not approved he will not charge for them. Owen delights in the work and the question of what personal advantage he might gain from it never occurs to him so that the 'question of profit [is] crowded out' (p. 143). In this he is typical of men of his kind, who believe that the virtue of work consists it doing it properly, to the best of their ability. In general, the men at 'The Cave' can take no pride in their work because they are always told to cut corners. Beyond this Tressell is keen to dismiss the conception 'of that lofty ideal of "work for work's sake", which is so popular with the people who do nothing' (p. 112), indeed the expression 'work for work's sake' sounds as a derisive echo of the rallying call of the Aesthetic Movement's 'Art for Art's sake'.

Another consequence of a working environment where men are without the protective cover of unionism is the want of rules about safety at work. The current Health and Safety at Work Act dates from as late as 1974, and though earlier rules applying to specific industries and occupations brought about by trade-union pressure were previously in place, they did not operate in the working environment described in this novel. Men were therefore exposed to risk from dangerous substances and careless practices. Two late chapters, 'The "Sixty-Five" ' and 'The Ghouls', illustrate this in the fate of Philpot who falls to his death when using the wrong type of ladder high on the outside of a house. Since Rushton's firm also operates as an undertakers, there follows a grotesque competition between him and another undertaker as to who will get the work of dealing with Philpot's corpse, and thus who will profit from Philpot's death.

Earlier Philpot had told how Hunter always enjoyed an epidemic of 'Small-pox, Hinfluenza, Chorlery morbus, or anything like that', and Crass replies with a chuckle, ' "I recollect we 'ad six children's funerals to do in one week. Ole Misery was as pleased as Punch, because of course as a rule there ain't many boxin'-up jobs in the summer. It's in winter as hundertakers reaps their 'arvest" ' (p. 146).

MONEY

One of the many occasions when Owen's companions are bewildered by his arguments is when he proposes that ' "Money *is* the principal cause of poverty" ' (p. 175). In the ironically titled Chapter 3, 'The Financiers', we get a detailed account of the domestic economy of the young painter and decorator Easton and his wife Ruth. Despite earnings which 'did not average a pound a week', he had enough as a single man to survive; now married and with a young child, the fear of being out of work haunts him and his income cannot meet their basic expenses. Working eight and a half hours a day for Rushton at sevenpence an hour his weekly income is one pound four and nine-pence-halfpenny. They owe four weeks' rent, eight shillings to the baker and twelve to the grocer, money for furniture bought on instalments and are threatened with legal action if they do not pay late council rates and the contribution levied on all workers by the administrators of the Poor Law. These figures are supported by evidence of wage rates for skilled workers and unskilled town labourers in histories of the period. Thus a skilled engineer in a Manchester engineering works in the years of the Boer War (1899–1902) was paid a weekly rate of £1 15*s.* 6*d.*, while a labourer working with him was paid £1, a distinction in reward common to all trades at that time between the skilled and unskilled.

Among the workers in The Cave there is resentment at Sawkins, an unskilled man who earns a lower hourly rate than the skilled man who should be doing that work, a dodge brought about by Hunter's always looking for ways to keep costs down for the benefit of Rushton. In Easton's case the solution they reach is to take a lodger, the appropriately named Slyme, who takes a room and board in their rented house. In order to keep on the right side of his employers, Easton takes to going to the pub after work to keep in the good books of Crass, the self-serving on-site foreman, and this leads to the neglect of his wife Ruth, and eventually to her sexual intimacy with Slyme, and the birth of an illegitimate child. The seduction of Ruth is echoed in the scene where Owen comes across Rushton fondling his secretary in his office, and chimes with several other occasions where a predatory male sexuality is jokingly aired among the men, including Crass's detailed description of sex with his wife. With Slyme, the connection between religious hypocrisy and sexual licence is here affirmed, and there may be something in this of Tressell's pain over his wife's infidelity. If the relation between income and expenditure is critical in Easton's case, it is even worse for Old Linden, sacked by Hunter and now responsible for the wife and children of his son Tom, killed in the Boer War. When Linden can get no other work and cannot pay his rent, he is expelled from the house he has rented from Sweater for several years, having paid 'six hundred pounds over the years for the privilege of living in it', a figure way beyond what Linden might have had to pay to buy the house in the first place, had this ever been possible for him.

The idea of Edwardian England as a golden age of peace and plenty brought about by the wealth created by the Industrial Revolution and the flourishing sale of exported British goods throughout the world concealed the reality of that age for the likes of Owen and his companions. A journal article in the *Nation* (1907) showed that

> half the total national income of Britain accrued to one-ninth of the population, and that half the national capital belonged to one-seventh . . . a product of the imperialist temper of the times in the service of the material interests of only a few, and was itself responsible for the debasing contrast between talk of the empire on which the sun never set and grim facts of the slums over which the sun never rose.[1]

Before her marriage to Easton, Ruth had been 'in service' with Mrs Starvem, a time she recalls with bitterness as 'a series of recollections of petty tyrannies, insults and indignities. Six years of cruelly excessive work, beginning every morning two or three hours before the rest of the household were awake and ceasing only when she went exhausted to bed, late at night . . . She had been what is called a "slavey" ' (p. 71). This was a term used of 'partial exemption scholars', applied to

> a child over twelve who was allowed by law, after attending school for half the day, to work for not more than twenty-seven and a half hours a week. Even in a middle-class home such a girl need be paid only 3s. a week; in poor districts she might get half a crown, but where regulations were not strictly enforced it was possible to

---

1 'The Political Scene' by Asa Briggs, in *Edwardian England 1901–1914*, edited and with a Preface by Simon Nowell-Smith, Oxford University Press, 1964, pp. 58–9

find children of more tender years working for far less: we hear of a girl of six who acted as nursemaid for twenty-nine hours a week at a wage of 2d. and her food.'[2]

Extraordinary as these figures are they go with the details of income and expenditure itemised for middle-class, urban working-class and rural families in the period. In the essay I have just cited, Marghanita Laski writes that

The Edwardian poor have attracted strangely little attention in imaginative literature and play almost no part in commonly held images of Edwardian England. But to look at the domestic lives of the poor, both urban and rural, is to shadow our pictures of upper- and middle-class life with horror and dismay.

One cannot fault Laski's point of view here, though she seems unaware of Tressell's contribution to the 'imaginative literature' on the Edwardian poor even though it had appeared in its full version in 1955, some nine years before her essay was published. Laski goes on to cite the view of the social historian Peter Laslett that 'the distribution of incomes in Edwardian England was just about as unequal as it has ever been anywhere'.[3] All these citations from histories of the period serve to validate Tressell's representation of the working-class poor in Edwardian England, a world he knew intimately and pictured with authority.[4]

It is men such as Adam Sweater and his companions on the town council who are part of that portion of the nation accumulating wealth at the expense of those who work for them. Sweater is named because he 'sweats' his workers, and by comparison with him Rushton is little more than a petty thief, who steals objects and materials from the houses he renovates, including The Cave. Then there is Sir Graball D'Englander, the local MP, whose salary is increased from five thousand to seven and a half thousand a year.[5]

---

2 'Domestic Life' by Marghanita Laski, p. 145, and pp. 166–7, 171–5, 177, 180, in *Edwardian England 1901–1914*, op. cit.

3 ibid., p. 142

4 See Jack London's *The People of the Abyss* (1903) for a contemporary account of working-class slum life and poverty in the East End of London.

5 These figures are inventions by Tressell: MPs did not receive salaries until 1911 when, under Labour Party pressure, it was agreed that a sum of £400 a year should be paid to MPs out of public funds.

Chapter 17 shows that what is good for the civic authorities also works for ministers of the Church in Mugsborough. The Reverend John Starr is brought in to address members of the Shining Light Chapel Sunday school meeting, where Sweater, Rushton and the others councillors are present, over the appeal for funds to provide its minister Mr Belcher, known for his gluttony, with funds for a recuperative holiday in the South of France. For his short address Starr is paid four guineas, an extraordinary sum by comparison with what Easton, Owen and others earn for a week's work, and a moment where Tressell cannot resist the temptation to add a conscious irony, 'But the Labourer is worthy of his hire' (p. 195). A similar case is that of the Reverend Mr Bosher, vicar of the fashionable Church of the Whited Sepulchre – how Tressell must have enjoyed coming up with that name – who runs a scam funded by 'a number of semi-imbecile old women who attended his church' for supplying fire-wood under the guise of a charitable concern: he then pockets a portion of the proceeds to buy himself 'a Newfoundland dog, an antique set of carved ivory chessmen, and a dozen bottles of whisky with the remainder of the cash' (p. 357). Tressell claims in the Preface that 'it will be evident that no attack is made upon sincere religion', and we should therefore see the animus here as directed at the institutions of the Church in Mugsborough. However, Owen is a rigorous atheist who repeatedly challenges his workmates un-thinking belief in God, their acceptance of the social order as some-thing given which they are powerless to change, and it is clear from this that the voice of Owen and that of his author are indistin-guishable. Yet the novel is full of quotations from the Bible, from familiar passages in the Gospels but also from less often cited books such as Joshua, Galatians and Jeremiah. Clearly, Tressell knew his Bible well and put this knowledge to good use in his critique of the religious community and the exploitative employers and councillors of Mugsborough. Tressell was an educated intelligent man, with a gift for languages occasionally evident in the novel, unlike Owen who was born into poverty, but who is a fine example of the autodidact, a man who, without the benefit of a sustained formal education, strives through reading and experience to understand the world he inhabits.

POVERTY AND CHARITY

These topics go together because the first invokes the second as a natural consequence, though of course there is a world of difference between private and public acts of charity. Charity, of course, is yoked to philanthropy, 'the disposition or active effort to promote the happiness and well-being of one's fellow men', and the use of the word is brilliantly ironic in the novel's title. In Chapter 4, 'The Placard', we get the back story of Frank Owen who left his wife Nora and their son Frankie for London, because he could no longer get work in Mugsborough. London is a bitter experience of failure for him as he 'walked the streets day after day; pawned or sold all his clothes save those he stood in, and stayed in London for six months, sometimes starving . . . The privations . . . and the foul atmosphere of the city combined to defeat him' (p. 86), and he returns to his native town a 'shadow of his former self', now suffering from the onset of consumption, the disease which killed his own father when Owen was a boy of five, a fatal condition which worsens on his return to Mugsborough. On the brink of destitution, his situation is redeemed by work at The Cave, and he forgets that he is ill, though he remains worse off than most of his companions because unlike them he cannot join a sick-benefit club because his ill-health 'rendered him ineligible for membership of such societies' (p. 245), a state of affairs which anticipates present-day health insurance companies who do not take on clients with pre-existing health issues. Owen's experience of London is authenticated by accounts of life there for the lowest strata of the working classes in histories of the period, the town labourers said to be the main canker in the nation's life, also reflected in the difficulty of recruiting men for service in the army in 1899 at the onset of the second phase of the Boer War in South Africa.[6]

---

6 *The Oxford History of England: England 1870–1914* by Sir Robert Ensor, p. 513, 'In Manchester in 1899 out of 12,000 men offering, 8,000 were rejected right off, and only 1,200 men accepted as fit in all respects, though army measurements had just been reduced to the lowest standard since Waterloo. In 1903 an official Memorandum by the director-general of the Army Medical Corps showed that during the decade 1893–1902 some 34.6 per cent had been rejected on medical examination, besides an uncounted number known to be very large, who had not been thought worth medically examining.'

The national instrument designed to address poverty was the Poor Law of 1834, though previous legislation of this kind dated back to Tudor England, and the nineteenth-century Act was not abolished until 1948. Despite attempts to reform the ways in which the Act was administered in the early years of the twentieth century, it remained a blunt instrument of social repair, signalled by the continued existence of the workhouse, an institution that by the end of the nineteenth century had become a refuge for the elderly, the infirm or the sick, rather than the able-bodied poor it was originally intended to assist. It was a brutal system. A savage irony of the implementation of the Poor Law is reflected on various occasions in this novel where men are sent to prison 'for not being able to pay their poor rates' (p. 443).

Non-governmental charities included Dr Barnardo's Homes originating in 1870 and William Booth's Salvation Army in 1880, and there were other charities operative in local contexts for the relief of poverty. One of these in Mugsborough is anatomised with particular venom in Chapter 36 on the 'Organised Benevolence Society', whose funds come from collections at a fancy-dress carnival, from church and chapel special services in aid of the unemployed, weekly collections by local firms, the proceeds of concerts, bazaars and entertainments, and subscriptions from members. However, its 'largest item of expenditure was the salary of the General Secretary, Mr Sawney Grinder – a most deserving case – who was paid one hundred pounds a year' (p. 358). There follows a list of the ways in which the society has responded to the 1,972 applications for assistance (one has been 'sent to Consumption Sanatorium'), although in 670 cases 'for various reasons the Society was unable to assist'. One of these 'cases' of total destitution the society is unable to assist may well have been that of the man whose suicide and the killing of his wife and two children is reported in Chapter 6, 'It is not My Crime'. It is described as 'one of the ordinary poverty crimes' (p. 108) and reported in the local newspaper as an act of 'temporary insanity', to which Owen responds, 'It seems to me that he would have been insane if he had *not* killed them' (p. 109).

There is a moment when, out of work and with no resources to provide for his family, and aware of his worsening consumptive condition, Owen also considers suicide, and the spectre of death brought about by poverty haunts the novel. In this chapter on the Organised Benevolent Society and elsewhere Tressell shows a marked antagonism to middle-class women 'who – after filling themselves with good things in their own luxurious homes – went flouncing into the poverty-stricken dwellings of their poor "sisters" and talked to them of "religion", lectured them about sobriety and thrift' (p. 359). He ends this chapter with the assertion that 'in spite of this and kindred organisations the condition of the under-paid poverty stricken and unemployed workers remained the same', and that '[i]f it were not for all this so-called charity the starving unemployed men all over the country would demand to be allowed to work and produce the things they are perishing for want of, instead of being – as they are now – content to wear their masters' cast-off clothing and to eat the crumbs that fall from his table' (pp. 362–3).

For Frank Owen the crucial issue is to expose the causes of poverty, to recognise it as a consequence of the capitalist system and not the irreversible reality of the way things are and always will be, the belief shared by most of his workmates. In this and other ways he is a discomfiting figure for them, a man with no interest in football, racing or drink, commonly supposed to be the natural consolations of the working-class man. Indeed, as Tressell makes clear, there was a widespread belief in middle-class England that poverty in the working classes was caused by drink. In contrast to the institutional forms of charity outlined above, what is marked in Owen's case is that he is a man of active charity whose benevolence to others is evident, despite his own poverty. This is shown in small acts such as when he sees Old Linden's grandchildren outside a sweet shop, imagining what they would choose to buy, and himself buys things for them. Earlier he visits Linden's house to tell the old man of a new work project in the town where a job might be had: Mrs Linden is disturbed by Owen's presence as a known atheist, and thinks it a terrible thing that a man who 'did not believe there was a Hell and said that the Bible was not the Word of God, should be here in the house sitting on one of their chairs, drinking from one of their cups, and talking to their children' (p. 94). Her view of Owen is shared by his middle-class neighbours in Lord Street, appalled by the presence of such a low-class non-believer living in their midst. Despite his atheism and his view that St Thomas 'was the only sensible man in the whole crowd of Apostles' (p. 104), he gives pennies to 'a ragged wreck of a man who was singing a hymn in the street' (p. 315). When Easton plans to leave his wife because of the illegitimate child she has had with Slyme, Owen offers to take the child off their hands into his own family, a gesture that ultimately encourages Easton to remain with Ruth. When Old Linden and his wife are forced into the workhouse, Owen encourages Easton to take Mary Linden and her children in as lodgers, an outcome of benefit to both families. And Owen takes a special interest in the untutored apprentice boy, Bert White, arranging for Bert to help him on the painting of the decorative ceiling at The Cave, and threatening Rushton with exposure to the Society for the Prevention of Cruelty to Children for his treatment of the boy.

Philpot is another man of charity: appalled at the amount of money he spends on beer while impoverished families are starving, he initiates a whip-round of cash among the workers for the benefit of Newman's family after Newman is sacked by Hunter for taking 'too much pains with his work', and unable to pay his poor rates, is sent to prison for a month. It is Philpot who gathers up the crumbs and crusts of bread from the floor when the men have finished their lunch and takes them up to the roof to feed the birds. This is a small moment in a very long novel, but one worth noting for its specificity. Against this, when Slyme buys a rattle for Easton's child after taking up lodgings with them, we know that this is not done out of charity, but out of self-interest, to ingratiate himself with Ruth. In the final chapter George Barrington leaves a letter for Owen enclosing a charitable gift of ten pounds for him, three pounds for Mrs Linden and two pounds for Bert White's mother, knowing, as he puts it, that Owen would have done the same for him 'if our positions were reversed' (p. 604). Barrington can do this because he is the son of a wealthy man, but this gesture of charity is validated by his shared commitment with Owen to the principles and practice of Socialism.

We have seen in the cases of Owen and Philpot that acts of charity do not necessarily involve money. In the final chapter Barrington comes across a public meeting of members of the Shining Light Chapel and the Church of the Whited Sepulchre, addressed by Rushton, who exhorts the 'half-starved, pale-faced working men and women' to join the community of the faithful. This is Tressell's final attack on the hypocrisy of the Forty Thieves and their like where he quotes Christ's admonitory words from St Luke's Gospel to those who make 'the accumulation of money the principal business of their lives': ' "Woe unto you that are rich" ' – and most famously – ' "it is easier for a camel to go through the eye of a needle than for a rich man to enter the kingdom of heaven" ' (p. 601– both slightly mis-quoted). Moments such as this go some way to justifying Tressell's claim that he intends no attack upon 'sincere religion'.

SOCIALISM

In his Author's Preface Tressell states that he 'intended to explain what Socialists understand by the word "Poverty": to define the Socialist theory of the causes of poverty, and to explain how Socialists propose to abolish poverty' (p. 33), and Owen is his spokesman, aided eventually by Barrington. Socialism is identified with the Labour Party in British politics, but when Tressell wrote this novel the Labour Party was in its infancy and without effective power in Parliament, though it won representation there in 1906 with 29 seats. It was formed out of the disparate agendas of the Independent Labour Party and the Social Democratic Federation, of which Tressell was a member. The need radically to improve the conditions of life for the working classes goes back at least to the early nineteenth century, as in the example of Robert Owen (1771–1858), whose idea of 'villages of cooperation', self-supporting communities run on socialist lines, which he believed would ultimately replace private ownership, briefly flourished in Scotland. The Chartist Movement of 1838–59 was the most dynamic attempt to reform Parliamentary democracy in Britain, and over the course of the century the Trade Union Movement became increasingly politicised. The drive for social reform towards the end of the nineteenth century drew upon several sources such as the writings of John Ruskin and William Morris, once a member of the Social Democratic Federation who later founded the Socialist League. Socialist ideology was thus informed by a variety of theories of social change, from the gradualist ideals of the Fabian Society to the revolutionary theories of Karl Marx and Friedrich Engels whose book *The Condition of the Working Class in England* of 1845 was translated into English in 1887. Tressell would have known much of this literature of Socialist thought, and was certainly familiar with the writings of Robert Blatchford (1851–1943), the author of *Merrie England* (1893), who founded a Socialist weekly newspaper, the *Clarion*, in 1891. Blatchford's use of a diagram to represent social classes and their respective proportions of national income is followed by Owen in two of the four chapters (7, 15, 21 and 25) in which he attempts to explain Socialism to his workmates. Barrington's 'great oration' in Chapter 45 is equally informed by Blatchford and other Socialist thinkers.

Owen is not a natural public speaker for his imagination is primarily visual rather than literary, as is appropriate for a signwriter. However, Owen is a reader of books with a small library of cheap paperback editions of new books, unlike his companions at work whose reading is confined to newspapers. Crass in particular challenges Owen's views on money, fiscal policy, tariff reform, free trade, protectionism, and the impact of foreign workers and machinery on the working classes, with opinions derived from the *Daily Obscurer*. The root of the problem for Owen is poverty, repeatedly defined by him in terms that often bewilder his listeners, as when he insists, 'Money *is* the principal cause of poverty' (p. 175). He thinks that the 'causes of poverty were so glaringly evident that he marvelled that any rational being should fail to perceive them; but at the same time he found it very difficult to define them himself' (p. 165). Hence his recourse to visual illustration of his arguments using a piece of board in Chapter 21 and a diagrammatic exposition in Chapter 25, 'The Oblong'. Whatever strategy he uses, his enterprise always fails, and the workers ridicule the idea that poverty could be abolished. They remain hostile, 'not to Owen, but to Socialism', are indeed 'savagely and malignantly opposed' to it, even those 'who had shown some symptoms of Socialism during the past winter when they were starving had now quite recovered and were stout defenders of the Present System' (p. 446). Their animosity to Socialism, widely shared in the middle-class community, is evident in the response to the Cycle Scouts associated with Blatchford's *Clarion* journal and their distribution of leaflets in Mugsborough where they are battered and reviled for their efforts to spread the gospel of Socialism. In his sociological history of England 'over the period which separates us from the pre-industrial past', *The World We Have Lost*, Peter Laslett writes: 'The great puzzle about the English working class may therefore seem to be why it was that the active, intelligent and well paid among them did not all draw the correct Marxian inference, why it is that there has been no violent social revolution in England in the twentieth century.'[7] There is no simple answer to this question, but if one may be drawn from Tressell's novel, it would surely be that apart from Owen, Barrington and their kind, the will to change was beyond them, as though they were all anaesthetised by poverty.

The passion and logic of Owen and Barrington's arguments for Socialism are countered by the adversarial forces aligned against the underclass of workers to the further advantage of those in power who have control over wages and working conditions, the relief of

7   Peter Laslett, *The World We Have Lost*, Methuen, 1965, p. 208

the poor, and so on. The antipathy to Owen and Barrington's Socialist ideas shown by their workmates indicates how far they are unwitting embodiments of ragged-trousered philanthropists, contributing to the wealth they create through their work but not sharing in it. 'The Golden Light that will be diffused throughout all the happy world from the rays of the risen sun of Socialism' (p. 606) remained a very distant prospect for Owen and his kind at the close of this novel.

LIONEL KELLY
University of Reading

NOTE ON THE TEXT

Wordsworth are pleased to publish this edition of *The Ragged Trousered Philanthropists* which reprints the Lawrence & Wishart edition of 1955, the first to be based faithfully on the author's manuscript. We would like to express our thanks to Mr Reg Johnson who has kindly given his permission on behalf of the Robert Tressell Estate for our use of this edition.

As the Foreword to the 1955 edition noted, Tressell's manuscript was incomplete:

The present edition follows Tressell's manuscript. Some manuscript pages were pasted over, corrected, paraphrased or summarised. Where they could not be restored, the original editor's paraphrases are given, and are printed within two square brackets. A few pages have been entirely lost, and gaps of this kind are indicated by a row of dots. Where necessary linking passages have been supplied by the present editor, and these are printed within [single] square brackets. The author's original grammar, spelling and punctuation, based on his quick apprehension of spoken idiom, as well as his somewhat inconsistent use of capital letters, are restored. Only the minimum of corrections have been made.

The arrangement and titles of chapters in this edition correspond to the list of chapters which the author attached to his manuscript in all except one particular. The original list includes fifty-five chapters, of which the third is entitled 'Mugsborough'. Corresponding to this there was attached to the manuscript a fragment, reproduced in this edition as an Appendix. The fifty-five chapters in the author's original list are therefore reduced to fifty-four.

The author's original Preface (uncompleted) has been restored. He designed his own title page, which is reproduced in this edition. It will be noted that he spelt his pen-name 'Tressell', and not 'Tressal', as it was rendered in the editions circulating hitherto.

SELECT BIBLIOGRAPHY

BIOGRAPHICAL

Ball, Fred, *Tressell of Mugsborough*, Lawrence and Wishart, London, 1951

Ball, Fred, *One of the Damned: The Life and Times of Robert Tressell, Author of 'The Ragged Trousered Philanthropists'*, Weidenfeld and Nicolson, 1973

Harker, Dave, *Tressell: The Real Story of 'The Ragged Trousered Philanthropists'*, Zed Books, London, 2003

CRITICAL STUDIES

Alfred, David (ed.), *The Robert Tressell Lectures 1981–1988*, Rochester, Workers' Educational Association, 1988

Eagleton, Mary and Pierce, David, *Attitudes to Class in the English Novel*, Thames & Hudson, London, 1979

Fox, Pamela, *Class Fictions: Shame and Resistance in the British Working-Class Novel, 1890-1945*, Duke University Press, London, 1995

Hawthorn, J., (ed.), *The British Working-Class Novel in the Twentieth Century*, London, 1984

Hunt, Tristram, Introduction to Robert Tressell, *The Ragged Trousered Philanthropists*, Penguin Classics, 2004

Hyslop, Jonathan, 'A Ragged Trousered Philanthropist and the Empire', in *History Workshop Journal*, 51 (2001), pp. 65–85

Ingle, Stephen, *Socialist Thought in Imaginative Literature*, Macmillan, London, 1979

Klaus, Gustav H., *The Socialist Novel in Britain*, Harvester, Brighton, 1982

Klaus, Gustav H. and Knight, Stephen (eds), *British Industrial Fictions*, University of Wales Press, Cardiff, 2000

Mayne, Brian, '*The Ragged Trousered Philanthropists*', in *Twentieth Century Literature*, 13/2 (1967), 73–85

McKibben, R., *The Ideologies of Class*, Oxford University Press, 1994

Miles, Peter, Introduction and Notes to Robert Tressell, *The Ragged Trousered Philanthropists*, Oxford University Press, Oxford World Classics, 2005

Mitchell, Jack, *Robert Tressell and 'The Ragged Trousered Philanthropists'*, Lawrence and Wishart, London, 1969

Nettleton, John, 'Robert Tressell and the Liverpool Connection', in *History Workshop Journal*, 12 (1981),163–71

Robert Tressell Workshop, *The Robert Tressell Papers*, Workers' Educational Association, Rochester, 1982

Rose, Jonathan, *The Intellectual Life of the British Working Classes*, Yale University Press, London, 2001

Sillitoe, Alan, Introduction to Robert Tressell, *The Ragged Trousered Philanthropists*, Panther, London, 1965, pp. 7–10

Smith, David, *Socialist Propaganda in the Twentieth-Century British Novel*, Macmillan, London, 1978

Stack, D. A., 'The First Darwinian Left: Radical and Socialist Responses to Darwin, 1859–1914', in *History of Political Thought*, 21/4, (2000), 682–710

Swingewood, A., *The Myth of Mass Culture*, London, 1977

Watts, Cedric, *Literature and Money*, Harvester, London, 1990

Young, James D., 'Militancy, English Socialism and *The Ragged Trousered Philanthropists*', in *Journal of Contemporary History*, 20/2 (1985), 282–303

THE
RAGGED TROUSERED
PHILANTHROPISTS.

Being the story of twelve months
in Hell, told by one of the
damned, and written down
by Robert Tressell.

The original title page drawn by the author

THE RAGGED TROUSERED
PHILANTHROPISTS

Preface

In writing this book my intention was to present, in the form of an interesting story, a faithful picture of working-class life – more especially of those engaged in the Building trades – in a small town in the south of England.

I wished to describe the relations existing between the workmen and their employers, the attitude and feelings of these two classes towards each other; the condition of the workers during the different seasons of the year, their circumstances when at work and when out of employment: their pleasures, their intellectual outlook, their religious and political opinions and ideals.

The action of the story covers a period of only a little over twelve months, but in order that the picture might be complete it was necessary to describe how the workers are circumstanced at all periods of their lives, from the cradle to the grave. Therefore the characters include women and children, a young boy – the apprentice – some improvers, journeymen in the prime of life, and worn-out old men.

I designed to show the conditions resulting from poverty and unemployment: to expose the futility of the measures taken to deal with them and to indicate what I believe to be the only real remedy, namely – Socialism. I intended to explain what Socialists understand by the word 'Poverty': to define the Socialist theory of the causes of poverty, and to explain how Socialists propose to abolish poverty.

It may be objected that, considering the number of books dealing with these subjects already existing, such a work as this was uncalled for. The answer is that not only are the majority of people opposed to Socialism, but a very brief conversation with an average anti-socialist is sufficient to show that he does not know what Socialism means. The same is true of all the anti-socialist writers and the 'great statesmen' who make anti-socialist speeches: unless we believe that they are all deliberate liars and impostors, who to serve their own interests labour to mislead other people, we must conclude that they do not understand Socialism. There is no other possible explanation of the extraordinary things they write and say. The thing they cry out against is not Socialism but a phantom of their own imagining.

Another answer is that 'The Philanthropists' is not a treatise or essay, but a novel. My main object was to write a readable story full of human interest and based on the happenings of everyday life, the subject of Socialism being treated incidentally.

This was the task I set myself. To what extent I have succeeded is for others to say; but whatever their verdict, the work possesses at least one merit – that of being true. I have invented nothing. There are no scenes or incidents in the story that I have not either witnessed myself or had conclusive evidence of. As far as I dared I let the characters express themselves in their own sort of language and consequently some passages may be considered objectionable. At the same time I believe that – because it is true – the book is not without its humorous side.

The scenes and characters are typical of every town in the South of England and they will be readily recognised by those concerned. If the book is published I think it will appeal to a very large number of readers. Because it is true it will probably be denounced as a libel on the working classes and their employers, and upon the religious-professing section of the community. But I believe it will be acknowledged as true by most of those who are compelled to spend their lives amid the surroundings it describes, and it will be evident that no attack is made upon sincere religion . . .

CHAPTER 1

An Imperial Banquet.
A Philosophical Discussion.
The Mysterious Stranger.
Britons Never shall be Slaves.

The house was named 'The Cave'. It was a large oldfashioned three-storied building standing in about an acre of ground, and situated about a mile outside the town of Mugsborough. It stood back nearly two hundred yards from the main road and was reached by means of a by-road or lane, on each side of which was a hedge formed of hawthorn trees and blackberry bushes. This house had been unoccupied for many years and it was now being altered and renovated for its new owner by the firm of Rushton & Co. Builders and Decorators.

There were, altogether, about twenty-five men working there, carpenters, plumbers, plasterers, bricklayers and painters, besides several unskilled labourers. New floors were being put in where the old ones were decayed, and upstairs two of the rooms were being made into one by demolishing the parting wall and substituting an iron girder. Some of the window frames and sashes were so rotten that they were being replaced. Some of the ceilings and walls were so cracked and broken that they had to be replastered. Openings were being cut through walls and doors were being put where no doors had ever been before. Old broken chimney pots were being taken down and new ones were being taken up and fixed in their places. All the old whitewash had to be washed off the ceilings and all the old paper had to be scraped off the walls preparatory to the house being repainted and decorated. The air was full of the sounds of hammering and sawing, the ringing of trowels, the rattle of pails, the splashing of water brushes, and the scraping of the stripping knives used by those who were removing the old wallpaper. Besides being full of these sounds the air was heavily laden with dust and disease germs, powdered mortar, lime, plaster, and the dirt that had been accumulating within the old house for years. In brief, those employed there might be said to be living in a Tariff Reform Paradise[1] – they had Plenty of Work.

At twelve o'clock Bob Crass – the painters' foreman – blew a prolonged blast upon a whistle and all hands assembled in the kitchen, where Bert the apprentice had already prepared the tea, which was ready in the large galvanised iron pail that he had placed in the middle of the floor. By the side of the pail were a number of old jam-jars, mugs, dilapidated tea-cups and one or two empty condensed milk tins. Each man on the 'job' paid Bert threepence a week for the tea and sugar – they did not have milk – and although they had tea at breakfast-time as well as at dinner, the lad was generally considered to be making a fortune.

Two pairs of steps, laid parallel on their sides at a distance of about eight feet from each other, with a plank laid across, in front of the fire, several upturned pails, and the drawers belonging to the dresser, formed the seating accommodation. The floor of the room was covered with all manner of debris, dust, dirt, fragments of old mortar and plaster. A sack containing cement was leaning against one of the walls, and a bucket containing some stale whitewash stood in one corner.

As each man came in he filled his cup, jam-jar or condensed milk tin with tea from the steaming pail, before sitting down. Most of them brought their food in little wicker baskets which they held on their laps or placed on the floor beside them.

At first there was no attempt at conversation and nothing was heard but the sounds of eating and drinking and the frizzling of the bloater[2] which Easton, one of the painters, was toasting on the end of a pointed stick at the fire.

'I don't think much of this bloody tea,' suddenly remarked Sawkins, one of the labourers.

'Well it oughter be all right,' retorted Bert; 'it's been bilin' ever since 'arf past eleven.'

Bert White was a frail-looking, weedy, pale-faced boy, fifteen years of age and about four feet nine inches in height. His trousers were part of a suit that he had once worn for best, but that was so long ago that they had become too small for him, fitting rather tightly and scarcely reaching the top of his patched and broken hobnailed boots. The knees and the bottoms of the legs of his trousers had been patched with square pieces of cloth, several shades darker than the original fabric, and these patches were now all in rags. His coat was several sizes too large for him and hung about him like a dirty ragged sack. He was a pitiable spectacle of neglect and wretchedness as he sat there on an upturned pail, eating his bread and cheese with fingers that, like his clothing, were grimed with paint and dirt.

'Well then, you can't have put enough tea in, or else you've bin usin' up wot was left yesterday,' continued Sawkins.

'Why the bloody 'ell don't you leave the boy alone?' said Harlow, another painter. 'If you don't like the tea you needn't drink it. For my part, I'm sick of listening to you about it every damn day.'

'It's all very well for you to say I needn't drink it,' answered Sawkins, 'but I've paid my share an' I've got a right to express an opinion. It's my belief that 'arf the money we gives 'im is spent in penny 'orribles: 'e's always got one in 'is hand, an' to make wot tea 'e does buy last, 'e collects all the slops wot's left and biles it up day after day.'

'No, I don't!' said Bert, who was on the verge of tears. 'It's not me wot buys the things at all. I gives all the money I gets to Crass, and 'e buys them 'imself, so there!'

At this revelation, some of the men furtively exchanged significant glances, and Crass, the foreman, became very red.

'You'd better keep your bloody thruppence and make your own tea after this week,' he said, addressing Sawkins, 'and then p'raps we'll 'ave a little peace at meal-times.'

'An' you needn't ask me to cook no bloaters or bacon for you no more,' added Bert, tearfully, 'cos I won't do it.'

Sawkins was not popular with any of the others. When, about twelve months previously, he first came to work for Rushton & Co., he was a simple labourer, but since then he had "picked up" a slight knowledge of the trade, and having armed himself with a putty-knife and put on a white jacket, regarded himself as a fully qualified painter. The others did not perhaps object to him trying to better his condition, but his wages – fivepence an hour – were twopence an hour less than the standard rate, and the result was that in slack times often a better workman was "stood off" when Sawkins was kept on. Moreover, he was generally regarded as a sneak who carried tales to the foreman and the "Bloke". Every new hand who was taken on was usually warned by his new mates 'not to let that b – r Sawkins see anything.'

The unpleasant silence which now ensued was at length broken by one of the men, who told a dirty story, and in the laughter and applause that followed, the incident of the tea was forgotten.

'How did you get on yesterday?' asked Crass, addressing Bundy, the plasterer, who was intently studying the sporting columns of the *Daily Obscurer*.

'No luck,' replied Bundy, gloomily. 'I had a bob each way on Stockwell, in the first race, but it was scratched before the start.'

This gave rise to a conversation between Crass, Bundy, and one or two others concerning the chances of different horses in the morrow's races. It was Friday, and no one had much money, so at the suggestion of Bundy, a Syndicate was formed, each member contributing threepence, for the purpose of backing a dead certainty given by the renowned Captain Kiddem of the *Obscurer*. One of those who did not join the syndicate was Frank Owen, who was as usual absorbed in a newspaper. He was generally regarded as a bit of a crank: for it was felt that there must be something wrong about a man who took no interest in racing or football and was always talking a lot of rot about religion and politics. If it had not been for the fact that he was generally admitted to be an exceptionally good workman, they would have had but little hesitation about thinking that he was mad. This man was about thirty-two years of age, and of medium height, but so slightly built that he appeared taller. There was a suggestion of refinement in his clean-shaven face, but his complexion was ominously clear, and an unnatural colour flushed the thin cheeks.[3]

There was a certain amount of justification for the attitude of his fellow workmen, for Owen held the most unusual and unorthodox opinions on the subjects mentioned.

The affairs of the world are ordered in accordance with orthodox opinions. If anyone [did not think in accordance with these he soon discovered this fact for himself. Owen saw that in the world a small class of people were] possessed of a great abundance and superfluity of the things that are produced by work. He saw also that a very great number – in fact, the majority of the people – lived on the verge of want; and that a smaller but still very large number lived lives of semi-starvation from the cradle to the grave; while a yet smaller but still very great number actually died of hunger, or, maddened by privation, killed themselves and their children in order to put a period to their misery. And strangest of all – in his opinion – he saw that the people who enjoyed abundance of the things that are made by work, were the people who did Nothing: and that the others, who lived in want or died of hunger, were the people who worked. And seeing all this he thought that it was wrong, that the system that produced such results was rotten and should be altered.

And he had sought out and eagerly read the writings of those who thought they knew how it might be done.

It was because he was in the habit of speaking of these subjects that his fellow workmen came to the conclusion that there was probably something wrong with his mind.

When all the members [of the syndicate] had handed over their contributions, Bundy went out to arrange matters with the bookie, and when he had gone Easton annexed the copy of the *Obscurer* that Bundy had thrown away, and proceeded to laboriously work through some carefully cooked statistics relating to Free Trade and Protection. Bert, his eyes starting out of his head and his mouth wide open, was devouring the contents of a paper called *The Chronicles of Crime*. Ned Dawson, a poor devil who was paid fourpence an hour for acting as mate or labourer to Bundy, or the bricklayers, or anyone else who wanted him, lay down on the dirty floor in a corner of the room and with his coat rolled up as a pillow, went to sleep. Sawkins, with the same intention, stretched himself at full length on the dresser. Another who took no part in the syndicate was Barrington, a labourer, who, having finished his dinner, placed the cup he brought for his tea back into his dinner basket and having closed and placed it on the mantelshelf above, took out an old briar pipe which he slowly filled, and proceeded to smoke in silence.

Some time previously the firm had done some work for a wealthy gentleman who lived in the country, some distance outside Mugsborough. This gentleman also owned some property in the town and it was commonly reported that he had used his influence with Rushton to induce the latter to give Barrington employment. It was whispered amongst the hands that the young man was a distant relative of the gentleman's, and that he had disgraced himself in some way and been disowned by his people. Rushton was supposed to have given him a job in the hope of currying favour with his wealthy client, from whom he hoped to obtain more work. Whatever the explanation of the mystery may have been, the fact remained that Barrington, who knew nothing of the work except what he had learned since he had been taken on, was employed as a painter's labourer at the usual wages – fivepence per hour.

He was about twenty-five years of age and a good deal taller than the majority of the others, being about five feet ten inches in height and slenderly though well and strongly built. He seemed very anxious to learn all that he could about the trade, and although rather reserved in his manner, he had contrived to make himself fairly popular with his workmates. He seldom spoke unless to answer when addressed, and it was difficult to draw him into conversation. At meal-times, as on the present occasion, he generally smoked, apparently lost in thought and unconscious of his surroundings.

Most of the others also lit their pipes and a desultory conversation ensued.

'Is the gent what's bought this 'ouse any relation to Sweater[4] the draper?' asked Payne, the carpenters' foreman.

'It's the same bloke,' replied Crass.

'Didn't he used to be on the Town Council or something?'

' 'E's bin on the Council for years,' returned Crass. ' 'E's on it now. 'E's mayor this year. 'E's bin mayor several times before.'

'Let's see,' said Payne, reflectively, ' 'E married old Grinder's sister, didn't 'e? You know who I mean, Grinder the green-grocer.'

'Yes, I believe he did,' said Crass.

'It wasn't Grinder's sister,' chimed in old Jack Linden. 'It was 'is niece. I know, because I remember working in their 'ouse just after they was married, about ten year ago.'

'Oh yes, I remember now,' said Payne. 'She used to manage one of Grinder's branch shops, didn't she?'

'Yes,' replied Linden. 'I remember it very well because there was a lot of talk about it at the time. By all accounts, ole Sweater used to be a regler 'ot un: no one never thought as he'd ever git married at all: there was some funny yarns about several young women what used to work for him.'

This important matter being disposed of, there followed a brief silence, which was presently broken by Harlow.

'Funny name to call a 'ouse, ain't it?' he said. ' "The Cave". I wonder what made 'em give it a name like that.'

'They calls 'em all sorts of outlandish names nowadays,' said old Jack Linden.

'There's generally some sort of meaning to it, though,' observed Payne. 'For instance, if a bloke backed a winner and made a pile, 'e might call 'is 'ouse "Epsom Lodge" or "Newmarket Villa".'

'Or sometimes there's a hoak tree or a cherry tree in the garding,' said another man; 'then they calls it "Hoak Lodge" or "Cherry Cottage".'

'Well, there's a cave up at the end of this garden,' said Harlow with a grin, 'you know, the cesspool, what the drains of the 'ouse runs into; praps they called it after that.'

'Talking about the drains,' said old Jack Linden when the laughter produced by this elegant joke had ceased, 'Talking about the drains, I wonder what they're going to do about them; the 'ouse aint fit to live in as they are now, and as for that bloody cesspool it ought to be done away with.'

'So it is going to be,' replied Crass. 'There's going to be a new set of drains altogether, carried right out to the road and connected with the main.'

Crass really knew no more about what was going to be done in this matter than did Linden, but he felt certain that this course would be adopted. He never missed an opportunity of enhancing his own prestige with the men by insinuating that he was in the confidence of the firm.

'That's goin' to cost a good bit,' said Linden.

'Yes, I suppose it will,' replied Crass, 'but money ain't no object to old Sweater. 'E's got tons of it; you know 'e's got a large wholesale business in London and shops all over the bloody country, besides the one 'e's got 'ere.'

Easton was still reading the *Obscurer*: he was not able to understand exactly what the compiler of the figures was driving at – probably the latter never intended that anyone should understand – but he was conscious of a growing feeling of indignation and hatred against foreigners of every description, who were ruining this country, and he began to think that it was about time we did something to protect ourselves. Still, it was a very difficult question: to tell the truth, he himself could not make head or tail of it. At length he said aloud, addressing himself to Crass:

'Wot do you think of this 'ere fissical policy,[5] Bob?'

'Aint thought much about it,' replied Crass. 'I don't never worry my 'ed about politics.'

'Much better left alone,' chimed in old Jack Linden sagely, 'argy-fying about politics generally ends up with a bloody row an' does no good to nobody.'

At this there was a murmur of approval from several of the others. Most of them were averse from arguing or disputing about politics. If two or three men of similar opinions happened to be together they might discuss such things in a friendly and superficial way, but in a mixed company it was better left alone. The 'Fissical Policy' emanated from the Tory party. That was the reason why some of them were strongly in favour of it, and for the same reason others were opposed to it. Some of them were under the delusion that they were Conservatives: similarly, others imagined themselves to be Liberals. As a matter of fact, most of them were nothing. They knew as much about the public affairs of their own country as they did of the condition of affairs in the planet Jupiter.

Easton began to regret that he had broached so objectionable a subject, when, looking up from his paper, Owen said:

'Does the fact that you never "trouble your heads about politics" prevent you from voting at election times?'

No one answered, and there ensued a brief silence. Easton however, in spite of the snub he had received, could not refrain from talking.

'Well, I don't go in for politics much, either, but if what's in this 'ere paper is true, it seems to me as we oughter take some interest in it, when the country is being ruined by foreigners.'

'If you're goin' to believe all that's in that bloody rag you'll want some salt,' said Harlow.

The *Obscurer* was a Tory paper and Harlow was a member of the local Liberal club. Harlow's remark roused Crass.

'Wot's the use of talkin' like that?' he said, 'you know very well that the country *is* being ruined by foreigners. Just go to a shop to buy something; look round the place an' you'll see that more than 'arf the damn stuff comes from abroad. They're able to sell their goods 'ere because they don't 'ave to pay no dooty, but they takes care to put 'eavy dooties on our goods to keep 'em out of their countries; and I say it's about time it was stopped.'

' 'Ear, 'ear,' said Linden, who always agreed with Crass, because the latter, being in charge of the job, had it in his power to put in a good – or a bad – word for a man to the boss. ' 'Ear, 'ear! Now that's wot I call common sense.'

Several other men, for the same reason as Linden, echoed Crass' sentiments, but Owen laughed contemptuously.

'Yes, it's quite true that we gets a lot of stuff from foreign countries,' said Harlow, 'but they buys more from us than we do from them.'

'Now you think you know a 'ell of a lot,' said Crass. 'Ow much more did they buy from us last year, than we did from them?'

Harlow looked foolish: as a matter of fact his knowledge of the subject was not much wider than Crass's. He mumbled something about not having no 'ed for figures, and offered to bring full particulars next day.

'You're wot I call a bloody windbag,' continued Crass; 'you've got a 'ell of a lot to say, but wen it comes to the point you don't know nothin'.'

'Wy, even 'ere in Mugsborough,' chimed in Sawkins – who though still lying on the dresser had been awakened by the shouting – 'We're overrun with 'em! Nearly all the waiters and the cook at the Grand Hotel where we was working last month is foreigners.'

'Yes,' said old Joe Philpot, tragically, 'and then thers all them Hitalian horgin grinders, an' the blokes wot sells 'ot chestnuts: an' wen I was goin' 'ome last night I see a lot of them Frenchies sellin' hunions, an' a little wile afterwards I met two more of 'em comin' up the street with a bear.'

Notwithstanding the disquieting nature of this intelligence, Owen again laughed, much to the indignation of the others, who thought it was a very serious state of affairs. It was a dam' shame that these people were allowed to take the bread out of English people's mouths: they ought to be driven into the bloody sea.

And so the talk continued, principally carried on by Crass and those who agreed with him. None of them really understood the subject: not one of them had ever devoted fifteen consecutive minutes to the earnest investigation of it. The papers they read were filled with vague and alarming accounts of the quantities of foreign merchandise imported into this country, the enormous number of aliens constantly arriving, and their destitute conditions, how they lived, the crimes they committed, and the injury they did to British trade. These were the seeds which, cunningly sown in their minds, caused to grow up within them a bitter undiscriminating hatred of foreigners. To them the mysterious thing they variously called the 'Friscal Policy', the 'Tistical Policy', or the 'Fissical Question' was a great Anti-Foreign Crusade. The country was in a hell of a state, poverty, hunger and misery in a hundred forms had already invaded thousands of homes and stood upon the thresholds of thousands more. How came these things to be? It was the bloody foreigner! Therefore, down with the foreigners and all their works. Out with them. Drive them b—s into the bloody sea! The country would be ruined if not protected in some way. This Friscal, Fistical, Fissical or whatever the hell policy it was called, *was* Protection, therefore no one but a bloody fool could hesitate to support it. It was all quite plain – quite simple. One did not need to think twice about it. It was scarcely necessary to think about it at all.

This was the conclusion reached by Crass and such of his mates who thought they were Conservatives – the majority of them could not have read a dozen sentences aloud without stumbling – it was not necessary to think or study or investigate anything. It was all as clear as daylight. The foreigner was the enemy, and the cause of poverty and bad trade.

When the storm had in some degree subsided,

'Some of you seem to think,' said Owen, sneeringly, 'that it was a great mistake on God's part to make so many foreigners. You ought to hold a mass meeting about it: pass a resolution something like this: "This meeting of British Christians hereby indignantly protests against the action of the Supreme Being in having created so many foreigners, and calls upon him to forth-with rain down fire, brimstone and mighty rocks upon the heads of all those Philistines, so that they may be utterly exterminated from the face of the earth, which rightly belongs to the British people".'

Crass looked very indignant, but could think of nothing to say in answer to Owen, who continued:

'A little while ago you made the remark that you never trouble yourself about what you call politics, and some of the rest agreed with you that to do so is not worth while. Well, since you never "worry" yourself about these things, it follows that you know nothing about them; yet you do not hesitate to express the most decided opinions concerning matters of which you admittedly know nothing. Presently, when there is an election, you will go and vote in favour of a policy of which you know nothing. I say that since you never take the trouble to find out which side is right or wrong you have no right to express any opinion. You are not fit to vote. You should not be allowed to vote.'

Crass was by this time very angry.

'I pays my rates and taxes,' he shouted, 'an' I've got as much right to express an opinion as you 'ave. I votes for who the bloody 'ell I likes. I shan't arst your leave nor nobody else's! Wot the 'ell's it got to do with you who I votes for?'

'It has a great deal to do with me. If you vote for Protection you will be helping to bring it about, and if you succeed, and if Protection is the evil that some people say it is, I shall be one of those who will suffer. I say you have no right to vote for a policy which may bring suffering upon other people, without taking the trouble to find out whether you are helping to make things better or worse.'

Owen had risen from his seat and was walking up and down the room emphasising his words with excited gestures.

'As for not trying to find out wot side is right,' said Crass, somewhat overawed by Owen's manner and by what he thought was the glare of madness in the latter's eyes, 'I reads the *Ananias* every week, and I generally takes the *Daily Chloroform*, or the *Hobscurer*,[6] so I ought to know summat about it.'

'Just listen to this,' interrupted Easton, wishing to create a diversion and beginning to read from the copy of the *Obscurer* which he still held in his hand: –

'GREAT DISTRESS IN MUGSBOROUGH.
HUNDREDS OUT OF EMPLOYMENT.
WORK OF THE CHARITY SOCIETY.
789 CASES ON THE BOOKS.

'Great as was the distress among the working classes last year, unfortunately there seems every prospect that before the winter which has just commenced is over the distress will be even more acute.

Already the Charity Society and kindred associations are relieving more cases than they did at the corresponding time last year. Applications to the Board of Guardians[7] have also been much more numerous, and the Soup Kitchen has had to open its doors on Nov. 7th a fortnight earlier than usual. The number of men, women and children provided with meals is three or four times greater than last year.'

Easton stopped: reading was hard work to him.

'There's a lot more,' he said, 'about starting relief works: two shillings a day for married men and one shilling for single and something about there's been 1,572 quarts of soup given to poor families wot was not even able to pay a penny, and a lot more. And 'ere's another thing, an advertisement.

'THE SUFFERING POOR

Sir: – Distress among the Poor is so acute that I earnestly ask you for aid for The Salvation Army's great Social work on their behalf. Some 6000 are being sheltered nightly. Hundreds are found work daily. Soup and bread are distributed in the midnight hours to homeless wanderers in London. Additional workshops for the unemployed have been established. Our Social Work for men, women and children, for the characterless and the outcast, is the largest and oldest organised effort of its kind in the country, and greatly needs help. £10,000 is required before Christmas day. Gifts may be made to any specific section or home, if desired. Can you please send us something to keep the work going? Please address cheques, crossed Bank of England (Law Courts Branch), to me at 101, Queen Victoria Street, E.C. Balance Sheets and Reports upon application.

BRAMWELL BOOTH.'

'Oh, that's part of the great 'appiness an' prosperity wot Owen makes out Free Trade brings,' said Crass with a jeering laugh.

'I never said Free Trade brought happiness or prosperity,' said Owen.

'Well, praps you didn't say exactly them words, but that's wot it amounts to.'

'I never said anything of the kind. We've had Free Trade for the last fifty years[8] and to-day most people are living in a condition of more or less abject poverty, and thousands are literally starving. When we had Protection things were worse still. Other countries have Protection and yet many of their people are glad to come here and work for starvation wages. The only difference between Free Trade and Protection is that under certain circumstances one might be a little worse than the other, but as remedies for Poverty, neither of them are of any real use whatever, for the simple reason that they do not deal with the real causes of Poverty.'

'The greatest cause of poverty is hover-population,' remarked Harlow.

'Yes,' said old Joe Philpot. 'If a boss wants two men, twenty goes after the job: ther's too many people and not enough work.'

'Over-population!' cried Owen, 'when there's thousands of acres of uncultivated land in England without a house or human being to be seen. Is overpopulation the cause of poverty in France? Is over-population[9] the cause of poverty in Ireland? Within the last fifty years the population of Ireland has been reduced by more than half. Four millions of people have been exterminated by famine or got rid of by emigration, but they haven't got rid of poverty. P'raps you think that half the people in this country ought to be exterminated as well.'

Here Owen was seized with a violent fit of coughing, and resumed his seat. When the cough had ceased he sat wiping his mouth with his handkerchief and listening to the talk that ensued.

'Drink is the cause of most of the poverty,' said Slyme.

This young man had been through some strange process that he called 'conversion'. He had had a 'change of 'art' and looked down with pious pity upon those he called 'worldly' people. He was not 'worldly', he did not smoke or drink and never went to the theatre. He had an extraordinary notion that total abstinence was one of the fundamental principles of the Christian religion. It never occurred to what he called his mind, that this doctrine is an insult to the Founder of Christianity.

'Yes,' said Crass, agreeing with Slyme, 'an' thers plenty of 'em wot's too lazy to work when they can get it. Some of the b—s who go about pleading poverty 'ave never done a fair day's work in all their bloody lives. Then thers all this new fangled machinery,' continued Crass. 'That's wot's ruinin' everything. Even in our trade ther's them machines for trimmin' wallpaper, an' now they've brought out a paintin' machine. Ther's a pump an' a 'ose pipe, an' they reckon two men can do as much with this 'ere machine as twenty could without it.'

'Another thing is women,' said Harlow, 'there's thousands of 'em nowadays doin' work wot oughter be done by men.'

'In my opinion ther's too much of this 'ere eddication, nowadays,' remarked old Linden. 'Wot the 'ell's the good of eddication to the likes of us?'

'None whatever,' said Crass, 'it just puts foolish idears into people's 'eds and makes 'em too lazy to work.'

Barrington, who took no part in the conversation, still sat silently smoking. Owen was listening to this pitiable farrago with feelings of contempt and wonder. Were they all hopelessly stupid? Had their intelligence never developed beyond the childhood stage? Or was he mad himself?

'Early marriages is another thing,' said Slyme: 'no man oughtn't to be allowed to get married unless he's in a position to keep a family.'

'How can marriage be a cause of poverty?' said Owen, contemptuously. 'A man who is not married is living an unnatural life. Why don't you continue your argument a little further and say that the practice of eating and drinking is the cause of poverty or that if people were to go barefoot and naked there would be no poverty? The man who is so poor that he cannot marry is in a condition of poverty already.'

'Wot I mean,' said Slyme, 'is that no man oughtn't to marry till he's saved up enough so as to 'ave some money in the bank; an' another thing, I reckon a man oughtn't to get married till 'e's got a 'ouse of 'is own. It's easy enough to buy one in a building society if you're in reg'lar work.'

At this there was a general laugh.

'Why, you bloody fool,' said Harlow, scornfully, 'most of us is walkin' about 'arf our time.[10] It's all very well for you to talk; you've got almost a constant job on this firm. If they're doin' anything at all you're one of the few wot gets a show in. And another thing,' he added with a sneer, 'we don't all go to the same chapel as old Misery.'

'Old Misery' was Rushton & Co.'s manager or walking foreman. 'Misery' was only one of the nicknames bestowed upon him by the hands: he was also known as 'Nimrod' and 'Pontius Pilate'.

'And even if it's not possible,' Harlow continued, winking at the others, 'what's a man to do during the years he's savin' up?'

'Well, he must conquer hisself,' said Slyme, getting red.

'Conquer hisself is right!' said Harlow and the others laughed again.

'Of course if a man tried to conquer hisself by his own strength,' replied Slyme, ' 'e would be sure to fail, but when you've got the Grace of God in you it's different.'

'Chuck it, fer Christ's sake!' said Harlow in a tone of disgust. 'We've only just 'ad our dinner!'

'And wot about drink?' demanded old Joe Philpot, suddenly.

' 'Ear, 'ear,' cried Harlow. 'That's the bleedin' talk. I wouldn't mind 'avin' 'arf a pint now, if somebody else will pay for it.'

Joe Philpot – or as he was usually called, 'Old Joe' – was in the habit of indulging rather freely in the cup that inebriates. He was not very old, being only a little over fifty, but he looked much older. He had lost his wife some five years ago and was now alone in the world, for his three children had died in their infancy. Slyme's reference to drink had roused Philpot's indignation; he felt that it was directed against himself. The muddled condition of his brain did not permit him to take up the cudgels in his own behalf, but he knew that although Owen was a tee-totaller himself, he disliked Slyme.

'There's no need for us to talk about drink or laziness,' returned Owen, impatiently, 'because they have nothing to do with the matter. The question is, what is the cause of the lifelong poverty of the majority of those who are not drunkards and who *do* work? Why, if all the drunkards and won't-works and unskilled or inefficient workers could be by some miracle transformed into sober, industrious and skilled workers tomorrow, it would, under the present conditions, be so much the worse for us, because there isn't enough work for all *now* and those people by increasing the competition for what work there is, would inevitably cause a reduction of wages and a greater scarcity of employment. The theories that drunkenness, laziness or in-efficiency are the causes of poverty are so many devices invented and fostered by those who are selfishly interested in maintaining the present state of affairs, for the purpose of preventing us from discovering the real causes of our present condition.'

'Well, if we're all wrong,' said Crass, with a sneer, 'praps you can tell us what the real cause is?'

'An' praps you think you know how it's to be altered,' remarked Harlow, winking at the others.

'Yes; I do think I know the cause,' declared Owen, 'and I do think I know how it could be altered – '

'It can't never be haltered,' interrupted old Linden. 'I don't see no sense in all this 'ere talk. There's always been rich and poor in the world, and there always will be.'

'Wot I always say is this 'ere,' remarked Philpot, whose principal characteristic – apart from thirst – was a desire to see everyone comfortable, and who hated rows of any kind. 'There ain't no use in the likes of us trubblin' our 'eds or quarrellin' about politics. It don't make a dam bit of difference who you votes for or who gets in. They're hall the same; workin' the horicle for their own benefit. You can talk till you're black in the face, but you won't never be able to alter it. It's no use worrying. The sensible thing is to try and make the best of things as we find 'em: enjoy ourselves, and do the best we can for each other. Life's too short to quarrel and we'll hall soon be dead!'

At the end of this lengthy speech, the philosophic Philpot abstractedly grasped a jam-jar and raised it to his lips; but suddenly remembering that it contained stewed tea and not beer, set it down again without drinking.

'Let us begin at the beginning,' continued Owen, taking no notice of these interruptions. 'First of all, what do you mean by Poverty?'

'Why, if you've got no money, of course,' said Crass impatiently.

The others laughed disdainfully. It seemed to them such a foolish question.

'Well, that's true enough as far as it goes,' returned Owen, 'that is, as things are arranged in the world at present. But money itself is not wealth: it's of no use whatever.'

At this there was another outburst of jeering laughter.

'Supposing for example that you and Harlow were ship-wrecked on a desolate island, and *you* had saved nothing from the wreck but a bag containing a thousand sovereigns, and he had a tin of biscuits and a bottle of water.'

'Make it beer!' cried Harlow appealingly.

'Who would be the richer man, you or Harlow?'

'But then you see we ain't shipwrecked on no dissolute island at all,' sneered Crass. 'That's the worst of your arguments. You can't never get very far without supposing some bloody ridiclus thing or other. Never mind about supposing things wot ain't true; let's 'ave facts and common sense.'

' 'Ear, 'ear,' said old Linden. 'That's wot we want – a little common sense.'

'What do *you* mean by poverty, then?' asked Easton.

'What I call poverty is when people are not able to secure for themselves all the benefits of civilisation; the necessaries, comforts, pleasures and refinements of life, leisure, books, theatres, pictures, music, holidays, travel, good and beautiful homes, good clothes, good and pleasant food.'

Everybody laughed. It was so ridiculous. The idea of the likes of *them* wanting or having such things! Any doubts that any of them had entertained as to Owen's sanity disappeared. The man was as mad as a March hare.

'If a man is only able to provide himself and his family with the bare necessaries of existence, that man's family is living in poverty. Since he cannot enjoy the advantages of civilisation he might just as well be a savage: better, in fact, for a savage knows nothing of what he is deprived. What we call civilisation – the accumulation of knowledge which has come down to us from our forefathers – is the fruit of thousands of years of human thought and toil. It is not the result of the labour of the ancestors of any separate class of people who exist today, and therefore it is by right the common heritage of all. Every little child that is born into the world, no matter whether he is clever or dull, whether he is physically perfect or lame, or blind; no matter how much he may excel or fall short of his fellows in other respects, in one thing at least he is their equal – he is one of the heirs of all the ages that have gone before.'

Some of them began to wonder whether Owen was not sane after all. He certainly must be a clever sort of chap to be able to talk like this. It sounded almost like something out of a book, and most of them could not understand one half of it.

'Why is it,' continued Owen, 'that we are not only deprived of our inheritance – we are not only deprived of nearly all the benefits of civilisation, but we and our children are also often unable to obtain even the bare necessaries of existence?'

No one answered.

'All these things,' Owen proceeded, 'are produced by those who work. We do our full share of the work, therefore we should have a full share of the things that are made by work.'

The others continued silent. Harlow thought of the overpopulation theory, but decided not to mention it. Crass, who could not have given an intelligent answer to save his life, for once had sufficient sense to remain silent. He did think of calling out the patent paint-pumping machine and bringing the hose-pipe to bear on the subject, but abandoned the idea; after all, he thought, what was the use of arguing with such a fool as Owen?

Sawkins pretended to be asleep.

Philpot, however, had suddenly grown very serious.

'As things are now,' went on Owen, 'instead of enjoying the advantages of civilisation we are really worse off than slaves, for if we were slaves our owners in their own interest would see to it that we always had food and – '

'Oh, I don't see that,' roughly interrupted old Linden, who had been listening with evident anger and impatience. 'You can speak for yourself, but I can tell yer I don't put *myself* down as a slave.'

'Nor me neither,' said Crass sturdily. 'Let them call theirselves slaves as wants to.'

At this moment a footstep was heard in the passage leading to the kitchen. Old Misery! or perhaps the Bloke himself! Crass hurriedly pulled out his watch.

'Jesus Christ!' he gasped. 'It's four minutes past one!'

Linden frantically seized hold of a pair of steps and began wandering about the room with them.

Sawkins scrambled hastily to his feet and, snatching a piece of sandpaper from the pocket of his apron, began furiously rubbing down the scullery door.

Easton threw down the copy of the *Obscurer* and scrambled hastily to his feet.

The boy crammed the *Chronicles of Crime* into his trousers pocket.

Crass rushed over to the bucket and began stirring up the stale whitewash it contained, and the stench which it gave forth was simply appalling.

Consternation reigned.

They looked like a gang of malefactors suddenly interrupted in the commission of a crime.

The door opened. It was only Bundy returning from his mission to the Bookie.

CHAPTER 2

Nimrod: A Mighty Hunter Before the Lord

Mr. Hunter, as he was called to his face and as he was known to his brethren at the Shining Light Chapel, where he was superintendent of the Sunday School, or 'Misery' or 'Nimrod', as he was named behind his back by the workmen over whom he tyrannised, was the general or walking foreman or 'manager' of the firm whose card is herewith presented to the reader:

RUSHTON & Co.
MUGSBOROUGH

Builders, Decorators, and General Contractors
FUNERALS FURNISHED
Estimates given for General Repairs to House Property
First-class Work only at Moderate Charges

There were a number of sub-foremen or 'coddies', but Hunter was *the* foreman.

He was a tall, thin man whose clothes hung loosely on the angles of his round-shouldered, bony form. His long, thin legs, about which the baggy trousers draped in ungraceful folds, were slightly knock-kneed and terminated in large, flat feet. His arms were very long even for such a tall man, and the huge, boney hands were gnarled and knotted. When he removed his bowler hat, as he frequently did to wipe away with a red hand-kerchief the sweat occasioned by furious bicycle riding, it was seen that his forehead was high, flat and narrow. His nose was a large, fleshy, hawklike beak, and from the side of each nostril a deep indentation extended downwards until it disappeared in the drooping moustache that concealed his mouth, the vast extent of which was perceived only when he opened it to bellow at the workmen his exhortations to greater exertions. His chin was large and extraordinarily long. The eyes were pale blue, very small and close together, surmounted by spare, light-coloured, almost invisible eyebrows, with a deep vertical cleft between them over the nose. His head, covered with thick, coarse brown hair, was very large at the back, the ears were small and laid close to the head. If one were to make a full-face drawing of his cadaverous visage it would be found that the outline resembled that of the lid of a coffin.

This man had been with Rushton – no one had ever seen the 'Co.' – for fifteen years, in fact almost from the time when the latter commenced business. Rushton had at that period realised the necessity of having a deputy who could be used to do all the drudgery and running about so that he himself might be free to attend to the more pleasant or more profitable matters. Hunter was then a journeyman, but was on the point of starting on his own account, when Rushton offered him a constant job as foreman, two pounds a week, and two and a half per cent. of the profits of all work done. On the face of it this appeared a generous offer. Hunter closed with it, gave up the idea of starting for himself, and threw himself heart and mind into the business. When an estimate was to be prepared it was Hunter who measured up the work and laboriously figured out the probable cost. When their tenders were accepted it was he who super-intended the work and schemed how to scamp it, where possible, using mud where mortar was specified, mortar where there ought to have been cement, sheet zinc where they were supposed to put sheet lead, boiled oil instead of varnish, and three coats of paint where five were paid for. In fact, scamping the work was with this man a kind of mania. It grieved him to see anything done properly. Even when it was more economical to do a thing well, he insisted from force of habit on having it scamped. Then he was almost happy, because he felt that he was doing someone down. If there were an architect superintending the work, Misery would square him or bluff him. If it were not possible to do either, at least he had a try; and in the intervals of watching, driving and bullying the hands, his vulture eye was ever on the look out for fresh jobs. His long red nose was thrust into every estate agent's office in the town in the endeavour to smell out what properties had recently changed hands or been let, in order that he might interview the new owners and secure the order for whatever alterations or repairs might be required. He it was who entered into unholy compacts with numerous charwomen and nurses of the sick, who in return for a small commission would let him know when some poor sufferer was passing away and would recommend Rushton & Co. to the bereaved and distracted relatives. By these means often – after first carefully enquiring into the financial position of the stricken family – Misery would contrive to wriggle his unsavoury carcase into the house of sorrow, seeking, even in the chamber of death, to further the interests of Rushton & Co. and to earn his miserable two and a half per cent.

It was to make possible the attainment of this object that Misery slaved and drove and schemed and cheated. It was for this that the workers' wages were cut down to the lowest possible point and their offspring went ill clad, ill shod and ill fed, and were driven forth to labour while they were yet children, because their fathers were unable to earn enough to support their homes.

Fifteen years!

Hunter realised now that Rushton had had considerably the best of the bargain. In the first place, it will be seen that the latter had bought over one who might have proved a dangerous competitor, and now, after fifteen years, the business that had been so laboriously built up, mainly by Hunter's energy, industry and unscrupulous cunning, belonged to Rushton & Co. Hunter was but an employee, liable to dismissal like any other workman, the only difference being that he was entitled to a week's notice instead of an hour's notice, and was but little better off financially than when he started for the firm.

Fifteen years!

Hunter knew now that he had been used, but he also knew that it was too late to turn back. He had not saved enough to make a successful start on his own account even if he had felt mentally and physically capable of beginning all over again, and if Rushton were to discharge him now he was too old to get a job as a journeyman. Further, in his zeal for Rushton & Co. and his anxiety to earn his commission, he had often done things that had roused the animosity of rival firms to such an extent that it was highly improbable that any of them would employ him, and even if they would, Misery's heart failed him at the thought of having to meet on an equal footing those workmen whom he had tyrannised over and oppressed. It was for these reasons that Hunter was as terrified of Rushton as the hands were of himself.

Over the men stood Misery, ever threatening them with dismissal and their wives and children with hunger. Behind Misery was Rushton, ever bullying and goading him on to greater excesses and efforts for the furtherance of the good cause – which was to enable the head of the firm to accumulate money.

Mr. Hunter, at the moment when the reader first makes his

acquaintance on the afternoon of the day when the incidents recorded in the first chapter took place, was executing a kind of strategical movement in the direction of the house where Crass and his mates were working. He kept to one side of the road because by so doing he could not be perceived by those within the house until the instant of his arrival. When he was within about a hundred yards of the gate he dismounted from his bicycle, there being a sharp rise in the road just there, and as he toiled up, pushing the bicycle in front, his breath showing in white clouds in the frosty air, he observed a number of men hanging about. Some of them he knew; they had worked for him at various times, but were now out of a job. There were five men altogether; three of them were standing in a group, the other two stood each by himself, being apparently strangers to each other and the first three. The three men who stood together were nearest to Hunter and as the latter approached, one of them advanced to meet him.

'Good morning, sir.'

Hunter replied by an inarticulate grunt, without stopping; the man followed.

'Any chance of a job, sir?'

'Full up,' replied Hunter, still without stopping. The man still followed, like a beggar soliciting charity.

'Be any use calling round in a day or so, sir?'

'Don't think so,' Hunter replied. 'Can if you like; but we're full up.'

'Thank you, sir,' said the man, and turned back to his friends.

By this time Hunter was within a few yards of one of the other two men, who also came to speak to him. This man felt there was no hope of getting a job; still, there was no harm in asking. Besides, he was getting desperate. It was over a month now since he had finished up for his last employer. It had been a very slow summer altogether. Sometimes a fortnight for one firm; then perhaps a week doing nothing; then three weeks or a month for another firm, then out again, and so on. And now it was November. Last winter they had got into debt; that was nothing unusual, but owing to the bad summer they had not been able, as in other years, to pay off the debts accumulated in winter. It was doubtful, too, whether they would be able to get credit again this winter. In fact this morning when his wife sent their little girl to the grocer's for some butter the latter had refused to let the child have it without the money. So although he felt it to be hopeless he accosted Hunter.

This time Hunter stopped: he was winded by his climb up the hill.

'Good morning, sir.'

Hunter did not return the salutation; he had not the breath to spare, but the man was not hurt; he was used to being treated like that.

'Any chance of a job, sir?'

Hunter did not reply at once. He was short of breath and he was thinking of a plan that was ever recurring to his mind, and which he had lately been hankering to put into execution. It seemed to him that the long waited for opportunity had come. Just now Rushton & Co. were almost the only firm in Mugsborough who had any work. There were dozens of good workmen out. Yes, this was the time. If this man agreed he would give him a start. Hunter knew the man was a good workman, he had worked for Rushton & Co. before. To make room for him old Linden and some other full-price man could be got rid of; it would not be difficult to find some excuse.

'Well,' Hunter said at last in a doubtful, hesitating kind of way, 'I'm afraid not, Newman. We're about full up.'

He ceased speaking and remained waiting for the other to say something more. He did not look at the man, but stooped down, fidgeting with the mechanism of the bicycle as if adjusting it.

'Things have been so bad this summer,' Newman went on. 'I've had rather a rough time of it. I would be very glad of a job even if it was only for a week or so.'

There was a pause. After a while, Hunter raised his eyes to the other's face, but immediately let them fall again.

'Well,' said he, 'I might – perhaps – be able to let you have a day or two. You can come here to this job,' and he nodded his head in the direction of the house where the men were working. 'Tomorrow at seven. Of course you know the figure?' he added as Newman was about to thank him. 'Six and a half.'

Hunter spoke as if the reduction were already an accomplished fact. The man was more likely to agree, if he thought that others were already working at the reduced rate.

Newman was taken by surprise and hesitated. He had never worked under price; indeed, he had sometimes gone hungry rather than do so; but now it seemed that others were doing it. And then he was so awfully hard up. If he refused this job he was not likely to get another in a hurry. He thought of his home and his family. Already they owed five weeks' rent, and last Monday the collector had hinted pretty plainly that the landlord would not wait much longer. Not only that, but if he did not get a job how were they to live? This morning he himself had had no breakfast to speak of, only a cup of tea and some dry bread. These thoughts crowded upon each other in his mind, but still he hesitated. Hunter began to move off.

'Well,' he said, 'if you like to start you can come here at seven in the morning.' Then as Newman still hesitated he added impatiently, 'Are you coming or not?'

'Yes, sir,' said Newman.

'All right,' said Hunter, affably. 'I'll tell Crass to have a kit ready for you.'

He nodded in a friendly way to the man, who went off feeling like a criminal.

As Hunter resumed his march, well satisfied with himself, the fifth man, who had been waiting all this time, came to meet him. As he approached, Hunter recognised him as one who had started work for Rushton & Co. early in the summer, but who had left suddenly of his own accord, having taken offence at some bullying remark of Hunter's.

Hunter was glad to see this man. He guessed that the fellow must be very hard pressed to come again and ask for work after what had happened.

'Any chance of a job, sir?'

Hunter appeared to reflect.

'I believe I have room for one,' he said at length. 'But you're such an uncertain kind of chap. You don't seem to care much whether you work or not. You're too independent, you know; one can't say two words to you but you must needs clear off.'

The man made no answer.

'We can't tolerate that kind of thing, you know,' Hunter added. 'If we were to encourage men of your stamp we should never know where we are.'

So saying, Hunter moved away and again proceeded on his journey.

When he arrived within about three yards of the gate he noise-lessly laid his machine against the garden fence. The high evergreens that grew inside still concealed him from the observation of anyone who might be looking out of the windows of the house. Then he carefully crept along till he came to the gate post, and bending down, he cautiously peeped round to see if he could detect anyone idling, or talking, or smoking. There was no one in sight except old Jack Linden, who was rubbing down the lobby doors with pumice-stone and water. Hunter noiselessly opened the gate and crept quietly along the grass border of the garden path. His idea was to reach the front door without being seen, so that Linden could not give notice of his approach to those within. In this he succeeded and passed silently into the house. He did not speak to Linden; to do so would have proclaimed his presence to the rest. He crawled stealthily over the house but was disappointed in his quest, for everyone he saw was hard at work. Upstairs he noticed that the door of one of the rooms was closed.

Old Joe Philpot had been working in this room all day, washing off the old whitewash from the ceiling and removing the old papers from the walls with a broad bladed, square topped knife called a stripper. Although it was only a small room, Joe had had to tear into the work pretty hard all the time, for the ceiling seemed to have had two or three coats of white-wash without ever having been washed off, and there were several thicknesses of paper on the walls. The difficulty of removing these papers was increased by the fact that there was a dado which had been varnished. In order to get this off it had been necessary to soak it several times with strong soda water,[11] and although Joe was as careful as possible he had not been able to avoid getting some of this stuff on his fingers. The result was that his nails were all burnt and discoloured and the flesh round them cracked and bleeding. However, he had got it all off at last, and he was not sorry, for his right arm and shoulder were aching from the prolonged strain and in the palm of the right hand there was a blister as large as a shilling, caused by the handle of the stripping knife.

All the old paper being off, Joe washed down the walls with water, and having swept the paper into a heap in the middle of the floor, he mixed with a small trowel some cement on a small board and proceeded to stop up the cracks and holes in the walls and ceiling. After a while, feeling very tired, it occurred to him that he deserved a spell and a smoke for five minutes. He closed the door and placed a pair of steps against it. There were two windows in the room almost opposite each other; these he opened wide in order that the smoke and smell of his pipe might be carried away. Having taken these precautions against surprise, he ascended to the top of the step ladder that he had laid against the door and sat down at ease. Within easy reach was the top of a cupboard where he had concealed a pint of beer in a bottle. To this he now applied himself. Having taken a long pull at the bottle, he tenderly replaced it on the top of the cupboard and proceeded to 'hinjoy' a quiet smoke, remarking to himself:

'This is where we get some of our own back.'

He held, however, his trowel in one hand, ready for immediate action in case of interruption.

Philpot was about fifty-five years old. He wore no white jacket, only an old patched apron; his trousers were old, very soiled with paint and ragged at the bottoms of the legs where they fell over the much-patched, broken and down-at-heel boots. The part of his waistcoat not protected by his apron was covered with spots of dried paint. He wore a coloured shirt and a 'dickey' which was very soiled and covered with splashes of paint, and one side of it was projecting from the opening of the waistcoat. His head was covered with an old cap, heavy and shining with paint. He was very thin and stooped slightly. Although he was really only fifty-five, he looked much older, for he was prematurely aged.

He had not been getting his own back for quite five minutes when Hunter softly turned the handle of the lock. Philpot immediately put out his pipe and descending from his perch opened the door. When Hunter entered Philpot closed it again and, mounting the steps, went on stopping the wall just above. Nimrod looked at him suspiciously, wondering why the door had been closed. He looked all round the room but could see nothing to complain of. He snuffed the air to try if he could detect the odour of tobacco, and if he had not been suffering from a cold in the head there is no doubt that he would have perceived it. However, as it was he could smell nothing, but all the same he was not quite satisfied, although he remembered that Crass always gave Philpot a good character.

'I don't like to have men working on a job like this with the door shut,' he said at length. 'It always gives me the idear that the man's 'avin a mike. You can do what you're doin' just as well with the door open.'

Philpot, muttering something about it being all the same to him – shut or open – got down from the steps and opened the door. Hunter went out again without making any further remark and once more began crawling over the house.

Owen was working by himself in a room on the same floor as Philpot. He was at the window, burning off with a paraffin torch-lamp those parts of the old paintwork that were blistered or cracked.

In this work the flame of the lamp is directed against the old paint, which becomes soft and is removed with a chisel knife, or a scraper called a shavehook. The door was ajar and he had opened the top sash of the window for the purpose of letting in some fresh air, because the atmosphere of the room was foul with the fumes of the lamp and the smell of the burning paint, besides being heavy with moisture. The ceiling had only just been water washed and the walls had just been stripped. The old paper, saturated with water, was piled up in a heap in the middle of the floor.

Presently, as he was working he began to feel conscious of some other presence in the room; he looked round. The door was open about six inches and in the opening appeared a long, pale face with a huge chin, surmounted by a bowler hat and ornamented with a large red nose, a drooping moustache and two small, glittering eyes set very close together. For some seconds this apparition regarded Owen intently, then it was silently withdrawn, and he was again alone. He had been so surprised and startled that he had nearly dropped the lamp, and now that the ghastly countenance was gone, Owen felt the blood surge into his own cheeks. He trembled with suppressed fury and longed to be able to go out there on the landing and hurl the lamp into Hunter's face.

Meanwhile, on the landing outside Owen's door, Hunter stood thinking. Someone must be got rid of to make room for the cheap man tomorrow. He had hoped to catch somebody doing something that would have served as an excuse for instant dismissal, but there was now no hope of that happening. What was to be done? He would like to get rid of Linden, who was now really too old to be of much use, but as the old man had worked for Rushton on and off for many years, Hunter felt that he could scarcely sack him off-hand without some reasonable pretext. Still, the fellow was really not worth the money he was getting. Sevenpence an hour was an absurdly large wage for an old man like him. It was preposterous: he would have to go, excuse or no excuse.

Hunter crawled downstairs again.

Jack Linden was about sixty-seven years old, but like Philpot, and as is usual with working men, he appeared older, because he had had to work very hard all his life, frequently without proper food and clothing. His life had been passed in the midst of a civilisation which he had never been permitted to enjoy the benefits of. But of course he knew nothing about all this. He had never expected or wished to be allowed to enjoy such things; he had always been of opinion that they were never intended for the likes of him. He called himself a Conservative and was very patriotic.

At the time when the Boer War commenced, Linden was an enthusiastic jingo:[12] his enthusiasm had been somewhat damped when his youngest son, a reservist, had to go to the front, where he died of fever and exposure. When this soldier son went away, he left his wife and two children, aged respectively four and five years at that time, in his father's care. After he died they stayed on with the old people. The young woman earned a little occasionally by doing needlework, but was really dependent on her father-in-law. Notwithstanding his poverty, he was glad to have them in the house, because of late years his wife had been getting very feeble, and, since the shock occasioned by the news of the death of her son, needed someone constantly with her.

Linden was still working at the vestibule doors when the manager came downstairs. Misery stood watching him for some minutes without speaking. At last he said loudly:

'How much longer are you going to be messing about those doors? Why don't you get them under colour? You were fooling about there when I was here this morning. Do you think it'll pay to have you playing about there hour after hour with a bit of pumice-stone? Get the work done! Or if you don't want to, I'll very soon find someone else who does! I've been noticing your style of doing things for some time past and I want you to understand that you can't play the fool with me. There's plenty of better men than you walking about. If you can't do more than you've been doing lately you can clear out; we can do without you even when we're busy.'

Old Jack trembled. He tried to answer, but was unable to speak. If he had been a slave and had failed to satisfy his master, the latter might have tied him up somewhere and thrashed him. Hunter could not do that; he could only take his food away. Old Jack was frightened – it was not only *his* food that might be taken away. At last, with a great effort, for the words seemed to stick in his throat, he said:

'I must clean the work down, sir, before I go on painting.'

'I'm not talking about what you're doing, but the time it takes you to do it!' shouted Hunter. 'And I don't want any back answers or argument about it. You just move yourself a bit quicker or leave it alone altogether.'

Linden did not answer: he went on with his work, his hand trembling to such an extent that he was scarcely able to hold the pumice stone.

Hunter shouted so loud that his voice filled all the house. Everyone heard and was afraid. Who would be the next? they thought.

Finding that Linden made no further answer, Misery again began walking about the house.

As he looked at them the men did their work in a nervous, clumsy, hasty sort of way. They made all sorts of mistakes and messes. Payne, the foreman carpenter, was putting some new boards in a part of the drawing-room floor: he was in such a state of panic that, while driving a nail, he accidentally struck the thumb of his left hand a severe blow with his hammer. Bundy was also working in the drawing-room putting some white-glazed tiles in the fireplace. Whilst cutting one of these in half in order to fit it into its place, he inflicted a deep gash on one of his fingers. He was afraid to leave off to bind it up while Hunter was there, and consequently as he worked the white tiles became all smeared and spattered with blood. Easton, who was working with Harlow on a plank, washing off the old distemper from the hall ceiling, was so upset that he was scarcely able to stand on the plank, and presently the brush fell from his trembling hand with a crash upon the floor.

Everyone was afraid. They knew that it was almost impossible to get a job for any other firm. They knew that this man had the power to deprive them of the means of earning a living; that he possessed the power to deprive their children of bread.

Owen, listening to Hunter over the banisters upstairs, felt that he would like to take him by the throat with one hand and smash his face in with the other.

And then?

Why then he would be sent to gaol, or at the best he would lose his employment: his food and that of his family would be taken away. That was why he only ground his teeth and cursed and beat the wall with his clenched fist. So! and so! and so!

If it were not for them!

Owen's imagination ran riot.

First he would seize him by the collar with his left hand, dig his knuckles into his throat, force him up against the wall and then, with his right fist, smash! smash! smash! until Hunter's face was all cut and covered with blood.

But then, what about those at home? Was it not braver and more manly to endure in silence?

Owen leaned against the wall, white-faced, panting and exhausted.

Downstairs, Misery was still going to and fro in the house and walking up and down in it. Presently he stopped to look at Sawkins' work. This man was painting the woodwork of the back staircase. Although the old paintwork here was very dirty and greasy, Misery had given orders that it was not to be [[cleaned before being painted.]]

[['Just dust it down and slobber the colour on,']] he had said. Consequently, when Crass made the paint, he had put into it an extra large quantity of dryers. To a certain extent this destroyed the 'body' of the colour: it did not cover well; it would require two coats. When Hunter perceived this he was furious. He was sure it could be made to do with one coat with a little care; he believed Sawkins was doing it like this on purpose. Really, these men seemed to have no conscience.

Two coats! and he had estimated for only three.

'Crass!'

'Yes, sir.'

'Come here!'

'Yes, sir.'

Crass came hurrying along.

'What's the meaning of this? Didn't I tell you to make this do with one coat? Look at it!'

'It's like this, sir,' said Crass. 'If it had been washed down – '

'Washed down be damned,' shouted Hunter. 'The reason is that the colour ain't thick enough. Take the paint and put a little more body in it and we'll soon see whether it can be done or not. I can make it cover if you can't.'

Crass took the paint, and, superintended by Hunter, made it thicker. Misery then seized the brush and prepared to demonstrate the possibility of finishing the work with one coat. Crass and Sawkins looked on in silence.

Just as Misery was about to commence he fancied he heard someone whispering somewhere. He laid down the brush and crawled stealthily upstairs to see who it was. Directly his back was turned Crass seized a bottle of oil that was standing near and, tipping about half a pint of it into the paint, stirred it up quickly. Misery returned almost immediately: he had not caught anyone; it must have been fancy. He took up the brush and began to paint. The result was worse than Sawkins!

He messed and fooled about for some time, but could not make it come right. At last he gave it up.

'I suppose it'll have to have two coats after all,' he said, mournfully. 'But it's a thousand pities.'

He almost wept.

The firm would be ruined if things went on like this.

'You'd better go on with it,' he said as he laid down the brush.

He began to walk about the house again. He wanted to go away now, but he did not want them to know that he was gone, so he sneaked out of the back door, crept round the house and out of the gate, mounted his bicycle and rode away.

No one saw him go.

For some time the only sounds that broke the silence were the noises made by the hands as they worked. The musical ringing of Bundy's trowel, the noise of the carpenters' hammers and saws and the occasional moving of a pair of steps.

No one dared to speak.

At last Philpot could stand it no longer. He was very thirsty.

He had kept the door of his room open since Hunter arrived.

He listened intently. He felt certain that Hunter must be gone: he looked across the landing and could see Owen working in the front room. Philpot made a little ball of paper and threw it at him to attract his attention. Owen looked round and Philpot began to make signals: he pointed downwards with one hand and jerked the thumb of the other over his shoulder in the direction of the town, winking grotesquely the while. This Owen interpreted to be an inquiry as to whether Hunter had departed. He shook his head and shrugged his shoulders to intimate that he did not know.

Philpot cautiously crossed the landing and peeped furtively over the banisters, listening breathlessly. 'Was it gorn or not?' he wondered.

He crept along on tiptoe towards Owen's room, glancing left and right, the trowel in his hand, and looking like a stage murderer. 'Do you think it's gorn?' he asked in a hoarse whisper when he reached Owen's door.

'I don't know,' replied Owen in a low tone.

Philpot wondered. He *must* have a drink, but it would never do for Hunter to see him with the bottle: he must find out somehow whether he was gone or not.

At last an idea came. He would go downstairs to get some more cement. Having confided this plan to Owen, he crept quietly back to the room in which he had been working, then he walked noisily across the landing again.

'Got a bit of stopping to spare, Frank?' he asked in a loud voice.

'No,' replied Owen. 'I'm not using it.'

'Then I suppose I'll have to go down and get some. Is there anything I can bring up for you?'

'No, thanks,' replied Owen.

Philpot marched boldly down to the scullery, which Crass had utilised as a paint-shop. Crass was there mixing some colour.

'I want a bit of stopping,' Philpot said as he helped himself to some.

'Is the b—r gorn?' whispered Crass.

'I don't know,' replied Philpot. 'Where's his bike?'

' 'E always leaves it outside the gate, so's we can't see it,' replied Crass.

'Tell you what,' whispered Philpot, after a pause, 'Give the boy a hempty bottle and let 'im go to the gate and look if the bike's there. If Misery sees him 'e can pretend to be goin' to the shop for some hoil.'

This was done. Bert went to the gate and returned immediately: the bike was gone. As the good news spread through the house a chorus of thanksgiving burst forth.

'Thank Gord!' said one.

'Hope the b—r falls orf and breaks 'is bloody neck,' said another.

'These Bible-thumpers are all the same; no one ever knew one to be any good yet,' cried a third.

Directly they knew for certain that he was gone, nearly everyone left off work for a few minutes to curse him. Then they again went on working and now that they were relieved of the embarrassment that Misery's presence inspired, they made better progress. A few of them lit their pipes and smoked as they worked.

One of these was old Jack Linden. He was upset by the bullying he had received, and when he noticed some of the others smoking he thought he would have a pipe; it might steady his nerves. As a rule he did not smoke when working; it was contrary to orders.

As Philpot was returning to work again he paused for a moment to whisper to Linden, with the result that the latter accompanied him upstairs.

On reaching Philpot's room the latter placed the step-ladder near the cupboard and, taking down the bottle of beer, handed it to Linden with the remark, 'Get some of that acrost yer, matey; it'll put yer right.'

While Linden was taking a hasty drink, Joe kept watch on the landing outside in case Hunter should suddenly and unexpectedly reappear.

When Linden was gone downstairs again, Philpot, having finished what remained of the beer and hidden the bottle up the chimney, resumed the work of stopping up the holes and cracks in the ceiling and walls. He must make a bit of a show tonight or there would be a hell of a row when Misery came in the morning.

Owen worked on in a disheartened, sullen way. He felt like a beaten dog.

He was more indignant on poor old Linden's account than on his own, and was oppressed by a sense of impotence and shameful degradation.

All his life it had been the same: incessant work under similar more or less humiliating conditions, and with no more result than being just able to avoid starvation.

And the future, as far as he could see, was as hopeless as the past; darker, for there would surely come a time, if he lived long enough, when he would be unable to work any more.

He thought of his child. Was he to be a slave and a drudge all his life also?

It would be better for the boy to die now.

As Owen thought of his child's future there sprung up within him a feeling of hatred and fury against the majority of his fellow workmen.

They were the enemy. Those who not only quietly submitted like so many cattle to the existing state of things, but defended it, and opposed and ridiculed any suggestion to alter it.

They were the real oppressors – the men who spoke of themselves as 'The likes of us,' who, having lived in poverty and degradation all their lives considered that what had been good enough for them was good enough for the children they had been the cause of bringing into existence.

He hated and despised them because they calmly saw their children condemned to hard labour and poverty for life, and deliberately refused to make any effort to secure for them better conditions than those they had themselves.

It was because they were indifferent to the fate of *their* children that he would be unable to secure a natural and human life for *his*. It was their apathy or active opposition that made it impossible to establish a better system of society under which those who did their fair share of the world's work would be honoured and rewarded. Instead of helping to do this, they abased themselves, and grovelled before their oppressors, and compelled and taught their children to do the same. *They* were the people who were really responsible for the continuance of the present system.

Owen laughed bitterly to himself. What a very comical system it was.

Those who worked were looked upon with contempt, and subjected to every possible indignity. Nearly everything they produced was taken away from them and enjoyed by the people who did nothing. And then the workers bowed down and grovelled before those who had robbed them of the fruits of their labour and were childishly grateful to them for leaving anything at all.

No wonder the rich despised them and looked upon them as dirt. They *were* despicable. They *were* dirt. They admitted it and gloried in it.

While these thoughts were seething in Owen's mind, his fellow workmen were still patiently toiling on downstairs. Most of them had by this time dismissed Hunter from their thoughts. They did not take things so seriously as Owen. They flattered themselves that they had more sense than that. It could not be altered. Grin and bear it. After all, it was only for life! Make the best of things, and get your own back whenever you get a chance.

Presently Harlow began to sing. He had a good voice and it was a good song, but his mates just then did not appreciate either one or the other. His singing was the signal for an outburst of exclamations and catcalls.

'Shut it, for Christ's sake!'

'That's enough of that bloody row!'

And so on. Harlow stopped.

'How's the enemy?' asked Easton presently, addressing no one in particular.

'Don't know,' replied Bundy. 'It must be about half past four. Ask Slyme; he's got a watch.'

It was a quarter past four.

'It gets dark very early now,' said Easton.

'Yes,' replied Bundy. 'It's been very dull all day. I think it's goin' to rain. Listen to the wind.'

'I 'ope not,' replied Easton. 'That means a wet shirt goin' 'ome.'

He called out to old Jack Linden, who was still working at the front doors:

'Is it raining, Jack?'

Old Jack, his pipe still in his mouth, turned to look at the weather. It was raining, but Linden did not see the large drops which splashed heavily upon the ground. He saw only Hunter, who was standing at the gate, watching him. For a few seconds the two men looked at each other in silence. Linden was paralysed with fear. Recovering himself, he hastily removed his pipe, but it was too late.

Misery strode up.

'I don't pay you for smoking,' he said, loudly. 'Make out your time sheet, take it to the office and get your money. I've had enough of you!'

Jack made no attempt to defend himself: he knew it was of no use. He silently put aside the things he had been using, went into the room where he had left his tool-bag and coat, removed his apron and white jacket, folded them up and put them into his tool-bag along with the tools he had been using – a chisel-knife and a shavehook – put on his coat, and, with the tool-bag slung over his shoulder, went away from the house.

Without speaking to anyone else, Hunter then hastily walked over the place, noting what progress had been made by each man during his absence. He then rode away, as he wanted to get to the office in time to give Linden his money.

It was now very cold and dark within the house, and as the gas was not yet laid on, Crass distributed a number of candles to the men, who worked silently, each occupied with his own gloomy thoughts. Who would be the next?

Outside, sombre masses of lead-coloured clouds gathered ominously in the tempestuous sky. The gale roared loudly round the old-fashioned house and the windows rattled discordantly. Rain fell in torrents.

They said it meant getting wet through going home, but all the same, Thank God it was nearly five o'clock!

CHAPTER 3

The Financiers

That night as Easton walked home through the rain he felt very depressed. It had been a very bad summer for most people and he had not fared better than the rest. A few weeks with one firm, a few days with another, then out of a job, then on again for a month perhaps, and so on.

William Easton was a man of medium height, about twenty-three years old, with fair hair and moustache and blue eyes. He wore a stand-up collar with a coloured tie and his clothes, though shabby, were clean and neat.

He was married: his wife was a young woman whose acquaintance he had made when he happened to be employed with others painting the outside of the house where she was a general servant. They had 'walked out' for about fifteen months. Easton had been in no hurry to marry, for he knew that, taking good times with bad, his wages did not average a pound a week. At the end of that time, however, he found that he could not honourably delay longer, so they were married.

That was twelve months ago.

As a single man he had never troubled much if he happened to be out of work; he always had enough to live on and pocket money besides, but now that he was married it was different; the fear of being 'out' haunted him all the time.

He had started for Rushton & Co. on the previous Monday after having been idle for three weeks, and as the house where he was working had to be done right through he had congratulated himself on having secured a job that would last till Christmas; but he now began to fear that what had befallen Jack Linden might also happen to himself at any time. He would have to be very careful not to offend Crass in any way. He was afraid the latter did not like him very much as it was. Easton knew that Crass could get him the sack at any time and would not scruple to do so if he wanted to make room for some crony of his own. Crass was the 'coddy' or foreman of the job. Considered as a workman he had no very unusual abilities; he was if anything inferior to the majority of his fellow workmen. But although he had but little real ability he pretended to know everything, and the vague references he was in the habit of making to 'tones', and 'shades', and 'harmony', had so impressed Hunter that the latter had a high opinion of him as a workman. It was by pushing himself forward in this way and by judicious toadying to Hunter that Crass managed to get himself put in charge of work.

Although Crass did as little work as possible himself he took care that the others worked hard. Any man who failed to satisfy him in this respect he reported to Hunter as being 'no good', or 'too slow for a funeral'. The result was that that man was dispensed with at the end of the week. The men knew this, and most of them feared the wily Crass accordingly, though there were a few whose known abilities placed them to a certain extent above the reach of his malice. Frank Owen was one of these.

There were others who by the judicious administration of pipefuls of tobacco and pints of beer, managed to keep in Crass's good graces and often retained their employment when better workmen were 'stood off'.

As he walked home through the rain thinking of these things, Easton realised that it was not possible to foresee what a day or even an hour might bring forth.

By this time he had arrived at his home; it was a small house, one of a long row of similar ones, and it contained altogether four rooms.

The front door opened into a passage about two feet six inches wide and ten feet in length, covered with oilcloth. At the end of the passage was a flight of stairs leading to the upper part of the house. The first door on the left led into the front sitting-room, an apartment about nine feet square, with a bay window. This room was very rarely used and was always very tidy and clean. The mantelpiece was of wood painted black and ornamented with jagged streaks of red and yellow, which were supposed to give it the appearance of marble. On the walls was a paper with a pale terra-cotta ground and a pattern consisting of large white roses with chocolate-coloured leaves and stalks.

There was a small iron fender with fire-irons to match, and on the mantelshelf stood a clock in a polished wood case, a pair of blue glass vases, and some photographs in frames. The floor was covered with oilcloth of a tile pattern in yellow and red. On the walls were two or three framed coloured prints such as are presented with Christmas numbers of illustrated papers. There was also a photograph of a group of Sunday School girls with their teachers, with the church for the background. In the centre of the room was a round deal table about three feet six inches across, with the legs stained red to look like mahogany. Against one wall was an old couch covered with faded cretonne, four chairs to match standing backs to wall in different parts of the room. The table was covered with a red cloth with a yellow crewel[13] work design in the centre and in each of the four corners, the edges being overcast[14] in the same material. On the table were a lamp and a number of brightly bound books.

Some of these things, as the couch and the chairs, Easton had bought second-hand and had done up himself. The table, oil-cloth, fender, hearthrug, etc., had been obtained on the hire system and were not yet paid for. The windows were draped with white lace curtains, and in the bay was a small bamboo table on which reposed a large Holy Bible, cheaply but showily bound.

If anyone had ever opened this book they would have found that its pages were as clean as the other things in the room, and on the flyleaf might have been read the following inscription: 'To dear Ruth, from her loving friend Mrs. Starvem with the prayer that

God's word may be her guide and that Jesus may be her very own Saviour. Oct. 12. 19—'

Mrs. Starvem was Ruth's former mistress, and this had been her parting gift when Ruth left to get married. It was supposed to be a keepsake, but as Ruth never opened the book and never willingly allowed her thoughts to dwell upon the scenes of which it reminded her, she had forgotten the existence of Mrs. Starvem almost as completely as that well-to-do and pious lady had forgotten hers.

For Ruth, the memory of the time she spent in the house of 'her loving friend' was the reverse of pleasant. It comprised a series of recollections of petty tyrannies, insults and indignities. Six years of cruelly excessive work, beginning every morning two or three hours before the rest of the household were awake and ceasing only when she went exhausted to bed, late at night.

She had been what is called a 'slavey', but if she had been really a slave her owner would have had some regard for her health and welfare: her 'loving friend' had had none. Mrs. Starvem's only thought had been to get out of Ruth the greatest possible amount of labour and to give her as little as possible in return.

When Ruth looked back upon that dreadful time she saw it, as one might say, surrounded by a halo of religion. She never passed by a chapel or heard the name of God, or the singing of a hymn, without thinking of her former mistress. To have looked into this Bible would have reminded her of Mrs. Starvem; that was one of the reasons why the book reposed, unopened and unread, a mere ornament on the table in the bay window.

The second door in the passage near the foot of the stairs led into the kitchen or living-room: from here another door led into the scullery. Upstairs were two bedrooms.

As Easton entered the house, his wife met him in the passage and asked him not to make a noise as the child had just gone to sleep. They kissed each other and she helped him to remove his wet overcoat. Then they both went softly into the kitchen.

This room was about the same size as the sitting-room. At one end was a small range with an oven and a boiler, [and] a high mantelpiece painted black. On the mantelshelf was a small round alarm clock and some brightly polished tin canisters. At the other end of the room, facing the fireplace, was a small dresser on the shelves of which were neatly arranged a number of plates and dishes. The walls were papered with oak paper.[15] On one wall, between two coloured almanacks, hung a tin lamp with a reflector behind the light. In the middle of the room was an oblong deal table with a white tablecloth upon which the tea things were set ready. There were four kitchen chairs, two of which were placed close to the table. Overhead, across the room, about eighteen inches down from the ceiling, were stretched several cords upon which were drying a number of linen or calico undergarments, a coloured shirt, and Easton's white apron and jacket. On the back of a chair at one side of the fire more clothes were drying. At the other side on the floor was a wicker cradle in which a baby was sleeping. Nearby stood a chair with a towel hung on the back, arranged so as to shade the infant's face from the light of the lamp. An air of homely comfort pervaded the room; the atmosphere was warm, and the fire blazed cheerfully over the whitened hearth.

They walked softly over and stood by the cradle side looking at the child; as they looked the baby kept moving uneasily in its sleep. Its face was very flushed and its eyes were moving under the half-closed lids. Every now and again its lips were drawn back slightly, showing part of the gums; presently it began to whimper, drawing up its knees as if in pain.

'He seems to have something wrong with him,' said Easton.

'I think it's his teeth,' replied the mother. 'He's been very restless all day and he was awake nearly all last night.'

'P'r'aps he's hungry.'

'No, it can't be that. He had the best part of an egg this morning and I've nursed him several times today. And then at dinner-time he had a whole saucer full of fried potatoes with little bits of bacon in it.'

Again the infant whimpered and twisted in its sleep, its lips drawn back showing the gums: its knees pressed closely to its body, the little fists clenched, and face flushed. Then after a few seconds it became placid: the mouth resumed its usual shape; the limbs relaxed and the child slumbered peacefully.

'Don't you think he's getting thin?' asked Easton. 'It may be fancy, but he don't seem to me to be as big now as he was three months ago.'

'No, he's not quite so fat,' admitted Ruth. 'It's his teeth what's wearing him out; he don't hardly get no rest at all with them.'

They continued looking at him a little longer. Ruth thought he was a very beautiful child: he would be eight months old on Sunday. They were sorry they could do nothing to ease his pain, but consoled themselves with the reflection that he would be all right once those teeth were through.

'Well, let's have some tea,' said Easton at last.

Whilst he removed his wet boots and socks and placed them in front of the fire to dry and put on dry socks and a pair of slippers in their stead, Ruth half filled a tin basin with hot water from the boiler and gave it to him, and he then went into the scullery, added some cold water and began to wash the paint off his hands. This done he returned to the kitchen and sat down at the table.

'I couldn't think what to give you to eat tonight,' said Ruth as she poured out the tea. 'I hadn't got no money left and there wasn't nothing in the house except bread and butter and that piece of cheese, so I cut some bread and butter and put some thin slices of cheese on it and toasted it on a plate in front of the fire. I hope you'll like it: it was the best I could do.'

'That's all right: it smells very nice anyway, and I'm very hungry.'

As they were taking their tea Easton told his wife about Linden's affair and his apprehensions as to what might befall himself. They were both very indignant, and sorry for poor old Linden, but their sympathy for him was soon almost forgotten in their fears for their own immediate future.

They remained at the table in silence for some time: then,

'How much rent do we owe now?' asked Easton.

'Four weeks, and I promised the collector the last time he called that we'd pay two weeks next Monday. He was quite nasty about it.'

'Well, I suppose you'll have to pay it, that's all,' said Easton.

'How much money will you have tomorrow?' asked Ruth.

He began to reckon up his time: he started on Monday and today was Friday; five days, from seven to five, less half an hour for breakfast and an hour for dinner, eight and a half hours a day – forty-two hours and a half. At sevenpence an hour that came to one pound four and ninepence halfpenny.

'You know I only started on Monday,' he said, 'so there's no back day to come. Tomorrow goes into next week.'

'Yes, I know,' replied Ruth.

'If we pay the two week's rent that'll leave us twelve shillings to live on.'

'But we won't be able to keep all that,' said Ruth, 'because there's other things to pay.'

'What other things?'

'We owe the baker eight shillings for the bread he let us have while you were not working, and there's about twelve shillings owing for groceries. We'll have to pay them something on account. Then we want some more coal; there's only about a shovelful left, and – '

'Wait a minit,' said Easton. 'The best way is to write out a list of everything we owe; then we shall know exactly where we are. You get me a piece of paper and tell me what to write. Then we'll see what it all comes to.'

'Do you mean everything we owe, or everything we must pay tomorrow.'

'I think we'd better make a list of all we owe first.'

While they were talking the baby was sleeping restlessly, occasionally uttering plaintive little cries. The mother now went and knelt at the side of the cradle, which she gently rocked with one hand, patting the infant with the other.

'Except the furniture people, the biggest thing we owe is the rent,' she said when Easton was ready to begin.

'It seems to me,' said he, as, after having cleared a space on the table and arranged the paper, he began to sharpen his pencil with a table-knife, 'that you don't manage things as well as you might. If you was to make out a list of just the things you *must* have before you went out of a Saturday, you'd find the money would go much farther. Instead of doing that you just take the money in your hand without knowing exactly what you're going to do with it, and when you come back it's all gone and next to nothing to show for it.'

His wife made no reply: her head was bent down over the child.

'Now, let's see,' went on her husband. 'First of all there's the rent. How much did you say we owe?'

'Four weeks. That's the three weeks you were out and this week.'

'Four sixes is twenty-four; that's one pound four,' said Easton as he wrote it down. 'Next?'

'Grocer, twelve shillings.'

Easton looked up in astonishment.

'Twelve shillings. Why, didn't you tell me only the other day that you'd paid up all we owed for groceries?'

'Don't you remember we owed thirty-five shillings last spring? Well, I've been paying that bit by bit all the summer. I paid the last of it the week you finished your last job. Then you were out three weeks – up till last Saturday – and as we had nothing in hand I had to get what we wanted without paying for it.'

'But do you mean to say it costs us three shillings a week for tea and sugar and butter?'

'It's not only them. There's been bacon and eggs and cheese and other things.'

The man was beginning to become impatient.

'Well,' he said. 'What else?'

'We owe the baker eight shillings. We did owe nearly a pound, but I've been paying it off a little at a time.'

This was added to the list.

'Then there's the milkman. I've not paid him for four weeks. He hasn't sent a bill yet, but you can reckon it up; we have two penn'orth every day.'

'That's four and eight,' said Easton, writing it down. 'Anything else?'

'One and seven to the greengrocer for potatoes, cabbage, and paraffin oil.'

'Anything else?'

'We owe the butcher two and sevenpence.'

'Why, we haven't had any meat for a long time,' said Easton. 'When was it?'

'Three weeks ago; don't you remember? A small leg of mutton.'

'Oh, yes,' and he added the item.

'Then there's the instalments for the furniture and oilcloth – twelve shillings. A letter came from them today. And there's something else.'

She took three letters from the pocket of her dress and handed them to him.

'They all came today. I didn't show them to you before as I didn't want to upset you before you had your tea.'

Easton drew the first letter from its envelope.

CORPORATION OF MUGSBOROUGH
General District and Special Rates

FINAL NOTICE

MR W. EASTON – I have to remind you that the amount due from you as under, in respect of the above Rates, has not been paid, and to request that you will forward the same within Fourteen Days from this date. You are hereby informed that after this notice no further call will be made, or intimation given, before legal proceedings are taken to enforce payment.

By order of the Council.

JAMES LEAH
Collector, No. 2 District.

	£–	13	11
District Rate			
Special Rate		10	2
	£1	4	1

The second communication was dated from the office of the Assistant Overseer of the Poor. It was also a Final Notice and was worded in almost exactly the same way as the other, the principal difference being that it was 'By order of the Overseers' instead of 'the Council'. It demanded the sum of £1 1s. 5½ for Poor Rate within fourteen days, and threatened legal proceedings in default.

Easton laid this down and began to read the third letter –

J. DIDLUM & CO. LTD.

Complete House Furnishers

QUALITY STREET, MUGSBOROUGH

MR W. EASTON,
  SIR:

    We have to remind you that three monthly payments of four shillings each (12/- in all) became due on the first of this month, and we must request you to let us have this amount *by return of post*.

    Under the terms of your agreement you guaranteed that the money should be paid on the Saturday of every fourth week. To prevent unpleasantness, we must request you for the future to forward the full amount punctually upon that day.

    Yours truly,

J. DIDLUM & CO. LTD.

He read these communications several times in silence and finally with an oath threw them down on the table.

'How much do we still owe for the oilcloth and the furniture?' he asked.

'I don't know exactly. It was seven pound odd, and we've had the things about six months. We paid one pound down and three or four instalments. I'll get you the card if you like.'

'No; never mind. Say we've paid one pound twelve; so we still owe about six pound.'

He added this amount to the list.

'I think it's a great pity we ever had the things at all,' he said, peevishly. 'It would have been much better to have gone without until we could pay cash for them: but you would have your way, of course. Now we'll have this bloody debt dragging on us for years, and before the dam stuff is paid for it'll be worn out.'

The woman did not reply at once. She was bending down over the cradle arranging the coverings which the restless movements of the child had disordered. She was crying silently, unnoticed by her husband.

For months past – in fact ever since the child was born – she had been existing without sufficient food. If Easton was unemployed they had to stint themselves so as to avoid getting further into debt than was absolutely necessary. When he was working they had to go short in order to pay what they owed; but of what there was Easton himself, without knowing it, always had the greater share. If he was at work she would pack into his dinner basket overnight the best there was in the house. When he was out of work she often pretended, as she gave him his meals, that she had had hers while he was out. And all this time the baby was draining her life away and her work was never done.

She felt very weak and weary as she crouched there, crying furtively and trying not to let him see.

At last she said, without looking round:

'You know quite well that you were just as much in favour of getting them as I was. If we hadn't got the oilcloth there would have been illness in the house because of the way the wind used to come up between the floorboards. Even now of a windy day the oilcloth moves up and down.'

'Well, I'm sure I don't know,' said Easton, as he looked alternatively at the list of debts and the three letters. 'I give you nearly every farthing I earn and I never interfere about anything, because I think it's your part to attend to the house, but it seems to me you don't manage things properly.'

The woman suddenly burst into a passion of weeping, laying her head on the seat of the chair that was standing near the cradle.

Easton started up in surprise.

'Why, what's the matter?' he said.

Then as he looked down upon the quivering form of the sobbing woman, he was ashamed. He knelt down by her, embracing her and apologising, protesting that he had not meant to hurt her like that.

'I always do the best I can with the money,' Ruth sobbed. 'I never spend a farthing on myself, but you don't seem to understand how hard it is. I don't care nothing about having to go without things myself, but I can't bear it when you speak to me like you do lately. You seem to blame me for everything. You usen't to speak to me like that before I – before – Oh, I am so tired – I am so tired, I wish I could lie down somewhere and sleep and never wake up any more.'

She turned away from him, half kneeling, half sitting on the floor, her arms folded on the seat of the chair, and her head resting upon them. She was crying in a heartbroken helpless way.

'I'm sorry I spoke to you like that,' said Easton, awkwardly. 'I didn't mean what I said. It's all my fault. I leave things too much to you, and it's more than you can be expected to manage. I'll help you to think things out in future; only forgive me, I'm very sorry. I know you try your best.'

She suffered him to draw her to him, laying her head on his shoulder as he kissed and fondled her, protesting that he would rather be poor and hungry with her than share riches with anyone else.

The child in the cradle – who had been twisting and turning restlessly all this time – now began to cry loudly. The mother took it from the cradle and began to hush and soothe it, walking about the room and rocking it in her arms. The child, however, continued to scream, so she sat down to nurse it: for a little while the infant refused to drink, struggling and kicking in its mother's arms, then for a few minutes it was quiet, taking the milk in a half-hearted, fretful way. Then it again began to scream and twist and struggle.

They both looked at it in a helpless manner. Whatever could be the matter with it? It must be those teeth.

Then suddenly as they were soothing and patting him, the child vomited all over its own and its mother's clothing a mass of undigested food. Mingled with the curdled milk were fragments of egg, little bits of bacon, bread and particles of potato.

Having rid his stomach of this unnatural burden, the unfortunate baby began to cry afresh, his face very pale, his lips colourless, and his eyes red-rimmed and running with water.

Easton walked about with him while Ruth cleaned up the mess and got ready some fresh clothing. They both agreed that it was the coming teeth that had upset the poor child's digestion. It would be a good job when they were through.

This work finished, Easton, who was still convinced in his own mind that with the aid of a little common sense and judicious management their affairs might be arranged more satisfactorily, said:

'We may as well make a list of all the things we must pay and buy tomorrow. The great thing is to think out exactly what you are going to do before you spend anything; that saves you from getting things you don't really need and prevents you forgetting the things you *must* have. Now, first of all, the rent; two weeks, twelve shillings.'

He took a fresh piece of paper and wrote this item down.

'What else is there that we must pay or buy tomorrow?'

'Well, you know I promised the baker and the grocer that I would begin to pay them directly you got a job, and if I don't keep my word they won't let us have anything another time, so you'd better put down two shillings each for them.'

'I've got that,' said Easton.

'Two and seven for the butcher. We must pay that. I'm ashamed to pass the shop, because when I got the meat I promised to pay him the next week, and it's nearly three weeks ago now.'

'I've put that down. What else?'

'A hundred of coal: one and six.'

'Next?'

'The instalment for the furniture and floor-cloth, twelve shillings.'

'Next?'

'We owe the milkman four weeks; we'd better pay one week on account; that's one and two.'

'Next?'

'The greengrocer; one shilling on account.'

'Anything else?'

'We shall want a piece of meat of some kind; we've had none for nearly three weeks. You'd better say one and six for that.'

'That's down.'

'One and nine for bread; that's one loaf a day.'

'But I've got two shillings down for bread already,' said Easton.

'Yes, I know, dear, but that's to go towards paying off what we owe, and what you have down for the grocer and milkman's the same.'

'Well, go on, for Christ's sake, and let's get it done,' said Easton, irritably.

'We can't say less than three shillings for groceries.'

Easton looked carefully at his list. This time he felt sure that the item was already down; but finding he was mistaken he said nothing and added the amount.

'Well, I've got that. What else?'

'Milk, one and two.'

'Next?'

'Vegetables, eightpence.'

'Yes.'

'Paraffin oil and firewood, sixpence.'

Again the financier scrutinised the list. He was positive that it was down already. However, he could not find it, so the sixpence was added to the column of figures.

'Then there's your boots; you can't go about with them old things in this weather much longer, and they won't stand mending again. You remember the man said they were not worth it when you had that patch put on a few weeks ago.'

'Yes. I was thinking of buying a new pair tomorrow. My socks was wet through tonight. If it's raining some morning when I'm going out and I have to work all day with wet feet I shall be laid up.'

'At that second-hand shop down in High Street I saw when I was out this afternoon a very good pair just your size, for two shillings.'

Easton did not reply at once. He did not much fancy wearing the cast-off boots of some stranger, who for all he knew might have suffered from some disease, but then remembering that his old ones were literally falling off his feet he realised that he had practically no choice.

'If you're quite sure they'll fit you'd better get them. It's better to do that than for me to catch cold and be laid up for God knows how long.'

So the two shillings were added to the list.

'Is there anything else?'

'How much does it come to now?' asked Ruth.

Easton added it all up. When he had finished he remained staring at the figures in consternation for a long time without speaking.

'Jesus Christ!' he ejaculated at last.

'What's it come to?' asked Ruth.

'Forty-four and tenpence.'

'I knew we wouldn't have enough,' said Ruth, wearily. 'Now if you think I manage so badly, praps you can tell me which of those things we ought to leave out.'

'We'd be all right if it wasn't for the debts,' said Easton, doggedly.

'When you're not working, we must either get into debt or starve.'

Easton made no answer.

'What'll we do about the rates?' asked Ruth.

'I'm sure I don't know: there's nothing left to pawn except my black coat and vest. You might get something on that.'

'It'll have to be paid somehow,' said Ruth, 'or you'll be taken off to jail for a month, the same as Mrs. Newman's husband was last winter.'

'Well, you'd better take the coat and vest and see what you can get on 'em tomorrow.'

'Yes,' said Ruth; 'and there's that brown silk dress of mine – you know, the one I wore when we was married – I might get something on that, because we won't get enough on the coat and vest. I don't like parting with the dress, although I never wear it; but we'll be sure to be able to get it out again, won't we?'

'Of course,' said Easton.

They remained silent for some time, Easton staring at the list of debts and the letters. She was wondering if he still thought she managed badly, and what he would do about it. She knew she had always done her best. At last she said, wistfully, trying hard to speak plainly for there seemed to be a lump in her throat: 'And what about tomorrow? Would you like to spend the money yourself, or shall I manage as I've done before, or will you tell me what to do?'

'I don't know, dear,' said Easton, sheepishly. 'I think you'd better do as you think best.'

'Oh, I'll manage all right, dear, you'll see,' replied Ruth, who seemed to think it a sort of honour to be allowed to starve herself and to wear shabby clothes.

The baby, who had been for some time quietly sitting upon his mother's lap, looking wonderingly at the fire – his teeth appeared to trouble him less since he got rid of the eggs and bacon and potatoes – now began to nod and doze, which Easton perceiving, suggested that the infant should not be allowed to go to sleep with an empty stomach, because it would probably wake up hungry in the middle of the night. He therefore woke him up as much as possible and mashed a little of the bread and toasted cheese with a little warm milk. Then taking the baby from Ruth he began to try to induce it to eat. As soon, however, as the child understood his object, it began to scream at the top of its voice, closing its lips firmly and turning its head rapidly from side to side every time the spoon approached its mouth. It made such a dreadful noise that Easton at last gave in. He began to walk about the room with it, and presently the child sobbed itself to sleep. After putting the baby into its cradle Ruth set about preparing Easton's breakfast and packing it into his basket. This did not take very long, there being only bread and butter – or, to be more correct, margarine.

Then she poured what tea was left in the tea-pot into a small saucepan and placed it on the top of the oven, but away from the fire; cut two more slices of bread and spread on them all the margarine that was left; then put them on a plate on the table, covering them with a saucer to prevent them getting hard and dry during the night. Near the plate she placed a clean cup and saucer and the milk and sugar.

In the morning Easton would light the fire and warm up the tea in the saucepan so as to have a cup of tea before going out. If Ruth was awake and he was not too pressed for time, he generally took a cup of tea to her in bed.

Nothing now remained to be done but to put some coal and wood ready in the fender so that there would be no unnecessary delay in the morning.

The baby was still sleeping and Ruth did not like to wake him up yet to dress him for the night. Easton was sitting by the fire smoking, so everything being done, Ruth sat down at the table and began sewing. Presently she spoke:

'I wish you'd let me try to let that back room upstairs: the woman next door has got hers let unfurnished to an elderly woman and her husband for two shillings a week. If we could get someone like that it would be better than having an empty room in the house.'

'And we'd always have them messing about down here, cooking and washing and one thing and another,' objected Easton; 'they'd be more trouble than they was worth.'

'Well, we might try and furnish it. There's Mrs. Crass across the road has got two lodgers in one room. They pay her twelve shillings a week each; board, lodging and washing. That's one pound four she has coming in reglar every week. If we could do the same we'd very soon be out of debt.'

'What's the good of talking? You'd never be able to do the work even if we had the furniture.'

'Oh, the work's nothing,' replied Ruth, 'and as for the furniture, we've got plenty of spare bedclothes, and we could easily manage without a washstand in our room for a bit, so the only thing we really want is a small bedstead and mattress; we could get them very cheap second-hand.'

'There ought to be a chest of drawers,' said Easton doubtfully.

'I don't think so,' replied Ruth. 'There's a cupboard in the room and whoever took it would be sure to have a box.'

'Well, if you think you can do the work I've no objection,' said Easton. 'It'll be a nuisance having a stranger in the way all the time, but I suppose we must do something of the sort or else we'll have to give up the house and take a couple of rooms somewhere. That would be worse than having lodgers ourselves.'

'Let's go and have a look at the room,' he added, getting up and taking the lamp from the wall.

They had to go up two flights of stairs before arriving at the top landing, where there were two doors, one leading into the front room – their bedroom – and the other into the empty back room. These two doors were at right angles to each other. The wallpaper in the back room was damaged and soiled in several places.

'There's nearly a whole roll of this paper on the top of the cupboard,' said Ruth. 'You could easily mend all those places. We could hang up a few almanacks on the walls; our washstand could go there by the window; a chair just there, and the bed along that wall behind the door. It's only a small window, so I can easily manage to make a curtain out of something. I'm sure I could make the room look quite nice without spending hardly anything.'

Easton reached down the roll of paper. It was the same pattern as that on the wall. The latter was a good deal faded, of course, but it would not matter much if the patches showed a little. They returned to the kitchen.

'Do you think you know anyone who would take it?' asked Ruth. Easton smoked thoughtfully.

'No,' he said at length. 'But I'll mention it to one or two of the chaps on the job; they might know of someone.'

'And I'll get Mrs. Crass to ask her lodgers: p'raps they might have a friend what would like to live near them.'

So it was settled; and as the fire was nearly out and it was getting late, they prepared to retire for the night. The baby was still sleeping, so Easton lifted it, cradle and all, and carried it up the narrow staircase into the front bedroom, Ruth leading the way, carrying the lamp and some clothes for the child. So that the infant might be within easy reach of its mother during the night, two chairs were arranged close to her side of the bed and the cradle placed on them.

'Now we've forgot the clock,' said Easton, pausing. He was half undressed and had already removed his slippers.

'I'll slip down and get it,' said Ruth.

'Never mind, I'll go,' said Easton, beginning to put his slippers on again.

'No, you get into bed. I've not started undressing yet, I'll get it,' replied Ruth who was already on her way down.

'I don't know as it was worth the trouble of going down,' said Ruth when she returned with the clock. 'It stopped three or four times today.'

'Well, I hope it don't stop in the night,' Easton said. 'It would be a bit of all right not knowing what time it was in the morning. I suppose the next thing will be that we'll have to buy a new clock.'

He woke several times during the night and struck a match to see if it was yet time to get up. At half past two the clock was still going and he again fell asleep. The next time he woke up the ticking had ceased. He wondered what time it was? It was still very dark, but that was nothing to go by, because it was always dark at six now. He was wide awake: it must be nearly time to get up. It would never do to be late; he might get the sack.

He got up and dressed himself. Ruth was asleep, so he crept quietly downstairs, lit the fire and heated the tea. When it was ready he went softly upstairs again. Ruth was still sleeping, so he decided not to disturb her. Returning to the kitchen, he poured out and drank a cup of tea, put on his boots, overcoat and hat and taking his basket went out of the house.

The rain was still falling and it was very cold and dark. There was no one else in the street. Easton shivered as he walked along wondering what time it could be. He remembered there was a clock over the front of a jeweller's shop a little way down the main road. When he arrived at this place he found that the clock being so high up he could not see the figures on the face distinctly, because it was still very dark. He stood staring for a few minutes vainly trying to see what time it was when suddenly the light of a bull's-eye lantern was flashed into his eyes.

'You're about very early,' said a voice, the owner of which Easton could not see. The light blinded him.

'What time is it?' said Easton. 'I've got to get to work at seven and our clock stopped during the night.'

'Where are you working?'

'At "The Cave" in Elmore Road. You know, near the old toll gate.'

'What are you doing there and who are you working for?' the policeman demanded.

Easton explained.

'Well,' said the constable, 'it's very strange that you should be wandering about at this hour. It's only about three-quarters of an hour's walk from here to Elmore Road. You say you've got to get there at seven, and it's only a quarter to four now. Where do you live? What's your name?' Easton gave his name and address and began repeating the story about the clock having stopped.

'What you say may be all right or it may not,' interrupted the policeman. 'I'm not sure but that I ought to take you to the station. All I know about you is that I find you loitering outside this shop. What have you got in that basket?'

'Only my breakfast,' Easton said, opening the basket and displaying its contents.

'I'm inclined to believe what you say,' said the policeman, after a pause. 'But to make quite sure I'll go home with you. It's on my beat, and I don't want to run you in if you're what you say you are, but I should advise you to buy a decent clock, or you'll be getting yourself into trouble.'

When they arrived at the house Easton opened the door, and after making some entries in his note-book the officer went away, much to the relief of Easton, who went upstairs, set the hands of the clock right and started it going again. He then removed his overcoat and lay down on the bed in his clothes, covering himself with the quilt. After a while he fell asleep, and when he awoke the clock was still ticking.

The time was exactly seven o'clock.

CHAPTER 4

The Placard

Frank Owen was the son of a journeyman carpenter who had died of consumption when the boy was only five years old. After that his mother earned a scanty living as a needle-woman. When Frank was thirteen he went to work for a master decorator who was a man of a type that has now almost disappeared, being not merely an employer but a craftsman of a high order.

He was an old man when Frank Owen went to work for him. At one time he had had a good business in the town, and used to boast that he had always done good work, had found pleasure in doing it and had been well paid for it. But of late years the number of his customers had dwindled considerably, for there had arisen a new generation which cared nothing about craftsmanship or art, and everything for cheapness and profit. From this man and by laborious study and practice in his spare time, aided by a certain measure of natural ability, the boy acquired a knowledge of decorative painting and design, and graining[16] and signwriting.

Frank's mother died when he was twenty-four, and a year afterwards he married the daughter of a fellow workman. In those days trade was fairly good and although there was not much demand for the more artistic kinds of work, still the fact that he was capable of doing them, if required, made it comparatively easy for him to obtain employment. Owen and his wife were very happy. They had one child – a boy – and for some years all went well. But gradually this state of things altered: broadly speaking, the change came slowly and imperceptibly, although there were occasional sudden fluctuations.

Even in summer he could not always find work: and in winter it was almost impossible to get a job of any sort. At last, about twelve months before the date that this story opens, he determined to leave his wife and child at home and go to try his fortune in London. When he got employment he would send for them.

It was a vain hope. He found London, if anything, worse than his native town. Wherever he went he was confronted with the legend: 'No hands wanted.' He walked the streets day after day; pawned or sold all his clothes save those he stood in, and stayed in London for six months, sometimes starving and only occasionally obtaining a few days or weeks work.

At the end of that time he was forced to give in. The privations he had endured, the strain on his mind and the foul atmosphere of the city combined to defeat him. Symptoms of the disease that had killed his father began to manifest themselves, and yielding to the repeated entreaties of his wife he returned to his native town, the shadow of his former self.

That was six months ago, and since then he had worked for Rushton & Co. Occasionally when they had no work in hand, he was 'stood off' until something came in.

Ever since his return from London, Owen had been gradually abandoning himself to hopelessness. Every day he felt that the disease he suffered from was obtaining a stronger grip on him. The doctor told him to 'take plenty of nourishing food', and prescribed costly medicines which Owen had not the money to buy.

Then there was his wife. Naturally delicate, she needed many things that he was unable to procure for her. And the boy – what hope was there for him? Often as Owen moodily thought of their circumstances and prospects he told himself that it would be far better if they could all three die now, together.

He was tired of suffering himself, tired of impotently watching the sufferings of his wife, and appalled at the thought of what was in store for the child.

Of this nature were his reflections as he walked homewards on the evening of the day when old Linden was dismissed. There was no reason to believe or hope that the existing state of things would be altered for a long time to come.

Thousands of people like himself dragged out a wretched existence on the very verge of starvation, and for the greater number of people life was one long struggle against poverty. Yet practically none of these people knew or even troubled themselves to enquire why they were in that condition; and for anyone else to try to explain to them was a ridiculous waste of time, for they did not want to know.

The remedy was so simple, the evil so great and so glaringly evident, that the only possible explanation of its continued existence was that the majority of his fellow workers were devoid of the power of reasoning. If these people were not mentally deficient they would of their own accord have swept this silly system away long ago. It would not have been necessary for anyone to teach them that it was wrong.

Why, even those who were successful or wealthy could not be sure that they would not eventually die of want. In every workhouse might be found people who had at one time occupied good positions; and their downfall was not in every case their own fault.

No matter how prosperous a man might be, he could not be certain that his children would never want for bread. There were thousands living in misery on starvation wages whose parents had been wealthy people.

As Owen strode rapidly along, his mind filled with these thoughts, he was almost unconscious of the fact that he was wet through to the skin. He was without an overcoat, it was pawned in London, and he had not yet been able to redeem it. His boots were leaky and sodden with mud and rain.

He was nearly home now. At the corner of the street in which he lived there was a newsagent's shop and on a board outside the door was displayed a placard:

TERRIBLE DOMESTIC TRAGEDY
DOUBLE MURDER AND SUICIDE

He went in to buy a copy of the paper. He was a frequent customer here, and as he entered the shopkeeper greeted him by name.

'Dreadful weather,' he remarked as he handed Owen the paper. 'It makes things pretty bad in your line, I suppose?'

'Yes,' responded Owen; 'there's a lot of men idle, but fortunately I happen to be working inside.'

'You're one of the lucky ones, then,' said the other. 'You know, there'll be a job here for some of 'em as soon as the weather gets a little better. All the outside of this block is going to be done up. That's a pretty big job, isn't it?'

'Yes,' returned Owen. 'Who's going to do it?'

'Makehaste and Sloggit. You know, they've got a place over at Windley.'

'Yes, I know the firm,' said Owen, grimly. He had worked for them once or twice himself.

'The foreman was in here today,' the shopkeeper went on. 'He said they're going to make a start Monday morning if it's fine.'

'Well, I hope it will be,' said Owen, 'because things are very quiet just now.'

Wishing the other 'Good night', Owen again proceeded homewards.

Halfway down the street he paused irresolutely: he was thinking of the news he had just heard and of Jack Linden.

As soon as it became generally known that this work was about to be started there was sure to be a rush after it, and it would be a case of first come, first served. If he saw Jack to-night the old man might be in time to secure a job.

Owen hesitated: he was wet through: it was a long way to Linden's place, nearly twenty minutes' walk. Still, he would like to let him know, because unless he was one of the first to apply, Linden would not stand such a good chance as a younger man. Owen said to himself that if he walked very fast there was not much risk of catching cold. Standing about in wet clothes might be dangerous, but so long as one kept moving it was all right.

He turned back and set off in the direction of Linden's house: although he was but a few yards from his own home, he decided not to go in because his wife would be sure to try to persuade him not to go out again.

As he hurried along he presently noticed a small dark object on the doorstep of an untenanted house. He stopped to examine it more closely and perceived that it was a small black kitten. The tiny creature came towards him and began walking about his feet, looking into his face and crying piteously. He stooped down and stroked it, shuddering as his hands came in contact with its emaciated body. Its fur was saturated with rain and every joint of its backbone was distinctly perceptible to the touch. As he caressed it, the starving creature mewed pathetically.

Owen decided to take it home to the boy, and as he picked it up and put it inside his coat the little outcast began to purr.

This incident served to turn his thoughts into another channel. If, as so many people pretended to believe, there was an infinitely loving God, how was it that this helpless creature that He had made was condemned to suffer? It had never done any harm, and was in no sense responsible for the fact that it existed. Was God unaware of the miseries of His creatures? If so, then He was not all-knowing. Was God aware of their sufferings, but unable to help them? Then He was not all-powerful. Had He the power but not the will to make His creatures happy? Then He was not good. No; it was impossible to believe in the existence of an individual, infinite God. In fact, no one did so believe; and least of all those who pretended for various reasons to be the disciples and followers of Christ. The anti-Christs who went about singing hymns, making long prayers and crying Lord, Lord, but never doing the things which He said, who were known by their works to be unbelievers and infidels, unfaithful to the Master they pretended to serve, their lives being passed in deliberate and systematic disregard of His teachings and Commandments. It was not necessary to call in the evidence of science, or to refer to the supposed inconsistencies, impossibilities, contradictions and absurdities contained in the Bible, in order to prove that there was no truth in the Christian religion. All that was necessary was to look at the conduct of the individuals who were its votaries.

CHAPTER 5

The Clock Case

Jack Linden lived in a small cottage in Windley. He had occupied this house ever since his marriage, over thirty years ago.

His home and garden were his hobby: he was always doing something; painting, whitewashing, papering and so forth. The result was that although the house itself was not of much account he had managed to get it into very good order, and as a result it was very clean and comfortable.

Another result of his industry was that – seeing the improved appearance of the place – the landlord had on two occasions raised the rent. When Linden first took the house the rent was six shillings a week. Five years after, it was raised to seven shillings, and after the lapse of another five years it had been increased to eight shillings.

During the thirty years of his tenancy he had paid altogether nearly six hundred pounds in rent, more than double the amount of the present value of the house. Jack did not complain of this – in fact, he was very well satisfied. He often said that Mr. Sweater was a very good landlord, because on several occasions when, being out of work, he had been a few weeks behind with his rent the agent acting for the benevolent Sweater had allowed Linden to pay off the arrears by instalments. As old Jack was in the habit of remarking, many a landlord would have sold up their furniture and turned them into the street.

As the reader is already aware, Linden's household consisted of his wife, his two grandchildren and his daughter-in-law, the widow and children of his youngest son, a reservist, who died while serving in the South African War. This man had been a plasterer, and just before the war he was working for Rushton & Co.

They had just finished their tea when Owen knocked at their front door. The young woman went to see who was there.

'Is Mr. Linden in?'

'Yes. Who is it?'

'My name's Owen.'

Old Jack, however, had already recognised Owen's voice, and came to the door, wondering what he wanted.

'As I was going home I heard that Makehaste and Sloggit are going to start a large job on Monday, so I thought I'd run over and let you know.'

'Are they?' said Linden. 'I'll go and see them in the morning. But I'm afraid I won't stand much chance, because a lot of their regular hands are waiting for a job; but I'll go and see 'em all the same.'

'Well, you know, it's a big job. All the outside of that block at the corner of Kerk Street and Lord Street. They're almost sure to want a few extra hands.'

'Yes, there's something in that,' said Linden. 'Anyhow, I'm much obliged to you for letting me know; but come in out of the rain. You must be wet through.'

'No; I won't stay,' responded Owen. 'I don't want to stand about any longer than I can help in these wet clothes.'

'But it won't take you a minit to drink a cup of tea,' Linden insisted. 'I won't ask you to stop longer than that.'

Owen entered; the old man closed the door and led the way into the kitchen. At one side of the fire, Linden's wife, a frail-looking old lady with white hair, was seated in a large armchair, knitting. Linden sat down in a similar chair on the other side. The two grandchildren, a boy and girl about seven and eight years, respectively, were still seated at the table.

Standing by the side of the dresser at one end of the room was a treadle sewing machine, and on one end of the dresser was a pile of sewing: ladies' blouses in process of making. This was another instance of the goodness of Mr. Sweater, from whom Linden's daughter-in-law obtained the work. It was not much, because she was only able to do it in her spare time, but then, as she often remarked, every little helped.

The floor was covered with linoleum: there were a number of framed pictures on the walls, and on the high mantelshelf were a number of brightly polished tins and copper utensils. The room had that indescribable homelike, cosy air that is found only in those houses in which the inhabitants have dwelt for a very long time.

The younger woman was already pouring out a cup of tea.

Old Mrs. Linden, who had never seen Owen before, although she had heard of him, belonged to the Church of England and was intensely religious. She looked curiously at the Atheist as he entered the room. He had taken off his hat and she was surprised to find that he was not repulsive to look at, rather the contrary. But then she remembered that Satan often appears as an angel of light.[17] Appearances are deceitful. She wished that John had not asked him into the house and hoped that no evil consequences would follow. As she looked at him, she was horrified to perceive a small black head with a pair of glistening green eyes peeping out of the breast of his coat, and immediately afterwards the kitten, catching sight of the cups and saucers on the table, began to mew frantically and scrambled suddenly out of its shelter, inflicting a severe scratch on Owen's restraining hands as it jumped to the floor.

It clambered up the tablecloth and began rushing all over the table, darting madly from one plate to another, seeking something to eat.

The children screamed with delight. Their grandmother was filled with a feeling of superstitious alarm. Linden and the young woman stood staring with astonishment at the unexpected visitor.

Before the kitten had time to do any damage, Owen caught hold of it and, despite its struggles, lifted it off the table.

'I found it in the street as I was coming along,' he said. 'It seems to be starving.'

'Poor little thing. I'll give it something,' exclaimed the young woman.

She put some milk and bread into a saucer for it and the kitten ate ravenously, almost upsetting the saucer in its eagerness, much to the amusement of the two children, who stood by watching it admiringly.

Their mother now handed Owen a cup of tea. Linden insisted on his sitting down and then began to talk about Hunter.

'You know I *had* to spend some time on them doors to make 'em look anything at all; but it wasn't the time I took, or even the smoking what made 'im go on like that. He knows very well the time it takes. The real reason is that he thinks I was gettin' too much money. Work is done so rough nowadays that chaps like Sawkins is good enough for most of it. Hunter shoved me off just because I was getting the top money, and you'll see I won't be the only one.'

'I'm afraid you're right,' returned Owen. 'Did you see Rushton when you went for your money?'

'Yes,' replied Linden. 'I hurried up as fast as I could, but Hunter was there first. He passed me on his bike before I got halfway, so I suppose he told his tale before I came. Anyway, when I started to speak to Mr. Rushton he wouldn't listen. Said he couldn't interfere between Mr. Hunter and the men.'

'Ah! they're a bad lot, them two,' said the old woman, shaking her head sagely. 'But it'll all come 'ome to 'em, you'll see. They'll never prosper. The Lord will punish them.'

Owen did not feel very confident of that. Most of the people he knew who had prospered were very similar in character to the two worthies in question. However, he did not want to argue with this poor old woman.

'When Tom was called up to go to the war,' said the young woman, bitterly, 'Mr. Rushton shook hands with him and promised to give him a job when he came back. But now that poor Tom's gone and they know that me and the children's got no one to look to but Father, they do *this*.'

Although at the mention of her dead son's name old Mrs. Linden was evidently distressed, she was still mindful of the Atheist's presence, and hastened to rebuke her daughter-in-law.

'You shouldn't say we've got no one to look to, Mary,' she said. 'We're not as them who are without God and without hope in the world. The Lord is our shepherd. He careth for the widow and the fatherless.'[18]

Owen was very doubtful about this also. He had seen so many badly cared-for children about the streets lately, and what he remembered of his own sorrowful childhood was all evidence to the contrary.

An awkward silence succeeded. Owen did not wish to continue this conversation: he was afraid that he might say something that would hurt the old woman. Besides, he was anxious to get away; he began to feel cold in his wet clothes.

As he put his empty cup on the table he said:

'Well, I must be going. They'll be thinking I'm lost, at home.'

The kitten had finished all the bread and milk and was gravely washing its face with one of its forepaws, to the great admiration of the two children, who were sitting on the floor beside it. It was an artful-looking kitten, all black, with a very large head and a very small body. It reminded Owen of a tadpole.

'Do you like cats?' he asked, addressing the children.

'Yes,' said the boy. 'Give it to us, will you, mister?'

'Oh, do leave it 'ere, mister,' exclaimed the little girl. 'I'll look after it.'

'So will I,' said the boy.

'But haven't you one of your own?' asked Owen.

'Yes; we've got a big one.'

'Well, if you have one already and I give you this, then you'd have two cats, and I'd have none. That wouldn't be fair, would it?'

'Well, you can 'ave a lend of our cat for a little while if you give us this kitten,' said the boy, after a moment's thought.

'Why would you rather have the kitten?'

'Because it would play: our cat don't want to play, it's too old.'

'Perhaps you're too rough with it,' returned Owen.

'No, it ain't that; it's just because it's old.'

'You know cats is just the same as people,' explained the little girl, wisely. 'When they're grown up I suppose they've got their troubles to think about.'

Owen wondered how long it would be before her troubles commenced. As he gazed at these two little orphans he thought of his own child, and of the rough and thorny way they would all three have to travel if they were so unfortunate as to outlive their childhood.

'Can we 'ave it, mister?' repeated the boy.

Owen would have liked to grant the children's request, but he wanted the kitten himself. Therefore he was relieved when their grandmother exclaimed:

'We don't want no more cats 'ere: we've got one already; that's quite enough.'

She was not yet quite satisfied in her mind that the creature was not an incarnation of the Devil, but whether it was or not she did not want it, or anything else of Owen's, in the house. She wished he would go, and take his kitten or his familiar or whatever it was, with him. No good could come of his being there. Was it not written in the Word: 'If any man love not the Lord Jesus Christ, let him be Anathema Maran-atha.'[19] She did not know exactly what Anathema Maran-atha meant, but there could be no doubt that it was something very unpleasant. It was a terrible thing that this blasphemer who – as she had heard – did not believe there was a Hell and said that the Bible was not the Word of God, should be here in the house sitting on one of their chairs, drinking from one of their cups, and talking to their children.

The children stood by wistfully when Owen put the kitten under his coat and rose to go away.

As Linden prepared to accompany him to the front door, Owen, happening to notice a timepiece standing on a small table in the recess at one side of the fireplace, exclaimed:

'That's a very nice clock.'

'Yes, it's all right, ain't it?' said old Jack, with a touch of pride. 'Poor Tom made that: not the clock itself, but just the case.'

It was the case that had attracted Owen's attention. It stood about two feet high and was made of fretwork in the form of an Indian mosque, with a pointed dome and pinnacles. It was a very beautiful thing and must have cost many hours of patient labour.

'Yes,' said the old woman, in a trembling, broken voice, and looking at Owen with a pathetic expression. 'Months and months he worked at it, and no one ever guessed who it were for. And then, when my birthday came round, the very first thing I saw when I woke up in the morning were the clock standing on a chair by the bed with a card:

'To dear mother, from her loving son, Tom.
Wishing her many happy birthdays.'

'But he never had another birthday himself, because just five months afterwards he were sent out to Africa, and he'd only been there five weeks when he died. Five years ago, come the fifteenth of next month.'

Owen, inwardly regretting that he had unintentionally broached so painful a subject, tried to think of some suitable reply, but had to content himself with murmuring some words of admiration of the work.

As he wished her good night, the old woman, looking at him, could not help observing that he appeared very frail and ill: his face was very thin and pale, and his eyes were unnaturally bright.

Possibly the Lord in His infinite loving kindness and mercy was chastening this unhappy castaway in order that He might bring him to Himself. After all, he was not altogether bad: it was certainly very thoughtful of him to come all this way to let John know about that job. She observed that he had no overcoat, and the storm was still raging fiercely outside, furious gusts of wind frequently striking the house and shaking it to its very foundations.

The natural kindliness of her character asserted itself; her better feelings were aroused, triumphing momentarily over the bigotry of her religious opinions.

'Why, you ain't got no overcoat!' she exclaimed. 'You'll be soaked goin' 'ome in this rain.' Then, turning to her husband, she continued: 'There's that old one of yours; you might lend him that; it would be better than nothing.'

But Owen would not hear of this: he thought, as he became very conscious of the clammy feel of his saturated clothing, that he could not get much wetter than he already was. Linden accompanied him as far as the front door, and Owen once more set out on his way homeward through the storm that howled around like a wild beast hungry for its prey.

CHAPTER 6

It is not My Crime

Owen and his family occupied the top floor of a house that had once been a large private dwelling but which had been transformed into a series of flats. It was situated in Lord Street, almost in the centre of the town.

At one time this had been a most aristocratic locality, but most of the former residents had migrated to the newer suburb at the west of the town. Notwithstanding this fact, Lord Street was still a most respectable neighbourhood, the inhabitants generally being of a very superior type: shop-walkers, shop assistants, barber's clerks, boarding house keepers, a coal merchant, and even two retired jerry-builders.

There were four other flats in the house in which Owen lived. No. 1 (the basement) was occupied by an estate agent's clerk. No. 2 – on a level with the street – was the habitat of the family of Mr. Trafaim, a cadaverous-looking gentleman who wore a top hat, boasted of his French descent, and was a shop-walker at Sweater's Emporium. No. 3 was tenanted by an insurance agent, and in No. 4 dwelt a tallyman's traveller.[20]

Lord Street – like most other similar neighbourhoods – supplied a striking answer to those futile theorists who prate of the equality of mankind, for the inhabitants instinctively formed themselves into groups, the more superior types drawing together, separating themselves from the inferior, and rising naturally to the top, while the others gathered themselves into distinct classes, grading downwards, or else isolated themselves altogether; being refused admission to the circles they desired to enter, and in their turn refusing to associate with their inferiors.

The most exclusive set consisted of the families of the coal merchant, the two retired jerry-builders and Mr. Trafaim, whose superiority was demonstrated by the fact that, to say nothing of his French extraction, he wore – in addition to the top hat aforesaid – a frock coat and a pair of lavender trousers every day. The coal merchant and the jerry-builders also wore top hats, lavender trousers, and frock coats, but only on Sundays and other special occasions. The estate agent's clerk and the insurance agent, though excluded from the higher circle, belonged to another select coterie from which they excluded in their turn all persons of inferior rank, such as shop assistants or barbers.

The only individual who was received with equal cordiality by all ranks, was the tallyman's traveller. But whatever differences existed amongst them regarding each other's social standing they were unanimous on one point at least: they were indignant at Owen's presumption in coming to live in such a refined locality.

This low fellow, this common workman, with his paint-bespattered clothing, his broken boots, and his generally shabby appearance, was a disgrace to the street; and as for his wife she was not much better, because although whenever she came out she was always neatly dressed, yet most of the neighbours knew perfectly well that she had been wearing the same white straw hat all the time she had been there. In fact, the only tolerable one of the family was the boy, and they were forced to admit that he was always very well dressed; so well indeed as to occasion some surprise, until they found out that all the boy's clothes were home-made. Then their surprise was changed into a somewhat grudging admiration of the skill displayed, mingled with contempt for the poverty which made its exercise necessary.

The indignation of the neighbours was increased when it became known that Owen and his wife were not Christians: then indeed everyone agreed that the landlord ought to be ashamed of himself for letting the top flat to such people.

But although the hearts of these disciples of the meek and lowly Jewish carpenter were filled with uncharitableness, they were powerless to do much harm. The landlord regarded their opinion with indifference. All he cared about was the money: although he also was a sincere Christian, he would not have hesitated to let the top flat to Satan himself, provided he was certain of receiving the rent regularly.

The only one upon whom the Christians were able to inflict any suffering was the child. At first when he used to go out into the street to play, the other children, acting on their parents' instructions, refused to associate with him, or taunted him with his parents' poverty. Occasionally he came home heartbroken and in tears because he had been excluded from some game.

At first, sometimes the mothers of some of the better-class children used to come out with a comical assumption of superiority and dignity and compel their children to leave off playing with Frankie and some other poorly dressed children who used to play in that street. These females were usually overdressed and wore a lot of jewellery. Most of them fancied they were ladies, and if they had only had the sense to keep their mouths shut, other people might possibly have shared the same delusion.

But this was now a rare occurrence, because the parents of the other children found it a matter of considerable difficulty to prevent their youngsters from associating with those of inferior rank, for when left to themselves the children disregarded all such distinctions. Frequently in that street was to be seen the appalling spectacle of the ten-year-old son of the refined and fashionable Trafaim dragging along a cart constructed of a sugar box and an old pair of perambulator wheels with no tyres, in which reposed the plebeian Frankie Owen, armed with a whip, and the dowdy daughter of a barber's clerk: while the nine-year-old heir of the coal merchant rushed up behind . . .

[[Owen's wife and little son were waiting for him in the living room.]] This room was about twelve feet square and the ceiling – which was low and irregularly shaped, showing in places the formation of the roof – had been decorated by Owen with painted ornaments.

There were three or four chairs, and an oblong table, covered with a clean white tablecloth, set ready for tea. In the recess at the right of the fireplace – an ordinary open grate – were a number of shelves filled with a miscellaneous collection of books, most of which had been bought second-hand.

There were also a number of new books, mostly cheap editions in paper covers.

Over the back of a chair at one side of the fire, was hanging an old suit of Owen's, and some underclothing, which his wife had placed there to air, knowing that he would be wet through by the time he arrived home . . .

The woman was half-sitting, half lying, on a couch by the other side of the fire. She was very thin, and her pale face bore the traces of much physical and mental suffering. She was sewing, a task which her reclining position rendered somewhat difficult. Although she was really only twenty-eight years of age, she appeared older.

The boy, who was sitting on the hearthrug playing with some toys, bore a strong resemblance to his mother. He also, appeared very fragile and in his childish face was reproduced much of the delicate prettiness which she had once possessed. His feminine appearance was increased by the fact that his yellow hair hung in long curls on his shoulders. The pride with which his mother regarded this long hair was by no means shared by Frankie himself, for he was always entreating her to cut it off.

Presently the boy stood up and walking gravely over to the window, looked down into the street, scanning the pavement for as far as he could see: he had been doing this at intervals for the last hour.

'I wonder wherever he's got to,' he said, as he returned to the fire.

'I'm sure I don't know,' returned his mother. 'Perhaps he's had to work overtime.'

'You know, I've been thinking lately,' observed Frankie, after a pause, 'that it's a great mistake for Dad to go out working at all. I believe that's the very reason why we're so poor.'

'Nearly everyone who works is more or less poor, dear, but if Dad didn't go out to work we'd be even poorer than we are now. We should have nothing to eat.'

'But Dad says that the people who do nothing get lots of everything.'

'Yes, and it's quite true that most of the people who never do any work get lots of everything, but where do they get it from? And how do they get it?'

'I'm sure I don't know,' replied Frankie, shaking his head in a puzzled fashion.

'Supposing Dad didn't go to work, or that he had no work to go to, or that he was ill and not able to do any work, then we'd have no money to buy anything. How should we get on then?'

'I'm sure I don't know,' repeated Frankie, looking round the room in a thoughtful manner. 'The chairs that's left aren't good enough to sell, and we can't sell the beds, or your sofa, but you might pawn my velvet suit.'

'But even if all the things were good enough to sell, the money we'd get for them wouldn't last very long, and what should we do then?'

'Well, I suppose we'd have to go without, that's all, the same as we did when Dad was in London.'

'But how do the people who never do any work manage to get lots of money then?' added Frankie.

'Oh, there's lots of different ways. For instance, you remember when Dad was in London, and we had no food in the house, I had to sell the easy chair.'

Frankie nodded. 'Yes,' he said, 'I remember you wrote a note and I took it to the shop, and afterwards old Didlum came up here and bought it, and then his cart came and a man took it away.'

'And do you remember how much he gave us for it?'

'Five shillings,' replied Frankie, promptly. He was well acquainted with the details of the transaction, having often heard his father and mother discuss it.

'And when we saw it in his shop window a little while afterwards, what price was marked on it?'

'Fifteen shillings.'

'Well, that's one way of getting money without working.'

Frankie played with his toys in silence for some minutes. At last he said:

'What other ways?'

'Some people who have some money already get more in this way: they find some people who have no money and say to them, "Come and work for us." Then the people who have the money pay the workers just enough wages to keep them alive whilst they are at work. Then, when the things that the working people have been making are finished, the workers are sent away, and as they still have no money, they are soon starving. In the meantime the people who had the money take all the things that the workers have made and sell them for a great deal more money than they gave to the workers for making them. That's another way of getting lots of money without doing any useful work.'

'But is there no way to get rich without doing such things as that?'

'It's not possible for anyone to become rich without cheating other people.'

'What about our schoolmaster then? He doesn't do any work.'

'Don't you think it's useful and necessary and also very hard work teaching all those boys every day? I don't think I should like to have to do it.'

'Yes, I suppose what he does *is* some use,' said Frankie thoughtfully, 'and it must be rather hard too, I should think. I've noticed he looks a bit worried sometimes, and sometimes he gets into a fine old wax when the boys don't pay proper attention.'

The child again went over to the window, and pulling back the edge of the blind looked down the deserted rain washed street.

'What about the vicar?' he remarked as he returned.

Although Frankie did not go to church or Sunday School, the day school that he had attended was that attached to the parish church, and the vicar was in the habit of looking in occasionally.

'Ah, he really is one of those who live without doing any necessary work, and of all the people who do nothing, the vicar is one of the very worst.'

Frankie looked up at his mother with some surprise, not because he entertained any very high opinion of clergymen in general, for, having been an attentive listener to many conversations between his parents, he had of course assimilated their opinions as far as his infant understanding permitted, but because at the school the scholars were taught to regard the gentleman in question with the most profound reverence and respect.

'Why, Mum?' he asked.

'For this reason, dearie. You know that all the beautiful things which the people who do nothing have are made by the people who work, don't you?'

'Yes.'

'And you know that those who work have to eat the very worst food, and wear the very worst clothes, and live in the very worst homes.'

'Yes,' said Frankie.

'And sometimes they have nothing to eat at all, and no clothes to wear except rags, and even no homes to live in.'

'Yes,' repeated the child.

'Well, the vicar goes about telling the Idlers that it's quite right for them to do nothing, and that God meant them to have nearly everything that is made by those who work. In fact, he tells them that God made the poor for the use of the rich. Then he goes to the workers and tells them that God meant them to work very hard and to give all the good things they make to those who do nothing, and that they should be very thankful to God and to the idlers for being allowed to have even the very worst food to eat and the rags, and broken boots to wear. He also tells them that they mustn't grumble, or be discontented because they're poor in this world, but that they must wait till they're dead, and then God will reward them by letting them go to a place called heaven.'

Frankie laughed.

'And what about the Idlers?' he asked.

'The vicar says that if they believe everything he tells them and give him some of the money they make out of the workers, then God will let them into heaven also.'

'Well, that's not fair dos, is it, Mum?' said Frankie with some indignation.

'It wouldn't be if it were true, but then you see it's not true, it can't be true.'

'Why can't it, Mum?'

'Oh, for many reasons: to begin with, the vicar doesn't believe it himself: he only pretends to. For instance, he pretends to believe the Bible, but if we read the Bible we find that Jesus said that God is our Father and that all the people in the world are His children, all brothers and sisters. But the vicar says that although Jesus said "brothers and sisters" He really ought to have said "masters and servants". Again, Jesus said that His disciples should not think of tomorrow, or save up a lot of money for themselves,[21] but they should be unselfish and help those who are in need. Jesus said that His disciples must not think about their own future needs at all, because God will provide for them if they only do as He commands. But the vicar says that is all nonsense.

'Jesus also said that if anyone tried to do His disciples harm,[22] they must never resist, but forgive those who injured them and pray God to forgive them also. But the vicar says this is all nonsense too. He says that the world would never be able to go on if we did as Jesus taught. The vicar teaches that the way to deal with those that injure us is to have them put into prison, or – if they belong to some other country – to take guns and knives and murder them, and burn their houses. So you see the vicar doesn't really believe or do any of the things that Jesus said: he only pretends.'

'But why does he pretend, and go about talking like that, Mum? What does he do it for?'

'Because he wishes to live without working himself, dear.'

'And don't the people know that he's only pretending?'

'Some of them do. Most of the idlers know that what the vicar says is not true, but they pretend to believe it, and give him money for saying it, because they want him to go on telling it to the workers so that they will go on working and keep quiet and be afraid to think for themselves.'

'And what about the workers? Do they believe it?'

'Most of them do, because when they were little children like you, their mothers taught them to believe, without thinking, whatever the vicar said, and that God made them for the use of the idlers. When they went to school, they were taught the same thing: and now that they're grown up they really believe it, and they go to work and give nearly everything they make to the idlers, and have next to nothing left for themselves and their children. That's the reason why the workers' children have very bad clothes to wear and some-times no food to eat; and that's how it is that the idlers and their children have more clothes than they need and more food than they can eat. Some of them have so many clothes that they are not able to wear them and so much food that they are not able to eat it. They just waste it or throw it away.'

'When I'm grown up into a man,' said Frankie, with a flushed face, 'I'm going to be one of the workers, and when we've made a lot of things, I shall stand up and tell the others what to do. If any of the idlers come to take our things away, they'll get something they won't like.'

In a state of suppressed excitement and scarcely conscious of what he was doing, the boy began gathering up the toys and throwing them violently one by one into the box.

'I'll teach 'em to come taking our things away,' he exclaimed, relapsing momentarily into his street style of speaking.

'First of all we'll all stand quietly on one side. Then when the idlers come in and start touching our things, we'll go up to 'em and say, " 'Ere, watcher doin' of? Just you put it down, will yer?" And if they don't put it down at once, it'll be the worse for 'em, I can tell you.'

All the toys being collected, Frankie picked up the box and placed it noisily in its accustomed corner of the room.

'I should think the workers will be jolly glad when they see me coming to tell them what to do, shouldn't you, Mum?'

'I don't know, dear; you see so many people have tried to tell them, but they won't listen, they don't want to hear. They think it's quite right that they should work very hard all their lives, and quite right that most of the things they help to make should be taken away from them by the people who do nothing. The workers think that their children are not as good as the children of the idlers, and they teach their children that as soon as ever they are old enough they must be satisfied to work very hard and to have only very bad food and clothes and homes.'

'Then I should think the workers ought to be jolly well ashamed of themselves, Mum, don't you?'

'Well, in one sense they ought, but you must remember that that's what they've always been taught themselves. First, their mothers and fathers told them so; then, their schoolteachers told them so; and then, when they went to church, the vicar and the Sunday School teacher told them the same thing. So you can't be surprised that they now really believe that God made them and their children to make things for the use of the people who do nothing.'

'But you'd think their own sense would tell them! How can it be right for the people who do nothing to have the very best and most of everything that's made, and the very ones who make everything to have hardly any. Why even I know better than that, and I'm only six and a half years old.'

'But then you're different, dearie, you've been taught to think about it, and Dad and I have explained it to you, often.'

'Yes, I know,' replied Frankie confidently. 'But even if you'd never taught me, I'm sure I should have tumbled to it all right by myself; I'm not such a juggins as you think I am.'

'So you might, but you wouldn't if you'd been brought up in the same way as most of the workers. They've been taught that it's very wicked to use their own judgement, or to think. And their children are being taught so now. Do you remember what you told me the other day, when you came home from school, about the Scripture lesson?'

'About St. Thomas?'

'Yes. What did the teacher say St. Thomas was?'

'She said he was a bad example; and she said I was worse than him because I asked too many foolish questions. She always gets in a wax if I talk too much.'

'Well, why did she call St. Thomas a bad example?'

'Because he wouldn't believe what he was told.'

'Exactly: well, when you told Dad about it what did he say?'

'Dad told me that really St. Thomas was the only sensible man in the whole crowd of Apostles. That is,' added Frankie, correcting himself, 'if there ever was such a man at all.'

'But did Dad say that there never was such a man?'

'No; he said *he* didn't believe there ever was, but he told me to just listen to what the teacher said about such things, and then to think about it in my own mind, and wait till I'm grown up and then I can use my own judgement.'

'Well, now, that's what *you* were told, but all the other children's mothers and fathers tell them to believe, without thinking, whatever the teacher says. So it will be no wonder if those children are not able to think for themselves when they're grown up, will it?'

'Don't you think it will be any use, then, for me to tell them what to do to the Idlers?' asked Frankie, dejectedly.

'Hark!' said his mother, holding up her finger.

'Dad!' cried Frankie, rushing to the door and flinging it open. He ran along the passage and opened the staircase door before Owen reached the top of the last flight of stairs.

'Why ever do you come up at such a rate,' reproachfully exclaimed Owen's wife as he came into the room exhausted from the climb upstairs and sank panting into the nearest chair.

'I al – ways – for – get,' he replied, when he had in some degree recovered. As he lay back in the chair, his face haggard and of a ghastly whiteness, and with the water dripping from his saturated clothing, Owen presented a terrible appearance.

Frankie noticed with childish terror the extreme alarm with which his mother looked at his father.

'You're always doing it,' he said with a whimper. 'How many more times will Mother have to tell you about it before you take any notice?'

'It's all right, old chap,' said Owen, drawing the child nearer to him and kissing the curly head. 'Listen, and see if you can guess what I've got for you under my coat.'

In the silence the purring of the kitten was distinctly audible.

'A kitten!' cried the boy, taking it out of its hiding-place. 'All black, and I believe it's half a Persian. Just the very thing I wanted.'

While Frankie amused himself playing with the kitten, which had been provided with another saucer of bread and milk, Owen went into the bedroom to put on the dry clothes, and then, those that he had taken off having been placed with his boots near the fire to dry, he explained as they were taking tea the reason of his late home-coming.

'I'm afraid he won't find it very easy to get another job,' he remarked, referring to Linden. 'Even in the summer nobody will be inclined to take him on. He's too old.'

'It's a dreadful prospect for the two children,' answered his wife.

'Yes,' replied Owen bitterly. 'It's the children who will suffer most. As for Linden and his wife, although of course one can't help feeling sorry for them, at the same time there's no getting away from the fact that they deserve to suffer. All their lives they've been working like brutes and living in poverty. Although they have done more than their fair share of the work, they have never enjoyed anything like a fair share of the things they have helped to produce. And yet, all their lives they have supported and defended the system that robbed them, and have resisted and ridiculed every proposal to alter it. It's wrong to feel sorry for such people; they deserve to suffer.'

After tea, as he watched his wife clearing away the tea things and rearranging the drying clothing by the fire, Owen for the first time noticed that she looked unusually ill.

'You don't look well to-night, Nora,' he said, crossing over to her and putting his arm around her.

'I don't feel well,' she replied, resting her head wearily against his shoulder. 'I've been very bad all day and I had to lie down nearly all the afternoon. I don't know how I should have managed to get the tea ready if it had not been for Frankie.'

'I set the table for you, didn't I, Mum?' said Frankie with pride; 'and tidied up the room as well.'

'Yes, darling, you helped me a lot,' she answered, and Frankie went over to her and kissed her hand.

'Well, you'd better go to bed at once,' said Owen. 'I can put Frankie to bed presently and do whatever else is necessary.'

'But there are so many things to attend to. I want to see that your clothes are properly dry and to put something ready for you to take in the morning before you go out, and then there's your breakfast to pack up – '

'I can manage all that.'

'I didn't want to give way to it like this,' the woman said, 'because I know you must be tired out yourself, but I really do feel quite done up now.'

'Oh, I'm all right,' replied Owen, who was really so fatigued that he was scarcely able to stand. 'I'll go and draw the blinds down and light the other lamp; so say good-night to Frankie and come at once.'

'I won't say good-night properly, now, Mum,' remarked the boy, 'because Dad can carry me into your room before he puts me into bed.'

A little later, as Owen was undressing Frankie, the latter remarked as he looked affectionately at the kitten, which was sitting on the hearthrug watching the child's every movement under the impression that it was part of some game:

'What name do you think we ought to call it, Dad?'

'You may give him any name you like,' replied Owen, absently.

'I know a dog that lives down the road,' said the boy, 'his name is Major. How would that do? Or we might call him Sergeant.'

The kitten, observing that he was the subject of their conversation, purred loudly and winked as if to intimate that he did not care what rank was conferred upon him so long as the commissariat department[23] was properly attended to.

'I don't know, though,' continued Frankie, thoughtfully. 'They're all right names for dogs, but I think they're too big for a kitten, don't you, Dad?'

'Yes, p'raps they are,' said Owen.

'Most cats are called Tom or Kitty, but I don't want a *common* name for him.'

'Well, can't you call him after someone you know?'

'I know; I'll call him after a little girl that comes to our school; a fine name, Maud! That'll be a good one, won't it, Dad?'

'Yes,' said Owen.

'I say, Dad,' said Frankie, suddenly realising the awful fact that he was being put to bed. 'You're forgetting all about my story, and you promised that you'd have a game of trains with me tonight.'

'I hadn't forgotten, but I was hoping that you had, because I'm very tired and it's very late, long past your usual bed-time, you know. You can take the kitten to bed with you tonight and I'll tell you two stories tomorrow and have the game as well. I shall have plenty of time tomorrow, because it's Saturday.'

'All right, then,' said the boy, contentedly; 'and I'll get the railway station built and I'll have the lines chalked on the floor, and the signals put up before you come home, so that there'll be no time wasted. And I'll put one chair at one end of the room and another chair at the other end, and tie some string across for telegraph wires. That'll be a very good idea, won't it, Dad?' and Owen agreed.

'But of course I'll come to meet you just the same as other Saturdays, because I'm going to buy a ha'porth of milk for the kitten out of my penny.'

After the child was in bed, Owen sat alone by the table in the draughty sitting-room, thinking. Although there was a bright fire, the room was very cold, being so close to the roof. The wind roared loudly round the gables, shaking the house in a way that threatened every moment to hurl it to the ground. The lamp on the table had a green glass reservoir which was half full of oil. Owen watched this with unconscious fascination. Every time a gust of wind struck the house the oil in the lamp was agitated and rippled against the glass like the waves of a miniature sea. Staring abstractedly at the lamp, he thought of the future.

A few years ago the future had seemed a region of wonderful and mysterious possibilities of good, but tonight the thought brought no such illusions, for he knew that the story of the future was to be much the same as the story of the past.

The story of the past would continue to repeat itself for a few years longer. He would continue to work and they would all three continue to do without most of the necessaries of life. When there was no work they would starve.

For himself he did not care much because he knew that at the best – or worst – it would only be a very few years. Even if he were to have proper food and clothing and be able to take reasonable care of himself, he could not live much longer; but when that time came, what was to become of *them*?

There would be some hope for the boy if he were more robust and if his character were less gentle and more selfish. Under the present system it was impossible for anyone to succeed in life without injuring other people and treating them and making use of them as one would not like to be treated and made use of oneself.

In order to succeed in the world it was necessary to be brutal, selfish and unfeeling: to push others aside and to take advantage of their misfortunes: to undersell and crush out one's competitors by fair means or foul: to consider one's own interests first in every case, absolutely regardless of the wellbeing of others.

That was the ideal character. Owen knew that Frankie's character did not come up to this lofty ideal. Then there was Nora, how would she fare?

Owen stood up and began walking about the room, oppressed with a kind of terror. Presently he returned to the fire and began re-arranging the clothes that were drying. He found that the boots, having been placed too near the fire, had dried too quickly and consequently the sole of one of them had begun to split away from the upper: he remedied this as well as he was able and then turned the wetter parts of the clothing to the fire. Whilst doing this he noticed the newspaper, which he had forgotten, in the coat pocket. He drew it out with an exclamation of pleasure. Here was something to distract his thoughts: if not instructive or comforting, it would at any rate be interesting and even amusing to read the reports of the self-satisfied, futile talk of the profound statesmen who with comical gravity presided over the working of the Great System which their combined wisdom pronounced to be the best that could possibly be devised. But tonight Owen was not to read of those things, for as soon as he opened the paper his attention was riveted by the staring headlines of one of the principal columns:

TERRIBLE DOMESTIC TRAGEDY
WIFE AND TWO CHILDREN KILLED
SUICIDE OF THE MURDERER

It was one of the ordinary poverty crimes. The man had been without employment for many weeks and they had been living by pawning or selling their furniture and other possessions. But even this resource must have failed at last, and when one day the neighbours noticed that the blinds remained down and that there was a strange silence about the house, no one coming out or going in, suspicions that something was wrong were quickly aroused. When the police entered the house, they found, in one of the upper rooms, the dead bodies of the woman and the two children, with their throats severed, laid out side by side upon the bed, which was saturated with their blood.

There was no bedstead and no furniture in the room except the straw mattress and the ragged clothes and blankets which formed the bed upon the floor.

The man's body was found in the kitchen, lying with outstretched arms face downwards on the floor, surrounded by the blood that had poured from the wound in his throat which had evidently been inflicted by the razor that was grasped in his right hand.

No particle of food was found in the house, and on a nail in the wall in the kitchen was hung a piece of blood-smeared paper on which was written in pencil:

'This is not *my* crime, but society's.'

The report went on to explain that the deed must have been perpetrated during a fit of temporary insanity brought on by the sufferings the man had endured.

'Insanity!' muttered Owen, as he read this glib theory. 'Insanity! It seems to me that he would have been insane if he had *not* killed them.'

Surely it was wiser and better and kinder to send them all to sleep, than to let them continue to suffer.

At the same time he thought it very strange that the man should have chosen to do it in that way, when there were so many other cleaner, easier and more painless ways of accomplishing the same object. He wondered why it was that most of these killings were done in more or less the same crude, cruel messy way. No; *he* would set about it in a different fashion. He would get some charcoal, then he would paste strips of paper over the joinings of the door and windows of the room and close the register of the grate.[24] Then he would kindle the charcoal on a tray or something in the middle of the room, and then they would all three just lie down together and sleep; and that would be the end of everything. There would be no pain, no blood, and no mess.

Or one could take poison. Of course, there was a certain amount of difficulty in procuring it, but it would not be impossible to find some pretext for buying some laudanum:[25] one could buy several small quantities at different shops until one had sufficient. Then he remembered that he had read somewhere that vermillion, one of the colours he frequently had to use in his work, was one of the most deadly poisons:[26] and there was some other stuff that photographers used, which was very easy to procure. Of course, one would have to be very careful about poisons, so as not to select one that would cause a lot of pain. It would be necessary to find out exactly how the stuff acted before using it. It would not be very difficult to do so. Then he remembered that among his books was one that probably contained some information about this subject. He went over to the book-shelf and presently found the volume; it was called *The Cyclopedia of Practical Medicine*, rather an old book, a little out of date, perhaps, but still it might contain the information he wanted. Opening it, he turned to the table of contents. Many different subjects were mentioned there and presently he found the one he sought:

> Poisons: chemically, physiologically
> and pathologically considered.
> Corrosive Poisons.
> Narcotic Poisons.
> Slow Poisons.
> Consecutive Poisons.
> Accumulative Poisons.

He turned to the chapter indicated and, reading it, he was astonished to find what a number of poisons there were within easy reach of whoever wished to make use of them: poisons that could be relied upon to do their work certainly, quickly and without pain. Why, it was not even necessary to buy them: one could gather them from the hedges by the road side and in the fields.

The more he thought of it the stranger it seemed that such a clumsy method as a razor should be so popular. Why almost any other way would be better and easier than that. Strangulation or even hanging, though the latter method could scarcely be adopted in that house, because there were no beams or rafters or anything from which it would be possible to suspend a cord. Still, he could drive some large nails or hooks into one of the walls. For that matter, there were already some clothes-hooks on some of the doors. He began to think that this would be an even more excellent way than poison or charcoal; he could easily pretend to Frankie that he was going to show him some new kind of play.

He could arrange the cord on the hook on one of the doors and then under pretence of play, it would be done. The boy would offer no resistance, and in a few minutes it would all be over.

He threw down the book and pressed his hands over his ears: he fancied he could hear the boy's hands and feet beating against the panels of the door as he struggled in his death agony.

Then, as his arms fell nervelessly by his side again, he thought that he heard Frankie's voice calling,

'Dad! Dad!'

Owen hastily opened the door.

'Are you calling, Frankie?'

'Yes. I've been calling you quite a long time.'

'What do you want?'

'I want you to come here. I want to tell you something.'

'Well, what is it, dear? I thought you were asleep a long time ago,' said Owen as he came into the room.

'That's just what I want to speak to you about: the kitten's gone to sleep all right, but I can't go. I've tried all different ways, counting and all, but it's no use, so I thought I'd ask you if you'd mind coming and staying with me, and letting me hold your hand for a little while and then p'raps I could go.'

The boy twined his arms round Owen's neck and hugged him very tightly.

'Oh, Dad, I love you so much!' he said. 'I love you so much, I could squeeze you to death.'

'I'm afraid you will, if you squeeze me so tightly as that.'

The boy laughed softly as he relaxed his hold. 'That *would* be a funny way of showing you how much I loved you, wouldn't it, Dad? Squeezing you to death!'

'Yes, I suppose it would,' replied Owen huskily, as he tucked the bedclothes round the child's shoulders. 'But don't talk any more, dear; just hold my hand and try to sleep.'

'All right,' said Frankie.

Lying there very quietly, holding his father's hand and occasionally kissing it, the child presently fell asleep. Then Owen got up very gently and, having taken the kitten out of the bed again and arranged the bedclothes, he softly kissed the boy's forehead and returned to the other room.

Looking about for a suitable place for the kitten to sleep in, he noticed Frankie's toy box, and having emptied the toys on to the floor in a corner of the room, he made a bed in the box with some rags and placed it on its side on the hearthrug, facing the fire, and with some difficulty persuaded the kitten to lie in it. Then, having placed the chairs on which his clothes were drying at a safe distance from the fire, he went into the bedroom. Nora was still awake.

'Are you feeling any better, dear?' he said.

'Yes. I'm ever so much better since I've been in bed, but I can't help worrying about your clothes. I'm afraid they'll never be dry enough for you to put on the first thing in the morning. Couldn't you stay at home till after breakfast, just for once?'

'No; I mustn't do that. If I did Hunter would probably tell me to stay away altogether. I believe he would be glad of an excuse to get rid of another full-price man just now.'

'But if it's raining like this in the morning, you'll be wet through before you get there.'

'It's no good worrying about that, dear: besides, I can wear this old coat that I have on now, over the other.'

'And if you wrap your old shoes in some paper, and take them with you, you can take off your wet boots as soon as you get to the place.'

'Yes, all right,' responded Owen. 'Besides,' he added, reassuringly, 'even if I do get a little wet, we always have a fire there, you know.'

'Well, I hope the weather will be a little better than this in the morning,' said Nora. 'Isn't it a dreadful night! I keep feeling afraid that the house is going to be blown down.'

Long after Nora was asleep, Owen lay listening to the howling of the wind and the noise of the rain as it poured heavily on the roof . . .

CHAPTER 7

The Exterminating Machines

'Come on, Saturday!' shouted Philpot, just after seven o'clock one Monday morning as they were getting ready to commence work.

It was still dark outside, but the scullery was dimly illuminated by the flickering light of two candles which Crass had lighted and stuck on the shelf over the fireplace in order to enable him to see to serve out the different lots of paint and brushes to the men.

'Yes, it do seem a 'ell of a long week, don't it?' remarked Harlow as he hung his overcoat on a nail and proceeded to put on his apron and blouse. 'I've 'ad bloody near enough of it already.'

'Wish to Christ it was breakfast-time,' growled the more easily satisfied Easton.

Extraordinary as it may appear, none of them took any pride in their work: they did not 'love' it. They had no conception of that lofty ideal of 'work for work's sake', which is so popular with the people who do nothing. On the contrary, when the workers arrived in the morning they wished it was breakfast-time. When they resumed work after breakfast they wished it was dinner-time. After dinner they wished it was one o'clock on Saturday.

So they went on, day after day, year after year, wishing their time was over and, without realising it, really wishing that they were dead.

How extraordinary this must appear to those idealists who believe in 'work for work's sake', but who themselves do nothing but devour or use and enjoy or waste the things that are produced by the labour of those others who are not themselves permitted to enjoy a fair share of the good things they help to create?

Cross poured several lots of colour into separate pots.

'Harlow,' he said, 'you and Sawkins, when he comes, can go up and do the top bedrooms out with this colour. You'll find a couple of candles up there. It's only goin' to 'ave one coat, so see that you make it cover all right, and just look after Sawkins a bit so as 'e doesn't make a bloody mess of it. You do the doors and windows, and let 'im do the cupboards and skirtings.'

'That's a bit of all right, I must say,' Harlow said, addressing the company generally. 'We've got to teach a b—r like 'im so as 'e can do us out of a job presently by working under price.'

'Well, I can't 'elp it,' growled Cross. 'You know 'ow it is: 'Unter sends 'im 'ere to do paintin', and I've got to put 'im on it. There ain't nothin' else for 'im to do.'

Further discussion on this subject was prevented by Sawkins' arrival, nearly a quarter of an hour late.

'Oh, you 'ave come, then,' sneered Cross. 'Thought p'raps you'd gorn for a 'oliday.'

Sawkins muttered something about oversleeping himself, and having hastily put on his apron, he went upstairs with Harlow.

'Now, let's see,' Cross said, addressing Philpot. 'You and Newman 'ad better go and make a start on the second floor: this is the colour, and 'ere's a couple of candles. You'd better not both go in one room or 'Unter will growl about it. You take one of the front and let Newman take one of the back rooms. Take a bit of stoppin' with you: they're goin' to 'ave two coats, but you'd better putty up the 'oles as well as you can, this time.'

'Only two coats!' said Philpot. 'Them rooms will never look nothing with two coats – a light colour like this.'

'It's only goin' to get two, anyway,' returned Cross, testily. ' 'Unter said so, so you'll 'ave to do the best you can with 'em, and get 'em smeared over middlin' sudden, too.'

Cross did not think it necessary to mention that according to the copy of the specification of the work which he had in his pocket the rooms in question were supposed to have four coats.

Cross now turned to Owen.

'There's that drorin'-room,' he said. 'I don't know what's goin' to be done with that yet. I don't think they've decided about it. Whatever's to be done to it will be an extra, because all that's said about it in the contract is to face it up with putty and give it one coat of white. So you and Easton 'ad better get on with it.'

Slyme was busy softening some putty by rubbing and squeezing it between his hands.

'I suppose I'd better finish the room I started on on Saturday?' he asked.

'All right,' replied Crass. 'Have you got enough colour?'

'Yes,' said Slyme.

As he passed through the kitchen on the way to his work, Slyme accosted Bert, the boy, who was engaged in lighting, with some pieces of wood, a fire to boil the water to make the tea for breakfast at eight o'clock.

'There's a bloater I want's cooked,' he said.

'All right,' replied Bert. 'Put it over there on the dresser along of Philpot's and mine.'

Slyme took the bloater from his food basket, but as he was about to put it in the place indicated, he observed that his was rather a larger one than either of the other two. This was an important matter. After they were cooked it would not be easy to say which was which: he might possibly be given one of the smaller ones instead of his own. He took out his pocket knife and cut off the tail of the large bloater.

' 'Ere it is, then,' he said to Bert. 'I've cut off the tail of mine so as you'll know which it is.'

It was now about twenty minutes past seven and all the other men having been started at work, Crass washed his hands under the tap. Then he went into the kitchen and having rigged up a seat by taking two of the drawers out of the dresser and placing them on the floor about six feet apart and laying a plank across, he sat down in front of the fire, which was now burning brightly under the pail, and, lighting his pipe, began to smoke. The boy went into the scullery and began washing up the cups and jars for the men to drink out of.

Bert was a lean, undersized boy about fifteen years of age and about four feet nine inches in height. He had light brown hair and hazel grey eyes, and his clothes were of many colours, being thickly encrusted with paint, the result of the unskilful manner in which he did his work, for he had only been at the trade about a year. Some of the men had nicknamed him 'the walking paint-shop', a title which Bert accepted good-humouredly.

This boy was an orphan. His father had been a railway porter who had worked very laboriously for twelve or fourteen hours every day for many years, with the usual result, namely, that he and his family lived in a condition of perpetual poverty. Bert, who was their only child and not very robust, had early shown a talent for drawing, so when his father died a little over a year ago, his mother readily assented when the boy said that he wished to become a decorator. It was a nice light trade, and she thought that a really good painter, such as she was sure he would become, was at least always able to earn a good living. Resolving to give the boy the best possible chance, she decided if possible to place him at Rushton's, that being one of the leading firms in the town. At first Mr. Rushton demanded ten pounds as a premium, the boy to be bound for five years, no wages the first year, two shillings a week the second, and a rise of one shilling every year for the remainder of the term. Afterwards, as a special favour – a matter of charity, in fact, as she was a very poor woman – he agreed to accept five pounds.

This sum represented the thrifty savings of years, but the poor woman parted with it willingly in order that the boy should become a skilled workman. So Bert was apprenticed – bound for five years to Rushton & Co.

For the first few months his life had been spent in the paint-shop at the yard, a place that was something between a cellar and a stable. There, surrounded by the poisonous pigments and materials of the trade, the youthful artisan worked, generally alone, cleaning the dirty paint-pots brought in by the workmen from finished 'jobs' outside, and occasionally mixing paint according to the instructions of Mr. Hunter, or one of the sub-foremen.

Sometimes he was sent out to carry materials to the places where the men were working – heavy loads of paint or white lead:[27] some-times pails of whitewash that his slender arms had been too feeble to carry more than a few yards at a time.

Often his fragile, childish figure was seen staggering manfully along, bending beneath the weight of a pair of steps or a heavy plank.

He could manage a good many parcels at once: some in each hand and some tied together with string and slung over his shoulders. Occasionally, however, there were more than he could carry; then they were put into a handcart which he pushed or dragged after him to the distant jobs.

That first winter the boy's days were chiefly spent in the damp, evil-smelling, stone-flagged paint-shop, without even a fire to warm the clammy atmosphere.

But in all this he had seen no hardship. With the unconsciousness of boyhood, he worked hard and cheerfully. As time went on, the goal of his childish ambition was reached – he was sent out to work with the men! And he carried the same spirit with him, always doing his best to oblige those with whom he was working.

He tried hard to learn, and to be a good boy, and he succeeded, fairly well.

He soon became a favourite with Owen, for whom he conceived a great respect and affection, for he observed that whenever there was any special work of any kind to be done it was Owen who did it. On such occasions, Bert, in his artful, boyish way, would scheme to be sent to assist Owen, and the latter whenever possible used to ask that the boy might be allowed to work with him.

Bert's regard for Owen was equalled in intensity by his dislike of Crass, who was in the habit of jeering at the boy's aspirations. 'There'll be plenty of time for you to think about doin' fancy work arter you've learnt to do plain painting,' he would say.

This morning, when he had finished washing up the cups and mugs, Bert returned with them to the kitchen.

'Now let's see,' said Crass, thoughtfully. 'You've put the tea in the pail, I s'pose.'

'Yes.'

'And now you want a job, don't you?'

'Yes,' replied the boy.

'Well, get a bucket of water and that old brush and a swab, and go and wash off the old whitewash and colouring orf the pantry ceiling and walls.'

'All right,' said Bert. When he got as far as the door leading into the scullery he looked round and said:

'I've got to git them three bloaters cooked by breakfast time.'

'Never mind about that,' said Crass. 'I'll do them.'

Bert got the pail and the brush, drew some water from the tap, got a pair of steps and a short plank, one end of which he rested on the bottom shelf of the pantry and the other on the steps, and proceeded to carry out Crass' instructions.

It was very cold and damp and miserable in the pantry, and the candle only made it seem more so. Bert shivered: he would like to have put his jacket on, but that was out of the question at a job like this. He lifted the bucket of water on to one of the shelves and, climbing up on to the plank, took the brush from the water and soaked about a square yard of the ceiling; then he began to scrub it with the brush.

He was not very skilful yet, and as he scrubbed the water ran down over the stock of the brush, over his hand and down his uplifted arm, wetting the turned-up sleeves of his shirt. When he had scrubbed it sufficiently he rinsed it off as well as he could with the brush, and then, to finish with, he thrust his hand into the pail of water and, taking out the swab, wrung the water out of it and wiped the part of the ceiling that he had washed. Then he dropped it back into the pail, and shook his numbed fingers to restore the circulation. Then he peeped into the kitchen, where Crass was still seated by the fire, smoking and toasting one of the bloaters at the end of a pointed stick. Bert wished he would go upstairs, or anywhere, so that he himself might go and have a warm at the fire.

' 'E might just as well 'ave let me do them bloaters,' he muttered to himself, regarding Crass malignantly through the crack of the door. 'This is a fine job to give anybody – a cold mornin' like this.'

He shifted the pail of water a little further along the shelf and went on with the work.

A little later, Crass, still sitting by the fire, heard footsteps approaching along the passage. He started up guiltily and, thrusting the hand holding his pipe into his apron pocket, retreated hastily into the scullery. He thought it might be Hunter, who was in the habit of turning up at all sorts of unlikely times, but it was only Easton.

'I've got a bit of bacon I want the young 'un to toast for me,' he said as Crass came back.

'You can do it yourself if you like,' replied Crass affably, looking at his watch. 'It's about ten to eight.'

Easton had been working for Rushton & Co. for a fortnight, and had been wise enough to stand Crass a drink on several occasions: he was consequently in that gentleman's good books for the time being.

'How are you getting on in there?' Crass asked, alluding to the work Easton and Owen were doing in the drawing-room. 'You ain't fell out with your mate yet, I s'pose?'

'No; 'e ain't got much to say this morning; 'is cough's pretty bad. I can generally manage to get on orl right with anybody, you know,' Easton added.

'Well, so can I as a rule, but I get a bit sick listening to that bloody fool. Accordin' to 'im, everything's wrong. One day it's religion, another it's politics, and the next it's something else.'

'Yes, it is a bit thick; too much of it,' agreed Easton, 'but I don't take no notice of the bloody fool: that's the best way.'

'Of course, we know that things is a bit bad just now,' Crass went on, 'but if the likes of 'im could 'ave their own way they'd make 'em a bloody sight worse.'

'That's just what I say,' replied Easton.

'I've got a pill ready for 'im, though, next time 'e starts yappin'.' Crass continued as he drew a small piece of printed paper from his waistcoat pocket. 'Just read that; it's out of the *Obscurer*.'

Easton took the newspaper cutting and read it: 'Very good,' he remarked as he handed it back.

'Yes, I think that'll about shut 'im up. Did yer notice the other day when we was talking about poverty and men bein' out of work, 'ow 'e dodged out of answerin' wot I said about machinery bein' the cause of it? 'e never answered me! Started talkin' about something else.'

'Yes, I remember 'e never answered it,' said Easton, who had really no recollection of the incident at all.

'I mean to tackle 'im about it at breakfast-time. I don't see why 'e should be allowed to get out of it like that. There was a bloke down at the "Cricketers" the other night talkin' about the same thing – a chap as takes a interest in politics and the like, and 'e said the very same as me. Why, the number of men what's been throwed out of work by all this 'ere new-fangled machinery is something chronic!'

'Of course,' agreed Easton, 'everyone knows it.'

'You ought to give us a look in at the "Cricketers" some night. There's a decent lot of chaps comes there.'

'Yes, I think I will.'

'What 'ouse do you usually use?' asked Crass after a pause.

Easton laughed. 'Well, to tell you the truth I've not used anywhere's lately. Been 'avin' too many 'ollerdays.'

'That do make a bit of difference, don't it?' said Crass. 'But you'll be all right 'ere, till this job's done. Just watch yerself a bit, and don't get comin' late in the mornin's. Ole Nimrod's dead nuts on that.'

'I'll see to that all right,' replied Easton. 'I don't believe in losing time when there *is* work to do. It's bad enough when you can't get it.'

'You know,' Crass went on, confidentially. 'Between me an' you an' the gatepost, as the sayin' is, I don't think Mr. bloody Owen will be 'ere much longer. Nimrod 'ates the sight of 'im.'

Easton had it in his mind to say that Nimrod seemed to hate the sight of all of them: but he made no remark, and Crass continued:

' 'E's 'eard all about the way Owen goes on about politics and religion, an' one thing an' another, an' about the firm scampin' the work. You know that sort of talk don't do, does it?'

'Of course not.'

' 'Unter would 'ave got rid of 'im long ago, but it wasn't 'im as took 'im on in the first place. It was Rushton 'imself as give 'im a start. It seems Owen took a lot of samples of 'is work an' showed 'em to the Bloke.'

'Is them the things wot's 'angin' up in the shop-winder?'

'Yes!' said Crass, contemptuously. 'But 'e's no good on plain work. Of course 'e does a bit of grainin' an' writin' – after a fashion – when there's any to do, and that ain't often, but on plain work, why, Sawkins is as good as 'im for most of it, any day!'

'Yes, I suppose 'e is,' replied Easton, feeling rather ashamed of himself for the part he was taking in this conversation.

Although he had for the moment forgotten the existence of Bert, Crass had instinctively lowered his voice, but the boy – who had left off working to warm his hands by putting them into his trousers pockets – managed, by listening attentively, to hear every word.

'You know there's plenty of people wouldn't give the firm no more work if they knowed about it,' Crass continued. 'Just fancy sendin' a b—r like that to work in a lady's or gentleman's 'ouse – a bloody Atheist!'

'Yes, it is a bit orf, when you look at it like that.'

'I know my missis – for one – wouldn't 'ave a feller like that in our place. We 'ad a lodger once and she found out that 'e was a free-thinker or something, and she cleared 'im out, bloody quick, I can tell yer!'

'Oh, by the way,' said Easton, glad of an opportunity to change the subject, 'you don't happen to know of anyone as wants a room, do you? We've got one more than we want, so the wife thought that we might as well let it.'

Crass thought for a moment. 'Can't say as I do,' he answered, doubtfully. 'Slyme was talking last week about leaving the place 'e's lodging at, but I don't know whether 'e's got another place to go to. You might ask him. I don't know of anyone else.'

'I'll speak to 'im,' replied Easton. 'What's the time? it must be nearly on it.'

'So it is: just on eight,' exclaimed Crass, and drawing his whistle he blew a shrill blast upon it to apprise the others of the fact.

'Has anyone seen old Jack Linden since 'e got the push?' enquired Harlow during breakfast.

'I seen 'im Saterdy,' said Slyme.

'Is 'e doin' anything?'

'I don't know: I didn't 'ave time to speak to 'im.'

'No, 'e ain't got nothing,' remarked Philpot. 'I seen 'im Saterdy night, an' 'e told me 'e's been walkin' about ever since.'

Philpot did not add that he had 'lent' Linden a shilling, which he never expected to see again.

' 'E won't be able to get a job again in a 'urry,' remarked Easton. ' 'E's too old.'

'You know, after all, you can't blame Misery for sackin' 'im,' said Crass after a pause. ' 'E was too slow for a funeral.'

'I wonder how much *you'll* be able to do when you're as old as he is?' said Owen.

'P'raps I won't want to do nothing,' replied Crass with a feeble laugh. 'I'm goin' to live on me means.'

'I should say the best thing old Jack could do would be to go in the union,'[28] said Harlow.

'Yes: I reckon that's what'll be the end of it,' said Easton in a matter-of-fact tone.

'It's a grand finish, isn't it?' observed Owen. 'After working hard all one's life to be treated like a criminal at the end.'

'I don't know what you call bein' treated like criminals,' exclaimed Crass. 'I reckon they 'as a bloody fine time of it, an' we've got to find the money.'

'Oh, for Gord's sake don't start no more arguments,' cried Harlow, addressing Owen. 'We 'ad enough of that last week. You can't expect a boss to employ a man when 'e's too old to work.'

'Of course not,' said Crass.

Philpot said – nothing.

'I don't see no sense in always grumblin',' Crass proceeded. 'These things can't be altered. You can't expect there can be plenty of work for everyone with all this 'ere labour-savin' machinery what's been invented.'

'Of course,' said Harlow, 'the people what used to be employed on the work what's now done by machinery, has to find something else to do. Some of 'em goes to our trade, for instance: the result is there's too many at it, and there ain't enough work to keep 'em all goin'.'

'Yes,' cried Crass, eagerly. 'That's just what I say. Machinery is the real cause of all the poverty. That's what I said the other day.'

'Machinery is undoubtedly the cause of unemployment,' replied Owen, 'but it's not the cause of poverty: that's another matter altogether.'

The others laughed derisively.

'Well, it seems to me to amount to the same thing,' said Harlow, and nearly everyone agreed.

'It doesn't seem to me to amount to the same thing,' Owen replied. 'In my opinion, we are all in a state of poverty even when we have employment – the condition we are reduced to when we're out of work is more properly described as destitution.'

'Poverty,' continued Owen after a short silence, 'consists in a shortage of the necessaries of life. When those things are so scarce or so dear that people are unable to obtain sufficient of them to satisfy all their needs, those people are in a condition of poverty. If you think that the machinery, which makes it possible to produce all the necessaries of life in abundance, is the cause of the shortage, it seems to me that there must be something the matter with your minds.'

'Oh, of course we're all bloody fools except you,' snarled Crass. 'When they was servin' out the sense, they give you such a 'ell of a lot, there wasn't none left for nobody else.'

'If there wasn't something wrong with your minds,' continued Owen, 'you would be able to see that we might have "Plenty of Work" and yet be in a state of destitution. The miserable wretches who toil sixteen or eighteen hours a day – father, mother and even the little children – making match-boxes, or shirts or blouses, have "plenty of work", but I for one don't envy them. Perhaps you think that if there was no machinery and we all had to work thirteen or fourteen hours a day in order to obtain a bare living, we should not be in a condition of poverty? Talk about there being something the matter with your minds! If there were not, you wouldn't talk one day about Tariff Reform as a remedy for unemployment and then the next day admit that Machinery is the cause of it! Tariff Reform won't do away with machinery, will it?'

'Tariff Reform is the remedy for bad trade,' returned Crass.

'In that case Tariff Reform is the remedy for a disease that does not exist. If you would only take the trouble to investigate for yourself you would find out that trade was never so good as it is at present: the output – the quantity of commodities of every kind – produced in and exported from this country is greater than it has ever been before. The fortunes amassed in business are larger than ever before: but at the same time – owing, as you have just admitted – to the continued introduction and extended use of wages-saving machinery, the number of human beings employed is steadily decreasing. I have here,' continued Owen, taking out his pocket book, 'some figures which I copied from the *Daily Mail Year Book* for 1907, page 33:

' "It is a very noticeable fact that although the number of factories and their value have vastly increased in the United Kingdom, there is an absolute decrease in the number of men and women employed in those factories between 1895 and 1901. This is doubtless due to the displacement of hand labour by machinery!"

'Will Tariff Reform deal with that? Are the good, kind capitalists going to abandon the use of wages-saving machinery if we tax all foreign-made goods? Does what you call "Free Trade" help us here? Or do you think that abolishing the House of Lords, or disestablishing the Church, will enable the workers who are displaced to obtain employment? Since it *is* true – as you admit – that machinery is the principal cause of unemployment, what are you going to do about it? What's your remedy?'

No one answered, because none of them knew of any remedy: and Crass began to feel sorry that he had re-introduced the subject at all.

'In the near future,' continued Owen, 'it is probable that horses will be almost entirely superseded by motor cars and electric trams. As the services of horses will be no longer required, all but a few of those animals will be caused to die out: they will no longer be bred to the same extent as formerly. We can't blame the horses for allowing themselves to be exterminated. They have not sufficient intelligence to understand what's being done. Therefore they will submit tamely to the extinction of the greater number of their kind.

'As we have seen, a great deal of the work which was formerly done by human beings is now being done by machinery. This machinery belongs to a few people: it is being worked for the benefit of those few, just the same as were the human beings it displaced. These Few have no longer any need of the services of so many human workers, so they propose to exterminate them! The unnecessary human beings are to be allowed to starve to death! And they are also to be taught that it is wrong to marry and breed children, because the Sacred Few do not require so many people to work for them as before!'

'Yes, and you'll never be able to prevent it, mate!' shouted Crass.

'Why can't we?'

'Because it can't be done!' cried Crass fiercely. 'It's impossible!'

'You're always sayin' that everything's all wrong,' complained

Harlow, 'but why the 'ell don't you tell us 'ow they're goin' to be put right?'

'It doesn't seem to me as if any of you really wish to know. I believe that even if it were proved that it could be done, most of you would be sorry and would do all you could to prevent it.'

' 'E don't know 'isself,' sneered Crass. 'Accordin' to 'im, Tariff Reform ain't no bloody good – Free Trade ain't no bloody good, and everybody else is wrong! But when you arst 'im what ought to be done – 'e's flummuxed.'

Crass did not feel very satisfied with the result of this machinery argument, but he consoled himself with the reflection that he would be able to flatten out his opponent on another subject. The cutting from the *Obscurer* which he had in his pocket would take a bit of answering! When you have a thing in print – in black and white – why there it is, and you can't get away from it! If it wasn't all right, a paper like that would never have printed it. However, as it was now nearly half-past eight, he resolved to defer this triumph till another occasion. It was too good a thing to be disposed of in a hurry.

CHAPTER 8

The Cap on the Stairs

After breakfast, when they were working together in the drawing-room, Easton, desiring to do Owen a good turn, thought he would put him on his guard, and repeated to him in a whisper the substance of the conversation he had held with Crass concerning him.

'Of course, you needn't mention that I told you, Frank,' he said, 'but I thought I ought to let you know: you can take it from me, Crass ain't no friend of yours.'

'I've known that for a long time, mate,' replied Owen. 'Thanks for telling me, all the same.'

'The bloody rotter's no friend of mine either, or anyone else's, for that matter,' Easton continued, 'but of course it doesn't do to fall out with 'im because you never know what he'd go and say to old 'Unter.'

'Yes, one has to remember that.'

'Of course we all know what's the matter with 'im as far as *you're* concerned,' Easton went on. 'He don't like 'avin' anyone on the firm wot knows more about the work that 'e does 'imself – thinks 'e might git worked out of 'is job.'

Owen laughed bitterly.

'He needn't be afraid of *me* on *that* account. I wouldn't have his job if it were offered to me.'

'But 'e don't think so,' replied Easton, 'and that's why 'e's got 'is knife into you.'

'I believe that what he said about Hunter is true enough,' said Owen. 'Every time he comes here he tries to goad me into doing or saying something that would give him an excuse to tell me to clear out. I might have done it before now if I had not guessed what he was after, and been on my guard.'

Meantime, Crass, in the kitchen, had resumed his seat by the fire with the purpose of finishing his pipe of tobacco. Presently he took out his pocket-book and began to write in it with a piece of blacklead pencil. When the pipe was smoked out he knocked the bowl against the grate to get rid of the ash, and placed the pipe in his waistcoat pocket. Then, having torn out the leaf on which he had been writing, he got up and went into the pantry, where Bert was still struggling with the old whitewash.

'Ain't yer nearly finished? I don't want yer to stop in 'ere all day, yer know.'

'I ain't got much more to do now,' said the boy. 'Just this bit under the bottom shelf and then I'm done.'

'Yes, and a bloody fine mess you've made, what I can see of it!' growled Crass. 'Look at all this water on the floor!'

Bert looked guiltily at the floor and turned very red.

'I'll clean it all up,' he stammered. 'As soon as I've got this bit of wall done, I'll wipe all the mess up with the swab.'

Crass now took a pot of paint and some brushes and, having put some more fuel on the fire, began in a leisurely way to paint some of the woodwork in the kitchen. Presently Bert came in.

'I've finished out there,' he said.

'About time, too. You'll 'ave to look a bit livelier than you do, you know, or me and you will fall out.'

Bert did not answer.

'Now I've got another job for yer. You're fond of drorin, ain't yer?' continued Crass in a jeering tone.

'Yes, a little,' replied the boy, shamefacedly.

'Well,' said Crass, giving him the leaf he had torn out of the pocketbook, 'you can go to the yard and git them things and put 'em on a truck and dror it up 'ere, and git back as soon as you can. Just look at the paper and see if you understand it before you go. I don't want you to make no mistakes.'

Bert took the paper and with some difficulty read as follows:

> 1 pare steppes 8 foot
> ½ galoon Plastor off perish
> 1 pale off witewosh
> 12 lbs wite led
> ½ galoon Linsede Hoil
> Do. Do. turps.

'I can make it out all right.'

'You'd better bring the big truck,' said Crass, 'because I want you to take the venetian blinds with you on it when you take it back tonight. They've got to be painted at the shop.'

'All right.'

When the boy had departed Crass took a stroll through the house to see how the others were getting on. Then he returned to the kitchen and proceeded with his work.

Crass was about thirty-eight years of age, rather above middle height and rather stout. He had a considerable quantity of curly black hair and wore a short beard of the same colour. His head was rather large, but low, and flat on the top. When among his cronies he was in the habit of referring to his obesity as the result of good nature and a contented mind. Behind his back other people attributed it to beer, some even going so far as to nickname him the 'tank'.

There was no work of a noisy kind being done this morning. Both the carpenters and the bricklayers having been taken away, temporarily, to another 'job'. At the same time there was not absolute silence: occasionally Crass could hear the voices of the other workmen as they spoke to each other, sometimes shouting from one room to another. Now and then Harlow's voice rang through the house as he sang snatches of music-hall songs or a verse of a Moody and Sankey hymn,[29] and occasionally some of the others joined in the chorus or interrupted the singer with squeals and catcalls. Once or twice Crass was on the point of telling them to make less row: there would be a fine to do if Nimrod came and heard them. Just as he had made up his mind to tell them to stop the noise, it ceased of itself and he heard loud whispers:

'Look out! Someone's comin'.'

The house became very quiet.

Crass put out his pipe and opened the window and the back door to get rid of the smell of the tobacco smoke. Then he shifted the pair of steps noisily, and proceeded to work more quickly than before. Most likely it was old Misery.

He worked on for some time in silence, but no one came to the kitchen: whoever it was must have gone upstairs. Crass listened attentively. Who could it be? He would have liked to go to see whom it was, but at the same time, if it were Nimrod, Crass wished to be discovered at work. He therefore waited a little longer and presently he heard the sound of voices upstairs but was unable to recognise them. He was just about to go out into the passage to listen, when whoever it was began coming downstairs. Crass at once resumed his work. The footsteps came along the passage leading to the kitchen: slow, heavy, ponderous footsteps, but yet the sound was not such as would be made by a man heavily shod. It was not Misery, evidently.

As the footsteps entered the kitchen, Crass looked round and beheld a very tall, obese figure, with a large, fleshy, coarse-featured, clean-shaven face, and a great double chin, the complexion being of the colour and appearance of the fat of uncooked bacon. A very large fleshy nose and weak-looking pale blue eyes, the slightly inflamed lids being almost destitute of eyelashes. He had large fat feet cased in soft calfskin boots, with drab-coloured spats. His overcoat, heavily trimmed with seal-skin, reached just below the knees, and although the trousers were very wide they were filled by the fat legs within, the shape of the calves being distinctly perceptible. Even as the feet seemed about to burst the uppers of the boots, so the legs appeared to threaten the trousers with disruption. This man was so large that his figure completely filled up the doorway, and as he came in he stooped slightly to avoid damaging the glittering silk hat on his head. One gloved hand was thrust into the pocket of the overcoat and in the other he carried a small Gladstone bag.

When Crass beheld this being, he touched his cap respectfully.

'Good morning, sir!'

'Good morning. They told me upstairs that I should find the foreman here. Are you the foreman?'

'Yes, sir.'

'I see you're getting on with the work here.'

'Ho yes, sir, we're beginning to make a bit hov a show now, sir,' replied Crass, speaking as if he had a hot potato in his mouth.

'Mr. Rushton isn't here yet, I suppose?'

'No, sir: 'e don't horfun come hon the job hin the mornin', sir; 'e generally comes hafternoons, sir, but Mr. 'Unter's halmost sure to be 'ere presently, sir.'

'It's Mr. Rushton I want to see: I arranged to meet him here at ten o'clock; but' – looking at his watch – 'I'm rather before my time.'

'He'll be here presently, I suppose,' added Mr. Sweater. 'I'll just take a look round till he comes.'

'Yes, sir,' responded Crass, walking behind him obsequiously as he went out of the room.

Hoping that the gentleman might give him a shilling, Crass followed him into the front hall and began explaining what progress had so far been made with the work, but as Mr. Sweater answered only by monosyllables and grunts, Crass presently concluded that his conversation was not appreciated and returned to the kitchen.

Meantime, upstairs, Philpot had gone into Newman's room and was discussing with him the possibility of extracting from Mr. Sweater the price of a little light refreshment.

'I think,' he remarked, 'that we oughter see-ise this 'ere tuner-opperty[30] to touch 'im for an allowance.'

'We won't git nothin' out of '*im*, mate,' returned Newman. ' 'E's a red-'ot teetotaller.'

'That don't matter. 'Ow's 'e to know that we buys beer with it? We might 'ave tea, or ginger ale, or lime-juice and glycerine for all 'e knows!'

Mr. Sweater now began ponderously re-ascending the stairs and presently came into the room where Philpot was. The latter greeted him with respectful cordiality:

'Good morning, sir.'

'Good morning. You've begun painting up here, then.'

'Yes, sir, we've made a start on it,' replied Philpot, affably.

'Is this door wet?' asked Sweater, glancing apprehensively at the sleeve of his coat.

'Yes, sir,' answered Philpot, and added, as he looked meaningly at the great man, 'the paint is wet, sir, but the *painters* is dry.'

'Confound it!' exclaimed Sweater, ignoring, or not hearing the latter part of Philpot's reply. 'I've got some of the beastly stuff on my coat sleeve.'

'Oh, that's nothing, sir,' cried Philpot, secretly delighted. 'I'll get that orf for yer in no time. You wait just 'arf a mo!'

He had a piece of clean rag in his tool bag, and there was a can of turps in the room. Moistening the rag slightly with turps he carefully removed the paint from Sweater's sleeve.

'It's all orf now, sir,' he remarked, as he rubbed the place with a dry part of the rag. 'The smell of the turps will go away in about a hour's time.'

'Thanks,' said Sweater.

Philpot looked at him wistfully, but Sweater evidently did not understand, and began looking about the room.

'I see they've put a new piece of skirting here,' he observed.

'Yes, sir,' said Newman, who came into the room just then to get the turps. 'The old piece was all to bits with dry-rot.'

'I feel as if I 'ad a touch of the dry-rot meself, don't you?' said Philpot to Newman, who smiled feebly and cast a sidelong glance at Sweater, who did not appear to notice the significance of the remark, but walked out of the room and began climbing up to the next floor, where Harlow and Sawkins were working.

'Well, there's a bleeder for yer!' said Philpot with indignation. 'After all the trouble I took to clean 'is coat! Not a bloody stiver![31] Well, it takes the cake, don't it?'

'I told you 'ow it would be, didn't I?' replied Newman.

'P'raps I didn't make it plain enough,' said Philpot, thoughtfully. 'We must try to get some of our own back somehow, you know.'

Going out on the landing he called softly upstairs:

'I say, Harlow.'

'Hallo,' said that individual, looking over the banisters.

'Ow are yer getting on up there?'

'Oh, all right, you know.'

'Pretty dry job, ain't it?' Philpot continued, raising his voice a little and winking at Harlow.

'Yes, it is, rather,' replied Harlow with a grin.

'I think this would be a very good time to take up the collection, don't you?'

'Yes, it wouldn't be a bad idear.'

'Well, I'll put me cap on the stairs,' said Philpot, suiting the action to the word. 'You never knows yer luck. Things is gettin' a bit serious on this floor, you know; my mate's fainted away once already!'

Philpot now went back to his room to await developments: but as Sweater made no sign, he returned to the landing and again hailed Harlow.

'I always reckon a man can work all the better after 'e's 'ad a drink: you can seem to get over more of it, like.'

'Oh, that's true enough,' responded Harlow. 'I've often noticed it meself.'

Sweater came out of the front bedroom and passed into one of the back rooms without any notice of either of the men.

'I'm afraid it's a frost, mate,' Harlow whispered, and Philpot, shaking his head sadly, returned to work; but in a little while he came out again and once more accosted Harlow.

'I knowed a case once,' he said in a melancholy tone, 'where a chap died – of thirst – on a job just like this; and at the inquest the doctor said as 'arf a pint would 'a saved 'im!'

'It must 'ave been a norrible death,' remarked Harlow.

' 'Orrible ain't the word for it, mate,' replied Philpot mournfully. 'It was something chronic!'

After this final heartrending appeal to Sweater's humanity they returned to work, satisfied that, whatever the result of their efforts, they had done their best. They had placed the matter fully and fairly before him: nothing more could be said: the issue now rested entirely with him.

But it was all in vain. Sweater either did not or would not understand, and when he came downstairs he took no notice whatever of the cap which Philpot had placed so conspicuously in the centre of the landing floor.

CHAPTER 9

Who is to Pay?

Sweater reached the hall almost at the same moment that Rushton entered by the front door. They greeted each other in a friendly way and after a few remarks concerning the work that was being done, they went into the drawing-room where Owen and Easton were and Rushton said:

'What about this room? Have you made up your mind what you're going to have done to it?'

'Yes,' replied Sweater; 'but I'll tell you about that afterwards. What I'm anxious about is the drains. Have you brought the plans?'

'Yes.'

'What's it going to cost?'

'Just wait a minute,' said Rushton, with a slight gesture calling Sweater's attention to the presence of the two workmen. Sweater understood.

'You might leave that for a few minutes, will you?' Rushton

continued, addressing Owen and Easton. 'Go and get on with something else for a little while.'

When they were alone, Rushton closed the door and remarked: 'It's always as well not to let these fellows know more than is necessary.'

Sweater agreed.

'Now this 'ere drain work is really two separate jobs,' said Rushton. 'First, the drains of the house: that is, the part of the work that's actually on your ground. When that's done, there will 'ave to be a pipe carried right along under this private road to the main road to connect the drains of the house with the town main. You follow me?'

'Perfectly. What's it going to cost for the lot?'

'For the drains of the house, £25 0. 0. and for the connecting pipe £30. 0. 0. £55. 0. 0. for the lot.'

' 'Um! That the lowest you can do it for, eh?'

'That's the lowest. I've figured it out most carefully, the time and materials, and that's practically all I'm charging you.'

The truth of the matter was that Rushton had had nothing whatever to do with estimating the cost of this work: he had not the necessary knowledge to do so. Hunter had drawn the plans, calculated the cost and prepared the estimate.

'I've been thinking over this business lately,' said Sweater, looking at Rushton with a cunning leer. 'I don't see why I should have to pay for the connecting pipe. The Corporation ought to pay for that. What do you say?'

Rushton laughed. 'I don't see why not,' he replied.

'I think we could arrange it all right, don't you?' Sweater went on. 'Anyhow, the work will have to be done, so you'd better let 'em get on with it. £55. 0. 0. covers both jobs, you say?'

'Yes.'

'Oh, all right, you get on with it and we'll see what can be done with the Corporation later on.'

'I don't suppose we'll find 'em very difficult to deal with,' said Rushton with a grin, and Sweater smiled agreement.

As they were passing through the hall they met Hunter, who had just arrived. He was rather surprised to see them, as he knew nothing of their appointment. He wished them 'Good morning' in an awkward hesitating undertone as if he were doubtful how his greeting would be received. Sweater nodded slightly, but Rushton ignored him altogether and Nimrod passed on looking and feeling like a disreputable cur that had just been kicked.

As Sweater and Rushton walked together about the house, Hunter hovered about them at a respectful distance, hoping that presently some notice might be taken of him. His dismal countenance became even longer than usual when he observed that they were about to leave the house without appearing even to know that he was there. However, just as they were going out, Rushton paused on the threshold and called him:

'Mr. Hunter!'

'Yes, sir.'

Nimrod ran to him like a dog taken notice of by his master: if he had possessed a tail, it is probable that he would have wagged it. Rushton gave him the plans with an intimation that the work was to be proceeded with.

For some time after they were gone, Hunter crawled silently about the house, in and out of the rooms, up and down the corridors and the staircases. After a while he went into the room where Newman was and stood quietly watching him for about ten minutes as he worked. The man was painting the skirting, and just then he came to a part that was split in several places, so he took his knife and began to fill the cracks with putty. He was so nervous under Hunter's scrutiny that his hand trembled to such an extent that it took him about twice as long as it should have done, and Hunter told him so with brutal directness.

'Never mind about puttying up such little cracks as them!' he shouted. 'Fill 'em up with the paint. We can't afford to pay you for messing about like that!'

Newman made no reply.

Misery found no excuse for bullying anyone else, because they were all tearing into it for all they were worth. As he wandered up and down the house like an evil spirit, he was followed by the furtively unfriendly glances of the men, who cursed him in their hearts as he passed.

He sneaked into the drawing-room and after standing with a malignant expression, silently watching Owen and Easton, he came out again without having uttered a word.

Although he frequently acted in this manner, yet somehow today the circumstance worried Owen considerably. He wondered uneasily what it meant, and began to feel vaguely apprehensive. Hunter's silence seemed more menacing than his speech.

CHAPTER 10

The Long Hill

Bert arrived at the shop and with as little delay as possible loaded up the handcart with the things he had been sent for and started on the return journey. He got on all right in the town, because the roads were level and smooth, being paved with wood blocks. If it had only been like that all the way it would have been easy enough, although he was a very small boy for such a large truck, and such a heavy load. While the wood road lasted the principal trouble he experienced was the difficulty of seeing where he was going, the handcart being so high and himself so short. The pair of steps on the cart of course made it all the worse in that respect. However, by taking great care he managed to get through the town all right, although he narrowly escaped colliding with several vehicles, including two or three motor cars and an electric tram, besides nearly knocking over an old woman who was carrying a large bundle of washing. From time to time he saw other small boys of his acquaintance, some of them former schoolmates. Some of these passed by carrying heavy loads of groceries in baskets, and others with wooden trays full of joints of meat.

Unfortunately, the wood paving ceased at the very place where the ground began to rise. Bert now found himself at the beginning of a long stretch of macadamised road which rose slightly and persistently throughout its whole length. Bert had pushed a cart up this road many times before and consequently knew the best method of tackling it. Experience had taught him that a frontal attack on this hill was liable to failure, so on this occasion he followed his usual plan of making diagonal movements, crossing the road repeatedly from right to left and left to right, after the fashion of a sailing ship tacking against the wind, and halting about every twenty yards to rest and take breath. The distance he was to go was regulated, not so much by his powers of endurance as by the various objects by the wayside – the lamp-posts, for instance. During each rest he used to look ahead and select a certain lamp-post or street corner as the next stopping-place, and when he started again he used to make the most strenuous and desperate efforts to reach it.

Generally the goal he selected was too distant, for he usually overestimated his strength, and whenever he was forced to give in he ran the truck against the kerb and stood there panting for breath and feeling profoundly disappointed at his failure.

On the present occasion, during one of these rests, it flashed upon him that he was being a very long time: he would have to buck up or he would get into a row: he was not even halfway up the road yet!

Selecting a distant lamp-post, he determined to reach it before resting again.

The cart had a single shaft with a cross-piece at the end, forming the handle: he gripped this fiercely with both hands and, placing his chest against it, with a mighty effort he pushed the cart before him.

It seemed to get heavier and heavier every foot of the way. His whole body, but especially the thighs and the calves of his legs, pained terribly, but still he strained and struggled and said to himself that he would not give in until he reached the lamp-post.

Finding that the handle hurt his chest, he lowered it to his waist, but that being even more painful he raised it again to his chest, and struggled savagely on, panting for breath and with his heart beating wildly.

The cart became heavier and heavier. After a while it seemed to the boy as if there were someone at the front of it trying to push him back down the hill. This was such a funny idea that for a moment he felt inclined to laugh, but the inclination went almost as soon as it came and was replaced by the dread that he would not be able to hold out long enough to reach the lamp-post, after all. Clenching his teeth, he made a tremendous effort and staggered forward two or three more steps and then – the cart stopped. He struggled with it despairingly for a few seconds, but all the strength had suddenly gone out of him: his legs felt so weak that he nearly collapsed on to the ground, and the cart began to move backwards down the hill. He was just able to stick to it and guide it so that it ran into and rested against the kerb, and then he stood holding it in a half-dazed way, very pale, saturated with perspiration, and trembling. His legs in particular shook so much that he felt that unless he could sit down for a little, he would *fall* down.

He lowered the handle very carefully so as not to spill the white-wash out of the pail which was hanging from a hook under the cart, then, sitting down on the kerbstone, he leaned wearily against the wheel.

A little way down the road was a church with a clock in the tower.

It was five minutes to ten by this clock. Bert said to himself that when it was ten he would make another start.

Whilst he was resting he thought of many things. Just behind that church was a field with several ponds in it where he used to go with other boys to catch effets.[32] If it were not for the cart he would go across now, to see whether there were any there still. He remembered that he had been very eager to leave school and go to work, but they used to be fine old times after all.

Then he thought of the day when his mother took him to Mr. Rushton's office to 'bind' him. He remembered that day very vividly: it was almost a year ago. How nervous he had been! His hand had trembled so that he was scarcely able to hold the pen. And even when it was all over, they had both felt very miserable, somehow. His mother had been very nervous in the office also, and when they got home she cried a lot and held him close to her and kissed him and called him her poor little fatherless boy, and said she hoped he would be good and try to learn. And then he cried as well, and promised her that he would do his best. He reflected with pride that he was keeping his promise about being a good boy and trying to learn: in fact, he knew a great deal about the trade already – he could paint back doors as well as anybody! and railings as well. Owen had taught him lots of things and had promised to do some patterns of graining for him so that he might practise copying them at home in the evenings. Owen was a fine chap. Bert resolved that he would tell him what Crass had been saying to Easton. Just fancy, the cheek of a rotter like Crass, trying to get Owen the sack! It would be more like it if Crass was to be sacked himself, so that Owen could be the foreman.

One minute to ten.

With a heavy heart Bert watched the clock. His legs were still aching very badly. He could not see the hands of the clock moving, but they were creeping on all the same. Now, the minute hand was over the edge of the number, and he began to deliberate whether he might not rest for another five minutes? But he had been such a long time already on his errand that he dismissed the thought. The minute hand was now upright and it was time to go on.

Just as he was about to get up a harsh voice behind him said:

'How much longer are you going to sit there?'

Bert started up guiltily, and found himself confronted by Mr. Rushton, who was regarding him with an angry frown, whilst close by towered the colossal figure of the obese Sweater, the expression on his greasy countenance betokening the pain he experienced on beholding such an appalling example of juvenile depravity.

'What do you mean by sich conduct?' demanded Rushton, indignantly. 'The idear of sitting there like that when most likely the men are waiting for them things?'

Crimson with shame and confusion, the boy made no reply.

'You've been there a long time,' continued Rushton, 'I've been watchin' you all the time I've been comin' down the road.'

Bert tried to speak to explain why he had been resting, but his mouth and his tongue had become quite parched from terror and he was unable to articulate a single word.

'You know, that's not the way to get on in life, my boy,' observed Sweater lifting his forefinger and shaking his fat head reproachfully.

'Get along with you at once!' Rushton said, roughly. 'I'm surprised at yer! The idear! Sitting down in my time!'

This was quite true. Rushton was not merely angry, but astonished at the audacity of the boy. That anyone in his employment should dare to have the impertinence to sit down in his time was incredible.

The boy lifted the handle of the cart and once more began to push it up the hill. It seemed heavier now than ever, but he managed to get on somehow. He kept glancing back after Rushton and Sweater, who presently turned a corner and were lost to view: then he ran the cart to the kerb again to have a breathe. He couldn't have kept up much further without a spell even if they had still been watching him, but he didn't rest for more than about half a minute this time, because he was afraid they might be peeping round the corner at him.

After this he gave up the lamp-post system and halted for a minute or so at regular short intervals. In this way, he at length reached the top of the hill, and with a sigh of relief congratulated himself that the journey was practically over.

Just before he arrived at the gate of the house, he saw Hunter sneak out and mount his bicycle and ride away. Bert wheeled his cart up to the front door and began carrying in the things. Whilst thus engaged he noticed Philpot peeping cautiously over the banisters of the staircase, and called out to him:

'Give us a hand with this bucket of whitewash, will yer, Joe?'

'Certinly, me son, with the greatest of hagony,' replied Philpot as he hurried down the stairs.

As they were carrying it in Philpot winked at Bert and whispered: 'Did yer see Pontius Pilate anywheres outside?'

' 'E went away on 'is bike just as I come in the gate.'

'Did 'e? Thank Gord for that! I don't wish 'im no 'arm,' said Philpot, fervently, 'but I 'opes 'e gets runned over with a motor.'

In this wish Bert entirely concurred, and similar charitable sentiments were expressed by all the others as soon as they heard that Misery was gone.

Just before four o'clock that afternoon Bert began to load up the truck with the venetian blinds, which had been taken down some days previously.

'I wonder who'll have the job of paintin' 'em?' remarked Philpot to Newman.

'P'raps's they'll take a couple of us away from 'ere.'

'I shouldn't think so. We're short-'anded 'ere already. Most likely they'll put on a couple of fresh 'ands. There's a 'ell of a lot of work in all them blinds, you know: I reckon they'll 'ave to 'ave three or four coats, the state they're in.'

'Yes. No doubt that's what will be done,' replied Newman, and added with a mirthless laugh:

'I don't suppose they'll have much difficulty in getting a couple of chaps.'

'No, you're right, mate. There's plenty of 'em walkin' about as a week's work would be a Gordsend to.'

'Come to think of it,' continued Newman after a pause, 'I believe the firm used to give all their blind work to old Latham, the venetian blind maker. Prap's they'll give 'im this lot to do.'

'Very likely,' replied Philpot, 'I should think 'e can do 'em cheaper even than us chaps, and that's all the firm cares about.'

How far their conjectures were fulfilled will appear later.

Shortly after Bert was gone it became so dark that it was necessary to light the candles, and Philpot remarked that although he hated working under such conditions, yet he was always glad when lighting up time came, because then knocking off time was not very far behind.

About five minutes to five, just as they were all putting their things away for the night, Nimrod suddenly appeared in the house. He had come hoping to find some of them ready dressed to go home before the proper time. Having failed in this laudable enterprise, he stood silently by himself for some seconds in the drawing-room. This was a spacious and lofty apartment with a large semicircular bay window. Round the ceiling was a deep cornice. In the semi-darkness the room appeared to be of even greater proportions than it really was. After standing thinking in this room for a little while, Hunter turned and strode out to the kitchen, where the men were preparing to go home.

Owen was taking off his blouse[33] and apron as the other entered. Hunter addressed him with a malevolent snarl:

'You can call at the office tonight as you go home.'

Owen's heart seemed to stop beating. All the petty annoyances he had endured from Hunter rushed into his memory, together with what Easton had told him that morning. He stood, still and speechless, holding his apron in his hand and staring at the manager.

'What for?' he ejaculated at length. 'What's the matter?'

'You'll find out what you're wanted for when you get there,' returned Hunter as he went out of the room and away from the house.

When he was gone a dead silence prevailed. The hands ceased their preparations for departure and looked at each other and at Owen in astonishment. To stand a man off like that – when the job was not half finished – and for no apparent reason: and of a Monday, too. It was unheard of. There was a general chorus of indignation. Harlow and Philpot especially were very wroth.

'If it comes to that,' Harlow shouted, 'they've got no bloody right to do it! We're intitled to an hour's notice.'

'Of course we are!' cried Philpot, his goggle eyes rolling wildly with wrath. 'And I should 'ave it too, if it was me. You take my tip, Frank: *Charge up to six o'clock* on yer time sheet and get some of your own back.'

Everyone joined in the outburst of indignant protest. Everyone, that is, except Crass and Slyme. But then they were not exactly in the kitchen: they were out in the scullery putting their things away, and so it happened that they said nothing, although they exchanged significant looks.

Owen had by this time recovered his self-possession. He collected all his tools and put them with his apron and blouse into his tool-bag with the purpose of taking them with him that night, but on reflection he resolved not to do so. After all, it was not absolutely certain that he was going to be 'stood off': possibly they were going to send him to some other job.

They kept all together – some walking on the pavement and some in the road – until they got down town, and then separated. Crass, Sawkins, Bundy and Philpot adjourned to the 'Cricketers' for a drink, Newman went on by himself, Slyme accompanied Easton, who had arranged with him to come that night to see the bedroom, and Owen went in the direction of the office.

CHAPTER 11

Hands and Brains

Rusgton & Co.'s premises were situated in one of the principal streets of Mugsborough and consisted of a double-fronted shop with plate glass windows. The shop extended right through to the narrow back street which ran behind it. The front part of the shop was stocked with wall-hangings, mouldings, stands showing patterns of embossed wall and ceiling decorations, cases of brushes, tins of varnish and enamel, and similar things.

The office was at the rear and was separated from the rest of the shop by a partition, glazed with muranese obscured glass.[34] This office had two doors, one in the partition, giving access to the front shop, and the other by the side of the window and opening on to the back street. The glass of the lower sash of the back window consisted of one large pane on which was painted 'Rushton & Co.' in black letters on a white ground.

Owen stood outside this window for two or three seconds before knocking. There was a bright light in the office. Then he knocked at the door, which was at once opened from the inside by Hunter, and Owen went in.

Rushton was seated in an armchair at his desk, smoking a cigar and reading one of several letters that were lying before him. At the back was a large unframed photograph of the size known as half-plate of the interior of some building. At another desk, or rather table, at the other side of the office, a young woman was sitting writing in a large ledger. There was a type-writing machine on the table at her side.

Rushton glanced up carelessly as Owen came in, but took no further notice of him.

'Just wait a minute,' Hunter said to Owen, and then, after conversing in a low tone with Rushton for a few minutes, the foreman put on his hat and went out of the office through the partition door which led into the front shop.

Owen stood waiting for Rushton to speak. He wondered why Hunter had sneaked off and felt inclined to open the door and call him back. One thing he was determined about: he meant to have some explanation: he would not submit tamely to be dismissed without any just reason.

When he had finished reading the letter, Rushton looked up, and, leaning comfortably back in his chair, he blew a cloud of smoke from his cigar, and said in an affable, indulgent tone, such as one might use to a child:

'You're a bit of a hartist, ain't yer?'

Owen was so surprised at this reception that he was for the moment unable to reply.

'You know what I mean,' continued Rushton; 'decorating work, something like them samples of yours what's hanging up there.'

He noticed the embarrassment of Owen's manner, and was gratified. He thought the man was confused at being spoken to by such a superior person as himself.

Mr. Rushton was about thirty-five years of age, with light grey eyes, fair hair and moustache, and his complexion was a whitey drab. He was tall – about five feet ten inches – and rather clumsily built; not corpulent, but fat – in good condition. He appeared to be very well fed and well cared for generally. His clothes were well made, of good quality, and fitted him perfectly. He was dressed in a grey Norfolk suit, dark brown boots and knitted woollen stockings reaching to the knee.

He was a man who took himself very seriously. There was an air of pomposity and arrogant importance about him which – considering who and what he was – would have been entertaining to any observer gifted with a sense of humour.

'Yes,' replied Owen at last. 'I can do a little of that sort of work, although of course I don't profess to be able to do it as well or as quickly as a man who does nothing else.'

'Oh, no, of course not, but I think you could manage this all right. It's that drawing-room at the "Cave". Mr. Sweater's been speaking to me about it. It seems that when he was over in Paris some time since he saw a room that took his fancy. The walls and ceiling was not papered, but painted: you know what I mean; sort of panelled out, and decorated with stencils and hand painting. This 'ere's a photer of it: it's done in a sort of *Japanese* fashion.'

He handed the photograph to Owen as he spoke. It represented a room, the walls and ceiling of which were decorated in a Moorish style.

'At first Mr. Sweater thought of getting a firm from London to do it, but 'e give up the idear on account of the expense; but if you can do it so that it doesn't cost too much, I think I can persuade 'im to go in for it. But if it's goin' to cost a lot it won't come off at all. 'E'll just 'ave a frieze put up and 'ave the room papered in the ordinary way.'

This was not true: Rushton said it in case Owen might want to be paid extra wages while doing the work. The truth was that Sweater was going to have the room decorated in any case, and intended to get a London firm to do it. He had consented rather unwillingly to let Rushton & Co. submit him an estimate, because he thought they would not be able to do the work satisfactorily.

Owen examined the photograph closely.

'Could you do anything like that in that room?'

'Yes, I think so,' replied Owen.

'Well, you know, I don't want you to start on the job and not be able to finish it. Can you do it or not?'

Rushton felt sure that Owen could do it, and was very desirous that he should undertake it, but he did not want him to know that. He wished to convey the impression that he was almost indifferent whether Owen did the work or not. In fact, he wished to seem to be conferring a favour upon him by procuring him such a nice job as this.

'I'll tell you what I *can* do,' Owen replied. 'I can make you a water-colour sketch – a design – and if you think it good enough, of course, I can reproduce it on the ceiling and the walls, and I can let you know, within a little, how long it will take.'

Rushton appeared to reflect. Owen stood examining the photograph and began to feel an intense desire to do the work.

Rushton shook his head dubiously.

'If I let you spend a lot of time over the sketches and then Mr. Sweater does not approve of your design, where do I come in?'

'Well, suppose we put it like this: I'll draw the design at home in the evenings – in my own time. If it's accepted, I'll charge you for the time I've spent upon it. If it's not suitable, I won't charge the time at all.'

Rushton brightened up considerably. 'All right. You can do so,' he said with an affectation of good nature, 'but you mustn't pile it on too thick, in any case, you know, because, as I said before, 'e don't want to spend too much money on it. In fact, if it's goin' to cost a great deal 'e simply won't 'ave it done at all.'

Rushton knew Owen well enough to be sure that no consideration of time or pains would prevent him from putting the very best that was in him into this work. He knew that if the man did the room at all there was no likelihood of his scamping it for the sake of getting it done quickly; and for that matter Rushton did not wish him to hurry over it. All that he wanted to do was to impress upon Owen from the very first that he must not charge too much time. Any profit that it was possible to make out of the work, Rushton meant to secure for himself. He was a smart man, this Rushton, he possessed the ideal character: the kind of character that is necessary for any man who wishes to succeed in business – to get on in life. In other words, his disposition was very similar to that of a pig – he was intensely selfish.

No one has any right to condemn him for this, because all who live under the present system practise selfishness, more or less. We must be selfish: the System demands it. We must be selfish or we shall be hungry and ragged and finally die in the gutter. The more selfish we are the better off we shall be. In the 'Battle of Life' only the selfish and cunning are able to survive: all others are beaten down and trampled under foot. No one can justly be blamed for acting selfishly – it is a matter of self-preservation – we must either injure or be injured. It is the system that deserves to be blamed. What those who wish to perpetuate the system deserve is another question.

'When do you think you'll have the drawings ready?' enquired Rushton. 'Can you get them done tonight?'

'I'm afraid not,' replied Owen, feeling inclined to laugh at the absurdity of the question. 'It will need a little thinking about.'

'When can you have them ready then? This is Monday. Wednesday morning?'

Owen hesitated.

'We don't want to keep ''im waiting too long, you know, or 'e may give up the idear altogether.'

'Well, say Friday morning, then,' said Owen, resolving that he would stay up all night if necessary to get it done.

Rushton shook his head.

'Can't you get it done before that? I'm afraid if we keeps ''im waiting all that time we may lose the job altogether.'

'I can't get them done any quicker in my spare time,' returned Owen, flushing. 'If you like to let me stay home tomorrow and charge the time the same as if I had gone to work at the house, I could go to my ordinary work on Wednesday and let you have the drawings on Thursday morning.'

'Oh, all right,' said Rushton, hastily. 'But all the same don't pile it on too thick, or we shall have to charge so much for the work that 'e won't 'ave it done at all. Good night.'

'I suppose I may take this photograph with me?'

'Yes; certainly,' said Rushton as he returned to the perusal of his letters.

That night, long after his wife and Frankie were asleep, Owen worked in the sitting-room, searching through old numbers of the *Decorators' Journal* and through the illustrations in other books of designs for examples of Moorish work, and making rough sketches in pencil.

He did not attempt to finish anything yet: it was necessary to think first; but he roughed out the general plan, and when at last he did go to bed he could not sleep for a long time. He almost fancied he was in the drawing-room at the 'Cave'. First of all it would be necessary to take down the ugly plaster centre flower with its crevices all filled up with old whitewash. The cornice was all right; it was fortunately a very simple one, with a deep cove and without many enrichments. Then, when the walls and the ceiling had been properly prepared, the ornamentation would be proceeded with. The walls, divided into panels and arches containing painted designs and lattice-work; the panels of the door decorated in a similar manner. The mouldings of the door and window frames picked out with colours and gold so as to be in character with the other work; the cove of the cornice, a dull yellow with a bold ornament in colour – gold was not advisable in the hollow because of the unequal distribution of the light, but some of the smaller mouldings of the cornice should be gold. On the ceiling there would be one large panel covered with an appropriate design in gold and colours and surrounded by a wide margin or border. To separate this margin from the centre panel there would be a narrow border, and another border – but wider – round the outer edge of the margin, where the ceiling met the cornice. Both these borders and the margin would be covered with ornamentation in colour and gold. Great care would be necessary when deciding what parts were to be gilded because – whilst large masses of gilding are apt to look garish and in bad taste – a lot of fine gold lines are ineffective, especially on a flat surface, where they do not always catch the light. Process by process he traced the work, and saw it advancing stage by stage until, finally, the large apartment was transformed and glorified. And then in the midst of the pleasure he experienced in the planning of the work there came the fear that perhaps they would not have it done at all.

The question, what personal advantage would he gain never once occurred to Owen. He simply wanted to do the work; and he was so fully occupied with thinking and planning how it was to be done that the question of profit was crowded out.

But although this question of what profit could be made out of the work never occurred to Owen, it would in due course be fully considered by Mr. Rushton. In fact, it was the only thing about the work that Mr. Rushton would think of at all: how much money could be made out of it. This is what is meant by the oft-quoted saying, 'The men work with their hands – the master works with his brains.'

CHAPTER 12

The Letting of the Room

It will be remembered that when the men separated, Owen going to the office to see Rushton, and the others on their several ways, Easton and Slyme went together.

During the day Easton had found an opportunity of speaking to him about the bedroom. Slyme was about to leave the place where he was at present lodging, and he told Easton that although he had almost decided on another place he would take a look at the room. At Easton's suggestion they arranged that Slyme was to accompany him home that night. As the former remarked, Slyme could come to see the place, and if he didn't like it as well as the other he was thinking of taking, there was no harm done.

Ruth had contrived to furnish the room. Some of the things she had obtained on credit from a second-hand furniture dealer. Exactly how she had managed, Easton did not know, but it was done.

'This is the house,' said Easton. As they passed through, the gate creaked loudly on its hinges and then closed of itself rather noisily.

Ruth had just been putting the child to sleep and she stood up as they came in, hastily fastening the bodice of her dress as she did so.

'I've brought a gentleman to see you,' said Easton.

Although she knew that he was looking out for someone for the room, Ruth had not expected him to bring anyone home in this sudden manner, and she could not help wishing that he had told her beforehand of his intention. It being Monday, she had been very busy all day and she was conscious that she was rather untidy in her appearance. Her long brown hair was twisted loosely into a coil behind her head. She blushed in an embarrassed way as the young man stared at her.

Easton introduced Slyme by name and they shook hands; and then at Ruth's suggestion Easton took a light to show him the room, and while they were gone Ruth hurriedly tidied her hair and dress.

When they came down again Slyme said he thought the room would suit him very well. What were the terms?

Did he wish to take the room only – just to lodge? enquired Ruth, or would he prefer to board as well?

Slyme intimated that he desired the latter arrangement.

In that case she thought twelve shillings a week would be fair. She believed that was about the usual amount. Of course that would include washing, and if his clothes needed a little mending she would do it for him.

Slyme expressed himself satisfied with these terms, which were as Ruth had said – about the usual ones. He would take the room, but he was not leaving his present lodgings until Saturday. It was therefore agreed that he was to bring his box on Saturday evening.

When he had gone, Easton and Ruth stood looking at each other in silence. Ever since this plan of letting the room first occurred to them they had been very anxious to accomplish it; and yet, now that it was done, they felt dissatisfied and unhappy, as if they had suddenly experienced some irreparable misfortune. In that moment they remembered nothing of the darker side of their life together. The hard times and the privations were far off and seemed insignificant beside the fact that this stranger was for the future to share their home. To Ruth especially it seemed that the happiness of the past twelve months had suddenly come to an end. She shrank with involuntary aversion and apprehension from the picture that rose before her of the future in which this intruder appeared the most prominent figure, dominating everything and interfering with every detail of their home life. Of course they had known all this before, but somehow it had never seemed so objectionable as it did now, and as Easton thought of it he was filled with an unreasonable resentment against Slyme, as if the latter had forced himself upon them against their will.

'Damn him!' he thought. 'I wish I'd never brought him here at all!'

Ruth did not appear to him to be very happy about it either.

'Well?' he said at last. 'What do you think of him?'

'Oh, he'll be all right, I suppose.'

'For my part, I wish he wasn't coming,' Easton continued.

'That's just what I was thinking,' replied Ruth dejectedly. 'I don't like him at all. I seemed to turn against him directly he came in the door.'

'I've a good mind to back out of it, somehow, tomorrow,' exclaimed Easton after another silence. 'I could tell him we've unexpectedly got some friends coming to stay with us.'

'Yes,' said Ruth eagerly. 'It would be easy enough to make some excuse or other.'

As this way of escape presented itself she felt as if a weight had been lifted from her mind, but almost in the same instant she remembered the reasons which had at first led them to think of letting the room, and she added, disconsolately:

'It's foolish for us to go on like this, dear. We must let the room and it might just as well be him as anyone else. We must make the best of it, that's all.'

Easton stood with his back to the fire, staring gloomily at her.

'Yes, I suppose that's the right way to look at it,' he replied at length. 'If we can't stand it, we'll give up the house and take a couple of rooms, or a small flat – if we can get one.'

Ruth agreed, although neither alternative was very inviting. The unwelcome alteration in their circumstances was after all not altogether without its compensations, because from the moment of arriving at this decision their love for each other seemed to be renewed and intensified. They remembered with acute regret that hitherto they had not always fully appreciated the happiness of that exclusive companionship of which there now remained to them but one week more. For once the present was esteemed at its proper value, being invested with some of the glamour which almost always envelops the past.

CHAPTER 13

Penal Servitude and Death

On Tuesday – the day after his interview with Rushton – Owen remained at home working at the drawings. He did not get them finished, but they were so far advanced that he thought he would be able to complete them after tea on Wednesday evening. He did not go to work until after breakfast on Wednesday and his continued absence served to confirm the opinion of the other workmen that he had been discharged. This belief was further strengthened by the fact that a new hand had been sent to the house by Hunter, who came himself also at about a quarter past seven and very nearly caught Philpot in the act of smoking.

During breakfast, Philpot, addressing Crass and referring to Hunter, enquired anxiously:

' 'Ow's 'is temper this mornin', Bob?'

'As mild as milk,' replied Crass. 'You'd think butter wouldn't melt in 'is mouth.'

'Seemed quite pleased with 'isself, didn't 'e?' said Harlow.

'Yes,' remarked Newman. ' 'E said good morning to me!'

'So 'e did to me!' said Easton. ' 'E come inter the drorin'-room an' 'e ses, "Oh, you're in 'ere, are yer, Easton," 'e ses – just like that, quite affable like. So I ses, "Yes sir." "Well," 'e ses, "get it slobbered over as quick as you can," 'e ses, " 'cos we ain't got much for this job: don't spend a lot of time puttying up. Just smear it over an' let it go!" '

' 'E certinly seemed very pleased about something,' said Harlow. 'I thought prap's there was a undertaking job in: one o' them generally puts 'im in a good humour.'

'I believe that nothing would please 'im so much as to see a epidemic break out,' remarked Philpot. 'Small-pox, Hinfluenza, Cholery morbus,[35] or anything like that.'

'Yes: don't you remember 'ow good-tempered 'e was last summer when there was such a lot of Scarlet Fever about?' observed Harlow.

'Yes,' said Crass with a chuckle. 'I recollect we 'ad six children's funerals to do in one week. Ole Misery was as pleased as Punch, because of course as a rule there ain't many boxin'-up jobs in the summer. It's in winter as hundertakers reaps their 'arvest.'

'We ain't 'ad very many this winter, though, so far,' said Harlow.

'Not so many as usual,' admitted Crass, 'but still, we can't grumble: we've 'ad one nearly every week since the beginning of October. That's not so bad, you know.'

Crass took a lively interest in the undertaking department of Rushton & Co.'s business. He always had the job of polishing or varnishing the coffin and assisting to take it home and to 'lift in' the corpse, besides acting as one of the bearers at the funeral. This work was more highly paid for than painting.

'But I don't think there's no funeral job in,' added Crass after a pause. 'I think it's because 'e's glad to see the end of Owen, if you ask me.'

'Praps that 'as got something to do with it,' said Harlow. 'But all the same I don't call that a proper way to treat anyone – givin' a man the push in that way just because 'e 'appened to 'ave a spite against 'im.'

'It's wot I call a bl—dy shame!' cried Philpot. 'Owen's a chap wots always ready to do a good turn to anybody, and 'e knows 'is work, although 'e is a bit of a nuisance sometimes, I must admit, when 'e gets on about Socialism.'

'I suppose Misery didn't say nothin' about 'im this mornin'?' enquired Easton.

'No,' replied Cross, and added: 'I only 'ope Owen don't think as I ever said anything against 'im. 'E looked at me very funny that night after Nimrod went away. Owen needn't think nothing like that about *me*, because I'm a chap like this – if I couldn't do nobody no good, I wouldn't never do 'em no 'arm!'

At this some of the others furtively exchanged significant glances, and Harlow began to smile, but no one said anything.

Philpot, noticing that the newcomer had not helped himself to any tea, called Bert's attention to the fact and the boy filled Owen's cup and passed it over to the new hand.

Their conjectures regarding the cause of Hunter's good humour were all wrong. As the reader knows, Owen had not been discharged at all, and there was nobody dead. The real reason was that, having decided to take on another man, Hunter had experienced no difficulty in getting one at the same reduced rate as that which Newman was working for, there being such numbers of men out of employment. Hitherto the usual rate of pay in Mugsborough had been sevenpence an hour for skilled painters. The reader will remember that Newman consented to accept a job at sixpence halfpenny. So far none of the other workmen knew that Newman was working under price: he had told no one, not feeling sure whether he was the only one or not. The man whom Hunter had taken on that morning also decided in his mind that he would keep his own counsel concerning what pay he was to receive, until he found out what the others were getting.

Just before half-past eight Owen arrived and was immediately assailed with questions as to what had transpired at the office. Cross listened with ill-concealed chagrin to Owen's account, but most of the others were genuinely pleased.

'But what a way to speak to anybody!' observed Harlow, referring to Hunter's manner on the previous Monday night.

'You know, I reckon if ole Misery 'ad four legs, 'e'd make a very good pig,' said Philpot, solemnly, 'and you can't expect nothin' from a pig but a grunt.'

During the morning, as Easton and Owen were working together in the drawing-room, the former remarked:

'Did I tell you I had a room I wanted to let, Frank?'

'Yes, I think you did.'

'Well, I've let it to Slyme. I think he seems a very decent sort of chap, don't you?'

'Yes, I suppose he is,' replied Owen, hesitatingly. 'I know nothing against him.'

'Of course, we'd rather 'ave the 'ouse to ourselves if we could afford it, but work is so scarce lately. I've been figuring out exactly what my money has averaged for the last twelve months and how much a week do you think it comes to?'

'God only knows,' said Owen. 'How much?'

'About eighteen bob.'

'So you see we had to do something,' continued Easton; 'and I reckon we're lucky to get a respectable sort of chap like Slyme, religious and teetotal and all that, you know. Don't you think so?'

'Yes, I suppose you are,' said Owen, who, although he intensely disliked Slyme, knew nothing definite against him.

They worked in silence for some time, and then Owen said:

'At the present time there are thousands of people so badly off that, compared with them, *we* are *rich*. Their sufferings are so great that compared with them, we may be said to be living in luxury. You know that, don't you?'

'Yes, that's true enough, mate. We really ought to be very thankful: we ought to consider ourselves lucky to 'ave a inside job like this when there's such a lot of chaps walkin' about doin' nothing.'

'Yes,' said Owen; 'we're lucky! Although we're in a condition of abject, miserable poverty we must consider ourselves lucky that we're not actually starving.'

Owen was painting the door; Easton was doing the skirting. This work caused no noise, so they were able to converse without difficulty.

'Do you think it's right for us to tamely make up our minds to live for the rest of our lives under such conditions as that?'

'No; certainly not,' replied Easton; 'but things are sure to get better presently. Trade hasn't always been as bad as it is now. Why, you can remember as well as I can a few years ago there was so much work that we was putting in fourteen and sixteen hours a day. I used to be so done up by the end of the week that I used to stay in bed nearly all day on Sunday.'

'But don't you think it's worth while trying to find out whether it's possible to so arrange things that we may be able to live like civilised human beings without being alternately worked to death or starved?'

'I don't see how we're goin' to alter things,' answered Easton. 'At the present time, from what I hear, work is scarce everywheres. *We* can't *make* work, can we?'

'Do you think, then, that the affairs of the world are something like the wind or the weather – altogether beyond our control? And that if they're bad we can do nothing but just sit down and wait for them to get better?'

'Well, I don't see 'ow we can odds it. If the people wot's got the money won't spend it, the likes of me and you can't make 'em, can we?'

Owen looked curiously at Easton.

'I suppose you're about twenty-six now,' he said. 'That means that you have about another thirty years to live. Of course, if you had proper food and clothes and hadn't to work more than a reasonable number of hours every day, there is no natural reason why you should not live for another fifty or sixty years: but we'll say thirty. Do you mean to say that you are able to contemplate with indifference the prospect of living for another thirty years under such conditions as those we endure at present?'

Easton made no reply.

'If you were to commit some serious breach of the law, and were sentenced next week to ten years' penal servitude, you'd probably think your fate a very pitiable one: yet you appear to submit quite cheerfully to this other sentence, which is – that you shall die a premature death after you have done another thirty years' hard labour.'

Easton continued painting the skirting.

'When there's no work,' Owen went on, taking another dip of paint as he spoke and starting on one of the lower panels of the door, 'when there's no work, you will either starve or get into debt. When – as at present – there is a little work, you will live in a state of semi-starvation. When times are what you call "good," you will work for twelve or fourteen hours a day and – if you're *very* lucky – occasionally all night. The extra money you then earn will go to pay your debts so that you may be able to get credit again when there's no work.'

Easton put some putty in a crack in the skirting.

'In consequence of living in this manner, you will die at least twenty years sooner than is natural, or, should you have an unusually strong constitution and live after you cease to be able to work, you will be put into a kind of jail[36] and treated like a criminal for the remainder of your life.'

Having faced up the cracks, Easton resumed the painting of the skirting.

'If it were proposed to make a law that all working men and women were to be put to death – smothered, or hung, or poisoned, or put into a lethal chamber – as soon as they reached the age of fifty years, there is not the slightest doubt that you would join in the uproar of protest that would ensue. Yet you submit tamely to have your life shortened by slow starvation, overwork, lack of proper boots and clothing, and through having often to turn out and go to work when you are so ill that you ought to be in bed receiving medical care.'

Easton made no reply: he knew that all this was true, but he was not without a large share of the false pride which prompts us to hide our poverty and to pretend that we are much better off than we really are. He was at that moment wearing the pair of second-hand boots that Ruth had bought for him, but he had told Harlow – who had passed some remark about them – that he had had them for years, wearing them only for best. He felt very resentful as he listened to the other's talk, and Owen perceived it, but nevertheless he continued:

'Unless the present system is altered, that is all we have to look forward to; and yet you're one of the upholders of the present system – you help to perpetuate it!'

' 'Ow do I help to perpetuate it?' demanded Easton.

'By not trying to find out how to end it – by not helping those who are trying to bring a better state of things into existence. Even if you are indifferent to your own fate – as you seem to be – you have no right to be indifferent to that of the child for whose existence in this world you are responsible. Every man who is not helping to bring about a better state of affairs for the future is helping to perpetuate the present misery, and is therefore the enemy of his own children. There is no such thing as being neutral: we must either help or hinder.'

As Owen opened the door to paint its edge, Bert came along the passage.

'Look out!' he cried, 'Misery's comin' up the road. 'E'll be 'ere in a minit.'

It was not often that Easton was glad to hear of the approach of

Nimrod, but on this occasion he heard Bert's message with a sigh of relief.

'I say,' added the boy in a whisper to Owen, 'if it comes orf – I mean if you gets the job to do this room – will you ask to 'ave me along of you?'

'Yes, all right, sonny,' replied Owen, and Bert went off to warn the others.

Unaware that he had been observed, Nimrod sneaked stealthily into the house and began softly crawling about from room to room, peeping round corners and squinting through the cracks of doors, and looking through keyholes. He was almost pleased to see that everybody was very hard at work, but on going into Newman's room Misery was not satisfied with the progress made since his last visit. The fact was that Newman had been forgetting himself again this morning. He had been taking a little pains with the work, doing it something like properly, instead of scamping and rushing it in the usual way. The result was that he had not done enough.

'You know, Newman, this kind of thing won't do!' Nimrod howled. 'You must get over a bit more than this or you won't suit me! If you can't move yourself a bit quicker I shall 'ave to get someone else. You've been in this room since seven o'clock this morning and it's dam near time you was out of it!'

Newman muttered something about being nearly finished now, and Hunter ascended to the next landing – the attics, where the cheap man – Sawkins, the labourer – was at work. Harlow had been taken away from the attics to go on with some of the better work, so Sawkins was now working alone. He had been slogging into it like a Trojan and had done quite a lot. He had painted not only the sashes of the windows, but also a large part of the glass, and when doing the skirting he had included part of the floors, sometimes an inch, sometimes half an inch.

The paint was of a dark drab colour and the surface of the newly painted doors bore a strong resemblance to corduroy cloth, and from the bottom corners of nearly every panel there was trickling down a large tear, as if the doors were weeping for the degenerate condition of the decorative arts. But these tears caused no throb of pity in the bosom of Misery: neither did the corduroy-like surface of the work grate upon his feelings. He perceived them not. He saw only that there was a Lot of Work done and his soul was filled with rapture as he reflected that the man who had accomplished all this was paid only fivepence an hour. At the same time it would never do to let

Sawkins know that he was satisfied with the progress made, so he said: –

'I don't want you to stand too much over this up 'ere, you know, Sawkins. Just mop it over anyhow, and get away from it as quick as you can.'

'All right, sir,' replied Sawkins, wiping the sweat from his brow as Misery began crawling downstairs again.

'Where's Harlow got to, then?' he demanded of Philpot. ' 'E wasn't 'ere just now, when I came up.'

' 'E's gorn downstairs, sir, out the back,' replied Joe, jerking his thumb over his shoulder and winking at Hunter. ' 'E'll be back in 'arf a mo.' And indeed at that moment Harlow was just coming upstairs again.

' 'Ere, we can't allow this kind of thing in workin' hours, you know,' Hunter bellowed. 'There's plenty of time for that in the dinner hour!'

Nimrod now went down to the drawing-room, which Easton and Owen had been painting. He stood here deep in thought for some time, mentally comparing the quantity of work done by the two men in this room with that done by Sawkins in the attics. Misery was not a painter himself: he was a carpenter, and he thought but little of the difference in the quality of the work: to him it was all about the same: just plain painting.

'I believe it would pay us a great deal better,' he thought to himself, 'if we could get hold of a few more lightweights like Sawkins.' And with his mind filled with this reflection he shortly afterwards sneaked stealthily from the house.

CHAPTER 14

Three Children. The Wages of Intelligence

Owen spent the greater part of the dinner hour by himself in the drawing-room making pencil sketches in his pocket-book and taking measurements. In the evening after leaving off, instead of going straight home as usual he went round to the Free Library[37] to see if he could find anything concerning Moorish decorative work in any of the books there. Although it was only a small and ill-equipped institution he was rewarded by the discovery of illustrations of several examples of which he made sketches. After about an hour spent in this way, as he was proceeding homewards he observed two children – a boy and a girl – whose appearance seemed familiar. They were standing at the window of a sweetstuff shop examining the wares exposed therein. As Owen came up the children turned round and they recognised each other simultaneously. They were Charley and Elsie Linden. Owen spoke to them as he drew near and the boy appealed to him for his opinion concerning a dispute they had been having.

'I say, mister. Which do you think is the best: a fardensworth of everlasting stickjaw torfee, or a prize packet?'[38]

'I'd rather have a prize packet,' replied Owen, unhesitatingly.

'There! I told you so!' cried Elsie, triumphantly.

'Well, I don't care. I'd soonest 'ave the torfee,' said Charley, doggedly.

'Why, can't you agree which of the two to buy?'

'Oh no, it's not that,' replied Elsie. 'We was only just *supposing* what we'd buy if we 'ad a fardin; but we're not really goin' to buy nothing, because we ain't got no money.'

'Oh, I see,' said Owen. 'But I think *I* have some money,' and putting his hand into his pocket he produced two half-pennies and gave one to each of the children, who immediately went in to buy the toffee and the prize packet, and when they came out he walked along with them, as they were going in the same direction as he was: indeed, they would have to pass by his house.

'Has your grandfather got anything to do yet?' he enquired as they went along.

'No. 'E's still walkin' about, mister,' replied Charley.

When they reached Owen's door he invited them to come up to see the kitten, which they had been enquiring about on the way. Frankie was delighted with these two visitors, and whilst they were eating some home-made cakes that Nora gave them, he entertained them by displaying the contents of his toy box, and the antics of the kitten, which was the best toy of all, for it invented new games all the time: acrobatic performances on the rails of chairs; curtain climbing; running slides up and down the oilcloth; hiding and peeping round corners and under the sofa. The kitten cut so many comical capers, and in a little while the children began to create such an uproar, that Nora had to interfere lest the people in the flat underneath should be annoyed.

However, Elsie and Charley were not able to stay very long, because their mother would be anxious about them, but they promised to come again some other day to play with Frankie.

'I'm going to 'ave a prize next Sunday at our Sunday School,' said Elsie as they were leaving.

'What are you going to get it for?' asked Nora.

' 'Cause I learned my text properly. I had to learn the whole of the first chapter of Matthew by heart and I never made one single mistake! So teacher said she'd give me a nice book next Sunday.'

'I 'ad one too, the other week, about six months ago, didn't I, Elsie?' said Charley.

'Yes,' replied Elsie and added: 'Do they give prizes at your Sunday School, Frankie?'

'I don't go to Sunday School.'

'Ain't you never been?' said Charley in a tone of surprise.

'No,' replied Frankie. 'Dad says I have quite enough of school all the week.'

'You ought to come to ours, man!' urged Charley. 'It's not like being in school at all! And we 'as a treat in the summer, and prizes and sometimes a magic lantern 'tainment. It ain't 'arf all right, I can tell you.'

Frankie looked enquiringly at his mother.

'Might I go, Mum?'

'Yes, if you like, dear.'

'But I don't know the way.'

'Oh, it's not far from 'ere,' cried Charley. 'We 'as to pass by your 'ouse when we're goin', so I'll call for you on Sunday if you like.'

'It's only just round in Duke Street; you know, the "Shining Light Chapel",' said Elsie. 'It commences at three o'clock.'

'All right,' said Nora. 'I'll have Frankie ready at a quarter to three. Now you must run home as fast as you can. Did you like those cakes?'

'Yes, thank you very much,' answered Elsie.

'Not 'arf!' said Charley.

'Does your mother make cakes for you sometimes?'

'She used to, but she's too busy now, making blouses and one thing and another,' Elsie answered.

'I suppose she hasn't much time for cooking,' said Nora, 'so I've wrapped up some more of those cakes in this parcel for you to take home for tomorrow. I think you can manage to carry it all right, can't you, Charley?'

'I think I'd better carry it myself,' said Elsie. 'Charley's *so* careless, he's sure to lose some of them.'

'I ain't no more careless than you are,' cried Charley, indignantly. 'What about the time you dropped the quarter of butter you was sent for in the mud?'

'That wasn't carelessness: that was an accident, and it wasn't butter at all: it was margarine, so there!'

Eventually it was arranged that they were to carry the parcel in turns, Elsie to have first innings. Frankie went downstairs to the front door with them to see them off, and as they went down the street he shouted after them:

'Mind you remember, next Sunday!'

'All right,' Charley shouted back. 'We shan't forget.'

*   *   *

On Thursday Owen stayed at home until after breakfast to finish the designs which he had promised to have ready that morning.

When he took them to the office at nine o'clock, the hour at which he had arranged to meet Rushton, the latter had not yet arrived, and he did not put in an appearance until half an hour later. Like the majority of the people who do brain work, he needed a great deal more rest than those who do only mere physical labour.

'Oh, you've brought them sketches, I suppose,' he remarked in a surly tone as he came in. 'You know, there was no need for you to wait: you could 'ave left 'em 'ere and gone on to your job.'

He sat down at his desk and looked carelessly at the drawing that Owen handed to him. It was on a sheet of paper about twenty-four by eighteen inches. The design was drawn with pencil and one half of it was coloured.

'That's for the ceiling,' said Owen. 'I hadn't time to colour all of it.'

With an affectation of indifference, Rushton laid the drawing down and took the other which Owen handed to him.

'This is for the large wall. The same design would be adapted for the other walls; and this one shows the door and the panels under the window.'

Rushton expressed no opinion about the merits of the drawings. He examined them carelessly one after the other, and then, laying them down, he enquired:

'How long would it take you to do this work – if we get the job?'

'About three weeks: say 150 hours. That is – the decorative work only. Of course, the walls and ceiling would have to be painted first: they will need three coats of white.'

Rushton scribbled a note on a piece of paper.

'Well,' he said, after a pause, 'you can leave these 'ere and I'll see Mr. Sweater about it and tell 'im what it will cost, and if he decides to have it done I'll let you know.'

He put the drawings aside with the air of a man who has other matters to attend to, and began to open one of the several letters that were on his desk. He meant this as an intimation that the audience was at an end and that he desired the 'hand' to retire from the presence. Owen understood this, but he did not retire, because it was necessary to mention one or two other things which Rushton would have to allow for when preparing the estimate.

'Of course I should want some help,' he said. 'I should need a man occasionally, and the boy most of the time. Then there's the gold leaf – say, fifteen books.'

'Don't you think it would be possible to use gold paint?'

'I'm afraid not.'

'Is there anything else?' enquired Rushton as he finished writing down these items.

'I think that's all, except a few sheets of cartridge paper for stencils and working drawings. The quantity of paint necessary for the decorative work will be very small.'

As soon as Owen was gone, Rushton took up the designs and examined them attentively.

'These are all right,' he muttered. 'Good enough for anywhere. If he can paint anything like as well as this on the walls and ceiling of the room, it will stand all the looking at that anyone in this town is likely to give it.'

'Let's see,' he continued. 'He said three weeks, but he's so anxious to do the job that he's most likely under-estimated the time; I'd better allow four weeks: that means about 200 hours: 200 hours at eightpence: how much is that? And say he has a painter to help him half the time, 100 hours at sixpence-ha'-penny.'

He consulted a ready reckoner that was on the desk.

'Time, £9. 7. 6. Materials: fifteen books of gold, say a pound. Then there's the cartridge paper and the colours – say another pound, at the outside. Boy's time? Well, he gets no wages as yet, so we needn't mention that at all. Then there's the preparing of the room. Three coats of white paint. I wish Hunter was here to give me an idea what it will cost.'

As if in answer to his wish, Nimrod entered the office at that moment, and in reply to Rushton's query said that to give the walls and ceiling three coats of paint would cost about three pounds five for time and material. Between them the two brain workers figured that fifteen pounds would cover the entire cost of the work – painting and decorating.

'Well, I reckon we can charge Sweater forty-five pounds for it,' said Rushton. 'It isn't like an ordinary job, you know. If he gets a London firm to do it, it'll cost him double that, if not more.'

Having arrived at this decision, Rushton rung up Sweater's Emporium on the telephone, and, finding that Mr. Sweater was there, he rolled up the designs and set out for that gentleman's office.

The men work with their hands, and the masters work with their brains. What a dreadful calamity it would be for the world and for mankind if all these brain workers were to go on strike.

CHAPTER 15

The Undeserving Persons and the Upper and Nether Millstones

Hunter had taken on three more painters that morning. Bundy and two labourers had commenced the work of putting in the new drains; the carpenters were back again doing some extra work, and there was also a plumber working in the house; so there was quite a little crowd in the kitchen at dinner-time. Crass had been waiting for a suitable opportunity to produce the newspaper cutting which it will be remembered he showed to Easton on Monday morning, but he had waited in vain, for there had been scarcely any 'political' talk at meal-times all the week, and it was now Thursday. As far as Owen was concerned, his thoughts were so occupied with the designs for the drawing-room that he had no time for anything else, and most of the others were only too willing to avoid a subject which frequently led to unpleasantness. As a rule Crass himself had no liking for such discussion, but he was so confident of being able to 'flatten out' Owen with the cutting from the *Obscurer* that he had several times tried to lead the conversation into the desired channel, but so far without success.

During dinner – as they called it – various subjects were discussed. Harlow mentioned that he had found traces of bugs in one of the bedrooms upstairs and this called forth a number of anecdotes of those vermin and of houses infested by them. Philpot remembered working in a house over at Windley; the people who lived in it were very dirty and had very little furniture; no bedsteads, the beds consisting of dilapidated mattresses and rags on the floor. He declared that these ragged mattresses used to wander about the rooms by themselves. The house was so full of fleas that if one placed a sheet of newspaper on the floor one could hear and see them jumping on it. In fact, directly one went into that house one was covered from head to foot with fleas! During the few days he worked at that place, he lost several pounds in weight, and of evenings as he walked homewards the children and the people in the streets, observing his ravaged countenance, thought he was suffering from some disease and used to get out of his way when they saw him coming.

There were several other of these narratives, four or five men talking at the top of their voices at the same time, each one telling a different story. At first each story-teller addressed himself to the company generally, but after a while, finding it impossible to make himself heard, he would select some particular individual who seemed disposed to listen and tell him the story. It sometimes happened that in the middle of the tale the man to whom it was being told would remember a somewhat similar adventure of his own, which he would immediately proceed to relate without waiting for the other to finish, and each of them was generally so interested in the gruesome details of his own story that he was unconscious of the fact that the other was telling one at all. In a contest of this kind the victory usually went to the man with the loudest voice, but sometimes a man who had a weak voice, scored by repeating the same tale several times until someone heard it.

Barrington, who seldom spoke and was an ideal listener, was appropriated by several men in succession, who each told him a different yarn. There was one man sitting on an up-ended pail in the far corner of the room and it was evident from the movements of his lips that he also was relating a story, although nobody knew what it was about or heard a single word of it, for no one took the slightest notice of him . . .

[When the uproar had subsided Harlow remembered the case of a family whose house got into such a condition that the landlord had given them notice and the father had committed] suicide because the painters had come to turn 'em out of house and home. There were a man and his wife and daughter – a girl about seventeen – living in the house, and all the three of 'em used to drink like hell. As for the woman, she *could* shift it and no mistake! Several times a day she used to send the girl with a jug to the pub at the corner. When the old man was out, one could have anything one liked to ask for from either of 'em for half a pint of beer, but for his part, said Harlow, he could never fancy it. They were both too ugly.

The finale of this tale was received with a burst of incredulous laughter by those who heard it.

'Do you 'ear what Harlow says, Bob?' Easton shouted to Crass.

'No. What was it?'

' 'E ses 'e once 'ad a chance to 'ave something but 'e wouldn't take it on because it was too ugly!'

'If it 'ad bin me, I should 'ave shut me bl—y eyes,' cried Sawkins. 'I wouldn't pass it for a trifle like that.'

'No,' said Crass amid laughter, 'and you can bet yer life 'e didn't lose it neither, although 'e tries to make 'imself out to be so innocent.'

'I always thought old Harlow was a bl—y liar,' remarked Bundy, 'but now we knows 'e is.'

Although everyone pretended to disbelieve him, Harlow stuck to his version of the story.

'It's not their faces you want, you know,' added Bundy as he helped himself to some more tea.

'I know it wasn't my old woman's face that I was after last night,' observed Crass; and then he proceeded amid roars of laughter to give a minutely detailed account of what had taken place between himself and his wife after they had retired for the night.

This story reminded the man on the pail of a very strange dream he had had a few weeks previously: 'I dreamt I was walkin' along the top of a 'igh cliff or some sich place, and all of a sudden the ground give way under me feet and I began to slip down and down and to save meself from going over I made a grab at a tuft of grass as was growin' just within reach of me 'and. And then I thought that some feller was 'ittin' me on the 'ead with a bl—y great stick, and tryin' to make me let go of the tuft of grass. And then I woke up to find my old woman shouting out and punchin' me with 'er fists. She said I was pullin' 'er 'air!'

While the room was in an uproar with the merriment induced by these stories, Crass rose from his seat and crossed over to where his overcoat was hanging on a nail in the wall, and took from the pocket a piece of card about eight inches by about four inches. One side of it was covered with printing, and as he returned to his seat Crass called upon the others to listen while he read it aloud. He said it was one of the best things he had ever seen: it had been given to him by a bloke at the 'Cricketers' the other night.

Crass was not a very good reader, but he was able to read this all right because he had read it so often that he almost knew it by heart. It was entitled 'The Art of Flatulence', and it consisted of a number of rules and definitions. Shouts of laughter greeted the reading of each paragraph, and when he had ended, the piece of dirty card was handed round for the benefit of those who wished to read it for themselves. Several of the men, however, when it was offered to them, refused to take it, and with evident disgust suggested that it should be put into the fire. This view did not commend itself to Crass, who, after the others had finished with it, put it back again in the pocket of his coat.

Meanwhile, Bundy stood up to help himself to some more tea. The cup he was drinking from had a large piece broken out of one side and did not hold much, so he usually had to have three or four helpings.

'Anyone else want any?' he asked.

Several cups and jars were passed to him. These vessels had been standing on the floor, and the floor was very dirty and covered with dust, so before dipping them into the pail, Bundy – who had been working at the drains all the morning – wiped the bottoms of the jars upon his trousers, on the same place where he was in the habit of wiping his hands when he happened to get some dirt on them. He filled the jars so full that as he held them by the rims and passed them to their owners part of the contents slopped over and trickled through his fingers. By the time he had finished the floor was covered with little pools of tea.

'They say that Gord made everything for some useful purpose,' remarked Harlow, reverting to the original subject, 'but I should like to know what the hell's the use of sich things as bugs and fleas and the like.'

'To teach people to keep theirselves clean, of course,' said Slyme.

'That's a very funny subject, ain't it?' continued Harlow, ignoring Slyme's answer. 'They say as all diseases is caused by little insects. If Gord 'adn't made no cancer germs or consumption microbes there wouldn't be no cancer or consumption.'

'That's one of the proofs that there *isn't* an individual God,' said Owen. 'If we were to believe that the universe and everything that lives was deliberately designed and created by God, then we must also believe that He made the disease germs you are speaking of for the purpose of torturing His other creatures.'

'You can't tell me a bloody yarn like that,' interposed Crass, roughly. 'There's a Ruler over us, mate, and so you're likely to find out.'

'If Gord didn't create the world, 'ow did it come 'ere?' demanded Slyme.

'I know no more about that than you do,' replied Owen. 'That is – I know nothing. The only difference between us is that you *think* you know. You think you know that God made the universe; how long it took Him to do it; why He made it; how long it's been in existence and how it will finally pass away. You also imagine you know that we shall live after we're dead; where we shall go, and the kind of existence we shall have. In fact, in the excess of your 'humility', you think you know all about it. But really you know no more of these things than any other human being does: that is, you know *nothing*.'

'That's only *your* opinion,' said Slyme.

'If we care to take the trouble to learn,' Owen went on, 'we can know a little of how the universe has grown and changed; but of the beginning we know nothing.'

'That's just my opinion, matey,' observed Philpot. 'It's just a bloody mystery, and that's all about it.'

'I don't pretend to 'ave no 'ead knowledge,' said Slyme, 'but 'ead knowledge won't save a man's soul: it's 'eart knowledge as does that. I knows in my 'eart as my sins is all hunder the Blood,[39] and it's knowin' that, wot's given 'appiness and the peace which passes all understanding[40] to me ever since I've been a Christian.'

'Glory, glory, hallelujah!' shouted Bundy, and nearly everyone laughed.

' 'Christian' is right,' sneered Owen. 'You've got some title to call yourself a Christian, haven't you? As for the happiness that passes all understanding, it certainly passes *my* understanding how you can be happy when you believe that millions of people are being tortured in Hell; and it also passes my understanding why you are not ashamed of yourself for being happy under such circumstances.'

'Ah, well, you'll find it all out when you comes to die, mate,' replied Slyme in a threatening tone. 'You'll think and talk different then!'

'That's just wot gets over *me*,' observed Harlow. 'It don't seem right that after living in misery and poverty all our bloody lives, workin' and slavin' all the hours that Gord A'mighty sends, that we're to be bloody well set fire to and burned in 'ell for all eternity! It don't seem feasible to me, you know.'

'It's my belief,' said Philpot, profoundly, 'that when you're dead, you're done for. That's the end of you.'

'That's what *I* say,' remarked Easton. 'As for all this religious business, it's just a money-making dodge. It's the parson's trade, just the same as painting is ours, only there's no work attached to it and the pay's a bloody sight better than ours is.'

'It's their livin', and a bloody good livin' too, if you ask me,' said Bundy.

'Yes,' said Harlow; 'they lives on the fat o' the land, and wears the best of everything, and they does nothing for it but talk a lot of twaddle two or three times a week. The rest of the time they spend cadgin' money orf silly old women who thinks it's a sorter fire insurance.'

'It's an old sayin' and a true one,' chimed in the man on the upturned pail. 'Parsons and publicans is the worst enemies the workin' man ever 'ad. There may be *some* good 'uns, but they're few and far between.'

'If I could only get a job like the Harchbishop of Canterbury,' said Philpot, solemnly, 'I'd leave this firm.'

'So would I,' said Harlow, 'if I was the Harchbishop of Canterbury, I'd take my pot and brushes down to the office and shy 'em through the bloody winder and tell ole Misery to go to 'ell.'

'Religion is a thing that don't trouble *me* much,' remarked Newman; 'and as for what happens to you after death, it's a thing I believes in leavin' till you comes to it – there's no sense in meetin' trouble 'arfway. All the things they tells us may be true or they may not, but it takes me all my time to look after *this* world. I don't believe I've been to church more than arf a dozen times since I've been married – that's over fifteen years ago now – and then it's been when the kids 'ave been christened. The old woman goes sometimes and of course the young 'uns goes; you've got to tell 'em something or other, and they might as well learn what they teaches at the Sunday School as anything else.'

A general murmur of approval greeted this. It seemed to be the almost unanimous opinion, that, whether it were true or not, 'religion' was a nice thing to teach children.

'I've not been even once since I was married,' said Harlow, 'and I sometimes wish to Christ I 'adn't gorn then.'

'I don't see as it matters a dam wot a man believes,' said Philpot, 'so long as you don't do no 'arm to nobody. If you see a poor b—r wot's down on 'is luck, give 'im a 'elpin' 'and. Even if you ain't got no money you can say a kind word. If a man does 'is work and looks arter 'is 'ome and 'is young 'uns, and does a good turn to a fellow creature when 'e can, I reckon 'e stands as much chance of getting into 'eaven – if there *is* sich a place – as some of these 'ere Bible-busters, whether 'e ever goes to church or chapel or not.'

These sentiments were echoed by everyone with the solitary exception of Slyme, who said that Philpot would find out his mistake after he was dead, when he would have to stand before the Great White Throne for judgement![41]

'And at the Last Day, when yer sees the moon turned inter Blood, you'll be cryin' hout for the mountings and the rocks to fall on yer and 'ide yer from the wrath of the Lamb!'[42]

The others laughed derisively.

'I'm a Bush Baptist meself,'[43] remarked the man on the upturned pail. This individual, Dick Wantley by name, was of what is usually termed a 'rugged' cast of countenance. He reminded one strongly of an ancient gargoyle, or a dragon.

Most of the hands had by now lit their pipes, but there were a few who preferred chewing their tobacco. As they smoked or chewed they expectorated upon the floor or into the fire. Wantley was one of those who preferred chewing and he had been spitting upon the floor to such an extent that he was by this time partly surrounded by a kind of semicircular moat of dark brown spittle.

'I'm a Bush Baptist!' he shouted across the moat, 'and you all knows wot that is.'

This confession of faith caused a fresh outburst of hilarity, because of course everyone knew what a Bush Baptist was.

'If evven's goin' to be full of sich b—r's as Hunter,' observed Easton, 'I think I'd rather go to the other place.'

'If ever ole Misery *does* get into 'eaven,' said Philpot, ' 'e won't stop there very long. I reckon 'e'll be chucked out of it before 'e's been there a week, because 'e's sure to start pinchin' the jewels out of the other saints' crowns.'

'Well, if they won't 'ave 'im in 'eaven, I'm sure I don't know wot's to become of 'im,' said Harlow with pretended concern, 'because I don't believe 'e'd be allowed into 'ell, now.'

'Why not?' demanded Bundy. 'I should think it's just the bloody place for sich b—r's as 'im.'

'So it used to be at one time o' day, but they've changed all that now. They've 'ad a revolution down there: deposed the Devil, elected a parson as President, and started puttin' the fire out.'

'From what I hears of it,' continued Harlow when the laughter had ceased, ' 'ell is a bloody fine place to live in just now. There's underground railways and 'lectric trams, and at the corner of nearly every street there's a sort of pub where you can buy ice-cream, lemon squash, four ale, and American cold drinks; and you're allowed to sit in a refrigerator for two hours for a tanner.'

Although they laughed at and made fun of these things the reader must not think that they really doubted the truth of the Christian religion, because – although they had all been brought up by 'Christian' parents and had been 'educated' in 'Christian' schools – none of them knew enough about Christianity to either really believe it or disbelieve it. The imposters who obtain a comfortable living by pretending to be the ministers and disciples of the Workman of Nazareth are too cunning to encourage their dupes to acquire any-thing approaching an intelligent understanding of the subject. They do not want people to know or understand anything: they want them to have Faith – to believe without knowledge, understanding, or evidence. For years Harlow and his mates – when children – had been 'taught' 'Christianity' in day school, Sunday School and in church or chapel, and now they knew practically nothing about it! But they were 'Christians' all the same. They believed that the Bible was the word of God, but they didn't know where it came from, how long it had been in existence, who wrote it, who translated it or how many different versions there were. Most of them were almost totally unacquainted with the contents of the book itself. But all the same, they believed it – after a fashion.

'But puttin' all jokes aside,' said Philpot, 'I can't believe there's sich a place as 'ell. There may be some kind of punishment, but I don't believe it's a real fire.'

'Nor nobody else, what's got any sense,' replied Harlow, con-temptuously.

'I believe as *this* world is 'ell,' said Crass, looking around with a philosophic expression. This opinion was echoed by most of the others, although Slyme remained silent and Owen laughed.

'Wot the bloody 'ell are *you* laughin' at?' Crass demanded in an indignant tone.

'I was laughing because you said you think this world is hell.'

'Well, I don't see nothing to laugh at in that,' said Crass.

'So it *is* a 'ell,' said Easton. 'There can't be anywheres much worse than this.'

' 'Ear, 'ear,' said the man behind the moat.

'What I was laughing at is this,' said Owen. 'The present system of managing the affairs of the world is so bad and has produced such dreadful results that you are of opinion that the earth is a hell: and yet you are a Conservative! You wish to preserve the present system – the system which has made the world into a hell!'

'I thought we shouldn't get through the dinner hour without politics if Owen was 'ere,' growled Bundy. 'Bloody sickenin' I call it.'

'Don't be 'ard on 'im,' said Philpot. ' 'E's been very quiet for the last few days.'

'We'll 'ave to go through it today, though,' remarked Harlow despairingly. 'I can see it comin'.'

'*I'm* not goin' through it,' said Bundy, 'I'm orf!' And he accordingly drank the remainder of his tea, closed his empty dinner basket and, having placed it on the mantelshelf, made for the door.

'I'll leave you to it,' he said as he went out. The others laughed.

Crass, remembering the cutting from the *Obscurer* that he had in his pocket, was secretly very pleased at the turn the conversation was taking. He turned roughly on Owen:

'The other day, when we was talkin' about the cause of poverty, you contradicted everybody. Everyone else was wrong! But you yourself couldn't tell us what's the cause of poverty, could yer?'

'I think I could.'

'Oh, of course, you think you know,' sneered Crass, 'and of course you think your opinion's right and everybody else's is wrong.'

'Yes,' replied Owen.

Several men expressed their abhorrence of this intolerant attitude of Owen's, but the latter rejoined:

'Of course I think that my opinions are right and that everyone who differs from me is wrong. If I didn't think their opinions were wrong I wouldn't differ from them. If I didn't think my own opinions right I wouldn't hold them.'

'But there's no need to keep on arguin' about it day after day,' said Crass. 'You've got your opinion and I've got mine. Let everyone enjoy his own opinion, I say.'

A murmur of approbation from the crowd greeted these sentiments; but Owen rejoined:

'But we can't both be right; if your opinions are right and mine are not, how am I to find out the truth if we never talk about them?'

'Well, wot do you reckon is the cause of poverty, then?' demanded Easton.

'The present system – competition – capitalism.'

'It's all very well to talk like that,' snarled Crass, to whom this statement conveyed no meaning whatever. 'But 'ow do you make it out?'

'Well, I put it like that for the sake of shortness,' replied Owen. 'Suppose some people were living in a house – '

'More supposin'!' sneered Crass.

'And suppose they were always ill, and suppose that the house was badly built, the walls so constructed that they drew and retained moisture, the roof broken and leaky, the drains defective, the doors and windows ill-fitting, and the rooms badly shaped and draughty. If you were asked to name, in a word, the cause of the ill-health of the people who lived there you would say – the house. All the tinkering in the world would not make that house fit to live in; the only thing to do with it would be to pull it down and build another. Well, we're all living in a house called the Money System;[44] and as a result most of us are suffering from a disease called poverty. There's so much the matter with the present system that it's no good tinkering at it. Everything about it is wrong and there's nothing about it that's right. There's only one thing to be done with it and that is to smash it up and have a different system altogether. We must get out of it.'

'It seems to me that that's just what you're trying to do,' remarked Harlow, sarcastically. 'You seem to be tryin' to get out of answering the question what Easton asked you.'

'Yes!' cried Crass, fiercely. 'Why don't you answer the bloody question? Wot's the cause of poverty?'

'What the 'ell's the matter with the present system?' demanded Sawkins.

'Ow's it goin' to be altered?' said Newman.

'Wot the bloody 'ell sort of a system do *you* think we ought to 'ave?' shouted the man behind the moat.

'It can't never be altered,' said Philpot. 'Human nature's human nature and you can't get away from it.'

'Never mind about human nature,' shouted Crass. 'Stick to the point. Wot's the cause of poverty?'

'Oh, b—r the cause of poverty!' said one of the new hands. 'I've 'ad enough of this bloody row.' And he stood up and prepared to go out of the room.

This individual had two patches on the seat of his trousers and the bottoms of the legs of that garment were frayed and ragged. He had been out of work for about six weeks previous to having been taken on by Rushton & Co. During most of that time he and his family had been existing in a condition of semi-starvation on the earnings of his wife as a charwoman and on the scraps of food she brought home from the houses where she worked. But all the same, the question of what is the cause of poverty had no interest for him.

'There are many causes,' answered Owen, 'but they are all part of and inseparable from the system. In order to do away with poverty, we must destroy the causes: to do away with the causes we must destroy the whole system.'

'What are the causes, then?'

'Well, money, for one thing.'

This extraordinary assertion was greeted with a roar of merriment, in the midst of which Philpot was heard to say that to listen to Owen was as good as going to a circus. Money the cause of poverty!

'I always thought it was the want of it!' said the man with the patches on the seat of his trousers as he passed out of the door.

'Other things,' continued Owen, 'are private ownership of land, private ownership of railways, tramways, gasworks, water-works, private ownership of factories, and of the other means of producing the necessaries and comforts of life. Competition in business – '

'But 'ow do you make it out?' demanded Crass, impatiently.

Owen hesitated. To his mind the thing appeared very clear and simple. The causes of poverty were so glaringly evident that he marvelled that any rational being should fail to perceive them; but at the same time he found it very difficult to define them himself. He could not think of words that would convey his thoughts clearly to these others who seemed so hostile and unwilling to understand, and who appeared to have made up their minds to oppose and reject whatever he said. They did not know what were the causes of poverty and apparently they did not *want* to know.

'Well, I'll try to show you one of the causes,' he said nervously at last.

He picked up a piece of charred wood that had fallen from the fire and knelt down and began to draw upon the floor. Most of the others regarded him with looks in which an indulgent, contemptuous kind of interest mingled with an air of superiority and patronage. There was no doubt, they thought, that Owen was a clever sort of chap: his work proved that: but he was certainly a little bit mad.

By this time Owen had drawn a circle about two feet in diameter. Inside this he had drawn two squares, one much larger than the other. These two squares he filled in solid black with the charcoal.

'Wot's it all about?' asked Crass with a sneer.

'Why, can't you see?' said Philpot with a wink. ' 'E's goin' to do some conjurin'! In a minit 'e'll make something pass out o' one o' them squares into the other and no one won't see 'ow it's done.'

When he had finished drawing, Owen remained for a few minutes awkwardly silent, oppressed by the anticipation of ridicule and a sense of his inability to put his thoughts into plain language. He began to wish that he had not undertaken this task. At last, with an effort, he began to speak in a halting, nervous way:

'This circle – or rather, the space inside the circle – is supposed to represent England.'

'Well, I never knowed it was round before,' jeered Crass. 'I've heard as the *world* is round – '

'I never said it was the shape – I said it was supposed to *represent* England.'

'Oh, I see. I thought we'd very soon begin supposin'.'

'The two black squares,' continued Owen, 'represent the people who live in the country. The small square represents a few thousand people. The large square stands for the remainder – about forty millions – that is, the majority.'

'We ain't sich bloody fools as to think that the largest number is the minority,' interrupted Crass.

'The greater number of the people represented by the large black square work for their living: and in return for their labour they receive money: some more, some less than others.'

'You don't think they'd be sich bloody fools as to work for nothing, do you?' said Newman.

'I suppose you think they ought all to get the same wages!' cried Harlow. 'Do you think it's right that a scavenger should get as much as a painter?'

'I'm not speaking about that at all,' replied Owen. 'I'm trying to show you what I think is one of the causes of poverty.'

'Shut up, can't you, Harlow,' remonstrated Philpot, who began to feel interested. 'We can't all talk at once.'

'I know we can't,' replied Harlow in an aggrieved tone; 'but 'e takes sich a 'ell of a time to say wot 'e's got to say. Nobody else can't get a word in edgeways.'

'In order that these people may live,' continued Owen, pointing to the large black square, 'it is first of all necessary that they shall have a *place* to live in – '

'Well! I should never a thought it!' exclaimed the man on the pail, pretending to be much impressed. The others laughed, and two or three of them went out of the room, contemptuously remarking to each other in an audible undertone as they went:

'Bloody rot!'

'Wonder wot the bloody 'ell 'e thinks 'e is? A sort of school-master?'

Owen's nervousness increased as he continued:

'Now, they can't live in the air or in the sea. These people are land animals, therefore they must live on the land.'

'Wot do yer mean by animals?' demanded Slyme.

'A human bean ain't a animal!' said Crass, indignantly.

'Yes, we are!' cried Harlow. 'Go into any chemist's shop you like and ask the bloke, and 'e'll tell you – '

'Oh, blow that!' interrupted Philpot. 'Let's 'ear wot Owen's sayin'.'

'They must live on the land: and that's the beginning of the trouble; because – under the present system – the majority of the people have really no right to be in the country at all! Under the present system the country belongs to a few – those who are here represented by this small black square. If it would pay them to do so, and if they felt so disposed, these few people have a perfect right – under the present system – to order everyone else to clear out!

'But they don't do that, they allow the majority to remain in the land on one condition – that is, they must pay rent to the few for the privilege of being permitted to live in the land of their birth. The amount of rent demanded by those who own this country is so large that, in order to pay it, the greater number of the majority have often to deprive themselves and their children, not only of the comforts, but even the necessaries of life. In the case of the working classes the rent absorbs at the lowest possible estimate, about one-third of their total earnings, for it must be remembered that the rent is an expense that goes on all the time, whether they are employed or not. If they get into arrears when out of work, they have to pay double when they get employment again.

'The majority work hard and live in poverty in order that the minority may live in luxury without working at all, and as the majority are mostly fools, they not only agree to pass their lives in incessant slavery and want, in order to pay this rent to those who own the country, but they say it is quite right that they should have to do so, and are very grateful to the little minority for allowing them to remain in the country at all.'

Owen paused, and immediately there arose a great clamour from his listeners.

'So it *is* right, ain't it?' shouted Crass. 'If you 'ad a 'ouse and let it to someone, you'd want your rent, wouldn't yer?'

'I suppose,' said Slyme with resentment, for he had some shares in a local building society, 'after a man's been careful, and scraping and saving and going without things he ought to 'ave 'ad all 'is life, and managed to buy a few 'ouses to support 'im in 'is old age – they ought all be took away from 'im? Some people,' he added, 'ain't got common honesty.'

Nearly everyone had something to say in reprobation of the views suggested by Owen. Harlow, in a brief but powerful speech, bristling with numerous sanguinary references to the bottomless pit, protested against any interference with the sacred rights of property. Easton listened with a puzzled expression, and Philpot's goggle eyes rolled horribly as he glared silently at the circle and the two squares.

'By far the greater part of the land,' said Owen when the row had ceased, 'is held by people who have absolutely no moral right to it. Possession of much of it was obtained by means of murder and theft perpetrated by the ancestors of the present holders. In other cases, when some king or prince wanted to get rid of a mistress of whom he had grown weary, he presented a tract of our country to some "nobleman" on condition that he would marry the female. Vast estates were also bestowed upon the remote ancestors of the present holders in return for real or alleged services. Listen to this,' he continued as he took a small newspaper cutting from his pocketbook.

Crass looked at the piece of paper dolefully. It reminded him of the one he had in his own pocket, which he was beginning to fear that he would not have an opportunity of producing today after all.

'Ballcartridge Rent Day.'[45]

'The hundredth anniversary of the Battle of Ballcartridge occurred yesterday and in accordance with custom the Duke of Ballcartridge handed to the authorities the little flag which he annually presents to the State in virtue of his tenure of the vast tract of this country which was presented to one of his ancestors – the first Duke – in addition to his salary, for his services at the battle of Ballcartridge.

'The flag – which is the only rent the Duke has to pay for the great estate which brings him in several hundred thousands of pounds per annum – is a small tricoloured one with a staff surmounted by an eagle.

'The Duke of Blankmind also presents the State with a little coloured silk flag every year in return for being allowed to retain possession of that part of England which was presented – in addition to his salary – to one of His Grace's very remote ancestors, for his services at the battle of Commissariat – in the Netherlands.'

'The Duke of Southward is another instance,' continued Owen. 'He 'owns' miles of the country we speak of as 'ours'. Much of his part consists of confiscated monastery lands which were stolen from the owners by King Henry VIII and presented to the ancestors of the present Duke.

'Whether it was right or wrong that these parts of our country should ever have been given to those people – the question whether those ancestor persons were really deserving cases or not – is a thing we need not trouble ourselves about now. But the present holders are certainly not deserving people. They do not even take the trouble to pretend that they are. They have done nothing and they do nothing to justify their possession of these "estates" as they call them. And in my opinion no man who is in his right mind can really think it's just that these people should be allowed to prey upon their fellow men as they are doing now. Or that it is right that their children should be allowed to continue to prey upon our children for ever! The thousands of people on those estates work and live in poverty in order that these three men and their families may enjoy leisure and luxury. Just think of the absurdity of it!' continued Owen, pointing to the drawings. 'All those people allowing themselves to be overworked and bullied and starved and robbed by this little crowd here!'

Observing signs of a renewal of the storm of protest, Owen hurriedly concluded:

'Whether it's right or wrong, you can't deny that the fact that this small minority possesses nearly all the land of the country is one of the principal causes of the poverty of the majority.'

'Well, that seems true enough,' said Easton, slowly. 'The rent's the biggest item a workin' man's got to pay. When you're out of work and you can't afford other things, you goes without 'em, but the rent 'as to be paid whether you're workin' or not.'

'Yes, that's true enough,' said Harlow impatiently; 'but you gets value for yer money: you can't expect to get a 'ouse for nothing.'

'Suppose we admits as it's wrong, just for the sake of argyment,' said Crass in a jeering tone. 'Wot then? Wot about it? 'Ow's it agoin' to be altered.'

'Yes!' cried Harlow triumphantly. 'That's the bloody question! 'Ow's it goin' to be altered? It can't be done!'

There was a general murmur of satisfaction. Nearly everyone seemed very pleased to think that the existing state of things could not possibly be altered.

'Whether it can be altered or not, whether it's right or wrong, landlordism is one of the causes of poverty,' Owen repeated. 'Poverty is not caused by men and women getting married; it's not caused by machinery; it's not caused by "over-production"; it's not caused by drink or laziness; and it's not caused by "over-population" It's caused by Private Monopoly. That is the present system. They have monopolised everything that it is possible to monopolise; they have got the whole earth, the minerals in the earth and the streams that water the earth. The only reason they have not monopolised the daylight and the air is that it is not possible to do it. If it were possible to construct huge gasometers and to draw together and compress within them the whole of the atmosphere, it would have been done long ago, and we should have been compelled to work for them in order to get money to buy air to breathe. And if that seemingly impossible thing were accomplished tomorrow, you would see thousands of people dying for want of air – or of the money to buy it – even as now thousands are dying for want of the other necessaries of life. You would see people going about gasping for breath, and telling each other that the likes of them could not expect to have air to breathe unless they had the money to pay for it. Most of you here, for instance, would think so and say so. Even as you think at present that it's right for a few people to own the Earth, the Minerals and the Water, which are all just as necessary as is the air. In exactly the same spirit as you now say: "It's Their Land," "It's Their Water," "It's Their Coal," "It's Their Iron," so you would say "It's Their Air," "These are Their gasometers, and what right have the likes of us to expect them to allow us to breathe for nothing?" [And even while he is doing this the air monopolist will be preaching sermons on the Brotherhood of Man; he will be dispensing advice on "Christian Duty" in the Sunday] magazines; he will give utterance to numerous more or less moral maxims for the guidance of the young. And meantime, all around, people will be dying for want of some of the air that he will have bottled up in his gasometers. And when you are all dragging out a miserable existence, gasping for breath or dying for want of air, if one of your number suggests smashing a hole in the side of one of the gasometers, you will all fall upon him in the name of law and order, and after doing your best to tear him limb from limb, you'll drag him, covered with blood, in triumph to the nearest Police Station and deliver him up to "justice" in the hope of being given a few half-pounds of air for your trouble.'

'I suppose you think the landlords ought to let people live in their 'ouses for nothing?' said Crass, breaking the silence that followed.

'Certainly,' remarked Harlow, pretending to be suddenly converted to Owen's views, 'I reckon the landlord ought to pay the rent to the tenant!'

'Of course, Landlordism is not the only cause,' said Owen, ignoring these remarks. 'The wonderful system fosters a great many others. Employers of labour, for instance, are as great a cause of poverty as landlords are.'

This extraordinary statement was received with astonished silence.

'Do you mean to say that if I'm out of work and a master gives me a job, that 'e's doin' me a injury?' said Crass at length.

'No, of course not,' replied Owen.

'Well, what the bloody 'ell *do* yer mean, then?'

'I mean this: supposing that the owner of a house wishes to have it repainted. What does he usually do?'

'As a rule, 'e goes to three or four master painters and asks 'em to give 'im a price for the job.'

'Yes; and those master painters are so eager to get the work that they cut the price down to what they think is the lowest possible point,' answered Owen, 'and the lowest usually gets the job. The successful tenderer has usually cut the price so fine that to make it pay he has to scamp the work, pay low wages, and drive and sweat the men whom he employs. He wants them to do two days' work for one day's pay. The result is that a job which – if it were done properly – would employ say twenty men for two months, is rushed and scamped in half that time with half that number of men.

'This means that – in one such case as this – ten men are deprived of one month's employment; and ten other men are deprived of two months' employment; and all because the employers have been cutting each other's throats to get the work.'

'And we can't 'elp ourselves, you nor me either,' said Harlow.

'Supposing one of us on this job was to make up 'is mind not to tear into it like we do, but just keep on steady and do a fair day's work: wot would 'appen?'

No one answered; but the same thought was in everyone's mind. Such a one would be quickly marked by Hunter; and even if the latter failed to notice him it would not be long before Crass reported his conduct.

'We can't 'elp ourselves,' said Easton, gloomily. 'If one man won't do it there's twenty others ready to take 'is place.'

'We could help ourselves to a certain extent if we would stand by each other. If, for instance, we all belonged to the Society,'[46] said Owen.

'I don't believe in the Society,' observed Crass. 'I can't see as it's right that a inferior man should 'ave the same wages as me.'

'They're a drunken lot of beer-swillers,' remarked Slyme. 'That's why they always 'as their meetings in public 'ouses.'

Harlow made no comment on this question. He had at one time belonged to the Union and he was rather ashamed of having fallen away from it.

'Wot good 'as the Society ever done 'ere?' said Easton. 'None that I ever 'eard of.'

'It might be able to do some good if most of us belonged to it; but after all, that's another matter. Whether we could help ourselves or not, the fact remains that we don't. But you must admit that this competition of the employers is one of the causes of unemployment and poverty, because it's not only in our line – exactly the same thing happens in every other trade and industry. Competing employers are the upper and nether millstones which grind the workers between them.'

'I suppose you think there oughtn't to be no employers at all?' sneered Crass. 'Or pr'aps you think the masters ought to do all the bloody work theirselves, and give us the money?'

'I don't see 'ow it's goin' to be altered,' remarked Harlow. 'There *must* be masters, and *someone* 'as to take charge of the work and do the thinkin'.'

'Whether it can be altered or not,' said Owen, 'Landlordism and Competing Employers are two of the causes of poverty. But of course they're only a small part of the system which produces luxury, refinement and culture for a few, and condemns the majority to a lifelong struggle with adversity, and many thousands to degradation, hunger and rags. This is the system you all uphold and defend, although you don't mind admitting that it has made the world into a hell.'

Crass slowly drew the *Obscurer* cutting from his waistcoat pocket, but after a moment's thought he replaced it, deciding to defer its production till a more suitable occasion.

'But you 'aven't told us yet 'ow you makes out that money causes poverty,' cried Harlow, winking at the others. 'That's what *I'm* anxious to 'ear about!'

'So am I,' remarked the man behind the moat. 'I was just wondering whether I 'adn't better tell ole Misery that I don't want no wages this week.'

'I think I'll tell 'im on Saterdy to keep *my* money and get 'imself a few drinks with it,' said Philpot. 'It might cheer 'im up a bit and make 'im a little more sociable and friendly like.'

'Money *is* the principal cause of poverty,' said Owen.

' 'Ow do yer make it out?' cried Sawkins.

But their curiosity had to remain unsatisfied for the time being because Crass announced that it was 'just on it.'

CHAPTER 16

True Freedom

About three o'clock that afternoon, Rushton suddenly appeared and began walking silently about the house, and listening outside the doors of rooms where the hands were working. He did not succeed in catching anyone idling or smoking or talking. The nearest approach to what the men called 'a capture' that he made was, as he stood outside the door of one of the upper rooms in which Philpot and Harlow were working, he heard them singing one of Sankey's hymns – 'Work! for the night is coming'. He listened to two verses and several repetitions of the chorus. Being a 'Christian,' he could scarcely object to this, especially as by peeping through the partly open door he could see that they were suiting the action to the word. When he went into the room they glanced round to see who it was, and stopped singing. Rushton did not speak, but stood in the middle of the floor, silently watching them as they worked, for about a quarter of an hour. Then, without having uttered a syllable, he turned and went out.

They heard him softly descend the stairs, and Harlow, turning to Philpot said in a hoarse whisper:

'What do you think of the b—r, standing there watchin' us like that, as if we was a couple of bloody convicts? If it wasn't that I've got someone else beside myself to think of, I would 'ave sloshed the bloody sod in the mouth with this pound brush!'

'Yes; it does make yer feel like that, mate,' replied Philpot, 'but of course we mustn't give way to it.'

'Several times,' continued Harlow, who was livid with anger, 'I was on the point of turnin' round and sayin' to 'im, "What the bloody 'ell do you mean by standin' there watchin' me, you bloody, psalm-singin' swine?" It took me all my time to keep it in, I can tell you.'

Meantime, Rushton was still going about the house, occasionally standing and watching the other men in the same manner as he had watched Philpot and Harlow.

None of the men looked round from their work or spoke either to Rushton or to each other. The only sounds heard were the noises made by the saws and hammers of the carpenters who were fixing the frieze rails and dado rails or repairing parts of the woodwork in some of the rooms.

Crass placed himself in Rushton's way several times with the hope of being spoken to, but beyond curtly acknowledging the 'foreman's' servile 'Good hafternoon, sir' the master took no notice of him.

After about an hour spent in this manner Rushton went away, but as no one saw him go, it was not until some considerable time after his departure that they knew that he was gone.

Owen was secretly very disappointed. 'I thought he had come to tell me about the drawing-room,' he said to himself, 'but I suppose it's not decided yet.'

Just as the 'hands' were beginning to breathe freely again, Misery arrived, carrying some rolled-up papers in his hand. He also flitted silently from one room to another, peering round corners and listening at doors in the hope of seeing or hearing something which would give him an excuse for making an example of someone. Disappointed in this, he presently crawled upstairs to the room where Owen was working and, handing to him the roll of papers he had been carrying, said:

'Mr. Sweater has decided to 'ave this work done, so you can start on it as soon as you like.'

It is impossible to describe, without appearing to exaggerate, the emotions experienced by Owen as he heard this announcement. For one thing it meant that the work at this house would last longer than it would otherwise have done; and it also meant that he would be paid for the extra time he had spent on the drawings, besides having his wages increased – for he was always paid an extra penny per hour when engaged on special work, such as graining or sign-writing or work of the present kind. But these considerations did not occur to him at the moment at all, for to him it meant much more. Since his first conversation on the subject with Rushton he had thought of little else than this work.

In a sense he had been *doing* it ever since. He had thought and planned and altered the details of the work repeatedly. The colours for the different parts had been selected and rejected and re-selected over and over again. A keen desire to do the work had grown within him, but he had scarcely allowed himself to hope that it would be done at all. His face flushed slightly as he took the drawings from Hunter.

'You can make a start on it tomorrow morning,' continued that gentleman. 'I'll tell Crass to send someone else up 'ere to finish this room.'

'I shan't be able to commence tomorrow, because the ceiling and walls will have to be painted first.'

'Yes: I know. You and Easton can do that. One coat tomorrow, another on Friday and the third on Saturday – that is, unless you can make it do with two coats. Even if it has to have the three, you will be able to go on with your decoratin' on Monday.'

'I won't be able to start it on Monday, because I shall have to make some working drawings first.'

'Workin' drorins!' ejaculated Misery with a puzzled expression. 'Wot workin' drorins? You've got *them*, ain't yer?' pointing to the roll of papers.

'Yes: but as the same ornaments are repeated several times, I shall have to make a number of full-sized drawings, with perforated outlines, to transfer the design to the walls,' said Owen, and he proceeded to laboriously explain the processes.

Nimrod looked at him suspiciously. 'Is all that really necessary?' he asked. 'Couldn't you just copy it on the wall, freehand?'

'No; that wouldn't do. It would take much longer that way.'

This consideration appealed to Misery.

'Ah, well,' he sighed. 'I s'pose you'll 'ave to do it the way you said; but for goodness sake don't spend too much time over it, because we've took it very cheap. We only took it on so as you could 'ave a job, not that we expect to make any profit out of it.'

'And I shall have to cut some stencils, so I shall need several sheets of cartridge paper.'

Upon hearing of this additional expense, Misery's long visage appeared to become several inches longer; but after a moment's thought he brightened up.

'I'll tell you what!' he exclaimed with a cunning leer, 'there's lots of odd rolls of old wallpaper down at the shop. Couldn't you manage with some of that?'

'I'm afraid it wouldn't do,' replied Owen doubtfully, 'but I'll have a look at it and if possible I'll use it.'

'Yes, do!' said Misery, pleased at the thought of saving something. 'Call at the shop on your way home tonight, and we'll see what we can find. 'Ow long do you think it'll take you to make the drorin's and the stencils?'

'Well, today's Thursday. If you let someone else help Easton to get the room ready, I think I can get them done in time to bring them with me on Monday morning.'

'Wot do yer mean, "bring them with you"?' demanded Nimrod.

'I shall have to do them at home, you know.'

'Do 'em at 'ome! Why can't you do 'em 'ere?'

'Well, there's no table, for one thing.'

'Oh, but we can soon fit you out with a table. You can 'ave a pair of paperhanger's tressels and boards, for that matter.'

'I have a lot of sketches and things at home that I couldn't very well bring here,' said Owen.

Misery argued about it for a long time, insisting that the drawings should be made either on the 'job' or at the paint-shop down at the yard. How, he asked, was he to know at what hour Owen commenced or left off working, if the latter did them at home?

'I shan't charge any more time than I really work,' replied Owen. 'I can't possibly do them here or at the paint-shop. I know I should only make a mess of them under such conditions.'

'Well, I s'pose you'll 'ave to 'ave your own way,' said Misery, dolefully. 'I'll let Harlow help Easton paint the room out, so as you can get your stencils and things ready. But for Gord's sake get 'em done as quick as you can. If you could manage to get done by Friday and come down and help Easton on Saturday, it would be so much the better. And when you do get a start on the decoratin', I shouldn't take too much care over it, you know, if I was you, because we 'ad to take the job for next to nothing or Mr. Sweater would never 'ave 'ad it done at all!'

Nimrod now began to crawl about the house, snarling and grumbling at everyone.

'Now then, you chaps. *Rouse yourselves!*' he bellowed, 'you seem to think this is a 'orspital. If some of you don't make a better show than this, I'll 'ave to 'ave a Alteration! There's plenty of chaps walkin' about doin' nothin' who'll be only too glad of a job!'

He went into the scullery, where Crass was mixing some colour.

'Look 'ere, Crass!' he said. 'I'm not at all satisfied with the way you're gettin' on with the work. You must push the chaps a bit more than you're doin'. There's not enough being done, by a long way. We shall lose money over this job before we're finished!'

Crass – whose fat face had turned a ghastly green with fright – mumbled something about getting on with it as fast as he could.

'Well, you'll 'ave to make 'em move a bit quicker than this!' Misery howled, 'or there'll 'ave to be a *Alteration!*'

By an 'alteration' Crass understood that he might get the sack, or that someone else might be put in charge of the job, and that would of course reduce him to the ranks and do away with his chance of being kept on longer than the others. He determined to try to ingratiate himself with Hunter and appease his wrath by sacrificing someone else. He glanced cautiously into the kitchen and up the passage and then, lowering his voice he said:

'They all shapes pretty well, except Newman. I would 'ave told you about 'im before, but I thought I'd give 'im a fair chance. I've spoke to 'im several times myself about not doin' enough, but it don't seem to make no difference.'

'I've 'ad me eye on 'im meself for some time,' replied Nimrod in the same tone. 'Anybody would think the work was goin' to be sent to a Exhibition, the way 'e messes about with it, rubbing it with glasspaper and stopping up every little crack! I can't understand where 'e gets all the glasspaper *from!*'

' 'E brings it 'isself!' said Crass hoarsely. 'I know for a fact that 'e bought two 'a'penny sheets of it, last week, out of 'is own money!'

'Oh, 'e did, did 'e?' snarled Misery. 'I'll give 'im glasspaper! I'll 'ave a Alteration!'

He went into the hall, where he remained alone for a considerable time, brooding. At last, with the manner of one who has resolved on a certain course of action, he turned and entered the room where Philpot and Harlow were working.

'You both get sevenpence an hour, don't you?' he said.

They both replied in the affirmative.

'I've never worked under price yet,' added Harlow.

'Nor me neither,' observed Philpot.

'Well, of course you can please yourselves,' Hunter continued, 'but after this week we've decided not to pay more than six and a half. Things is cut so fine nowadays that we can't afford to go on payin' sevenpence any longer. You can work up till tomorrow night on the old terms, but if you're not willin' to accept six and a half you needn't come on Saterday morning. Please yourselves. Take it or leave it.'

Harlow and Philpot were both too much astonished to say anything in reply to this cheerful announcement, and Hunter, with the final remark, 'You can think it over,' left them and went to deliver the same ultimatum to all the other full-price men, who took it in the same way as Philpot and Harlow had done. Crass and Owen were the only two whose wages were not reduced.

It will be remembered that Newman was one of those who were already working for the reduced rate. Misery found him alone in one of the upper rooms, to which he was giving the final coat. He was at his old tricks. The woodwork of the cupboard he was doing was in a rather damaged condition, and he was facing up the dents with white-lead putty before painting it. He knew quite well that Hunter objected to any but very large holes or cracks being stopped, and yet somehow or other he could not scamp the work to the extent that he was ordered to; and so, almost by stealth, he was in the habit of doing it – not properly – but as well as he dared. He even went to the length of occasionally buying a few sheets of glasspaper with his own money, as Crass had told Hunter. When the latter came into the room he stood with a sneer on his face, watching Newman for about five minutes before he spoke. The workman became very nervous and awkward under this scrutiny.

'You can make out yer time-sheet and come to the office for yer money at five o'clock,' said Nimrod at last. 'We shan't require your valuable services no more after tonight.'

Newman went white.

'Why, what's wrong?' said he. 'What have I done?'

'Oh, it's not wot you've *done*,' replied Misery. 'It's wot you've *not* done. That's wot's wrong! You've not done enough, that's all!' And without further parley he turned and went out.

Newman stood in the darkening room feeling as if his heart had turned to lead. There rose before his mind the picture of his home and family. He could see them as they were at this very moment, the wife probably just beginning to prepare the evening meal, and the children setting the cups and saucers and other things on the kitchen table – a noisy work, enlivened with many a frolic and childish dispute. Even the two-year-old baby insisted on helping, although she always put everything in the wrong place and made all sorts of funny mistakes. They had all been so happy lately because they knew that he had work that would last till nearly Christmas – if not longer. And now *this* had happened – to plunge them back into that abyss of wretchedness from which they had so recently escaped. They still owed several weeks' rent, and were already so much in debt to the baker and the grocer that it was hopeless to expect any further credit.

'My God!' said Newman, realising the almost utter hopelessness of the chance of obtaining another 'job' and unconsciously speaking aloud. 'My God! How can I tell them? What *will* become of us?'

Having accomplished the objects of his visit, Hunter shortly afterwards departed, possibly congratulating himself that he had not been hiding his light under a bushel, but that he had set it upon a candlestick and given light unto all that were within that house.[47]

As soon as they knew that he was gone, the men began to gather into little groups, but in a little while they nearly all found themselves in the kitchen, discussing the reduction. Sawkins and the other 'light-weights'[48] remained at their work. Some of them got only fourpence halfpenny – Sawkins was paid fivepence – so none of these were affected by the change. The other two fresh hands – the journeymen – joined the crowd in the kitchen, being anxious to conceal the fact that they had agreed to accept the reduced rate before being 'taken on.' Owen also was there, having heard the news from Philpot.

There was a lot of furious talk. At first several of them spoke of 'chucking up' at once; but others were more prudent, for they knew that if they did leave there were dozens of others who would be eager to take their places.

'After all, you know,' said Slyme, who had – stowed away somewhere at the back of his head – an idea of presently starting business on his own account: he was only waiting until he had saved enough money, 'after all, there's something in what 'Unter says. It's very 'ard to get a fair price for work nowadays. Things *is* cut very fine.'

'Yes! We knows all about that!' shouted Harlow. 'And who the bloody 'ell is it cuts 'em? Why, sich b—rs as 'Unter and Rushton! If this firm 'adn't cut *this* job so fine, some other firm would 'ave 'ad it for more money. Rushton's cuttin' it fine didn't *make* this job, did it? It would 'ave been done just the same if they 'adn't tendered for it at all! The only difference is that we should 'ave been workin' for some other master.'

'I don't believe the bloody job's cut fine at all!' said Philpot. 'Rushton is a pal of Sweater's and they're both members of the Town Council.'

'That may be,' replied Slyme; 'but all the same I believe Sweater got several other prices besides Rushton's – friend or no friend; and you can't blame 'im: it's only business. But pr'aps Rushton got the preference – Sweater may 'ave told 'im the others' prices.'

'Yes, and a bloody fine lot of prices they was, too, if the truth was known!' said Bundy. 'There was six other firms after this job to my knowledge – Pushem and Sloggem, Bluffum and Doemdown, Dodger and Scampit, Snatcham and Graball, Smeeriton and Leavit, Makehaste and Sloggitt, and Gord only knows 'ow many more.'

At this moment Newman came into the room. He looked so white and upset that the others involuntarily paused in their conversation.

'Well, what do *you* think of it?' asked Harlow.

'Think of what?' said Newman.

'Why, didn't 'Unter tell you?' cried several voices, whose owners looked suspiciously at him. They thought – if Hunter had not spoken to Newman, it must be because he was already working under price. There had been a rumour going about the last few days to that effect. 'Didn't Misery tell you? They're not goin' to pay more than six and a half after this week.'

'That's not what 'e said to me. 'E just told me to knock off. Said I didn't do enough for 'em.'

'Jesus Christ!' exclaimed Crass, pretending to be overcome with surprise.

Newman's account of what had transpired was listened to in gloomy silence. Those who – a few minutes previously – had been talking loudly of chucking up the job became filled with apprehension that they might be served in the same manner as he had been. Crass was one of the loudest in his expression of astonishment and indignation, but he rather overdid it and only succeeded in confirming the secret suspicions of the others that he had had something to do with Hunter's action.

The result of the discussion was that they decided to submit to Misery's terms for the time being, until they could see a chance of getting work elsewhere.

As Owen had to go to the office to see the wallpaper spoken of by Hunter, he accompanied Newman when the latter went to get his wages. Nimrod was waiting for them, and had the money ready in an envelope, which he handed to Newman, who took it without speaking and went away.

Misery had been rummaging amongst the old wallpapers, and had got out a great heap of odd rolls, which he now submitted to Owen, but after examining them the latter said that they were unsuitable for the purpose, so after some argument Misery was compelled to sign an order for some proper cartridge paper, which Owen obtained at a stationer's on his way home.

The next morning, when Misery went to the 'Cave', he was in a fearful rage, and he kicked up a terrible row with Crass. He said that Mr. Rushton had been complaining of the lack of discipline on the job, and he told Crass to tell all the hands that for the future singing in working hours was strictly forbidden, and anyone caught breaking this rule would be instantly dismissed.

*   *   *

Several times during the following days Nimrod called at Owen's flat to see how the work was progressing and to impress upon him the necessity of not taking too much trouble over it.

CHAPTER 17

The Rev. John Starr

'What time is it now, Mum?' asked Frankie as soon as he had finished dinner on the following Sunday. 'Two o'clock.'

'Hooray! Only one more hour and Charlie will be here! Oh, I wish it was three o'clock now, don't you, Mother?'

'No, dear, I don't. You're not dressed yet, you know.'

Frankie made a grimace.

'You're surely not going to make me wear my velvets, are you, Mum? Can't I go just as I am, in my old clothes?'

The 'velvets' was a brown suit of that material that Nora had made out of the least worn parts of an old costume of her own.

'Of course not: if you went as you are now, you'd have everyone staring at you.'

'Well, I suppose I'll have to put up with it,' said Frankie, re-signedly. 'And I think you'd better begin to dress me now, don't you?'

'Oh, there's plenty of time yet; you'd only make yourself untidy and then I should have the trouble all over again. Play with your toys a little while, and when I've done the washing up I'll get you ready.'

Frankie obeyed, and for about ten minutes his mother heard him in the next room rummaging in the box where he stored his collection of 'things'. At the end of that time, however, he returned to the kitchen.

'Is it time to dress me yet, Mum?'

'No, dear, not yet. You needn't be afraid; you'll be ready in plenty of time.'

'But I can't help being afraid; you might forget.'

'Oh, I shan't forget. There's lots of time.'

'Well, you know, I should be much easier in my mind if you would dress me now, because perhaps our clock's wrong, or p'r'aps when you begin dressing me you'll find some buttons off or something, and then there'll be a lot of time wasted sewing them on; or p'r'aps you won't be able to find my clean stockings or something and then while you're looking for it Charlie might come, and if he sees I'm not ready he mightn't wait for me.'

'Oh, dear!' said Nora, pretending to be alarmed at this appalling list of possibilities. 'I suppose it will be safer to dress you at once. It's very evident you won't let me have much peace until it is done, but mind when you're dressed you'll have to sit down quietly and wait till he comes, because I don't want the trouble of dressing you twice.'

'Oh, I don't mind sitting still,' returned Frankie, loftily. 'That's very easy.'

'I don't mind having to take care of my clothes,' said Frankie as his mother – having washed and dressed him, was putting the finishing touches to his hair, brushing and combing and curling the long yellow locks into ringlets round her fingers, 'the only thing I don't like is having my hair done. You know all these curls are quite unnecessary. I'm sure it would save you a lot of trouble if you wouldn't mind cutting them off.'

Nora did not answer: somehow or other she was unwilling to comply with this often-repeated entreaty. It seemed to her that when this hair was cut off the child would have become a different individual – more separate and independent.

'If you don't want to cut it off for your own sake, you might do it for my sake, because I think it's the reason some of the big boys don't want to play with me, and some of them shout after me and say I'm a girl, and sometimes they sneak up behind me and pull it. Only yesterday I had to have a fight with a boy for doing it: and even Charlie Linden laughs at me, and he's my best friend – except you and Dad of course.

'Why don't you cut it off, Mum?'

'I am going to cut it as I promised you, after your next birthday.'

'Then I shall be jolly glad when it comes. Won't you? Why, what's the matter, Mum? What are you crying for?' Frankie was so concerned that he began to cry also, wondering if he had done or said something wrong. He kissed her repeatedly, stroking her face with his hand. 'What's the matter, Mother?'

'I was thinking that when you're over seven and you've had your hair cut short you won't be a baby any more.'

'Why, I'm not a baby now, am I? Here, look at this!'

He strode over to the wall and, dragging out two chairs, he placed them in the middle of the room, back to back, about fifteen inches apart, and before his mother realised what he was doing he had climbed up and stood with one leg on the back of each chair.

'I should like to see a baby who could do this,' he cried, with his face wet with tears. 'You needn't lift me down. I can get down by myself. Babies can't do tricks like these or even wipe up the spoons and forks or sweep the passage. But you needn't cut it off if you don't want to. I'll bear it as long as you like. Only don't cry any more, because it makes me miserable. If I cry when I fall down or when you pull my hair when you're combing it you always tell me to bear it like a man and not be a baby, and now you're crying yourself just because I'm not a baby. You ought to be jolly glad that I'm nearly grown up into a man, because you know I've promised to build you a house with the money I earn, and then you needn't do no more work. We'll have a servant the same as the people downstairs, and Dad can stop at home and sit by the fire and read the paper or play with me and Maud and have pillow fights and tell stories and – '

'It's all right, dearie,' said Nora, kissing him. 'I'm not crying now, and you mustn't either, or your eyes will be all red and you won't be able to go with Charlie at all.'

When she had finished dressing him, Frankie sat for some time in silence, apparently lost in thought. At last he said:

'Why don't you get a baby, Mother? You could nurse it, and I could have it to play with instead of going out in the street.'

'We can't afford to keep a baby, dear. You know, even as it is, sometimes we have to go without things we want because we haven't the money to buy them. Babies need many things that cost lots of money.'

'When I build our house when I'm a man, I'll take jolly good care not to have a gas-stove in it. That's what runs away with all the money; we're always putting pennies in the slot. And that reminds me: Charlie said I'll have to take a ha'penny to put in the mishnery box. Oh, dear, I'm tired of sitting still. I wish he'd come. What time is it now, Mother?'

Before she could answer both Frankie's anxiety and the painful ordeal of sitting still were terminated by a loud peal at the bell announcing Charlie's arrival, and Frankie, without troubling to observe the usual formality of looking out of the window to see if it was a runaway ring, had clattered halfway downstairs before he heard his mother calling him to came back for the halfpenny; then he clattered up again and then down again at such a rate and with so much noise as to rouse the indignation of all the respectable people in the house.

When he arrived at the bottom of the stairs he remembered that he had omitted to say goodbye, and as it was too far to go up again he rang the bell and then went into the middle of the road and looked up at the window that Nora opened.

'Goodbye, Mother,' he shouted. 'Tell Dad I forgot to say it before I came down.'

The School was not conducted in the chapel itself, but in a large lecture hall under it. At one end was a small platform raised about six inches from the floor; on this was a chair and a small table. A number of groups of chairs and benches were arranged at intervals round the sides and in the centre of the room, each group of seats accommodating a separate class. On the walls – which were painted a pale green – were a number of coloured pictures: Moses striking the Rock, the Israelites dancing round the Golden Calf,[49] and so on. As the reader is aware, Frankie had never been to a Sunday School of any kind before, and he stood for a moment looking in at the door and half afraid to enter. The lessons had already commenced, but the scholars had not yet settled down to work.

The scene was one of some disorder: some of the children talking, laughing or playing, and the teachers alternately threatening and coaxing them. The girls' and the very young children's classes were presided over by ladies: the boys' teachers were men.

The reader already has some slight knowledge of a few of these people. There was Mr. Didlum, Mr. Sweater, Mr. Rushton and Mr. Hunter and Mrs. Starvem (Ruth Easton's former mistress). On this occasion, in addition to the teachers and other officials of the Sunday School there were also present a considerable number of prettily dressed ladies and a few gentlemen, who had come in the hope of meeting the Rev. John Starr, the young clergyman who was going to be their minister for the next few weeks during the absence of their regular shepherd, Mr. Belcher, who was going away for a holiday for the benefit of his health. Mr. Belcher was not suffering from any particular malady, but was merely 'run down', and rumour had it that this condition had been brought about by the rigorous asceticism of his life and his intense devotion to the arduous labours of his holy calling.

Mr. Starr had conducted the service in the Shining Light Chapel that morning, and a great sensation had been produced by the young minister's earnest and eloquent address, which was of a very different style from that of their regular minister. Although perhaps they had not quite grasped the real significance of all that he had said, most of them had been favourably impressed by the young clergyman's appearance and manner in the morning: but that might have arisen from prepossession and force of habit, for they were accustomed, as a matter of course, to think well of any minister. There were, however, one or two members of the congregation who were not without some misgivings and doubts as to the soundness of his doctrines.

Mr. Starr had promised that he would look in some time during the afternoon to say a few words to the Sunday School children, and consequently on this particular afternoon all the grown-ups were looking forward so eagerly to hearing him again that not much was done in the way of lessons. Every time a late arrival entered all eyes were directed towards the door in the hope and expectation that it was he.

When Frankie, standing at the door, saw all these people looking at him he drew back timidly.

'Come on, man,' said Charlie. 'You needn't be afraid; it's not like a week-day school; they can't do nothing to us, not even if we don't behave ourselves. There's our class over in that corner, and that's our teacher, Mr. Hunter. You can sit next to me. Come on!'

Thus encouraged, Frankie followed Charlie over to the class, and both sat down. The teacher was so kind and spoke so gently to the children that in a few minutes Frankie felt quite at home.

When Hunter noticed how well cared for and well dressed he was, he thought the child must belong to well-to-do, respectable parents.

Frankie did not pay much attention to the lesson, for he was too much interested in the pictures on the walls and in looking at the other children. He also noticed a very fat man who was not teaching at all, but drifted aimlessly about the room from one class to another. After a time he came and stood by the class where Frankie was, and, after nodding to Hunter, remained near, listening and smiling patronisingly at the children. He was arrayed in a long garment of costly black cloth, a sort of frock coat, and by the rotundity of his figure he seemed to be one of those accustomed to sit in the chief places at feasts. This was the Rev. Mr. Belcher, minister of the Shining Light Chapel. His short, thick neck was surrounded by a collar, apparently studless and buttonless, being fastened in some mysterious way known only to himself, and he showed no shirt front.

The long garment before-mentioned was unbuttoned and through the opening there protruded a vast expanse of waistcoat and trousers, distended almost to bursting by the huge globe of flesh they contained. A gold watch-chain with a locket extended partly across the visible portion of the envelope of the globe. He had very large feet which were carefully encased in soft calfskin boots. If he had removed the long garment, this individual would have resembled a balloon: the feet representing the car and the small head that surmounted the globe, the safety valve; as it was it did actually serve the purpose of a safety valve, the owner being, in consequence of gross overfeeding and lack of natural exercise, afflicted with chronic flatulence, which manifested itself in frequent belchings forth through the mouth of the foul gases generated in the stomach by the decomposition of the foods with which it was generally loaded. But as the Rev. Mr. Belcher had never been seen with his coat off, no one ever noticed the resemblance. It was not necessary for him to take his coat off: his part in life was not to help to produce, but to help to devour the produce of the labour of others.

After exchanging a few words and grins with Hunter, he moved on to another class, and presently Frankie with a feeling of awe noticed that the confused murmuring sound that had hitherto pervaded the place was hushed. The time allotted for lessons had expired, and the teachers were quietly distributing hymn-books to the children.

Meantime, the balloon had drifted up to the end of the hall and had ascended the platform, where it remained stationary by the side of the table, occasionally emitting puffs of gas through the safety valve.

On the table were several books, and also a pile of folded cards. These latter were about six inches by three inches; there was some printing on the outside: one of them was lying open on the table, showing the inside, which was ruled and had money columns.

Presently Mr. Belcher reached out a flabby white hand and, taking up one of the folded cards, he looked around upon the underfed, ill-clad children with a large, sweet, benevolent, fatherly smile, and then in a drawling voice occasionally broken by explosions of flatulence, he said:

'My dear children. This afternoon as I was standing near Brother Hunter's class I heard him telling them of the wanderings of the Children of Israel in the wilderness, and of all the wonderful things that were done for them; and I thought how sad it was that they were so ungrateful.

'Now those ungrateful Israelites had received many things, but we have even more cause to be grateful than they had, for we have received even more abundantly than they did.' (Here the good man's voice was stifled by a succession of explosions.) 'And I am sure,' he resumed, 'that none of you would like to be even as those Israelites, ungrateful for all the good things you have received. Oh, how thankful you should be for having been made happy English children. Now, I am sure that you are grateful and that you will all be very glad of an opportunity of showing your gratitude by doing something in return.

'Doubtless some of you have noticed the unseemly condition of the interior of our Chapel. The flooring is broken in countless places, the walls are sadly in need of cleansing and distempering, and they also need cementing externally to keep out the draught. The seats and benches and the chairs are also in a most unseemly condition and need varnishing.

'Now, therefore, after much earnest meditation and prayer, it has been decided to open a Subscription List, and although times are very hard just now, we believe we shall succeed in getting enough to have the work done; so I want each one of you to take one of these cards and go round to all your friends to see how much you can collect. It doesn't matter how trifling the amounts are, because the smallest donations will be thankfully received.

'Now, I hope you will all do your very best. Ask everyone you know; do not refrain from asking people because you think that they are too poor to give a donation, but remind them that if they cannot give their thousands they can give the widow's mite.[50] Ask Everyone! First of all ask those whom you feel certain will give: then ask all those whom you think may *possibly* give: and, finally, ask all those whom you feel certain will *not* give: and you will be surprised to find that many of these last will donate abundantly.

'If your friends are very poor and unable to give a large donation at one time, a good plan would be to arrange to call upon them every Saturday afternoon with your card to collect their donations. And while you are asking others, do not forget to give what you can yourselves. Just a little self-denial, and those pennies and halfpennies which you so often spend on sweets and other unnecessary things might be given – as a donation – to the good cause.'

Here the holy man paused again, and there was a rumbling, gurgling noise in the interior of the balloon, followed by several escapes of gas through the safety valve. The paroxysm over, the apostle of self-denial continued:

'All those who wish to collect donations will stay behind for a few minutes after school, when Brother Hunter – who has kindly consented to act as secretary to the fund – will issue the cards.

'I would like here to say a few words of thanks to Brother Hunter for the great interest he has displayed in this matter, and for all the trouble he is taking to help us to gather in the donations.'

This tribute was well deserved; Hunter in fact had originated the whole scheme in the hope of securing the job for Rushton & Co., and two-and-a-half per cent. of the profits for himself.

Mr. Belcher now replaced the collecting card on the table and, taking up one of the hymn-books, gave out the words and afterwards conducted the singing, flourishing one fat, flabby white hand in the air and holding the book in the other.

As the last strains of the music died away, he closed his eyes and a sweet smile widened his mouth as he stretched forth his right hand, open, palm down, with the fingers close together, and said:

'Let us pray.'

With much shuffling of feet everyone knelt down. Hunter's lanky form was distributed over a very large area; his body lay along one of the benches, his legs and feet sprawled over the floor, and his huge hands clasped the sides of the seat. His eyes were tightly closed and an expression of the most intense misery pervaded his long face.

Mrs. Starvem, being so fat that she knew if she once knelt down she would never be able to get up again, compromised by sitting on the extreme edge of her chair, resting her elbows on the back of the seat in front of her, and burying her face in her hands. It was a very large face, but her hands were capacious enough to receive it.

In a seat at the back of the hall knelt a pale-faced, weary-looking little woman about thirty-six years of age, very shabbily dressed, who had come in during the singing. This was Mrs. White, the caretaker, Bert White's mother. When her husband died, the committee of the Chapel, out of charity, gave her this work, for which they paid her six shillings a week. Of course, they could not offer her full employment; the idea was that she could get other work as well, charing and things of that kind, and do the Chapel work in between. There wasn't much to do: just the heating furnace to light when necessary; the Chapel, committee rooms, classrooms and Sunday School to sweep and scrub out occasionally; the hymn-books to collect, etc. Whenever they had a tea meeting – which was on an average about twice a week – there were the trestle tables to fix up, the chairs to arrange, the table to set out, and then, supervised by Miss Didlum or some other lady, the tea to make. There was rather a lot to do on the days following these functions: the washing up, the tables and chairs to put away, the floor to sweep, and so on; but the extra work was supposed to be compensated by the cakes and broken victuals generally left over from the feast, which were much appreciated as a welcome change from the bread and dripping or margarine that constituted Mrs. White's and Bert's usual fare.

There were several advantages attached to the position: the caretaker became acquainted with the leading members and their wives, some of whom, out of charity, occasionally gave her a day's work as charwoman, the wages being on about the same generous scale as those she earned at the Chapel, sometimes supplemented by a parcel of broken victuals or some cast off clothing.

An evil-minded, worldly or unconverted person might possibly sum up the matter thus: These people required this work done: they employed this woman to do it, taking advantage of her poverty to impose upon her conditions of price and labour that they would not have liked to endure themselves. Although she worked very hard, early and late, the money they paid her as wages was insufficient to enable her to provide herself with the bare necessaries of life. Then her employers, being good, kind, generous, Christian people, came to the rescue and bestowed charity, in the form of cast-off clothing and broken victuals.

Should any such evil-minded, worldly or unconverted persons happen to read these lines, it is a sufficient answer to their impious and malicious criticisms to say that no such thoughts ever entered the simple mind of Mrs. White herself: on the contrary, this very afternoon as she knelt in the Chapel, wearing an old mantle that some years previously had adorned the obese person of the saintly Mrs. Starvem, her heart was filled with gratitude towards her generous benefactors.

During the prayer the door was softly opened: a gentleman in clerical dress entered on tiptoe and knelt down next to Mr. Didlum. He came in very softly, but all the same most of those present heard him and lifted their heads or peeped through their fingers to see who it was, and when they recognised him a sound like a sigh swept through the hall.

At the end of the prayer, amid groans and cries of 'Amen', the balloon slowly descended from the platform, and collapsed into one of the seats, and everyone rose up from the floor. When all were seated and the shuffling, coughing and blowing of noses had ceased Mr. Didlum stood up and said:

'Before we sing the closin' 'ymn, the genelman hon my left, the Rev. Mr. John Starr, will say a few words.'

An expectant murmur rippled through the hall. The ladies lifted their eyebrows and nodded, smiled and whispered to each other; the gentlemen assumed various attitudes and expressions; the children were very quiet. Everyone was in a state of suppressed excitement as John Starr rose from his seat and, stepping up on to the platform, stood by the side of the table, facing them.

He was about twenty-six years of age, tall and slenderly built. His clean-cut, intellectual face, with its lofty forehead, and his air of refinement and culture were in striking contrast to the coarse appearance of the other adults in the room: the vulgar, ignorant, uncultivated crowd of profit-mongers and hucksters in front of him. But it was not merely his air of good breeding and the general comeliness of his exterior that attracted and held one. There was an indefinable something about him – an atmosphere of gentleness and love that seemed to radiate from his whole being, almost compelling confidence and affection from all those with whom he came in contact.

As he stood there facing the others with an inexpressibly winning smile upon his comely face, it seemed impossible that there could be any fellowship between him and them.

There was nothing in his appearance to give anyone even an inkling of the truth, which was: that he was there for the purpose of bolstering up the characters of the despicable crew of sweaters and slave-drivers who paid his wages.

He did not give a very long address this afternoon – only just a Few Words: but they were very precious, original and illuminating. He told them of certain Thoughts that had occurred to his mind on his way there that afternoon; and as they listened, Sweater, Rushton, Didlum, Hunter, and the other disciples exchanged significant looks and gestures. Was it not magnificent! Such power! Such reasoning! In fact, as they afterwards modestly admitted to each other, it was so profound that even *they* experienced great difficulty in fathoming the speaker's meaning.

As for the ladies, they were motionless and dumb with admiration. They sat with flushed faces, shining eyes and palpitating hearts, looking hungrily at the dear man as he proceeded:

'Unfortunately, our time this afternoon does not permit us to dwell at length upon these Thoughts. Perhaps at some future date we may have the blessed privilege of so doing; but this afternoon I have been asked to say a Few Words on another subject. The failing health of your *dear* minister has for some time past engaged the anxious attention of the congregation.'

Sympathetic glances were directed towards the interesting invalid; the ladies murmured, 'Poor dear!' and other expressions of anxious concern.

'Although naturally robust,' continued Starr, 'long, continued Overwork, the loving solicitude for Others that often prevented him taking even necessary repose, and a too rigorous devotion to the practice of Self-denial have at last brought about the inevitable Breakdown, and rendered a period of Rest absolutely imperative.'

The orator paused to take breath, and the silence that ensued was disturbed only by faint rumblings in the interior of the ascetic victim of overwork.

'With this laudable object,' proceeded Starr, 'a Subscription List was quietly opened about a month ago, and those dear children who had cards and assisted in the good work of collecting donations will be pleased to hear that altogether a goodly sum was gathered, but as it was not quite enough, the committee voted a further amount out of the General Fund, and at a special meeting held last Friday evening, your *dear* Shepherd was presented with an illuminated address, and a purse of gold sufficient to defray the expenses of a month's holiday in the South of France.

'Although, of course, he regrets being separated from you even for such a brief period he feels that in going he is choosing the lesser of two evils. It is better to go to the South of France for a month than to continue Working in spite of the warnings of exhausted nature and perhaps be taken away from you altogether – to Heaven.'

'God forbid!' fervently ejaculated several disciples, and a ghastly pallor overspread the features of the object of their prayers.

'Even as it is there is a certain amount of danger. Let us hope and pray for the best, but if the worst *should* happen, and he *is* called upon to Ascend, there will be some satisfaction in knowing that you have done what you could to avert the dreadful calamity.'

Here, probably as a precaution against the possibility of an involuntary ascent, a large quantity of gas was permitted to escape through the safety valve of the balloon.

'He sets out on his pilgrimage tomorrow,' concluded Starr, 'and I am sure he will be followed by the good wishes and prayers of all the members of his flock.'

The reverend gentleman resumed his seat, and almost immediately it became evident from the oscillations of the balloon that Mr. Belcher was desirous of rising to say a Few Words in acknowledgement, but he was restrained by the entreaties of those near him, who besought him not to exhaust himself. He afterwards said that he would not have been able to say much even if they had permitted him to speak, because he felt too full.

'During the absence of our beloved pastor,' said Brother Didlum, who now rose to give out the closing hymn, 'his flock will not be left hentirely without a shepherd, for we 'ave arranged with Mr. Starr to come and say a Few Words to us hevery Sunday.'

From the manner in which they constantly referred to themselves, it might have been thought that they were a flock of sheep instead of being what they really were – a pack of wolves.

When they heard Brother Didlum's announcement a murmur of intense rapture rose from the ladies, and Mr. Starr rolled his eyes and smiled sweetly. Brother Didlum did not mention the details of the 'arrangement'; to have done so at that time would have been most unseemly, but the following extract from the accounts of the chapel will not be out of place here: 'Paid to Rev. John Starr for

Sunday, Nov. 14 – £4. 4. 0. per the treasurer.' It was not a large sum considering the great services rendered by Mr. Starr, but, small as it was, it is to be feared that many worldly, unconverted persons will think it was far too much to pay for a Few Words, even such wise words as Mr. John Starr's admittedly always were. But the Labourer is worthy of his hire.[51]

After the 'service' was over, most of the children, including Charley and Frankie, remained to get collecting cards. Mr. Starr was surrounded by a crowd of admirers, and a little later, when he rode away with Mr. Belcher and Mr. Sweater in the latter's motor car, the ladies looked hungrily after that conveyance, listening to the melancholy 'pip, pip' of its hooter and trying to console themselves with the reflection that they would see him again in a few hours' time at the evening service.

CHAPTER 18

The Lodger

In accordance with his arrangement with Hunter, Owen commenced the work in the drawing-room on the Monday morning. Harlow and Easton were distempering some of the ceilings, and about ten o'clock they went down to the scullery to get some more whitewash. Crass was there as usual, pretending to be very busy mixing colours.

'Well, wot do you think of it?' he said as he served them with what they required.

'Think of what?' asked Easton.

'Why, hour speshul hartist,' replied Crass with a sneer. 'Do you think 'e's goin' to get through with it?'

'Shouldn't like to say,' replied Easton guardedly.

'You know it's one thing to draw on a bit of paper and colour it with a penny box of paints, and quite another thing to do it on a wall or ceiling,' continued Crass. 'Ain't it?'

'Yes; that's true enough,' said Harlow.

'Do you believe they're 'is own designs?' Crass went on.

'Be rather 'ard to tell,' remarked Easton, embarrassed.

Neither Harlow nor Easton shared Crass's sentiments in this matter, but at the same time they could not afford to offend him by sticking up for Owen.

'If you was to ast *me*, quietly,' Crass added, 'I should be more inclined to say as 'e copied it all out of some book.'

'That's just about the size of it, mate,' agreed Harlow.

'It would be a bit of all right if 'e was to make a bloody mess of it, wouldn't it?' Crass continued with a malignant leer.

'Not arf!' said Harlow.

When the two men regained the upper landing on which they were working they exchanged significant glances and laughed quietly. Hearing these half-suppressed sounds of merriment, Philpot, who was working alone in a room close by, put his head out of the doorway.

'Wot's the game?' he enquired in a low voice.

'Ole Crass ain't arf wild about Owen doin' that room,' replied Harlow, and repeated the substance of Crass' remarks.

'It is a bit of a take-down for the bleeder, ain't it, 'avin' to play second fiddle,' said Philpot with a delighted grin.

' 'E's 'opin' Owen'll make a mess of it,' Easton whispered.

'Well, 'e'll be disappointed, mate,' answered Philpot. 'I was workin' along of Owen for Pushem and Sloggem about two year ago, and I seen 'im do a job down at the Royal 'Otel – the smokin'-room ceilin' it was – and I can tell you it looked a bloody treat!'

'I've heard tell of it,' said Harlow.

'There's no doubt Owen knows 'is work,' remarked Easton, 'although 'e *is* a bit orf is onion about Socialism.'

'I don't know so much about that, mate,' returned Philpot. 'I agree with a lot that 'e ses. I've often thought the same things meself, but I can't talk like 'im, 'cause I ain't got no 'ead for it.'

'I agree with some of it too,' said Harlow with a laugh, 'but all the same 'e does say some bloody silly things, you must admit. For instance, that cuff about money bein' the cause of poverty.'

'Yes. I can't exactly see that meself,' agreed Philpot.

'We must tackle 'im about that at dinner-time,' said Harlow. 'I should rather like to 'ear 'ow 'e makes it out.'

'For Gord's sake don't go startin' no arguments at dinner-time,' said Easton. 'Leave 'im alone when 'e *is* quiet.'

'Yes; let's 'ave our dinner in peace, if possible,' said Philpot. 'Sh!!' he added, hoarsely, suddenly holding up his hand warningly.

They listened intently. It was evident from the creaking of the stairs that someone was crawling up them. Philpot instantly disappeared. Harlow lifted up the pail of whitewash and set it down again noisily.

'I think we'd better 'ave the steps and the plank over this side, Easton,' he said in a loud voice.

'Yes. I think that'll be the best way,' replied Easton.

While they were arranging their scaffold to do the ceiling Crass arrived on the landing. He made no remark at first, but walked into the rooms to see how many ceilings they had done.

'You'd better look alive, you chaps,' he said as he went downstairs again. 'If we don't get these ceilings finished by dinner-time, Nimrod's sure to ramp.'

'All right,' said Harlow, gruffly. 'We'll bloody soon slosh 'em over.'

'Slosh' was a very suitable word; very descriptive of the manner in which the work was done. The cornices of the staircase ceilings were enriched with plaster ornaments. These ceilings were supposed to have been washed off, but as the men who were put to do that work had not been allowed sufficient time to do it properly, the crevices of the ornaments were still filled up with old whitewash, and by the time Harlow and Easton had 'sloshed' a lot more whitewash on to them they were mere formless unsightly lumps of plaster. The 'hands' who did the 'washing off' were not to blame. They had been hunted away from the work before it was half done.

While Harlow and Easton were distempering these ceilings, Philpot and the other hands were proceeding with the painting in different parts of the inside of the house, and Owen, assisted by Bert, was getting on with the work in the drawing-room, striking chalk lines and measuring and setting out the different panels.

There were no 'political' arguments that day at dinner-time, to the disappointment of Crass, who was still waiting for an opportunity to produce the *Obscurer* cutting. After dinner, when the others had all gone back to their work, Philpot unobtrusively returned to the kitchen and gathered up the discarded paper wrappers in which some of the men had brought their food. Spreading one of these open, he shook the crumbs from the others upon it. In this way and by picking up particles of bread from the floor, he collected a little pile of crumbs and crusts. To these he added some fragments that he had left from his own dinner. He then took the parcel upstairs and opening one of the windows threw the crumbs on to the roof of the portico. He had scarcely closed the window when two starlings fluttered down and began to eat. Philpot watching them furtively from behind the shutter.

The afternoon passed uneventfully. From one till five seemed a very long time to most of the hands, but to Owen and his mate, who were doing something in which they were able to feel some interest and pleasure, the time passed so rapidly that they both regretted the approach of evening.

'Other days,' remarked Bert, 'I always keeps on wishin' it was time to go 'ome, but today seems to 'ave gorn like lightnin'!'

After leaving off that night, all the men kept together till they arrived down town, and then separated. Owen went by himself: Easton, Philpot, Crass and Bundy adjourned to the 'Cricketers Arms' to have a drink together before going home, and Slyme, who was a teetotaler, went by himself, although he was now lodging with Easton.

'Don't wait for me,' said the latter as he went off with Crass and the others. 'I shall most likely catch you up before you get there.'

'All right,' replied Slyme.

This evening Slyme did not take the direct road home. He turned into the main street, and, pausing before the window of a toy shop, examined the articles displayed therein attentively. After some minutes he appeared to have come to a decision, and entering the shop he purchased a baby's rattle for fourpence halfpenny. It was a pretty toy made of white bone and coloured wool, with a number of little bells hanging upon it, and a ring of white bone at the end of the handle.

When he came out of the shop Slyme set out for home, this time walking rapidly. When he entered the house Ruth was sitting by the fire with the baby on her lap. She looked up with an expression of disappointment as she perceived that he was alone.

'Where's Will got to again?' she asked.

'He's gone to 'ave a drink with some of the chaps. He said he wouldn't be long,' replied Slyme as he put his food basket on the dresser and went upstairs to his room to wash and to change his clothes.

When he came down again, Easton had not yet arrived.

'Everything's ready, except just to make the tea,' said Ruth, who was evidently annoyed at the continued absence of Easton, 'so you may as well have yours now.'

'I'm in no hurry. I'll wait a little and see if he comes. He's sure to be here soon.'

'If you're sure you don't mind, I shall be glad if you will wait,' said Ruth, 'because it will save me making two lots of tea.'

They waited for about half an hour, talking at intervals in a constrained, awkward way about trivial subjects. Then as Easton did not come, Ruth decided to serve Slyme without waiting any longer. With this intention she laid the baby in its cot, but the child resented this arrangement and began to cry, so she had to hold him under her left arm while she made the tea. Seeing her in this predicament, Slyme exclaimed, holding out his hands:

'Here, let me hold him while you do that.'

'Will you?' said Ruth, who, in spite of her instinctive dislike of the man, could not help feeling gratified with this attention. 'Well, mind you don't let him fall.'

But the instant Slyme took hold of the child it began to cry even louder than it did when it was put into the cradle.

'He's always like that with strangers,' apologised Ruth as she took him back again.

'Wait a minute,' said Slyme. 'I've got something upstairs in my pocket that will keep him quiet. I'd forgotten all about it,'

He went up to his room and presently returned with the rattle. When the baby saw the bright colours and heard the tinkling of the bells he crowed with delight, and reached out his hands eagerly towards it and allowed Slyme to take him without a murmur of protest. Before Ruth had finished making and serving the tea the man and the child were on the very best of terms with each other, so much so indeed that when Ruth had finished and went to take him again, the baby seemed reluctant to part from Slyme, who had been dancing him in the air and tickling him in the most delightful way.

Ruth, too, began to have a better opinion of Slyme, and felt inclined to reproach herself for having taken such an unreasonable dislike to him at first. He was evidently a very good sort of fellow after all.

The baby had by this time discovered the use of the bone ring at the end of the handle of the toy and was biting it energetically.

'It's a very beautiful rattle,' said Ruth. 'Thank you very much for it. It's just the very thing he wanted.'

'I heard you say the other day that he wanted something of the kind to bite on to help his teeth through,' answered Slyme, 'and when I happened to notice that in the shop I remembered what you said and thought I'd bring it home.'

The baby took the ring out of its mouth and shaking the rattle frantically in the air laughed and crowed merrily, looking at Slyme.

'Dad! Dad! Dad!' he cried, holding out his arms.

Slyme and Ruth burst out laughing.

'That's not your dad, you silly boy,' she said, kissing the child as she spoke. 'Your dad ought to be ashamed of himself for staying out like this. We'll give him dad, dad, dad, when he does come home, won't we?'

But the baby only shook the rattle and rang the bells and laughed and crowed and laughed again, louder than ever.

CHAPTER 19

The Filling of the Tank

Viewed from outside, the 'Cricketers Arms' was a pretentious-looking building with plate-glass windows and a profusion of gilding. The pilasters were painted in imitation of different marbles and the doors grained to represent costly woods. There were panels containing painted advertisements of wines and spirits and beer, written in gold, and ornamented with gaudy colours. On the lintel over the principal entrance was inscribed in small white letters:

'A. Harpy.[52] Licensed to sell wines, spirits and malt liquors by retail to be consumed either on or off the premises.'

The bar was arranged in the usual way, being divided into several compartments. First there was the 'Saloon Bar': on the glass of the door leading into this was fixed a printed bill: 'No four ale served in this bar.' Next to the saloon bar was the jug and bottle department,[53] much appreciated by ladies who wished to indulge in a drop of gin on the quiet. There were also two small 'private' bars, only capable of holding two or three persons, where nothing less than four-pennyworth of spirits or glasses of ale at threepence were served. Finally, the public bar, the largest compartment of all. At each end, separating it from the other departments, was a wooden partition, painted and varnished.

Wooden forms fixed across these partitions and against the walls under the windows provided seating accommodation for the customers. A large automatic musical instrument – a 'penny in the slot' polyphone[54] – resembling a grandfather's clock in shape – stood against one of the partitions and close up to the counter, so that those behind the bar could reach to wind it up. Hanging on the partition near the polyphone was a board about fifteen inches square, over the surface of which were distributed a number of small hooks, numbered. At the bottom of the board was a net made of fine twine, extended by means of a semicircular piece of wire. In this net several indiarubber rings about three inches in diameter were lying. There was no table in the place but jutting out from the other partition was a hinged flap about three feet long by twenty inches wide, which could be folded down when not in use. This was the shove-ha'penny board. The coins – old French pennies[55] – used in playing this game were kept behind the bar and might be borrowed on application. On the partition, just above the shove-ha'penny board was a neatly printed notice, framed and glazed:

NOTICE
Gentlemen using this house are requested to refrain
from using obscene language.

Alongside this notice were a number of gaudily-coloured bills advertising the local theatre and the music-hall, and another of a travelling circus and menagerie, then visiting the town and encamped on a piece of waste ground about halfway on the road to Windley.

The fittings behind the bar, and the counter, were of polished mahogany, with silvered plate glass at the back of the shelves. On these shelves were rows of bottles and cut-glass decanters, gin, whisky, brandy and wines and liqueurs of different kinds.

When Crass, Philpot, Easton and Bundy entered, the landlord, a well-fed, prosperous-looking individual in white shirt-sleeves, and a bright maroon fancy waistcoat with a massive gold watch-chain and a diamond ring, was conversing in an affable, friendly way with one of his regular customers, who was sitting on the end of the seat close to the counter, a shabbily dressed, bleary-eyed, degraded, beer-sodden, trembling wretch, who spent the greater part of every day, and all his money, in this bar. He was a miserable-looking wreck of a man about thirty years of age, supposed to be a carpenter, although he never worked at that trade now. It was commonly said that some years previously he had married a woman considerably his senior, the landlady of a third-rate lodging-house. This business was evidently sufficiently prosperous to enable him to exist without working and to maintain himself in a condition of perpetual semi-intoxication. This besotted wretch practically lived at the 'Cricketers'. He came regularly every morning and sometimes earned a pint of beer by assisting the barman to sweep up the sawdust or clean the windows. He usually remained in the bar until closing time every night. He was a very good customer; not only did he spend whatever money he could get hold of himself, but he was the cause of others spending money, for he was acquainted with most of the other regular customers, who, knowing his impecunious condition, often stood him a drink 'for the good of the house.'

The only other occupant of the public bar – previous to the entrance of Crass and his mates – was a semi-drunken man, who appeared to be a house-painter, sitting on the form near the shove-ha'penny board. He was wearing a battered bowler hat and the usual shabby clothes. This individual had a very thin, pale face, with a large, high-bridged nose, and bore a striking resemblance to the portraits of the first Duke of Wellington. He was not a regular customer here, having dropped in casually about two o'clock and had remained ever since. He was beginning to show the effects of the drink he had taken during that time.

As Crass and the others came in they were hailed with enthusiasm by the landlord and the Besotted Wretch, while the semi-drunk workman regarded them with fishy eyes and stupid curiosity.

'Wot cheer, Bob?' said the landlord, affably, addressing Crass, and nodding familiarly to the others. ' 'Ow goes it?'

'All reet, me ole dear!' replied Crass, jovially. ' 'Ow's yerself?'

'A.1,' replied the "Old Dear", getting up from his chair in readiness to execute their orders.

'Well, wot's it to be?' enquired Philpot of the others generally.

'Mine's a pint o' beer,' said Crass.

'Half for me,' said Bundy.

'Half o' beer for me too,' replied Easton.

'That's one pint, two 'arves, and a pint o' porter[56] for meself,' said Philpot, turning and addressing the Old Dear.

While the landlord was serving these drinks the Besotted Wretch finished his beer and set the empty glass down on the counter, and Philpot observing this, said to him:

' 'Ave one along o' me?'

'I don't mind if I do,' replied the other.

When the drinks were served, Philpot, instead of paying for them, winked significantly at the landlord, who nodded silently and unobtrusively made an entry in an account book that was lying on one of the shelves. Although it was only Monday and he had been at work all the previous week, Philpot was already stony broke. This was accounted for by the fact that on Saturday he had paid his landlady something on account of the arrears of board and lodging money that had accumulated while he was out of work; and he had also paid the Old Dear four shillings for drinks obtained on tick during the last week.

'Well, 'ere's the skin orf yer nose,' said Crass, nodding to Philpot, and taking a long pull at the pint glass which the latter had handed to him.

Similar appropriate and friendly sentiments were expressed by the others and suitably acknowledged by Philpot, the founder of the feast.

The Old Dear now put a penny in the slot of the polyphone, and winding it up started it playing. It was some unfamiliar tune, but when the Semi-drunk Painter heard it he rose unsteadily to his feet and began shuffling and dancing about, singing:

> 'Oh, we'll inwite you to the wedding,
>   An' we'll 'ave a glorious time!
> Where the boys an' the girls is a-dancing,
>   An' we'll all get drunk on wine.'

' 'Ere! that's quite enough o' that!' cried the landlord, roughly. 'We don't want that row 'ere.'

The Semi-drunk stopped, and looking stupidly at the Old Dear, sank abashed on to the seat again.

'Well, we may as well sit as stand – for a few minutes,' remarked Crass, suiting the action to the word. The others followed his example.

At frequent intervals the bar was entered by fresh customers, most of them working men on their way home, who ordered and drank their pint or half-pint of ale or porter and left at once. Bundy began reading the advertisement of the circus and menageries and a conversation ensued concerning the wonderful performances of the trained animals. The Old Dear said that some of them had as much sense as human beings, and the manner with which he made this statement implied that he thought it was a testimonial to the sagacity of the brutes. He further said that he had heard – a little earlier in the evening – a rumour that one of the wild animals, a bear or something, had broken loose and was at present at large. This was what he had heard – he didn't know if it were true or not. For his own part he didn't believe it, and his hearers agreed that it was highly improbable. Nobody ever knew how these silly yarns got about.

Presently the Besotted Wretch got up and, taking the india-rubber rings out of the net with a trembling hand, began throwing them one at a time at the hooks on the board. The rest of the company watched him with much interest, laughing when he made a very bad shot and applauding when he scored.

' 'E's a bit orf tonight,' remarked Philpot aside to Easton, 'but as a rule 'e's a fair knock-out at it. Throws a splendid ring.'

The Semi-drunk regarded the proceedings of the Besotted Wretch with an expression of profound contempt.

'You can't play for nuts,' he said, scornfully.

'Can't I? I can play *you*, anyway.'

'Right you are! I'll play you for drinks round!' cried the Semi-drunk.

For a moment the Besotted Wretch hesitated. He had not money enough to pay for drinks round. However, feeling confident of winning, he replied:

'Come on then. What's it to be? Fifty up?'

'Anything you like! Fifty or a 'undred or a bloody million!'

'Better make it fifty for a start.'

'All right!'

'You play first if you like.'

'All right,' agreed the Semi-drunk, anxious to distinguish himself.

Holding the six rings in his left hand, the man stood in the middle of the floor at a distance of about three yards from the board, with his right foot advanced. Taking one of the rings between the forefinger and thumb of his right hand, and closing his left eye, he carefully 'sighted' the centre hook, No. 13; then he slowly extended his arm to its full length in the direction of the board: then, bending his elbow, he brought his hand back again until it nearly touched his chin, and slowly extended his arm again. He repeated these movements several times, whilst the others watched with bated breath. Getting it right at last he suddenly shot the ring at the board, but it did not go on No. 13; it went over the partition into the private bar.

This feat was greeted with a roar of laughter. The player stared at the board in a dazed way, wondering what had become of the ring. When someone in the next bar threw it over the partition again, he realised what had happened and, turning to the company with a sickly smile, remarked:

'I ain't got properly used to this board yet: that's the reason of it.'

He now began throwing the other rings at the board rather wildly, without troubling to take aim. One struck the partition to the right of the board: one to the left: one underneath: one went over the counter, one on the floor, the other – the last – hit the board, and amid a shout of applause, caught on the centre hook No. 13, the highest number it was possible to score with a single throw.

'I shall be all right now that I've got the range,' observed the Semi-drunk as he made way for his opponent.

'You'll see something now,' whispered Philpot to Easton. 'This bloke is a dandy!'

The Besotted Wretch took up his position and with an affectation of carelessness began throwing the rings. It was really a remarkable exhibition, for notwithstanding the fact that his hand trembled like the proverbial aspen leaf, he succeeded in striking the board almost in the centre every time; but somehow or other most of them failed to catch on the hooks, and fell into the net. When he finished his innings, he had only scored 4, two of the rings having caught on the No. 2 hook.

' 'Ard lines,' remarked Bundy as he finished his beer and put the glass down on the counter.

'Drink up and 'ave another,' said Easton as he drained his own glass.

'I don't mind if I do,' replied Crass, pouring what remained of the pint down his throat.

Philpot's glass had been empty for some time.

'Same again,' said Easton, addressing the Old Dear and putting six pennies on the counter.

By this time the Semi-drunk had again opened fire on the board, but he seemed to have lost the range, for none of the rings scored. They flew all over the place, and he finished his innings without increasing his total.

The Besotted Wretch now sailed in and speedily piled up 37. Then the Semi-drunk had another go, and succeeded in getting 8. His case appeared hopeless, but his opponent in his next innings seemed to go all to pieces. Twice he missed the board altogether, and when he did hit it he failed to score, until the very last throw, when he made 1. Then the Semidrunk went in again, and got 10.

The scores were now:

Besotted Wretch	.	.	.	42
Semi-drunk	.	.	.	31

So far it was impossible to foresee the end. It was anybody's game. Crass became so excited that he absentmindedly opened his mouth and shot his second pint down into his stomach with a single gulp, and Bundy also drained his glass and called upon Philpot and Easton to drink up and have another, which they accordingly did.

While the Semi-drunk was having his next innings, the Besotted Wretch placed a penny on the counter and called for half a pint, which he drank in the hope of steadying his nerves for a great effort. His opponent meanwhile threw the rings at the board and missed it every time, but all the same he scored, for one ring, after striking the partition about a foot above the board, fell down and caught on the hook.

The other man now began his innings, playing very carefully, and nearly every ring scored. As he played, the others uttered exclamations of admiration and called out the result of every throw.

'One!'

'One again!'

'Miss! No! Got 'im! Two!'

'Miss!'

'Miss!'

'Four!'

The Semi-drunk accepted his defeat with a good grace, and after explaining that he was a bit out of practice, placed a shilling on the counter and invited the company to give their orders. Everyone asked for 'the same again,' but the landlord served Easton, Bundy and the Besotted Wretch with pints instead of half-pints as before, so there was no change out of the shilling.

'You know, there's a great deal in not bein' used to the board,' said the Semi-drunk.

'There's no disgrace in bein' beat by a man like 'im, mate,' said Philpot. ' 'E's a champion!'

'Yes, there's no mistake about it. 'E throws a splendid ring!' said Bundy.

This was the general verdict. The Semi-drunk, though beaten, was not disgraced: and he was so affected by the good feeling manifested by the company that he presently produced a six-pence and insisted on paying for another half-pint all round.

Crass had gone outside during this conversation, but he returned in a few minutes. 'I feel a bit easier now,' he remarked with a laugh as he took the half-pint glass that the Semi-drunk passed to him with a shaking hand. One after the other, within a few minutes, the rest followed Crass's example, going outside and returning almost immediately: and as Bundy, who was the last to return, came back he exclaimed:

'Let's 'ave a game of shove-'a'penny.'

'All right,' said Easton, who was beginning to feel reckless. 'But drink up first, and let's 'ave another.'

He had only sevenpence left, just enough to pay for another pint for Crass and half a pint for everyone else.

The shove-ha'penny table was a planed mahogany board with a number of parallel lines scored across it. The game is played by placing the coin at the end of the board – the rim slightly over-hanging the edge – and striking it with the back part of the palm of the hand, regulating the force of the blow according to the distance it is desired to drive the coin.

'What's become of Alf tonight?' inquired Philpot of the landlord, whilst Easton and Bundy were playing. Alf was the barman.

' 'E's doing a bit of a job down in the cellar; some of the valves gone a bit wrong. But the missus is comin' down to lend me a hand presently. 'Ere she is now.'

The landlady – who at this moment entered through the door at the back of the bar – was a large woman with a highly-coloured countenance and a tremendous bust, incased in a black dress with a shot silk blouse. She had several jewelled gold rings on the fingers of each fat white hand, and a long gold watch guard hung round her fat neck. She greeted Crass and Philpot with condescension, smiling affably upon them.

Meantime the game of shove-ha'penny proceeded merrily, the Semi-drunk taking a great interest in it and tendering advice to both players impartially. Bundy was badly beaten, and then Easton suggested that it was time to think of going home. This proposal – slightly modified – met with general approval, the modification being suggested by Philpot, who insisted on standing one final round of drinks before they went.

While they were pouring this down their throats, Crass took a penny from his waistcoat pocket and put it in the slot of the poly-phone. The landlord put a fresh disc into it and wound it up and it began to play 'The Boys of the Bulldog Breed.' The Semi-drunk happened to know the words of the chorus of this song, and when he heard the music he started unsteadily to his feet and with many fierce looks and gestures began to roar at the top of his voice:

'They may build their ships, my lads,
And try to play the game,
But they can't build the boys of the Bulldog breed,
Wot made ole Hingland's – '

' 'Ere! Stop that, will yer?' cried the Old Dear, fiercely. 'I told you once before that I don't allow that sort of thing in my 'ouse!'

The Semi-drunk stopped in confusion.

'I didn't mean no 'arm,' he said unsteadily, appealing to the company.

'I don't want no chin from you!' said the Old Dear with a ferocious scowl. 'If you want to make that row you can go somewheres else, and the sooner you goes the better. You've been 'ere long enough.'

This was true. The man had been there long enough to spend every penny he had been possessed of when he first came: he had no money left now, a fact that the observant and experienced landlord had divined some time ago. He therefore wished to get rid of the fellow before the drink affected him further and made him helplessly drunk. The Semi-drunk listened with indignation and wrath to the landlord's insulting words.

'I shall go when the bloody 'ell I like!' he shouted. 'I shan't ask you nor nobody else! Who the bloody 'ell are you? You're nobody! See? Nobody! It's orf the likes of me that you gets your bloody livin'! I shall stop 'ere as long as I bloody well like, and if you don't like it you can go to 'ell!'

'Oh! Yer will, will yer?' said the Old Dear. 'We'll soon see about that.' And, opening the door at the back of the bar, he roared out:

'Alf!'

'Yes, sir,' replied a voice, evidently from the basement.

'Just come up 'ere.'

'All right,' replied the voice, and footsteps were heard ascending some stairs.

'You'll see some fun in a minute,' gleefully remarked Crass to Easton.

The polyphone continued to play 'The Boys of the Bulldog Breed.'

Philpot crossed over to the Semi-drunk. 'Look 'ere, old man,' he whispered, 'take my tip and go 'ome quietly. You'll only git the worst of it, you know.'

'Not me, mate,' replied the other, shaking his head doggedly. ' 'Ere I am, and 'ere I'm goin' to bloody well stop.'

'No, you ain't,' replied Philpot coaxingly. 'Look 'ere. I'll tell you wot we'll do. You 'ave just one more 'arf-pint along of me, and then we'll both go 'ome together. I'll see you safe 'ome.'

'See me safe 'ome! Wotcher mean?' indignantly demanded the other. 'Do you think I'm *drunk* or wot?'

'No. Certainly not,' replied Philpot, hastily. 'You're all right, as right as I am myself. But you know wot I mean. Let's go 'ome. You don't want to stop 'ere all night, do you?'

By this time Alf had arrived at the door of the back of the bar. He was a burly young man about twenty-two or twenty-three years of age.

'Put it outside,' growled the landlord, indicating the culprit.

The barman instantly vaulted over the counter, and, having opened wide the door leading into the street, he turned to the half-drunken man and, jerking his thumb in the direction of the door, said:

'Are yer goin'?'

'I'm goin' to 'ave 'arf a pint along of this genelman first – '

'Yes. It's all right,' said Philpot to the landlord. 'Let's 'ave two 'arf-pints, and say no more about it.'

'You mind your own business,' shouted the landlord, turning savagely on him. ' 'E'll get no more 'ere! I don't want no drunken men in my 'ouse. Who asked *you* to interfere?'

'Now, then!' exclaimed the barman to the cause of the trouble, 'Outside!'

'Not me!' said the Semi-drunk, firmly. 'Not before I've 'ad my 'arf – '

But before he could conclude, the barman had clutched him by the collar, dragged him violently to the door and shot him into the middle of the road, where he fell in a heap almost under the wheels of a brewer's dray[57] that happened to be passing. This accomplished, Alf shut the door and retired behind the counter again.

'Serve 'im bloody well right,' said Crass.

'I couldn't 'elp laughin' when I seen 'im go flyin' through the bloody door,' said Bundy.

'You oughter 'ave more sense that to go interferin' like that,' said Crass to Philpot. 'It was nothing to do with you.'

Philpot made no reply. He was standing with his back to the others, peeping out into the street over the top of the window casing. Then he opened the door and went out into the street. Crass and the others – through the window – watched him assist the Semi-drunk to his feet and rub some of the dirt off his clothes, and presently after some argument they saw the two go away together arm in arm.

Crass and the others laughed, and returned to their half-finished drinks.

'Why, old Joe ain't drunk 'ardly 'arf of '*is*!' cried Easton, seeing Philpot's porter on the counter. 'Fancy going away like that!'

'More fool 'im,' growled Crass. 'There was no need for it: the man's all right.'

The Besotted Wretch gulped his beer down as quickly as he could, with his eyes fixed greedily on Philpot's glass. He had just finished his own and was about to suggest that it was a pity to waste the porter when Philpot unexpectedly reappeared.

'Hullo! What 'ave you done with 'im?' inquired Crass.

'I think 'e'll be all right,' replied Philpot. 'He wouldn't let me go no further with 'im: said if I didn't go away, 'e'd go for me! But I believe 'e'll be all right. I think the fall sobered 'im a bit.'

'Oh, 'e's all right,' said Crass offhandedly. 'There's nothing the matter with 'im.'

Philpot now drank his porter, and bidding 'good night' to the Old Dear, the landlady and the Besotted Wretch, they all set out for home.

As they went along the dark and lonely thoroughfare that led over the hill to Windley, they heard from time to time the weird roaring of the wild animals in the menagerie that was encamped in the adjacent field. Just as they reached a very gloomy and deserted part, they suddenly observed a dark object in the middle of the road some distance in front of them. It seemed to be a large animal of some kind and was coming slowly and stealthily towards them.

They stopped, peering in a half-frightened way through the darkness. The animal continued to approach. Bundy stooped down to the ground, groping about in search of a stone, and – with the exception of Crass, who was too frightened to move – the others followed his example. They found several large stones and stood waiting for the creature – whatever it was – to come a little nearer so as to get a fair shot at it. They were about to let fly when the creature fell over on its side and moaned as if in pain. Observing this, the four men advanced cautiously towards it. Bundy struck a match and held it over the prostrate figure. It was the Semi-drunk.

After parting from Philpot, the poor wretch had managed to walk all right for some distance. As Philpot had remarked, the fall had to some extent sobered him; but he had not gone very far before the drink he had taken began to affect him again and he had fallen down. Finding it impossible to get up, he began crawling along on his hands and knees, unconscious of the fact that he was travelling in the wrong direction. Even this mode of progression failed him at last, and he would probably have been run over if they had not found him. They raised him up, and Philpot, exhorting him to 'pull himself together' enquired where he lived. The man had sense enough left to be able to tell them his address, which was fortunately at Windley, where they all resided.

Bundy and Philpot took him home, separating from Crass and Easton at the corner of the street where both the latter lived.

Crass felt very full and satisfied with himself. He had had six and a half pints of beer, and had listened to two selections on the polyphone at a total cost of one penny.

Easton had but a few yards to go before reaching his own house after parting from Crass, but he paused directly he heard the latter's door close, and leaning against a street lamp yielded to the feeling of giddiness and nausea that he had been fighting against all the way home. All the inanimate objects around him seemed to be in motion. The lights of the distant street lamps appeared to be floating about and the pavement and the roadway rose and fell like the surface of a troubled sea. He searched his pockets for his handkerchief and having found it wiped his mouth, inwardly congratulating himself that Crass was not there to see him. Resuming his walk, after a few minutes he reached his own home. As he passed through, the gate closed of itself after him, clanging loudly. He went rather unsteadily up the narrow path that led to his front door and entered.

The baby was asleep in the cradle. Slyme had gone up to his own room, and Ruth was sitting sewing by the fireside. The table was still set for two persons, for she had not yet taken her tea.

Easton lurched in noisily. ' 'Ello, old girl!' he cried, throwing his dinner basket carelessly on the floor with an affectation of joviality and resting his hands on the table to support himself. 'I've come at last, you see.'

Ruth left off sewing, and, letting her hands fall into her lap, sat looking at him. She had never seen him like this before. His face was ghastly pale, the eyes bloodshot and red-rimmed, the lips tremulous and moist, and the ends of the hair of his fair moustache, stuck together with saliva and stained with beer, hung untidily round his mouth in damp clusters.

Perceiving that she did not speak or smile, Easton concluded that she was angry and became grave himself.

'I've come at last, you see, my dear; better late than never.'

He found it very difficult to speak plainly, for his lips trembled and refused to form the words.

'I don't know so much about that,' said Ruth, inclined to cry and trying not to let him see the pity she could not help feeling for him. 'A nice state you're in. You ought to be ashamed of yourself.'

Easton shook his head and laughed foolishly. 'Don't be angry, Ruth. It's no good, you know.'

He walked clumsily towards her, still leaning on the table to steady himself.

'Don't be angry,' he mumbled as he stooped over her, putting his arm round her neck and his face close to hers. 'It's no good being angry, you know, dear.'

She shrank away, shuddering with involuntary disgust as he pressed his wet lips and filthy moustache upon her mouth. His fetid breath, foul with the smell of tobacco and beer, and the odour of the stale tobacco smoke that exuded from his clothes filled her with loathing. He kissed her repeatedly and when at last he released her she hastily wiped her face with her handkerchief and shivered.

Easton said he did not want any tea, and went upstairs to bed almost immediately. Ruth did not want any tea either now, although she had been very hungry before he came home. She sat up very late, sewing, and when at length she did go upstairs she found him lying on his back, partly undressed on the outside of the bedclothes, with his mouth wide open, breathing stertorously.

CHAPTER 20

The Forty Thieves. The Battle: Brigands versus Bandits

This is an even more than unusually dull and uninteresting chapter, and introduces several matters that may appear to have nothing to do with the case. The reader is nevertheless entreated to peruse it, because it contains certain information necessary to an understanding of this history.

The town of Mugsborough was governed by a set of individuals called the Municipal Council. Most of these 'representatives of the people' were well-to-do or retired tradesmen. In the opinion of the inhabitants of Mugsborough, the fact that a man had succeeded in accumulating money in business was a clear demonstration of his fitness to be entrusted with the business of the town.

Consequently, when that very able and successful man of business Mr. George Rushton was put up for election to the Council he was returned by a large majority of the votes of the working men who thought him an ideal personage . . .

These Brigands did just as they pleased. No one ever interfered with them. They never consulted the ratepayers in any way. Even at election times they did not trouble to hold meetings: each one of them just issued a kind of manifesto setting forth his many noble qualities and calling upon the people for their votes: and the latter never failed to respond. They elected the same old crew time after time . . .

[The Brigands committed their depredations almost unhindered, for the voters were engaged in the Battle of Life. Take the public park for instance. Like.] so many swine around a trough – they were so busily engaged in this battle that most of them had no time to go to the park, or they might have noticed that there were not so many costly plants there as there should have been. And if they had enquired further they would have discovered that nearly all the members of the Town Council had very fine gardens. There was reason for these gardens being so grand, for the public park was systematically robbed of its best to make them so.

There was a lake in the park where large numbers of ducks and geese were kept at the ratepayers' expense. In addition to the food provided for these fowl with public money, visitors to the park used to bring them bags of biscuits and bread crusts. When the ducks and geese were nicely fattened the Brigands used to carry them off and devour them at home. When they became tired of eating duck or goose, some of the Councillors made arrangements with certain butchers and traded away the birds for meat.

One of the most energetic members of the Band was Mr. Jeremiah Didlum, the house-furnisher, who did a large hire system trade. He had an extensive stock of second-hand furniture that he had resumed possession of when the unfortunate would-be purchasers failed to pay the instalments regularly. Other of the second-hand things had been purchased for a fraction of their real value at Sheriff's sales[58] or from people whom misfortune or want of employment had reduced to the necessity of selling their household possessions.

Another notable member of the Band was Mr. Amos Grinder, who had practically monopolised the greengrocery trade and now owned nearly all the fruiterers' shops in the town. As for the other shops, if they did not buy their stocks from him – or, rather, the company of which he was managing director and principal share-holder – if these other fruiterers and greengrocers did not buy their stuff from his company, he tried to smash them by opening branches in their immediate neighbourhood and selling below cost. He was a self-made man: an example of what may be accomplished by cunning and selfishness.

Then there was the Chief of the Band – Mr. Adam Sweater, the Mayor. He was always the Chief, although he was not always Mayor, it being the rule that the latter 'honour' should be enjoyed by all the members of the Band in turn. A bright 'honour', forsooth! to be the first citizen in a community composed for the most part of ignorant semi-imbeciles, slaves, slave-drivers and psalm-singing hypocrites.

Mr. Sweater was the managing director and principal shareholder of a large drapery business in which he had amassed a considerable fortune. This was not very surprising, considering that he paid none of his workpeople fair wages and many of them no wages at all. He employed a great number of girls and young women who were supposed to be learning dressmaking, mantle-making or millinery. These were all indentured apprentices, some of whom had paid premiums of from five ten pounds. They were 'bound' for three years. For the first two years they received no wages: the third year they got a shilling or eighteenpence a week. At the end of the third year they usually got the sack, unless they were willing to stay on as improvers at from three shillings to four and sixpence per week.

They worked from half-past eight in the morning till eight at night, with an interval of an hour for dinner, and at half-past four they ceased work for fifteen minutes for tea. This was provided by the firm – half a pint for each girl, but they had to bring their own milk and sugar and bread and butter.

Few of these girls ever learned their trades thoroughly. Some were taught to make sleeves: others cuffs or button-holes, and so on. The result was that in a short time each one became very expert and quick *at one thing*; and although their proficiency in this one thing would never enable them to earn a decent living, it enabled Mr. Sweater to make money during the period of their apprenticeship, and that was all he cared about.

Occasionally a girl of intelligence and spirit would insist on the fulfilment of the terms of her indentures, and sometimes the parents would protest. If this were persisted in those girls got on better: but even these were turned to good account by the wily Sweater, who induced the best of them to remain after their time was up by paying them what appeared – by contrast with the other girls' money – good wages, sometimes even seven or eight shillings a week! and liberal promises of future advancement. These girls then became a sort of reserve who could be called up to crush any manifestation of discontent on the part of the leading hands.

The greater number of the girls, however, submitted tamely to the conditions imposed upon them. They were too young to realise the wrong that was being done them. As for their parents, it never occurred to them to doubt the sincerity of so good a man as Mr. Sweater, who was always prominent in every good and charitable work.

At the expiration of a girl's apprenticeship, if the parents complained of her want of proficiency, the pious Sweater would attribute it to idleness or incapacity, and as the people were generally poor he seldom or never had any trouble with them. This was how he fulfilled the unctuous promise made to the confiding parents at the time the girl was handed over to his tender mercy – that he would 'make a woman of her.'

This method of obtaining labour by false pretences and without payment, which enabled him to produce costly articles for a mere fraction of the price for which they were eventually sold, was adopted in other departments of his business. He procured shop assistants of both sexes on the same terms. A youth was indentured, usually for five years, to be 'Made a Man of' and 'Turned out fit to take a Position in any House'. If possible, a premium, five, ten, or twenty pounds – according to their circumstances – would be extracted from the parents. For the first three years, no wages: after that, perhaps two or three shillings a week.

At the end of the five years the work of 'Making a Man of him' would be completed. Mr. Sweater would then congratulate him and assure him that he was qualified to assume a 'position' in any House, but regret that there was no longer any room for him in *his*. Business was so bad. Still, if the Man wished he might stay on until he secured a better 'position' and, as a matter of generosity, although he did not really need the Man's services, he would pay him ten shillings per week!

Provided he was not addicted to drinking, smoking, gambling on the Stock Exchange, or going to theatres, the young man's future was thus assured. Even if he were unsuccessful in his efforts to obtain another position he could save a portion of his salary and eventually commence business on his own account.

However, the branch of Mr. Sweater's business to which it is desired to especially direct the reader's attention was the Homeworkers Department. He employed a large number of women making ladies' blouses, fancy aprons and children's pinafores. Most of these articles were disposed of wholesale in London and elsewhere, but some were retailed at 'Sweaters' Emporium' in Mugsborough and at the firm's other retail establishments throughout the country. Many of the women workers were widows with children, who were glad to obtain any employment that did not take them away from their homes and families.

The blouses were paid for at the rate of from two shillings to five shillings a dozen, the woman having to provide her own machine and cotton, besides calling for and delivering the work. These poor women were able to clear from six to eight shillings a week: and to earn even that they had to work almost incessantly for fourteen or sixteen hours a day. There was no time for cooking and very little to cook, for they lived principally on bread and margarine and tea. Their homes were squalid, their children half-starved and raggedly clothed in grotesque garments hastily fashioned out of the cast-off clothes of charitable neighbours.

But it was not in vain that these women toiled every weary day until exhaustion compelled them to cease. It was not in vain that they passed their cheerless lives bending with aching shoulders over the thankless work that barely brought them bread. It was not in vain that they and their children went famished and in rags, for after all, the principal object of their labour was accomplished: the Good Cause was advanced. Mr. Sweater waxed rich and increased in goods and respectability.

Of course, none of those women were *compelled* to engage in that glorious cause. No one is compelled to accept any particular set of conditions in a free country like this. Mr. Trafaim – the manager of Sweater's Homework Department – always put the matter before them in the plainest, fairest possible way. There was the work: that was the figure! And those who didn't like it could leave it. There was no compulsion.

Sometimes some perverse creature belonging to that numerous class who are too lazy to work *did* leave it! But as the manager said, there were plenty of others who were only too glad to take it. In fact, such was the enthusiasm amongst these women – especially such of them as had little children to provide for – and such was their zeal for the Cause, that some of them have been known to positively beg to be allowed to work!

By these and similar means Adam Sweater had contrived to lay up for himself a large amount of treasure upon earth, besides attaining undoubted respectability; for that he was respectable no one questioned. He went to chapel twice every Sunday, his obese figure arrayed in costly apparel, consisting – with other things – of grey trousers, a long garment called a frock-coat, a tall silk hat, a quantity of jewellery and a morocco-bound gilteged Bible. He was an official of some sort of the Shining Light Chapel. His name appeared in nearly every published list of charitable subscriptions. No starving wretch had ever appealed to him in vain for a penny soup ticket.

Small wonder that when this good and public-spirited man offered his services to the town – free of charge – the intelligent working men of Mugsborough accepted his offer with enthusiastic applause. The fact that he had made money in business was a proof of his intellectual capacity. His much-advertised benevolence was a guarantee that his abilities would be used to further not his own private interests, but the interests of every section of the community, especially those of the working classes, of whom the majority of his constituents was composed.

As for the shopkeepers, they were all so absorbed in their own business – so busily engaged chasing their employees, adding up their accounts, and dressing themselves up in feeble imitation of the 'Haristocracy' – that they were incapable of taking a really intelligent interest in anything else. They thought of the Town Council as a kind of Paradise reserved exclusively for jerry-builders and successful tradesmen. Possibly, some day, if they succeeded in making money, they might become town councillors themselves! but in the meantime public affairs were no particular concern of theirs. So some of them voted for Adam Sweater because he was a Liberal and some of them voted against him for the same 'reason'.

Now and then, when details of some unusually scandalous proceeding of the Council's leaked out, the townspeople – roused for a brief space from their customary indifference – would discuss the matter in a casual, half-indignant, half-amused, helpless sort of way; but always as if it were something that did not directly concern them. It was during some such nine days' wonder that the title of 'The Forty Thieves' was bestowed on the members of the Council by their semi-imbecile constituents, who, not possessing sufficient intelligence to devise means of punishing the culprits, affected to regard the manœuvres of the Brigands as a huge joke.

There was only one member of the Council who did not belong to the Band – Councillor Weakling, a retired physician; but unfortunately he also was a respectable man. When he saw something going forwards that he did not think was right, he protested and voted against it and then – he collapsed! There was nothing of the low agitator about *him*. As for the Brigands, they laughed at his protests and his vote did not matter.

With this one exception, the other members of the band were very similar in character to Sweater, Rushton, Didlum and Grinder. They had all joined the Band with the same objects, self-glorification and the advancement of their private interests. These were the real reasons why they besought the ratepayers to elect them to the Council, but of course none of them ever admitted that such was the case. No! When these noble-minded altruists offered their services to the town they asked the people to believe that they were actuated by a desire to give their time and abilities for the purpose of furthering the interests of Others, which was much the same as asking them to believe that it is possible for the leopard to change his spots.

*   *   *

Owing to the extraordinary apathy of the other inhabitants, the Brigands were able to carry out their depredations undisturbed. Daylight robberies were of frequent occurrence.

For many years these Brigands had looked with greedy eyes upon the huge profits of the Gas Company. They thought it was a beastly shame that those other bandits should be always raiding the town and getting clear away with such rich spoils.

At length – about two years ago – after much study and many private consultations, a plan of campaign was evolved; a secret council of war was held, presided over by Mr. Sweater, and the Brigands formed themselves into an association called 'The Mugsborough Electric Light Supply and Installation Coy. Ltd.', and bound themselves by a solemn oath to do their best to drive the Gas Works Bandits out of the town and to capture the spoils at present enjoyed by the latter for themselves.

There was a large piece of ground, the property of the town, that was a suitable site for the works; so in their character of directors of the Electric Light Coy. they offered to buy this land from the Municipality – or, in other words, from themselves – for about half its value.

At the meeting of the Town Council when this offer was considered, all the members present, with the solitary exception of Dr. Weakling, being shareholders in the newly formed company, Councillor Rushton moved a resolution in favour of accepting it.

He said that every encouragement should be given to the promoters of the Electric Light Coy., those public-spirited citizens who had come forward and were willing to risk their capital in an undertaking that would be a benefit to every class of residents in the town that they all loved so well. (Applause.) There could be no doubt that the introduction of the electric light would be a great addition to the attractions of Mugsborough, but there was another and more urgent reason that disposed him to do whatever he could to encourage the Company to proceed with this work. Unfortunately, as was usual at that time of the year (Mr. Rushton's voice trembled with emotion) the town was full of unemployed. (The Mayor, Alderman Sweater, and all the other Councillors shook their heads sadly; they were visibly affected.) There was no doubt that the starting of that work at that time would be an inestimable boon to the working-classes. As the representative of a working-class ward he was in favour of accepting the offer of the Company. (Hear. Hear.)

Councillor Didlum seconded. In his opinion, it would be nothing short of a crime to oppose anything that would provide work for the unemployed.

Councillor Weakling moved that the offer be refused. (Shame.) He admitted that the electric light would be an improvement to the town, and in view of the existing distress he would be glad to see the work started, but the price mentioned was altogether too low. It was not more than half the value of the land. (Derisive laughter.)

Councillor Grinder said he was astonished at the attitude taken up by Councillor Weakling. In his (Grinder's) opinion it was disgraceful that a member of the council should deliberately try to wreck a project which would do so much towards relieving the unemployed.

The Mayor, Alderman Sweater, said that he could not allow the amendment to be discussed until it was seconded: if there were no seconder he would put the original motion.

There was no seconder, because everyone except Weakling was in favour of the resolution, which was carried amid loud cheers, and the representatives of the ratepayers proceeded to the consideration of the next business.

Councillor Didlum proposed that the duty on all coal brought into the borough be raised from two shillings to three shillings per ton.

Councillor Rushton seconded. The largest consumer of coal was the Gas Coy. and, considering the great profits made by that company, they were quite justified in increasing the duty to the highest figure the Act permitted.

After a feeble protest from Weakling, who said it would only increase the price of gas and coal without interfering with the profits of the Gas Coy., this was also carried, and after some other business had been transacted, the Band dispersed.

That meeting was held two years ago, and since that time the Electric Light Works had been built and the war against the gas-works carried on vigorously. After several encounters, in which they lost a few customers and a portion of the public lighting, the Gas-works Bandits retreated out of the town and entrenched themselves in a strong position beyond the borough boundary, where they erected a number of gasometers. They were thus enabled to pour gas into the town at long range without having to pay the coal dues.

This masterly stragem created something like a panic in the ranks of the Forty Thieves. At the end of two years they found themselves exhausted with the protracted campaign, their movements hampered by a lot of worn-out plant and antiquated machinery, and harassed on every side by the lower charges of the Gas Coy. They were reluctantly constrained to admit that the attempt to undermine the Gasworks was a melancholy failure, and that the Mugsborough Electric Light and Installation Coy. was a veritable white elephant. They began to ask themselves what they should do with it; and some of them even urged unconditional surrender, or an appeal to the arbitration of the Bankruptcy Court.

In the midst of all the confusion and demoralisation there was, however, one man who did not lose his presence of mind, who in this dark hour of disaster remained calm and immovable, and like a vast mountain of flesh reared his head above the storm, whose mighty intellect perceived a way to turn this apparently hopeless defeat into a glorious victory. That man was Adam Sweater, the Chief of the Band.

CHAPTER 21

The Reign of Terror.[59] *The Great MoneyTrick.*

During the next four weeks the usual reign of terror continued at 'The Cave'. The men slaved like so many convicts under the vigilant surveillance of Crass, Misery and Rushton. No one felt free from observation for a single moment. It happened frequently that a man who was working alone – as he thought – on turning round would find Hunter or Rushton standing behind him: or one would look up from his work to catch sight of a face watching him through a door or a window or over the banisters. If they happened to be working in a room on the ground floor, or at a window on any floor, they knew that both Rushton and Hunter were in the habit of hiding among the trees that surrounded the house, and spying upon them thus.

There was a plumber working outside repairing the guttering that ran round the bottom edge of the roof. This poor wretch's life was a perfect misery: he fancied he saw Hunter or Rushton in every bush. He had two ladders to work from, and since these ladders had been in use Misery had thought of a new way of spying on the men. Finding that he never succeeded in catching anyone doing anything wrong when he entered the house by one of the doors, Misery adopted the plan of crawling up one of the ladders, getting in through one of the upper windows and creeping softly downstairs and in and out of the rooms. Even then he never caught anyone, but that did not matter, for he accomplished his principal purpose – every man seemed afraid to cease working for even an instant.

The result of all this was, of course, that the work progressed rapidly towards completion. The hands grumbled and cursed, but all the same every man tore into it for all he was worth. Although he did next to nothing himself, Crass watched and urged on the others. He was 'in charge of the job': he knew that unless he succeeded in making this work pay he would not be put in charge of another job. On the other hand, if he did make it pay he would be given the preference over others and be kept on as long as the firm had any work. The firm would give him the preference only as long as it paid them to do so.

As for the hands, each man knew that there was no chance of obtaining work anywhere else at present; there were dozens of men out of employment already. Besides, even if there had been a chance of getting another job somewhere else, they knew that the conditions were more or less the same on every firm. Some were even worse than this one. Each man knew that unless he did as much as ever he could, Crass would report him for being slow. They knew also that when the job began to draw to a close the number of men employed upon it would be reduced, and when that time came the hands who did the most work would be kept on and the slower ones discharged. It was therefore in the hope of being one of the favoured few that while inwardly cursing the rest for 'tearing into it', everyone as a matter of self-preservation went and 'tore into it' themselves.

They all cursed Crass, but most of them would have been very glad to change places with him: and if any one of them *had* been in his place they would have been compelled to act in the same way – or lose the job.

They all reviled Hunter, but most of them would have been glad to change places with him also: and if any one of them *had* been in his place they would have been compelled to do the same things, or lose the job.

They all hated and blamed Rushton. Yet if they had been in Rushton's place they would have been compelled to adopt the same methods, or become bankrupt: for it is obvious that the only way to compete successfully against other employers who are sweaters is to be a sweater yourself. Therefore no one who is an upholder of the present system can consistently blame any of these men. Blame the system.

If you, reader, had been one of the hands, would you have slogged? Or would you have preferred to starve and see your family starve? If you had been in Crass's place, would you have resigned rather than do such dirty work? If you had had Hunter's berth, would you have given it up and voluntarily reduced yourself to the level of the hands? If you had been Rushton, would you rather have become bankrupt than treat your 'hands' and your customers in the same way as your competitors treated theirs? It may be that, so placed, you – being the noble-minded paragon that you are – would behave unselfishly. But no one has any right to expect you to sacrifice yourself for the benefit of other people, who would only call you a fool for your pains.

It may be true that if any one of the hands – Owen, for instance – had been an employer of labour, he would have done the same as other employers. Some people seem to think that proves that the present system is all right! But really it only proves that the present system compels selfishness. One must either trample upon others or be trampled upon oneself. Happiness might be possible if everyone were unselfish; if everyone thought of the welfare of his neighbour before thinking of his own. But as there is only a very small percentage of such unselfish people in the world, the present system has made the earth into a sort of hell. Under the present system there is not sufficient of anything for everyone to have enough. Consequently there is a fight – called by Christians the 'Battle of Life'. In this fight some get more than they need, some barely enough, some very little, and some none at all. The more aggressive, cunning, unfeeling and selfish you are the better it will be for you.

As long as this 'Battle of Life' System endures, we have no right to blame other people for doing the same things that we are ourselves compelled to do. Blame the system.

But that *is* just what the hands did not do. They blamed each other; they blamed Crass, and Hunter, and Rushton, but with the Great System of which they were all more or less the victims they were quite content, being persuaded that it was the only one possible and the best that human wisdom could devise. The reason why they all believed this was because not one of them had ever troubled to enquire whether it would not be possible to order things differently. They were content with the present system. If they had not been content they would have been anxious to find out some way to alter it. But they had never taken the trouble to seriously enquire whether it was possible to find some better way, and although they all knew in a hazy fashion that other methods of managing the affairs of the world had already been proposed, they neglected to enquire whether these other methods were possible or practicable, and they were ready and willing to oppose with ignorant ridicule or brutal force any man who was foolish or quixotic enough to try to explain to them the details of what he thought was a better way. They accepted the present system in the same way as they accepted the alternating seasons. They knew that there was spring and summer and autumn and winter. As to how these different seasons came to be, or what caused them, they hadn't the remotest notion, and it is extremely doubtful whether the question had ever occurred to any of them: but there is no doubt whatever about the fact that none of them knew. From their infancy they had been trained to distrust their own intelligence, and to leave the management of the affairs of the world – and for that matter of the next world too – to their betters; and now most of them were absolutely incapable of thinking of any abstract subject whatever. Nearly all their betters – that is, the people who do nothing – were unanimous in agreeing that the present system is a very good one and that it is impossible to alter or improve it. Therefore Crass and his mates, although they knew nothing whatever about it themselves, accepted it as an established, incontrovertible fact that the existing state of things is immutable. They believed it because someone else told them so. They would have believed anything: on one condition – namely, that they were told to believe it by their betters. They said it was surely not for the Likes of Them to think that they knew better than those who were more educated and had plenty of time to study.

As the work in the drawing-room proceeded, Crass abandoned

the hope that Owen was going to make a mess of it. Some of the rooms upstairs being now ready for papering, Slyme was started on that work, Bert being taken away from Owen to assist Slyme as paste boy, and it was arranged that Crass should help Owen whenever he needed someone to lend him a hand.

Sweater came frequently during these four weeks, being interested in the progress of the work. On these occasions Crass always managed to be present in the drawing-room and did most of the talking. Owen was very satisfied with this arrangement, for he was always ill at ease when conversing with a man like Sweater, who spoke in an offensively patronising way and expected common people to kowtow to and 'Sir' him at every second word. Crass, however, seemed to enjoy doing that kind of thing. He did not exactly grovel on the floor, when Sweater spoke to him, but he contrived to convey the impression that he was willing to do so if desired.

Outside the house Bundy and his mates had dug deep trenches in the damp ground in which they were laying new drains. This work, like that of the painting of the inside of the house, was nearly completed. It was a miserable job. Owing to the fact that there had been a spell of bad weather the ground was sodden with rain and there was mud everywhere, the men's clothing and boots being caked with it. But the worst thing about the job was the smell. For years the old drain-pipes had been defective and leaky. The ground a few feet below the surface was saturated with fetid moisture and a stench as of a thousand putrefying corpses emanated from the opened earth. The clothing of the men who were working in the trenches became saturated with this fearful odour, and for that matter, so did the men themselves.

They said they could smell and taste it all the time, even when they were away from the work, at home, and when they were at meals. Although they smoked their pipes all the time they were at work, Misery having ungraciously given them permission, several times Bundy and one or other of his mates were attacked with fits of vomiting.

But, as they began to realise that the finish of the job was in sight, a kind of panic seized upon the hands, especially those who had been taken on last and who would therefore be the first to be 'stood still'. Easton, however, felt pretty confident that Crass would do his best to get him kept on till the end of the job, for they had become quite chummy lately, usually spending a few evenings together at the Cricketers every week.

'There'll be a bloody slaughter 'ere soon,' remarked Harlow to Philpot one day as they were painting the banisters of the staircase. 'I reckon next week will about finish the inside.'

'And the outside ain't goin' to take very long, you know,' replied Philpot.

'They ain't got no other work in, have they?'

'Not that I knows of,' replied Philpot gloomily; 'and I don't think anyone else has either.'

'You know that little place they call the "Kiosk" down on the Grand Parade, near the bandstand,' asked Harlow after a pause.

'Where they used to sell refreshments?'

'Yes; it belongs to the Corporation, you know.'

'It's been closed up lately, ain't it?'

'Yes; the people who 'ad it couldn't make it pay; but I 'eard last night that Grinder the fruit-merchant is goin' to open it again. If it's true, there'll be a bit of a job there for someone, because it'll 'ave to be done up.'

'Well, I hope it does come orf,' replied Philpot. 'It'll be a job for some poor b—rs.'

'I wonder if they've started anyone yet on the Venetian blinds for this 'ouse?' remarked Easton after a pause.

'I don't know,' replied Philpot.

They relapsed into silence for a while.

'I wonder what time it is?' said Philpot at length. 'I don't know 'ow you feel, but I begin to want my dinner.'

'That's just what I was thinking; it can't be very far off it now. It's nearly 'arf an hour since Bert went down to make the tea. It seems a 'ell of a long morning to me.'

'So it does to me,' said Philpot; 'slip upstairs and ask Slyme what time it is.'

Harlow laid his brush across the top of his paint-pot and went upstairs. He was wearing a pair of cloth slippers, and walked softly, not wishing that Crass should hear him leaving his work, so it happened that without any intention of spying on Slyme, Harlow reached the door of the room in which the former was working without being heard and, entering suddenly, surprised Slyme – who was standing near the fireplace – in the act of breaking a whole roll of wallpaper across his knee as one might break a stick. On the floor beside him was what had been another roll, now broken into two pieces. When Harlow came in, Slyme started, and his face became crimson with confusion. He hastily gathered the broken rolls together and, stooping down, thrust the pieces up the flue of the grate and closed the register.

'Wot's the bloody game?' enquired Harlow.

Slyme laughed with an affectation of carelessness, but his hands trembled and his face was now very pale.

'We must get our own back somehow, you know, Fred,' he said.

Harlow did not reply. He did not understand. After puzzling over it for a few minutes, he gave it up.

'What's the time?' he asked.

'Fifteen minutes to twelve,' said Slyme and added, as Harlow was going away: 'Don't mention anything about that paper to Cross or any of the others.'

'I shan't say nothing,' replied Harlow.

Gradually, as he pondered over it, Harlow began to comprehend the meaning of the destruction of the two rolls of paper. Slyme was doing the paperhanging piecework – so much for each roll hung. Four of the rooms upstairs had been done with the same pattern, and Hunter – who was not over-skilful in such matters – had evidently sent more paper than was necessary. By getting rid of these two rolls, Slyme would be able to make it appear that he had hung two rolls more than was really the case. He had broken the rolls so as to be able to take them away from the house without being detected, and he had hidden them up the chimney until he got an opportunity of so doing. Harlow had just arrived at this solution of the problem when, hearing the lower flight of stairs creaking, he peeped over and observed Misery crawling up. He had come to see if anyone had stopped work before the proper time. Passing the two workmen without speaking, he ascended to the next floor, and entered the room where Slyme was.

'You'd better not do this room yet,' said Hunter. 'There's to be a new grate and mantelpiece put in.'

He crossed over to the fireplace and stood looking at it thoughtfully for a few minutes.

'It's not a bad little grate, you know, is it?' he remarked. 'We'll be able to use it somewhere or other.'

'Yes; it's all right,' said Slyme, whose heart was beating like a steam-hammer.

'Do for a front room in a cottage,' continued Misery, stooping down to examine it more closely. 'There's nothing broke that I can see.'

He put his hand against the register and vainly tried to push it open.

'H'm, there's something wrong 'ere,' he remarked, pushing harder.

'Most likely a brick or some plaster fallen down,' gasped Slyme, coming to Misery's assistance. 'Shall I try to open it?'

'Don't trouble,' replied Nimrod, rising to his feet. 'It's most likely what you say. I'll see that the new grate is sent up after dinner. Bundy can fix it this afternoon and then you can go on papering as soon as you like.'

With this, Misery went out of the room, downstairs and away from the house, and Slyme wiped the sweat from his forehead with his handkerchief. Then he knelt down and, opening the register, he took out the broken rolls of paper and hid them up the chimney of the next room. While he was doing this the sound of Crass's whistle shrilled through the house.

'Thank Gord!' exclaimed Philpot fervently as he laid his brushes on the top of his pot and joined in the general rush to the kitchen. The scene here is already familiar to the reader. For seats, the two pairs of steps laid on their sides parallel to each other, about eight feet apart and at right angles to the fireplace, with the long plank placed across; and the upturned pails and the drawers of the dresser. The floor unswept and littered with dirt, scraps of paper, bits of plaster, pieces of lead pipe and dried mud; and in the midst, the steaming bucket of stewed tea and the collection of cracked cups, jam-jars and condensed milk tins. And on the seats the men in their shabby and in some cases ragged clothing sitting and eating their coarse food and cracking jokes.

It was a pathetic and wonderful and at the same time a despicable spectacle. Pathetic that human beings should be condemned to spend the greater part of their lives amid such surroundings, because it must be remembered that most of their time was spent on some job or other. When 'The Cave' was finished they would go to some similar 'job', if they were lucky enough to find one. Wonderful, because although they knew that they did more than their fair share of the great work of producing the necessaries and comforts of life, they did not think they were entitled to a fair share of the good things they helped to create! And despicable, because although they saw their children condemned to the same life of degradation, hard labour and privation, yet they refused to help to bring about a better state of affairs. Most of them thought that what had been good enough for themselves was good enough for their children.

It seemed as if they regarded their own children with a kind of contempt, as being only fit to grow up to be the servants of the children of such people as Rushton and Sweater. But it must be remembered that they had been taught self-contempt when they were children. In the so-called 'Christian' schools they attended then they were taught to 'order themselves lowly and reverently towards their betters', and they were now actually sending their own children to learn the same degrading lessons in their turn! They had a vast amount of consideration for their betters, and for the children of their betters, but very little for their own children, for each other, or for themselves.

That was why they sat there in their rags and ate their coarse food, and cracked their coarser jokes, and drank the dreadful tea, and were content! So long as they had Plenty of Work and plenty of – Something – to eat, and somebody else's cast-off clothes to wear, they were content! And they were proud of it. They gloried in it. They agreed and assured each other that the good things of life were not intended for the 'Likes of them', or their children.

'Wot's become of the Professor?' asked the gentleman who sat on the upturned pail in the corner, referring to Owen, who had not yet come down from his work.

'P'raps 'e's preparing 'is sermon,' remarked Harlow with a laugh.

'We ain't 'ad no lectures from 'im lately, since 'e's been on that room,' observed Easton. ' 'Ave we?'

'Dam good job too!' exclaimed Sawkins. 'It gives me the pip to 'ear 'im, the same old thing over and over again.'

'Poor ole Frank,' remarked Harlow. ' 'E does upset 'isself about things, don't 'e?'

'More fool 'im!' said Bundy. 'I'll take bloody good care I don't go worryin' myself to death like 'e's doin', about such dam rot as that.'

'I do believe that's wot makes 'im look so bad as 'e does,' observed Harlow. 'Several times this morning I couldn't help noticing the way 'e kept on coughing.'

'I thought 'e seemed to be a bit better lately,' Philpot observed; 'more cheerful and happier like, and more inclined for a bit of fun.'

'He's a funny sort of chap, ain't he?' said Bundy. 'One day quite jolly, singing and cracking jokes and tellin' yarns, and the next you can't hardly get a word out of 'im.'

'Bloody rot, I call it,' chimed in the man on the pail. 'Wot the 'ell's the use of the likes of us troublin' our 'eads about politics?'

'Oh, I don't see *that*,' replied Harlow. 'We've got votes and we're really the people what control the affairs of the country, so I reckon we ought to take *some* interest in it, but at the same time I can't see no sense in this 'ere Socialist wangle that Owen's always talkin' about.'

'Nor nobody else neither,' said Crass with a jeering laugh.

'Even if all the bloody money in the world *was* divided out equal,' said the man on the pail, profoundly, 'it wouldn't do no good! In six months' time it would be all back in the same 'ands again.'

'Of course,' said everybody.

'But 'e 'ad a cuff the other day about money bein' no good at all!' observed Easton. 'Don't you remember 'e said as money was the principal cause of poverty?'

'So it is the principal cause of poverty,' said Owen, who entered at that moment.

'Hooray!' shouted Philpot, leading off a cheer which the others took up. 'The Professor 'as arrived and will now proceed to say a few remarks.'

A roar of merriment greeted this sally.

'Let's 'ave our bloody dinner first, for Christ's sake,' appealed Harlow, with mock despair.

As Owen, having filled his cup with tea, sat down in his usual place, Philpot rose solemnly to his feet, and, looking round upon the company, said:

'Genelmen, with your kind permission, as soon as the Professor 'as finished 'is dinner 'e will deliver 'is well-known lecture, entitled, "Money the Principal Cause of being 'ard up," proving as money ain't no good to nobody. At the hend of the lecture a collection will be took up to provide the lecturer with a little encouragement.' Philpot resumed his seat amid cheers.

As soon as they had finished eating, some of the men began to make remarks about the lecture, but Owen only laughed and went on reading the piece of newspaper that his dinner had been wrapped in. Usually most of the men went out for a walk after dinner, but as it happened to be raining that day they were determined, if possible, to make Owen fulfil the engagement made in his name by Philpot.

'Let's 'oot 'im,' said Harlow, and the suggestion was at once acted upon; howls, groans and catcalls filled the air, mingled with cries of 'Fraud!' 'Imposter!' 'Give us our money back!' 'Let's wreck the 'all!' and so on.

'Come on 'ere,' cried Philpot, putting his hand on Owen's shoulder. 'Prove that money is the cause of poverty.'

'It's one thing to say it and another to prove it,' sneered Crass, who was anxious for an opportunity to produce the long-deferred *Obscurer* cutting.

'Money *is* the real cause of poverty,' said Owen.

'Prove it,' repeated Crass.

'Money is the cause of poverty because it is the device by which those who are too lazy to work are enabled to rob the workers of the fruits of their labour.'

'Prove it,' said Crass.

Owen slowly folded up the piece of newspaper he had been reading and put it into his pocket.

'All right,' he replied. 'I'll show you how the Great Money Trick is worked.'

Owen opened his dinner basket and took from it two slices of bread, but as these were not sufficient, he requested that anyone who had some bread left would give it to him. They gave him several pieces, which he placed in a heap on a clean piece of paper, and, having borrowed the pocket knives they used to cut and eat their dinners with from Easton, Harlow and Philpot, he addressed them as follows:

'These pieces of bread represent the raw materials which exist naturally in and on the earth for the use of mankind; they were not made by any human being, but were created by the Great Spirit for the benefit and sustenance of all, the same as were the air and the light of the sun.'

'You're about as fair-speakin' a man as I've met for some time,' said Harlow, winking at the others.

'Yes, mate,' said Philpot. 'Anyone would agree to that much! It's as clear as mud.'

'Now,' continued Owen, 'I am a capitalist; or, rather, I represent the landlord and capitalist class. That is to say, all these raw materials belong to me. It does not matter for our present argument how I obtained possession of them, or whether I have any real right to them; the only thing that matters now is the admitted fact that all the raw materials which are necessary for the production of the necessaries of life are now the property of the Landlord and Capitalist class. I am that class: all these raw materials belong to me.'

'Good enough!' agreed Philpot.

'Now you three represent the Working Class: you have nothing – and for my part, although I have all these raw materials, they are of no use to me – what I need is – the things that can be made out of these raw materials by Work: but as I am too lazy to work myself, I have invented the Money Trick to make you work *for* me. But first I must explain that I possess something else beside the raw materials. These three knives represent – all the machinery of production; the factories, tools, railways, and so forth, without which the necessaries of life cannot be produced in abundance. And these three coins' – taking three halfpennies from his pocket – 'represent my Money Capital.'

'But before we go any further,' said Owen, interrupting himself, 'it is most important that you remember that I am not supposed to be merely 'a' capitalist. I represent the whole Capitalist Class. You are not supposed to be just three workers – you represent the whole Working Class.'

'All right, all right,' said Crass, impatiently, 'we all understand that. Git on with it.'

Owen proceeded to cut up one of the slices of bread into a number of little square blocks.

'These represent the things which are produced by labour, aided by machinery, from the raw materials. We will suppose that three of these blocks represent – a week's work. We will suppose that a week's work is worth – one pound: and we will suppose that each of these ha'pennies is a sovereign. We'd be able to do the trick better if we had real sovereigns, but I forgot to bring any with me.'

'I'd lend you some,' said Philpot, regretfully, 'but I left me purse on our grand pianner.'

As by a strange coincidence nobody happened to have any gold with them, it was decided to make shift with the halfpence.

'Now this is the way the trick works – '

'Before you goes on with it,' interrupted Philpot, apprehensively, 'don't you think we'd better 'ave someone to keep watch at the gate in case a Slop[60] comes along? We don't want to get runned in, you know.'

'I don't think there's any need for that,' replied Owen, 'there's only one slop who'd interfere with us for playing this game, and that's Police Constable Socialism.'

'Never mind about Socialism,' said Crass, irritably. 'Get along with the bloody trick.'

Owen now addressed himself to the working classes as represented by Philpot, Harlow and Easton.

'You say that you are all in need of employment, and as I am the kind-hearted capitalist class I am going to invest all my money in various industries, so as to give you Plenty of Work. I shall pay each of you one pound per week, and a week's work is – you must each produce three of these square blocks. For doing this work you will each receive your wages; the money will be your own, to do as you like with, and the things you produce will of course be mine, to do as I like with. You will each take one of these machines and as soon as you have done a week's work, you shall have your money.'

The Working Classes accordingly set to work, and the Capitalist class sat down and watched them. As soon as they had finished, they passed the nine little blocks to Owen, who placed them on a piece of paper by his side and paid the workers their wages.

'These blocks represent the necessaries of life. You can't live without some of these things, but as they belong to me, you will have to buy them from me: my price for these blocks is – one pound each.'

As the working classes were in need of the necessaries of life and as they could not eat, drink or wear the useless money, they were compelled to agree to the kind Capitalist's terms. They each bought back and at once consumed one-third of the produce of their labour. The capitalist class also devoured two of the square blocks, and so the net result of the week's work was that the kind capitalist had consumed two pounds worth of the things produced by the labour of the others, and reckoning the squares at their market value of one pound each, he had more than doubled his capital, for he still possessed the three pounds in money and in addition four pounds worth of goods. As for the working classes, Philpot, Harlow and Easton, having each consumed the pound's worth of necessaries they had bought with their wages, they were again in precisely the same condition as when they started work – they had nothing.

This process was repeated several times: for each week's work the producers were paid their wages. They kept on working and spending all their earnings. The kind-hearted capitalist consumed twice as much as any one of them and his pile of wealth continually increased. In a little while – reckoning the little squares at their market value of one pound each – he was worth about one hundred pounds, and the working classes were still in the same condition as when they began, and were still tearing into their work as if their lives depended upon it.

After a while the rest of the crowd began to laugh, and their merriment increased when the kind-hearted capitalist, just after having sold a pound's worth of necessaries to each of his workers, suddenly took their tools – the Machinery of Production – the knives – away from them, and informed them that as owing to Over

Production all his store-houses were glutted with the necessaries of life, he had decided to close down the works.

'Well, and wot the bloody 'ell are we to do now?' demanded Philpot.

'That's not my business,' replied the kind-hearted capitalist. 'I've paid you your wages, and provided you with Plenty of Work for a long time past. I have no more work for you to do at present. Come round again in a few months' time and I'll see what I can do for you.'

'But what about the necessaries of life?' demanded Harlow. 'We must have something to eat.'

'Of course you must,' replied the capitalist, affably; 'and I shall be very pleased to sell you some.'

'But we ain't got no bloody money!'

'Well, you can't expect me to give you my goods for nothing! You didn't work for me for nothing, you know. I paid you for your work and you should have saved something: you should have been thrifty like me. Look how I have got on by being thrifty!'

The unemployed looked blankly at each other, but the rest of the crowd only laughed; and then the three unemployed began to abuse the kind-hearted Capitalist, demanding that he should give them some of the necessaries of life that he had piled up in his warehouses, or to be allowed to work and produce some more for their own needs; and even threatened to take some of the things by force if he did not comply with their demands. But the kind-hearted Capitalist told them not to be insolent, and spoke to them about honesty, and said if they were not careful he would have their faces battered in for them by the police, or if necessary he would call out the military and have them shot down like dogs, the same as he had done before at Featherstone and Belfast.[61]

'Of course,' continued the kind-hearted capitalist, 'if it were not for foreign competition I should be able to sell these things that you have made, and then I should be able to give you Plenty of Work again: but until I have sold them to somebody or other, or until I have used them myself, you will have to remain idle.'

'Well, this takes the bloody biskit, don't it?' said Harlow.

'The only thing as I can see for it,' said Philpot mournfully, 'is to 'ave a unemployed procession.'

'That's the idear,' said Harlow, and the three began to march about the room in Indian file, singing:

'We've got no work to do-oo-oo!
We've got no work to do-oo-oo!
Just because we've been workin' a dam sight too hard,

Now we've got no work to do.'

As they marched round, the crowd jeered at them and made offensive remarks. Crass said that anyone could see that they were a lot of lazy, drunken loafers who had never done a fair day's work in their lives and never intended to.

'We shan't never get nothing like this, you know,' said Philpot. 'Let's try the religious dodge.'

'All right,' agreed Harlow. 'What shall we give 'em?'

'I know!' cried Philpot after a moment's deliberation. ' 'Let my lower lights be burning.' That always makes 'em part up.'

The three unemployed accordingly resumed their march round the room, singing mournfully and imitating the usual whine of street-singers:

> 'Trim your fee-bil lamp me brither-in,
> Some poor sail-er tempest torst,
> Strugglin' 'ard to save the 'arb-er,
> Hin the dark-niss may be lorst,
> So let my lower lights be burning,
> Send 'er gleam acrost the wave,
> Some poor shipwrecked, struggling seaman,
> You may rescue, you may save.'

'Kind frens,' said Philpot, removing his cap and addressing the crowd, 'we're hall honest British workin' men, but we've been hout of work for the last twenty years on account of foreign competition and over-production. We don't come hout 'ere because we're too lazy to work; it's because we can't get a job. If it wasn't for foreign competition, the kind-'earted Hinglish capitalists would be able to sell their goods and give us Plenty of Work, and if they could, I assure you that we should hall be perfectly willing and contented to go on workin' our bloody guts out for the benefit of our masters for the rest of our lives. We're quite willin' to work: that's hall we arst for – Plenty of Work – but as we can't get it we're forced to come out 'ere and arst you to spare a few coppers towards a crust of bread and a night's lodgin'.'

As Philpot held out his cap for subscriptions, some of them attempted to expectorate into it, but the more charitable put in pieces of cinder or dirt from the floor, and the kind-hearted capitalist was so affected by the sight of their misery that he gave them one of the sovereigns he had in his pocket: but as this was of no use to them they immediately returned it to him in exchange for one of the small squares of the necessaries of life, which they divided and greedily devoured. And when they had finished eating they gathered round the philanthropist and sang, 'For he's a jolly good fellow,' and afterwards Harlow suggested that they should ask him if he would allow them to elect him to Parliament.

CHAPTER 22

The Phrenologist

The following morning – Saturday – the men went about their work in gloomy silence; there were but few attempts at conversation and no jests or singing. The terror of the impending slaughter pervaded the house. Even those who were confident of being spared and kept on till the job was finished shared the general depression, not only out of sympathy for the doomed, but because they knew that a similar fate awaited themselves a little later on.

They all waited anxiously for Nimrod to come, but hour after hour dragged slowly by and he did not arrive. At half-past eleven some of those who had made up their minds that they were to be 'stood still' began to hope that the slaughter was to be deferred for a few days: after all, there was plenty of work still to be done: even if all hands were kept on, the job could scarcely be finished in another week. Anyhow, it would not be very long now before they would know one way or the other. If he did not come before twelve, it was all right: all the hands were paid by the hour and were therefore entitled to an hour's notice.

Easton and Harlow were working together on the staircase, finishing the doors and other woodwork with white enamel. The men had not been allowed to spend the time necessary to prepare this work in a proper manner, it had not been rubbed down smooth or properly filled up, and it had not had a sufficient number of coats of paint to make it solid white. Now that the glossy enamel was put on, the work looked rather rough and shady.

'It ain't 'arf all right, ain't it?' remarked Harlow, sarcastically, indicating the door he had just finished.

Easton laughed: 'I can't understand how people pass such work,' he said.

'Old Sweater did make some remark about it the other day,'

replied Harlow, 'and I heard Misery tell 'im it was impossible to make a perfect job of such old doors.'

'I believe that man's the biggest liar Gord ever made,' said Easton, an opinion in which Harlow entirely concurred.

'I wonder what the time is?' said the latter after a pause.

'I don't know exactly,' replied Easton, 'but it can't be far off twelve.'

' 'E don't seem to be comin', does 'e?' Harlow continued.

'No: and I shouldn't be surprised if 'e didn't turn up at all, now. P'raps 'e don't mean to stop nobody today after all.'

They spoke in hushed tones and glanced cautiously about them fearful of being heard or observed.

'This is a bloody life, ain't it?' Harlow said, bitterly. 'Workin' our guts out like a lot of slaves for the benefit of other people, and then as soon as they've done with you, you're chucked aside like a dirty rag.'

'Yes: and I begin to think that a great deal of what Owen says is true. But for my part I can't see 'ow it's ever goin' to be altered, can you?'

'Blowed if I know, mate. But whether it can be altered or not, there's one thing very certain; it won't be done in *our* time.'

Neither of them seemed to think that if the 'alteration' they spoke of were to be accomplished at all they themselves would have to help to bring it about.

'I wonder what they're doin' about the venetian blinds?' said Easton. 'Is there anyone doin' 'em yet?'

'I don't know; ain't 'eard nothing about 'em since the boy took 'em to the shop.'

There was quite a mystery about these blinds. About a month ago they were taken to the paint-shop down at the yard to be repainted and re-harnessed, and since then nothing had been heard of them by the men working at the 'Cave'.

'P'rap's a couple of us will be sent there to do 'em next week,' remarked Harlow.

'P'rap's so. Most likely they'll 'ave to be done in a bloody 'urry at the last minute.'

Presently Harlow – who was very anxious to know what time it was – went downstairs to ask Slyme. It was twenty minutes to twelve.

From the window of the room where Slyme was papering, one could see into the front garden. Harlow paused a moment to watch Bundy and the labourers, who were still working in the trenches at the drains, and as he looked out he saw Hunter approaching the house. Harlow drew back hastily and returned to his work, and as he went he passed the word to the other men, warning them of the approach of Misery.

Hunter entered in his usual manner and, after crawling quietly about the house for about ten minutes, he went into the drawing-room.

'I see you're putting the finishing touches on at last,' he said.

'Yes,' replied Owen. 'I've only got this bit of outlining to do now.'

'Ah, well, it looks very nice, of course,' said Misery in a voice of mourning, 'but we've lost money over it. It's taken you a week longer to do than we allowed for; you said three weeks and it's taken you a month; and we only allowed for fifteen books of gold, but you've been and used twenty-three.'

'You can hardly blame me for that, you know,' answered Owen. 'I could have got it done in the three weeks, but Mr. Rushton told me not to hurry for the sake of a day or two, because he wanted a good job. He said he would rather lose a little over it than spoil it; and as for the extra gold, that was also his order.'

'Well, I suppose it can't be helped,' whined Misery. 'Anyhow, I'm very glad it's done, because this kind of work don't pay. We'll 'ave you back on the brush on Monday morning; we want to get the outside done next week if it keeps fine.'

The 'brush' alluded to by Nimrod was the large 'pound' brush used in ordinary painting.

Misery now began wandering about the house, in and out of the rooms, sometimes standing for several minutes silently watching the hands as they worked. As he watched them the men became nervous and awkward, each one dreading that he might be one of those who were to be paid off at one o'clock.

At about five minutes to twelve Hunter went down to the paint-shop – the scullery – where Crass was mixing some colour, and getting ready some 'empties' to be taken to the yard.

'I suppose the b—r's gone to ask Crass which of us is the least use,' whispered Harlow to Easton.

'I wouldn't be surprised if it was you and me, for two,' replied the latter in the same tone. 'You can't trust Crass you know, for all 'e seems so friendly to our faces. You never know what 'e ses behind our backs.'

'You may be sure it won't be Sawkins or any of the other light-weights, because Nimrod won't want to pay us sixpence ha'penny for painting guttering and rainpipes when *they* can do it near enough for fourpence ha'penny and fivepence. They won't be able to do the sashes, though, will they?'

'I don't know so much about that,' replied Easton. 'Anything seems to be good enough for Hunter.'

'Look out! 'Ere 'e comes!' said Harlow, and they both relapsed into silence and busied themselves with their work. Misery stood watching them for some time without speaking, and then went out of the house. They crept cautiously to the window of a room that overlooked the garden and, peeping furtively out, they saw him standing on the brink of one of the trenches, moodily watching Bundy and his mates as they toiled at the drains. Then, to their surprise and relief, he turned and went out of the gate! They just caught sight of one of the wheels of his bicycle as he rode away.

The slaughter was evidently to be put off until next week! It seemed too good to be true.

'P'rap's 'e's left a message for some of us with Crass?' suggested Easton. 'I don't think it's likely, but it's just possible.'

'Well, I'm goin' down to ask 'im,' said Harlow, desperately. 'We may as well know the worst at once.'

He returned in a few minutes with the information that Hunter had decided not to stop anyone that day because he wanted to get the outside finished during the next week, if possible.

The hands received this intelligence with mixed feelings, because although it left them safe for the present, it meant that nearly everybody would certainly be stopped next Saturday, if not before; whereas if a few had been sacked today it would have made it all the better for the rest. Still, this aspect of the business did not greatly interfere with the relief that they all felt at knowing that the immediate danger was over; and the fact that it was Saturday – pay-day – also served to revive their drooping spirits. They all felt pretty certain that Misery would return no more that day, and presently Harlow began to sing the old favourite, 'Work! for the night is coming!' the refrain of which was soon taken up by nearly everyone in the house:

> 'Work! for the night is coming,
>   Work in the morning hours.
> Work! for the night is coming,
>   Work 'mid springing flowers!
> 'Work while the dew is sparkling,
>   Work in the noonday sun!
> Work! for the night is coming,
>   When man's work is done!'

whichever way they took it was equally amusing to Crass and the rest, who were like a crowd of boys just let out of school.

It will be remembered that there was a back door to Rushton's office; in this door was a small sliding panel or trap-door with a little shelf at the bottom. The men stood in the road and on the pavement outside the closed door, their money being passed out to them through the sliding panel. As there was no shelter, when it rained they occasionally got wet through while waiting to be paid. With some firms it is customary to call out the names of the men and pay them in order of seniority or ability, but there was no such system here; the man who got to the aperture first was paid first, and so on. The result was that there was always a sort of miniature 'Battle of Life', the men pushing and struggling against each other as if their lives depended upon their being paid by a certain time.

On the ledge of the little window through which their money was passed there was always a Hospital collecting-box. Every man put either a penny or twopence into this box. Of course, it was not compulsory to do so, but they all did, because they felt that any man who omitted to contribute might be 'marked'. They did not all agree with contributing to the Hospital, for several reasons. They knew that the doctors at the Hospital made a practice of using the free patients to make experiments upon, and they also knew that the so-called 'free' patients who contribute so very largely directly to the maintenance of such institutions, get scant consideration when they apply for the 'free' treatment, and are plainly given to understand that they are receiving 'charity'. Some of the men thought that, considering the extent to which they contributed, they should be entitled to attention as a right.

After receiving their wages, Crass, Easton, Bundy, Philpot, Harlow and a few others adjourned to the 'Cricketers' for a drink. Owen went away alone, and Slyme also went on by himself. There was no use waiting for Easton to come out of the public house, because there was no knowing how long he would be; he might stay half an hour or two hours.

On his way home, in accordance with his usual custom, Slyme called at the Post Office to put some of his wages in the bank. Like most other 'Christians', he believed in taking thought for the morrow, what he should eat and drink and wherewithal he was to be clothed. He thought it wise to lay up for himself as much treasure upon earth as possible. The fact that Jesus said that His disciples were not to do these things made no more difference to Slyme's

When this hymn was finished, someone else, imitating the
of a street-singer, started, 'Oh, where is my wandering boy ton
and then Harlow – who by some strange chance had a penny –
it out of his pocket and dropped it on the floor, the ringing
coin being greeted with shouts of 'Thank you, kind lady,'
several of the singers. This little action of Harlow's was the n
of bringing a most extraordinary circumstance to light. Althou
was Saturday morning, several of the others had pennies or
pence! and at the conclusion of each verse they all followed Harl
example and the house resounded with the ringing of falling c
cries of 'Thank you, kind lady,' 'Thank you, sir,' and 'Gord
you,' mingled with shouts of laughter.

'My wandering boy' was followed by a choice selection of chor
of well-known music-hall songs, including 'Good-bye, my Blueb
'The Honeysuckle and the Bee', 'I've got 'em!' and 'The Chu
Parade', the whole being tastefully varied and interspersed w
howls, shrieks, curses, catcalls, and downward explosions
flatulence.

In the midst of the uproar Crass came upstairs.

' 'Ere!' he shouted. 'For Christ's sake make less row! Supp
Nimrod was to come back!'

'Oh, he ain't comin' any more today,' said Harlow, recklessly.

'Besides, what if 'e does come?' cried Easton. 'Oo cares for '*in*

'Well, we never know; and for that matter Rushton or Swe
might come at any minit.'

With this, Crass went muttering back to the scullery, and the
relapsed into their usual silence.

At ten minutes to one they all ceased work, put away their co
and locked up the house. There were a number of 'empties'
taken away and left at the yard on their way to the office;
Crass divided amongst the others – carrying nothing himself
then they all set out for the office to get their money, cracking
as they went along. Harlow and Easton enlivened the journ
coughing significantly whenever they met a young woman
audibly making some complimentary remark about her pe
appearance. If the girl smiled, each of them eagerly claimed t
'seen her first', but if she appeared offended or 'stuck up'
suggested that she was cross-cut[62] or that she had been
vinegar with a fork. Now and then they kissed their
affectionately to servant-girls whom they saw looking
windows. Some of these girls laughed, others looked indigna

conduct than it does to the conduct of any other 'Christian'. They are all agreed that when Jesus said this He meant something else; and all the other inconvenient things that Jesus said are disposed of in the same way. For instance, these 'disciples' assure us that when Jesus said, 'Resist not evil',[63] 'If a man smite thee upon the right cheek turn unto him also the left', He really meant 'Turn on to him a Maxim gun; disembowel him with a bayonet or batter in his skull with the butt end of a rifle!' When He said, 'If one take thy coat, give him thy cloak also,' the 'Christians' say that what He really meant was: 'If one take thy coat, give him six months' hard labour.' A few of the followers of Jesus admit that He really did mean just what He said, but they say that the world would never be able to go on if they followed out His teachings! That is true. It is probably the effect that Jesus intended His teachings to produce. It is altogether improbable that He wished the world to continue along its present lines. But, if these pretended followers really think – as they say that they do – that the teachings of Jesus are ridiculous and impracticable, why continue the hypocritical farce of calling themselves 'Christians' when they don't really believe in or follow Him at all?

As Jesus himself pointed out, there's no sense in calling Him 'Lord, Lord'[64] when they do not the things that He said.

This banking transaction finished, Slyme resumed his homeward way, stopping only to purchase some sweets at a confectioner's. He spent a whole sixpence at once in this shop on a glass jar of sweets for the baby.

Ruth was not surprised when she saw him come in alone; it was the usual thing since Easton had become so friendly with Crass. She made no reference to his absence, but Slyme noticed with secret chagrin that she was annoyed and disappointed. She was just finishing scrubbing the kitchen floor and little Freddie was sitting up in a baby's high chair that had a little shelf or table fixed in front of it. To keep him amused while she did her work, Ruth had given him a piece of bread and raspberry jam, which the child had rubbed all over his face and into his scalp, evidently being under the impression that it was something for the improvement of the complexion, or a cure for baldness. He now looked as if he had been in a fight or a railway accident. The child hailed the arrival of Slyme with enthusiasm, being so overcome with emotion that he began to shed tears, and was only pacified when the man gave him the jar of sweets and took him out of the chair.

Slyme's presence in the house had not proved so irksome as Easton and Ruth had dreaded it would be. Indeed, at first, he made a point of retiring to his own room after tea every evening, until they invited him to stay downstairs in the kitchen. Nearly every Wednesday and Saturday he went to a meeting, or an open-air preaching, when the weather permitted, for he was one of a little zealous band of people connected with the Shining Light Chapel who carried on the 'open-air' work all the year round. After a while, the Eastons not only became reconciled to his presence in the house, but were even glad of it. Ruth especially would often have been very lonely if he had not been there, for it had lately become Easton's custom to spend a few evenings every week with Crass at the 'Cricketers'.

When at home Slyme passed his time playing a mandoline or making fretwork photo frames. Ruth had the baby's photograph taken a few weeks after Slyme came, and the frame he made for it was now one of the ornaments of the sitting-room. The instinctive, unreasoning aversion she had at first felt for him had passed away. In a quiet, unobtrusive manner he did her so many little services that she found it impossible to dislike him. At first, she used to address him as 'Mr.' but after a time she fell naturally into Easton's practice of calling him by his first name.

As for the baby, *he* made no secret of his affection for the lodger, who nursed and played with him for hours at a stretch.

'I'll serve your dinner now, Alf,' said Ruth when she had finished scrubbing the floor, 'but I'll wait for mine for a little while. Will may come.'

'I'm in no hurry,' replied Slyme. 'I'll go and have a wash; he may be here by then.'

As he spoke, Slyme – who had been sitting by the fire nursing the baby – who was trying to swallow the jar of sweets – put the child back into the high chair, giving him one of the sticks of sweet out of the jar to keep him quiet; and went upstairs to his own room. He came down again in about a quarter of an hour, and Ruth proceeded to serve his dinner, for Easton was still absent.

'If I was you, I wouldn't wait for Will,' said Slyme, 'he may not come for another hour or two. It's after two o'clock now, and I'm sure you must be hungry.'

'I suppose I may as well,' replied Ruth, hesitatingly. 'He'll most likely get some bread and cheese at the "Cricketers", same as he did last Saturday.'

'Almost sure to,' responded Slyme.

The baby had had his face washed while Slyme was upstairs. Directly he saw his mother eating he threw away the sugar-stick and began to cry, holding out his arms to her. She had to take him on her lap whilst she ate her dinner, and feed him with pieces from her plate.

Slyme talked all the time, principally about the child. He was very fond of children, he said, and always got on well with them, but he had really never known such an intelligent child – for his age – as Freddie. His fellow-workmen would have been astonished had they been present to hear him talking about the shape of the baby's head. They would have been astonished at the amount of knowledge he appeared to possess of the science of Phrenology.[65] Ruth, at any rate, thought he was very clever.

After a time the child began to grow fretful and refused to eat; when his mother gave him a fresh piece of sugar-stick out of the jar he threw it peevishly on the floor and began to whimper, rubbing his face against his mother's bosom and pulling at her dress with his hands. When Slyme first came Ruth had made a practice of withdrawing from the room if he happened to be present when she wanted to nurse the child, but lately she had been less sensitive. She was sitting with her back to the window and she partly covered the baby's face with a light shawl that she wore. By the time they finished dinner the child had dozed off to sleep. Slyme got up from his chair and stood with his back to the fire, looking down at them; presently he spoke, referring, of course, to the baby:

'He's very like you, isn't he?'

'Yes,' replied Ruth. 'Everyone says he takes after me.'

Slyme moved a little closer, bending down to look at the slumbering infant.

'You know, at first I thought he was a girl,' he continued after a pause. 'He seems almost too pretty for a boy, doesn't he?'

Ruth smiled. 'People always take him for a girl at first,' she said. 'Yesterday I took him with me to the Monopole Stores[66] to buy some things, and the manager would hardly believe it wasn't a girl.'

The man reached out his hand and stroked the baby's face.

Although Slyme's behaviour had hitherto always been very correct, yet there was occasionally an indefinable something in his manner when they were alone that made Ruth feel conscious and embarrassed. Now, as she glanced up at him and saw the expression on his face she crimsoned with confusion and hastily lowered her eyes without replying to his last remark. He did not speak again either, and they remained for several minutes in silence, as if spellbound, Ruth oppressed with instinctive dread, and Slyme scarcely less agitated, his face flushed and his heart beating wildly. He trembled as he stood over her, hesitating and afraid.

And then the silence was suddenly broken by the creaking and clanging of the front gate, heralding the tardy coming of Easton. Slyme went out into the scullery and, taking down the blacking brushes from the shelf, began cleaning his boots.

It was plain from Easton's appearance and manner that he had been drinking, but Ruth did not reproach him in any way; on the contrary, she seemed almost feverishly anxious to attend to his comfort.

When Slyme finished cleaning his boots he went upstairs to his room, receiving a careless greeting from Easton as he passed through the kitchen. He felt nervous and apprehensive that Ruth might say something to Easton, and was not quite able to reassure himself with the reflection that, after all, there was nothing to tell. As for Ruth, she had to postpone the execution of her hastily formed resolution to tell her husband of Slyme's strange behaviour, for Easton fell asleep in his chair before he had finished his dinner, and she had some difficulty in waking him sufficiently to persuade him to go upstairs to bed, where he remained until tea-time. Probably he would not have come down even then if it had not been for the fact that he had made an appointment to meet Crass at the 'Cricketers'.

Whilst Easton was asleep, Slyme had been downstairs in the kitchen, making a fretwork frame. He played with Freddie while Ruth prepared the tea, and he appeared to her to be so unconscious of having done anything unusual that she began to think that she must have been mistaken in imagining that he had intended any-hing wrong.

After tea, Slyme put on his best clothes to go to his usual 'open-air' meeting. As a rule Easton and Ruth went out marketing together every Saturday night, but this evening he could not wait for her because he had promised to meet Crass at seven o'clock; so he arranged to see her down town at eight.

CHAPTER 23

The 'Open Air'

During the last few weeks ever since he had been engaged on the decoration of the drawing-room, Owen had been so absorbed in his work that he had no time for other things. Of course, all he was paid for was the time he actually worked, but really every waking moment of his time was given to the task. Now that it was finished he felt something like one aroused from a dream to the stern realities and terrors of life. By the end of next week, the inside of the house and part of the outside would be finished, and as far as he knew the firm had nothing else to do at present. Most of the other employers in the town were in the same plight, and it would be of no use to apply even to such of them as had something to do, for they were not likely to take on a fresh man while some of their regular hands were idle.

For the last month he had forgotten that he was ill; he had forgotten that when the work at 'The Cave' was finished he would have to stand off with the rest of the hands. In brief, he had forgotten for the time being that, like the majority of his fellow workmen, he was on the brink of destitution, and that a few weeks of unemployment or idleness meant starvation. As far as illness was concerned, he was even worse off than most others, for the greater number of them were members of some sick benefit club, but Owen's ill-health rendered him ineligible for membership of such societies.

As he walked homewards after being paid, feeling unutterably depressed and weary, he began once more to think of the future; and the more he thought of it the more dreadful it appeared. Even looking at it in the best possible light – supposing he did not fall too ill to work, or lose his employment from some other cause – what was there to live for? He had been working all this week. These few coins that he held in his hand were the result, and he laughed bitterly as he thought of all they had to try to do with this money, and of all that would have to be left undone.

As he turned the corner of Kerk Street he saw Frankie coming to meet him, and the boy catching sight of him at the same moment began running and leapt into his arms with a joyous whoop.

'Mother told me to tell you to buy something for dinner before you come home, because there's nothing in the house.'

'Did she tell you what I was to get?'

'She did tell me something, but I forget what it was. But I know she said to get anything you like if you couldn't get what she told me to tell you.'

'Well, we'll go and see what we can find,' said Owen.

'If I were you, I'd get a tin of salmon or some eggs and bacon,' suggested Frankie as he skipped along holding his father's hand. 'We don't want anything that's a lot of trouble to cook, you know, because Mum's not very well today.'

'Is she up?'

'She's been up all the morning, but she's lying down now. We've done all the work, though. While she was making the beds I started washing up the cups and saucers without telling her, but when she came in and saw what a mess I'd made on the floor, she had to stop me doing it, and she had to change nearly all my clothes as well, because I was almost wet through; but I managed the wiping up all right when she did the washing, and I swep the passage and put all my things tidy and made the cat's bed. And that just reminds me: will you please give me my penny now? I promised the cat that I'd bring him back some meat.'

Owen complied with the boy's request, and while the latter went to the butcher's for the meat, Owen went into the grocer's to get something for dinner, it being arranged that they were to meet again at the corner of the street. Owen was at the appointed place first and after waiting some time and seeing no sign of the boy he decided to go towards the butcher's to meet him. When he came in sight of the shop he saw the boy standing outside in earnest conversation with the butcher, a jolly-looking, stoutly built man, with a very red face. Owen perceived at once that the child was trying to explain something, because Frankie had a habit of holding his head sideways and supplementing his speech by spreading out his fingers and making quaint gestures with his hands whenever he found it difficult to make himself understood. The boy was doing this now, waving one hand about with the fingers and thumb extended wide, and with the other flourishing a paper parcel which evidently contained the pieces of meat. Presently the man laughed heartily and after shaking hands with Frankie went into the shop to attend to a customer, and Frankie rejoined his father.

'That butcher's a very decent sort of chap, you know, Dad,' he said. 'He wouldn't take the penny for the meat.'

'Is that what you were talking to him about?'

'No; we were talking about Socialism. You see, this is the second time he wouldn't take the money, and the first time he did it I thought he must be a Socialist, but I didn't ask him then. But when he did it again this time I asked him if he was. So he said, No. He said he wasn't quite mad yet. So I said, "If you think that Socialists are all mad, you're very much mistaken, because I'm a Socialist myself, and I'm quite sure *I'm* not mad." So he said he knew I was all right, but he didn't understand anything about Socialism himself – only that it meant sharing out all the money so that everyone could have the same. So then I told him that's not Socialism at all! And when I explained it to him properly and advised him to be one, he said he'd think about it. So I said if he'd only do *that* he'd be *sure* to change over to our side; and then he laughed and promised to let me know next time he sees me, and I promised to lend him some literature. You won't mind, will you, Dad?'

'Of course not; when we get home we'll have a look through what we've got and you can take him some of them.'

'I know!' cried Frankie eagerly. 'The two very best of all. *Happy Britain* and *England for the English.*'

He knew that these were 'two of the best' because he had often heard his father and mother say so, and he had noticed that whenever a Socialist friend came to visit them, he was also of the same opinion.

* * *

As a rule on Saturday evenings they all three went out together to do the marketing, but on this occasion, in consequence of Nora being unwell, Owen and Frankie went by themselves. The frequent recurrence of his wife's illness served to increase Owen's pessimism with regard to the future, and the fact that he was unable to procure for her the comforts she needed was not calculated to dispel the depression that filled his mind as he reflected that there was no hope of better times.

In the majority of cases, for a workman there is no hope of advancement. After he has learnt his trade and become a 'journeyman' all progress ceases. He is at the goal. After he has been working ten or twenty years he commands no more than he did at first – a bare living wage – sufficient money to purchase fuel to keep the human machine working. As he grows older he will have to be content with even less; and all the time he holds his employment at the caprice and by the favour of his masters, who regard him merely as a piece of mechanism that enables them to accumulate money – a thing which they are justified in casting aside as soon as it becomes unprofitable. And the workman must not only be an efficient money-producing machine, but he must also be the servile subject of his masters. If he is not abjectly civil and humble, if he will not submit tamely to insult, indignity, and every form of contemptuous treatment that occasion makes possible, he can be dismissed, and replaced in a moment by one of the crowd of unemployed who are always waiting for his job. This is the status of the majority of the 'Heirs of all the ages' under the present system.

As he walked through the crowded streets holding Frankie by the hand, Owen thought that to voluntarily continue to live such a life as this betokened a degraded mind. To allow one's child to grow up to suffer it in turn was an act of callous, criminal cruelty.

In this matter he held different opinions from most of his fellow workmen. The greater number of them were quite willing and content that their children should be made into beasts of burden for the benefit of other people. As he looked down upon the little, frail figure trotting along by his side, Owen thought for the thousandth time that it would be far better for the child to die now: he would never be fit to be a soldier in the ferocious Christian Battle of Life.

Then he remembered Nora. Although she was always brave, and never complained, he knew that her life was one of almost incessant physical suffering; and as for himself he was tired and sick of it all. He had been working like a slave all his life and there was nothing to show for it – there never would be anything to show for it. He thought of the man who had killed his wife and children. The jury had returned the usual verdict, 'Temporary Insanity'. It never seemed to occur to these people that the truth was that to continue to suffer hopelessly like this was evidence of permanent insanity.

But supposing that bodily death was not the end. Suppose there was some kind of a God? If there were, it wasn't unreasonable to think that the Being who was capable of creating such a world as this and who seemed so callously indifferent to the unhappiness of His creatures, would also be capable of devising and creating the other Hell that most people believed in.

Although it was December the evening was mild and clear. The full moon deluged the town with silvery light, and the cloudless sky was jewelled with myriads of glittering stars.

Looking out into the unfathomable infinity of space, Owen wondered what manner of Being or Power it was that had originated and sustained all this? Considered as an explanation of the existence of the universe, the orthodox Christian religion was too absurd to merit a second thought. But, then, every other conceivable hypothesis was also – ultimately – unsatisfactory and even ridiculous. To believe that the universe as it is now has existed from all eternity without any Cause is surely ridiculous. But to say that it was created by a Being who existed without a Cause from all eternity is equally ridiculous. In fact, it was only postponing the difficulty one stage. Evolution was not more satisfactory, because although it was undoubtedly true as far as it went, it only went part of the way, leaving the great question still unanswered by assuming the existence – in the beginning – of the elements of matter, without a cause! This question remained unanswered because it was unanswerable. Regarding this problem man was but –

> 'An infant crying in the night,
> An infant crying for the light
> And with no language but a cry.'

All the same, it did not follow, because one could not explain the mystery oneself, that it was right to try to believe an unreasonable explanation offered by someone else.

But although he reasoned like this, Owen could not help longing for something to believe, for some hope for the future; something to compensate for the unhappiness of the present. In one sense, he thought, how good it would be if Christianity were true, and after all the sorrow there was to be an eternity of happiness such as it had never entered into the heart of man to conceive? If only that were true, nothing else would matter. How contemptible and insignificant the very worst that could happen here would be if one knew that this life was only a short journey that was to terminate at the beginning of an eternity of joy? But no one really believed this; and as for those who pretended to do so – their lives showed that they did not believe it at all. Their greed and inhumanity – their ferocious determination to secure for themselves the good things of *this* world – were conclusive proofs of their hypocrisy and infidelity.

'Dad,' said Frankie, suddenly, 'let's go over and hear what that man's saying.' He pointed across the way to where – a little distance back from the main road, just round the corner of a side street – a group of people were standing encircling a large lantern fixed on the top of a pole about seven feet high, which was being held by one of the men. A bright light was burning inside this lantern and on the pane of white, obscured glass which formed the sides, visible from where Owen and Frankie were standing, was written in bold plain letters that were readable even at that distance, the text:

'Be not deceived: God is not mocked!'[67]

The man whose voice had attracted Frankie's attention was reading out a verse of a hymn:

'I heard the voice of Jesus say,
    Behold, I freely give,
The living water, thirsty one,
    Stoop down and drink, and live.
I came to Jesus and I drank,
    Of that life giving stream,
My thirst was quenched,
    My soul revived,
And now I live in Him.'

The individual who gave out this hymn was a tall, thin man whose clothes hung loosely on the angles of his round-shouldered, bony form. His long, thin legs – about which the baggy trousers hung in ungraceful folds – were slightly knock-kneed, and terminated in large, flat feet. His arms were very long even for such a tall man, and the huge, bony hands were gnarled and knotted. Regardless of the season, he had removed his bowler hat, revealing his forehead, which was high, flat and narrow. His nose was a large, fleshy, hawklike beak, and from the side of each nostril a deep indentation extended downwards until it disappeared in the drooping moustache that concealed his mouth when he was not speaking, but the vast extent of which was perceptible now as he opened it to call out the words of the hymn. His chin was large and extraordinarily long: the eyes were pale blue, very small and close together, surmounted by spare, light-coloured, almost invisible eyebrows with a deep vertical cleft between them over the nose. His head – covered with thick, coarse brown hair – was very large, especially at the back; the ears were small and laid close to the head. If one were to make a full-face drawing of his cadaverous visage, it would be found that the outline resembled that of the lid of a coffin.

As Owen and Frankie drew near, the boy tugged at his father's hand and whispered: 'Dad! that's the teacher at the Sunday School where I went that day with Charley and Elsie.'

[[Owen looked quickly and saw that it was Hunter.]]

As Hunter ceased reading out the words of the hymn, the little company of evangelists began to sing, accompanied by the strains of a small but peculiarly sweet-toned organ. A few persons in the crowd joined in, the words being familiar to them. During the singing their faces were a study, they all looked so profoundly solemn and miserable, as if they were a gang of condemned criminals waiting to be led forth to execution. The greater number of the people standing around appeared to be listening more out of idle curiosity than anything else, and two well-dressed young men – evidently strangers and visitors to the town – amused themselves by making audible remarks about the texts on the lantern. There was also a shabbily dressed, semi-drunken man in a battered bowler hat who stood on the inner edge of the crowd, almost in the ring, itself, with folded arms and an expression of scorn. He had a very thin, pale face with a large, high-bridged nose, and bore a striking resemblance to the first Duke of Wellington.

As the singing proceeded, the scornful expression faded from the visage of the Semi-drunk, and he not only joined in, but unfolded his arms and began waving them about as if he were conducting the music.

By the time the singing was over a considerable crowd had gathered, and then one of the evangelists, the same man who had given out the hymn, stepped into the middle of the ring. He had evidently been offended by the unseemly conduct of the two well-dressed young men, for after a preliminary glance round upon the crowd, he fixed his gaze upon the pair, and immediately launched out upon a long tirade against what he called 'Infidelity'. Then, having heartily denounced all those who – as he put it – 'refused' to believe, he proceeded to ridicule those half-and-half believers who, while professing to believe the Bible, rejected the doctrine of Hell. That the existence of a place of eternal torture is taught in the Bible, he tried to prove by a long succession of texts. As he proceeded he became very excited, and the contemptuous laughter of the two unbelievers seemed to make him worse. He shouted and raved, literally foaming at the mouth and glaring in a frenzied manner around upon the faces of the crowd.

'There *is* a Hell!' he shouted. 'And understand this clearly – 'The wicked *shall* be turned into hell'[68] – 'He that believeth not *shall* be damned.' '

'Well, then, *you'll* stand a very good chance of being damned also,' exclaimed one of the two young men.

' 'Ow do you make it out?' demanded the preacher, wiping the froth from his lips and the perspiration from his forehead with his handkerchief.

'Why, because you don't believe the Bible yourselves.'

Nimrod and the other evangelists laughed, and looked pityingly at the young man.

'Ah, my dear brother,' said Misery. 'That's your delusion. I thank God I do believe it, every word!'

'Amen,' fervently ejaculated Slyme and several of the other disciples.

'Oh no, you don't,' replied the other. 'And I can prove you don't.'

'Prove it, then,' said Nimrod.

'Read out the 17th and 18th verses of the XVIth chapter of Mark,' said the disturber of the meeting. The crowd began to close in on the centre, the better to hear the dispute. Misery, standing close to the lantern, found the verse mentioned and read aloud as follows:

'And these signs shall follow them that believe. In my name shall they cast out devils: they shall speak with new tongues. They shall take up serpents; and if they drink any deadly thing it shall not hurt them: they shall lay hands on the sick, and they shall recover.'

'Well, you can't heal the sick, neither can you speak new languages or cast out devils: but perhaps you can drink deadly things without suffering harm.' The speaker here suddenly drew from his waistcoat pocket a small glass bottle and held it out towards Misery, who shrank from it with horror as he continued: 'I have here a most deadly poison. There is in this bottle sufficient strychnine to kill a dozen unbelievers. Drink it! And if it doesn't harm you, we'll know that you really are a believer and that what you believe is the truth!'

' 'Ear, 'ear!' said the Semi-drunk, who had listened to the progress of the argument with great interest. ' 'Ear, 'ear! That's fair enough. Git it acrost yer chest.'

Some of the people in the crowd began to laugh, and voices were heard from several quarters calling upon Misery to drink the strychnine.

'Now, if you'll allow me, I'll explain to you what that there verse means,' said Hunter. 'If you read it carefully – *with* the context – '

'I don't want you to tell me what it means,' interrupted the other. 'I am able to read for myself. Whatever you may say, or pretend to think it means, I know what it *says*.'

'Hear, Hear,' shouted several voices, and angry cries of 'Why don't you drink the poison?' began to be heard from the outskirts of the crowd.

'Are you going to drink it or not?' demanded the man with the bottle.

'No! I'm not such a fool!' retorted Misery, fiercely, and a loud shout of laughter broke from the crowd.

'P'raps some of the other "believers" would like to,' said the young man sneeringly, looking round upon the disciples. As no one seemed desirous of availing himself of this offer, the man returned the bottle regretfully to his pocket.

'I suppose,' said Misery, regarding the owner of the strychnine with a sneer, 'I suppose you're one of them there hired critics wot's goin' about the country doin' the Devil's work?'

'Wot I wants to know is this 'ere,' said the Semi-drunk, suddenly advancing into the middle of the ring and speaking in a loud voice. 'Where did Cain get 'is wife from?'[69]

'Don't answer 'im, Brother 'Unter,' said Mr. Didlum, one of the disciples. This was rather an unnecessary piece of advice, because Misery did not know the answer.

An individual in a long black garment – the 'minister' – now whispered something to Miss Didlum, who was seated at the organ, whereupon she began to play, and the 'believers' began to sing, as loud as they could so as to drown the voices of the disturbers of the meeting, a song called 'Oh, that will be Glory for me!'

After this hymn the 'minister' invited a shabbily dressed 'brother' – a working-man member of the P.S.A., to say 'a few words', and the latter accordingly stepped into the centre of the ring and held forth as follows:

'My dear frens, I thank Gord tonight that I can stand 'ere tonight, hout in the hopen hair and tell hall you dear people tonight of hall wot's been done for *me*. Ho my dear frens hi ham so glad tonight as I can stand 'ere tonight and say as hall my sins is hunder the blood tonight and wot 'E's done for me 'E can do for you tonight. If you'll honly do as I done and just acknowledge yourself a lost sinner – '

'Yes! that's the honly way!' shouted Nimrod.

'Amen,' cried all the other believers.

' – If you'll honly come to 'im tonight hin the same way as I done you'll see that wot 'E's done for me 'E can do for you. Ho my dear frens, don't go on puttin' it orf from day to day like a door turnin' on its 'inges, don't put of it orf to some more convenient time because you may never 'ave another chance. 'Im that bein' orfen reproved 'ardeneth 'is neck[70] shall be suddenly cut orf and that without remedy. Ho come to 'im tonight, for 'Is name's sake and to 'Im we'll give hall the glory. Amen.'

'Amen,' said the believers, fervently, and then the man who was dressed in the long garment entreated all those who were not yet true believers – and doers – of the word to join earnestly and *meaningly* in the singing of the closing hymn, which he was about to read out to them.

The Semi-drunk obligingly conducted as before, and the crowd faded away with the last notes of the music.

Chapter 24

Ruth

AS has already been stated, hitherto Slyme had passed the greater number of his evenings at home, but during the following three weeks a change took place in his habits in this respect. He now went out nearly every night and did not return until after ten o'clock. On meeting nights he always changed his attire, dressing himself as on Sundays, but on the other occasions he went out in his week-day clothes. Ruth often wondered where he went on those nights, but he never volunteered the information and she never asked him.

Easton had chummed up with a lot of the regular customers at the 'Cricketers', where he now spent most of his spare time, drinking beer, telling yarns or playing shove-ha'penny or hooks and rings. When he had no cash the Old Dear gave him credit until Saturday. At first, the place had not had much attraction for him, and he really went there only for the purpose of 'keeping in' with Crass: but after a time he found it a very congenial way of passing his evenings . . .

[One evening, Ruth saw Slyme] meet Crass as if by appointment and as the two men went away together she returned to her housework wondering what it meant.

Meantime, Crass and Slyme proceeded on their way down town. It was about half-past six o'clock: the shops and streets were brilliantly lighted, and as they went along they saw numerous groups of men talking together in a listless way. Most of them were artisans and labourers out of employment and evidently in no great hurry to go home. Some of them had neither tea nor fire to go to, and stayed away from home as long as possible so as not to be compelled to look upon the misery of those who were waiting for them there. Others hung about hoping against all probability that they might even yet – although it was so late – hear of some job to be started somewhere or other.

As they passed one of these groups they recognised and nodded to Newman and old Jack Linden, and the former left the others and came up to Crass and Slyme, who did not pause, so Newman walked along with them.

'Anything fresh in, Bob?' he asked.

'No; we ain't got 'ardly anything,' replied Crass. 'I reckon we shall finish up at "The Cave" next week, and then I suppose we shall all be stood orf. We've got several plumbers on, and I believe there's a little gas-fitting work in, but next to nothing in our line.'

'I suppose you don't know of any other firm what's got anything?'

'No, I don't, mate. Between you and me, I don't think any of 'em has; they're all in about the same fix.'

'I've not done anything since I left, you know,' said Newman, 'and we've just about got as far as we can get, at home.'

Slyme and Crass said nothing in reply to this. They wished that Newman would take himself off, because they did not want him to know where they were going.

However, Newman continued to accompany them and an awkward silence succeeded. He seemed to wish to say something more, and they both guessed what it was. So they walked along as rapidly as possible in order not to give him any encouragement. At last Newman blurted out:

'I suppose – you don't happen – either of you – to have a tanner you could lend me? I'll let you have it back – when I get a job.'

'I ain't mate,' replied Crass. 'I'm sorry; if I 'ad one on me, you should 'ave it, with pleasure.'

Slyme also expressed his regret that he had no money with him, and at the corner of the next street Newman – ashamed of having asked – wished them 'good night' and went away.

Slyme and Crass hurried along and presently arrived at Rushton & Co.'s shop. The windows were lit up with electric light, displaying an assortment of wallpapers, gas and electric light fittings, glass shades, globes, tins of enamel, paint and varnish. Several framed show-cards – 'Estimates Free', 'First class work only, at moderate charges', 'Only First Class Workmen Employed' and several others of the same type. On one side wall of the window was a large shield-shaped board covered with black velvet on which a number of brass

fittings for coffins were arranged. The shield was on an oak mount
with the inscription: 'Funerals conducted on modern principles.'

Slyme waited outside while Crass went in. Mr. Budd, the shopman,
was down at the far end near the glazed partition which separated
Mr. Rushton's office from the front shop. As Crass entered, Budd –
who was a pale-faced, unhealthy-looking, undersized youth about
twenty years of age – looked round and, with a grimace, motioned
him to walk softly. Crass paused, wondering what the other meant;
but the shopman beckoned him to advance, grinning and winking
and jerking his thumb over his shoulder in the direction of the office.
Crass hesitated, fearing that possibly the miserable Budd had gone –
or been driven – out of his mind; but as the latter continued to
beckon and grin and point towards the office Crass screwed up his
courage and followed him behind one of the showcases, and applying
his eye to a crack in the woodwork of the partition indicated by
Budd, he could see Mr. Rushton in the act of kissing and embracing
Miss Wade, the young lady clerk. Crass watched them for some
time and then whispered to Budd to call Slyme, and when the latter
came they all three took turns at peeping through the crack in the
partition.

When they had looked their fill they came out from behind the
showcase, almost bursting with suppressed merriment. Budd reached
down a key from where it was hanging on a hook on the wall and
gave it to Crass and the two resumed their interrupted journey. But
before they had proceeded a dozen yards from the shop, they were
accosted by a short, elderly man with grey hair and a beard. This
man looked about sixty-five years of age, and was very shabbily
dressed. The ends of the sleeves of his coat were frayed and ragged,
and the elbows were worn threadbare. His boots were patched,
broken, and down at heel, and the knees and bottoms of the legs of
his trousers were in the same condition as the sleeves of his coat.
This man's name was Latham; he was a venetian blind maker and
repairer. With his son, he was supposed to be 'in business' on his
own account, but as most of their work was done for 'the trade', that
is, for such firms as Rushton & Co., they would be more correctly
described as men who did piece-work at home.

He had been 'in business' – as he called it – for about forty years
working, working, always working; and ever since his son became
old enough to labour he had helped his father in the philanthropic
task of manufacturing profits for the sweaters who employed them.
They had been so busy running after work, and working for the

benefit of others, that they had overlooked the fact that they were only earning a bare living for themselves and now, after forty years' hard labour, the old man was clothed in rags and on the verge of destitution.

'Is Rushton there?' he asked.

'Yes, I think so,' replied Crass, attempting to pass on; but the old man detained him.

'He promised to let us know about them blinds for "The Cave". We gave 'im a price for 'em about a month ago. In fact, we gave 'im two prices, because he said the first was too high. Five and six a set I asked 'im! take 'em right through the 'ole 'ouse! one with another – big and little. Two coats of paint, and new tapes and cords. That wasn't too much, was it?'

'No,' said Crass, walking on; 'that was cheap enough!'

'*He* said it was too much,' continued Latham. 'Said as 'e could get 'em done cheaper! But I say as no one can't do it and make a living.'

As he walked along, talking, between Crass and Slyme, the old man became very excited.

'But we 'adn't nothing to do to speak of, so my son told 'im we'd do 'em for five bob a set, and 'e said 'e'd let us know, but we ain't 'eard nothing from 'im yet, so I thought I'd try and see 'im tonight.'

'Well, you'll find 'im in there now,' said Slyme with a peculiar look, and walking faster. 'Good night.'

'I won't take 'em on for no less!' cried the old man as he turned back. 'I've got my livin' to get, and my son's got 'is wife and little 'uns to keep. We can't work for nothing!'

'Certainly not,' said Crass, glad to get away at last. 'Goodnight, and good luck to you.'

As soon as they were out of hearing, they both burst out laughing at the old man's vehemence.

'Seemed quite upset about it,' said Slyme; and they laughed again.

They now left the main road and pursued their way through a number of badly lighted, mean-looking streets, and finally turning down a kind of alley, arrived at their destination. On one side of this street was a row of small houses; facing these were a number of buildings of a miscellaneous description – sheds and stables; and beyond these a plot of waste ground on which could be seen, looming weirdly through the dusk, a number of empty carts and waggons with their shafts resting on the ground or reared up into the air. Threading their way carefully through these and avoiding as much as possible the mud, pools of water, and rubbish which covered the ground, they arrived at a large gate fastened with a padlock. Applying the key, Crass swung back the gate and they found themselves in a large yard filled with building materials and plant, ladders, huge tressels, planks and beams of wood, hand-carts, and wheelbarrows, heaps of sand and mortar and innumerable other things that assumed strange fantastic shapes in the semi-darkness. Crates and packing cases, lengths of iron guttering and rain-pipes, old doorframes and other woodwork that had been taken from buildings where alterations had been made. And over all these things, a gloomy, indistinct and shapeless mass, rose the buildings and sheds that comprised Rushton & Co.'s workshops.

Crass struck a match, and Slyme, stooping down, drew a key from a crevice in the wall near one of the doors, which he unlocked, and they entered. Crass struck another match and lit the gas at a jointed bracket fixed to the wall. This was the paint-shop. At one end was a fireplace without a grate but with an iron bar fixed across the blackened chimney for the purpose of suspending pails or pots over the fire, which was usually made of wood on the hearthstone. All round the walls of the shop – which had once been whitewashed, but were now covered with smears of paint of every colour where the men had 'rubbed out' their brushes – were rows of shelves with kegs of paint upon them. In front of the window was a long bench covered with an untidy litter of dirty paint-pots, including several earthenware mixing vessels or mortars, the sides of these being thickly coated with dried paint. Scattered about the stone floor were a number of dirty pails, either empty or containing stale whitewash; and standing on a sort of low platform or shelf at one end of the shop were four large round tanks fitted with taps and labelled 'Boiled Oil', 'Turps', 'Linseed Oil', 'Turps Substitute'. The lower parts of the walls were discoloured with moisture. The atmosphere was cold and damp and foul with the sickening odours of the poisonous materials.

It was in this place that Bert – the apprentice – spent most of his time, cleaning out pots and pails, during slack periods when there were no jobs going on outside.

In the middle of the shop, under a two-armed gas pendant, was another table or bench, also thickly coated with old, dried paint, and by the side of this were two large stands on which were hanging up to dry some of the lathes of the venetian blinds belonging to 'The Cave', which Crass and Slyme were painting – piecework – in their spare time. The remainder of the lathes were leaning against the walls or piled in stacks on the table.

Crass shivered with cold as he lit the two gas-jets. 'Make a bit of a fire, Alf,' he said, 'while I gets the colour ready.'

Slyme went outside and presently returned with his arms full of old wood, which he smashed up and threw into the fireplace; then he took an empty paint-pot and filled it with turpentine from the big tank and emptied it over the wood. Amongst the pots on the mixing bench he found one full of old paint, and he threw this over the wood also, and in a few minutes he had made a roaring fire.

Meantime, Crass had prepared the paint and brushes and taken down the lathes from the drying frames. The two men now proceeded with the painting of the blinds, working rapidly, each lathe being hung on the wires of the drying frame after being painted. They talked freely as they worked, having no fear of being overheard by Rushton or Nimrod. This job was piecework, so it didn't matter whether they talked or not. They waxed hilarious over Old Latham's discomfiture and wondered what he would say if he could see them now. Then the conversation drifted to the subject of the private characters of the other men who were employed by Rushton & Co., and an impartial listener – had there been one there – would have been forced to come to the same conclusion as Crass and Slyme did: namely, that they themselves were the only two decent fellows on the firm. There was something wrong or shady about everybody else. That bloke Barrington, for instance – it was a very funny business, you know, for a chap like 'im to be workin' as a labourer, it looked very suspicious. Nobody knowed exactly who 'e was or where 'e come from, but anyone could tell 'e'd been a toff. It was very certain 'e'd never bin brought up to work for 'is livin'. The most probable explanation was that 'e'd committed some crime and bin disowned by 'is family – pinched some money, or forged a cheque or something like that. Then there was that Sawkins. He was no class whatever. It was a well-known fact that he used to go round to Misery's house nearly every night to tell him every little thing that had happened on the job during the day! As for Payne, the foreman carpenter, the man was a perfect fool: he'd find out the difference if ever he got the sack from Rushton's and went to work for some other firm! He didn't understand his trade, and he couldn't make a coffin properly to save 'is life! Then there was that rotter Owen; there was a bright specimen for yer! An Atheist! didn't believe in no God or Devil or nothing else. A pretty state of things there would be if these Socialists could have their own way: for one thing, nobody would be allowed to work overtime!

Crass and Slyme worked and talked in this manner till ten o'clock, and then they extinguished the fire by throwing some water on it – put out the gas and locked up the shop and the yard, dropping the key of the latter into the letter-box at Rushton's office on their way home.

In this way they worked at the blinds nearly every night for three weeks.

When Saturday arrived the men working at 'The Cave' were again surprised that nobody was sacked, and they were divided in opinion as to the reason, some thinking that Nimrod was determined to keep them all on till the job was finished, so as to get it done as quickly as possible; and others boldly asserting the truth of a rumour that had been going about for several days that the firm had another big job in. Mr. Sweater had bought another house; Rushton had to do it up, and they were all to be kept on to start this other work as soon as 'the Cave' was finished. Crass knew no more than anyone else and he maintained a discreet silence, but the fact that he did not contradict the rumour served to strengthen it. The only foundation that existed for this report was that Rushton and Misery had been seen looking over the garden gate of a large empty house near 'The Cave'. But although it had such an insignificant beginning, the rumour had grown and increased in detail and importance day by day. That very morning at breakfast-time, the man on the pail had announced that he had heard on the very best authority that Mr. Sweater had sold all his interest in the great business that bore his name, and was about to retire into private life, and that he intended to buy up all the house property in the neighbourhood of 'The Cave'. Another individual – one of the new hands – said that he had heard someone else – in a public house – say that Rushton was about to marry one of Sweater's daughters, and that Sweater intended to give the couple a house to live in, as a wedding present: but the fact that Rushton was already married and the father of four children, rather knocked the bottom out of this story, so it was regretfully dismissed. Whatever the reason, the fact remained that nobody had been discharged, and when pay-time arrived they set out for the office in high spirits.

That evening, the weather being fine, Slyme went out as usual to his open-air meeting, but Easton departed from *his* usual custom of rushing off to the 'Cricketers' directly he had had his tea, having on this occasion promised to wait for Ruth and to go with her to do the marketing. The baby was left at home alone, asleep in the cradle.

By the time they had made all their purchases they had a fairly heavy load. Easton carried the string-bag containing the potatoes, and other vegetables, and the meat, and Ruth, the groceries. On their way home, they had to pass the 'Cricketers' and just before they reached that part of their journey they met Mr. and Mrs. Crass, who were also out marketing. They both insisted on Easton and Ruth going in to have a drink with them. Ruth did not want to go, but she allowed herself to be persuaded for she could see that Easton was beginning to get angry with her for refusing. Crass had on a new overcoat and a new hat, with dark grey trousers and yellow boots, and a 'stand-up' collar with a bright blue tie. His wife – a fat, vulgar-looking, well-preserved woman about forty – was arrayed in a dark red 'motor' costume, with hat to match. Both Easton and Ruth – whose best clothes had all been pawned to raise the money to pay the poor rate – felt very mean and shabby before them.

When they got inside, Crass paid for the first round of drinks, a pint of Old Six for himself; the same for Easton, half a pint for Mrs. Easton and threepenny-worth of gin for Mrs. Crass.

The Besotted Wretch was there, just finishing a game of hooks and rings with the Semi-drunk – who had called round on the day after he was thrown out, to apologise for his conduct to the Old Dear, and had since then become one of the regular customers. Philpot was absent. He had been there that afternoon, so the Old Dear said, but he had gone home about five o'clock, and had not been back since. He was almost sure to look in again in the course of the evening.

Although the house was not nearly so full as it would have been if times had been better, there was a large number of people there, for the 'Cricketers' was one of the most popular houses in the town. Another thing that helped to make them busy was the fact that two other public houses in the vicinity had recently been closed up. There were people in all the compartments. Some of the seats in the public bar were occupied by women, some young and accompanied by their husbands, some old and evidently sodden with drink. In one corner of the public bar, drinking beer or gin with a number of young fellows, were three young girls who worked at a steam laundry in the neighbourhood. Two large, fat, gipsy-looking women: evidently hawkers, for on the floor beside them were two baskets containing bundles of flowers – chrysanthemums and Michaelmas daisies. There were also two very plainly and shabbily dressed women about thirty-five years of age, who were always to be found there on Saturday nights, drinking with any man who was willing to pay for them. The behaviour of these two women was very quiet and their manners unobtrusive. They seemed to realise that they were there only on sufferance, and their demeanour was shamefaced and humble.

The majority of the guests were standing. The floor was sprinkled with sawdust which served to soak up the beer that slopped out of the glasses of those whose hands were too unsteady to hold them upright. The air was foul with the smell of beer, spirits and tobacco smoke, and the uproar was deafening, for nearly everyone was talking at the same time, their voices clashing discordantly with the strains of the Polyphone, which was playing 'The Garden of Your Heart'. In one corner a group of men convulsed with laughter at the details of a dirty story related by one of their number. Several impatient customers were banging the bottoms of their empty glasses or pewters on the counter and shouting their orders for more beer. Oaths, curses and obscene expressions resounded on every hand, coming almost as frequently from the women as the men. And over all the rattle of money, the ringing of the cash register, the clinking and rattling of the glasses and pewter pots as they were being washed, and the gurgling noise made by the beer as it poured into the drinking vessels from the taps of the beer engine, whose handles were almost incessantly manipulated by the barman, the Old Dear and the glittering landlady, whose silken blouse, bejewelled hair, ears, neck and fingers scintillated gloriously in the blaze of the gaslight.

The scene was so novel and strange to Ruth that she felt dazed and bewildered. Previous to her marriage she had been a total abstainer, but since then she had occasionally taken a glass of beer with Easton for company's sake with their Sunday dinner at home; but it was generally Easton who went out and bought the beer in a jug. Once or twice she had bought it herself at an Off Licence beer-shop near where they lived, but she had never before been in a public house to drink. She was so confused and ill at ease that she scarcely heard or understood Mrs. Crass, who talked incessantly, principally about their other residents in North Street where they both resided; and about Mr. Crass. She also promised Ruth to introduce her presently – if he came in, as he was almost certain to do – to Mr. Partaker, one of her two lodgers, a most superior young man, who had been with them now for over three years and would not leave on any account. In fact, he had been their lodger in their old house, and when they moved he came with them to North Street, although it was farther away from his place of business than their former residence. Mrs. Crass talked a lot more of the same sort of stuff, to which Ruth listened like one in a dream, and answered with an occasional yes or no.

Meantime, Crass and Easton – the latter had deposited the string-bag on the seat at Ruth's side – and the Semi-drunk and the Besotted Wretch, arranged to play a match of Hooks and Rings, the losers to pay for drinks for all the party, including the two women. Crass and the Semi-drunk tossed up for sides. Crass won and picked the Besotted Wretch, and the game began. It was a one-sided affair from the first, for Easton and the Semi-drunk were no match for the other two. The end of it was that Easton and his partner had to pay for the drinks. The four men had a pint each of four ale, and Mrs. Crass had another threepennyworth of gin. Ruth protested that she did not want any more to drink, but the others ridiculed this, and both the Besotted Wretch and the Semi-drunk seemed to regard her unwillingness as a personal insult, so she allowed them to get her another half-pint of beer, which she was compelled to drink, because she was conscious that the others were watching her to see that she did so.

The Semi-drunk now suggested a return match. He wished to have his revenge. He was a little out of practice, he said, and was only just getting his hand in as they were finishing the other game. Crass and his partner readily assented, and in spite of Ruth's whispered entreaty that they should return home without further delay, Easton insisted on joining the game.

Although they played more carefully than before, and notwithstanding the fact that the Besotted Wretch was very drunk, Easton and his partner were again beaten and once more had to pay for the drinks. The men had a pint each as before. Mrs. Crass – upon whom the liquor so far seemed to have no effect – had another threepennyworth of gin; and Ruth consented to take another glass of beer on condition that Easton would come away directly their drinks were finished. Easton agreed to do so, but instead of keeping his word he began to play a four-handed game of shove-ha'penny with the other three, the sides and stakes being arranged as before.

The liquor was by this time beginning to have some effect upon Ruth: she felt dizzy and confused. Whenever it was necessary to reply to Mrs. Crass's talk she found some difficulty in articulating the words and she knew she was not answering very intelligently. Even when Mrs. Crass introduced her to the interesting Mr. Partaker, who arrived about this time, she was scarcely able to collect herself sufficiently to decline that fascinating gentleman's invitation to have another drink with himself and Mrs. Crass.

After a time a kind of terror took possession of her, and she resolved that if Easton would not come when he had finished the game he was playing, she would go home without him.

Meantime the game of shove-ha'penny proceeded merrily, the majority of the male guests crowding round the board, applauding or censuring the players as occasion demanded. The Semi-drunk was in high glee, for Crass was not much of a hand at this game, and the Besotted Wretch, although playing well, was not able to make up for his partner's want of skill. As the game drew near its end and it became more and more certain that his opponents would be defeated, the joy of the Semi-drunk was unbounded, and he challenged them to make it double or quits – a generous offer which they wisely declined, and shortly afterwards, seeing that their position was hopeless, they capitulated and prepared to pay the penalty of the vanquished.

Crass ordered the drinks and the Besotted Wretch paid half the damage – a pint of four ale for each of the men and the same as before for the ladies. The Old Dear executed the order, but by mistake, being very busy, he served two 'threes' of gin instead of one. Ruth did not want any more at all, but she was afraid to say so, and she did not like to make any fuss about it being the wrong drink, especially as they all assured her that the spirits would do her more good than beer. She did not want either; she wanted to get away, and would have liked to empty the stuff out of the glass on to the floor, but she was afraid that Mrs. Crass or one of the others might see her doing so, and there might be some trouble about it. Anyway, it seemed easier to drink this small quantity of spirits and water than a big glass of beer, the very thought of which now made her feel ill. She drank the stuff which Easton handed to her at a single draught and, handing back the empty glass with a shudder, stood up resolutely.

'Are you coming home now? You promised you would,' she said.

'All right: presently,' replied Easton. 'There's plenty of time; it's not nine yet.'

'That doesn't matter; it's quite late enough. You know we've left the child at home alone in the house. You promised you'd come as soon as you'd finished that other game.'

'All right, all right,' answered Easton impatiently. 'Just wait a minute, I want to see this, and then I'll come.'

'This' was a most interesting problem propounded by Crass, who had arranged eleven matches side by side on the shove-ha'penny board. The problem was to take none away and yet leave only nine. Nearly all the men in the bar were crowding round the shove-ha'penny board, some with knitted brows and drunken gravity trying to solve the puzzle and others waiting curiously for the result. Easton crossed over to see how it was done, and as none of the crowd were able to do the trick, Crass showed that it could be accomplished by simply arranging the eleven matches so as to form the word NINE. Everybody said it was very good indeed, very clever and interesting. Both the Semi-drunk and the Besotted Wretch were reminded by this trick of several others equally good, and they proceeded to do them; and then the men had another pint each all round as a reviver after the mental strain of the last few minutes.

Easton did not know any tricks himself, but he was an interested spectator of those done by several others until Ruth came over and touched his arm.

'Aren't you coming?'

'Wait a minute, can't you?' cried Easton roughly. 'What's your hurry?'

'I don't want to stay here any longer,' said Ruth, hysterically. 'You said you'd come as soon as you saw that trick. If you don't come, I shall go home by myself. I don't want to stay in this place any longer.'

'Well, go by yourself if you want to!' shouted Easton fiercely, pushing her away from him. 'I shall stop 'ere as long as I please, and if you don't like it you can do the other thing.'

Ruth staggered and nearly fell from the force of the push he gave her, and the man turned again to the table to watch the Semi-drunk, who was arranging six matches so as to form the numeral XII, and who said he could prove that this was equal to a thousand.

Ruth waited a few minutes longer, and then as Easton took no further notice of her, she took up the string-bag and the other parcels, and without staying to say good-night to Mrs. Crass – who was earnestly conversing with the interesting Partaker – she with some difficulty opened the door and went out into the street. The cold night air felt refreshing and sweet after the foul atmosphere of the public house, but after a little while she began to feel faint and dizzy, and was conscious also that she was walking unsteadily, and she fancied that people stared at her strangely as they passed. The parcels felt very heavy and awkward to carry, and the string-bag seemed as if it were filled with lead.

Although under ordinary circumstances it was only about ten minutes' walk home from here, she resolved to go by one of the trams which passed by the end of North Street. With this intention, she put down her bag on the pavement at the stopping-place, and waited, resting her hand on the iron pillar at the corner of the street, where a little crowd of people were standing evidently with the same object as herself. Two trams passed without stopping, for they were already full of passengers, a common circumstance on Saturday nights. The next one stopped, and several persons alighted, and then ensued a fierce struggle amongst the waiting crowd for the vacant seats. Men and women pushed, pulled and almost fought, shoving their fists and elbows into each other's sides and breasts and faces. Ruth was quickly thrust aside and nearly knocked down, and the tram, having taken aboard as many passengers as it had accommodation for, passed on. She waited for the next one, and the same scene was enacted with the same result for her, and then, reflecting that if she had not stayed for these trams she might have been home by now, she determined to resume her walk. The parcels felt heavier than ever, and she had not proceeded very far before she was compelled to put the bag down again upon the pavement, outside an empty house.

Leaning against the railings, she felt very tired and ill. Everything around her – the street, the houses, the traffic – seemed vague and shadowy and unreal. Several people looked curiously at her as they passed, but by this time she was scarcely conscious of their scrutiny.

Slyme had gone that evening to the usual 'open-air' conducted by the Shining Light Mission. The weather being fine, they had a most successful meeting, the disciples, including Hunter, Rushton, Sweater, Didlum, and Mrs. Starvem – Ruth's former mistress – assembled in great force so as to be able to deal more effectively with any infidels or hired critics or drunken scoffers who might try to disturb the proceedings; and – possibly as an evidence of how much real faith there was in them – they had also arranged to have a police officer in attendance, to protect them from what they called the 'Powers of Darkness'. One might be excused for thinking that – if they really believed – they would have relied rather upon those powers of Light which they professed to represent on this planet to protect them without troubling to call in the aid of such a 'worldly' force as the police. However, it came to pass that on this occasion the only infidels present were those who were conducting the meeting, but as these consisted for the most part of members of the chapel, it will be seen that the infidel fraternity was strongly represented.

On his way home after the meeting Slyme had to pass by the 'Cricketers' and as he drew near the place he wondered if Easton were there, but he did not like to go and look in, because he was afraid someone might see him coming away and perhaps think he had been in to drink. Just as he arrived opposite the house another man opened the door of the public bar and entered, enabling Slyme to catch a momentary glimpse of the interior, where he saw Easton and Crass with a number of others who were strangers to him, laughing and drinking together.

Slyme hurried away; it had turned very cold, and he was anxious to get home. As he approached the place where the trams stopped to take up passengers and saw that there was a tram in sight he resolved to wait for it and ride home: but when the tram arrived there were only one or two seats vacant, and although he did his best to secure one of these he was unsuccessful, and after a moment's hesitation he decided that it would be quicker to walk than to wait for the next one. He accordingly resumed his journey, but he had not gone very far when he saw a small crowd of people on the pavement on the other side of the road outside an unoccupied house, and although he was in a hurry to get home he crossed over to see what was the matter. There were about twenty people standing there, and in the centre close to the railing there were three or four women whom Slyme could not see although he could hear their voices.

'What's up?' he enquired of a man on the edge of the crowd.

'Oh, nothing much,' returned the other. 'Some young woman; she's either ill, come over faint, or something – or else she's had a drop too much.'

'Quite a respectable-looking young party, too,' said another man.

Several young fellows in the crowd were amusing themselves by making suggestive jokes about the young woman and causing some laughter by the expressions of mock sympathy.

'Doesn't anyone know who she is?' said the second man who had spoken in reply to Slyme's enquiry.

'No,' said a woman who was standing a little nearer the middle of the crowd. 'And she won't say where she lives.'

'She'll be all right now she's had that glass of soda,' said another man, elbowing his way out of the crowd. As this individual came out, Slyme managed to work himself a little further into the group of people, and he uttered an involuntary cry of astonishment as he caught sight of Ruth, very pale, and looking very ill, as she stood clasping one of the railings with her left hand and holding the packages of groceries in the other. She had by this time recovered sufficiently to feel overwhelmed with shame and confusion before the crowd of strangers who hemmed her in on every side, and some of whom she could hear laughing and joking about her. It was therefore with a sensation of intense relief and gratitude that she saw Slyme's familiar face and heard his friendly voice as he forced his way through to her side.

'I can walk home all right now,' she stammered in reply to his anxious questioning. 'If you wouldn't mind carrying some of these things for me.'

He insisted on taking all the parcels, and the crowd, having jumped to the conclusion that he was the young woman's husband, began to dwindle away, one of the jokers remarking 'It's all over!' in a loud voice as he took himself off.

It was only about seven minutes' walk home from there, and as the streets along which they had to pass were not very brilliantly lighted, Ruth was able to lean on Slyme's arm most of the way. When they arrived home, after she had removed her hat, he made her sit down in the armchair by the fire, which was burning brightly, and the kettle was singing on the hob, for she had banked up the fire with cinders and small coal before she went out.

The baby was still asleep in the cradle, but his slumbers had evidently not been of the most restful kind, for he had kicked all the bedclothes off him and was lying all uncovered. Ruth obeyed passively when Slyme told her to sit down, and, lying back languidly in the armchair, she watched him through half-closed eyes and with a slight flush on her face as he deftly covered the sleeping child with the bedclothes and settled him more comfortably in the cot.

Slyme now turned his attention to the fire, and as he placed the kettle upon it he remarked: 'As soon as the water boils I'll make you some strong tea.'

During their walk home she had acquainted Slyme with the cause of her being in the condition in which he found her in the street, and as she reclined in the armchair, drowsily watching him, she wondered what would have happened to her if he had not passed by when he did.

'Are you feeling better?' he asked, looking down at her.

'Yes, thanks. I feel quite well now; but I'm afraid I've given you a lot of trouble.'

'No, you haven't. Nothing I can do for *you* is a trouble to me. But don't you think you'd better take your jacket off? Here, let me help you.'

It took a very long time to get this jacket off, because whilst he was helping her, Slyme kissed her repeatedly and passionately as she lay limp and unresisting in his arms.

CHAPTER 25

The Oblong

During the following week the work at 'The Cave' progressed rapidly towards completion, although, the hours of daylight being so few, the men worked only from 8 a.m. till 4 p.m. and they had their breakfasts before they came. This made 40 hours a week, so that those who were paid sevenpence an hour earned £1. 3. 4. Those who got sixpence-halfpenny drew £1. 1. 8. Those whose wages were fivepence an hour were paid the princely sum of 16/8d. for their week's hard labour, and those whose rate was fourpence-halfpenny 'picked up' 15/-.

And yet there are people who have the insolence to say that Drink is the cause of poverty.

And many of the persons who say this, spend more money than that on drink themselves – every day of their useless lives.

By Tuesday night all the inside was finished with the exception of the kitchen and scullery. The painting of the kitchen had been delayed owing to the non-arrival of the new cooking range, and the scullery was still used as the paint shop. The outside work was also nearly finished: all the first coating was done and the second coating was being proceeded with. According to the specification, all the outside woodwork was supposed to have three coats, and the guttering, rain-pipes and other ironwork two coats, but Crass and Hunter had arranged to make two coats do for most of the windows and woodwork, and all the ironwork was to be made to do with one coat only. The windows were painted in two colours: the sashes dark green and the frames white. All the rest – gables, doors, railings, guttering, etc. – was dark green; and all the dark green paint was made with boiled linseed oil and varnish; no turpentine being allowed to be used on this part of the work.

'This is some bloody fine stuff to 'ave to use, ain't it?' remarked Harlow to Philpot on Wednesday morning. 'It's more like a lot of treacle than anything else.'

'Yes: and it won't arf blister next summer when it gets a bit of sun on it,' replied Philpot with a grin.

'I suppose they're afraid that if they was to put a little turps in, it wouldn't bear out, and they'd 'ave to give it another coat.'

'You can bet yer life that's the reason,' said Philpot. 'But all the same I mean to pinch a drop to put in mine as soon as Cross is gorn.'

'Gorn where?'

'Why, didn't you know? there's another funeral on today? Didn't you see that corfin plate[71] what Owen was writing in the drorin'-room last Saturday mornin'?'

'No. I wasn't 'ere. Don't you remember I was sent away to do a ceilin' and a bit of painting over at Windley?'

'Oh, of course; I forgot,' exclaimed Philpot.

'I reckon Cross and Slyme must be making a small fortune out of all these funerals,' said Harlow. 'This makes the fourth in the last fortnight. What is it they gets for 'em?'

'A shillin' for takin' 'ome the corfin and liftin' in the corpse, and four bob for the funeral – five bob altogether.'

'That's a bit of all right, ain't it?' said Harlow. 'A couple of them in a week besides your week's wages, eh? Five bob for two or three hours work!'

'Yes, the money's all right, mate, but they're welcome to it for my part. I don't want to go messin' about with no corpses,' replied Philpot with a shudder.

'Who is this last party what's dead?' asked Harlow after a pause.

'It's a parson what used to belong to the "Shining Light" Chapel. He'd been abroad for 'is 'ollerdays – to Monte Carlo. It seems 'e was ill before 'e went away, but the change did 'im a lot of good; in fact, 'e was quite recovered, and 'e was coming back again. But while 'e was standin' on the platform at Monte Carlo Station waitin' for the train, a porter runned into 'im with a barrer load o' luggage, and 'e blowed up.'

'Blowed up?'

'Yes,' repeated Philpot. 'Blowed up! Busted! Exploded! All into pieces. But they swep' 'em all up and put it in a corfin and it's to be planted this afternoon.'

Harlow maintained an awestruck silence, and Philpot continued:

'I had a drink the other night with a butcher bloke what used to serve this parson with meat, and we was talkin' about what a strange sort of death[72] it was, but 'e said 'e wasn't at all surprised to 'ear of it; the only thing as 'e wondered at was that the man didn't blow up long ago, considerin' the amount of grub as 'e used to make away with. He ses the quantities of stuff as 'e's took there and seen other tradesmen take was something chronic. Tons of it!'

'What was the parson's name?' asked Harlow.

'Belcher. You must 'ave noticed 'im about the town. A very fat chap,' replied Philpot. 'I'm sorry you wasn't 'ere on Saturday to see the corfin plate. Frank called me in to see the wordin' when 'e'd finished it. It had on: "Jonydab Belcher. Born January 1st 1849. Ascended, December 8th 19—"[73]

'Oh, I know the bloke now!' cried Harlow. 'I remember my youngsters bringin' 'ome a subscription list what they'd got up at the Sunday School to send 'im away for a 'ollerday because 'e was ill, and I gave 'em a penny each to put on their cards because I didn't want 'em to feel mean before the other young 'uns.'

'Yes, it's the same party. Two or three young 'uns asked me to give 'em something to put on at the time. And I see they've got another subscription list on now. I met one of Newman's children yesterday and she showed it to me. It's for an entertainment and a Christmas Tree for all the children what goes to the Sunday School, so I didn't mind giving just a trifle for anything like that.' . . .

'Seems to be gettin' colder, don't it?'

'It's enough to freeze the ears orf a brass monkey!' remarked Easton as he descended from a ladder close by and, placing his pot of paint on the ground, began to try to warm his hands by rubbing and beating them together.

He was trembling, and his teeth were chattering with cold.

'I could just do with a nice pint of beer, now,' he said as he stamped his feet on the ground.

'That's just what I was thinkin',' said Philpot, wistfully, 'and what's more, I mean to 'ave one, too, at dinner-time. I shall nip down to the "Cricketers". Even if I don't get back till a few minutes after one, it won't matter, because Crass and Nimrod will be gorn to the funeral.'

'Will you bring me a pint back with you, in a bottle?' asked Easton.

'Yes, certainly,' said Philpot.

Harlow said nothing. He also would have liked a pint of beer, but, as was usual with him, he had not the necessary cash. Having restored the circulation to a certain extent, they now resumed their work, and only just in time, for a few minutes afterwards they observed Misery peeping round the corner of the house at them and they wondered how long he had been there, and whether he had overheard their conversation.

At twelve o'clock Crass and Slyme cleared off in a great hurry, and a little while afterwards, Philpot took off his apron and put on his coat to go to the 'Cricketers'. When the others found out where he was going, several of them asked him to bring back a drink for them, and then someone suggested that all those who wanted some beer should give twopence each. This was done: one shilling and four-pence was collected and given to Philpot, who was to bring back a gallon of beer in a jar. He promised to get back as soon as ever he could, and some of the shareholders decided not to drink any tea with their dinners, but to wait for the beer, although they knew that it would be nearly time to resume work before he could get back. It would be a quarter to one at the very earliest.

The minutes dragged slowly by, and after a while the only man on the job who had a watch began to lose his temper and refused to answer any more enquiries concerning the time. So presently Bert was sent up to the top of the house to look at a church clock which was visible therefrom, and when he came down he reported that it was ten minutes to one.

Symptoms of anxiety now began to manifest themselves amongst the shareholders, several of whom went down to the main road to see if Philpot was yet in sight, but each returned with the same report – they could see nothing of him.

No one was formally 'in charge' of the job during Crass's absence, but they all returned to their work promptly at one because they feared that Sawkins or some other sneak might report any irregularity to Crass or Misery.

At a quarter-past one, Philpot was still missing and the uneasiness of the shareholders began to develop into a panic. Some of them plainly expressed the opinion that he had gone on the razzle with the money. As the time wore on, this became the general opinion. At two o'clock, all hope of his return having been abandoned, two or three of the shareholders went and drank some of the cold tea.

Their fears were only too well founded, for they saw no more of Philpot till the next morning, when he arrived looking very sheepish and repentant and promised to refund all the money on Saturday. He also made a long, rambling statement from which it appeared that on his way to the 'Cricketers' he met a couple of chaps whom he knew who were out of work, and he invited them to come and have a drink. When they got to the pub, they found there the Semi-drunk and the Besotted Wretch. One drink led to another, and then they started arguing, and he had forgotten all about the gallon of beer until he woke up this morning.

Whilst Philpot was making this explanation they were putting on their aprons and blouses, and Crass was serving out the lots of colour.

Slyme took no part in the conversation, but got ready as quickly as possible and went outside to make a start. The reason for this haste soon became apparent to some of the others, for they noticed that he had selected and commenced painting a large window that was so situated as to be sheltered from the keen wind that was blowing.

The basement of the house was slightly below the level of the ground and there was a sort of a trench or area about three feet deep in front of the basement windows. The banks of this trench were covered with rose trees and evergreens, and the bottom was a mass of slimy, evil-smelling, rain-sodden earth, foul with the excrement of nocturnal animals. To second-coat these basement windows, Philpot and Harlow had to get down into and stand in all this filth, which soaked through the worn and broken soles of their boots. As they worked, the thorns of the rose trees caught and tore their clothing and lacerated the flesh of their half-frozen hands.

Owen and Easton were working on ladders doing the windows immediately above Philpot and Harlow, Sawkins, on another ladder, was painting one of the gables, and the other men were working at different parts of the outside of the house. The boy Bert was painting the iron railings of the front fence. The weather was bitterly cold, the sun was concealed by the dreary expanse of grey cloud that covered the wintry sky.

As they stood there working most of the time they were almost perfectly motionless, the only part of their bodies that were exercised being their right arms. The work they were now doing required to be done very carefully and deliberately, otherwise the glass would be 'messed up' or the white paint of the frames would 'run into' the dark green of the sashes, both colours being wet at the same time, each man having two pots of paint and two sets of brushes. The wind was not blowing in sudden gusts, but swept by in a strong, persistent current that penetrated their clothing and left them trembling and numb with cold. It blew from the right; and it was all the worse on that account, because the right arm, being in use, left that side of the body fully exposed. They were able to keep their left hands in their trousers pockets and the left arm close to the side most of the time. This made a lot of difference.

Another reason why it is worse when the wind strikes upon one from the right side is that the buttons on a man's coat are always on the right side, and consequently the wind gets underneath. Philpot realised this all the more because some of the buttons on his coat and waistcoat were missing.

As they worked on, trembling with cold, and with their teeth chattering, their faces and hands became of that pale violet colour generally seen on the lips of a corpse. Their eyes became full of water and the lids were red and inflamed. Philpot's and Harlow's boots were soon wet through, with the water they absorbed from the damp ground, and their feet were sore and intensely painful with cold.

Their hands, of course, suffered the most, becoming so numbed that they were unable to feel the brushes they held; in fact, presently, as Philpot was taking a dip of colour, the brush fell from his hand into the pot; and then, finding that he was unable to move his fingers, he put his hand into his trousers pocket to thaw, and began to walk about, stamping his feet upon the ground. His example was quickly followed by Owen, Easton and Harlow, and they all went round the corner to the sheltered side of the house where Slyme was working, and began walking up and down, rubbing their hands, stamping their feet and swinging their arms to warm themselves.

'If I thought Nimrod wasn't comin', I'd put my overcoat on and work in it,' remarked Philpot, 'but you never knows when to expect the b—r, and if 'e saw me in it, it would mean the bloody push.'

'It wouldn't interfere with our workin' if we did wear 'em,' said Easton; 'in fact, we'd be able to work all the quicker if we wasn't so cold.'

'Even if Misery didn't come, I suppose Crass would 'ave something to say if we did put 'em on,' continued Philpot.

'Well, yer couldn't blame 'im if 'e did say something, could yer?' said Slyme, offensively. 'Crass would get into a row 'imself if 'Unter came and saw us workin' in overcoats. It would look ridiclus.'

Slyme suffered less from the cold than any of them, not only because he had secured the most sheltered window, but also because he was better clothed than most of the rest.

'What's Crass supposed to be doin' inside?' asked Easton as he tramped up and down, with his shoulders hunched up and his hands thrust deep into the pockets of his trousers.

'Blowed if I know,' replied Philpot. 'Messin' about touchin' up or makin' colour. He never does 'is share of a job like this; 'e knows 'ow to work things all right for 'isself.'

'What if 'e does? We'd do the same if we was in 'is place, and so would anybody else,' said Slyme, and added sarcastically: 'Or p'raps you'd give all the soft jobs to other people and do all the rough yerself!'

Slyme knew that, although they were speaking of Crass, they were also alluding to himself, and as he replied to Philpot he looked slyly at Owen, who had so far taken no part in the conversation.

'It's not a question of what we would do,' chimed in Harlow. 'It's a question of what's fair. If it's not fair for Crass to pick all the soft jobs for 'imself, and leave all the rough for others, the fact that we might do the same if we 'ad the chance don't make it right.'

'No one can be blamed for doing the best he can for himself under existing circumstances,' said Owen in reply to Slyme's questioning look. 'That is the principle of the present system – every man for himself and the devil take the rest. For my own part I don't pretend to practise unselfishness. I don't pretend to guide my actions by the rules laid down in the Sermon on the Mount. But it's certainly surprising to hear you who profess to be a follower of Christ – advocating selfishness. Or, rather, it would be surprising if it were not that the name of "Christian" has ceased to signify one who follows Christ, and has come to mean only liar and hypocrite.'

Slyme made no answer. Possibly the fact that he *was* a true believer enabled him to bear this insult with meekness and humility.

'I wonder what time it is?' interposed Philpot.

Slyme looked at his watch. It was nearly ten o'clock.

'Jesus Christ! Is that all?' growled Easton as they returned to work. 'Two hours more before dinner!'

Only two more hours, but to these miserable, half-starved, ill-clad wretches, standing here in the bitter wind that pierced their clothing and seemed to be tearing at their very hearts and lungs with icy fingers, it appeared like an eternity. To judge by the eagerness with which they longed for dinner-time, one might have thought they had some glorious banquet to look forward to instead of bread and cheese and onions, or bloaters – and stewed tea.

Two more hours of torture before dinner; and three more hours after that. And then, thank God, it would be too dark to see to work any longer.

It would have been much better for them if, instead of being 'Freemen', they had been slaves, and the property, instead of the hirelings, of Mr. Rushton. As it was, *he* would not have cared if one or all of them had become ill or died from the effects of exposure. It would have made no difference to him. There were plenty of others out of work and on the verge of starvation who would be very glad to take their places. But if they had been Rushton's property, such work as this would have been deferred until it could be done without danger to the health and lives of the slaves; or at any rate, even if it were proceeded with during such weather, their owner would have seen to it that they were properly clothed and fed; he would have taken as much care of them as he would of his horse.

People always take great care of their horses. If they were to overwork a horse and make it ill, it would cost something for medicine and the veterinary surgeon, to say nothing of the animal's board and lodging. If they were to work their horses to death, they would have to buy others. But none of these considerations applies to workmen. If they work a man to death they can get another for nothing at the corner of the next street. They don't have to buy him; all they have to do is to give him enough money to provide him with food and clothing – of a kind – while he is working for them. If they only make him ill, they will not have to feed him or provide him with medical care while he is laid up. He will either go without these things or pay for them himself. At the same time it must be admitted that the workman scores over both the horse and the slave, inasmuch as he enjoys the priceless blessing of Freedom. If he does not like the hirer's conditions he need not accept them. He can refuse to work, and he can go and starve. There are no ropes on him. He is a Free man. He is the Heir of all the Ages. He enjoys perfect Liberty. He has the right to choose freely which he will do – Submit or Starve. Eat dirt, or eat nothing.

The wind blew colder and colder. The sky, which at first had shown small patches of blue through rifts in the masses of clouds, had now become uniformly grey. There was every indication of an impending fall of snow.

The men perceived this with conflicting feelings. If it did commence to snow, they would not be able to continue this work, and therefore they found themselves involuntarily wishing that it *would* snow, or rain, or hail, or anything that would stop the work. But on the other hand, if the weather prevented them getting on with the outside, some of them would have to 'stand off', because the inside was practically finished. None of them wished to lose any time if they could possibly help it, because there were only ten days more before Christmas.

The morning slowly wore away and the snow did not fall. The hands worked on in silence, for they were in no mood for talking, and not only that, but they were afraid that Hunter or Rushton or Crass might be watching them from behind some bush or tree, or through some of the windows. This dread possessed them to such an extent that most of them were almost afraid even to look round, and kept steadily on at work. None of them wished to spoil his chance of being kept on to help to do the other house that it was reported Rushton & Co. were going to 'do up' for Mr. Sweater.

Twelve o'clock came at last, and Crass's whistle had scarcely ceased to sound before they all assembled in the kitchen before the roaring fire. Sweater had sent in two tons of coal and had given orders that fires were to be lit every day in nearly every room to make the house habitable by Christmas.

'I wonder if it's true as the firm's got another job to do for old Sweater?' remarked Harlow as he was toasting a bloater on the end of a pointed stick.

'True? No!' said the man on the pail scornfully. 'It's all bogy. You know that empty 'ouse as they said Sweater 'ad bought – the one that Rushton and Nimrod was seen lookin' at?'

'Yes,' replied Harlow. The other men listened with evident interest.

'Well, they wasn't pricing it up at all! The landlord of that 'ouse is abroad, and there was some plants in the garden as Rushton thought 'e'd like, and 'e was tellin' Misery which ones 'e wanted. And afterwards old Pontius Pilate came up with Ned Dawson and a truck. They made two or three journeys and took bloody near everything in the garden as was worth takin'. What didn't go to Rushton's place went to 'Unter's.'

The disappointment of their hopes for another job was almost forgotten in their interest in this story.

'Who told you about it?' said Harlow.

'Ned Dawson 'imself. It's right enough what I say. Ask 'im.'

Ned Dawson, usually called 'Bundy's mate', had been away from the house for a few days down at the yard doing odd jobs, and had only come back to the 'Cave' that morning. On being appealed to, he corroborated Dick Wantley's statement.

'They'll be gettin' theirselves into trouble if they ain't careful,' remarked Easton.

'Oh, no they won't. Rushton's too artful for that. It seems the agent[74] is a pal of 'is, and they worked it between 'em.'

'Wot a bloody cheek, though!' exclaimed Harlow.

'Oh, that's nothing to some of the things I've knowed 'em do before now,' said the man on the pail. 'Why, don't you remember, back in the summer, that carved hoak hall table as Rushton pinched out of that 'ouse on Grand Parade?'

'Yes; that was a bit of all right too, wasn't it?' cried Philpot, and several of the others laughed.

'You know, that big 'ouse we did up last summer – No. 596,' Wantley continued, for the benefit of those not 'in the know'. 'Well, it 'ad bin empty for a long time and we found this 'ere table in a cupboard under the stairs. A bloody fine table it was too. One of them bracket tables what you fix to the wall, without no legs. It 'ad a 'arf-round marble top to it, and underneath was a carved hoak figger, a mermaid, with 'er arms up over 'er 'ead 'oldin' up the table top – something splendid!' The man on the pail waxed enthusiastic as he thought of it. 'Must 'ave been worth at least five quid. Well, just as we pulled this 'ere table out, who should come in but Rushton, and when 'e seen it, 'e tells Crass to cover it over with a sack and not to let nobody see it. And then 'e clears orf to the shop and sends the boy down with the truck and 'as it took up to 'is own 'ouse, and it's there now, fixed in the front 'all. I was sent up there a couple of months ago to paint and varnish the lobby doors and I seen it meself. There's a pitcher called "The Day of Judgement" 'angin' on the wall just over it – thunder and lightning and earthquakes and corpses gettin' up out o' their graves – something bloody 'orrible! And underneath the picture is a card with a tex out of the Bible – "Christ is the 'ead of this 'ouse: the unknown guest at every meal. The silent listener to every conversation." I was workin' there for three or four days and I got to know it orf by 'eart.'

'Well, that takes the biskit, don't it?' said Philpot.

'Yes: but the best of it was,' the man on the pail proceeded, 'the best of it was, when ole Misery 'eard about the table, 'e was so bloody wild because 'e didn't get it 'imself that 'e went upstairs and pinched one of the venetian blinds and 'ad it took up to 'is own 'ouse by the boy, and a few days arterwards one of the carpenters 'ad to go and fix it up in 'is bedroom.'

'And wasn't it never found out?' enquired Easton.

'Well, there was a bit of talk about it. The agent wanted to know where it was, but Pontius Pilate swore black and white as there 'adn't been no blind in that room, and the end of it was that the firm got the order to supply a new one.'

'What I can't understand is, who did the table belong to?' said Harlow.

'It was a fixture belongin' to the 'ouse,' replied Wantley. 'But I suppose the former tenants had some piece of furniture of their own that they wanted to put in the 'all where this table was fixed, so they took it down and stored it away in this 'ere cupboard, and when they left the 'ouse I suppose they didn't trouble to put it back again.

Anyway, there was the mark on the wall where it used to be fixed, but when we did the staircase down, the place was papered over, and I suppose the landlord or the agent never give the table a thought. Anyhow, Rushton got away with it all right.'

A number of similar stories were related by several others concerning the doings of different employers they had worked for, but after a time the conversation reverted to the subject that was uppermost in their thoughts – the impending slaughter, and the improbability of being able to obtain another job, considering the large number of men who were already out of employment.

'I can't make it out, myself,' remarked Easton. 'Things seems to get worse every year. There don't seem to be 'arf the work about that there used to be, and even what there is is messed up anyhow, as if the people who 'as it done can't afford to pay for it.'

'Yes,' said Harlow; 'that's true enough. Why, just look at the work that's in one o' them 'ouses on the Grand Parade. People must 'ave 'ad more money to spend in those days, you know; all those massive curtain cornishes over the drawing- and dining-room winders – gilded solid! Why, nowadays they'd want all the bloody 'ouse done down right through – inside and out, for the money it cost to gild one of them.'

'It seems that nearly everybody is more or less 'ard up nowadays,' said Philpot. 'I'm jiggered if I can understand it, but there it is.'

'You should ast Owen to explain it to yer,' remarked Cross with a jeering laugh. ' 'E knows all about wot's the cause of poverty, but 'e won't tell nobody. 'E's been *goin'* to tell us wot it is for a long time past, but it don't seem to come orf.'

Crass had not yet had an opportunity of producing the *Obscurer* cutting, and he made this remark in the hope of turning the conversation into a channel that would enable him to do so. But Owen did not respond, and went on reading his newspaper.

'We ain't 'ad no lectures at all lately, 'ave we?' said Harlow in an injured tone. 'I think it's about time Owen explained what the real cause of poverty is. I'm beginning to get anxious about it.'

The others laughed.

*　　*　　*

When Philpot had finished eating his dinner he went out of the kitchen and presently returned with a small pair of steps, which he opened and placed in a corner of the room, with the back of the steps facing the audience.

'There you are, me son!' he exclaimed to Owen. 'There's a pulpit for yer.'

'Yes! come on 'ere!' cried Crass, feeling in his waistcoat pocket for the cutting. 'Tell us wot's the real cause of poverty.'

'Ear, 'ear,' shouted the man on the pail. 'Git up into the bloody pulpit and give us a sermon.'

As Owen made no response to the invitations, the crowd began to hoot and groan.

'Come on, man,' whispered Philpot, winking his goggle eye persuasively at Owen. 'Come on, just for a bit of fun, to pass the time away.'

Owen accordingly ascended the steps – much to the secret delight of Crass – and was immediately greeted with a round of enthusiastic applause.

'There you are, you see,' said Philpot, addressing the meeting. 'It's no use booin' and threatenin', because 'e's one of them lecturers wot can honly be managed with kindness. If it 'adn't a bin fer me, 'e wouldn't 'ave agreed to speak at all.'

Philpot having been unanimously elected chairman, proposed by Harlow and seconded by the man on the pail, Owen commenced:

'Mr. Chairman and gentlemen:

'Unaccustomed as I am to public speaking, it is with some degree of hesitation that I venture to address myself to such a large, distinguished, fashionable, and intelligent looking audience as that which I have the honour of seeing before me on the present occasion.' (Applause.)

'One of the finest speakers I've ever 'eard!' remarked the man on the pail in a loud whisper to the chairman, who motioned him to be silent.

Owen continued:

'In some of my previous lectures I have endeavoured to convince you that money is in itself of no value and of no real use whatever. In this I am afraid I have been rather unsuccessful.'

'Not a bit of it, mate,' cried Crass, sarcastically. 'We all agrees with it.'

' 'Ear, 'ear,' shouted Easton. 'If a bloke was to come in 'ere now and orfer to give me a quid – I'd refuse it!'

'So would I,' said Philpot.

'Well, whether you agree or not, the fact remains. A man might possess so much money that, in England, he would be comparatively rich, and yet if he went to some country where the cost of living is very high he would find himself in a condition of poverty. Or one might conceivably be in a place where the necessaries of life could not be bought for money at all. Therefore it is more conducive to an intelligent understanding of the subject if we say that to be rich consists not necessarily in having much money, but in being able to enjoy an abundance of the things that are made by work; and that poverty consists not merely in being without money, but in being short of the necessaries and comforts of life – or in other words in being short of the Benefits of Civilisation, the things that are all, without exception, produced by work. Whether you agree or not with anything else that I say, you will all admit that that is our condition at the present time. We do not enjoy a full share of the benefits of civilisation – we are all in a state of more or less abject poverty.'

'Question!' cried Crass, and there were loud murmurs of indignant dissent from several quarters as Owen proceeded:

'How does it happen that we are so short of the things that are made by work?'

'The reason why we're short of the things that's made by work,' interrupted Crass, mimicking Owen's manner, 'is that we ain't got the bloody money to buy 'em.'

'Yes,' said the man on the pail; 'and as I said before, if all the money in the country was shared out equal today according to Owen's ideas – in six months' time it would be all back again in the same 'ands as it is now, and what are you goin' to do then?'

'Share again, of course.'

This answer came derisively from several places at the same instant, and then they all began speaking at once, vying with each other in ridiculing the foolishness of 'them there Socialists', whom they called 'The Sharers Out'.

Barrington was almost the only one who took no part in the conversation. He was seated in his customary place and, as usual, silently smoking, apparently oblivious of his surroundings.

'I never said anything about "sharing out all the money",' said Owen during a lull in the storm, 'and I don't know of any Socialist who advocates anything of the kind. Can any of you tell me the name of someone who proposes to do so?'

No one answered, so Owen repeated his enquiry, this time addressing himself directly to Crass, who had been one of the loudest in denouncing and ridiculing the 'Sharers Out'. Thus cornered, Crass – who knew absolutely nothing about the subject – for a few moments looked rather foolish. Then he began to talk in a very loud voice:

'Why, it's a well-known fact. Everybody knows that's what they wants. But they take bloody good care they don't act up to it theirselves, though. Look at them there Labour members of Parliament[75] – a lot of b—rs what's too bloody lazy to work for their livin'! What the bloody 'ell was they before they got there? Only workin' men, the same as you and me! But they've got the gift o' the gab and – '

'Yes, we know all about that,' said Owen, 'but what I'm asking you is to tell us who advocates taking all the money in the country and sharing it out equally?'

'And I say that everybody knows that's what they're after!' shouted Crass. 'And you know it as well as I do. A fine thing!' he added indignantly. 'Accordin' to that idear, a bloody scavenger or a farm labourer ought to get as much wages as you or me!'

'We can talk about that some other time. What I want to know at present is – what authority have you for saying that Socialists believe in sharing out all the money equally amongst all the people?'

'Well, that's what I've always understood they believed in doing,' said Crass rather lamely.

'It's a well-known fact,' said several others.

'Come to think of it,' continued Crass as he drew the *Obscurer* cutting from his waistcoat pocket, 'I've got a little thing 'ere that I've been goin' to read to yer. It's out of the *Obscurer*. I'd forgotten all about it.'

Remarking that the print was too small for his own eyes, he passed the slip of paper to Harlow, who read aloud as follows:

PROVE YOUR PRINCIPLES; OR, LOOK AT BOTH SIDES

'I wish I could open your eyes to the true misery of our condition: injustice, tyranny and oppression!' said a discontented hack to a weary-looking cob as they stood side by side in unhired cabs.

'I'd rather have them opened to something pleasant, thank you,' replied the cob.

'I am sorry for you. If you could enter into the noble aspirations – ' the hack began.

'Talk plain. What would you have?' said the cob, interrupting him.

'What would I have? Why, equality, and share and share alike all over the world,' said the hack.

'You *mean* that?' said the cob.

'Of course I do. What right have those sleek, pampered hunters and racers to their warm stables and high feed, their grooms and jockeys? It is really heart-sickening to think of it,' replied the hack.

'I don't know but you may be right,' said the cob, 'and to show I'm in earnest, as no doubt you are, let me have half the good beans you have in your bag, and you shall have half the musty oats and chaff I have in mine. There's nothing like proving one's principles.'

Original Parables. By Mrs. Prosser.

'There you are!' cried several voices.

'What does *that* mean?' cried Crass, triumphantly. 'Why don't you go and share your wages with the chaps what's out of work?'

'What does it mean?' replied Owen contemptuously. 'It means that if the Editor of the *Obscurer* put that in his paper as an argument against Socialism, either he is of feeble intellect himself or else he thinks that the majority of his readers are. That isn't an argument against Socialism – it's an argument against the hypocrites who pretend to be Christians – the people who profess to "Love their neighbours as themselves"[76] – who pretend to believe in Universal Brotherhood, and that they do not love the world or the things of the world and say that they are merely "Pilgrims on their way to a better land". As for why *I* don't do it – why should I? I don't pretend to be a Christian. But you're all "Christians" – why don't *you* do it?'

'We're not talkin' about religion,' exclaimed Crass, impatiently.

'Then what *are* you talking about? I never said anything about "Sharing Out" or "Bearing one another's burdens". I don't profess to "Give to everyone who asks of me" or to "Give my cloak to the man who takes away my coat".[77] I have read that Christ taught that His followers must do all these things, but as I do not pretend to be one of His followers I don't do them. But you believe in Christianity: why don't you do the things that He said?'

As nobody seemed to know the answer to this question, the lecturer proceeded:

'In this matter the difference between so-called "Christians" and Socialists is this: Christ taught the Fatherhood of God and the Brotherhood of Men. Those who today pretend to be Christ's followers hypocritically profess to carry out those teachings *now*. But they don't. They have arranged "The Battle of Life" system instead!

'The Socialist – very much against his will – finds himself in the midst of this horrible battle, and he appeals to the other combatants to cease from fighting and to establish a system of Brotherly Love and Mutual Helpfulness, but he does not hypocritically pretend to practise brotherly love towards those who will not agree to his appeal, and who compel him to fight with them for his very life. He knows that in this battle he must either fight or go under. Therefore, in self-defence, he fights; but all the time he continues his appeal for the cessation of the slaughter. He pleads for the changing of the system. He advocates Co-operation instead of Competition: but how can he co-operate with people who insist on competing with him? No individual can practise co-operation by himself! Socialism can only be practised by the Community – that is the meaning of the word. At present, the other members of the community – the "Christians" – deride and oppose the Socialist's appeal.

'It is these pretended Christians who do not practise what they preach, because, all the time they are singing their songs of Brother-hood and Love, they are fighting with each other, and strangling each other, and trampling each other under foot in their horrible "Battle of Life"!

'No Socialist suggests "Sharing out" money or anything else in the manner you say. And another thing: if you only had a little more sense you might be able to perceive that this stock "argument" of yours is really an argument against the present system, inasmuch as it proves that Money is in itself of no use whatever. Supposing all the money *was* shared out equally; and suppose there was enough of it for everyone to have ten thousand pounds; and suppose they then all thought they were rich and none of them would work. What would they live on? Their money? Could they eat it or drink it or wear it? It wouldn't take them very long to find out that this wonderful money – which under the present system is the most powerful thing in existence – is really of no more use than so much dirt. They would speedily perish, not from lack of money, but from lack of wealth – that is, from lack of the things that are made by work. And further, it is quite true that if all the money were dis-tributed equally amongst all the people tomorrow, it would all be up in heaps again in a very short time. But that only proves that while the present Money System remains, it will be impossible to do away with poverty, for heaps in some places mean little or nothing in other places. Therefore while the money system lasts we are bound to have poverty and all the evils it brings in its train.'

'Oh, of course everybody's an idjit except you,' sneered Crass, who was beginning to feel rather fogged.

'I rise to a pint of order,' said Easton.

'And I rise to order a pint,' cried Philpot.

'Order what the bloody 'ell you like,' remarked Harlow, 'so long as I 'aven't got to pay for it.'

'Mine's a pint of porter,' observed the man on the pail.

'The pint is,' proceeded Easton, 'when does the lecturer intend to explain to us what is the real cause of poverty.'

' 'Ear, 'ear,' cried Harlow. 'That's what *I* want to know, too.'

'And what *I* should like to know is, who is supposed to be givin' this 'ere lecture?' enquired the man on the pail.

'Why, Owen, of course,' replied Harlow.

'Well, why don't you try to keep quiet for a few minutes and let 'im get on with it?'

'The next b—r wot interrupts,' cried Philpot, rolling up his shirt-sleeves and glaring threateningly round upon the meeting. 'The next b—r wot interrupts goes out through the bloody winder!'

At this, everybody pretended to be very frightened, and edged away as far as possible from Philpot. Easton, who was sitting next to him, got up and crossed over to Owen's vacant seat. The man on the pail was the only one who did not seem nervous; perhaps he felt safer because he was, as usual, surrounded by a moat.

'Poverty,' resumed the lecturer, 'consists in a shortage of the necessaries of life – or rather, of the benefits of civilisation.'

'You've said that about a 'undred times before,' snarled Crass.

'I know I have; and I have no doubt I shall have to say it about five hundred times more before you understand what it means.'

'Get on with the bloody lecture,' shouted the man on the pail. 'Never mind arguin' the point.'

'Well, keep horder, can't you?' cried Philpot, fiercely, 'and give the man a chance.'

'All these things are produced in the same way,' proceeded Owen. 'They are made from the Raw materials by those who work – aided by machinery. When we enquire into the cause of the present shortage of these things, the first question we should ask is – Are there not sufficient of the raw materials in existence to enable us to produce enough to satisfy the needs of all?

'The answer to this question is – There are undoubtedly more than sufficient of all the raw materials.

'Insufficiency of raw material is therefore not the cause. We must look in another direction.

'The next question is – Are we short of labour? Is there not a sufficient number of people able and willing to work? Or is there not enough machinery?

'The answers to these questions are – There are plenty of people able and willing to work, and there is plenty of machinery!

'These things being so, how comes this extraordinary result? How is it that the benefits of civilisation are not produced in sufficient quantity to satisfy the needs of all? How is it that the majority of the people always have to go without most of the refinements, comforts, and pleasure of life, and very often without even the bare necessaries of existence?

'Plenty of materials – Plenty of Labour – Plenty of Machinery – and, nearly everybody going short of nearly everything!

'The cause of this extraordinary state of affairs is that although we possess the means of producing more than abundance for all, we also have an imbecile system of managing our affairs.

'The present Money System prevents us from doing the necessary work, and consequently causes the majority of the population to go short of the things that can be made by work. They suffer want in the midst of the means of producing abundance. They remain idle because they are bound and fettered with a chain of gold.

'Let us examine the details of this insane, idiotic, imbecile system.'

Owen now asked Philpot to pass him a piece of charred wood from under the grate, and having obtained what he wanted, he drew upon the wall a quadrangular figure about four feet in length and one foot deep. The walls of the kitchen had not yet been cleaned off, so it did not matter about disfiguring them.

This represents the whole of the adult population of the country.

'To find out the cause of the shortage in this country of the things that can be made by work it is first of all necessary to find out how people spend their time. Now this square represents the whole of the adult population of this country. There are many different classes of people, engaged in a great number of different occupations. Some of them are helping to produce the benefits of civilisation, and some are not. All these people help to consume these things, but when we enquire into their occupations we shall find that although the majority are workers, only a comparatively small number are engaged in actually producing either the benefits of civilisation or the necessaries of life.' . . .

Order being once more restored, the lecturer turned again to the drawing on the wall and stretched out his hand, evidently with the intention of making some addition to it, but instead of doing so he paused irresolutely, and faltering, let his arm drop down again by his side.

An absolute, disconcerting silence reigned. His embarrassment and nervousness increased. He knew that they were unwilling to hear or talk or think about such subjects as the cause of poverty at all. They preferred to make fun of and ridicule them. He knew they would refuse to try to see the meaning of what he wished to say if it were at all difficult or obscure. How was he to put it to them so that they would *have* to understand it whether they wished to or not. It was almost impossible.

It would be easy enough to convince them if they would only take a *little* trouble and try to understand, but he knew that they certainly would not 'worry' themselves about such a subject as this; it was not as if it were some really important matter, such as a smutty story, a game of hooks and rings or shove-ha'penny, something concerning football or cricket, horse-racing or the doings of some Royal personage or aristocrat.

The problem of the cause of poverty was only something that concerned their own and their children's future welfare. Such an unimportant matter, being undeserving of any earnest attention, must be put before them so clearly and plainly that they would be compelled to understand it at a glance; and it was almost impossible to do it.

Observing his hesitation, some of the men began to snigger.

' 'E seems to 'ave got 'isself into a bit of a fog,' remarked Crass in a loud whisper to Slyme, who laughed.

The sound roused Owen, who resumed:

'All these people help to consume the things produced by labour. We will now divide them into separate classes. Those who help to produce; those who do nothing, those who do harm, and those who are engaged in unnecessary work.'

'And,' sneered Crass, 'those who are engaged in unnecessary talk.'

'First we will separate those who not only do nothing, but do not even pretend to be of any use; people who would consider themselves disgraced if they by any chance did any useful work. This class includes, tramps, beggars, the "Aristocracy", "Society" people, great

landowners, and generally all those possessed of hereditary wealth.'
As he spoke he drew a vertical line across one end of the oblong.

1	
Tramps, Beggars, Society People, the 'Aristocracy', Great Landowners, All those possessed of hereditary Wealth.	

'These people do absolutely nothing except devour or enjoy the things produced by the labour of others.

'Our next division represents those who do work of a kind – "mental" work if you like to call it so – work that benefits themselves and harms other people. Employers – or rather Exploiters of Labour; Thieves, Swindlers, Pickpockets; profit seeking shareholders; burglars; Bishops; Financiers; Capitalists, and those persons humorously called "Ministers" of religion. If you remember that the word "minister" means "servant" you will be able to see the joke.

1	2	
Tramps, Beggars, Society People, the 'Aristocracy', Great Landowners, All those possessed of hereditary Wealth.	Exploiters of Labour, Thieves, Swindlers, Pickpockets, Burglars, Bishops, Financiers, Capitalists, Shareholders, 'Ministers' of Religion.	

'None of these people produce anything themselves, but by means of cunning and scheming they contrive between them to obtain possession of a very large portion of the things produced by the labour of others.

'Number three stands for those who work for wages or salaries, doing *unnecessary* work. That is, producing things or doing things which – though useful and necessary to the Imbecile System – cannot be described as the necessaries of life or the benefits of civilisation.

This is the largest section of all. It comprises Commercial Travellers, Canvassers, Insurance agents, commission agents, the greater number of Shop Assistants, the majority of clerks, workmen employed in the construction and adornment of business premises, people occupied with what they call "Business", which means being very busy without producing anything. Then there is a vast army of people engaged in designing, composing, painting or printing advertisements, things which are for the most part of no utility whatever, the object of most advertisements is merely to persuade people to buy from one firm rather than from another. If you want some butter it doesn't matter whether you buy it from Brown or Jones or Robinson.'

1	2	3	
Tramps, Beggars, Society People, the 'Aristocracy,' Great Landowners, All those possessed of hereditary Wealth.	Exploiters of Labour, Thieves, Swindlers, Pickpockets, Burglars, Bishops, Financiers, Capitalists, Shareholders, 'Ministers' of Religion.	All those engaged in unnecessary work.	

During the delivery of this part of the lecture, the audience began to manifest symptoms of impatience and dissent. Perceiving this, Owen, speaking very rapidly, continued:

'If you go down town, you will see half a dozen drapers' shops within a stone's-throw of each other – often even next door to each other – all selling the same things. You can't possibly think that all those shops are really necessary? You know that one of them would serve the purpose for which they are all intended – to store and serve as a centre for the distribution of the things that are made by work. If you will admit that five out of the six shops are not really necessary, you must also admit that the men who built them, and the salesmen and women or other assistants engaged in them, and the men who design and write and print their advertisements are all doing unnecessary work; all really wasting their time and labour, time and labour that might be employed in helping to produce these things that we are at present short of. You must admit that none of these people are engaged in producing either the necessaries of life or the benefits of civilisation. They buy them, and sell them, and handle them, and haggle over them, and display them, in the plateglass windows of "Stores" and "Emporiums" and make profit out of them, and use them, but these people themselves produce nothing that is necessary to life or happiness, and the things that some of them do produce are only necessary to the present imbecile system.'

'What the 'ell sort of a bloody system do you think we ought to 'ave, then?' interrupted the man on the pail.

'Yes: you're very good at finding fault,' sneered Slyme, 'but why don't you tell us 'ow it's all going to be put right?'

'Well, that's not what we're talking about now, is it?' replied Owen. 'At present we're only trying to find out how it is that there is not sufficient produced for everyone to have enough of the things that are made by work. Although most of the people in number three work very hard, they produce Nothing.'

'This is a lot of bloody rot!' exclaimed Crass, impatiently.

'Even if there is more shops than what's actually necessary,' cried Harlow, 'it all helps people to get a livin'! If half of 'em was shut up, it would just mean that all them what works there would be out of a job. Live and let live, I say: all these things makes work.'

' 'Ear, 'ear,' shouted the man behind the moat.

'Yes, I know it makes "work",' replied Owen, 'but we can't live on mere "work", you know. To live in comfort we need a sufficiency of the things that can be made by work. A man might work very hard and yet be wasting his time if he were not producing something necessary or useful.

'Why are there so many shops and stores and emporiums? Do you imagine they exist for the purpose of giving those who build them, or work in them, a chance to earn a living? Nothing of the sort. They are carried on, and exorbitant prices are charged for the articles they sell, to enable the proprietors to amass fortunes, and to pay extortionate rents to the landlords. That is why the wages and salaries of nearly all those who do the work created by these businesses are cut down to the lowest possible point.'

'We knows all about that,' said Crass, 'but you can't get away from it that all these things makes Work; and that's what we wants – Plenty of Work.'

Cries of ' 'Ear, 'ear,' and expressions of dissent from the views expressed by the lecturer resounded through the room, nearly everyone speaking at the same time. After a while, when the row had in some measure subsided, Owen resumed:

'Nature has not provided ready-made all the things necessary for the life and happiness of mankind. In order to obtain these things we have to Work. The only rational labour is that which is directed to the creation of those things. Any kind of work which does not help us to attain this object is a ridiculous, idiotic, criminal, imbecile, waste of time.

'That is what the great army of people represented by division number three are doing at present: they are all very busy – working very hard – but to all useful intents and purposes they are doing Nothing.'

'Well, all right,' said Harlow. ' 'Ave it yer own way, but there's no need to keep on repeating the same thing over an' over again.'

'The next division,' resumed Owen, 'stands for those who are engaged in really useful work – the production of the benefits of civilisation – the necessaries, refinements and comforts of life.'

1	2	3	4	
Tramps, Beggars, Society People, the 'Aristocracy', Great Landowners, All those possessed of hereditary Wealth.	Exploiters of Labour, Thieves, Swindlers, Pickpockets, Burglars, Bishops, Financiers, Capitalists, Shareholders, 'Ministers' of Religion.	All those engaged in unnecessary work.	All those engaged in necessary work – the production of the benefits of civilisation.	UNEMPLOYED.

'Hooray!' shouted Philpot, leading off a cheer which was taken up enthusiastically by the crowd, 'Hooray! This is where *we* comes in,' he added, nodding his head and winking his goggle eyes at the meeting.

'I wish to call the chairman to horder,' said the man on the pail.

When Owen had finished writing in the list of occupations several members of the audience rose to point out that those engaged in the production of beer had been omitted. Owen rectified this serious oversight and proceeded:

'As most of the people in number four are out of work at least one quarter of their time, we must reduce the size of this division by one fourth – so. The grey part represents the unemployed.'

'But some of those in number three are often unemployed as well,' said Harlow.

'Yes: but as *they* produce nothing even when they are at work we need not trouble to classify them unemployed, because our present purpose is only to discover the reason why there is not enough produced for everyone to enjoy abundance; and this – the Present System of conducting our affairs – is the reason of the shortage – the cause of poverty. When you reflect that all the other people are devouring the things produced by those in number four – can you wonder that there is not plenty for all?'

' 'Devouring' is a good word,' said Philpot, and the others laughed.

The lecturer now drew a small square upon the wall below the other drawing. This square he filled in solid black.

1	2	3	4	
Tramps, Beggars, Society People, the 'Aristocracy', Great Landowners, All those possessed of hereditary Wealth.	Exploiters of Labour, Thieves, Swindlers, Pickpockets, Burglars, Bishops, Financiers, Capitalists, Shareholders, 'Ministers' of Religion.	All those engaged in unnecessary work.	All those engaged in necessary work – the production of the benefits of civilisation.	UNEMPLOYED.

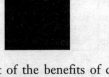

This represents the total of the things produced by the people in division 4.

'This represents the total amount of the benefits of civilisation and necessaries of life produced by the people in number four. We now proceed to "Share Out" the things in the same way as they are actually divided amongst the different classes of the population under the present imbecile system.

'As the people in divisions one and two are universally considered to be the most worthy and deserving we give them – two thirds of the whole.

'The remainder we give to be "Shared Out" amongst the people represented by divisions three and four.

1	2	3	4	
Tramps, Beggars, Society People, the 'Aristocracy', Great Landowners, All those possessed of hereditary Wealth.	Exploiters of Labour, Thieves, Swindlers, Pickpockets, Burglars, Bishops, Financiers, Capitalists, Shareholders, 'Ministers' of Religion.	All those engaged in unnecessary work.	All those engaged in necessary work – the production of the benefits of civilisation.	UNEMPLOYED.

How the things produced by the people in division 4 are 'shared out'
amongst the different classes of the population.

'Now you mustn't run away with the idea that the people in three and four take their share quietly and divide the things equally between them. Not at all. Some get very little, some none, some more than a fair share. It is in these two divisions that the ferocious "Battle of Life" rages most fiercely; and of course in this battle the weak and the virtuous fare the worst. Even those whose exceptional abilities or opportunities enable them to succeed, are compelled to practise selfishness, because a man of exceptional ability who was not selfish would devote his abilities to relieving the manifest sufferings of others, and not to his own profit, and if he did the former he would not be successful in the sense that the world understands the word. All those who really seek to "Love their neighbour as themselves", or to return good for evil, the gentle, the kind, and all those who refrain from doing to others the things they would not like to suffer themselves; all these are of necessity found amongst the vanquished; because only the worst – only those who are aggressive, cunning, selfish and mean are fitted to survive. And all these people in numbers three and four are so fully occupied in this dreadful struggle to secure a little, that but few of them pause to enquire why there are not more of the things they are fighting for, or why it is necessary to fight like this at all!'

For a few minutes silence prevailed, each man's mind being busy trying to think of some objection to the lecturer's arguments.

'How could the small number of people in number one and two consume as much as you've given 'em in your drorin'?' demanded Crass.

'They don't actually consume all of it,' replied Owen. 'Much of it is wantonly wasted. They also make fortunes by selling some of it in foreign countries; but they consume a great part of it themselves, because the amount of labour expended on the things enjoyed by these people is greater than that expended in the production of the things used by the workers. Most of the people who do nothing get the best of everything. More than three-quarters of the time of the working classes is spent in producing the things used by the wealthy. Compare the quality and quantity of the clothing possessed by the wife or daughter of a rich man with that of the wife or daughter of a worker. The time and labour spent on producing the one is twenty times greater in one case than in the other; and it's the same with everything else. Their homes, their clothing, boots, hats, jewellery, and their food. Everything must be of the very best that art or long and painful labour can produce. But for most of those whose labour produces all these good things – anything is considered good enough. For themselves, the philanthropic workers manufacture shoddy cloth – that is, cheap cloth made of old rags and dirt; and shoddy, uncomfortable ironclad boots. If you see a workman wearing a really good suit of clothes you may safely conclude that he is either leading an unnatural life – that is, he is not married – or that he has obtained it from a tallyman on the hire system and has not yet paid for it – or that it is someone else's cast-off suit that he has bought second-hand or had given to him by some charitable person. It's the same with the food. All the ducks and geese, pheasants, partridges, and all the very best parts of the very best meat – all the soles and the finest plaice and salmon and trout – '

' 'Ere, chuck it,' cried Harlow, fiercely. 'We don't want to 'ear no more of it,' and several others protested against the lecturer wasting time on such mere details.

' – all the very best of everything is reserved exclusively for the enjoyment of the people in divisions one and two, while the workers subsist on block ornaments,[78] margarine, adulterated tea, mysterious beer, and are content – only grumbling when they are unable to obtain even such fare as this.'

Owen paused and a gloomy silence followed, but suddenly Crass brightened up. He detected a serious flaw in the lecturer's argument.

'You say the people in one and two gets all the best of everything, but what about the tramps and beggars? You've got them in division one.'

'Yes, I know. You see, that's the proper place for them. They belong to a loafer class. They are no better mentally or morally than any of the other loafers in that division; neither are they of any more use. Of course, when we consider them in relation to the amount they consume of the things produced by others, they are not so harmful as the other loafers, because they consume comparatively little. But all the same they are in their right place in that division. All those people don't get the same share. The section represents not individuals – but the Loafer class.'

'But I thought you said you was goin' to prove that money was the cause of poverty,' said Easton.

'So it is,' said Owen. 'Can't you see that it's money that's caused all these people to lose sight of the true purpose of labour – the production of the things we need? All these people are suffering from the delusion that it doesn't matter what kind of work they do – or whether they merely do nothing – so long as they get *money* for doing it. Under the present extraordinary system, that's the only object they have in view – to get money. Their ideas are so topsy-turvy that they regard with contempt those who are engaged in useful work! With the exception of criminals and the poorer sort of loafers, the working classes are considered to be the lowest and least worthy in the community. Those who manage to get money for doing something other than productive work are considered more worthy of respect on that account. Those who do nothing themselves, but get money out of the labour of others, are regarded as being more worthy still! But the ones who are esteemed most of all and honoured above all the rest, are those who obtain money for doing absolutely nothing!'

'But I can't see as that proves that money is the cause of poverty,' said Easton.

'Look here,' said Owen. 'The people in number four produce everything, don't they?'

'Yes; we knows all about that,' interrupted Harlow. 'But they gets paid for it, don't they? They gets their wages.'

'Yes, and what does their wages consist of?' said Owen.

'Why, money, of course,' replied Harlow, impatiently.

'And what do they do with their money when they get it? Do they eat it, or drink it, or wear it?'

At this apparently absurd question several of those who had hitherto been attentive listeners laughed derisively; it was really very difficult to listen patiently to such nonsense.

'Of course they don't,' answered Harlow scornfully. 'They buy the things they want with it.'

'Do you think that most of them manage to save a part of their wages – put it away in the bank.'

'Well, I can speak for meself,' replied Harlow amid laughter. 'It takes me all my bloody time to pay my rent and other expenses and to keep my little lot in shoe leather, and it's dam little I spend on beer; p'r'aps a tanner or a bob a week at the most.'

'A single man can save money if he likes,' said Slyme.

'I'm not speaking of single men,' replied Owen. 'I'm referring to those who live natural lives.'

'What about all the money what's in the Post Office Savings Bank, and Building and Friendly Societies?' said Crass.

'A very large part of that belongs to people who are in business, or who have some other source of income than their own wages. There are some exceptionally fortunate workers who happen to have good situations and higher wages than the ordinary run of workmen. Then there are some who are so placed – by letting lodgings, for instance – that they are able to live rent free. Others whose wives go out to work; and others again who have exceptional jobs and work a lot of overtime – but these are all exceptional cases.'

'I say as no married workin' man can save any money at all!' shouted Harlow, 'not unless 'e goes without some of even the few things we *are* able to get – and makes 'is wife and kids go without as well.'

' 'Ear, 'ear,' said everybody except Crass and Slyme, who were both thrifty working men, and each of them had some money saved in one or other of the institutions mentioned.

'Then that means,' said Owen, 'that means that the wages the people in division four receive is not equivalent to the work they do.'

'Wotcher mean, quiverlent?' cried Crass. 'Why the 'ell don't yer talk plain English without draggin' in a lot of long words wot nobody can't understand?'

'I mean this,' replied Owen, speaking very slowly. 'Everything is produced by the people in number four. In return for their work they are given – Money, and the things they have made become the property of the people who do nothing. Then, as the money is of no use, the workers go to shops and give it away in exchange for some of the things they themselves have made. They spend – or give back – *All* their wages; but as the money they got as wages is not equal in value to the things they produced, they find that they are only able to buy back a *very small part*. So you see that these little discs of metal – this Money – is a device for enabling those who do not work to rob the workers of the greater part of the fruits of their toil.'

The silence that ensued was broken by Crass.

'It sounds very pretty,' he sneered, 'but I can't make no 'ead or tail of it, meself.'

'Look here!' cried Owen. 'The producing class – these people in number four are supposed to be paid for their work. Their wages are supposed to be equal in value to their work. But it's not so. If it were, by spending all their wages, the producing class would be able to buy back All they had produced.'

Owen ceased speaking and silence once more ensued. No one gave any sign of understanding, or of agreeing or of disagreeing with what he had said. Their attitude was strictly neutral. Barrington's pipe had gone out during the argument. He relit it from the fire with a piece of twisted paper.

'If their wages were really equal in value to the product of their labour,' Owen repeated, 'they would be able to buy back not a small part – but the Whole.' . . .

[At this, a remark from Bundy caused a shout of laughter, and when Wantley added point] to the joke by making a sound like the discharge of a pistol the merriment increased tenfold.

'Well, that's done it,' remarked Easton, as he got up and opened the window.

'It's about time you was buried, if the smell's anything to go by,' said Harlow, addressing Wantley, who laughed and appeared to think he had distinguished himself . . .

'But even if we include the whole of the working classes,' continued Owen, 'that is, the people in number three as well as those in number four, we find that their combined wages are insufficient to buy the things made by the producers. The total value of the wealth produced in this country during the last year was £1,800,000,000, and the total amount paid in wages during the same period was only £600,000,000. In other words, by means of the Money Trick, the workers were robbed of two-thirds of the value of their labour. All the people in numbers three and four are working and suffering and starving and fighting in order that the rich people in numbers one and two may live in luxury, and do nothing. These are the wretches who cause poverty: they not only devour or waste or hoard the things made by the worker, but as soon as their own wants are supplied – they compel the workers to cease working and prevent them producing the things they need. Most of these people!' cried Owen, his usually pale face flushing red and his eyes shining with sudden anger, 'most of these people do not deserve to be called human beings at all! They're devils! They know that whilst they are indulging in pleasures of every kind – all around them men and women and little children are existing in want or dying of hunger.'

The silence which followed was at length broken by Harlow:

'You say the workers is entitled to all they produce, but you forget there's the raw materials to pay for. They don't make *them*, you know.'

'Of course the workers don't *create* the raw materials,' replied Owen. 'But I am not aware that the capitalists or the landlords do so either. The raw materials exist in abundance in and on the earth, but they are of no use until labour has been applied to them.'

'But then, you see, the earth belongs to the landlords!' cried Crass, unguardedly.

'I know that; and of course *you* think it's right that the whole country should belong to a few people – '

'I must call the lecturer to horder,' interrupted Philpot. 'The land question is not before the meeting at present.'

'You talk about the producers being robbed of most of the value of what they produce,' said Harlow, 'but you must remember that it ain't all produced by hand labour. What about the things what's made by machinery?'

'The machines themselves were made by the workers,' returned Owen, 'but of course they do not belong to the workers, who have been robbed of them by means of the Money Trick.'

'But who invented all the machinery?' cried Crass.

'That's more than you or I or anyone else can say,' returned Owen, 'but it certainly wasn't the wealthy loafer class, or the landlords, or the employers. Most of the men who invented the machinery lived and died unknown in poverty and often in actual want. [The inventors too were robbed by the] exploiter-of-labour class.

'There are no men living at present who can justly claim to have invented the machinery that exists today. The most they can truthfully say is that they have added to or improved upon the ideas of those who lived and worked before them. Even Watt and Stevenson merely improved upon steam engines and locomotives already existing. Your question has really nothing to do with the subject we are discussing: we are only trying to find out why the majority of people have to go short of the benefits of civilisation. One of the causes is – the majority of the population are engaged in work that does not produce those things; and most of what *is* produced is appropriated and wasted by those who have no right to it . . .

'The workers produce Everything! If you walk through the streets of a town or a city, and look around, Everything that you can see – Factories, Machinery, Houses, Railways, Tramways, Canals, Furniture, Clothing, Food and the very road or pavement you stand upon were all made by the working class, who spend all their wages in buying back only a very small part of the things they produce. Therefore what remains in the possession of their masters represents the difference between the value of the work done and the wages paid for doing it. This systematic robbery has been going on for generations, the value of the accumulated loot is enormous, and all of it, all the wealth at present in the possession of the rich, is rightly the property of the working class – it has been stolen from them by means of the Money Trick.' . . .

For some moments an oppressive silence prevailed. The men stared with puzzled, uncomfortable looks alternately at each other and at the drawings on the wall. They were compelled to do a little thinking on their own account, and it was a process to which they were unaccustomed. In their infancy they had been taught to distrust their own intelligence and to leave 'thinking' to their 'pastors' and masters and to their 'betters' generally. All their lives they had been true to this teaching, they had always had blind, unreasoning faith in the wisdom and humanity of their pastors and masters. That was the reason why they and their children had been all their lives on the verge of starvation and nakedness, whilst their 'betters' – who did nothing but the thinking – went clothed in purple and fine linen and fared sumptuously every day.

Several men had risen from their seats and were attentively studying the diagrams Owen had drawn on the wall; and nearly all the others were making the same mental effort – they were trying to think of something to say in defence of those who robbed them of the fruits of their toil.

'I don't see no bloody sense in always runnin' down the rich,' said Harlow at last. 'There's always been rich and poor in the world and there always will be.'

'Of course,' said Slyme. 'It says in the Bible that the poor shall always be with us.'[79]

'What the bloody 'ell kind of system do you think we ought to 'ave?' demanded Crass. 'If everything's wrong, 'ow's it goin' to be altered?'

At this, everybody brightened up again, and exchanged looks of satisfaction and relief. Of course! It wasn't necessary to think about these things at all! Nothing could ever be altered: it had always been more or less the same, and it always would be.

'It seems to me that you all *hope* it is impossible to alter it,' said Owen. 'Without trying to find out whether it could be done, you persuade yourselves that it is impossible, and then, instead of being sorry, you're glad!'

Some of them laughed in a silly, half-ashamed way.

'How do *you* reckon it could be altered?' said Harlow.

'The way to alter it is, first to enlighten the people as to the real cause of their sufferings, and then – '

'Well,' interrupted Crass, with a self-satisfied chuckle, 'it'll take a better bloody man than you to enlighten *me*!'

'I don't want to be henlightened into Darkness!' said Slyme, piously.

'But what sort of a System do you propose, then?' repeated Harlow. 'After you've got 'em all enlightened – if you don't believe in sharing out all the money equal, how *are* you goin' to alter it?'

'I don't know 'ow 'e's goin' to alter it,' sneered Crass, looking at his watch and standing up, 'but I do know what the time is – two minits past one!'

'The next lecture,' said Philpot, addressing the meeting as they all prepared to return to work, 'the next lecture will be postponded till tomorrer at the usual time, when it will be my painful dooty to call upon Mr. Owen to give 'is well-known and most hobnoxious [[address entitled "Work, and how to avoid it." Hall them as wants to be henlightened kindly attend.'

'Or hall them as don't get the sack tonight,' remarked Easton grimly.]]

CHAPTER 26

The Slaughter

During the afternoon, Rushton and Sweater visited the house, the latter having an appointment to meet there a gardener to whom he wished to give instructions concerning the laying out of the grounds, which had been torn up for the purpose of putting in the new drains. Sweater had already arranged with the head gardener of the public park to steal some of the best plants from that place and have them sent up to 'The Cave'. These plants had been arriving in small lots for about a week. They must have been brought there either in the evening after the men left off or very early in the morning before they came. The two gentlemen remained at the house for about half an hour and as they went away the mournful sound of the Town Hall bell – which was always tolled to summon meetings of the Council – was heard in the distance, and the hands remarked to each other that another robbery was about to be perpetrated.

Hunter did not come to the job again that day: he had been sent by Rushton to price some work for which the firm was going to tender an estimate. There was only one person who felt any regret at his absence, and that was Mrs. White – Bert's mother, who had been working at 'The Cave' for several days, scrubbing the floors. As a rule, Hunter paid her wages every night, and on this occasion she happened to need the money even more than usual. As leaving off time drew near, she mentioned the matter to Crass, who advised her to call at the office on her way home and ask the young lady clerk for the money. As Hunter did not appear, she followed the foreman's advice.

When she reached the shop Rushton was just coming out. She explained to him what she wanted and he instructed Mr. Budd to tell Miss Wade to pay her. The shopman accordingly escorted her to the office at the back of the shop, and the young lady book-keeper – after referring to former entries to make quite certain of the amount, paid her the sum that Hunter had represented as her wages, the same amount that Miss Wade had on the previous occasions given to him to pay the char-woman. When Mrs. White got outside she found that she held in her hand half a crown instead of the two shillings she usually received from Mr. Hunter. At first she felt inclined to take it back, but after some hesitation she thought it better to wait until she saw Hunter, when she could tell him about it; but the next morning when she saw that disciple at 'The Cave' he broached the subject first, and told her that Miss Wade had made a mistake. And that evening when he paid her, he deducted the sixpence from the usual two shillings . . .

[The lecture announced by Philpot was not delivered. Anxiously awaiting the impending slaughter the men kept tearing into it as usual, for they] generally keep working in the usual way, each one trying to outdo the others so as not to lose his chance of being one of the lucky ones . . .

Misery now went round and informed all the men with the exception of Crass, Owen, Slyme and Sawkins – that they would have to stand off that night. He told them that the firm had several jobs in view – work they had tendered for and hoped to get, and said they could look round after Christmas and he might – possibly – be able to start some of them again. They would be paid at the office tomorrow – Saturday – at one o'clock as usual, but if any of them wished they could have their money tonight. The men thanked him, and most of them said they would come for their wages at the usual pay-time, and would call round as he suggested, after the holidays, to see if there was anything to do.

In all, fifteen men – including Philpot, Harlow, Easton and Ned Dawson, were to 'stand off' that night. They took their dismissal stolidly, without any remark, some of them even with an affectation of indifference, but there were few attempts at conversation afterwards. The little work that remained to be done they did in silence, every man oppressed by the same terror – the dread of the impending want, the privation and unhappiness that they knew they and their families would have to suffer during the next few months.

Bundy and his mate Dawson were working in the kitchen fixing the new range in place of the old one which they had taken out. They had been engaged on this job all day, and their hands and faces and clothes were covered with soot, which they had also contrived to smear and dab all over the surfaces of the doors and other woodwork in the room, much to the indignation of Crass and Slyme, who had to wash it all off before they could put on the final coat of paint.

'You can't help makin' a little mess on a job of this kind, you know,' remarked Bundy, as he was giving the finishing touches to the work, making good the broken parts of the wall with cement, whilst his mate was clearing away the debris.

'Yes; but there's no need to claw 'old of the bloody doors every time you goes in and out,' snarled Crass, 'and you could 'ave put yer tools on the floor instead of makin' a bench of the dresser.'

'You can 'ave the bloody place all to yerself in about five minutes,' replied Bundy, as he assisted to lift a sack of cement weighing about two hundred weight on to Dawson's back. 'We're finished now.'

When they had cleared away all the dirt and fragments of bricks and mortar, while Crass and Slyme proceeded with the painting, Bundy and Dawson loaded up their hand-cart with the old range and the bags of unused cement and plaster, which they took back to the yard. Meantime, Misery was wandering about the house and grounds like an evil spirit seeking rest and finding none. He stood for some time gloomily watching the four gardeners, who were busily at work laying strips of turf, mowing the lawn, rolling the gravel paths and trimming the trees and bushes. The boy Bert, Philpot, Harlow, Easton and Sawkins were loading a hand-cart with ladders and empty paint-pots to return to the yard. Just as they were setting out, Misery stopped them, remarking that the cart was not half loaded – he said it would take a month to get all the stuff away if they went on like that; so by his directions they placed another long ladder on top of the pile and once more started on their way, but before they had gone two dozen yards one of the wheels of the cart collapsed and the load was scattered over the roadway. Bert was at the same side of the cart as the wheel that broke and he was thrown violently to the ground, where he lay half stunned, in the midst of the ladders and planks. When they got him out they were astonished to find that, thanks to the special Providence that watches over all small boys, he was almost unhurt – just a little dazed, that was all; and by the time Sawkins returned with another cart, Bert was able to help to gather up the fallen paint-pots and to accompany the men with the load to the yard. At the corner of the road they paused to take a last look at the 'job'.

'There it stands!' said Harlow, tragically, extending his arm towards the house. 'There it stands! A job that if they'd only have let us do it properly, couldn't 'ave been done with the number of 'ands we've 'ad, in less than four months; and there it is, finished, messed up, slobbered over and scamped, in nine weeks!'

'Yes, and now we can all go to 'ell,' said Philpot, gloomily.

At the yard they found Bundy and his mate, Ned Dawson, who

helped them to hang up the ladders in their usual places. Philpot was glad to get out of assisting to do this, for he had contracted a rather severe attack of rheumatism when working outside at the 'Cave'. Whilst the others were putting the ladders away he assisted Bert to carry the paint-pots and buckets into the paint shop, and while there he filled a small medicine bottle he had brought with him for the purpose, with turpentine from the tank. He wanted this stuff to rub into his shoulders and legs, and as he secreted the bottle in the inner pocket of his coat, he muttered: 'This is where we gets some of our own back.'

They took the key of the yard to the office and as they separated to go home Bundy suggested that the best thing they could do would be to sew their bloody mouths up for a few months, because there was not much probability of their getting another job until about March.

The next morning while Crass and Slyme were finishing inside, Owen wrote the two gates. On the front entrance 'The Cave' and on the back 'Tradesmens Entrance', in gilded letters. In the meantime, Sawkins and Bert made several journeys to the Yard with the hand-cart.

Crass – working in the kitchen with Slyme – was very silent and thoughtful. Ever since the job was started, every time Mr. Sweater had visited the house to see what progress was being made, Crass had been grovelling to him in the hope of receiving a tip when the work was finished. He had been very careful to act upon any suggestions that Sweater had made from time to time and on several occasions had taken a lot of trouble to get just the right tints of certain colours, making up a number of different shades and combinations, and doing parts of the skirtings or mouldings of rooms in order that Mr. Sweater might see exactly – before they went on with it – what it would look like when finished. He made a great pretence of deferring to Sweater's opinion, and assured him that he did not care how much trouble he took as long as he – Sweater – was pleased. In fact, it was no trouble at all: it was a pleasure. As the work neared completion, Crass began to speculate upon the probable amount of the donation he would receive as the reward of nine weeks of cringing, fawning, abject servility. He thought it quite possible that he might get a quid: it would not be too much, considering all the trouble he had taken. It was well worth it. At any rate, he felt certain that he was sure to get ten bob; a gentleman like Mr. Sweater would never have the cheek to offer less. The more he thought about it the more improbable it appeared that the amount would be less than a quid, and he made up his mind that whatever he got he would take good care that none of the other men knew anything about it. *He* was the one who had had all the worry of the job, and he was the only one entitled to anything there was to be had. Besides, even if he got a quid, by the time you divided that up amongst a dozen – or even amongst two or three – it would not be worth having.

At about eleven o'clock Mr. Sweater arrived and began to walk over the house, followed by Crass, who carried a pot of paint and a small brush and made believe to be 'touching up' and finishing off parts of the work. As Sweater went from one room to another Crass repeatedly placed himself in the way in the hope of being spoken to, but Sweater took no notice of him whatever. Once or twice Crass's heart began to beat quickly as he furtively watched the great man and saw him thrust his thumb and finger into his waistcoat pocket, but on each occasion Sweater withdrew his hand with nothing in it. After a while, observing that the gentleman was about to depart without having spoken, Crass determined to break the ice himself.

'It's a little better weather we're 'avin' now, sir.'

'Yes,' replied Sweater.

'I was beginnin' to be afraid as I shouldn't be hable to git hevery-thing finished in time for you to move in before Christmas, sir,' Crass continued, 'but it's hall done now, sir.'

Sweater made no reply.

'I've kept the fires agoin' in hall the rooms has you told me, sir,' resumed Crass after a pause. 'I think you'll find as the place is nice and dry, sir; the honly places as is a bit damp is the kitching and scullery and the other rooms in the basement, sir, but of course that's nearly halways the case, sir, when the rooms is partly hunder-ground, sir.

'But of course it don't matter so much about the basement, sir, because it's honly the servants what 'as to use it, sir, and even down there it'll be hall right hin the summer, sir.'

One would scarcely think, from the contemptuous way in which he spoke of 'servants' that Crass's own daughter was 'in service', but such was the case.

'Oh, yes, there's no doubt about that,' replied Sweater as he moved towards the front door; 'there's no doubt it will be dry enough in the summer. Good morning.'

'Good morning to *you*, sir,' said Crass, following him. 'I 'opes as you're pleased with all the work, sir; everything satisfactory, sir.'

'Oh, yes. I think it looks very nice; very nice indeed; I'm very pleased with it,' said Sweater affably. 'Good morning.'

'Good morning, sir,' replied the foreman with a sickly smile as Sweater departed.

When the other was gone, Crass sat down dejectedly on the bottom step of the stairs, overwhelmed with the ruin of his hopes and expectations. He tried to comfort himself with the reflection that all hope was not lost, because he would have to come to the house again on Monday and Tuesday to fix the venetian blinds; but all the same he could not help thinking that it was only a very faint hope, for he felt that if Sweater had intended giving anything he would have done so today; and it was very improbable that he would see Sweater on Monday or Tuesday at all, for the latter did not usually visit the job in the early part of the week. However, Crass made up his mind to hope for the best, and, pulling himself together, he presently returned to the kitchen, where he found Slyme and Sawkins waiting for him. He had not mentioned his hopes of a tip to either of them, but they did not need any telling and they were both determined to have their share of whatever he got. They eyed him keenly as he entered.

'What did 'e give yer?' demanded Sawkins, going straight to the point.

'Give me?' replied Crass. 'Nothing!'

Slyme laughed in a sneering, incredulous way, but Sawkins was inclined to be abusive. He averred that he had been watching Crass and Sweater and had seen the latter put his thumb and finger into his waistcoat pocket as he walked into the dining-room, followed by Crass. It took the latter a long time to convince his two workmates of the truth of his own account, but he succeeded at last, and they all three agreed that Old Sweater was a sanguinary rotter, and they lamented over the decay of the good old-fashioned customs.

'Why, at one time o' day,' said Crass, 'only a few years ago, if you went to a gentleman's 'ouse to paint one or two rooms you could always be sure of a bob or two when you'd finished.'

By half-past twelve everything was squared up, and, having loaded up the hand-cart with all that remained of the materials, dirty paint-pots and plant, they all set out together for the yard, to put all the things away before going to the office for their money. Sawkins took the handle of the cart, Slyme and Crass walked at one side and Owen and Bert at the other. There was no need to push, for the road was downhill most of the way; so much so that they had all to help to hold back the cart, which travelled so rapidly that Bert found it difficult to keep pace with the others and frequently broke into a trot to recover lost ground, and Crass – being fleshy and bloated with beer, besides being unused to much exertion – began to perspire and soon appealed to the others not to let it go so fast – there was no need to get done before one o'clock.

CHAPTER 27

The March of the Imperialists

It was an unusually fine day for the time of year, and as they passed along the Grand Parade – which faced due south – they felt quite warm. The Parade was crowded with richly dressed and bejewelled loafers, whose countenances in many instances bore unmistakable signs of drunkenness and gluttony. Some of the females had tried to conceal the ravages of vice and dissipation by coating their faces with powder and paint. Mingling with and part of this crowd were a number of well-fed-looking individuals dressed in long garments of black cloth of the finest texture, and broad-brimmed soft felt hats. Most of these persons had gold rings on their soft white fingers and glove-like kid or calfskin boots on their feet. They belonged to the great army of impostors who obtain an easy living by taking advantage of the ignorance and simplicity of their fellow-men, and pretending to be the 'followers' and 'servants' of the lowly Carpenter of Nazareth – the Man of Sorrows, who had not where to lay His head.[80]

None of these black-garbed 'disciples' were associating with the groups of unemployed carpenters, bricklayers, plasterers, and painters who stood here and there in the carriage-way dressed in mean and shabby clothing and with faces pale with privation. Many of these latter were known to our friends with the cart, and nodded to them as they passed. Now and then some of them came over and walked a little distance by their side, enquiring whether there was any news of another job at Rushton's.

When they were about halfway down the Parade, just near the Fountain, Crass and his mates encountered a number of men on whose arms were white bands with the word 'Collector' in black letters. They carried collecting boxes and accosted the people in the street, begging for money for the unemployed. These men were a kind of skirmishers for the main body, which could be seen some distance behind.

As the procession drew near, Sawkins steered the cart into the kerb and halted as they went past. There were about three hundred men altogether, marching four abreast. They carried three large white banners with black letters, 'Thanks to our Subscribers', 'In aid of Genuine Unemployed', 'The Children must be Fed'. Although there were a number of artisans in the procession, the majority of the men belonged to what is called the unskilled labourer class. The skilled artisan does not as a rule take part in such a procession except as a very last resource . . . And all the time he strives to keep up an appearance of being well-to-do, and would be highly indignant if anyone suggested that he was really in a condition of abject, miserable poverty. Although he knows that his children are often not so well fed as are the pet dogs and cats of his 'betters', he tries to bluff his neighbours into thinking that he has some mysterious private means of which they know nothing, and conceals his poverty as if it were a crime. Most of this class of men would rather starve than beg. Consequently not more than a quarter of the men in the procession were skilled artisans; the majority were labourers.

There was also a sprinkling of those unfortunate outcasts of society – tramps and destitute, drunken loafers. If the self-righteous hypocrites who despise these poor wretches had been subjected to the same conditions, the majority of them would inevitably have become the same as these.

Haggard and pale, shabbily or raggedly dressed, their boots broken and down at heel, they slouched past. Some of them stared about with a dazed or half-wild expression, but most of them walked with downcast eyes or staring blankly straight in front of them. They appeared utterly broken-spirited, hopeless and ashamed . . .

[['Anyone can see what *they* are,' sneered Crass, 'there isn't fifty genuine tradesmen in the whole]] crowd, and most of 'em wouldn't work if they 'ad the offer of it.'

'That's just what I was thinkin',' agreed Sawkins with a laugh.

'There will be plenty of time to say that when they have been offered work and have refused to do it,' said Owen.

'This sort of thing does the town a lot of 'arm,' remarked Slyme; 'it oughtn't to be allowed; the police ought to stop it. It's enough to drive all the gentry out of the place!'

'Bloody disgraceful, I call it,' said Crass, 'marchin' along the Grand

Parade on a beautiful day like this, just at the very time when most of the gentry is out enjoyin' the fresh hair.'

'I suppose you think they ought to stay at home and starve quietly,' said Owen. 'I don't see why these men should care what harm they do to the town; the town doesn't seem to care much what becomes of *them*.'

'Do you believe in this sort of thing, then?' asked Slyme.

'No; certainly not. I don't believe in begging as a favour for what one is entitled to demand as a right [[from the thieves who have robbed them and who are now enjoying the fruits of their labour. From the look of shame on their faces you might think that *they* were the criminals instead of being the victims.']]

'Well you must admit that most of them is very inferior men,' said Crass with a self-satisfied air. 'There's very few mechanics amongst 'em.'

'What about it if they are? What difference does that make?' replied Owen. 'They're human beings, and they have as much right to live as anyone else. What is called unskilled labour is just as necessary and useful as yours or mine. I am no more capable of doing the 'unskilled' labour that most of these men do than most of them would be capable of doing my work.'

'Well, if they was skilled tradesmen, they might find it easier to get a job,' said Crass.

Owen laughed offensively.

'Do you mean to say you think that if all these men could be transformed into skilled carpenters, plasterers, bricklayers, and painters, that it would be easier for all those other chaps whom we passed a little while ago to get work? Is it possible that you or any other sane man can believe anything so silly as that?'

Crass did not reply.

'If there is not enough work to employ all the mechanics whom we see standing idle about the streets, how would it help these labourers in the procession if they could all become skilled workmen?'

Still Crass did not answer, and neither Slyme nor Sawkins came to his assistance.

'If that could be done,' continued Owen, 'it would simply make things worse for those who are already skilled mechanics. A greater number of skilled workers – keener competition for skilled workmen's jobs – a larger number of mechanics out of employment, and consequently, improved opportunities for employers to reduce wages. That is probably the reason why the Liberal Party – which consists for the most part of exploiters of labour – procured the great Jim Scalds to tell us that improved technical education is the remedy for unemployment and poverty.'

'I suppose you think Jim Scalds is a bloody fool, the same as everybody else what don't see things *your* way?' said Sawkins.

'I should think he was a fool if I thought he believed what he says. But I don't think he believes it. He says it because he thinks the majority of the working classes are such fools that they will believe him. If he didn't think that most of us are fools he wouldn't tell us such a yarn as that.'

'And I suppose you think as 'is opinion ain't far wrong,' snarled Crass.

'We shall be better able to judge of that after the next General Election,' replied Owen. 'If the working classes again elect a majority of Liberal or Tory landlords and employers to rule over them, it will prove that Jim Scalds' estimate of their intelligence is about right.'

'Well, anyhow,' persisted Slyme, 'I don't think it's a right thing that they should be allowed to go marchin' about like that – driving visitors out of the town.'

'What do you think they ought to do, then?' demanded Owen.

'Let the b—rs go to the bloody workhouse!' shouted Crass.

'But before they could be received there they would have to be absolutely homeless and destitute, and then the ratepayers would have to keep them. It costs about twelve shillings a week for each inmate, so it seems to me that it would be more sensible and economical for the community to employ them on some productive work.'

They had by this time arrived at the yard. The steps and ladders were put away in their places and the dirty paint-pots and pails were placed in the paint-shop on the bench and on the floor. With what had previously been brought back there were a great many of these things, all needing to be cleaned out, so Bert at any rate stood in no danger of being out of employment for some time to come.

When they were paid at the office, Owen on opening his envelope found it contained as usual, a time sheet for the next week, which meant that he was not 'stood off' although he did not know what work there would be to do. Crass and Slyme were both to go to the 'Cave' to fix the venetian blinds, and Sawkins also was to come to work as usual.

CHAPTER 28

The Week before Christmas

During the next week Owen painted a sign on the outer wall of one of the workshops at the yard, and he also wrote the name of the firm on three of the handcarts. These and other odd jobs kept him employed a few hours every day, so that he was not actually out of work.

One afternoon – there being nothing to do – he went home at three o'clock, but almost as soon as he reached the house Bert White came with a coffin-plate which had to be written at once. The lad said he had been instructed to wait for it.

Nora gave the boy some tea and bread and butter to eat whilst Owen was doing the coffin-plate, and presently Frankie – who had been playing out in the street – made his appearance. The two boys were already known to each other, for Bert had been there several times before – on errands similar to the present one, or to take lessons on graining and letter-painting from Owen.

'I'm going to have a party next Monday – after Christmas,' remarked Frankie. 'Mother told me I might ask you if you'll come?'

'All right,' said Bert; 'and I'll bring my Pandoramer.'[81]

'What is it? Is it alive?' asked Frankie with a puzzled look.

'Alive! No, of course not,' replied Bert with a superior air. 'It's a show, like they have at the Hippodrome or the Circus.'

'How big is it?'

'Not very big: it's made out of a sugar-box. I made it myself. It's not quite finished yet, but I shall get it done this week. There's a band as well, you know. I do that part with this.'

'This' was a large mouth organ which he produced from the inner pocket of his coat.

'Play something now.'

Bert accordingly played, and Frankie sang at the top of his voice a selection of popular songs, including 'The Old Bull and Bush', 'Has Anyone seen a German Band?', 'Waiting at the Church', and finally – possibly as a dirge for the individual whose coffin-plate Owen was writing – 'Goodbye, Mignonette' and 'I wouldn't leave my little wooden hut for you'.

'You don't know what's in that,' said Frankie, referring to a large earthenware bread-pan which Nora had just asked Owen to help her to lift from the floor on to one of the chairs. The vessel in question was covered with a clean white cloth.

'Christmas pudding,' replied Bert, promptly.

'Guessed right first time!' cried Frankie. 'We got the things out of the Christmas Club on Saturday. We've been paying in ever since last Christmas. We're going to mix it now, and you can have a stir too if you like, for luck.'

Whilst they were stirring the pudding, Frankie several times requested the others to feel his muscle: he said he felt sure that he would soon be strong enough to go out to work, and he explained to Bert that the extraordinary strength he possessed was to be attributed to the fact that he lived almost exclusively on porridge and milk.

*   *   *

For the rest of the week, Owen continued to work down at the yard with Sawkins, Crass, and Slyme, painting some of the ladders, steps and other plant belonging to the firm. These things had to have two coats of paint and the name Rushton & Co. written on them. As soon as they had got some of them second-coated, Owen went on with the writing, leaving the painting for the others, so as to share the work as fairly as possible. Several times during the week one or other of them was taken away to do some other work; once Crass and Slyme had to go and wash off and whiten a ceiling somewhere, and several times Sawkins was sent out to assist the plumbers.

Every day some of the men who had been 'stood off' called at the yard to ask if any other 'jobs' had 'come in'. From these callers they heard all the news. Old Jack Linden had not succeeded in getting anything to do at the trade since he was discharged from Rushton's, and it was reported that he was trying to earn a little money by hawking bloaters from house to house. As for Philpot, *he* said that he had been round to nearly all the firms in the town and none of them had any work to speak of.

Newman – the man whom the reader will remember was sacked for taking too much pains with his work – had been arrested and sentenced to a month's imprisonment because he had not been able to pay his poor rates, and the Board of Guardians were allowing his wife three shillings a week to maintain herself and the three children. Philpot had been to see them, and she told him that the landlord was threatening to turn them into the street; he would have seized their furniture and sold it if it had been worth the expense of the doing.

'I feel ashamed of meself,' Philpot added in confidence to Owen, 'when I think of all the money I chuck away on beer. If it wasn't for that, I shouldn't be in such a hole meself now, and I might be able to lend 'em a 'elpin' 'and.'

'It ain't so much that I likes the beer, you know,' he continued; 'it's the company. When you ain't got no 'ome, in a manner o' speakin', like me, the pub's about the only place where you can get a little enjoyment. But you ain't very welcome there unless you spends your money.'

'Is the three shillings all they have to live on?'

'I think she goes out charin' when she can get it,' replied Philpot, 'but I don't see as she can do a great deal o' that with three young 'uns to look after, and from what I hear of it she's only just got over a illness and ain't fit to do much.'

'My God!' said Owen.

'I'll tell you what,' said Philpot. 'I've been thinking we might get up a bit of a subscription for 'em. There's several chaps in work what knows Newman, and if they was each to give a trifle we could get enough to pay for a Christmas dinner, anyway. I've brought a sheet of foolscap with me, and I was goin' to ask you to write out the heading for me.'

As there was no pen available at the workshop, Philpot waited till four o'clock and then accompanied Owen home, where the heading of the list was written. Owen put his name down for a shilling and Philpot his for a similar amount.

Philpot stayed to tea and accepted an invitation to spend Christmas Day with them, and to come to Frankie's party on the Monday after.

The next morning Philpot brought the list to the yard and Crass and Slyme put their names down for a shilling each, and Sawkins for threepence, it being arranged that the money was to be paid on pay-day – Christmas Eve. In the meantime, Philpot was to see as many as he could of those who were in work at other firms and get as many subscriptions as possible.

At pay-time on Christmas Eve Philpot turned up with the list and Owen and the others paid him the amounts they had put their names down for. From other men he had succeeded in obtaining nine and sixpence, mostly in sixpences and threepences. Some of this money he had already received, but for the most part he had made appointments with the subscribers to call at their homes that evening. It was decided that Owen should accompany him and also go with him to hand over the money to Mrs. Newman.

It took them nearly three hours to get in all the money, for the places they had to go to were in different localities, and in one or two cases they had to wait because their man had not yet come home, and sometimes it was not possible to get away without wasting a little time in talk. In three instances those who had put their names for threepence increased the amount to sixpence and one who had promised sixpence gave a shilling. There were two items of three-pence each which they did not get at all, the individuals who had put their names down having gone upon the drunk. Another cause of delay was that they met or called on several other men who had not yet been asked for a subscription, and there were several others – including some members of the Painters' Society whom Owen had spoken to during the week – who had promised him to give a sub-scription. In the end they succeeded in increasing the total amount to nineteen and ninepence, and they then put threehalfpence each to make it up to a pound.

The Newmans lived in a small house the rent of which was six shillings per week and taxes. To reach the house one had to go down a dark and narrow passage between two shops, the house being in a kind of well, surrounded by the high walls of the back parts of larger buildings – chiefly business premises and offices. The air did not circulate very freely in this place, and the rays of the sun never reached it. In the summer the atmosphere was close and foul with the various odours which came from the back-yards of the adjoining buildings, and in the winter it was dark and damp and gloomy, a culture-ground for bacteria and microbes. The majority of those who profess to be desirous of preventing and curing the disease called consumption must be either hypocrites or fools, for they ridicule the suggestion that it is necessary first to cure and prevent the poverty that compels badly clothed and half-starved human beings to sleep in such dens as this.

The front door opened into the living-room or, rather, kitchen, which was dimly lighted by a small paraffin lamp on the table, where were also some tea-cups and saucers, each of a different pattern, and the remains of a loaf of bread. The wallpaper was old and discoloured; a few almanacs and unframed prints were fixed to the walls, and on the mantelshelf were some cracked and worthless vases and ornaments. At one time they had possessed a clock and an overmantel and some framed pictures, but they had all been sold to obtain money to buy food. Nearly everything of any value had been parted with for the same reason – the furniture, the pictures, the bedclothes, the carpet and the oil-cloth, piece by piece, nearly everything that had once constituted the home – had been either pawned or sold to buy food or to pay rent during the times when Newman was out of work – periods that had recurred during the last few years with constantly increasing frequency and duration. Now there was nothing left but these few old broken chairs and the deal table which no one would buy; and upstairs, the wretched bedsteads and mattresses whereon they slept at night, covering themselves with worn-out remnants of blankets and the clothes they wore during the day.

In answer to Philpot's knock, the door was opened by a little girl about seven years old, who at once recognised Philpot, and called out his name to her mother, and the latter came also to the door, closely followed by two other children, a little, fragile-looking girl about three, and a boy about five years of age, who held on to her skirt and peered curiously at the visitors. Mrs. Newman was about thirty, and her appearance confirmed the statement of Philpot that she had only just recovered from an illness; she was very white and thin and dejected-looking. When Philpot explained the object of their visit and handed her the money, the poor woman burst into tears, and the two smaller children – thinking that this piece of paper betokened some fresh calamity – began to cry also. They remembered that all their troubles had been preceded by the visits of men who brought pieces of paper, and it was rather difficult to reassure them.

That evening, after Frankie was asleep, Owen and Nora went out to do their Christmas marketing. They had not much money to spend, for Owen had brought home only seventeen shillings. He had worked thirty-three hours – that came to nineteen and threepence – one shilling and threehalfpence had gone on the subscription list, and he had given the rest of the coppers to a ragged wreck of a man who was singing a hymn in the street. The other shilling had been deducted from his wages in repayment of a 'sub' he had had during the week.

There was a great deal to be done with this seventeen shillings. First of all there was the rent – seven shillings – that left ten. Then there was the week's bread bill – one and threepence. They had a pint of milk every day, chiefly for the boy's sake – that came to one and two. Then there was one and eight for a hundredweight of coal that had been bought on credit. Fortunately, there were no groceries to buy, for the things they had obtained with their Christmas Club money would be more than sufficient for the ensuing week.

Frankie's stockings were all broken and beyond mending, so it was positively necessary to buy him another pair for fivepence three-farthings. These stockings were not much good – a pair at double the price would have been much cheaper, for they would have lasted three or four times longer; but they could not afford to buy the dearer kind. It was just the same with the coal: if they had been able to afford it, they could have bought a ton of the same class of coal for twenty-six shillings, but buying it as they did, by the hundredweight, they had to pay at the rate of thirty-three shillings and fourpence a ton. It was just the same with nearly everything else. This is how the working classes are robbed. Although their incomes are the lowest, they are compelled to buy the most expensive articles – that is, the lowest-priced articles. Everybody knows that good clothes, boots or furniture are really the cheapest in the end, although they cost more money at first; but the working classes can seldom or never afford to buy good things; they have to buy cheap rubbish which is dear at any price.

Six weeks previously Owen bought a pair of second-hand boots for three shillings and they were now literally falling to pieces. Nora's shoes were in much the same condition, but, as she said, it did not matter so much about hers because there was no need for her to go out if the weather were not fine.

In addition to the articles already mentioned, they had to spend fourpence for half a gallon of paraffin oil, and to put sixpence into the slot of the gas-stove. This reduced the money to five and seven-pence farthing, and of this it was necessary to spend a shilling on potatoes and other vegetables.

They both needed some new underclothing, for what they had was so old and worn that it was quite useless for the purpose it was supposed to serve; but there was no use thinking of these things, for they had now only four shillings and sevenpence farthing left, and all that would be needed for toys. They had to buy something special for Frankie for Christmas, and it would also be necessary to buy something for each of the children who were coming to the party on the following Monday. Fortunately, there was no meat to buy, for Nora had been paying into the Christmas Club at the butcher's as well as at the grocer's. So this necessary was already paid for.

They stopped to look at the display of toys at Sweater's Emporium. For several days past Frankie had been talking of the wonders contained in these windows, so they wished if possible to buy him something here. They recognised many of the things from the description the boy had given of them, but nearly everything was so dear that for a long time they looked in vain for something it would be possible to buy.

'That's the engine he talks so much about,' said Nora, indicating a model railway locomotive; 'that one marked five shillings.'

'It might just as well be marked five pounds as far as we're concerned,' replied Owen.

As they were speaking, one of the salesmen appeared at the back of the window and, reaching forward, removed the engine. It was probably the last one of the kind and had evidently just been sold. Owen and Nora experienced a certain amount of consolation in knowing that even if they had the money they would not have been able to buy it.

After lengthy consideration, they decided on a clockwork engine at a shilling, but the other toys they resolved to buy at a cheaper shop. Nora went into the Emporium to get the toy and whilst Owen was waiting for her Mr. and Mrs. Rushton came out. They did not appear to see Owen, who observed that the shape of one of several parcels they carried suggested that it contained the engine that had been taken from the window a little while before.

When Nora returned with her purchase, they went in search of a cheaper place and after a time they found what they wanted. For sixpence they bought a cardboard box that had come all the way from Japan and contained a whole family of dolls – father, mother and four children of different sizes. A box of paints, threepence: a sixpenny tea service, a threepenny drawing slate, and a rag doll, sixpence.

On their way home they called at a greengrocer's where Owen had ordered and paid for a small Christmas tree a few weeks before; and as they were turning the corner of the street where they lived they met Crass, half-drunk, with a fine fat goose slung over his shoulder by its neck. He greeted Owen jovially and held up the bird for their inspection.

'Not a bad tanner's-worth, eh?' he hiccoughed. 'This makes two we've got. I won this and a box of cigars – fifty – for a tanner, and the other one I got out of the Club at our Church Mission 'all: threepence a week for twenty-eight weeks; that makes seven bob. But,' he added, confidentially, 'you couldn't buy 'em for that price in a shop, you know. They costs the committee a good bit more nor that – wholesale; but we've got some rich gents on our committee and they makes up the difference,' and with a nod and a cunning leer he lurched off.

Frankie was sleeping soundly when they reached home, and so was the kitten, which was curled up on the quilt on the foot of the bed. After they had had some supper, although it was after eleven o'clock, Owen fixed the tree in a large flower-pot that had served a similar purpose before, and Nora brought out from the place where it had been stored away since last Christmas a cardboard box containing a lot of glittering tinsel ornaments – globes of silvered or gilded or painted glass, birds, butterflies and stars. Some of these things had done duty three Christmases ago and although they were in some instances slightly tarnished most of them were as good as new. In addition to these and the toys they had bought that evening they had a box of bon-bons and a box of small coloured wax candles, both of which had formed part of the things they got from the grocer's with the Christmas Club money; and there were also a lot of little coloured paper bags of sweets, and a number of sugar and chocolate toys and animals which had been bought two or three at a time for several weeks past and put away for this occasion. There was something suitable for each child that was coming, with the exception of Bert White; they had intended to include a six-penny pocket knife for him in their purchases that evening, but as they had not been able to afford this Owen decided to give him an old set of steel graining combs which he knew the lad had often longed to possess. The tin case containing these tools was accordingly wrapped in some red tissue paper and hung on the tree with the other things.

They moved about as quietly as possible so as not to disturb those who were sleeping in the rooms beneath, because long before they were finished the people in the other parts of the house had all retired to rest, and silence had fallen on the deserted streets outside. As they were putting the final touches to their work the profound stillness of the night was suddenly broken by the voices of a band of carol-singers.

The sound overwhelmed them with memories of other and happier times, and Nora stretched out her hands impulsively to Owen, who drew her close to his side.

They had been married just over eight years, and although during all that time they had never been really free from anxiety for the future, yet on no previous Christmas had they been quite so poor as now. During the last few years periods of unemployment had gradually become more frequent and protracted, and the attempt he had made in the early part of the year to get work elsewhere had only resulted in plunging them into even greater poverty than before. But all the same there was much to be thankful for: poor though they were, they were far better off than many thousands of others: they still had food and shelter, and they had each other and the boy.

Before they went to bed Owen carried the tree into Frankie's bedroom and placed it so that he would be able to see it in all its glittering glory as soon as he awoke on Christmas morning.

CHAPTER 29

The Pandora

Although the party was not supposed to begin till six o'clock, Bert turned up at half-past four, bringing the 'Pandoramer' with him.

At about half-past five the other guests began to arrive. Elsie and Charley Linden came first, the girl in a pretty blue frock trimmed with white lace, and Charley resplendent in a new suit, which, like his sister's dress, had been made out of somebody's cast-off clothes that had been given to their mother by a visiting lady. It had taken Mrs. Linden many hours of hard work to contrive these garments; in fact, more time than the things were worth, for although they looked all right – especially Elsie's – the stuff was so old that it would not wear very long: but this was the only way in which she could get clothes for the children at all: she certainly could not afford to buy them any. So she spent hours and hours making things that she knew would fall to pieces almost as soon as they were made.

After these came Nellie, Rosie and Tommy Newman. These presented a much less prosperous appearance than the other two. Their mother was not so skilful at contriving new clothes out of old. Nellie was wearing a grown-up woman's blouse, and by way of ulster she had on an old-fashioned jacket of thick cloth with large pearl buttons. This was also a grown-up woman's garment: it was shaped to fit the figure of a tall woman with wide shoulders and a small waist; consequently, it did not fit Nellie to perfection. The waist reached below the poor child's hips.

Tommy was arrayed in the patched remains of what had once been a good suit of clothes. They had been purchased at a second-hand shop last summer and had been his 'best' for several months, but they were now much too small for him.

Little Rosie – who was only just over three years old – was better off than either of the other two, for she had a red cloth dress that fitted her perfectly: indeed, as the district visitor who gave it to her mother had remarked, it looked as if it had been made for her.

'It's not much to look at,' observed Nellie, referring to her big jacket, 'but all the same we was very glad of it when the rain came on.'

The coat was so big that by withdrawing her arms from the sleeves and using it as a cloak or shawl she had managed to make it do for all three of them.

Tommy's boots were so broken that the wet had got in and saturated his stockings, so Nora made him take them all off and wear some old ones of Frankie's whilst his own were drying at the fire.

Philpot, with two large paper bags full of oranges and nuts, arrived just as they were sitting down to tea – or rather cocoa – for with the exception of Bert all the children expressed a preference for the latter beverage. Bert would have liked to have cocoa also, but hearing that the grown-ups were going to have tea, he thought it would be more manly to do the same. This question of having tea or cocoa for tea became a cause of much uproarious merriment on the part of the children, who asked each other repeatedly which they liked best, 'tea tea?' or 'cocoa tea?' They thought it so funny that they said it over and over again, screaming with laughter all the while, until Tommy got a piece of cake stuck in his throat and became nearly black in the face, and then Philpot had to turn him upside down and punch him in the back to save him from choking to death. This rather sobered the others, but for some time afterwards whenever they looked at each other they began to laugh afresh because they thought it was such a good joke.

When they had filled themselves up with the 'cocoa-tea' and cakes and bread and jam, Elsie Linden and Nellie Newman helped to clear away the cups and saucers, and then Owen lit the candles on the Christmas tree and distributed the toys to the children, and a little while afterward Philpot – who had got a funny-looking mask out of one of the bon-bons – started a fine game pretending to be a dreadful wild animal which he called a Pandroculus, and crawling about on all fours, rolled his goggle eyes and growled out he must have a little boy or girl to eat for his supper.

He looked so terrible that although they knew it was only a joke they were almost afraid of him, and ran away laughing and screaming to shelter themselves behind Nora or Owen; but all the same, whenever Philpot left off playing, they entreated him to 'be it again', and so he had to keep on being a Pandroculus, until exhaustion compelled him to return to his natural form.

After this they all sat round the table and had a game of cards; 'Snap', they called it, but nobody paid much attention to the rules of the game: everyone seemed to think that the principal thing to do was to kick up as much row as possible. After a while Philpot suggested a change to 'Beggar my neighbour', and won quite a lot of cards before they found out that he had hidden all the jacks in the pocket of his coat, and then they mobbed him for a cheat. He might have been seriously injured if it had not been for Bert, who created a diversion by standing on a chair and announcing that he was about to introduce to their notice 'Bert White's World-famed Pandorama' as exhibited before all the nobility and crowned heads of Europe, England, Ireland and Scotland, including North America and Wales.

Loud cheers greeted the conclusion of Bert's speech. The box was placed on the table, which was then moved to the end of the room, and the chairs were ranged in two rows in front.

The 'Pandorama' consisted of a stage-front made of painted cardboard and fixed on the front of a wooden box about three feet long by two feet six inches high, and about one foot deep from back to front. The 'Show' was a lot of pictures cut out of illustrated weekly papers and pasted together, end to end, so as to form a long strip or ribbon. Bert had coloured all the pictures with water-colours.

Just behind the wings of the stage-front at each end of the box – was an upright roller, and the long strip of pictures was rolled up on this. The upper ends of the rollers came through the top of the box and had handles attached to them. When these handles were turned the pictures passed across the stage, unrolling from one roller and rolling on to the other, and were illuminated by the light of three candles placed behind.

The idea of constructing this machine had been suggested to Bert by a panorama entertainment he had been to see some time before.

'The Style of the decorations,' he remarked, alluding to the painted stage-front, 'is Moorish.'

He lit the candles at the back of the stage and, having borrowed a tea-tray from Nora, desired the audience to take their seats. When they had all done so, he requested Owen to put out the lamp and the candles on the tree, and then he made another speech, imitating the manner of the lecturer at the panorama entertainment before mentioned.

'Ladies and Gentlemen: with your kind permission I am about to hinterduce to your notice some pitchers of events in different parts of the world. As each pitcher appears on the stage I will give a short explanation of the subject, and afterwards the band will play a suitable collection of appropriated music, consisting of hymns and all the latest and most popular songs of the day, and the audience is kindly requested to join in the chorus.

'Our first scene,' continued Bert as he turned the handles and brought the picture into view, 'represents the docks at Southampton; the magnificent steamer which you see lying alongside the shore is the ship which is waiting to take us to foreign parts. As we have already paid our fare, we will now go on board and set sail.'

As an accompaniment to this picture Bert played the tune of 'Goodbye, Dolly, I must leave you', and by the time the audience had finished singing the chorus he had rolled on another scene, which depicted a dreadful storm at sea, with a large ship evidently on the point of foundering. The waves were running mountains high and the inky clouds were riven by forked lightning. To increase the terrifying effect, Bert rattled the tea tray and played 'The Bay of Biscay', and the children sung the chorus whilst he rolled the next picture into view. This scene showed the streets of a large city; mounted police with drawn swords were dispersing a crowd: several men had been ridden down and were being trampled under the hoofs of the horses, and a number of others were bleeding profusely from wounds on the head and face.

'After a rather stormy passage we arrives safely at the beautiful city of Berlin, in Germany, just in time to see a procession of unemployed workmen being charged by the military police. This picture is hintitled "Tariff Reform means Work for All".'

As an appropriate musical selection Bert played the tune of a well-known song, and the children sang the words:

> 'To be there! to be there!
> Oh, I knew what it was to be there!
> And when they tore me clothes,
> Blacked me eyes and broke me nose,
> Then I knew what it was to be there!'

During the singing Bert turned the handles backwards and again brought on the picture of the storm at sea.

'As we don't want to get knocked on the 'ed, we clears out of Berlin as soon as we can – whiles we're safe – and once more embarks on our gallint ship, and after a few more turns of the 'andle we finds ourselves back once more in Merry Hingland, where we see the inside of a blacksmith's shop with a lot of half-starved women making iron chains. They work seventy hours a week for seven shillings. Our next scene is hintitled "The Hook and Eye Carders". 'Ere we see the inside of a room in Slumtown, with a mother and three children and the old grandmother sewin' hooks and eyes on cards to be sold in drapers' shops. It ses underneath the pitcher that 384 hooks and 384 eyes has to be joined together and sewed on cards for one penny.'

While this picture was being rolled away the band played and the children sang with great enthusiasm:

> 'Rule, Brittania, Brittania rules the waves!
> Britons, never, never, never shall be slaves!'

'Our next picture is called "An Englishman's Home". 'Ere we see the inside of another room in Slumtown, with the father and mother and four children sitting down to dinner – bread and drippin' and tea. It ses underneath the pitcher that there's Thirteen millions of people in England always on the verge of starvation. These people that you see in the pitcher might be able to get a better dinner than this if it wasn't that most of the money wot the bloke earns 'as to go to pay the rent. Again we turns the 'andle and presently we comes to another very beautiful scene – "Early Morning in Trafalgar Square". 'Ere we see a lot of Englishmen who have been sleepin' out all night because they ain't got no 'omes to go to.'

As a suitable selection for this picture, Bert played the tune of a music-hall song, the words of which were familiar to all the youngsters, who sang at the top of their voices:

> 'I live in Trafalgar Square,
> With four lions to guard me,
> Pictures and statues all over the place,
> Lord Nelson staring me straight in the face,
> Of course it's rather draughty,
> But still I'm sure you'll agree,
> If it's good enough for Lord Nelson,
> It's quite good enough for me.'

'Next we 'ave a view of the dining-hall at the Topside Hotel in London, where we see the tables set for a millionaires' banquet.

The forks and spoons is made of solid gold and the plates is made of silver. The flowers that you see on the tables and 'angin' down from the ceilin' and on the walls is worth £2,000 and it cost the bloke wot give the supper over £30,000 for this one beano. A few more turns of the 'andle shows us another glorious banquet – the King of Rhineland being entertained by the people of England. Next we finds ourselves looking on at the Lord Mayor's supper at the Mansion House. All the fat men that you see sittin' at the tables is Liberal and Tory Members of Parlimint. After this we 'ave a very beautiful pitcher hintitled "Four footed Haristocrats". 'Ere you see Lady Slumrent's pet dogs sittin' up on chairs at their dinner table with white linen napkins tied round their necks, eatin' orf silver plates like human people and being waited on by real live waiters in hevening dress. Lady Slumrent is very fond of her pretty pets and she does not allow them to be fed on anything but the very best food; they gets chicken, rump steak, mutton chops, rice pudding, jelly and custard.'

'I wished *I* was a pet dog, don't you?' remarked Tommy Newman to Charley Linden.

'Not arf!' replied Charley.

'Here we see another unemployed procession,' continued Bert as he rolled another picture into sight; '2,000 able-bodied men who are not allowed to work. Next we see the hinterior of a Hindustrial 'Ome – Blind children and cripples working for their living. Our next scene is called "Cheap Labour". 'Ere we see a lot of small boys about twelve and thirteen years old bein' served out with their Labour Stifficats,[82] which gives 'em the right to go to work and earn money to help their unemployed fathers to pay the slum rent.

'Once more we turns the 'andle and brings on one of our finest scenes. This lovely pitcher is hintitled "The Hangel of Charity", and shows us the beautiful Lady Slumrent seated at the table in a cosy corner of 'er charmin' boodore, writin' out a little cheque for the relief of the poor of Slumtown.

'Our next scene is called "The Rival Candidates, or, a Scene during the General Election". On the left you will observe, standin' up in a motor car, a swell bloke with a eyeglass stuck in one eye, and a overcoat with a big fur collar and cuffs, addressing the crowd: this is the Honourable Augustus Slumrent, the Conservative candidate. On the other side of the road we see another motor car and another swell bloke with a round pane of glass in one eye and a overcoat with a big fur collar and cuffs, standing up in the car and addressin' the crowd. This is Mr. Mandriver, the Liberal candidate. The crowds of shabby-lookin' chaps standin' round the motor cars wavin' their 'ats and cheerin' is workin' men. Both the candidates is tellin' 'em the same old story, and each of 'em is askin' the workin' men to elect 'im to Parlimint, and promisin' to do something or other to make things better for the lower horders.'

As an appropriate selection to go with this picture, Bert played the tune of a popular song, the words being well known to the children, who sang enthusiastically, clapping their hands and stamping their feet on the floor in time with the music:

> 'We've both been there before,
> Many a time, many a time!
> We've both been there before,
> Many a time!
> Where many a gallon of beer has gone,
> To colour his nose and mine,
> We've both been there before,
> Many a time, many a time!'

At the conclusion of the singing, Bert turned another picture into view.

' 'Ere we 'ave another election scene. At each side we see the two candidates the same as in the last pitcher. In the middle of the road we see a man lying on the ground, covered with blood, with a lot of Liberal and Tory working men kickin' 'im, jumpin' on 'im, and stampin' on 'is face with their 'obnailed boots. The bloke on the ground is a Socialist, and the reason why they're kickin' 'is face in is because 'e said that the only difference between Slumrent and Mandriver was that they was both alike.'

Whilst the audience were admiring this picture, Bert played another well-known tune, and the children sang the words:

> 'Two lovely black eyes,
>   Oh what a surprise!
> Only for telling a man he was wrong,
>   Two lovely black eyes.'

Bert continued to turn the handles of the rollers and a long succession of pictures passed across the stage, to the delight of the children, who cheered and sang as occasion demanded, but the most enthusiastic outburst of all greeted the appearance of the final picture, which was a portrait of the King. Directly the children saw it – without waiting for the band – they gave three cheers and began to sing the chorus of the National Anthem.

A round of applause for Bert concluded the Pandorama performance; the lamp and the candles of the Christmas tree were re-lit – for although all the toys had been taken off, the tree still made a fine show with the shining glass ornaments – and then they had some more games; blind man's buff, a tug-of-war – in which Philpot was defeated with great slaughter – and a lot of other games. And when they were tired of these, each child 'said a piece' or sung a song, learnt specially for the occasion. The only one who had not come prepared in this respect was little Rosie, and even she – so as to be the same as the others – insisted on reciting the only piece she knew. Kneeling on the hearthrug, she put her hands together, palm to palm, and shutting her eyes very tightly she repeated the verse she always said every night before going to bed:

> 'Gentle Jesus, meek and mild,
> Look on me, a little child.
> Pity my simplicity,
> Suffer me to come to Thee.'

Then she stood up and kissed everyone in turn, and Philpot crossed over and began looking out of the window, and coughed, and blew his nose, because a nut that he had been eating had gone down the wrong way.

Most of them were by this time quite tired out, so after some supper the party broke up. Although they were nearly all very sleepy, none of them were very willing to go, but they were consoled by the thought of another entertainment to which they were going later on in the week – the Band of Hope[83] Tea and Prize Distribution at the Shining Light Chapel.

Bert undertook to see Elsie and Charley safely home, and Philpot volunteered to accompany Nellie and Tommy Newman, and to carry Rosie, who was so tired that she fell asleep on his shoulder before they left the house.

As they were going down the stairs Frankie held a hurried consultation with his mother, with the result that he was able to shout after them an invitation to come again next Christmas.

CHAPTER 30

The Brigands Hold a Council of War

It being now what is usually called the festive season – possibly because at this period of the year a greater number of people are suffering from hunger and cold than at any other time – the reader will not be surprised at being invited to another little party which took place on the day after the one we have just left. The scene was Mr. Sweater's office. Mr. Sweater was seated at his desk, but with his chair swung round to enable him to face his guests – Messrs. Rushton, Didlum, and Grinder, who were also seated.

'Something will 'ave to be done, and that very soon,' Grinder was saying. 'We can't go on much longer as we're doing at present. For my part, I think the best thing to do is to chuck up the sponge at once; the company is practically bankrupt now, and the longer we waits the worser it will be.'

'That's just my opinion,' said Didlum dejectedly. 'If we could supply the electric light at the same price as gas, or a little cheaper, we might have some chance; but we can't do it. The fact is that the machinery we've got is no dam good; it's too small and it's wore out, consequently the light we supply is inferior to gas and costs more.'

'Yes, I think we're fairly beaten this time,' said Rushton. 'Why, even if the Gas Coy. hadn't moved their works beyond the borough boundary, still we shouldn't 'ave been hable to compete with 'em.'

'Of course not,' said Grinder. 'The truth of the matter is just wot Didlum says. Our machinery is too small, it's worn hout, and good for nothing but to be throwed on the scrap-heap. So there's only one thing left to do and that is – go into liquidation.'

'I don't see it,' remarked Sweater.

'Well, what *do* you propose, then?' demanded Grinder. 'Reconstruct the company? Ask the shareholders for more money? Pull down the works and build fresh, and buy some new machinery? And then most likely not make a do of it after all? Not for me, old chap! I've 'ad enough. You won't catch me chuckin' good money after bad in that way.'

'Nor me neither,' said Rushton.

'Dead orf!' remarked Didlum, very decidedly.

Sweater laughed quietly. 'I'm not such a fool as to suggest anything of that sort,' he said. 'You seem to forget that I am one of the largest shareholders myself. No. What I propose is that we Sell Out.'

'Sell out!' replied Grinder with a contemptuous laugh in which the others joined. 'Who's going to buy the shares of a concern that's practically bankrupt and never paid a dividend?'

'I've tried to sell my little lot several times already,' said Didlum with a sickly smile, 'but nobody won't buy 'em.'

'Who's to buy?' repeated Sweater, replying to Grinder. 'The municipality of course! The ratepayers. Why shouldn't Mugsborough go in for Socialism as well as other towns?'

Rushton, Didlum and Grinder fairly gasped for breath: the audacity of the chief's proposal nearly paralysed them.

'I'm afraid we should never git away with it,' ejaculated Didlum, as soon as he could speak. 'When the people tumbled to it, there'd be no hend of a row.'

'*People! Row!*' replied Sweater, scornfully. 'The majority of the people will never know anything about it! Listen to me – '

'Are you quite sure as we can't be over'eard?' interrupted Rushton, glancing nervously at the door and round the office.

'It's all right,' answered Sweater, who nevertheless lowered his voice almost to a whisper, and the others drew their chairs closer and bent forward to listen.

'You know we still have a little money in hand: well, what I propose is this: At the annual meeting, which, as you know, comes off next week, we'll arrange for the Secretary to read a highly satisfactory report, and we'll declare a dividend of 15 per cent. – we can arrange it somehow between us. Of course, we'll have to cook the accounts a little, but I'll see that it's done properly. The other shareholders are not going to ask any awkward questions, and we all understand each other.'

Sweater paused, and regarded the other three brigands intently. 'Do you follow me?' he asked.

'Yes, yes,' said Didlum eagerly. 'Go on with it.' And Rushton and Grinder nodded assent.

'Afterwards,' resumed Sweater, 'I'll arrange for a good report of the meeting to appear in the *Weekly Ananias*. I'll instruct the Editor to write it himself, and I'll tell him just what to say. I'll also get him to write a leading article about it, saying that electricity is sure to supersede gas for lighting purposes in the very near future. Then the article will go on to refer to the huge profits made by the Gas

Coy. and to say how much better it would have been if the town had bought the gasworks years ago, so that those profits might have been used to reduce the rates, the same as has been done in other towns. Finally, the article will declare that it's a great pity that the Electric Light Supply should be in the hands of a private company, and to suggest that an effort be made to acquire it for the town.

'In the meantime we can all go about – in a very quiet and judicious way, of course – bragging about what a good thing we've got, and saying we don't mean to sell. We shall say that we've overcome all the initial expenses and difficulties connected with the installation of the works – that we are only just beginning to reap the reward of our industry and enterprise, and so on.

'Then,' continued the Chief, 'we can arrange for a proposal in the Council that the Town should purchase the Electric Light Works.'

'But not by one of us four, you know,' said Grinder with a cunning leer.

'Certainly not; that would give the show away at once. There are, as you know – several members of the Band who are not shareholders in the company; we'll get some of them to do most of the talking. We, being the directors of the company, must pretend to be against selling, and stick out for our own price; and when we do finally consent we must make out that we are sacrificing our private interests for the good of the Town. We'll get a committee appointed – we'll have an expert engineer down from London – I know a man that will suit our purpose admirably – we'll pay him a trifle and he'll say whatever we tell him to – and we'll rush the whole business through before you can say "Jack Robinson", and before the ratepayers have time to realise what's being done. Not that we need worry ourselves much about *them*. Most of them take no interest in public affairs, but even if there is something said, it won't matter much to us once we've got the money. It'll be a nine days' wonder and then we'll hear no more of it.'

As the Chief ceased speaking, the other brigands also remained silent, speechless with admiration of his cleverness.

'Well, what do you think of it?' he asked.

'Think of it!' cried Grinder, enthusiastically. 'I think it's splendid! Nothing could be better. If we can honly git away with it, I reckon it'll be one of the smartest things we've ever done.'

'Smart ain't the word for it,' observed Rushton.

'There's no doubt it's a grand idear!' exclaimed Didlum, 'and I've just thought of something else that might be done to help it along.

We could arrange to 'ave a lot of letters sent "To the Editor of the *Obscurer*" and "To the Editor of the *Ananias*" and "To the Editor of the *Weekly Chloroform*" in favour of the scheme.'

'Yes, that's a very good idear,' said Grinder. 'For that matter the editors could write them to themselves and sign them "Progress", "Ratepayer", "Advance Mugsborough", and sich-like.'

'Yes, that's all right,' said the Chief, thoughtfully, 'but we must be careful not to overdo it; of course there will have to be a certain amount of publicity, but we don't want to create too much interest in it.'

'Come to think of it,' observed Rushton arrogantly, 'why should we trouble ourselves about the opinion of the ratepayers at all? Why should we trouble to fake the books, or declare a dividend or 'ave the harticles in the papers or anything else? We've got the game in our own 'ands; we've got a majority in the Council, and, as Mr. Sweater ses, very few people even take the trouble to read the reports of the meetings.'

'Yes, that's right enough,' said Grinder. 'But it's just them few wot would make a lot of trouble and talk; *they're* the very people we 'as to think about. If we can only manage to put *them* in a fog we'll be all right, and the way to do it is as Mr. Sweater proposes.'

'Yes, I think so,' said the Chief. 'We must be very careful. I can work it all right in the *Ananias* and the *Chloroform*, and of course you'll see that the *Obscurer* backs us up.'

'I'll take care of that,' said Grinder, grimly.

The three local papers were run by limited companies. Sweater held nearly all the shares of the *Ananias* and of the *Weekly Chloroform*, and controlled their policy and contents. Grinder occupied the same position with regard to the *Obscurer*. The editors were a sort of marionettes who danced as Sweater and Grinder pulled the strings.

'I wonder how Dr. Weakling will take it?' remarked Rushton.

'That's the very thing I was just thinkin' about,' cried Didlum. 'Don't you think it would be a good plan if we could arrange to 'ave somebody took bad – you know, fall down in a fit or something in the street just outside the Town 'All just before the matter is brought forward in the Council, and then 'ave someone to come and call 'im out to attend to the party wot's ill, and keep 'im out till the business is done.'

'Yes, that's a capital idear,' said Grinder thoughtfully. 'But who could we get to 'ave the fit? It would 'ave to be someone we could trust, you know.'

' 'Ow about Rushton? You wouldn't mind doin' it, would yer?' enquired Didlum.

'I should strongly object,' said Rushton haughtily. He regarded the suggestion that he should act such an undignified part, as a kind of sacrilege.

'Then I'll do it meself if necessary,' said Didlum. 'I'm not proud when there's money to be made; anything for an honest living.'

'Well, I think we're all agreed, so far,' remarked Sweater. The others signified assent.

'And I think we all deserve a drink,' the Chief continued, producing a decanter and a box of cigars from a cupboard by the side of his desk. 'Pass that water bottle from behind you, Didlum.'

'I suppose nobody won't be comin' in?' said the latter, anxiously. 'I'm a teetotaller, you know.'

'Oh, it's all right,' said Sweater, taking four glasses out of the cupboard and pouring out the whisky. 'I've given orders that we're not to be disturbed for anyone. Say when.'

'Well, 'ere's success to Socialism,' cried Grinder, raising his glass, and taking a big drink.

'Amen – 'ear, 'ear, I mean,' said Didlum, hastily correcting himself.

'Wot I likes about this 'ere business is that we're not only doin' ourselves a bit of good,' continued Grinder with a laugh, 'we're not only doin' ourselves a bit of good, but we're likewise doin' the Socialists a lot of 'arm. When the ratepayers 'ave bought the Works, and they begins to kick up a row because they're losin' money over it – we can tell 'em that it's Socialism! And then they'll say that if that's Socialism they don't want no more of it.'

The other brigands laughed gleefully, and some of Didlum's whisky went down the wrong way and nearly sent him into a fit.

'You might as well kill a man at once,' he protested as he wiped the tears from his eyes, 'you might as well kill a man at once as choke 'im to death.'

'And now I've got a bit of good news for you,' said the Chief as he put his empty glass down.

The others became serious at once.

'Although we've had a very rough time of it in our contest with the Gasworks Company, and although we've got the worst of it, it hasn't been all lavender for them, you know. They've not enjoyed themselves either: we hit them pretty hard when we put up the coal dues.'

'A dam good job too,' said Grinder malignantly.

'Well,' continued Sweater, 'they're just as sick of the fight as they want to be, because of course they don't know exactly how badly we've been hit. For all they know, we could have continued the struggle indefinitely: and – well, to make a long story short, I've had a talk with the managing director and one or two others, and they're willing to let us in with them. So that we can put the money we get for the Electric Light Works into gas shares!'

This was such splendid news that they had another drink on the strength of it, and Didlum said that one of the first things they would have to do would be to totally abolish the Coal Dues, because they pressed so hard on the poor.

CHAPTER 31

The Deserter

About the end of January, Slyme left Easton's. The latter had not succeeded in getting anything to do since the work at 'The Cave' was finished, and latterly the quality of the food had been falling off. The twelve shillings Slyme paid for his board and lodging was all that Ruth had to keep house with. She had tried to get some work to do herself, but generally without success; there were one or two jobs that she might have had if she had been able to give her whole time to them, but of course that was not possible; the child and the housework had to be attended to, and Slyme's meals had to be prepared. Nevertheless, she contrived to get away several times when she had a chance of earning a few shillings by doing a day's charing for some lady or other, and then she left everything in such order at home that Easton was able to manage all right while she was away. On these occasions, she usually left the baby with Owen's wife, who was an old schoolmate of hers. Nora was the more willing to render her this service because Frankie used to be so highly delighted whenever it happened. He never tired of playing with the child, and for several days afterwards he used to worry his mother with entreaties to buy a baby of their own.

Easton earned a few shillings occasionally; now and then he got a job to clean windows, and once or twice he did a few days' or hours' work with some other painter who had been fortunate enough to get a little job 'on his own' – such as a ceiling to wash and whiten, or a room or two to paint; but such jobs were few.

Sometimes, when they were very hard up, they sold something; the Bible that used to lie on the little table in the bay window was one of the first things to be parted with. Ruth erased the inscription from the fly-leaf and then they sold the book at a second-hand shop for two shillings. As time went on, they sold nearly everything that was saleable, except of course, the things that were obtained on the hire system.

Slyme could see that they were getting very much into debt and behind with the rent, and on two occasions already Easton had borrowed five shillings from him, which he might never be able to pay back. Another thing was that Slyme was always in fear that Ruth – who had never wholly abandoned herself to wrongdoing – might tell Easton what had happened; more than once she had talked of doing so, and the principal reason why she refrained was that she knew that even if he forgave her, he could never think the same of her as before. Slyme repeatedly urged this view upon her, pointing out that no good could result from such a confession.

Latterly the house had become very uncomfortable. It was not only that the food was bad and that sometimes there was no fire, but Ruth and Easton were nearly always quarrelling about something or other. She scarcely spoke to Slyme at all, and avoided sitting at the table with him whenever possible. He was in constant dread that Easton might notice her manner towards him, and seek for some explanation. Altogether the situation was so unpleasant that Slyme determined to clear out. He made the excuse that he had been offered a few weeks' work at a place some little distance outside the town. After he was gone they lived for several weeks in semi-starvation on what credit they could get and by selling the furniture or anything else they possessed that could be turned into money. The things out of Slyme's room were sold almost directly he left.

CHAPTER 32

The Veteran

Old Jack Linden had tried hard to earn a little money by selling bloaters, but they often went bad, and even when he managed to sell them all the profit was so slight that it was not worth doing.

Before the work at 'The Cave' was finished, Philpot was a good friend to them; he frequently gave old Jack sixpence or a shilling and often brought a bag of cakes or buns for the children. Sometimes he came to tea with them on Sundays as an excuse for bringing a tin of salmon.

Elsie and Charley frequently went to Owen's house to take tea with Frankie; in fact, whilst Owen had anything to do, they almost lived there, for both Owen and Nora, knowing that the Lindens had nothing to live on except the earnings of the young woman, encouraged the children to come often.

Old Jack made some hopeless attempts to get work – work of any kind, but nobody wanted him; and to make things worse, his eyesight, which had been failing for a long time, became very bad. Once he was given a job by a big provision firm to carry an advertisement about the streets. The man who had been carrying it before – an old soldier – had been sacked the previous day for getting drunk while on duty. The advertisement was not an ordinary pair of sandwich boards, but a sort of box without any bottom or lid, a wooden frame, four sides covered with canvas, on which were pasted printed bills advertising margarine. Each side of this box or frame was rather larger than an ordinary sandwich board.

Old Linden had to get inside this thing and carry it about the streets; two straps fixed across the top of the frame and passing one over each of his shoulders enabled him to carry it. It swayed about a good deal as he walked along, especially when the wind caught it, but there were two handles inside to hold it steady by. The pay was eighteenpence a day, and he had to travel a certain route, up and down the busiest streets.

At first the frame did not feel very heavy, but the weight seemed to increase as the time went on, and the straps hurt his shoulders. He felt very much ashamed, also, whenever he encountered any of his old mates, some of whom laughed at him.

In consequence of the frame requiring so much attention to keep it steady, and being unused to the work, and his sight so bad, he several times narrowly escaped being run over. Another thing that added to his embarrassment was the jeering of the other sandwichmen, the loafers outside the public houses, and the boys, who shouted 'Old Jack in the box' after him. Sometimes the boys threw refuse at the frame, and once a decayed orange thrown by one of them knocked his hat off.

By the time evening came he was scarcely able to stand for weariness. His shoulders, his legs and his feet ached terribly, and as he was taking the thing back to the shop he was accosted by a ragged, dirty-looking, beer-sodden old man whose face was inflamed with drink and fury. This was the old soldier who had been discharged the previous day. He cursed and swore in the most awful manner and accused Linden of 'taking the bread out of his mouth', and, shaking his fist fiercely at him, shouted that he had a good mind to knock his face through his head and out of the back of his neck. He might possibly have tried to put this threat into practice but for the timely appearance of a policeman, when he calmed down at once and took himself off.

Jack did not go back the next day; he felt that he would rather starve than have any more of the advertisement frame, and after this he seemed to abandon all hope of earning money: wherever he went it was the same – no one wanted him. So he just wandered about the streets aimlessly, now and then meeting an old workmate who asked him to have a drink, but this was not often, for nearly all of them were out of work and penniless.

CHAPTER 33

The Soldier's Children

During most of this time, Jack Linden's daughter-in-law had 'Plenty of Work', making blouses and pinafores for Sweater & Co. She had so much to do that one might have thought that the Tory Millennium had arrived, and that Tariff Reform was already an accomplished fact.

She had Plenty of Work.

At first they had employed her exclusively on the cheapest kind of blouses – those that were paid for at the rate of two shillings a dozen, but they did not give her many of that sort now. She did the work so neatly that they kept her busy on the better qualities, which did not pay her so well, because although she was paid more per dozen, there was a great deal more work in them than in the cheaper kinds. Once she had a very special one to make, for which she was paid six shillings; but it took her four and a half days – working early and late – to do it. The lady who bought this blouse was told that it came from Paris, and paid three guineas for it. But of course Mrs. Linden knew nothing of that, and even if she had known, it would have made no difference to her.

Most of the money she earned went to pay the rent, and sometimes there was only two or three shillings left to buy food for all of them: sometimes not even so much, because although she had Plenty of Work she was not always able to do it. There were times when the strain of working the machine was unendurable: her shoulders ached, her arms became cramped, and her eyes pained so that it was impossible to continue. Then for a change she would leave the sewing and do some housework.

Once, when they owed four weeks' rent, the agent was so threatening that they were terrified at the thought of being sold up and turned out of the house, and so she decided to sell the round mahogany table and some of the other things out of the sitting-room. Nearly all the furniture that was in the house now belonged to her, and had formed her home before her husband died. The old people had given most of their things away at different times to their other sons since she had come to live there. These men were all married and all in employment. One was a fitter at the gas-works; the second was a railway porter, and the other was a butcher; but now that the old man was out of work they seldom came to the house. The last time they had been there was on Christmas Eve, and then there had been such a terrible row between them that the children had been awakened by it and frightened nearly out of their lives. The cause of the row was that some time previously they had mutually agreed to each give a shilling a week to the old people. They had done this for three weeks and after that the butcher had stopped his contribution: it had occurred to him that he was not to be expected to help to keep his brother's widow and her children. If the old people liked to give up the house and go to live in a room somewhere by themselves, he would continue paying his shilling a week, but not otherwise. Upon this the railway porter and the gas-fitter also ceased paying. They said it wasn't fair that they should pay a shilling a week each when the butcher – who was the eldest and earned the best wages – paid nothing. Provided he paid, they would pay; but if he didn't pay anything, neither would they. On Christmas Eve they all happened to come to the house at the same time; each denounced the others, and after nearly coming to blows they all went away raging and cursing and had not been near the place since.

As soon as she decided to sell the things, Mary went to Didlum's second-hand furniture store, and the manager said he would ask Mr. Didlum to call and see the table and other articles. She waited anxiously all the morning, but he did not appear, so she went once more to the shop to remind him. When he did come at last he was very contemptuous of the table and of everything else she offered to sell. Five shillings was the very most he could think of giving for the table, and even then he doubted whether he would ever get his money back. Eventually he gave her thirty shillings for the table, the overmantel, the easy chair, three other chairs and the two best pictures – one a large steel engraving of 'The Good Samaritan' and the other 'Christ Blessing Little Children'.

He paid the money at once; half an hour afterwards the van came to take the things away, and when they were gone, Mary sank down on the hearthrug in the wrecked room and sobbed as if her heart would break.

This was the first of several similar transactions. Slowly, piece by piece, in order to buy food and to pay the rent, the furniture was sold. Every time Didlum came he affected to be doing them a very great favour by buying the things at all. Almost an act of charity. He did not want them. Business was so bad: it might be years before he could sell them again, and so on. Once or twice he asked Mary if she did not want to sell the clock – the one that her late husband had made for his mother, but Mary shrank from the thought of selling this, until at last there was nothing else left that Didlum would buy, and one week, when Mary was too ill to do any needlework – it had to go. He gave them ten shillings for it.

Mary had expected the old woman to be heartbroken at having to part with this clock, but she was surprised to see her almost in-different. The truth was, that lately both the old people seemed stunned, and incapable of taking an intelligent interest in what was happening around them, and Mary had to attend to everything.

From time to time nearly all their other possessions – things of inferior value that Didlum would not look at, she carried out and sold at small second-hand shops in back streets or pledged at the pawnbroker's. The feather pillows, sheets, and blankets: bits of carpet or oilcloth, and as much of their clothing as was saleable or pawnable.

They felt the loss of the bedclothes more than anything else, for although all the clothes they wore during the day, and all the old clothes and dresses in the house, and even an old coloured table-cloth, were put on the beds at night, they did not compensate for the blankets, and they were often unable to sleep on account of the intense cold.

A lady district visitor who called occasionally sometimes gave Mary an order for a hundredweight of coal or a shillingsworth of groceries, or a ticket for a quart of soup, which Elsie fetched in the evening from the Soup Kitchen. But this was not very often, because, as the lady said, there were so many cases similar to theirs that it was impossible to do more than a very little for any one of them.

Sometimes Mary became so weak and exhausted through over-work, worry, and lack of proper food that she broke down altogether for the time being, and positively could not do any work at all. Then she used to lie down on the bed in her room and cry.

Whenever she became like this, Elsie and Charley used to do the housework when they came home from school, and make tea and toast for her, and bring it to the bedside on a chair so that she could eat lying down. When there was no margarine or dripping to put on the toast, they made it very thin and crisp and pretended it was biscuit.

The children rather enjoyed these times; the quiet and leisure was so different from other days when their mother was so busy she had no time to speak to them.

[[They would sit on the side of the bed, the old grandmother in her chair opposite,]] with the cat beside her listening to the conversation and purring or mewing whenever they stroked it or spoke to it. They talked principally of the future. Elsie said she was going to be a teacher and earn a lot of money to bring home to her mother to buy things with. Charley was thinking of opening a grocer's shop and having a horse and cart. When one has a grocer's shop, there is always plenty to eat; even if you have no money, you can take as much as you like out of your shop – good stuff, too, tins of salmon, jam, sardines, eggs, cakes, biscuits and all those sorts of things – and one was almost certain to have some money every day, because it wasn't likely that a whole day would go by without someone or other coming into the shop to buy something. When delivering the groceries with the horse and cart, he would give rides to all the boys he knew, and in the summertime, after the work was done and the shop shut up, Mother and Elsie and Granny could also come for long rides into the country.

The old grandmother – who had latterly become quite childish – used to sit and listen to all this talk with a superior air. Sometimes she argued with the children about their plans, and ridiculed them. She used to say with a chuckle that she had heard people talk like that before – lots of times – but it never came to nothing in the end.

One week about the middle of February, when they were in very sore straits indeed, old Jack applied to the secretary of the Organised Benevolence Society for assistance. It was about eleven o'clock in the morning when he turned the corner of the street where the office of the society was situated and saw a crowd of about thirty men waiting for the doors to be opened in order to apply for soup tickets. Some of these men were of the tramp or the drunken loafer class; some were old, broken-down workmen like himself, and others were labourers wearing corduroy or moleskin trousers with straps round their legs under their knees.

Linden waited at a distance until all these were gone before he went in. The secretary received him sympathetically and gave him a big form to fill up, but as Linden's eyes were so bad and his hand so unsteady the secretary very obligingly wrote in the answers himself, and informed him that he would enquire into the case and lay his application before the committee at the next meeting, which was to be held on the following Thursday – it was then Monday.

Linden explained to him that they were actually starving. He had been out of work for sixteen weeks, and during all that time they had lived for the most part on the earnings of his daughter-in-law, but she had not done anything for nearly a fortnight now, because the firm she worked for had not had any work for her to do. There was no food in the house and the children were crying for something to eat. All last week they had been going to school hungry, for they had had nothing but dry bread and tea every day: but this week – as far as he could see – they would not get even that. After some further talk the secretary gave him two soup tickets and an order for a loaf of bread, and repeated his promise to enquire into the case and bring it before the committee.

As Jack was returning home he passed the Soup Kitchen, where he saw the same lot of men who had been to the office of the Organised Benevolence Society for the soup tickets. They were waiting in a long line to be admitted. The premises being so small, the proprietor served them in batches of ten at a time.

On Wednesday the secretary called at the house, and on Friday Jack received a letter from him to the effect that the case had been duly considered by the committee, who had come to the conclusion that as it was a 'chronic' case they were unable to deal with it, and advised him to apply to the Board of Guardians. This was what Linden had hitherto shrunk from doing, but the situation was desperate. They owed five weeks' rent, and to crown their misfortune his eyesight had become so bad that even if there had been any prospect of obtaining work it was very doubtful if he could have managed to do it. So Linden, feeling utterly crushed and degraded, swallowed all that remained of his pride and went like a beaten dog to see the relieving officer, who took him before the Board, who did not think it a suitable case for out-relief, and after some preliminaries it was arranged that Linden and his wife were to go into the work-house, and Mary was to be allowed three shillings a week to help her to support herself and the two children. As for Linden's sons, the Guardians intimated their intention of compelling them to con-tribute towards the cost of their parents' maintenance.

Mary accompanied the old people to the gates of their future dwelling-place, and when she returned home she found there a letter addressed to J. Linden. It was from the house agent and contained a notice to leave the house before the end of the ensuing week. Nothing was said about the rent that was due. Perhaps Mr. Sweater thought that as he had already received nearly six hundred pounds in rent from Linden he could afford to be generous about the five weeks that were still owing – or perhaps he thought there was no possibility of getting the money. However that may have been, there was no reference to it in the letter – it was simply a notice to clear out, addressed to Linden, but meant for Mary.

It was about half-past three o'clock in the afternoon when she returned home and found this letter on the floor in the front passage. She was faint with fatigue and hunger, for she had had nothing but a cup of tea and a slice of bread that day, and her fare had not been much better for many weeks past. The children were at school, and the house – now almost destitute of furniture and without carpets or oilcloth on the floors – was deserted and cold and silent as a tomb. On the kitchen table were a few cracked cups and saucers, a broken knife, some lead teaspoons, a part of a loaf, a small basin containing some dripping and a brown earthenware teapot with a broken spout. Near the table were two broken kitchen chairs, one with the top cross piece gone from the back, and the other with no back to the seat at all. The bareness of the walls was relieved only by a coloured almanac and some paper pictures which the children had tacked upon them, and by the side of the fireplace was the empty wicker chair where the old woman used to sit. There was no fire in the grate, and the cold hearth was untidy with an accumulation of ashes, for during the trouble of these last few days she had not had time or heart to do any housework. The floor was unswept and littered with scraps of paper and dust: in one corner was a heap of twigs and small branches of trees that Charley had found somewhere and brought home for the fire.

The same disorder prevailed all through the house: all the doors were open, and from where she stood in the kitchen she could see the bed she shared with Elsie, with its heterogeneous heap of coverings. The sitting-room contained nothing but a collection of odds and ends of rubbish which belonged to Charley – his 'things' as he called them – bits of wood, string and rope; one wheel of a perambulator, a top, an iron hoop and so on. Through the other door was visible the dilapidated bedstead that had been used by the old people, with a similar lot of bedclothes to those on her own bed, and the torn, ragged covering of the mattress through the side of which the flock was protruding and falling in particles on to the floor.

As she stood there with the letter in her hand – faint and weary in the midst of all this desolation, it seemed to her as if the whole world were falling to pieces and crumbling away all around her.

CHAPTER 34

The Beginning of the End

During the months of January and February, Owen, Crass, Slyme and Sawkins continued to work at irregular intervals for Rushton & Co., although – even when there was anything to do – they now put in only six hours a day, commencing in the morning and leaving off at four, with an hour's interval for dinner between twelve and one. They finished the 'plant' and painted the front of Rushton's shop. When all this was completed, as no other work came in, they all had to 'stand off' with the exception of Sawkins, who was kept on because he was cheap and able to do all sorts of odd jobs, such as unstopping drains, repairing leaky roofs, rough painting or lime-washing, and he was also useful as a labourer for the plumbers, of whom there were now three employed at Rushton's, the severe weather which had come in with January having made a lot of work in that trade. With the exception of this one branch, practically all work was at a standstill.

During this time Rushton & Co. had had several 'boxing-up' jobs to do, and Crass always did the polishing of the coffins on these occasions, besides assisting to take the 'box' home when finished and to 'lift in' the corpse, and afterwards he always acted as one of the bearers at the funerals. For an ordinary class funeral he usually put in about three hours for the polishing; that came to one and nine. Taking home the coffin and lifting in the corpse, one shilling – usually there were two men to do this besides Hunter, who always accompanied them to superintend the work – attending the funeral and acting as bearer, four shillings: so that altogether Crass made six shillings and ninepence out of each funeral, and sometimes a little more. For instance, when there was an unusually good-class corpse they had a double coffin and then of course there were two 'lifts in', for the shell was taken home first and the outer coffin perhaps a day or two later: this made another shilling. No matter how expensive the funeral was, the bearers never got any more money. Sometimes the carpenter and Crass were able to charge an hour or two more on the making and polishing of a coffin for a good job, but that was all. Sometimes, when there was a very cheap job, they were paid only three shillings for attending as bearers, but this was not often: as a rule they got the same amount whether it was a cheap funeral or an expensive one. Slyme earned only five shillings out of each funeral, and Owen only one and six – for writing the coffin plate.

Sometimes there were three or four funerals in a week, and then Crass did very well indeed. He still had the two young men lodgers at his house, and although one of them was out of work he was still able to pay his way because he had some money in the bank.

One of the funeral jobs led to a terrible row between Crass and Sawkins. The corpse was that of a well-to-do woman who had been ill for a long time with cancer of the stomach, and after the funeral Rushton & Co. had to clean and repaint and paper the room she had occupied during her illness. Although cancer is not supposed to be an infectious disease, they had orders to take all the bedding away and have it burnt. Sawkins was instructed to take a truck to the house and get the bedding and take it to the town Refuse Destructor to be destroyed. There were two feather beds, a bolster and two pillows: they were such good things that Sawkins secretly resolved that instead of taking them to the Destructor he would take them to a second-hand dealer and sell them.

As he was coming away from the house with the things he met Hunter, who told him that he wanted him for some other work; so he was to take the truck to the yard and leave it there for the present; he could take the bedding to the Destructor later on in the day.

Sawkins did as Hunter ordered, and in the meantime Crass, who happened to be working at the yard painting some venetian blinds, saw the things on the truck, and, hearing what was to be done with them, he also thought it was a pity that such good things should be destroyed: so when Sawkins came in the afternoon to take them away Crass told him he need not trouble; 'I'm goin' to 'ave that lot,' he said; 'they're too good to chuck away; there's nothing wrong with 'em.'

This did not suit Sawkins at all. He said he had been told to take them to the Destructor, and he was going to do so. He was dragging the cart out of the yard when Crass rushed up and lifted the bundle off and carried it into the paint-shop. Sawkins ran after him and they began to curse and swear at each other; Crass accusing Sawkins of intending to take the things to the marine stores and sell them. Sawkins seized hold of the bundle with the object of replacing it on the cart, but Crass got hold of it as well and they had a tussle for it – a kind of tug of war – reeling and struggling all over the shop, cursing and swearing horribly all the time. Finally, Sawkins – being the better man of the two – succeeded in wrenching the bundle away and put it on the cart again, and then Crass hurriedly put on his coat and said he was going to the office to ask Mr. Rushton if he might have the things. Upon hearing this, Sawkins became so infuriated that he lifted the bundle off the cart and, throwing it upon the muddy ground, right into a pool of dirty water, trampled it underfoot; and then, taking out his clasp knife, began savagely hacking and ripping the ticking so that the feathers all came falling out. In a few minutes he had damaged the things beyond hope of repair, while Crass stood by, white and trembling, watching the proceedings but lacking the courage to interfere.

'Now go to the office and ask Rushton for 'em, if you like!' shouted Sawkins. 'You can 'ave 'em now, if you want 'em.'

Crass made no answer and, after a moment's hesitation, went back to his work, and Sawkins piled the things on the cart once more and took them away to the Destructor. He would not be able to sell them now, but at any rate he had stopped that dirty swine Crass from getting them.

When Crass went back to the paint-shop he found there one of the pillows which had fallen out of the bundle during the struggle. He took it home with him that evening and slept upon it. It was a fine pillow, much fuller and softer and more cosy than the one he had been accustomed to.

A few days afterwards when he was working at the room where the woman died, they gave him some other things that had belonged to her to do away with, and amongst them was a kind of wrap of grey knitted wool. Crass kept this for himself: it was just the thing to wrap round one's neck when going to work on a cold morning, and he used it for that purpose all through the winter. In addition to the funerals, there was a little other work: sometimes a room or two to be painted and papered and ceilings whitened, and once they had the outside of two small cottages to paint – doors and windows – two coats. All four of them worked at this job and it was finished in two days. And so they went on.

Some weeks Crass earned a pound or eighteen shillings; sometimes a little more, generally less and occasionally nothing at all.

There was a lot of jealousy and ill-feeling amongst them about the work. Slyme and Crass were both aggrieved about Sawkins whenever they were idle, especially if the latter were painting or whitewashing, and their indignation was shared by all the others who were 'off'. Harlow swore horribly about it, and they all agreed that it was disgraceful that a bloody labourer should be employed doing what ought to be skilled work for fivepence an hour, while properly qualified men were 'walking about'. These other men were also incensed against Slyme and Crass because the latter were given the preference whenever there was a little job to do, and it was darkly insinuated that in order to secure this preference these two were working for sixpence an hour. There was no love lost between Crass and Slyme either: Crass was furious whenever it happened that Slyme had a few hours' work to do if he himself were idle, and if ever Crass was working while Slyme was 'standing still' the latter went about amongst the other unemployed men saying ugly things about Crass, whom he accused of being a 'crawler'. Owen also came in for his share of abuse and blame: most of them said that a man like him should stick out for higher wages whether employed on special work or not, and then he would not get any preference. But all the same, whatever they said about each other behind each other's backs, they were all most friendly to each other when they met face to face.

Once or twice Owen did some work – such as graining a door or writing a sign – for one or other of his fellow workmen who had managed to secure a little job 'on his own', but putting it all together, the coffin plates and other work at Rushton's and all, his earnings had not averaged ten shillings a week for the last six weeks. Often they had no coal and sometimes not even a penny to put into the gas

meter, and then, having nothing left good enough to pawn, he sometimes obtained a few pence by selling some of his books to second-
hand book dealers. However, bad as their condition was, Owen knew
that they were better off than the majority of the others, for whenever he went out he was certain to meet numbers of men whom he
had worked with at different times, who said – some of them – that
they had been idle for ten, twelve, fifteen and in some cases for
twenty weeks without having earned a shilling.

Owen used to wonder how they managed to continue to exist.
Most of them were wearing other people's cast-off clothes, hats, and
boots, which had in some instances been given to their wives by
'visiting ladies', or by the people at whose houses their wives went to
work, charing. As for food, most of them lived on such credit as they
could get, and on the scraps of broken victuals and meat that their
wives brought home from the places they worked at. Some of them
had grown-up sons and daughters who still lived with them and
whose earnings kept their homes together, and the wives of some of
them eked out a miserable existence by letting lodgings.

The week before old Linden went into the workhouse Owen
earned nothing, and to make matters worse the grocer from whom
they usually bought their things suddenly refused to let them have
any more credit. Owen went to see him, and the man said he was
very sorry, but he could not let them have anything more without
the money; he did not mind waiting a few weeks for what was
already owing, but he could not let the amount get any higher; his
books were full of bad debts already. In conclusion, he said that he
hoped Owen would not do as so many others had done and take his
ready money elsewhere. People came and got credit from him when
they were hard up, and afterwards spent their ready money at the
Monopole Company's stores on the other side of the street, because
their goods were a trifle cheaper, and it was not fair. Owen admitted
that it was not fair, but reminded him that they always bought their
things at his shop. The grocer, however, was inexorable; he repeated
several times that his books were full of bad debts and his own
creditors were pressing him. During their conversation the shopkeeper's eyes wandered continually to the big store on the other
side of the street; the huge, gilded letters of the name 'Monopole
Stores' seemed to have an irresistible attraction for him. Once he
interrupted himself in the middle of a sentence to point out to
Owen a little girl who was just coming out of the Stores with a
small parcel in her hand.

'Her father owes me nearly thirty shillings,' he said, 'but they spend their ready money there.'

The front of the grocer's shop badly needed repainting, and the name on the fascia, 'A. Smallman', was so faded as to be almost indecipherable. It had been Owen's intention to offer to do this work – the cost to go against his account – but the man appeared to be so harassed that Owen refrained from making the suggestion.

They still had credit at the baker's, but they did not take much bread: when one has had scarcely anything else but bread to eat for nearly a month one finds it difficult to eat at all. That same day, when he returned home after his interview with the grocer, they had a loaf of beautiful fresh bread, but none of them could eat it, although they were hungry: it seemed to stick in their throats, and they could not swallow it even with the help of a drink of tea. But they drank the tea, which was the one thing that enabled them to go on living.

The next week Owen earned eight shillings altogether: a few hours he put in assisting Crass to wash off and whiten a ceiling and paint a room, and there was one coffin-plate. He wrote the latter at home, and while he was doing it he heard Frankie – who was out in the scullery with Nora – say to her:

'Mother, how many more days do you think we'll have to have only dry bread and tea?'

Owen's heart seemed to stop as he heard the child's question and listened for Nora's answer, but the question was not to be answered at all just then, for at that moment they heard someone running up the stairs and presently the door was unceremoniously thrown open and Charley Linden rushed into the house, out of breath, hatless, and crying piteously. His clothes were old and ragged; they had been patched at the knees and elbows, but the patches were tearing away from the rotting fabric into which they had been sewn. He had on a pair of black stockings full of holes through which the skin was showing. The soles of his boots were worn through at one side right to the uppers, and as he walked the sides of his bare heels came into contact with the floor, the front part of the sole of one boot was separated from the upper, and his bare toes, red with cold and covered with mud, protruded through the gap. Some sharp substance – a nail or a piece of glass or flint – had evidently lacerated his right foot, for blood was oozing from the broken heel of his boot on to the floor.

They were unable to make much sense of the confused story he told them through his sobs as soon as he was able to speak. All that was clear was that there was something very serious the matter at home: he thought his mother must be either dying or dead, because she did not speak or move or open her eyes, and 'please, please, *please* will you come home with me and see her?'

*   *   *

While Nora was getting ready to go with the boy, Owen made him sit on a chair, and having removed the boot from the foot that was bleeding, washed the cut with some warm water and bandaged it with a piece of clean rag, and then they tried to persuade him to stay there with Frankie while Nora went to see his mother, but the boy would not hear of it. So Frankie went with them instead. Owen could not go because he had to finish the coffin-plate, which was only just commenced.

It will be remembered that we left Mary Linden alone in the house after she returned from seeing the old people away. When the children came home from school, about half an hour afterwards, they found her sitting in one of the chairs with her head resting on her arms on the table, unconscious. They were terrified, because they could not awaken her and began to cry, but presently Charley thought of Frankie's mother and, telling his sister to stay there while he was gone, he started off at a run for Owen's house, leaving the front door wide open after him.

When Nora and the two boys reached the house they found there two other women neighbours, who had heard Elsie crying and had come to see what was wrong. Mary had recovered from her faint and was lying down on the bed. Nora stayed with her for some time after the other women went away. She lit the fire and gave the children their tea – there was still some coal and food left of what had been bought with the three shillings obtained from the Board of Guardians – and afterwards she tidied the house.

Mary said that she did not know exactly what she would have to do in the future. If she could get a room somewhere for two or three shillings a week, her allowance from the Guardians would pay the rent, and she would be able to earn enough for herself and the children to live on.

This was the substance of the story that Nora told Owen when she returned home. He had finished writing the coffin-plate, and as it was now nearly dry he put on his [[coat and took it down to the carpenter's shop at the yard.]]

On his way back he met Easton, who had been hanging about in the vain hope of seeing Hunter, and finding out if there was any chance of a job. As they walked along together, Easton confided to Owen that he had earned scarcely anything since he had been stood off at Rushton's, and what he had earned had gone, as usual, to pay the rent. Slyme had left them some time ago. Ruth did not seem able to get on with him; she had been in a funny sort of temper altogether, but since he had gone she had had a little work at a boarding-house on the Grand Parade. But things had been going from bad to worse. They had not been able to keep up the payments for the furniture they had hired, so the things had been seized and carted off. They had even stripped the oilcloth from the floor. Easton remarked he was sorry he had not tacked the bloody stuff down in such a manner that they would not have been able to take it up without destroying it. He had been to see Didlum, who said he didn't want to be hard on them, and that he would keep the things together for three months, and if Easton had paid up arrears by that time he could have them back again, but there was, in Easton's opinion, very little chance of that.

Owen listened with contempt and anger. Here was a man who grumbled at the present state of things, yet took no trouble to think for himself and try to alter them, and who at the first chance would vote for the perpetuation of the System which produced his misery.

'Have you heard that old Jack Linden and his wife went to the workhouse today,' he said.

'No,' replied Easton, indifferently. 'It's only what I expected.'

Owen then suggested it would not be a bad plan for Easton to let his front room, now that it was empty, to Mrs. Linden, who would be sure to pay her rent, which would help Easton to pay his. Easton agreed and said he would mention it to Ruth, and a few minutes later they parted.

The next morning Nora found Ruth talking to Mary Linden [[about the room]] and as the Eastons lived only about five minutes' walk away, they all three went round there in order that Mary might see the room. The appearance of the house from outside was unaltered: the white lace curtains still draped the windows of the front room; and in the centre of the bay was what appeared to be a small round table covered with a red cloth, and upon it a geranium in a flowerpot standing in a saucer with a frill of coloured tissue paper round it. These things and the curtains, which fell close together, made it impossible for anyone to see that the room was, otherwise, unfurnished. The 'table' consisted of an empty wooden box – procured from the grocer's – stood on end, with the lid of the scullery copper[84] placed upside down upon it for a top and covered with an old piece of red cloth. The purpose of this was to prevent the neighbours from thinking that they were hard up; although they knew that nearly all those same neighbours were in more or less similar straits.

It was not a very large room, considering that it would have to serve all purposes for herself and the two children, but Mrs. Linden knew that it was not likely that she would be able to get one as good elsewhere for the same price, so she agreed to take it from the following Monday at two shillings a week.

As the distance was so short they were able to carry most of the smaller things to their new home during the next few days, and on the Monday evening, when it was dark, Owen and Easton brought the remainder on a truck they borrowed for the purpose from Hunter.

During the last weeks of February the severity of the weather increased. There was a heavy fall of snow on the 20th followed by a hard frost which lasted several days.

About ten o'clock one night a policeman found a man lying unconscious in the middle of a lonely road. At first he thought the man was drunk, and after dragging him on to the footpath out of the way of passing vehicles he went for the stretcher. They took the man to the station and put him into a cell, which was already occupied by a man who had been caught in the act of stealing a swede turnip from a barn. When the police surgeon came he pronounced the supposed drunken man to be dying from bronchitis and want of food; and he further said that there was nothing to indicate that the man was addicted to drink. When the inquest was held a few days afterwards, the coroner remarked that it was the third case of death from destitution that had occurred in the town within six weeks.

The evidence showed that the man was a plasterer who had walked from London with the hope of finding work somewhere in the country. He had no money in his possession when he was found by the policeman; all that his pockets contained being several pawn-tickets and a letter from his wife, which was not found until after he died, because it was in an inner pocket of his waistcoat. A few days before this inquest was held, the man who had been arrested for stealing the turnips had been taken before the magistrates. The poor wretch said he did it because he was starving, but Aldermen Sweater and Grinder, after telling him that starvation was no excuse for dishonesty, sentenced him to pay a fine of seven shillings and costs, or go to prison for seven days with hard labour. As the convict had neither money nor friends, he had to go to jail, where he was, after all, better off than most of those who were still outside because they lacked either the courage or the opportunity to steal something to relieve their sufferings.

As time went on the long-continued privation began to tell upon Owen and his family. He had a severe cough: his eyes became deeply sunken and of remarkable brilliancy, and his thin face was always either deathly pale or dyed with a crimson flush.

Frankie also began to show the effects of being obliged to go so often without his porridge and milk; he became very pale and thin and his long hair came out in handfuls when his mother combed or brushed it. This was a great trouble to the boy, who, since hearing the story of Samson[85] read out of the Bible at school, had ceased from asking to have his hair cut short, lest he should lose his strength in consequence. He used to test himself by going through a certain exercise he had himself invented, with a flat iron, and he was always much relieved when he found that, notwithstanding the loss of the porridge, he was still able to lift the iron the proper number of times. But after a while, as he found that it became increasingly difficult to go through the exercise, he gave it up altogether, secretly resolving to wait until 'Dad' had more work to do, so that he could have the porridge and milk again. He was sorry to have to discontinue the exercise, but he said nothing about it to his father or mother, because he did not want to 'worry' them . . .

[Sometimes Nora managed to get a small job of needlework. On one occasion a woman with a small son brought a parcel] of garments belonging to herself or her husband, an old ulster, several coats, and so on – things that although they were too old-fashioned or shabby to wear, yet might look all right if turned and made up for the boy.

Nora undertook to do this, and after working several hours every day for a week she earned four shillings: and even then the woman thought it was so dear that she did not bring any more.

Another time Mrs. Easton got her some work at a boarding-house where she herself was employed. The servant was laid up, and they wanted some help for a few days. The pay was to be two shillings a day, and dinner. Owen did not want her to go because he feared she was not strong enough to do the work, but he gave way at last and Nora went. She had to do the bedrooms, and on the evening of the second day, as a result of the constant running up and down the stairs carrying heavy cans and pails of water, she was in such intense pain that she was scarcely able to walk home, and for several days afterwards had to lie in bed through a recurrence of her old illness, which caused her to suffer untold agony whenever she tried to stand.

Owen was alternately dejected and maddened by the knowledge of his own helplessness: when he was not doing anything for Rushton he went about the town trying to find some other work, but usually with scant success. He did some samples of show-card and window tickets and endeavoured to get some orders by canvassing the shops in the town, but this was also a failure, for these people generally had a ticket-writer to whom they usually gave their work. He did get a few trifling orders, but they were scarcely worth doing at the price he got for them. He used to feel like a criminal when he went into the shops to ask them for the work, because he realised fully that, in effect, he was saying to them: 'Take your work away from the other man, and employ *me*.' He was so conscious of this that it gave him a shamefaced manner, which, coupled as it was with his shabby clothing, did not create a very favourable impression upon those he addressed, who usually treated him with about as much courtesy as they would have extended to any other sort of beggar. Generally, after a day's canvassing, he returned home unsuccessful and faint with hunger and fatigue.

Once, when there was a bitterly cold east wind blowing, he was out on one of these canvassing expeditions and contracted a severe cold: his chest became so bad that he found it almost impossible to speak, because the effort to do so often brought on a violent fit of coughing. It was during this time that a firm of drapers, for whom he had done some showcards, sent him an order for one they wanted in a hurry, it had to be delivered the next morning, so he stayed up by himself till nearly midnight to do it. As he worked, he felt a strange sensation in his chest: it was not exactly a pain, and he would have found it difficult to describe it in words – it was just a sensation. He did not attach much importance to it, thinking it an effect of the cold he had taken, but whatever it was he could not help feeling conscious of it all the time.

Frankie had been put to bed that evening at the customary hour, but did not seem to be sleeping as well as usual. Owen could hear him twisting and turning about and uttering little cries in his sleep.

He left his work several times to go into the boy's room and cover him with the bedclothes which his restless movements had disordered.

As the time wore on, the child became more tranquil, and about eleven o'clock, when Owen went in to look at him, he found him in a deep sleep, lying on his side with his head thrown back on the pillow, breathing so softly through his slightly parted lips that the sound was almost imperceptible. The fair hair that clustered round his forehead was damp with perspiration, and he was so still and pale and silent that one might have thought he was sleeping the sleep that knows no awakening.

About an hour later, when he had finished writing the show-card, Owen went out into the scullery to wash his hands before going to bed: and whilst he was drying them on the towel, the strange sensation he had been conscious of all the evening became more intense, and a few seconds afterwards he was terrified to find his mouth suddenly filled with blood.

For what seemed an eternity he fought for breath against the suffocating torrent, and when at length it stopped, he sank trembling into a chair by the side of the table, holding the towel to his mouth and scarcely daring to breathe, whilst a cold sweat streamed from every pore and gathered in large drops upon his forehead.

Through the deathlike silence of the night there came from time to time the chimes of the clock of a distant church, but he continued to sit there motionless, taking no heed of the passing hours, and possessed with an awful terror.

So this was the beginning of the end! And afterwards the other two would be left by themselves at the mercy of the world. In a few years' time the boy would be like Bert White, in the clutches of some psalm-singing devil like Hunter or Rushton, who would use him as if he were a beast of burden. He imagined he could see him now as he would be then: worked, driven, and bullied, carrying loads, dragging carts, and running here and there, trying his best to satisfy the brutal tyrants, whose only thought would be to get profit out of him for themselves. If he lived, it would be to grow up with his body deformed and dwarfed by unnatural labour and with his mind stultified, degraded and brutalised by ignorance and poverty. As this vision of the child's future rose before him, Owen resolved that it should never be! He would not leave them alone and defence-less in the midst of the 'Christian' wolves who were waiting to rend them as soon as he was gone. If he could not give them happiness, he could at least put them out of the reach of further suffering. If he could not stay with them, they would have to come with him. It would be kinder and more merciful.[86]

CHAPTER 35

Facing the 'Problem'

Nearly every other firm in the town was in much the same plight as Rushton & Co.; none of them had anything to speak of to do, and the workmen no longer troubled to go to the different shops asking for a job. They knew it was of no use. Most of them just walked about aimlessly or stood talking in groups in the streets, principally in the neighbourhood of the Wage Slave Market near the fountain on the Grand Parade. They congregated here in such numbers that one or two residents wrote to the local papers complaining of the 'nuisance', and pointing out that it was calculated to drive the 'better-class' visitors out of the town. After this two or three extra policemen were put on duty near the fountain with instructions to 'move on' any groups of unemployed that formed. They could not stop them from coming there, but they prevented them standing about.

The processions of unemployed continued every day, and the money they begged from the public was divided equally amongst those who took part. Sometimes it amounted to one and sixpence each, sometimes it was a little more and sometimes a little less. These men presented a terrible spectacle as they slunk through the dreary streets, through the rain or the snow, with the slush soaking into their broken boots, and, worse still, with the bitterly cold east wind penetrating their rotten clothing and freezing their famished bodies.

The majority of the skilled workers still held aloof from these processions, although their haggard faces bore involuntary testimony to their sufferings. Although privation reigned supreme in their desolate homes, where there was often neither food nor light nor fire, they were too 'proud' to parade their misery before each other or the world. They secretly sold or pawned their clothing and their furniture and lived in semi-starvation on the proceeds, and on credit, but they would not beg. Many of them even echoed the sentiments of those who had written to the papers, and with a strange lack of class-sympathy blamed those who took part in the processions. They said it was that sort of thing that drove the 'better class' away, injured the town, and caused all the poverty and unemployment. However, some of them accepted charity in other ways; district visitors distributed tickets for coal and groceries. Not that that sort of thing made much difference; there was usually a great deal of fuss and advice, many quotations of Scripture, and very little groceries. And even what there was generally went to the least-deserving people, because the only way to obtain any of this sort of 'charity' is by hypocritically pretending to be religious: and the greater the hypocrite, the greater the quantity of coal and groceries. These 'charitable' people went into the wretched homes of the poor and – in effect – said: 'Abandon every particle of self-respect: cringe and fawn: come to church: bow down and grovel to us, and in return we'll give you a ticket that you can take to a certain shop and exchange for a shillingsworth of groceries. And, if you're very servile and humble we may give you another one next week.'

They never gave the 'case' the money. The ticket system[87] serves three purposes. It prevents the 'case' abusing the 'charity' by spending the money on drink. It advertises the benevolence of the donors: and it enables the grocer – who is usually a member of the church – to get rid of any stale or damaged stock he may have on hand.

When these visiting 'ladies' went into a workman's house and found it clean and decently furnished, and the children clean and tidy, they came to the conclusion that those people were not suitable 'cases' for assistance. Perhaps the children had had next to nothing to eat, and would have been in rags if the mother had not worked like a slave washing and mending their clothes. But these were not the sort of cases that the visiting ladies assisted; they only gave to those who were in a state of absolute squalor and destitution, and then only on condition that they whined and grovelled.

In addition to this district visitor business, the well-to-do inhabitants and the local authorities attempted – or rather, pretended – to grapple with the poverty 'problem' in many other ways, and the columns of the local papers were filled with letters from all sorts of cranks who suggested various remedies. One individual, whose income was derived from brewery shares, attributed the prevailing distress to the drunken and improvident habits of the lower orders. Another suggested that it was a Divine protest against the growth of Ritualism and what he called 'fleshly religion', and suggested a day of humiliation and prayer. A great number of well-fed persons thought this such an excellent proposition that they proceeded to put it into practice. They prayed, whilst the unemployed and the little children fasted.

If one had not been oppressed by the tragedy of Want and Misery, one might have laughed at the farcical, imbecile measures that were taken to relieve it. Several churches held what they called 'Rummage' or 'Jumble' sales. They sent out circulars something like this:

JUMBLE SALE
IN AID OF THE UNEMPLOYED.

If you have any articles of any description which are of no further use to you, we should be grateful for them, and if you will kindly fill in annexed form and post it to us, we will send and collect them.

On the day of the sale the parish room was transformed into a kind of Marine Stores, filled with all manner of rubbish, with the parson and the visiting ladies grinning in the midst. The things were sold for next to nothing to such as cared to buy them, and the local rag-and-bone man reaped a fine harvest. The proceeds of these sales were distributed in 'charity' and it was usually a case of much cry and little wool.[88]

There was a religious organisation, called 'The Mugsborough Skull and Crossbones Boys', which existed for the purpose of perpetuating the great religious festival of Guy Fawkes. This association also came to the aid of the unemployed and organised a Grand Fancy Dress Carnival and Torchlight Procession. When this took place, although there was a slight sprinkling of individuals dressed in tawdry costumes as cavaliers of the time of Charles I, and a few more as highwaymen or footpads, the majority of the processionists were boys in women's clothes, or wearing sacks with holes cut in them for their heads and arms, and with their faces smeared with soot. There were also a number of men carrying frying-pans in which they burnt red and blue fire. The procession – or rather, mob – was headed by a band, and the band was headed by two men, arm in arm, one very tall, dressed to represent Satan, in red tights, with horns on his head, and smoking a large cigar, and the other attired in the no less picturesque costume of a bishop of the Established Church.

This crew paraded the town, howling and dancing, carrying flaring torches, burning the blue and red fire, and some of them singing silly or obscene songs; whilst the collectors ran about with the boxes begging for money from people who were in most cases nearly as poverty-stricken as the unemployed they were asked to assist. The money thus obtained was afterwards handed over to the Secretary of the Organised Benevolence Society, Mr. Sawney Grinder.

Then there was the Soup Kitchen, which was really an inferior eating-house in a mean street. The man who ran this was a relative of the secretary of the O.B.S. He cadged all the ingredients for the soup from different tradespeople: bones and scraps of meat from butchers: pea meal and split peas from provision dealers: vegetables from greengrocers: stale bread from bakers, and so on. Well-intentioned, charitable old women with more money than sense sent him donations in cash, and he sold the soup for a penny a basin – or a penny a quart to those who brought jugs.

He had a large number of shilling books printed, each containing thirteen penny tickets. The Organised Benevolence Society bought a lot of these books and resold them to benevolent persons, or gave them away to 'deserving cases'. It was this connection with the O.B.S. that gave the Soup Kitchen a semi-official character in the estimation of the public, and furnished the proprietor with the excuse for cadging the materials and money donations.

In the case of the Soup Kitchen, as with the unemployed processions, most of those who benefited were unskilled labourers or derelicts: with but few exceptions the unemployed artisans – although their need was just as great as that of the others – avoided the place as if it were infected with the plague. They were afraid even to pass through the street where it was situated lest anyone seeing them coming from that direction should think they had been there. But all the same, some of them allowed their children to go there by stealth, by night, to buy some of this charity-tainted food.

Another brilliant scheme, practical and statesmanlike, so different from the wild projects of demented Socialists, was started by the Rev. Mr. Bosher, a popular preacher, the Vicar of the fashionable Church of the Whited Sepulchre.[89] He collected some subscriptions from a number of semi-imbecile old women who attended his church. With some of this money he bought a quantity of timber and opened what he called a Labour Yard, where he employed a number of men sawing firewood. Being a clergyman, and because he said he wanted it for a charitable purpose, of course he obtained the timber very cheaply – for about half what anyone else would have had to pay for it.

The wood-sawing was done piecework. A log of wood about the size of a railway sleeper had to be sawn into twelve pieces, and each of these had to be chopped into four. For sawing and chopping one log in this manner the worker was paid ninepence. One log made two bags of firewood, which were sold for a shilling each – a trifle under the usual price. The men who delivered the bags were paid three-halfpence for each two bags.

As there were such a lot of men wanting to do this work, no one was allowed to do more than three logs in one day – that came to two shillings and threepence – and no one was allowed to do more than two days in one week.

The Vicar had a number of bills printed and displayed in shop windows calling attention to what he was doing, and informing the public that orders could be sent to the Vicarage by post and would receive prompt attention and the fuel could be delivered at any address – Messrs. Rushton & Co. having very kindly lent a handcart for the use of the men employed at the Labour Yard.

As a result of the appearance of this bill, and of the laudatory notices in the columns of the *Ananias*, the *Obscurer*, and the *Chloroform* – the papers did not mind giving the business a free advertisement, because it was a charitable concern – many persons withdrew their custom from those who usually supplied them with firewood, and gave their orders to the Yard; and they had the satisfaction of getting their fuel cheaper than before and of performing a charitable action at the same time.

As a remedy for unemployment this scheme was on a par with the method of the tailor in the fable who thought to lengthen his cloth by cutting a piece off one end and sewing it on to the other; but there was one thing about it that recommended it to the Vicar – it was self-supporting. He found that there would be no need to use all the money he had extracted from the semi-imbecile old ladies for timber, so he bought himself a Newfoundland dog, an antique set of carved ivory chessmen, and a dozen bottles of whiskey with the remainder of the cash.

The reverend gentleman hit upon yet another means of helping the poor. He wrote a letter to the *Weekly Chloroform* appealing for cast-off boots for poor children. This was considered such a splendid idea that the editors of all the local papers referred to it in leading articles, and several other letters were written by prominent citizens extolling the wisdom and benevolence of the profound Bosher. Most of the boots that were sent in response to this appeal had been worn until they needed repair – in a very large proportion of instances, until they were beyond repair. The poor people to whom they were given could not afford to have them mended before using them, and the result was that the boots generally began to fall to pieces after a few days' wear.

This scheme amounted to very little. It did not increase the number of cast-off boots, and most of the people who 'cast off' their boots generally gave them to someone or other. The only difference it can have made was that possibly a few persons who usually threw their boots away or sold them to second-hand dealers may have been induced to send them to Mr. Bosher instead. But all the same nearly everybody said it was a splendid idea: its originator was applauded as a public benefactor, and the pettifogging busybodies who amused themselves with what they were pleased to term 'charitable work' went into imbecile ecstasies over him.

CHAPTER 36

The O. B. S.

One of the most important agencies for the relief of distress was the Organised Benevolence Society. This association received money from many sources. The proceeds of the fancy-dress carnival; the collections from different churches and chapels which held special services in aid of the unemployed; the weekly collections made by the employees of several local firms and business houses; the proceeds of concerts, bazaars, and entertainments, donations from charitable persons, and the subscriptions of the members. The society also received large quantities of cast-off clothing and boots, and tickets of admission to hospitals, convalescent homes and dispensaries from subscribers to those institutions, or from people like Rushton & Co., who had collecting-boxes in their workshops and offices.

Altogether during the last year the Society had received from various sources about three hundred pounds in hard cash. This money was devoted to the relief of cases of distress.

The largest item in the expenditure of the Society was the salary of the General Secretary, Mr. Sawney Grinder – a most deserving case – who was paid one hundred pounds a year.

After the death of the previous secretary there were so many candidates for the vacant post that the election of the new secretary was a rather exciting affair. The excitement was all the more intense because it was restrained. A special meeting of the society was held: the Mayor, Alderman Sweater, presided, and amongst those present were Councillors Rushton, Didlum and Grinder, Mrs. Starvem,

Rev. Mr. Bosher, a number of the rich, semi-imbecile old women who had helped to open the Labour Yard, and several other 'ladies'. Some of these were the district visitors already alluded to, most of them the wives of wealthy citizens and retired tradesmen, richly dressed, ignorant, insolent, overbearing frumps, who – after filling themselves with good things in their own luxurious homes – went flouncing into the poverty-stricken dwellings of their poor 'sisters' and talked to them of 'religion', lectured them about sobriety and thrift, and – sometimes – gave them tickets for soup or orders for shillingsworths of groceries or coal. Some of these overfed females – the wives of tradesmen, for instance – belonged to the Organised Benevolence Society, and engaged in this 'work' for the purpose of becoming acquainted with people of superior social position – one of the members was a colonel, and Sir Graball D'Encloseland – the Member of Parliament for the borough – also belonged to the Society and occasionally attended its meetings. Others took up district visiting as a hobby; they had nothing to do, and being densely ignorant and of inferior mentality, they had no desire or capacity for any intellectual pursuit. So they took up this work for the pleasure of playing the grand lady and the superior person at a very small expense. Other of these visiting ladies were middle-aged, unmarried women with small private incomes – some of them well-meaning, compassionate, gentle creatures who did this work because they sincerely desired to help others, and they knew of no better way. These did not take much part in the business of the meetings; they paid their subscriptions and helped to distribute the cast-off clothing and boots to those who needed them, and occasionally obtained from the secretary an order for provisions or coal or bread for some poverty-stricken family; but the poor, toil-worn women whom they visited welcomed them more for their sisterly sympathy than for the gifts they brought. Some of the visiting ladies were of this character – but they were not many. They were as a few fragrant flowers amidst a dense accumulation of noxious weeds. They were examples of humility and kindness shining amidst a vile and loathsome mass of hypocrisy, arrogance, and cant.

When the Chairman had opened the meeting, Mr. Rushton moved a vote of condolence with the relatives of the late secretary whom he eulogised in the most extraordinary terms.

'The poor of Mugsborough had lost a kind and sympathetic friend', 'One who had devoted his life to helping the needy', and so on and so forth. (As a matter of fact, most of the time of the defunct had been passed in helping himself, but Rushton said nothing about that.)

Mr. Didlum seconded the vote of condolence in similar terms, and it was carried unanimously. Then the Chairman said that the next business was to elect a successor to the departed paragon; and immediately no fewer than nine members rose to propose a suitable person – they each had a noble-minded friend or relative willing to sacrifice himself for the good of the poor.

The nine Benevolent stood looking at each other and at the Chairman with sickly smiles upon their hypocritical faces. It was a dramatic moment. No one spoke. It was necessary to be careful. It would never do to have a contest. The Secretary of the O.B.S. was usually regarded as a sort of philanthropist by the outside public, and it was necessary to keep this fiction alive.

For one or two minutes an awkward silence reigned. Then, one after another they all reluctantly resumed their seats with the exception of Mr. Amos Grinder, who said he wished to propose his nephew, Mr. Sawney Grinder, a young man of a most benevolent disposition who was desirous of immolating himself upon the altar of charity for the benefit of the poor – or words to that effect.

Mr. Didlum seconded, and there being no other nomination – for they all knew that it would give the game away to have a contest – the Chairman put Mr. Grinder's proposal to the meeting and declared it carried unanimously.

Another considerable item in the expenditure of the society was the rent of the offices – a house in a back street. The landlord of this place was another very deserving case.

There were numerous other expenses: stationery and stamps, printing, and so on, and what was left of the money was used for the purpose for which it had been given – a reasonable amount being kept in hand for future expenses. All the details were of course duly set forth in the Report and Balance Sheet at the annual meetings. No copy of this document was ever handed to the reporters for publication; it was read to the meeting by the Secretary; the representatives of the Press took notes, and in the reports of the meeting that subsequently appeared in the local papers the thing was so mixed up and garbled together that the few people who read it could not make head or tail of it. The only thing that was clear was that the society had been doing a great deal of good to someone or other, and that more money was urgently needed to carry on the work. It usually appeared something like this:

HELPING THE NEEDY

MUGSBOROUGH ORGANISED BENEVOLENCE SOCIETY.

Annual Meeting at the Town Hall.

A Splendid record of Miscellaneous and Valuable Work.

The annual meeting of the above Society was held yesterday at the Town Hall. The Mayor, Alderman Sweater, presided, and amongst those present were Sir Graball D'Encloseland, Lady D'Encloseland, Lady Slumrent, Rev. Mr. Bosher, Mr. Cheeseman, Mrs. Bilder, Mrs. Grosare, Mrs. Daree, Mrs. Butcher, Mrs. Taylor, Mrs. Baker, Mrs. Starvem, Mrs. Slodging, Mrs. M. B. Sile, Mrs. Knobrane, Mrs. M. T. Head, Mr. Rushton, Mr. Didlum, Mr. Grinder and (here followed about a quarter of a column of names of other charitable persons, all subscribers to the Society).

The Secretary read the annual report which contained the following amongst other interesting items:

During the year, 1,972 applications for assistance have been received, and of this number 1,302 have been assisted as follows: Bread or grocery orders, 273. Coal or coke orders, 57. Nourishment 579.* (Applause.) Pairs of boots granted, 29, Clothing, 105. Crutch granted to poor man, 1. Nurses provided, 2. Hospital tickets, 26. Sent to Consumption Sanatorium, 1. Twenty-nine persons, whose cases being chronic, were referred to the Poor Law Guardians. Work found for 19 persons. (Cheers.) Pedlar's licences, 4. Dispensary tickets, 24. Bedding redeemed, 1. Loans granted to people to enable them to pay their rent, 8. (Loud cheers.) Dental tickets, 2. Railway fares for men who were going away from the town to employment else-where, 12. (Great cheering.) Loans granted, 5. Advertisements for employment, 4 – and so on.

There was about another quarter of a column of these details, the reading of which was punctuated with applause and concluded with: 'Leaving 670 cases which for various reasons the Society was unable to assist.' The report then went on to explain that the work of enquiring into the genuineness of the applications entailed a lot of labour on the part of the Secretary, some cases taking several days.

---

*   This was the Secretary's way of saying that Soup tickets had been given.

No fewer than 649 letters had been sent out from the office, and 97 postcards. (Applause.) Very few cash gifts were granted, as it was most necessary to guard against the Charity being abused. (Hear, hear.)

Then followed a most remarkable paragraph headed 'The Balance Sheet', which – as it was put – 'included the following'. 'The following' was a jumbled list of items of expenditure, subscriptions, donations, legacies, and collections, winding up with 'the general summary showed a balance in hand of £178. 4. 6'. (They always kept a good balance in hand because of the Secretary's salary and the rent of the offices.)

After this very explicit financial statement came the most important part of the report: 'Thanks are expressed to Sir Graball D'Encloseland for a donation of 2 guineas. Mrs. Grosare, 1 guinea. Mrs. Starvem, Hospital tickets. Lady Slumrent, letter of admission to Convalescent Home. Mrs. Knobrane, 1 guinea. Mrs. M. B. Sile, 1 guinea. Mrs. M. T. Head, 1 guinea. Mrs. Slodging, gifts of clothing – and so on for another quarter of a column, the whole concluding with a vote of thanks to the Secretary and an urgent appeal to the charitable public for more funds to enable the Society to continue its noble work.

Meantime, in spite of this and kindred organisations the conditions of the under-paid poverty stricken and unemployed workers remained the same. Although the people who got the grocery and coal orders, the 'Nourishment', and the cast-off clothes and boots, were very glad to have them, yet these things did far more harm than good. They humiliated, degraded and pauperised those who received them, and the existence of the societies prevented the problem being grappled with in a sane and practical manner. The people lacked the necessaries of life: the necessaries of life are produced by Work: these people were willing to work, but were prevented from doing so by the idiotic system of society which these 'charitable' people are determined to do their best to perpetuate.

If the people who expect to be praised and glorified for being charitable were never to give another farthing it would be far better for the industrious poor, because then the community as a whole would be compelled to deal with the absurd and unnecessary state of affairs that exists today – millions of people living and dying in wretchedness and poverty in an age when science and machinery have made it possible to produce such an abundance of everything that everyone might enjoy plenty and comfort. If it were not for all this so-called charity the starving unemployed men all over the country would demand to be allowed to work and produce the things they are perishing for want of, instead of being – as they are now – content to wear their masters' cast-off clothing and to eat the crumbs that fall from his table.

CHAPTER 37

A Brilliant Epigram

All through the winter, the wise, practical, philanthropic, fat persons whom the people of Mugsborough had elected to manage their affairs – or whom they permitted to manage them without being elected – continued to grapple or, to pretend to grapple, with the 'problem' of unemployment and poverty. They continued to hold meetings, rummage and jumble sales, entertainments and special services. They continued to distribute the rotten cast-off clothing and boots, and the nourishment tickets. They were all so sorry for the poor, especially for the 'dear little children'. They did all sorts of things to help the children. In fact, there was nothing that they would not do for them except levy a halfpenny rate. It would never do to do that. It might pauperise the parents and destroy parental responsibility. They evidently thought that it would be better to destroy the health or even the lives of the 'dear little children' than to pauperise the parents or undermine parental responsibility. These people seemed to think that the children were the property of their parents. They did not have sense enough to see that the children are not the property of their parents at all, but the property of the community. When they attain to manhood and womanhood they will be, if mentally or physically inefficient, a burden on the community; if they become criminals, they will prey upon the community, and if they are healthy, educated and brought up in good surroundings, they will become useful citizens, able to render valuable service, not merely to their parents, but to the community. Therefore the children are the property of the community, and it is the business and to the interest of the community to see that their constitutions are not undermined by starvation. The Secretary of the local Trades Council, a body formed of delegates from all the different trades unions in the town, wrote a letter to the *Obscurer*, setting forth this view. He pointed out that a halfpenny rate in that town would produce a sum of £800, which would be more than sufficient to provide food for all the hungry schoolchildren. In the next issue of the paper several other letters appeared from leading citizens, including, of course, Sweater, Rushton, Didlum and Grinder, ridiculing the proposal of the Trades Council, who were insultingly alluded to as 'pothouse politicians', 'beer-sodden agitators' and so forth. Their right to be regarded as representatives of the working men was denied, and Grinder, who, having made inquiries amongst working men, was acquainted with the facts, stated that there was scarcely one of the local branches of the trades unions which had more than a dozen members; and as Grinder's statement was true, the Secretary was unable to contradict it. The majority of the working men were also very indignant when they heard about the Secretary's letter: they said the rates were quite high enough as it was, and they sneered at him for presuming to write to the papers at all.

'Who the bloody 'ell was 'e?' they said. ' 'E was not a Gentleman! 'E was only a workin' man the same as themselves – a common carpenter! What the 'ell did 'e know about it? Nothing. 'E was just trying to make 'isself out to be Somebody, that was all. The idea of one of the likes of them writing to the papers!'

One day, having nothing better to do, Owen was looking at some books that were exposed for sale on a table outside a second-hand furniture shop. One book in particular took his attention: he read several pages with great interest, and regretted that he had not the necessary sixpence to buy it. The title of the book was: *Consumption: Its Causes and Its Cure*. The author was a well-known physician who devoted his whole attention to the study of that disease. Amongst other things, the book gave rules for the feeding of delicate children, and there were also several different dietaries recommended for adult persons suffering from the disease. One of these dietaries amused him very much, because as far as the majority of those who suffer from consumption are concerned, the good doctor might just as well have prescribed a trip to the moon:

'Immediately on waking in the morning, half a pint of milk – this should be hot, if possible – with a small slice of bread and butter.

'At breakfast: half a pint of milk, with coffee, chocolate, or oatmeal: eggs and bacon, bread and butter, or dry toast.

'At eleven o'clock: half a pint of milk with an egg beaten up in it or some beef tea and bread and butter.

'At one o'clock: half a pint of warm milk with a biscuit or sandwich.

'At two o'clock: fish and roast mutton, or a mutton chop, with as much fat as possible: poultry, game, etc., may be taken with vegetables, and milk pudding.

'At five o'clock: hot milk with coffee or chocolate, bread and butter, watercress, etc.

'At eight o'clock: a pint of milk, with oatmeal or chocolate, and gluten bread, or two lightly boiled eggs with bread and butter.

'Before retiring to rest: a glass of warm milk.

'During the night: a glass of milk with a biscuit or bread and butter should be placed by the bedside and be eaten if the patient awakes.'

Whilst Owen was reading this book, Crass, Harlow, Philpot and Easton were talking together on the other side of the street, and presently Crass caught sight of him. They had been discussing the Secretary's letter *re* the halfpenny rate, and as Owen was one of the members of the Trades Council, Crass suggested that they should go across and tackle him about it.

'How much is your house assessed at?' asked Owen after listening for about a quarter of an hour to Crass's objection.

'Fourteen pound,' replied Crass.

'That means that you would have to pay sevenpence per year if we had a halfpenny rate. Wouldn't it be worth sevenpence a year to you to know that there were no starving children in the town?'

'Why should I 'ave to 'elp to keep the children of a man who's too lazy to work, or spends all 'is money on drink?' shouted Crass. ' 'Ow are yer goin' to make out about the likes o' them?'

'If his children are starving we should feed them first, and punish him afterwards.'

'The rates is quite high enough as it is,' grumbled Harlow, who had four children himself.

'That's quite true, but you must remember that the rates the working classes at present pay are spent mostly for the benefit of other people. Good roads are maintained for people who ride in motor cars and carriages; the Park and the Town Band for those who have leisure to enjoy them; the Police force to protect the property of those who have something to lose, and so on. But if we pay this rate we shall get something for our money.'

'We gets the benefit of the good roads when we 'as to push a 'andcart with a load o' paint and ladders,' said Easton.

'Of course,' said Crass, 'and besides, the workin' class gets the benefit of all the other things too, because it all makes work.'

'Well, for my part,' said Philpot, 'I wouldn't mind payin' my share towards a 'appeny rate, although I ain't got no kids o' me own.'

The hostility of most of the working men to the proposed rate was almost as bitter as that of the 'better' classes – the noble-minded philanthropists who were always gushing out their sympathy for the 'dear little ones', the loathsome hypocrites who pretended that there was no need to levy a rate because they were willing to give sufficient money in the form of charity to meet the case: but the children continued to go hungry all the same.

'Loathsome hypocrites' may seem a hard saying, but it was a matter of common knowledge that the majority of the children attending the local elementary schools were insufficiently fed. It was admitted that the money that could be raised by a half-penny rate would be more than sufficient to provide them all with one good meal every day. The charity-mongers who professed such extravagant sympathy with the 'dear little children' resisted the levying of the rate 'because it would press so heavily on the poorer ratepayers', and said that they were willing to give more in voluntary charity than the rate would amount to: but, the 'dear little children' – as they were so fond of calling them – continued to go to school hungry all the same.

To judge them by their professions and their performances, it appeared that these good kind persons were willing to do any mortal thing for the 'dear little children' except allow them to be fed.

If these people had really meant to do what they pretended, they would not have cared whether they paid the money to a rate-collector or to the secretary of a charity society and they would have preferred to accomplish their object in the most efficient and economical way.

But although they would not allow the children to be fed, they went to church and to chapel, glittering with jewellery, their fat carcases clothed in rich raiment, and sat with smug smiles upon their faces listening to the fat parsons reading out of a Book that none of them seemed able to understand, for this was what they read:

'And Jesus called a little child unto Him,[90] and set him in the midst of them, and said: Whosoever shall receive one such little child in My name, receiveth Me. But whoso shall offend one of these little ones, it were better for him that a millstone were hanged about his neck and that he were drowned in the depth of the sea.

'Take heed that ye despise not one of these little ones, for I say unto you that in heaven their angels do always behold the face of My Father.'

And this: 'Then shall He say unto them: Depart from me, ye cursed, into the everlasting fire prepared for the devil and his angels:

for I was an hungred and ye gave Me no meat: I was thirsty, and ye gave Me no drink: I was a stranger and ye took Me not in; naked, and ye clothed Me not.

'Then shall they answer: "Lord, when saw we Thee an hungred or athirst or a stranger or naked, or sick, and did not minister unto Thee?' and He shall answer them, 'Verily I say unto you, inasmuch as ye did it not to one of the least of these, ye did it not to Me." '[90]

These were the sayings that the infidel parsons mouthed in the infidel temples to the richly dressed infidel congregations, who heard but did not understand, for their hearts were become gross and their ears dull of hearing.[90] And meantime, all around them, in the alley and the slum, and more terrible still – because more secret – in the better sort of streets where lived the respectable class of skilled artisans, the little children became thinner and paler day by day for lack of proper food, and went to bed early because there was no fire.

Sir Graball D'Encloseland, the Member of Parliament for the borough, was one of the bitterest opponents of the halfpenny rate, but as he thought it was probable that there would soon be another General Election and he wanted the children's fathers to vote for him again, he was willing to do something for them in another way. He had a little ten-year-old daughter whose birthday was in that month, so the kind-hearted Baronet made arrangements to give a Tea to all the school children in the town in honour of the occasion. The tea was served in the schoolrooms, and each child was presented with a gilt-edged card on which was a printed portrait of the little hostess, with 'From your loving little friend, Honoria D'Encloseland', in gold letters. During the evening the little girl, accompanied by Sir Graball and Lady D'Encloseland, motored round to all the schools where the tea was being consumed: the Baronet made a few remarks, and Honoria made a pretty little speech, specially learnt for the occasion, at each place, and they were loudly cheered and greatly admired in response. The enthusiasm was not confined to the boys and girls, for while the speechmaking was going on inside, a little crowd of grown-up children were gathered round outside the entrance, worshipping the motor car: and when the little party came out the crowd worshipped them also, going into imbecile ecstasies of admiration of their benevolence and their beautiful clothes.

For several weeks everybody in the town was in raptures over this tea – or, rather, everybody except a miserable little minority of Socialists, who said it was bribery, an electioneering dodge, that it did no real good, and who continued to clamour for a halfpenny rate.

Another specious fraud was the 'Distress Committee'.[91] This body – or corpse, for there was not much vitality in it – was supposed to exist for the purpose of providing employment for 'deserving cases'. One might be excused for thinking that any man – no matter what his past may have been – who is willing to work for his living is a 'deserving case': but this was evidently not the opinion of the persons who devised the regulations for the working of this committee. Every applicant for work was immediately given a long job, and presented with a double sheet of foolscap paper to do it with. Now, if the object of the committee had been to furnish the applicant with material for the manufacture of an appropriate head-dress for himself, no one could reasonably have found fault with them: but the foolscap was not to be utilised in that way; it was called a 'Record Paper', three pages of it were covered with insulting, inquisitive, irrelevant questions concerning the private affairs and past life of the 'case' who wished to be permitted to work for his living, and all these had to be answered to the satisfaction of Messrs. D'Encloseland, Bosher, Sweater, Rushton, Didlum, Grinder and the other members of the committee, before the case stood any chance of getting employment.

However, notwithstanding the offensive nature of the questions on the application form, during the five months that this precious committee was in session, no fewer than 1,237 broken-spirited and humbled 'lion's whelps' filled up the forms and answered the questions as meekly as if they had been sheep. The funds of the committee consisted of £500, obtained from the Imperial Exchequer, and about £250 in charitable donations. This money was used to pay wages for certain work – some of which would have had to be done even if the committee had never existed – and if each of the 1,237 applicants had had an equal share of the work, the wages they would have received would have amounted to about twelve shillings each. This was what the 'practical' persons, the 'business-men', called 'dealing with the problem of unemployment'. Imagine having to keep your family for five months with twelve shillings!

And, if you like, imagine that the Government grant had been four times as much as it was, and that the charity had amounted to four times as much as it did, and then fancy having to keep your family for five months with two pounds eight shillings!

It is true that some of the members of the committee would have been very glad if they had been able to put the means of earning a living within the reach of every man who was willing to work; but they simply did not know what to do, or how to do it. They were not ignorant of the reality of the evil they were supposed to be 'dealing with' – appalling evidences of it faced them on every side, and as, after all, these committee men were human beings and not devils, they would have been glad to mitigate it if they could have done so without hurting themselves: but the truth was that they did not know what to do!

These are the 'practical' men; the monopolists of intelligence, the wise individuals who control the affairs of the world: it is in accordance with the ideas of such men as these that the conditions of human life are regulated.

This is the position:

It is admitted that never before in the history of mankind was it possible to produce the necessaries of life in such abundance as at present.

The management of the affairs of the world – the business of arranging the conditions under which we live – is at present in the hands of Practical, Level-headed, Sensible Business-men.

The result of their management is, that the majority of the people find it a hard struggle to live. Large numbers exist in perpetual poverty: a great many more periodically starve: many actually die of want: hundreds destroy themselves rather than continue to live and suffer.

When the Practical, Level-headed, Sensible Business-men are asked why they do not remedy this state of things, they reply that they do not know what to do! or, that it is impossible to remedy it!

And yet it is admitted that it is now possible to produce the necessaries of life, in greater abundance than ever before!

With lavish kindness, the Supreme Being had provided all things necessary for the existence and happiness of his creatures. To suggest that it is not so is a blasphemous lie: it is to suggest that the Supreme Being is not good or even just. On every side there is an over-flowing superfluity of the materials requisite for the production of all the necessaries of life: from these materials everything we need may be produced in abundance – by Work. Here was an army of people lacking the things that may be made by work, standing idle. Willing to work; able to work; clamouring to be allowed to work, and the Practical, Level-headed, Sensible Business-men did not know what to do!

Of course, the real reason of the difficulty is that the raw materials that were created for the use and benefit of all have been stolen by a small number, who refuse to allow them to be used for the purposes for which they were intended. This numerically insignificant minority refused to allow the majority to work and produce the things they need; and what work they do graciously permit to be done is not done with the object of producing the necessaries of life for those who work, but for the purpose of creating profit for their masters.

And then, strangest fact of all, the people who find it a hard struggle to live, or who exist in dreadful poverty and sometimes starve, instead of trying to understand the causes of their misery and to find out a remedy themselves, spend all their time applauding the Practical, Sensible, Level-headed Business-men, who bungle and mismanage their affairs, and pay them huge salaries for doing so. Sir Graball D'Encloseland, for instance, was a 'Secretary of State' and was paid £5,000 a year. When he first got the job the wages were only a beggarly £2,000, but as he found it impossible to exist on less than £100 a week he decided to raise his salary to that amount; and the foolish people who find it a hard struggle to live paid it willingly, and when they saw the beautiful motor car and the lovely clothes and jewellery he purchased for his wife with the money, and heard the Great Speech he made – telling them how the shortage of everything was caused by Over-production and Foreign Competition, they clapped their hands and went frantic with admiration. Their only regret was that there were no horses attached to the motor car, because if there had been, they could have taken them out and harnessed themselves to it instead.

Nothing delighted the childish minds of these poor people so much as listening to or reading extracts from the speeches of such men as these; so in order to amuse them, every now and then, in the midst of all the wretchedness, some of the great statesmen made 'great speeches' full of cunning phrases intended to hoodwink the fools who had elected them. The very same week that Sir Graball's salary was increased to £5,000 a year, all the papers were full of a very fine one that he made. They appeared with large headlines like this:

GREAT SPEECH BY SIR GRABALL D'ENCLOSELAND.
Brilliant Epigram!
None should have more than they need, whilst
any have less than they need!

The hypocrisy of such a saying in the mouth of a man who was drawing a salary of five thousand pounds a year did not appear to occur to anyone. On the contrary, the hired scribes of the capitalist Press wrote columns of fulsome admiration of the miserable claptrap, and the working men who had elected this man went into raptures over the 'Brilliant Epigram' as if it were good to eat. They cut it out of the papers and carried it about with them: they showed it to each other: they read it and repeated it to each other: they wondered at it and were delighted with it, grinning and gibbering at each other in the exuberance of their imbecile enthusiasm.

The Distress Committee was not the only body pretending to 'deal' with the poverty 'problem': its efforts were supplemented by all the other agencies already mentioned – the Labour Yard, the Rummage Sales, the Organised Benevolence Society, and so on, to say nothing of a most benevolent scheme originated by the management of Sweater's Emporium, who announced in a letter that was published in the local Press that they were prepared to employ fifty men for one week to carry sandwich boards at one shilling – and a loaf of bread – per day.

They got the men; some unskilled labourers, a few old, wornout artisans whom misery had deprived of the last vestiges of pride or shame; a number of habitual drunkards and loafers, and a nondescript lot of poor ragged old men – old soldiers and others of whom it would be impossible to say what they had once been.

The procession of sandwich men was headed by the Semi-drunk and the Besotted Wretch, and each board was covered with a printed poster: 'Great Sale of Ladies' Blouses now Proceeding at Adam Sweater's Emporium.'

Besides this artful scheme of Sweater's for getting a good advertisement on the cheap numerous other plans for providing employment or alleviating the prevailing misery were put forward in the columns of the local papers and at the various meetings that were held. Any foolish, idiotic, useless suggestion was certain to receive respectful attention; any crafty plan devised in his own interest or for his own profit by one or other of the crew of sweaters and landlords who controlled the town was sure to be approved of by the other inhabitants of Mugsborough, the majority of whom were persons of feeble intellect who not only allowed themselves to be robbed and exploited by a few cunning scoundrels, but venerated and applauded them for doing it.

CHAPTER 38

The Brigands' Cave

One evening in the drawing-room at 'The Cave' there was a meeting of a number of the 'Shining Lights' to arrange the details of a Rummage Sale, that was to be held in aid of the unemployed. It was an informal affair, and while they were waiting for the other luminaries, the early arrivals, Messrs. Rushton, Didlum and Grinder, Mr. Oyley Sweater, the Borough Surveyor, Mr. Wireman, the electrical engineer who had been engaged as an 'expert' to examine and report on the Electric Light Works, and two or three other gentlemen – all members of the Band – took advantage of the opportunity to discuss a number of things they were mutually interested in, which were to be dealt with at the meeting of the Town Council the next day. First, there was the affair of the untenanted Kiosk on the Grand Parade. This building belonged to the corporation, and 'The Cosy Corner Refreshment Coy.' of which Mr. Grinder was the managing director, was thinking of hiring it [[to open as a high-class refreshment lounge, provided the Corporation would make certain alterations and let the place at a reasonable rent. Another item which was to be discussed at the Council meeting was Mr. Sweater's generous offer to the Corporation respecting the new drain connecting 'The Cave' with the Town Main.

The report of Mr. Wireman, the electrical expert, was also to be dealt with, and afterwards a resolution in favour of the purchase of the Mugsborough Electric Light and Installation Co. Ltd. by the town, was to be proposed.

In addition to these matters, several other items, including a proposal by Mr. Didlum for an important reform in the matter of conducting the meetings of the Council, formed subjects for animated conversation between the brigands and their host.]]

[During this discussion other luminaries arrived, including several ladies and the Rev. Mr. Bosher, of the Church of the Whited Sepulchre.]

[[The drawing-room of 'The Cave' was now elaborately furnished. A large mirror in a richly gilt frame reached from the carved marble mantelpiece to the cornice.]] A magnificent clock in an alabaster case stood in the centre of the mantelpiece and was flanked by two exquisitely painted and gilded vases of Dresden ware. The windows were draped with costly hangings, the floor was covered with a luxurious carpet and expensive rugs. Sumptuously upholstered couches and easy chairs added to the comfort of the apartment, which was warmed by the immense fire of coal and oak logs that blazed and crackled in the grate.

The conversation now became general and at times highly philosophical in character, although Mr. Bosher did not take much part, being too busily engaged gobbling up the biscuits and tea, and only occasionally spluttering out a reply when a remark or question was directly addressed to him.

This was Mr. Grinder's first visit at the house, and he expressed his admiration of the manner in which the ceiling and the walls were decorated, remarking that he had always liked this 'ere Japanese style.

Mr. Bosher, with his mouth full of biscuit, mumbled that it was sweetly pretty – charming – beautifully done – must have cost a lot of money.

'Hardly wot you'd call Japanese, though, is it?' observed Didlum, looking round with the air of a connoisseur. 'I should be inclined to say it was rather more of the – er – Chinese or Egyptian.'

'Moorish,' explained Mr. Sweater with a smile. 'I got the idear at the Paris Exhibition. It's simler to the decorations in the "Halambara", the palace of the Sultan of Morocco. That clock there is in the same style.'

The case of the clock referred to – which stood on a table in a corner of the room – was of fretwork, in the form of an Indian Mosque, with a pointed dome and pinnacles. This was the case that Mary Linden had sold to Didlum; the latter had had it stained a dark colour and polished and further improved it by substituting a clock of more suitable design than the one it originally held. Mr. Sweater had noticed it in Didlum's window and, seeing that the design was similar in character to the painted decorations on the ceiling and walls of his drawing-room, had purchased it.

'I went to the Paris Exhibition meself,' said Grinder, when everyone had admired the exquisite workmanship of the clock-case. 'I remember 'avin' a look at the moon through that big telescope. I was never so surprised in me life: you can see it quite plain, and it's round!'

'Round?' said Didlum with a puzzled look. 'Round? Of course it's round! You didn't used to think it was square, did yer?'

'No, of course not, but I always used to think it was flat – like a plate, but it's round like a football.'

'Certainly: the moon is a very simler body to the earth,' explained Didlum, describing an aerial circle with a wave of his hand. 'They moves through the air together, but the earth is always nearest to the sun and consequently once a fortnight the shadder of the earth falls on the moon and darkens it so that it's invisible to the naked eye. The new moon is caused by the moon movin' away a little bit out of the earth's shadder, and it keeps on comin' out more and more until we gets the full moon; and then it goes back again into the shadder; and so it keeps on.'

For about a minute everyone looked very solemn, and the profound silence was disturbed only by the crunching of the biscuits between the jaws of Mr. Bosher, and by certain gurglings in the interior of that gentleman.

'Science is a wonderful thing,' said Mr. Sweater at length, wagging his head gravely, 'wonderful!'

'Yes: but a lot of it is mere theory, you know,' observed Rushton. 'Take this idear that the world is round, for instance; I fail to see it! and then they say as Hawstralia is on the other side of the globe, underneath our feet. In my opinion it's ridiculous, because if it was true, wot's to prevent the people droppin' orf?'

'Yes: well, of course it's very strange,' admitted Sweater. 'I've often thought of that myself. If it was true, we ought to be able to walk on the ceiling of this room, for instance; but of course we know that's impossible, and I really don't see that the other is any more reasonable.'

'I've often noticed flies walkin' on the ceilin',' remarked Didlum, who felt called upon to defend the globular theory.

'Yes; but they're different,' replied Rushton. 'Flies is provided by nature with a gluey substance which oozes out of their feet for the purpose of enabling them to walk upside down.'

'There's one thing that seems to me to finish that idear once for all,' said Grinder, 'and that is – water always finds its own level. You can't get away from that; and if the world was round, as they want us to believe, all the water would run off except just a little at the top. To my mind, that settles the whole argymint.'

'Another thing that gets over me,' continued Rushton, 'is this: according to science, the earth turns round on its axle at the rate of twenty miles a minit. Well, what about when a lark goes up in the sky and stays there about a quarter of an hour? Why, if it was true that the earth was turnin' round at that rate all the time, when the bird came down it would find itself 'undreds of miles away from the place where it went up from! But that doesn't 'appen at all; the bird always comes down in the same spot.'

'Yes, and the same thing applies to balloons and flyin' machines,' said Grinder, 'if it was true that the world is spinnin' round on its axle so quick as that, if a man started out from Calais to fly to Dover, by the time he got to England he'd find 'imself in North America, or p'r'aps farther off still.'

'And if it was true that the world goes round the sun at the rate they makes out, when a balloon went up, the earth would run away from it! They'd never be able to get back again!' remarked Rushton.

This was so obvious that nearly everyone said there was probably something in it, and Didlum could think of no reply. Mr. Bosher upon being appealed to for his opinion, explained that science was alright in its way, but unreliable: the things scientists said yesterday they contradicted today, and what they said today they would probably repudiate tomorrow. It was necessary to be very cautious before accepting any of their assertions.

'Talking about science,' said Grinder, as the holy man relapsed into silence and started on another biscuit and a fresh cup of tea. 'Talking about science reminds me of a conversation I 'ad with Dr. Weakling the other day. You know, he believes we're hall descended from monkeys.'[92]

Everyone laughed; the thing was so absurd: the idea of placing intellectual beings on a level with animals!

'But just wait till you hear how nicely I flattened 'im out,' continued Grinder. 'After we'd been arguin' a long time about wot 'e called everlution or some sich name, and a lot more tommy-rot that I couldn't make no 'ed or tail of – and to tell you the truth I don't believe 'e understood 'arf of it 'imself – I ses to 'im, "Well," I ses, "if it's true that we're hall descended from monkeys," I ses, "I think your famly must 'ave left orf where mine begun." '

In the midst of the laughter that greeted the conclusion of Grinder's story it was seen that Mr. Bosher had become black in the face. He was waving his arms and writhing about like one in a fit, his goggle eyes bursting from their sockets, whilst his huge stomach, quivering spasmodically, alternately contracted and expanded as if it were about to explode.

In the exuberance of his mirth, the unfortunate disciple had swallowed two biscuits at once. Everybody rushed to his assistance,

Grinder and Didlum seized an arm and a shoulder each and forced his head down, Rushton punched him in the back and the ladies shrieked with alarm. They gave him a big drink of tea to help to get the biscuits down, and when he at last succeeded in swallowing them he sat in the armchair with his eyes red-rimmed and full of tears, which ran down over his white, flabby face.

The arrival of the other members of the committee put an end to the interesting discussion, and they shortly afterwards proceeded with the business for which the meeting had been called – the arrangements for the forthcoming Rummage Sale.

CHAPTER 39

The Brigands at Work

The next day, at the meeting of the Town Council, Mr. Wireman's report concerning the Electric Light Works was read. The expert's opinion was so favourable – and it was endorsed by the Borough Engineer, Mr. Oyley Sweater – that a resolution was unanimously carried in favour of acquiring the Works for the town, and a secret committee was appointed to arrange the preliminaries. Alderman Sweater then suggested that a suitable honorarium be voted to Mr. Wireman for his services. This was greeted with a murmur of approval from most of the members, and Mr. Didlum rose with the intention of proposing a resolution to that effect when he was interrupted by Alderman Grinder, who said he couldn't see no sense in giving the man a thing like that. 'Why not give him a sum of money?'

Several members said 'Hear, hear,' to this, but some of the others laughed.

'I can't see nothing to laugh at,' cried Grinder angrily. 'For my part I wouldn't give you tuppence for all the honorariums in the country. I move that we pay 'im a sum of money.'

'I'll second that,' said another member of the band – one of those who had cried 'Hear, Hear.'

Alderman Sweater said that there seemed to be a little misunderstanding and explained that an honorarium *was* a sum of money.

'Oh, well, in that case I'll withdraw my resolution,' said Grinder. 'I thought you wanted to give 'im a 'luminated address or something like that.'

Didlum now moved that a letter of thanks and a fee of fifty guineas be voted to Mr. Wireman, and this was also unanimously agreed to. Dr. Weakling said that it seemed rather a lot, but he did not go so far as to vote against it.

The next business was the proposal that the Corporation should take over the drain connecting Mr. Sweater's house with the town main. Mr. Sweater – being a public-spirited man – proposed to hand this connecting drain – which ran through a private road – over to the corporation to be theirs and their successors for ever, on condition that they would pay him the cost of construction – £55 – and agree to keep it in proper repair. After a brief discussion it was decided to take over the drain on the terms offered, and then Councillor Didlum proposed a vote of thanks to Alderman Sweater for his generosity in the matter: this was promptly seconded by Councillor Rushton and would have been carried nem. con. but for the disgraceful conduct of Dr. Weakling, who had the bad taste to suggest that the amount was about double what the drain could possibly have cost to construct, that it was of no use to the corporation at all, and that they would merely acquire the liability to keep it in repair.

However, no one took the trouble to reply to Weakling, and the band proceeded to the consideration of the next business, which was Mr. Grinder's offer – on behalf of the 'Cosy Corner Refreshment Company' – to take the Kiosk on the Grand Parade. Mr. Grinder submitted a plan of certain alterations that he would require the Corporation to make at the Kiosk, and, provided the Council agreed to do this work he was willing to take a lease of the place for five years at £20 per year.

Councillor Didlum proposed that the offer of the 'Cosy Corner Refreshment Co. Ltd.' be accepted and the required alterations proceeded with at once. The Kiosk had brought in no rent for nearly two years, but, apart from that consideration, if they accepted this offer they would be able to set some of the unemployed to work. (Applause.)

Councillor Rushton seconded.

Dr. Weakling pointed out that as the proposed alterations would cost about £175 – according to the estimate of the Borough Engineer – and, the rent being only £20 a year, it would mean that the Council would be £75 out of pocket at the end of the five years; to say nothing of the expense of keeping the place in repair during all that time. (Disturbance.) He moved as an amendment that the alterations be made, and that they then invite tenders, and let the place to the highest bidder. (Great uproar.)

Councillor Rushton said he was disgusted with the attitude taken up by that man Weakling. (Applause.) Perhaps it was hardly right to call him a man. (Hear! Hear!) In the matter of these alterations they had had the use of Councillor Grinder's brains: it was he who first thought of making these improvements in the Kiosk, and therefore he – or rather the company he represented – had a moral right to the tenancy. (Loud cheers.)

Dr. Weakling said that he thought it was understood that when a man was elected to that Council it was because he was supposed to be willing to use his brains for the benefit of his constituents. (Sardonic laughter.)

The Mayor asked if there was any seconder to Weakling's amendment, and as there was not the original proposition was put and carried.

Councillor Rushton suggested that a large shelter with seating accommodation for about two hundred persons should be erected on the Grand Parade near the Kiosk. The shelter would serve as a protection against rain, or the rays of the sun in summer. It would add materially to the comfort of visitors and would be a notable addition to the attractions of the town.

Councillor Didlum said it was a very good idear, and proposed that the Surveyor be instructed to get out the plans.

Dr. Weakling opposed the motion. (Laughter.) It seemed to him that the object was to benefit, not the town, but Mr. Grinder. (Disturbance.) If this shelter were erected, it would increase the value of the Kiosk as a refreshment bar by a hundred per cent. If Mr. Grinder wanted a shelter for his customers he should pay for it himself. (Uproar.) He (Dr. Weakling) was sorry to have to say it, but he could not help thinking that this was a put-up job. (Loud cries of 'Withdraw' 'Apologise' 'Cast 'im out' and terrific uproar.)

Weakling did not apologise or withdraw, but he said no more. Didlum's proposition was carried, and the 'Band' went on to the next item on the agenda, which was a proposal by Councillor Didlum to increase the salary of Mr. Oyley Sweater, the Borough Engineer, from fifteen pounds to seventeen pounds per week.

Councillor Didlum said that when they had a good man they ought to appreciate him. (Applause.) Compared with other officials, the Borough Engineer was not fairly paid. (Hear, hear.) The magistrates' clerk received seventeen pounds a week. The Town

Clerk seventeen pounds per week. He did not wish it to be understood that he thought those gentlemen were overpaid – far from it. (Hear, hear.) It was not that they got too much, but that the Engineer got too little. How could they expect a man like that to exist on a paltry fifteen pounds a week? Why, it was nothing more or less than sweating! (Hear, hear.) He had much pleasure in moving that the Borough Engineer's salary be increased to seventeen pounds a week, and that his annual holiday be extended from a fortnight to one calendar month with hard la— he begged pardon – with full pay. (Loud cheers.)

Councillor Rushton said that he did not propose to make a long speech – it was not necessary. He would content himself with formally seconding Councillor Didlum's excellent proposition. (Applause.)

Councillor Weakling, whose rising was greeted with derisive laughter, said he must oppose the resolution. He wished it to be understood that he was not actuated by any feeling of personal animosity towards the Borough Engineer, but at the same time he considered it his duty to say that in his (Dr. Weakling's) opinion, that official would be dear at half the price they were now paying him. (Disturbance.) He did not appear to understand his business, nearly all the work that was done cost in the end about double what the Borough Engineer estimated it could be done for. (Liar.) He considered him to be a grossly incompetent person (uproar) and was of opinion that if they were to advertise they could get dozens of better men who would be glad to do the work for five pounds a week. He moved that Mr. Oyley Sweater be asked to resign and that they advertise for a man at five pounds a week. (Great uproar.)

Councillor Grinder rose to a point of order. He appealed to the Chairman to squash the amendment. (Applause.)

Councillor Didlum remarked that he supposed Councillor Grinder meant 'quash': in that case, he would support the suggestion.

Councillor Grinder said it was about time they put a stopper on that feller Weakling. He (Grinder) did not care whether they called it squashing or quashing; it was all the same so long as they nipped him in the bud. (Cheers.) The man was a disgrace to the Council; always interfering and hindering the business.

The Mayor – Alderman Sweater – said that he did not think it consistent with the dignity of that Council to waste any more time over this scurrilous amendment. (Applause.) He was proud to say that it had not even been seconded, and therefore he would put Mr. Didlum's resolution – a proposition which he had no hesitation in saying reflected the highest credit upon that gentleman and upon all those who supported it. (Vociferous cheers.)

All those who were in favour signified their approval in the customary manner, and as Weakling was the only one opposed, the resolution was carried and the meeting proceeded to the next business.

Councillor Rushton said that several influential ratepayers and employers of labour had complained to him about the high wages of the Corporation workmen, some of whom were paid sevenpence-halfpenny an hour. Sevenpence an hour was the maximum wage paid to skilled workmen by private employers in that town, and he failed to see why the Corporation should pay more. (Hear, hear.) It had a very bad effect on the minds of the men in the employment of private firms, tending to make them dissatisfied with their wages. The same state of affairs prevailed with regard to the unskilled labourers in the Council's employment. Private employers could get that class of labour for fourpence-halfpenny or fivepence an hour, and yet the corporation paid fivepence-halfpenny and even sixpence for the same class of work. (Shame.) It was not fair to the ratepayers. (Hear, hear.) Considering that the men in the employment of the Corporation had almost constant work, if there was to be a difference at all, they should get not more, but less, than those who worked for private firms. (Cheers.) He moved that the wages of the Corporation workmen be reduced in all cases to the same level as those paid by private firms.

Councillor Grinder seconded. He said it amounted to a positive scandal. Why, in the summer-time some of these men drew as much as 35/- in a single week! (Shame.) and it was quite common for unskilled labourers – fellers who did nothing but the very hardest and most laborious work, sich as carrying sacks of cement, or digging up the roads to get at the drains, and sich-like easy jobs – to walk of with 25/- a week! (Sensation.) He had often noticed some of these men swaggering about the town on Sundays, dressed like millionaires and cigared up! They seemed quite a different class of men from those who worked for private firms, and to look at the way some of their children was dressed you'd think their fathers was Cabinet Minstrels! No wonder the ratepayers complained of the high rates. Another grievance was that all the corporation workmen were allowed two days' holiday every year, in addition to the Bank Holidays, and were paid for them! (Cries of 'Shame', 'Scandalous', 'Disgraceful', etc.) No private contractor paid his men for Bank Holidays, and why should the Corporation do so? He had much pleasure in seconding Councillor Rushton's resolution.

Councillor Weakling opposed the motion. He thought that 35/-
a week was little enough for a man to keep a wife and family with
(Rot), even if all the men got it regularly, which they did not.
Members should consider what was the average amount per week
throughout the whole year, not merely the busy time, and if they
did that they would find that even the skilled men did not average
more than 25/- a week, and in many cases not so much. If this
subject had not been introduced by Councillor Rushton, he (Dr.
Weakling) had intended to propose that the wages of the Corporation workmen should be increased to the standard recognised by
the Trades Unions. (Loud laughter.) It had been proved that the
notoriously short lives of the working people – whose average span
of life was about twenty years less than that of the well-to-do
classes – their increasingly inferior physique, and the high rate
of mortality amongst their children was caused by the wretched
remuneration they received for hard and tiring work, the excessive
number of hours they have to work, when employed, the bad quality
of their food, the badly constructed and insanitary homes their
poverty compels them to occupy, and the anxiety, worry, and
depression of mind they have to suffer when out of employment.
(Cries of 'Rot', 'Bosh', and loud laughter.) Councillor Didlum said,
'Rot'. It was a very good word to describe the disease that was
sapping the foundations of society and destroying the health and
happiness and the very lives of so many of their fellow countrymen
and women. (Renewed merriment and shouts of 'Go and buy a red
tie.') He appealed to the members to reject the resolution. He was
very glad to say that he believed it was true that the workmen in the
employ of the Corporation were a little better off than those in the
employ of private contractors, and if it were so, it was as it should
be. They had need to be better off than the poverty-stricken, half-
starved poor wretches who worked for private firms.

Councillor Didlum said that it was very evident that Dr. Weakling
had obtained his seat on that Council by false pretences. If he had
told the ratepayers that he was a Socialist, they would never have
elected him. (Hear, hear.) Practically every Christian minister in the
country would agree with him (Didlum) when he said that the poverty
of the working classes was caused not by the 'wretched remuneration
they receive as wages', but by Drink. (Loud applause.) And he was
very sure that the testimony of the clergy of all denominations was
more to be relied upon than the opinion of a man like Dr. Weakling.
(Hear, hear.)

Dr. Weakling said that if some of the clergymen referred to or some of the members of the council had to exist and toil amid the same sordid surroundings, overcrowding and ignorance as some of the working classes, they would probably seek to secure some share of pleasure and forgetfulness in drink themselves! (Great uproar and shouts of 'Order', 'Withdraw', 'Apologise'.)

Councillor Grinder said that even if it was true that the haverage lives of the working classes was twenty years shorter than those of the better classes, he could not see what it had got to do with Dr. Weakling. (Hear, hear.) So long as the working class was contented to die twenty years before their time, he failed to see what it had got to do with other people. They was not runnin' short of workers, was they? There was still plenty of 'em left. (Laughter.) So long as the workin' class was satisfied to die orf – let 'em die orf! It was a free country. (Applause.) The workin' class 'adn't arst Dr. Weakling to stick up for them, had they? If they wasn't satisfied, they would stick up for theirselves! The working men didn't want the likes of Dr. Weakling to stick up for them, and they would let 'im know it when the next election came round. If he (Grinder) was a worldly man, he would not mind betting that the workin' men of Dr. Weakling's ward would give him 'the dirty kick out' next November. (Applause.)

Councillor Weakling, who knew that this was probably true, made no further protest. Rushton's proposition was carried, and then the Clerk announced that the next item was the resolution Mr. Didlum had given notice of at the last meeting, and the Mayor accordingly called upon that gentleman.

Councillor Didlum, who was received with loud cheers, said that unfortunately a certain member of that Council seemed to think he had a right to oppose nearly everything that was brought forward.

(The majority of the members of the Band glared malignantly at Weakling.)

He hoped that for once the individual he referred to would have the decency to restrain himself, because the resolution he (Didlum) was about to have the honour of proposing was one that he believed no right-minded man – no matter what his politics or religious opinions – could possibly object to; and he trusted that for the credit of the Council it would be entered on the records as an unopposed motion. The resolution was as follows:

'That from this date all the meetings of this Council shall be opened with prayer and closed with the singing of the Doxology.'[93] (Loud applause.)

Councillor Rushton seconded the resolution, which was also supported by Mr. Grinder, who said that at a time like the present, when there was sich a lot of infiddles about who said that we all came from monkeys, the Council would be showing a good example to the working classes by adopting the resolution.

Councillor Weakling said nothing, so the new rule was carried *nem. con.*, and as there was no more business to be done it was put into operation for the first time there and then, Mr. Sweater conducting the singing with a roll of paper – the plan of the drain of 'The Cave' – and each member singing a different tune.

Weakling withdrew during the singing, and afterwards, before the Band dispersed, it was agreed that a certain number of them were to meet the Chief at the Cave, on the following evening to arrange the details of the proposed raid on the finances of the town in connection with the sale of the Electric Light Works.

CHAPTER 40

Vive la System!

The alterations which the Corporation had undertaken to make in the Kiosk on the Grand Parade provided employment for several carpenters and plasterers for about three weeks, and afterwards for several painters. This fact was sufficient to secure the working men's unqualified approval of the action of the Council in letting the place to Grinder, and Councillor Weakling's opposition – the reasons of which they did not take the trouble to enquire into or understand – they as heartily condemned. All they knew or cared was that he had tried to prevent the work being done, and that he had referred in insulting terms to the working men of the town. What right had he to call them half-starved, poverty-stricken, poor wretches? If it came to being poverty-stricken, according to all accounts, he wasn't any too well orf hisself. Some of those blokes who went swaggering about in frock-coats and pot-'ats was just as 'ard-up as anyone else if the truth was known.

As for the Corporation workmen, it was quite right that their wages should be reduced. Why should they get more money than anyone else?

'It's us what's got to find the money,' they said. 'We're the rate-payers, and why should we have to pay them more wages than we gets ourselves? And why should they be paid for holidays any more than us?'

During the next few weeks the dearth of employment continued, for, of course, the work at the Kiosk and the few other jobs that were being done did not make much difference to the general situation. Groups of workmen stood at the corners or walked aimlessly about the streets. Most of them no longer troubled to go to the different firms to ask for work, for they were usually told that they would be sent for if wanted.

During this time Owen did his best to convert the other men to his views. He had accumulated a little library of Socialist books and pamphlets which he lent to those he hoped to influence. Some of them took these books and promised, with the air of men who were conferring a great favour, that they would read them. As a rule, when they returned them it was with vague expressions of approval, but they usually evinced a disinclination to discuss the contents in detail because, in nine instances out of ten, they had not attempted to read them. As for those who did make a half-hearted effort to do so, in the majority of cases their minds were so rusty and stultified by long years of disuse, that, although the pamphlets were generally written in such simple language that a child might have understood, the argument was generally too obscure to be grasped by men whose minds were addled by the stories told them by their Liberal and Tory masters. Some, when Owen offered to lend them some books or pamphlets refused to accept them, and others who did him the great favour of accepting them, afterwards boasted that they had used them as toilet paper.

Owen frequently entered into long arguments with the other men, saying that it was the duty of the State to provide productive work for all those who were willing to do it. Some few of them listened like men who only vaguely understood, but were willing to be convinced.

'Yes, mate. It's right enough what you say,' they would remark. 'Something ought to be done.'

Others ridiculed this doctrine of State employment: It was all very fine, but where was the money to come from? And then those who had been disposed to agree with Owen would relapse into their old apathy.

There were others who did not listen so quietly, but shouted with many curses that it was the likes of such fellows as Owen who were responsible for all the depression in trade. All this talk about

Socialism and State employment was frightening Capital out of the country. Those who had money were afraid to invest it in industries, or to have any work done for fear they would be robbed. When Owen quoted statistics to prove that as far as commerce and the quantity produced of commodities of all kinds was concerned, the last year had been a record one, they became more infuriated than ever, and talked threateningly of what they would like to do to those bloody Socialists who were upsetting everything.

One day Crass, who was one of these upholders of the existing system, scored off Owen finely. A little group of them were standing talking in the Wage Slave Market near the Fountain. In the course of the argument, Owen made the remark that under existing conditions life was not worth living, and Crass said that if he really thought so, there was no compulsion about it; if he wasn't satisfied – if he didn't want to live – he could go and die. Why the hell didn't he go and make a hole in the water, or cut his bloody throat?

On this particular occasion the subject of the argument was – at first – the recent increase of the Borough Engineer's salary to seventeen pounds per week. Owen had said it was robbery, but the majority of the others expressed their approval of the increase. They asked Owen if he expected a man like that to work for nothing! It was not as if he were one of the likes of themselves. They said that, as for it being robbery, Owen would be very glad to have the chance of getting it himself. Most of them seemed to think the fact that anyone would be glad to have seventeen pounds a week, proved that it was right for them to pay that amount to the Borough Engineer!

Usually whenever Owen reflected upon the gross injustices and inhumanity of the existing social disorder, he became convinced that it could not possibly last; it was bound to fall to pieces because of it own rottenness. It was not just, it was not common sense, and therefore it could not endure. But always after one of these arguments – or, rather, disputes – with his fellow workmen, he almost relapsed into hopelessness and despondency, for then he realised how vast and how strong are the fortifications that surround the present system; the great barriers and ramparts of invincible ignorance, apathy and self-contempt, which will have to be broken down before the system of society of which they are the defences, can be swept away.

At other times as he thought of this marvellous system, it presented itself to him in such an aspect of almost comical absurdity that he was forced to laugh and to wonder whether it really existed at all, or if it were only an illusion of his own disordered mind.

One of the things that the human race needed in order to exist was shelter; so with much painful labour they had constructed a large number of houses. Thousands of these houses were now standing unoccupied, while millions of the people who had helped to build the houses were either homeless or herding together in overcrowded hovels.

These human beings had such a strange system of arranging their affairs that if anyone were to go and burn down a lot of the houses he would be conferring a great boon upon those who had built them, because such an act would 'Make a lot more work!'

Another very comical thing was that thousands of people wore broken boots and ragged clothes, while millions of pairs of boots and abundance of clothing, which they had helped to make, were locked up in warehouses, and the System had the keys.

Thousands of people lacked the necessaries of life. The necessaries of life are all produced by work. The people who lacked begged to be allowed to work and create those things of which they stood in need. But the System prevented them from so doing.

If anyone asked the System why it prevented these people from producing the things of which they were in want, the System replied:

'Because they have already produced too much. The markets are glutted. The warehouses are filled and overflowing, and there is nothing more for them to do.'

There was in existence a huge accumulation of everything necessary. A great number of the people whose labour had produced that vast store were now living in want, but the System said that they could not be permitted to partake of the things they had created. Then, after a time, when these people, being reduced to the last extreme of misery, cried out that they and their children were dying of hunger, the System grudgingly unlocked the doors of the great warehouses, and taking out a small part of the things that were stored within, distributed it amongst the famished workers, at the same time reminding them that it was Charity, because all the things in the warehouses, although they had been made by the workers, were now the property of the people who do nothing.

And then the starving, bootless, ragged, stupid wretches fell down and worshipped the System, and offered up their children as living sacrifices upon its altars, saying:

'This beautiful System is the only one possible, and the best that human wisdom can devise. May the System live for ever! Cursed be those who seek to destroy the System!'

As the absurdity of the thing forced itself upon him, Owen, in spite of the unhappiness he felt at the sight of all the misery by which he was surrounded, laughed aloud and said to himself that if he was sane, then all these people must be mad.

In the face of such colossal imbecility it was absurd to hope for any immediate improvement. The little already accomplished was the work of a few self-sacrificing enthusiasts, battling against the opposition of those they sought to benefit, and the results of their labours were, in many instances, as pearls cast before the swine who stood watching for opportunities to fall upon and rend their benefactors.

There was only one hope. It was possible that the monopolists, encouraged by the extraordinary stupidity and apathy of the people, would proceed to lay upon them even greater burdens, until at last, goaded by suffering, and not having sufficient intelligence to understand any other remedy, these miserable wretches would turn upon their oppressors and drown both them and their System in a sea of blood.

Besides the work at the Kiosk, towards the end of March things gradually began to improve in other directions. Several firms began to take on a few hands. Several large empty houses that were relet had to be renovated for their new tenants, and there was a fair amount of inside work arising out of the annual spring-cleaning in other houses. There was not enough work to keep everyone employed, and most of those who were taken on as a rule only managed to make a few hours a week, but still it was better than absolute idleness, and there also began to be talk of several large outside jobs that were to be done as soon as the weather was settled.

This bad weather, by the way, was a sort of boon to the defenders of the present system, who were hard-up for sensible arguments to explain the cause of poverty. One of the principal causes was, of course, the weather, which was keeping everything back. There was not the slightest doubt that if only the weather would allow there would always be plenty of work, and poverty would be abolished.

Rushton & Co. had a fair share of what work there was, and Crass, Sawkins, Slyme and Owen were kept employed pretty regularly, although they did not start until half-past eight and left off at four. At different houses in various parts of the town they had ceilings to wash off and distemper, to strip the old paper from the walls, and to repaint and paper the rooms, and sometimes there were the venetian blinds to repair and repaint. Occasionally a few extra hands were taken on for a few days, and discharged again as soon as the job they were taken on to do was finished.

The defenders of the existing system may possibly believe that the knowledge that they would be discharged directly the job was done was a very good incentive to industry, that they would naturally under these circumstances do their best to get the work done as quickly as possible. But then it must be remembered that most of the defenders of the existing system are so constituted, that they can believe anything provided it is not true and sufficiently silly.

All the same, it was a fact that the workmen did do their very best to get over this work in the shortest possible time, because although they knew that to do so was contrary to their own interests, they also knew that it would be very much more contrary to their interests not to do so. Their only chance of being kept on if other work came in was to tear into it for all they were worth. Consequently, most of the work was rushed and botched and slobbered over in about half the time that it would have taken to do it properly. Rooms for which the customers paid to have three coats of paint were scamped with one or two. What Misery did not know about scamping and faking the work, the men suggested to and showed him in the hope of currying favour with him in order that they might get the preference over others and be sent for when the next job came in. This is the principal incentive provided by the present system, the incentive to cheat. These fellows cheated the customers of their money. They cheated themselves and their fellow workmen of work, and their children of bread, but it was all for a good cause – to make profit for their master.

Harlow and Slyme did one job – a room that Rushton & Co. had contracted to paint three coats. It was finished with two and the men cleared away their paints. The next day, when Slyme went there to paper the room, the lady of the house said that the painting was not yet finished – it was to have another coat. Slyme assured her that it had already had three, but, as the lady insisted, Slyme went to the shop and sought out Misery. Harlow had been stood off, as there was not another job in just then, but fortunately he happened to be standing in the street outside the shop, so they called him and then the three of them went round to the job and swore that the room had had three coats. The lady protested that it was not so. She had watched the progress of the work. Besides, it was impossible; they had only been there three days. The first day they had not put any paint on at all; they had done the ceiling and stripped the walls; the painting was not started till the second day. How then could it have had three coats? Misery explained the mystery: he said that for first coating they had an extra special very fast-drying paint – paint that dried so quickly that they were able to give the work two coats in one day. For instance, one man did the window, the other the door: when these were finished both men did the skirting; by the time the skirting was finished the door and window were dry enough to second coat; and then, on the following day – the finishing coat!

Of course, this extra special quick-drying paint was very expensive, but the firm did not mind that. They knew that most of their customers wished to have their work finished as quickly as possible, and their study was to give satisfaction to the customers. This explanation satisfied the lady – a poverty-stricken widow making a precarious living by taking in lodgers – who was the more easily deceived because she regarded Misery as a very holy man, having seen him preaching in the street on many occasions.

There was another job at another boarding-house that Owen and Easton did – two rooms which had to be painted three coats of white paint and one of enamel, making four coats altogether. That was what the firm had contracted to do. As the old paint in these rooms was of a rather dark shade it was absolutely necessary to give the work three coats before enamelling it. Misery wanted them to let it go with two, but Owen pointed out that if they did so it would be such a ghastly mess that it would never pass. After thinking the matter over for a few minutes, Misery told them to go on with the third coat of paint. Then he went downstairs and asked to see the lady of the house. He explained to her that, in consequence of the old paint being so dark, he found that it would be necessary, in order to make a good job of it, to give the work four coats before enamelling it. Of course, they had agreed for only three, but as they always made a point of doing their work in a first-class manner rather than not make a good job, they would give it the extra coat for nothing, but he was sure she would not wish them to do that. The lady said that she did not want them to work for nothing, and she wanted it done properly. If it were necessary to give it an extra coat, they must do so and she would pay for it. How much would it be? Misery told her. The lady was satisfied, and Misery was in the seventh heaven. Then he went upstairs again and warned Owen and Easton to be sure to say, if they were asked, that the work had had four coats.

It would not be reasonable to blame Misery or Rushton for not wishing to do good, honest work – there was no incentive. When they secured a contract, if they had thought first of making the very best possible job of it, they would not have made so much profit. The incentive was not to do the work as well as possible, but to do as little as possible. The incentive was not to make good work, but to make good profit.

The same rule applied to the workers. They could not justly be blamed for not doing good work – there was no incentive. To do good work requires time and pains. Most of them would have liked to take time and pains, because all those who are capable of doing good work find pleasure and happiness in doing it, and have pride in it when done: but there was no incentive, unless the certainty of getting the sack could be called an incentive, for it was a moral certainty that any man who was caught taking time and pains with his work would be promptly presented with the order of the boot. But there was plenty of incentive to hurry and scamp and slobber and botch.

There was another job at a lodging-house – two rooms to be painted and papered. The landlord paid for the work, but the tenant had the privilege of choosing the paper. She could have any pattern she liked so long as the cost did not exceed one shilling per roll, Rushton's estimate being for paper of that price. Misery sent her several patterns of sixpenny papers, marked at a shilling, to choose from, but she did not fancy any of them, and said that she would come to the shop to make her selection. So Hunter tore round to the shop in a great hurry to get there before her. In his haste to dismount, he fell off his bicycle into the muddy road, and nearly smashed the plate-glass window with the handle-bar of the machine as he placed it against the shop front before going in.

Without waiting to clean the mud off his clothes, he ordered Budd, the pimply-faced shopman, to get out rolls of all the sixpenny papers they had, and then they both set to work and altered the price marked upon them from sixpence to a shilling. Then they got out a number of shilling papers and altered the price marked upon them, changing it from a shilling to one and six.

When the unfortunate woman arrived, Misery was waiting for her with a benign smile upon his long visage. He showed her all the sixpenny ones, but she did not like any of them, so after a while Nimrod suggested that perhaps she would like a paper of a little better quality, and she could pay the trifling difference out of her own pocket. Then he showed her the shilling papers that he had marked up to one and sixpence, and eventually the lady selected one of these and paid the extra sixpence per roll herself, as Nimrod suggested. There were fifteen rolls of paper altogether – seven for one room and eight for the other – so that in addition to the ordinary profit on the sale of the paper – about two hundred and seventy-five per cent. – the firm made seven and sixpence on this transaction. They might have done better out of the job itself if Slyme had not been hanging the paper piece-work, for, the two rooms being of the same pattern, he could easily have managed to do them with fourteen rolls; in fact, that was all he did use, but he cut up and partly destroyed the one that was over so that he could charge for hanging it.

Owen was working there at the same time, for the painting of the rooms was not done before Slyme papered them; the finishing coat was put on after the paper was hung. He noticed Slyme destroying the paper and, guessing the reason, asked him how he could reconcile such conduct as that with his profession of religion.

Slyme replied that the fact that he was a Christian did not imply that he never did anything wrong: if he committed a sin, he was a Christian all the same, and it would be forgiven him for the sake of the Blood. As for this affair of the paper, it was a matter between himself and God, and Owen had no right to set himself up as a Judge.

In addition to all this work, there were a number of funerals. Crass and Slyme did very well out of it all, working all day whitewashing or painting, and sometimes part of the night painting Venetian blinds or polishing coffins and taking them home, to say nothing of the lifting in of the corpses and afterwards acting as bearers.

As time went on, the number of small jobs increased, and as the days grew longer the men were allowed to put in a greater number of hours. Most of the firms had some work, but there was never enough to keep all the men in the town employed at the same time. It worked like this: Every firm had a certain number of men who were regarded as the regular hands. When there was any work to do, they got the preference over strangers or outsiders. When things were busy, outsiders were taken on temporarily. When the work fell off, these casual hands were the first to be 'stood still'. If it continued to fall off, the old hands were also stood still in order of seniority, the older hands being preferred to strangers – so long, of course, as they were not old in the sense of being aged or inefficient.

This kind of thing usually continued all through the spring and summer. In good years the men of all trades, carpenters, bricklayers, plasterers, painters and so on, were able to keep almost regularly at work, except in wet weather.

The difference between a good and bad spring and summer is that in good years it is sometimes possible to make a little overtime, and the periods of unemployment are shorter and less frequent than in bad years. It is rare even in good years for one of the casual hands to be employed by one firm for more than one, two or three months without a break. It is usual for them to put in a month with one firm, then a fortnight with another, then perhaps six weeks somewhere else, and often between there are two or three days or even weeks of enforced idleness. This sort of thing goes on all through spring, summer and autumn.

CHAPTER 41

The Easter Offering. The Beano Meeting.

By the beginning of April, Rushton & Co. were again working nine hours a day, from seven in the morning till five-thirty at night, and after Easter they started working full time from 6 a.m. till 5.30 p.m., eleven and a half hours – or, rather, ten hours, for they had to lose half an hour at breakfast and an hour at dinner.

Just before Easter several of the men asked Hunter if they might be allowed to work on Good Friday and Easter Monday, as, they said, they had had enough holidays during the winter; they had no money to spare for holiday-making, and they did not wish to lose two days' pay when there was work to be done. Hunter told them that there was not sufficient work in to justify him in doing as they requested: things were getting very slack again, and Mr. Rushton had decided to cease work from Thursday night till Tuesday morning. They were thus prevented from working on Good Friday, but it is true that not more than one working man in fifty went to any religious service on that day or on any other day during the Easter festival. On the contrary, this festival was the occasion of much cursing and blaspheming on the part of those whose penniless, poverty-stricken condition it helped to aggravate by enforcing unprofitable idleness which they lacked the means to enjoy.

During these holidays some of the men did little jobs on their own account and others put in the whole time – including Good Friday and Easter Sunday – gardening, digging and planting their plots of allotment ground.

When Owen arrived home one evening during the week before Easter, Frankie gave him an envelope which he had brought home from school. It contained a printed leaflet:

CHURCH OF THE WHITED SEPULCHRE, MUGSBOROUGH.

Easter 19—

Dear Sir (or Madam),

In accordance with the usual custom we invite you to join with us in presenting the Vicar, the Rev. Habbakuk Bosher, with an Easter Offering, as a token of affection and regard.

Yours faithfully,

A. Cheeseman } *Churchwardens.*
W. Taylor

Mr. Bosher's income from various sources connected with the church was over six hundred pounds a year, or about twelve pounds per week, but as that sum was evidently insufficient, his admirers had adopted this device for supplementing it. Frankie said all the boys had one of these letters, and were going to ask their fathers for some money to give towards the Easter Offering. Most of them expected to get twopence.

As the boy had evidently set his heart on doing the same as the other children, Owen gave him the twopence, and they afterwards learned that the Easter Offering for that year was one hundred and twenty-seven pounds, which was made up of the amounts collected from the parishioners by the children, the district visitors and the verger, the collection at a special Service, and donations from the feeble-minded old females elsewhere referred to.

By the end of April nearly all the old hands were back at work, and several casual hands had also been taken on, the Semi-drunk being one of the number. In addition to these, Misery had taken on a number of what he called 'lightweights', men who were not really skilled workmen, but had picked up sufficient knowledge of the simpler parts of the trade to be able to get over it passably. These were paid fivepence or fivepence-halfpenny, and were employed in preference to those who had served their time, because the latter wanted more money and therefore were only employed when absolutely necessary. Besides the lightweights there were a few young fellows called improvers, who were also employed because they were cheap.

Crass now acted as colourman, having been appointed possibly because he knew absolutely nothing about the laws of colour. As most of the work consisted of small jobs, all the paint and distemper was mixed up at the shop and sent out ready for use to the various jobs.

Sawkins or some of the other lightweights generally carried the heavier lots of colour or scaffolding, but the smaller lots of colour or such things as a pair of steps or a painter's plank were usually sent by the boy, whose slender legs had become quite bowed since he had been engaged helping the other philanthropists to make money for Mr. Rushton.

Crass's work as colourman was simplified, to a certain extent, by the great number of specially prepared paints and distempers[94] in all colours, supplied by the manufacturers ready for use. Most of these new-fangled concoctions were regarded with an eye of suspicion and dislike by the hands, and Philpot voiced the general opinion about them one day during a dinner-hour discussion when he said they might appear to be all right for a time, but they would probably not last, because they was mostly made of kimicles.

One of these new-fashioned paints was called 'Petrifying Liquid', and was used for first-coating decaying stone or plaster work. It was also supposed to be used for thinning up a certain kind of patent distemper, but when Misery found out that it was possible to thin the latter with water, the use of 'Petrifying Liquid' for that purpose was discontinued. This 'Petrifying Liquid' was a source of much innocent merriment to the hands. The name was applied to the tea that they made in buckets on some of the jobs, and also to the four-ale that was supplied by certain pubs.

One of the new inventions was regarded with a certain amount of indignation by the hands: it was a white enamel, and they objected to it for two reasons – one was because, as Philpot remarked, it dried so quickly that you had to work like greased lightning; you had to be all over the door directly you started it.

The other reason was that, because it dried so quickly, it was necessary to keep closed the doors and windows of the room where it was being used, and the smell was so awful that it brought on fits of dizziness and sometimes vomiting. Needless to say, the fact that it compelled those who used it to work quickly recommended the stuff to Misery.

As for the smell, he did not care about that; he did not have to inhale the fumes himself.

*   *   *

It was just about this time that Crass, after due consultation with several of the others, including Philpot, Harlow, Bundy, Slyme, Easton and the Semi-drunk, decided to call a meeting of the hands for the purpose of considering the advisability of holding the usual Beano[95] later on in the summer. The meeting was held in the carpenter's shop down at the yard one evening at six o'clock, which allowed time for those interested to attend after leaving work.

The hands sat on the benches or carpenter's stools, or reclined upon heaps of shavings. On a pair of tressels in the centre of the workshop stood a large oak coffin which Crass had just finished polishing.

When all those who were expected to turn up had arrived, Payne, the foreman carpenter – the man who made the coffins – was voted to the chair on the proposition of Crass, seconded by Philpot, and then a solemn silence ensued, which was broken at last by the chairman, who, in a lengthy speech, explained the object of the meeting. Possibly with a laudable desire that there should be no mistake about it, he took the trouble to explain several times, going over the same ground and repeating the same words over and over again, whilst the audience waited in a deathlike and miserable silence for him to leave off. Payne, however, did not appear to have any intention of leaving off, for he continued, like a man in a trance, to repeat what he had said before, seeming to be under the impression that he had to make a separate explanation to each individual member of the audience. At last the crowd could stand it no longer, and began to shout 'Hear, hear' and to bang bits of wood and hammers on the floor and the benches; and then, after a final repetition of the statement, that the object of the meeting was to consider the advisability of holding an outing, or beanfeast, the chairman collapsed on to a carpenter's stool and wiped the sweat from his forehead.

Crass then reminded the meeting that the last year's Beano had been an unqualified success, and for his part he would be very sorry if they did not have one this year. Last year they had four brakes,[96] and they went to Tubberton Village.

It was true that there was nothing much to see at Tubberton, but there was one thing they could rely on getting there that they could not be sure of getting for the same money anywhere else, and that was – a good feed. (Applause.) Just for the sake of getting on with the business, he would propose that they decide to go to Tubberton, and that a committee be appointed to make arrangements – about the dinner – with the landlord of the Queen Elizabeth's Head at that place.

Philpot seconded the motion, and Payne was about to call for a show of hands when Harlow rose to a point of order. It appeared to him that they were getting on a bit too fast. The proper way to do this business was first to take the feeling of the meeting as to whether they wished to have a Beano at all, and then, if the meeting was in favour of it, they could decide where they were to go, and whether they would have a whole day or only half a day.

The Semi-drunk said that he didn't care a dreadful expression where they went: he was willing to abide by the decision of the majority. (Applause.) It was a matter of indifference to him whether they had a day, or half a day, or two days; he was agreeable to anything.

Easton suggested that a special saloon carriage might be engaged, and they could go and visit Madame Tussaud's Waxworks. He had never been to that place and had often wished to see it. But Philpot objected that if they went there, Madame Tussaud's might be unwilling to let them out again.

Bundy endorsed the remarks that had fallen from Crass with reference to Tubberton. He did not care where they went, they would never get such a good spread for the money as they did last year at the Queen Elizabeth. (Cheers.)

The chairman said that he remembered the last Beano very well. They had half a day – left off work on Saturday at twelve instead of one – so there was only one hour's wages lost – they went home, had a wash and changed their clothes, and got up to the Cricketers, where the brakes was waiting, at one. Then they had the two hours' drive to Tubberton, stopping on the way for drinks at the Blue Lion, The Warrior's Head, the Bird in Hand, the Dewdrop Inn and the World Turned Upside Down. (Applause.) They arrived at the Queen Elizabeth at three-thirty, and the dinner was ready; and it was one of the finest blow-outs he had ever had. (Hear, hear.) There was soup, vegetables, roast beef, roast mutton, lamb and mint sauce, plum duff, Yorkshire, and a lot more. The landlord of the Elizabeth kept as good a drop of beer as anyone could wish to drink, and as for the teetotallers, they could have tea, coffee or ginger beer.

Having thus made another start, Payne found it very difficult to leave off, and was proceeding to relate further details of the last Beano when Harlow again rose up from his heap of shavings and said he wished to call the chairman to order. (Hear, hear.) What the hell was the use of all this discussion before they had even decided to have a Beano at all! Was the meeting in favour of a Beano or not? That was the question.

A prolonged and awkward silence followed. Everybody was very uncomfortable, looking stolidly on the ground or staring straight in front of them.

At last Easton broke the silence by suggesting that it would not be a bad plan if someone was to make a motion that a Beano be held. This was greeted with a general murmur of 'Hear, hear,' followed by another awkward pause, and then the chairman asked Easton if he would move a resolution to that effect. After some hesitation, Easton agreed, and formally moved: 'That this meeting is in favour of a Beano.'

The Semi-drunk said that, in order to get on with the business, he would second the resolution. But meantime, several arguments had broken out between the advocates of different places, and several men began to relate anecdotes of previous Beanos. Nearly everyone was speaking at once and it was some time before the chairman was able to put the resolution. Finding it impossible to make his voice heard above the uproar, he began to hammer on the bench with a wooden mallet, and to shout requests for order, but this only served to increase the din. Some of them looked at him curiously and wondered what was the matter with him, but the majority were so interested in their own arguments that they did not notice him at all.

Whilst the chairman was trying to get the attention of the meeting in order to put the question, Bundy had become involved in an argument with several of the new hands who claimed to know of an even better place than the Queen Elizabeth, a pub called 'The New Found Out', at Mirkfield, a few miles further on than Tubberton, and another individual joined in the dispute, alleging that a house called 'The Three Loggerheads' at Slushton-cum-Dryditch was the finest place for a Beano within a hundred miles of Mugsborough. He went there last year with Pushem and Driver's crowd, and they had roast beef, goose, jam tarts, mince pies, sardines, blancmange, calves' feet jelly and one pint for each man was included in the cost of the dinner. In the middle of the discussion, they noticed that most of the others were holding up their hands, so to show there was no ill feeling they held up theirs also and then the chairman declared it was carried unanimously.

Bundy said he would like to ask the chairman to read out the resolution which had just been passed, as he had not caught the words.

The chairman replied that there was no written resolution. The motion was just to express the feeling of this meeting as to whether there was to be an outing or not.

Bundy said he was only asking a civil question, a point of information: all he wanted to know was, what was the terms of the resolution? Was they in favour of the Beano or not?

The chairman responded that the meeting was unanimously in favour. (Applause.)

Harlow said that the next thing to be done was to decide upon the date. Crass suggested the last Saturday in August. That would give them plenty of time to pay in.

Sawkins asked whether it was proposed to have a day or only half a day. He himself was in favour of the whole day. It would only mean losing a morning's work. It was hardly worth going at all if they only had half the day.

The Semi-drunk remarked that he had just thought of a very good place to go if they decided to have a change. Three years ago he was working for Dauber and Botchit and they went to 'The First In and the Last Out' at Bashford. It was a very small place, but there was a field where you could have a game of cricket or football, and the dinner was A1 at Lloyds. There was also a skittle alley attached to the pub and no charge was made for the use of it. There was a bit of a river there, and one of the chaps got so drunk that he went orf his onion and jumped into the water, and when they got him out the village policeman locked him up, and the next day he was took before the beak and fined two pounds or a month's hard labour for trying to commit suicide.

Easton pointed out that there was another way to look at it: supposing they decided to have the Beano, he supposed it would come to about six shillings a head. If they had it at the end of August and started paying in now, say a tanner a week, they would have plenty of time to make up the amount, but supposing the work fell off and some of them got the push?

Crass said that in that case a man could either have his money back or he could leave it, and continue his payments even if he were working for some other firm; the fact that he was off from Rushton's would not prevent him from going to the Beano.

Harlow proposed that they decide to go to the Queen Elizabeth the same as last year, and that they have half a day.

Philpot said that, in order to get on with the business, he would second the resolution.

Bundy suggested – as an amendment – that it should be a whole day, starting from the Cricketers at nine in the morning, and Sawkins said that, in order to get on with the business, he would second the amendment.

One of the new hands said he wished to move another amendment. He proposed to strike out the Queen Elizabeth and substitute the Three Loggerheads.

The Chairman – after a pause – enquired if there were any seconder to this, and the Semi-drunk said that, although he did not care much where they went, still, to get on with the business, he would second the amendment, although for his own part he would prefer to go to the 'First In and Last Out' at Bashford.

The new hand offered to withdraw his suggestion *re* the Three Loggerheads in favour of the Semi-drunk's proposition, but the latter said it didn't matter; it could go as it was.

As it was getting rather late, several men went home, and cries of 'Put the question' began to be heard on all sides; the chairman accordingly was proceeding to put Harlow's proposition when the new hand interrupted him by pointing out that it was his duty as chairman to put the amendments first. This produced another long discussion, in the course of which a very tall, thin man who had a harsh, metallic voice gave a long rambling lecture about the rules of order and the conduct of public meetings. He spoke very slowly and deliberately, using very long words and dealing with the subject in an exhaustive manner. A resolution was a resolution, and an amendment was an amendment; then there was what was called an amendment to an amendment; the procedure of the House of Commons differed very materially from that of the House of Lords – and so on.

This man kept on talking for about ten minutes, and might have continued for ten hours if he had not been rudely interrupted by Harlow, who said that it seemed to him that they were likely to stay there all night if they went on like they were going. He wanted his tea, and he would also like to get a few hours' sleep before having to resume work in the morning. He was getting about sick of all this talk. (Hear, hear.) In order to get on with the business, he would withdraw his resolution if the others would withdraw their amendments. If they would agree to do this, he would then propose another resolution which – if carried – would meet all the requirements of the case. (Applause.)

The man with the metallic voice observed that it was not necessary to ask the consent of those who had moved amendments: if the original proposition was withdrawn, all the amendments fell to the ground.

'Last year,' observed Crass, 'when we was goin' out of the room after we'd finished our dinner at the Queen Elizabeth, the landlord pointed to the table and said, "There's enough left over for you all to 'ave another lot." ' (Cheers.)

Harlow said that he would move that it be held on the last Saturday in August; that it be for half a day, starting at one o'clock so that they could work up till twelve, which would mean that they would only have to lose one hour's pay: that they go to the same place as last year – the Queen Elizabeth. (Hear, hear.) That the same committee that acted last year – Crass and Bundy – be appointed to make all the arrangements and collect the subscriptions. (Applause.)

The tall man observed that this was what was called a compound resolution, and was proceeding to explain further when the chairman exclaimed that it did not matter a dam' what it was called – would anyone second it? The Semi-drunk said that he would – in order to get on with the business.

Bundy moved, and Sawkins seconded, as an amendment, that it should be a whole day.

The new hand moved to substitute the Loggerheads for the Queen Elizabeth.

Easton proposed to substitute Madame Tussaud's Waxworks for the Queen Elizabeth. He said he moved this just to test the feeling of the meeting.

Harlow point out that it would cost at least a pound a head to defray the expenses of such a trip. The railway fares, tram fares in London, meals – for it would be necessary to have a whole day – and other incidental expenses; to say nothing of the loss of wages. It would not be possible for any of them to save the necessary amount during the next four months. (Hear, hear.)

Philpot repeated his warning as to the danger of visiting Madame Tussaud's. He was certain that if she once got them in there she would never let them out again. He had no desire to pass the rest of his life as an image in a museum.

One of the new hands – a man with a red tie – said that they would look well, after having been soaked for a month or two in petrifying liquid, chained up in the Chamber of Horrors with labels round their necks – 'Specimens of Liberal and Conservative upholders of the Capitalist System, 20 century'.

Crass protested against the introduction of politics into that meeting. (Hear, hear.) The remarks of the last speaker were most uncalled-for.

Easton said that he would withdraw his amendment.

Acting under the directions of the man with the metallic voice, the chairman now proceeded to put the amendment to the vote. Bundy's proposal that it should be a whole day was defeated, only himself, Sawkins and the Semi-drunk being in favour. The motion to substitute the Loggerheads for the Queen Elizabeth was also defeated, and the compound resolution proposed by Harlow was then carried *nem. con.*

Philpot now proposed a hearty vote of thanks to the chairman for the very able manner in which he had conducted the meeting. When this had been unanimously agreed to, the Semi-drunk moved a similar tribute of gratitude to Crass for his services to the cause and the meeting dispersed.

CHAPTER 42

June

During the early part of May the weather was exceptionally bad, with bitterly cold winds. Rain fell nearly every day, covering the roads with a slush that penetrated the rotten leather of the cheap or second-hand boots worn by the workmen. This weather had the effect of stopping nearly all outside work, and also caused a lot of illness, for those who were so fortunate as to have inside jobs frequently got wet through on their way to work in the morning and had to work all day in damp clothing, and with their boots saturated with water. It was also a source of trouble to those of the men who had allotments, because if it had been fine they would have been able to do something to their gardens while they were out of work.

Newman had not succeeded in getting a job at the trade since he came out of prison, but he tried to make a little money by hawking bananas. Philpot – when he was at work – used often to buy a tanner's or a bob's worth from him and give them to Mrs. Linden's children. On Saturdays Old Joe used to waylay these children and buy them bags of cakes at the bakers. One week when he knew that Mrs. Linden had not had much work to do, he devised a very cunning scheme to help her. He had been working with Slyme, who was papering a large boarded ceiling in a shop. It had to be covered with unbleached calico before it could be papered and when the work was done there were a number of narrow pieces of calico left over. These he collected and tore into strips about six inches wide which he took round to Mrs. Linden, and asked her to sew them together, end to end, so as to make one long strip: then this long strip had to be cut into four pieces of equal length and the edges sewn together in such a manner that it would form a long tube. Philpot told her that it was required for some work that Rushton's were doing, and said he had undertaken to get the sewing done. The firm would have to pay for it, so she could charge a good price.

'You see,' he said with a wink, 'this is one of those jobs where we gets a chance to get some of our own back.'

Mary thought it was rather a strange sort of job, but she did as Philpot directed and when he came for the stuff and asked how much it was she said threepence: it had only taken about half an hour. Philpot ridiculed this: it was not nearly enough. *They* were not supposed to know how long it took: it ought to be a bob at the very least. So, after some hesitation she made out a bill for that amount on a half-sheet of note-paper. He brought her the money the next Saturday afternoon and went off chuckling to himself over the success of the scheme. It did not occur to him until the next day that he might just as well have got her to make him an apron or two: and when he did think of this he said that after all it didn't matter, because if he had done that it would have been necessary to buy new calico, and anyhow, it could be done some other time.

Newman did not make his fortune out of the bananas – seldom more than two shillings a day – and consequently he was very glad when Philpot called at his house one evening and told him there was a chance of a job at Rushton's. Newman accordingly went to the yard the next morning, taking his apron and blouse and his bag of tools with him, ready to start work. He got there at about quarter to six and was waiting outside when Hunter arrived. The latter was secretly very glad to see him, for there was a rush of work in and they were short of men. He did not let this appear, of course, but hesitated for a few minutes when Newman repeated the usual formula: 'Any chance of a job, sir?'

'We wasn't at all satisfied with you last time you was on, you know,' said Misery. 'Still, I don't mind giving you another chance. But if you want to hold your job you'll have to move yourself a bit quicker than you did before.'

Towards the end of the month things began to improve all round. The weather became finer and more settled. As time went on the improvement was maintained and nearly everyone was employed. Rushton's were so busy that they took on several other old hands who had been sacked the previous year for being too slow.

Thanks to the influence of Crass, Easton was now regarded as one of the regular hands. He had recently resumed the practice of spending some of his evenings at the Cricketers. It is probable that even if it had not been for his friendship with Crass, he would still have continued to frequent the public house, for things were not very comfortable at home. Somehow or other, Ruth and he seemed to be always quarrelling, and he was satisfied that it was not always his fault. Sometimes, after the day's work was over he would go home resolved to be good friends with her: he would plan on his way homewards to suggest to her that they should have their tea and then go out for a walk with the child. Once or twice she agreed, but on each occasion, they quarrelled before they got home again. So after a time he gave up trying to be friends with her and went out by himself every evening as soon as he had had his tea.

Mary Linden, who was still lodging with them, could not help perceiving their unhappiness: she frequently noticed that Ruth's eyes were red and swollen as if with crying, and she gently sought to gain her confidence, but without success. On one occasion when Mary was trying to advise her, Ruth burst out into a terrible fit of weeping, but she would not say what was the cause – except that her head was aching – she was not well, that was all.

Sometimes Easton passed the evening at the 'Cricketers' but frequently he went over to the allotments, where Harlow had a plot of ground. Harlow used to get up about four o'clock in the morning and put in an hour or so at his garden before going to work; and every evening as soon as he had finished tea he used to go there again and work till it was dark. Sometimes he did not go home to tea at all, but went straight from work to the garden, and his children used to bring his tea to him there in a glass bottle, with something to eat in a little basket. He had four children, none of whom were yet old enough to go to work, and as may be imagined, he found it a pretty hard struggle to live. He was not a teetotaller, but as he often remarked, 'what the publicans got from him wouldn't make them very fat', for he often went for weeks together without tasting the stuff, except a glass or two with the Sunday dinner, which he did not regard as an unnecessary expense, because it was almost as cheap as tea or coffee.

Fortunately his wife was a good needlewoman, and as sober and industrious as himself; by dint of slaving incessantly from morning till night she managed to keep her home fairly comfortable and the children clean and decently dressed; they always looked respectable, although they did not always have enough proper food to eat. They looked so respectable that none of the 'visiting ladies' ever regarded them as deserving cases.

Harlow paid fifteen shillings a year for his plot of ground, and although it meant a lot of hard work it was also a source of pleasure and some profit. He generally made a few shillings out of the flowers, besides having enough potatoes and other vegetables to last them nearly all the year.

Sometimes Easton went over to the allotments and lent Harlow a hand with this gardening work, but whether he went there or to the 'Cricketers', he usually returned home about half-past nine, and then went straight to bed, often without speaking a single word to Ruth, who for her part seldom spoke to him except to answer something he said, or to ask some necessary question. At first, Easton used to think that it was all because of the way he had behaved to her in the public house, but when he apologised – as he did several times – and begged her to forgive him and forget about it, she always said it was all right; there was nothing to forgive. Then, after a time, he began to think it was on account of their poverty and the loss of their home, for nearly all their furniture had been sold during the last winter. But whenever he talked of trying to buy some more things to make the place comfortable again, she did not appear to take any interest: the house was neat enough as it was: they could manage very well, she said, indifferently.

One evening, about the middle of June, when he had been over to the allotments, Easton brought her home a bunch of flowers that Harlow had given him – some red and white roses and some pansies. When he came in, Ruth was packing his food basket for the next day. The baby was asleep in its cot on the floor near the window. Although it was nearly nine o'clock the lamp had not yet been lighted and the mournful twilight that entered the room through the open window increased the desolation of its appearance. The fire had burnt itself out and the grate was filled with ashes. On the hearth was an old rug made of jute that had once been printed in bright colours which had faded away till the whole surface had become almost uniformly drab, showing scarcely any trace of the original pattern. The rest of the floor was bare except for two or three small pieces of old carpet that Ruth had bought for a few pence at different times at some inferior second-hand shop. The chairs and the table were almost the only things that were left of the original furniture of the room, and except for three or four plates of different patterns and sizes and a few cups and saucers, the shelves of the dresser were bare.

The stillness of the atmosphere was disturbed only by the occasional sound of the wheels of a passing vehicle and the strangely distinct voices of some children who were playing in the street.

'I've brought you these,' said Easton, offering her the flowers. 'I thought you'd like them. I got them from Harlow. You know I've been helping him a little with his garden.'

At first he thought she did not want to take them. She was standing at the table with her back to the window, so that he was unable to see the expression of her face, and she hesitated for a moment before she faltered out some words of thanks and took the flowers, which she put down on the table almost as soon as she touched them.

Offended at what he considered her contemptuous indifference, Easton made no further attempt at conversation, but went into the scullery to wash his hands, and then went up to bed.

Downstairs, for a long time after he was gone, Ruth sat alone by the fireless grate, in the silence and the gathering shadows, holding the bunch of flowers in her hand, living over again the events of the last year, and consumed with an agony of remorse.

The presence of Mary Linden and the two children in the house probably saved Ruth from being more unhappy than she was. Little Elsie had made an arrangement with her to be allowed to take the baby out for walks, and in return Ruth did Elsie's housework. As for Mary, she had not much time to do anything but sew, almost the only relaxation she knew being when she took the work home, and on Sunday, which she usually devoted to a general clean-up of the room, and to mending the children's clothes. Sometimes on Sunday evening she used to go with Ruth and the children to see Mrs. Owen, who, although she was not ill enough to stay in bed, seldom went out of the house. She had never really recovered from the attack of illness which was brought on by her work at the boarding house. The doctor had been to see her once or twice and had prescribed – rest. She was to lie down as much as possible, not to do any heavy work – not to carry or lift any heavy articles, scrub floors, make beds, or anything of that sort: and she was to take plenty of nourishing food, beef tea, chicken, a little wine and so on. He did not suggest a trip round the world in a steam yacht or a visit to Switzerland – perhaps he thought they might not be able to afford it. Sometimes she was so ill that she had to observe one at least of the doctor's instructions – to lie down: and then she would worry and fret because she was not able to do the housework and because Owen had to prepare his own tea when he came home at night. On one of these occasions it would have been necessary for Owen to stay at home from work if it had not been for Mrs. Easton, who came for several days in succession to look after her and attend to the house.

Fortunately, Owen's health was better since the weather had become warmer. For a long time after the attack of haemorrhage he had while writing the show-card he used to dread going to sleep at night for fear it should recur. He had heard of people dying in their sleep from that cause. But this terror gradually left him. Nora knew nothing of what occurred that night: to have told her would have done no good, but on the contrary would have caused her a lot of useless anxiety. Sometimes he doubted whether it was right not to tell her, but as time went by and his health continued to improve he was glad he had said nothing about it.

Frankie had lately resumed his athletic exercises with the flat iron: his strength was returning since Owen had been working regularly, because he had been having his porridge and milk again and also some Parrish's Food[97] which a chemist at Windley was selling large bottles of for a shilling. He used to have what he called a 'party' two or three times a week with Elsie, Charley and Easton's baby as the guests. Sometimes, if Mrs. Owen were not well, Elsie used to stay in with her after tea and do some housework while the boys went out to play, but more frequently the four children used to go together to the park to play or sail boats on the lake. Once one of the boats was becalmed about a couple of yards from shore and whilst trying to reach it with a stick Frankie fell into the water, and when Charley tried to drag him out he fell in also. Elsie put the baby down on the bank and seized hold of Charley and while she was trying to get him out, the baby began rolling down, and would probably have tumbled in as well if a man who happened to be passing by had not rushed up in time to prevent it. Fortunately the water at that place was only about two feet deep, so the boys were not much the worse for their ducking. They returned home wet through, smothered with mud, and feeling very important, like boys who had distinguished themselves.

After this, whenever she could manage to spare the time, Ruth Easton used to go with the children to the park. There was a kind of summer-house near the shore of the lake, only a few feet away from the water's edge, surrounded and shaded by trees, whose branches arched over the path and drooped down to the surface of the water. While the children played Ruth used to sit in this arbour and sew, but often her work was neglected and forgotten as she gazed pensively at the water, which just there looked very still, and dark, and deep, for it was sheltered from the wind and overshadowed by the trees that lined the banks at that end of the lake.

Sometimes, if it happened to be raining, instead of going out the children used to have some games in the house. On one such occasion Frankie produced the flat iron and went through the exercise, and Charley had a go as well. But although he was slightly older and taller than Frankie he could not lift the iron so often or hold it out so long as the other, a failure that Frankie attributed to the fact that Charley had too much tea and bread and butter instead of porridge and milk and Parrish's Food. Charley was so upset about his lack of strength that he arranged with Frankie to come home with him the next day after school to see his mother about it. Mrs. Linden had a flat iron, so they gave a demonstration of their respective powers before her, Mrs. Easton being also present, by request, because Frankie said that the diet in question was suitable for babies as well as big children. He had been brought up on it ever since he could remember, and it was almost as cheap as bread and butter and tea.

The result of the exhibition was that Mrs. Linden promised to make porridge for Charley and Elsie whenever she could spare the time, and Mrs. Easton said she would try it for the baby also.

CHAPTER 43

The Good Old Summer-Time

All through the summer the crowd of ragged-trousered philan-thropists continued to toil and sweat at their noble and unselfish task of making money for Mr. Rushton.

Painting the outsides of houses and shops, washing off and dis-tempering ceilings, stripping old paper off walls, painting and papering rooms and staircases, building new rooms or other additions to old houses or business premises, digging up old drains, repairing leaky roofs and broken windows.

Their zeal and enthusiasm in the good cause was unbounded. They were supposed to start work at six o'clock, but most of them were usually to be found waiting outside the job at about a quarter to that hour, sitting on the kerbstones or the doorstep.

Their operations extended all over the town: at all hours of the day they were to be seen either going or returning from 'jobs', carrying ladders, planks, pots of paint, pails of whitewash, earthen-ware, chimney pots, drainpipes, lengths of guttering, closet pans, grates, bundles of wallpaper, buckets of paste, sacks of cement, and loads of bricks and mortar. Quite a common spectacle – for gods and men – was a procession consisting of a handcart loaded up with such materials being pushed or dragged through the public streets by about half a dozen of these Imperialists in broken boots and with battered, stained, discoloured bowler hats, or caps splashed with paint and whitewash; their 'stand-up' collars dirty, limp and crumpled, and their rotten second-hand misfit clothing saturated with sweat and plastered with mortar.

Even the assistants in the grocers' and drapers' shops laughed and ridiculed and pointed the finger of scorn at them as they passed.

The superior classes – those who do nothing – regarded them as a sort of lower animals. A letter appeared in the *Obscurer* one week from one of these well-dressed loafers, complaining of the annoyance caused to the better-class visitors by workmen walking on the pave-ment as they passed along the Grand Parade in the evening on their way home from work, and suggesting that they should walk in the roadway. When they heard of the letter a lot of the workmen adopted the suggestion and walked in the road so as to avoid contaminating the idlers.

This letter was followed by others of a somewhat similar kind, and one or two written in a patronising strain in defence of the working classes by persons who evidently knew nothing about them. There was also a letter from an individual who signed himself 'Morpheus'[98] complaining that he was often awakened out of his beauty sleep in the middle of the night by the clattering noise of the workmen's boots as they passed his house on their way to work in the morning. 'Morpheus' wrote that not only did they make a dreadful noise with their horrible iron-clad boots, but they were in the habit of coughing and spitting a great deal, which was very unpleasant to hear, and they conversed in loud tones. Sometimes their conversation was not at all edifying, for it consisted largely of bad language, which 'Morpheus' assumed to be attributable to the fact that they were out of temper because they had to rise so early.

As a rule they worked till half-past five in the evening, and by the time they reached home it was six o'clock. When they had taken their evening meal and had a wash it was nearly eight: about nine most of them went to bed so as to be able to get up about half-past four the next morning to make a cup of tea before leaving home at half-past five to go to work again. Frequently it happened that they had to leave home earlier than this, because their 'job' was more than half an hour's walk away. It did not matter how far away the 'job' was from the shop, the men had to walk to and fro in their own time, for Trades Union rules were a dead letter in Mugsborough. There were no tram fares or train fares or walking time allowed for the likes of them.

Ninety-nine out of every hundred of them did not believe in such things as those: they had much more sense than to join Trades Unions: on the contrary, they believed in placing themselves entirely at the mercy of their good, kind Liberal and Tory masters.

Very frequently it happened, when only a few men were working together, that it was not convenient to make tea for breakfast or dinner, and then some of them brought tea with them ready made in bottles and drank it cold; but most of them went to the nearest pub and ate their food there with a glass of beer. Even those who would rather have had tea or coffee had beer, because if they went to a temperance restaurant or coffee tavern it generally happened that they were not treated very civilly unless they bought something to eat as well as to drink, and the tea at such places was really dearer than beer, and the latter was certainly quite as good to drink as the stewed tea or the liquid mud that was sold as coffee at cheap 'Workmen's' Eating Houses.

There were some who were – as they thought – exceptionally lucky: the firms they worked for were busy enough to let them work two hours' overtime every night – till half past seven – without stopping for tea. Most of these arrived home about eight, completely flattened out. Then they had some tea and a wash and before they knew where they were it was about half-past nine. Then they went to sleep again till half-past four or five the next morning.

They were usually so tired when they got home at night that they never had any inclination for study or any kind of self-improvement, even if they had had the time. They had plenty of time to study during the winter: and their favourite subject then was, how to preserve themselves from starving to death.

This overtime, however, was the exception, for although in former years it had been the almost invariable rule to work till half-past seven in summer, most of the firms now made a practice of ceasing work at five-thirty. The revolution which had taken place in this matter was a favourite topic of conversation amongst the men, who spoke regretfully of the glorious past, when things were busy, and they used to work fifteen, sixteen and even eighteen hours a day. But nowadays there were nearly as many chaps out of work in the summer as in the winter. They used to discuss the causes of the change. One was, of course, the fact that there was not so much building going on as formerly, and another was the speeding up and slave-driving, and the manner in which the work was now done, or rather scamped. As old Philpot said, he could remember the time, when he was a nipper, when such a 'job' as that at 'The Cave' would have lasted at least six months, and they would have had more hands on it too! But it would have been done properly, not messed up like that was: all the woodwork would have been rubbed down with pumice stone and water: all the knots cut out and the holes properly filled up, and the work properly rubbed down with glasspaper between every coat. But nowadays the only place you'd see a bit of pumice stone was in a glass case in a museum, with a label on it: 'Pumice Stone: formerly used by house-painters.'

Most of them spoke of those bygone times with poignant regret, but there were a few – generally fellows who had been contaminated by contact with Socialists or whose characters had been warped and degraded by the perusal of Socialist literature – who said that they did not desire to work overtime at all – ten hours a day were quite enough for them – in fact they would rather do only eight. What they wanted, they said, was not more work, but more grub, more clothes, more leisure, more pleasure and better homes. They wanted to be able to go for country walks or bicycle rides, to go out fishing or to go to the seaside and bathe and lie on the beach and so forth. But these were only a very few; there were not many so selfish as this. The majority desired nothing but to be allowed to work, and as for their children, why, 'what was good enough for themselves oughter be good enough for the kids'.

They often said that such things as leisure, culture, pleasure and the benefits of civilisation were never intended for 'the likes of us'.

They did not – all – actually say this, but that was what their conduct amounted to; for they not only refused to help to bring about a better state of things for their children, but they ridiculed and opposed and cursed and abused those who were trying to do it for them. The foulest words that came out of their mouths were directed against the men of their own class in the House of Commons – the Labour Members – and especially the Socialists, whom they spoke of as fellows who were too bloody lazy to work for a living, and who wanted the working classes to keep them.

Some of them said that they did not believe in helping their children to become anything better than their parents had been because in such cases the children, when they grew up, 'looked down' upon and were ashamed of their fathers and mothers! They seemed to think that if they loved and did their duty to their children, the probability was that the children would prove ungrateful: as if even if that were true, it would be any excuse for their indifference.

Another cause of the shortage of work was the intrusion into the trade of so many outsiders: fellows like Sawkins and the other light-weights. Whatever other causes there were, there could be no doubt that the hurrying and scamping was a very real one. Every 'job' had to be done at once! as if it were a matter of life or death! It must be finished by a certain time. If the 'job' was at an empty house, Misery's yarn was that it was let! the people were coming in at the end of the week! therefore everything must be finished by Wednesday night. All the ceilings had to be washed off, the walls stripped and re-papered, and two coats of paint inside and outside the house. New drains were to be put in, and all broken windows and locks and broken plaster repaired. A number of men – usually about half as many as there should have been – would be sent to do the work, and one man was put in charge of the 'job'. These sub-foremen or 'coddies' knew that if they 'made their jobs pay' they would be put in charge of others and be kept on in preference to other men as long as the firm had any work; so they helped Misery to scheme and scamp the work and watched and drove the men under their charge; and these latter poor wretches, knowing that their only chance of retaining their employment was to 'tear into it', tore into it like so many maniacs. Instead of cleaning any parts of the woodwork that were greasy or very dirty, they brushed them over with a coat of spirit varnish before painting to make sure that the paint would dry: places where the plaster of the walls was damaged were repaired with what was humorously called 'garden cement' – which was the technical term for dirt out of the garden – and the surface was skimmed over with proper material. Ceilings that were not very dirty were not washed off, but dusted, and lightly gone over with a thin coat of whitewash. The old paper was often left upon the walls of rooms that were supposed to be stripped before being repapered, and to conceal this the joints of the old paper were rubbed down so that they should not be perceptible through the new paper. As far as possible, Misery and the sub-foremen avoided doing the work the customers paid for, and even what little they did was hurried over anyhow.

*   *   *

A reign of terror – the terror of the sack – prevailed on all the 'jobs', which were carried on to the accompaniment of a series of alarums and excursions: no man felt safe for a moment: at the most unexpected times Misery would arrive and rush like a whirlwind all over the 'job'. If he happened to find a man having a spell the culprit was immediately discharged, but he did not get the opportunity of doing this very often for everybody was too terrified to leave off working even for a few minutes' rest.

From the moment of Hunter's arrival until his departure, a state of panic, hurry, scurry and turmoil reigned. His strident voice rang through the house as he bellowed out to them to 'Rouse themselves! Get it done! Smear it on anyhow! Tar it over! We've got another job to start when you've done this!'

Occasionally, just to keep the others up to concert pitch, he used to sack one of the men for being too slow. They all trembled before him and ran about whenever he spoke to or called them, because they knew that there were always a lot of other men out of work who would be willing and eager to fill their places if they got the sack.

Although it was now summer, and the Distress Committee and all the other committees had suspended operations, there was still always a large number of men hanging about the vicinity of the Fountain on the Parade – The Wage Slave Market. When men finished up for the firm they were working for they usually made for that place. Any master in want of a wage slave for a few hours, days or weeks could always buy one there. The men knew this and they also knew that if they got the sack from one firm it was no easy matter to get another job, and that was why they were terrified.

When Misery was gone – to repeat the same performance at some other job – the sub-foreman would have a crawl round to see how the chaps were getting on: to find out if they had used up all their paint yet, or to bring them some putty so that they should not have to leave their work to go to get anything themselves: and then very often Rushton himself would come and stalk quietly about the house or stand silently behind the men, watching them as they worked. He seldom spoke to anyone, but just stood there like a graven image, or walked about like a dumb animal – a pig, as the men used to say. This individual had a very exalted idea of his own importance and dignity. One man got the sack for presuming to stop him in the street to ask some question about some work that was being done.

Misery went round to all the jobs the next day and told all the 'coddies' to tell all the hands that they were never to speak to Mr. Rushton if they met him in the street, and the following Saturday the man who had so offended was given his back day,[99] ostensibly because there was nothing for him to do, but really for the reason stated above.

There was one job, the outside of a large house that stood on elevated ground overlooking the town. The men who were working there were even more than usually uncomfortable, for it was said that Rushton used to sit in his office and watch them through a telescope.

Sometimes, when it was really necessary to get a job done by a certain time, they had to work late, perhaps till eight or nine o'clock. No time was allowed for tea, but some of them brought sufficient food with them in the morning to enable them to have a little about six o'clock in the evening. Others arranged for their children to bring them some tea from home. As a rule, they partook of this without stopping work: they had it on the floor beside them and ate and drank and worked at the same time – a paint-brushful of white lead in one hand, and a piece of bread and margarine in the other. On some jobs, if the 'coddy' happened to be a decent sort, they posted a sentry to look out for Hunter or Rushton while the others knocked off for a few minutes to snatch a mouthful of grub; but it was not safe always to do this, for there was often some crawling sneak with an ambition to become a 'coddy' who would not scruple to curry favour with Misery by reporting the crime.

As an additional precaution against the possibility of any of the men idling or wasting their time, each one was given a time-sheet on which he was required to account for every minute of the day. The form of these sheets vary slightly with different firms: that of Rushton & Co. was is shown opposite.

One Monday morning Misery gave each of the sub-foremen an envelope containing one of the firm's memorandum forms. Crass opened his and found the following:

Crass

When you are on a job with men under you, check and initial their time sheets every night.

If they are called away and sent to some other job, or stood off, check and initial their time sheets as they leave your job.

Any man coming on your job during the day, you must take note of the exact time of his arrival, and see that his sheet is charged right.

Any man who is slow or lazy, or any man that you notice talking more than is necessary during working hours, you must report him to Mr. Hunter.

We expect you and the other foremen to help us to carry out these rules, *and any information given us about any man is treated in confidence*.

Rushton & Co.

Note: This applies to all men of all trades who come on the jobs of which you are the foreman.

Every week the time sheets were scrutinised, and every now and then a man would be 'had up on the carpet' in the office before Rushton and Misery, and interrogated as to why he had taken fifteen hours to do ten hours work? In the event of the accused being unable to give a satisfactory explanation of his conduct he was usually sacked on the spot.

Misery was frequently called 'up on the carpet' himself.

If he made a mistake in figuring out a 'job', and gave in too high a tender for it, so that the firm did not get the work, Rushton

TIME SHEET

OF WORK DONE BY _____ IN THE EMPLOY OF

RUSHTON & CO.

BUILDERS & DECORATORS : MUGSBOROUGH

NO SMOKING OR INTOXICANTS ALLOWED DURING WORKING HOURS.

EACH PIECE OF WORK MUST BE FULLY DESCRIBED, WHAT IT WAS,
AND HOW LONG IT TOOK TO DO.

	Where Working	Time When Started	Time When Finished	Hours	What Doing
Sat.					
Mon.					
Tues.					
Wed.					
Thur.					
Fri.					
			Total Hours		

grumbled. If the price was so low that there was not enough profit, Rushton was very unpleasant about it, and whenever it happened that there was not only no profit but an actual loss, Rushton created such a terrible disturbance that Misery was nearly frightened to death and used to get on his bicycle and rush off to the nearest 'job' and howl and bellow at the 'chaps' to get it done.

All the time the capabilities of the men – especially with regard to speed – were carefully watched and noted: and whenever there was a slackness of work and it was necessary to discharge some hands those that were slow or took too much pains were weeded out: this of course was known to the men and it had the desired effect upon them.

In justice to Rushton and Hunter, it must be remembered that there was a certain amount of excuse for all this driving and cheating, because they had to compete with all the other firms, who conducted their business in precisely the same way. It was not their fault, but the fault of the system.

A dozen firms tendered for every 'job', and of course the lowest tender usually obtained the work. Knowing this, they all cut the price down to the lowest possible figure and the workmen had to suffer.

The trouble was that there were too many 'masters'. It would have been far better for the workmen if nine out of every ten of the employers had never started business. Then the others would have been able to get a better price for their work, and the men might have had better wages and conditions. The hands, however, made no such allowances or excuses as these for Misery and Rushton. They never thought or spoke of them except with hatred and curses. But whenever either of them came to the 'job' the 'coddies' cringed and grovelled before them, greeting them with disgustingly servile salutations, plentifully interspersed with the word 'Sir', greetings which were frequently either ignored altogether or answered with an inarticulate grunt. They said 'Sir' at nearly every second word: it made one feel sick to hear them, because it was not courtesy: they were never courteous to each other, it was simply abject servility and self-contempt.

One of the results of all the frenzied hurrying was that every now and then there was an accident: somebody got hurt: and it was strange that accidents were not more frequent, considering the risks that were taken. When they happened to be working on ladders in busy streets they were not often allowed to have anyone to stand at the foot, and the consequence was that all sorts and conditions of people came into violent collision with the bottoms of the ladders. Small boys playing in the reckless manner characteristic of their years rushed up against them. Errand boys, absorbed in the perusal of penny instalments of the adventures of Claude Duval,[100] and carrying large baskets of greengroceries, wandered into them. Blind men fell foul of them. Adventurous schoolboys climbed up them. People with large feet became entangled in them. Fat persons of both sexes who thought it unlucky to walk underneath, tried to negotiate the narrow strip of pavement between the foot of the ladder and the kerb, and in their passage knocked up against the ladder and sometimes fell into the road. Nursemaids wheeling perambulators – lolling over the handle, which they usually held with their left hands, the right holding a copy of *Orange Blossoms* or some halfpenny paper, and so interested in the story of the Marquis of Lymejuice – a young man of noble presence and fabulous wealth, with a drooping golden moustache and very long legs, who, notwithstanding the diabolical machinations of Lady Sibyl Malvoise, who loves him as well as a woman with a name like that is capable of loving anyone, is determined to wed none other than the scullery-maid at the Village Inn – inevitably bashed the perambulators into the ladders. Even when the girls were not reading they nearly always ran into the ladders, which seemed to possess a magnetic attraction for perambulators and go-carts of all kinds, whether propelled by nurses or mothers. Sometimes they would advance very cautiously towards the ladder: then, when they got very near, hesitate a little whether to go under or run the risk of falling into the street by essaying the narrow passage: then they would get very close up to the foot of the ladder, and dodge and dance about, and give the cart little pushes from side to side, until at last the magnetic influence exerted itself and the perambulator crashed into the ladder, perhaps at the very moment that the man at the top was stretching out to do some part of the work almost beyond his reach.

Once Harlow had just started painting some rainpipes from the top of a 40-ft. ladder when one of several small boys who were playing in the street ran violently against the foot. Harlow was so startled that he dropped his brushes and clutched wildly at the ladder, which turned completely round and slid about six feet along the parapet into the angle of the wall, with Harlow hanging beneath by his hands. The paint pot was hanging by a hook from one of the rungs, and the jerk scattered the brown paint it contained all over Harlow and all over the brickwork of the front of the house. He managed to descend safely by clasping his legs round the sides of the ladder and sliding down. When Misery came there was a row about what he called carelessness. And the next day Harlow had to wear his Sunday trousers to work.

On another occasion they were painting the outside of a house called 'Gothic Lodge'. At one corner it had a tower surmounted by a spire or steeple, and this steeple terminated with an ornamental wrought-iron pinnacle which had to be painted. The ladder they had was not quite long enough, and besides that, as it had to stand in a sort of a courtyard at the base of the tower, it was impossible to slant it sufficiently: instead of lying along the roof of the steeple, it was sticking up in the air.

When Easton went up to paint the pinnacle he had to stand on almost the very top rung of the ladder, to be exact, the third from the top, and lean over to steady himself by holding on to the pinnacle with his left hand while he used the brush with his right. As it was only about twenty minutes' work there were two men to hold the foot of the ladder.

It was cheaper to do it this way than to rig up a proper scaffold, which would have entailed perhaps two hours' work for two or three men. Of course it was very dangerous, but that did not matter at all, because even if the man fell it would make no difference to the firm – all the men were insured and somehow or other, although they frequently had narrow escapes, they did not often come to grief.

On this occasion, just as Easton was finishing he felt the pinnacle that he was holding on to giving way, and he got such a fright that his heart nearly stopped beating. He let go his hold and steadied himself on the ladder as well as he was able, and when he had descended three or four steps – into comparative safety – he remained clinging convulsively to the ladder and feeling so limp that he was unable to go down any further for several minutes. When he arrived at the bottom and the others noticed how white and trembling he was, he told them about the pinnacle being loose, and the 'coddy' coming along just then, they told him about it, and suggested that it should be repaired, as otherwise it might fall down and hurt someone: but the 'coddy' was afraid that if they reported it they might be blamed for breaking it, and the owner might expect the firm to put it right for nothing, so they decided to say nothing about it. The pinnacle is still on the apex of the steeple waiting for a sufficiently strong wind to blow it down on somebody's head.

When the other men heard of Easton's 'narrow shave', most of them said that it would have served him bloody well right if he *had* fallen and broken his neck: he should have refused to go up at all without a proper scaffold. That was what *they* would have done. If Misery or the coddy had ordered any of *them* to go up and paint the pinnacle off that ladder, they would have chucked their tools down and demanded their ha'pence!

That was what they said, but somehow or other it never happened that any of them ever 'chucked their tools down' at all, although such dangerous jobs were of very frequent occurrence.

The scamping business was not confined to houses or properties of an inferior class: it was the general rule. Large good-class houses, villas and mansions, the residences of wealthy people, were done in exactly the same way. Generally in such places costly and beautiful materials were spoilt in the using.

There was a large mansion where the interior woodwork – the doors, windows and staircase – had to be finished in white enamel. It was rather an old house and the woodwork needed rubbing down and filling up before being repainted, but of course there was not time for that, so they painted it without properly preparing it and when it was enamelled the rough, uneven surface of the wood looked horrible: but the owner appeared quite satisfied because it was nice and shiny. The dining-room of the same house was papered with a beautiful and expensive plush paper. The ground of this wall-hanging was made to imitate crimson watered silk, and it was covered with a raised pattern in plush of the same colour. The price marked on the back of this paper in the pattern book was eighteen shillings a roll. Slyme was paid sixpence a roll for hanging it: the room took ten rolls, so it cost nine pounds for the paper and five shillings to hang it! To fix such a paper as this properly the walls should first be done with a plain lining paper of the same colour as the ground of the wall paper itself, because unless the paperhanger 'lapps' the joints – which should not be done – they are apt to open a little as the paper dries and to show the white wall underneath – Slyme suggested this lining to Misery, who would not entertain the idea for a moment – they had gone to quite enough expense as it was, stripping the old paper off!

So Slyme went ahead, and as he had to make his wages, he could not spend a great deal of time over it. Some of the joints were 'lapped' and some were butted, and two or three weeks after the owner of the house moved in, as the paper became more dry, the joints began to open and to show the white plaster of the wall, and then Owen had to go there with a small pot of crimson paint and a little brush, and touch out the white line.

While he was doing this he noticed and touched up a number of other faults; places where Slyme – in his haste to get the work done –

had slobbered and smeared the face of the paper with finger-marks and paste.

The same ghastly mess was made of several other 'jobs' besides this one, and presently they adopted the plan of painting strips of colour on the wall in the places where the joints would come, so that if they opened the white wall would not show: but it was found that the paste on the back of the paper dragged the paint off the wall, and when the joints opened the white streaks showed all the same, so Misery abandoned all attempts to prevent joints showing, and if a customer complained, he sent someone to 'touch it up': but the lining paper was never used, unless the customer or the architect knew enough about the work to insist upon it.

In other parts of the same house the ceilings, the friezes, and the dados, were covered with 'embossed' or 'relief' papers. These hangings require very careful handling, for the raised parts are easily damaged; but the men who fixed them were not allowed to take the pains and time necessary to make good work: consequently in many places – especially at the joints – the pattern was flattened out and obliterated.

The ceiling of the drawing-room was done with a very thick high-relief paper that was made in sheets about two feet square. These squares were not very true in shape: they had evidently warped in drying after manufacture: to make them match anything like properly would need considerable time and care. But the men were not allowed to take the necessary time. The result was that when it was finished it presented a sort of 'higgledy-piggledy' appearance. But it didn't matter: nothing seemed to matter except to get it done. One would think from the way the hands were driven and chivvied and hurried over the work that they were being paid five or six shillings an hour instead of as many pence.

'Get it done!' shouted Misery from morning till night. 'For God's sake get it done! Haven't you finished yet? We're losing money over this 'job'! If you chaps don't wake up and move a bit quicker, I shall see if I can't get somebody else who will.'

These costly embossed decorations were usually finished in white; but instead of carefully coating them with specially prepared paint or patent distemper, which would need two or three coats, they slobbered one thick coat of common whitewash on to it with ordinary whitewash brushes.

This was a most economical way to get over it, because it made it unnecessary to stop up the joints beforehand – the whitewash filled up all the cracks: and it also filled up the hollow parts, the crevices and interstices of the ornament, destroying the sharp outlines of the beautiful designs and reducing the whole to a lumpy, formless mass. But that did not matter either, so long as they got it done.

The architect didn't notice it, because he knew that the more Rushton & Co. made out of the 'job', the more he himself would make.

The man who had to pay for the work didn't notice it; he had the fullest confidence in the architect.

At the risk of wearying the long-suffering reader, mention must be made of an affair that happened at this particular 'job'.

The windows were all fitted with venetian blinds. The gentleman for whom all the work was being done had only just purchased the house, but he preferred roller blinds: he had had roller blinds in his former residence – which he had just sold – and as these roller blinds were about the right size, he decided to have them fitted to the windows of his new house: so he instructed Mr. Rushton to have all the venetian blinds taken down and stored away up in the loft under the roof. Mr. Rushton promised to have this done; but they were not *all* put away under the roof: he had four of them taken to his own place and fitted up in the conservatory. They were a little too large, so they had to be narrowed before they were fixed.

The sequel was rather interesting, for it happened that when the gentleman attempted to take the roller blinds from his old house, the person to whom he had sold it refused to allow them to be removed; claiming that when he bought the house, he bought the blinds also. There was a little dispute, but eventually it was settled that way and the gentleman decided that he would have the venetian blinds in his new house after all, and instructed the people who moved his furniture to take the venetians down again from under the roof, and refix them, and then, of course, it was discovered that four of the blinds were missing. Mr. Rushton was sent for, and he said that he couldn't understand it at all! The only possible explanation that he could think of was that some of his workmen must have stolen them! He would make inquiries, and endeavour to discover the culprits, but in any case, as this had happened while things were in his charge, if he did not succeed in recovering them, he would replace them.

As the blinds had been narrowed to fit the conservatory he had to have four new ones made.

The customer was of course quite satisfied, although very sorry for Mr. Rushton. They had a little chat about it. Rushton told the gentleman that he would be astonished if he knew all the facts: the difficulties one has to contend with in dealing with working men: one has to watch them continually! directly one's back is turned they leave off working! They come late in the morning, and go home before the proper time at night, and then unless one actually happens to catch them – they charge the full number of hours on their time sheets! Every now and then something would be missing, and of course Nobody knew anything about it. Sometimes one would go unexpectedly to a 'job' and find a lot of them drunk. Of course one tried to cope with these evils by means of rules and restrictions and organisation, but it was very difficult – one could not be everywhere or have eyes at the back of one's head. The gentleman said that he had some idea of what it was like: he had had something to do with the lower orders himself at one time and another, and he knew they needed a lot of watching.

Rushton felt rather sick over this affair, but he consoled himself by reflecting that he had got clear away with several valuable rose trees and other plants which he had stolen out of the garden, and that a ladder which had been discovered in the hayloft over the stable and taken – by his instructions – to the 'yard' when the 'job' was finished had not been missed.

Another circumstance which helped to compensate for the blinds was that the brass fittings throughout the house, finger-plates, sash-lifts and locks, bolts and door handles, which were supposed to be all new and which the customer had paid a good price for – were really all the old ones which Misery had had re-laquered and re-fixed.

There was nothing unusual about this affair of the blinds, for Rushton and Misery robbed everybody. They made a practice of annexing every thing they could lay their hands upon, provided it could be done without danger to themselves. They never did anything of a heroic or dare-devil character: they had not the courage to break into banks or jewellers' shops in the middle of the night, or to go out picking pockets: all their robberies were of the sneak-thief order.

At one house that they 'did up' Misery made a big haul. He had to get up into the loft under the roof to see what was the matter with the water tank. When he got up there he found a very fine hall gas lamp, made of wrought brass and copper with stained and painted glass sides. Although covered with dust, it was otherwise in perfect condition, so Misery had it taken to his own house and cleaned up and fixed in the hall.

In the same loft there were a lot of old brass picture rods and other fittings, and three very good planks, each about ten feet in length; these latter had been placed across the rafters so that one could walk easily and safely over to the tank. But Misery thought they would be very useful to the firm for whitewashing ceilings and other work, so he had them taken to the yard along with the old brass, which was worth about fourpence a pound.

There was another house that had to be painted inside: the people who used to live there had only just left: they had moved to some other town, and the house had been re-let before they vacated it. The new tenant had agreed with the agent that the house was to be renovated throughout before he took possession.

The day after the old tenants moved away, the agent gave Rushton the key so that he could go to see what was to be done and give an estimate for the work.

While Rushton and Misery were looking over the house they discovered a large barometer hanging on the wall behind the front door: it had been overlooked by those who removed the furniture. Before returning the key to the agent, Rushton sent one of his men to the house for the barometer, which he kept in his office for a few-weeks to see if there would be any enquiries about it. If there had been, it would have been easy to say that he had brought it there for safety – to take care of till he could find the owner. The people to whom it belonged thought the thing had been lost or stolen in transit, and afterwards one of the workmen who had assisted to pack and remove the furniture was dismissed from his employment on suspicion of having had something to do with its disappearance. No one ever thought of Rushton in connection with the matter, so after about a month he had it taken to his own dwelling and hung up in the hall near the carved oak marble-topped console table that he had sneaked last summer from 596 Grand Parade.

And there it hangs unto this day: and close behind it, supported by cords of crimson silk, is a beautiful bevelled-edged card about a foot square, and upon this card is written, in letters of gold: 'Christ is the head of this house; the unseen Guest at every meal, the silent Listener to every conversation.'

And on the other side of the barometer is another card of the same kind and size which says: 'As for me and my house we will serve the Lord.'[101]

From another place they stole two large brass chandeliers. This house had been empty for a very long time, and its owner – who did not reside in the town – wished to sell it. The agent, to improve the chances of a sale, decided to have the house overhauled and re-decorated. Rushton & Co.'s tender being the lowest, they got the work. The chandeliers in the drawing-room and the dining-room were of massive brass, but they were all blackened and tarnished. Misery suggested to the agent that they could be cleaned and re-lacquered, which would make them equal to new: in fact, they would be better than new ones, for such things as these were not made now, and for once Misery was telling the truth. The agent agreed and the work was done: it was an extra, of course, and as the firm got twice as much for the job as they paid for having it done, they were almost satisfied.

When this and all the other work was finished they sent in their account and were paid.

Some months afterwards the house was sold, and Nimrod inter-viewed the new proprietor with the object of securing the order for any work that he might want done. He was successful. The papers on the walls of several of the rooms were not to the new owner's taste, and, of course, the woodwork would have to be re-painted to harmonise with the new paper. There was a lot of other work besides this: a new conservatory to build, a more modern bath and heating apparatus to be put in, and the electric light to be installed, the new people having an objection to the use of gas.

The specifications were prepared by an architect, and Rushton secured the work. When the chandeliers were taken down, the men, instructed by Misery, put them on a handcart, and covered them over with sacks and dust-sheets and took them to the front shop, where they were placed for sale with the other stock.

When all the work at the house was finished, it occurred to Rushton and Nimrod that when the architect came to examine and pass the work before giving them the certificate that would enable them to present their account, he might remember the chandeliers and enquire what had become of them. So they were again placed on the handcart, covered with sacks and dust-sheets, taken back to the house and put up in the loft under the roof so that, if he asked for them, there they were.

The architect came, looked over the house, passed the work, and gave his certificate; he never mentioned or thought of the chandeliers. The owner of the house was present and asked for Rushton's bill, for which he at once gave them a cheque and Rushton and Misery almost grovelled and wallowed on the ground before him.

Throughout the whole interview the architect and the 'gentleman' had kept their hats on, but Rushton and Nimrod had been respectfully uncovered all the time, and as they followed the other two about the house their bearing had been expressive of the most abject servility.

When the architect and the owner were gone the two chandeliers were taken down again from under the roof, put upon a handcart, covered over with sacks and dust-sheets and taken back to the shop and again placed for sale with the other stock.

These are only a few of the petty thefts committed by these people. To give anything approaching a full account of all the rest would require a separate volume.

* * *

As a result of all the hurrying and scamping, every now and again the men found that they had worked themselves out of a job.

Several times during the summer the firm had scarcely anything to do, and nearly everybody had to stand off for a few days or weeks.

When Newman got his first start in the early part of the year he had only been working for about a fortnight when – with several others – he was 'stood off'. Fortunately, however, the day after he left Rushtons, he was lucky enough to get a start for another firm, Driver and Botchit, where he worked for nearly a month, and then he was again given a job at Rushton's, who happened to be busy again.

He did not have to lose much time, for he 'finished up' for Driver and Botchit on a Thursday night and on the Friday he interviewed Misery, who told him they were about to commence a fresh 'job' on the following Monday morning at six o'clock, and that he could start with them. So this time Newman was only out of work the Friday and Saturday, which was another stroke of luck, because it often happens that a man has to lose a week or more after 'finishing up' for one firm before he gets another 'job'.

All through the summer Crass continued to be the general 'colour-man', most of his time being spent at the shop mixing up colours for all the different 'jobs'. He also acted as a sort of lieutenant to Hunter, who, as the reader has already been informed, was not a practical painter. When there was a price to be given for some painting work, Misery sometimes took Crass with him to look over it and help him to estimate the amount of time and material it would take. Crass was thus in a position of more than ordinary importance, not only being superior to the 'hands', but also ranking above the other sub-foremen who had charge of the 'jobs'.

It was Crass and these sub-foremen who were to blame for most of the scamping and driving, because if it had not been for them neither Rushton nor Hunter would have known how to scheme the work.

Of course, Hunter and Rushton wanted to drive and scamp, but not being practical men they would not have known how if it had not been for Crass and the others, who put them up to all the tricks of the trade.

Crass knew that when the men stayed till half-past seven they were in the habit of ceasing work for a few minutes to eat a mouthful of grub about six o'clock, so he suggested to Misery that as it was not possible to stop this, it would be a good plan to make the men stop work altogether from half-past five till six, and lose half an hour's pay; and to make up the time, instead of leaving off at seven-thirty, they could work till eight.

Misery had known of and winked at the former practice, for he knew that the men could not work all that time without something to eat, but Crass's suggestion seemed a much better way, and it was adopted.

When the other masters in Mugsborough heard of this great reform they all followed suit, and it became the rule in that town, whenever it was necessary to work overtime, for the men to stay till eight instead of half-past seven as formerly, and they got no more pay than before.

Previous to this summer it had been the almost invariable rule to have two men in each room that was being painted, but Crass pointed out to Misery that under such circumstances they wasted time talking to each other, and they also acted as a check on one another: each of them regulated the amount of work he did by the amount the other did, and if the 'job' took too long it was always difficult to decide which of the two was to blame: but if they were made to work alone, each of them would be on his mettle; he would not know how much the others were doing, and the fear of being considered slow in comparison with others would make them all tear into it all they could.

Misery thought this a very good idea, so the solitary system was introduced, and as far as practicable, one room, one man became the rule.

They even tried to make the men distemper large ceilings single-handed, and succeeded in one or two cases, but after several ceilings had been spoilt and had to be washed off and done over again, they gave that up: but nearly all the other work was now arranged on the 'solitary system', and it worked splendidly: each man was constantly in a state of panic as to whether the others were doing more work than himself.

Another suggestion that Crass made to Misery was that the sub-foremen should be instructed never to send a man into a room to prepare it for painting.

'If you sends a man into a room to get it ready,' said Crass, ' 'e makes a meal of it! 'E spends as much time messin' about rubbin' down and stoppin' up as it would take to paint it. But,' he added, with a cunning leer, 'give 'em a bit of putty and a little bit of glass-paper, *and* the paint at the *start*, and then 'e gits it in 'is mind as 'e's going in there to paint it! And 'e doesn't mess about much over the preparing of it.'

These and many other suggestions – all sorts of devices for scamping and getting over the work – were schemed out by Crass and the other sub-foremen, who put them into practice and showed them to Misery and Rushton in the hope of currying favour with them and being 'kept on'. And between the lot of them they made life a veritable hell for themselves, and the hands, and everybody else around them. And the mainspring of it all was – the greed and selfishness of one man, who desired to accumulate money! For this was the only object of all the driving and bullying and hatred and cursing and unhappiness – to make money for Rushton, who evidently considered himself a deserving case.

It is sad and discreditable, but nevertheless true, that some of the more selfish of the philanthropists often became weary of well-doing, and lost all enthusiasm in the good cause. At such times they used to say that they were 'Bloody well fed up' with the whole business, and 'Tired of tearing their bloody guts out for the benefit of other people' and every now and then some of these fellows would 'chuck up' work, and go on the booze, sometimes stopping away for two or three days or a week at a time. And then, when it was all over, they came back, very penitent, to ask for another 'start', but they generally found that their places had been filled.

If they happened to be good 'sloggers' – men who made a practice of 'tearing their guts out' when they *did* work – they were usually forgiven, and after being admonished by Misery, permitted to resume work, with the understanding that if ever it occurred again they would get the 'infernal' – which means the final and irrevocable – sack.

* * *

There was once a job at a shop that had been a high-class restaurant kept by a renowned Italian chef. It had been known as

'MACARONI'S ROYAL ITALIAN CAFE'

Situated on the Grand Parade, it was a favourite resort of the 'Elite', who frequented it for afternoon tea and coffee and for little suppers after the theatre.

It had plate-glass windows, resplendent with gilding, marble-topped tables with snow white covers, vases of flowers, and all the other appurtenances of glittering cut glass and silver. The obsequious waiters were in evening dress, the walls were covered with lofty plate-glass mirrors in carved and gilded frames, and at certain hours of the day and night an orchestra consisting of two violins and a harp discoursed selections of classic music.

But of late years the business had not been paying, and finally the proprietor went bankrupt and was sold out. The place was shut up for several months before the shop was let to a firm of dealers in fancy articles, and the other part was transformed into flats.

Rushton had the contract for the work. When the men went there to 'do it up' they found the interior of the house in a state of indescribable filth: the ceilings discoloured with smoke and hung with cobwebs, the wallpapers smeared and black with grease, the hand-rails and the newel posts of the staircase were clammy with filth, and the edges of the doors near the handles were blackened with greasy dirt and finger-marks. The tops of the skirtings, the mouldings of the doors, the sashes of the windows and the corners of the floors were thick with the accumulated dust of years.

In one of the upper rooms which had evidently been used as a nursery or playroom for the children of the renowned chef, the wallpaper for about two feet above the skirting was blackened with grease and ornamented with childish drawings made with burnt sticks and black lead pencils, the door being covered with similar artistic efforts, to say nothing of some rude attempts at carving, evidently executed with an axe or a hammer. But all this filth was nothing compared with the unspeakable condition of the kitchen and scullery, a detailed description of which would cause the blood of the reader to curdle, and each particular hair of his head to stand on end.

Let it suffice to say that the walls, the ceiling, the floor, the paint-work, the gas-stove, the kitchen range, the dresser and everything else were uniformly absolutely and literally – black. And the black was composed of soot and grease.

In front of the window there was a fixture – a kind of bench or table, deeply scored with marks of knives like a butcher's block. The sill of the window was about six inches lower than the top of the table, so that between the glass of the lower sash of the window, which had evidently never been raised, and the back of the table, there was a long narrow cavity or trough, about six inches deep, four inches wide and as long as the width of the window, the sill forming the bottom of the cavity.

This trough was filled with all manner of abominations: fragments of fat and decomposed meat, legs of rabbits and fowls, vegetable matter, broken knives and forks, and hair: and the glass of the window was caked with filth of the same description.

This job was the cause of the sacking of the Semi-drunk and another man named Bill Bates, who were sent into the kitchen to clean it down and prepare it for painting and distempering.

They commenced to do it, but it made them feel so ill that they went out and had a pint each, and after that they made another start at it. But it was not long before they felt that it was imperatively necessary to have another drink. So they went over to the pub, and this time they had two pints each. Bill paid for the first two and then the Semi-drunk refused to return to work unless Bill would consent to have another pint with him before going back. When they had drunk the two pints, they decided – in order to save themselves the trouble and risk of coming away from the job – to take a couple of quarts back with them in two bottles, which the landlord of the pub lent them, charging twopence on each bottle, to be refunded when they were returned.

When they got back to the job they found the 'coddy' in the kitchen, looking for them and he began to talk and grumble, but the Semi-drunk soon shut him up: he told him he could either have a drink out of one of the bottles or a punch in the bloody nose – whichever he liked! Or if he did not fancy either of these alternatives, he could go to hell!

As the 'coddy' was a sensible man he took the beer and advised them to pull themselves together and try to get some work done before Misery came, which they promised to do.

When the 'coddy' was gone they made another attempt at the work.

Misery came a little while afterwards and began shouting at them because he said he could not see what they had done. It looked as if they had been asleep all the morning: Here it was nearly ten o'clock, and as far as he could see, they had done Nothing!

When he was gone they drank the rest of the beer and then they began to feel inclined to laugh. What did they care for Hunter or Rushton either? To hell with both of 'em! They left off scraping and scrubbing, and began throwing buckets of water over the dresser and the walls, laughing uproariously all the time.

'We'll show the b—s how to wash down paintwork!' shouted the Semi-drunk, as he stood in the middle of the room and hurled a pailful of water over the door of the cupboard. 'Bring us another bucket of water, Bill.'

Bill was out in the scullery filling his pail under the tap, and laughing so much that he could scarcely stand. As soon as it was full he passed it to the Semi-drunk, who threw it bodily, pail and all, on to the bench in front of the window, smashing one of the panes of glass. The water poured off the table and all over the floor.

Bill brought the next pailful in and threw it at the kitchen door, splitting one of the panels from top to bottom, and then they threw about half a dozen more pailfuls over the dresser.

'We'll show the b—rs how to clean paintwork,' they shouted, as they hurled the buckets at the walls and doors.

By this time the floor was deluged with water, which mingled with the filth and formed a sea of mud.

They left the two taps running in the scullery and as the waste pipe of the sink was choked up with dirt, the sink filled up and overflowed like a miniature Niagara.

The water ran out under the doors into the back-yard, and along the passage out to the front door. But Bill Bates and the Semi-drunk remained in the kitchen, smashing the pails at the walls and doors and the dresser, and cursing and laughing hysterically.

They had just filled the two buckets and were bringing them into the kitchen when they heard Hunter's voice in the passage, shouting out inquiries as to where all that water came from. Then they heard him advancing towards them and they stood waiting for him with the pails in their hands, and directly he opened the door and put his head into the room they let fly the two pails at him. Unfortunately, they were too drunk and excited to aim straight. One pail struck the middle rail of the door and the other the wall by the side of it.

Misery hastily shut the door again and ran upstairs, and presently the 'coddy' came down and called out to them from the passage.

They went out to see what he wanted, and he told them that Misery had gone to the office to get their wages ready: they were to make out their time sheets and go for their money at once. Misery had said that if they were not there in ten minutes he would have the pair of them locked up.

The Semi-drunk said that nothing would suit them better than to have all their pieces at once – they had spent all their money and wanted another drink. Bill Bates concurred, so they borrowed a piece of blacklead pencil from the 'coddy' and made out their time sheets, took off their aprons, put them into their tool bags, and went to the office for their money, which Misery passed out to them through the trap-door.

The news of this exploit spread all over the town during that day and evening, and although it was in July, the next morning at six o'clock there were half a dozen men waiting at the yard to ask Misery if there was 'any chance of a job'.

Bill Bates and the Semi-drunk had had their spree and had got the sack for it and most of their chaps said it served them right. Such conduct as that was going too far.

Most of them would have said the same thing no matter what the circumstances might have been. They had very little sympathy for each other at any time.

Often, when, for instance, one man was sent away from one 'job' to another, the others would go into his room and look at the work he had been doing, and pick out all the faults they could find and show them to each other, making all sorts of ill-natured remarks about the absent one meanwhile. 'Jist run yer nose over that door, Jim,' one would say in a tone of disgust. 'Wotcher think of it? Did yer ever see sich a mess in yer life? Calls hisself a painter!' And the other man would shake his head sadly and say that although the one who had done it had never been up to much as a workman, he could do it a bit better than that if he liked, but the fact was that he never gave himself time to do anything properly: he was always tearing his bloody guts out! Why, he'd only been in this room about four hours from start to finish! He ought to have a watering cart to follow him about, because he worked at such a hell of a rate you couldn't see him for dust! And then the first man would reply that other people could do as they liked, but for his part, *he* was not going to tear *his* guts out for nobody!

The second man would applaud these sentiments and say that he wasn't going to tear his out either: and then they would both go back to their respective rooms and tear into the work for all they were worth, making the same sort of 'job' as the one they had been criticising, and afterwards, when the other's back was turned, each of them in turn would sneak into the other's room and criticise it and point out the faults to anyone else who happened to be near at hand.

Harlow was working at the place that had been Macaroni's Café when one day a note was sent to him from Hunter at the shop. It was written on a scrap of wallpaper, and worded in the usual manner of such notes – as if the writer had studied how to avoid all suspicion of being unduly civil:

> Harlow go to the yard at once take your tools with you Crass will tell you where you have to go.
>
> J. H.

They were just finishing their dinners when the boy brought this note; and after reading it aloud for the benefit of the others, Harlow remarked that it was worded in much the same way in which one would speak to a dog. The others said nothing; but after he was gone the other men – who all considered that it was ridiculous for the 'likes of us' to expect or wish to be treated with common civility – laughed about it, and said that Harlow was beginning to think he was Somebody: they supposed it was through readin' all those books what Owen was always lendin' 'im. And then one of them got a piece of paper and wrote a note to be given to Harlow at the first opportunity. This note was properly worded written in a manner suitable for a gentleman like him, neatly folded and addressed:

> Mr. Harlow Esq.,
>   c/o Macoroni's Royal Café
>   till called for.
> Mister Harlow,
>   Dear Sir: Wood you kinely oblige me bi cummin to the paint shop as soon as you can make it convenient as there is a sealin' to be wite-woshed hoppin this is not trubbling you to much
>
> I remane
> Yours respeckfully
Pontius Pilate.

This note was read out for the amusement of the company and afterwards stored away in the writer's pocket till such a time as an opportunity should occur of giving it to Harlow.

As the writer of the note was on his way back to his room to resume work he was accosted by a man who had gone into Harlow's room to criticise it, and had succeeded in finding several faults which he pointed out to the other, and of course they were both very much disgusted with Harlow.

'I can't think why the coddy keeps him on the job,' said the first man. 'Between you and me, if I had charge of a job, and Misery sent Harlow there – I'd send 'im back to the shop.'

'Same as you,' agreed the other as he went back to tear into his own room. 'Same as you, old man: I shouldn't 'ave 'im neither.'

It must not be supposed from this that either of these two men were on exceptionally bad terms with Harlow; they were just as good friends with him – to his face – as they were with each other – to each other's faces – and it was just their way: that was all.

If it had been one or both of these two who had gone away instead of Harlow, just the same things would have been said about them by the others who remained – it was merely their usual way of speaking about each other behind each other's backs.

It was always the same: if any one of them made a mistake or had an accident or got into any trouble he seldom or never got any sympathy from his fellow workmen. On the contrary, most of them at such times seemed rather pleased than otherwise.

There was a poor devil – a stranger in the town; he came from London – who got the sack for breaking some glass. He had been sent to 'burn off' some old paint of the woodwork of a window. He was not very skilful in the use of the burning-off lamp, because on the firm where he had been working in London it was a job that the ordinary hands were seldom or never called upon to do. There were one or two men who did it all. For that matter, not many of Rushton's men were very skilful at it either. It was a job everybody tried to get out of, because nearly always the lamp went wrong and there was a row about the time the work took. So they worked this job on to the stranger.

This man had been out of work for a long time before he got a start at Rushton's, and he was very anxious not to lose the job, because he had a wife and family in London. When the 'coddy' told him to go and burn off this window he did not like to say that he was not used to the work: he hoped to be able to do it. But he was very nervous, and the end was that although he managed to do the burning off all right, just as he was finishing he accidentally allowed the flame of the lamp to come into contact with a large pane of glass and broke it.

They sent to the shop for a new pane of glass, and the man stayed late that night and put it in in his own time, thus bearing half the cost of repairing it.

Things were not very busy just then, and on the following Saturday two of the hands were 'stood off'. The stranger was one of them, and nearly everybody was very pleased. At mealtimes the story of the broken window was repeatedly told amid jeering laughter. It really seemed as if a certain amount of indignation was felt that a stranger – especially such an inferior person as this chap who did not know how to use a lamp – should have had the cheek to try to earn his living at all! One thing was very certain – they said, gleefully – he would never get another job at Rushton's: that was one good thing.

And yet they all knew that this accident might have happened to any one of them.

Once a couple of men got the sack because a ceiling they distempered had to be washed off and done again. It was not really the men's fault at all: it was a ceiling that needed special treatment and they had not been allowed to do it properly.

But all the same, when they got the sack most of the others laughed and sneered and were glad. Perhaps because they thought that the fact that these two unfortunates had been disgraced, increased their own chances of being 'kept on'. And so it was with nearly everything. With a few exceptions, they had an immense amount of respect for Rushton and Hunter, and very little respect or sympathy for each other.

Exactly the same lack of feeling for each other prevailed amongst the members of all the different trades. Everybody seemed glad if anybody got into trouble for any reason whatever.

There was a garden gate that had been made at the carpenter's shop: it was not very well put together, and for the usual reason; the man had not been allowed the time to do it properly. After it was fixed, one of his shopmates wrote upon it with lead pencil in big letters: 'This is good work for a joiner. Order one ton of putty.'

But to hear them talking in the pub of a Saturday afternoon just after pay-time one would think them the best friends and mates and the most independent spirits in the world, fellows whom it would be very dangerous to trifle with, and who would stick up for each other through thick and thin. All sorts of stories were related of the wonderful things they had done and said; of jobs they had 'chucked up', and masters they had 'told off': of pails of whitewash thrown over offending employers, and of horrible assaults and batteries committed upon the same. But strange to say, for some reason or other, it seldom happened that a third party ever witnessed any of these prodigies. It seemed as if a chivalrous desire to spare the feelings of their victims had always prevented them from doing or saying anything to them in the presence of witnesses.

When he had drunk a few pints, Crass was a very good hand at these stories. Here is one that he told in the bar of the Cricketers on the Saturday afternoon of the same week that Bill Bates and the Semi-drunk got the sack. The Cricketers was only a few minutes' walk from the shop and at pay-time a number of the men used to go in there to take a drink before going home.

'Last Thursday night about five o'clock, 'Unter comes inter the paint-shop an' ses to me, "I wants a pail o' wash made up tonight, Crass," 'e ses, "ready for fust thing in the mornin'," 'e ses. "Oh," I ses, lookin' 'im straight in the bloody eye, "Oh, yer do, do yer?" – just like that. "Yes," 'e ses. "Well, you can bloody-well make it yerself!" I ses, " 'cos I ain't agoin' to," I ses – just like that. "Wot the 'ell do yer mean," I ses, "by comin' 'ere at this time o' the night with a order like that?" I ses. You'd a larfed,' continued Crass, as he wiped his mouth with the back of his hand after taking another drink out of his glass, and looking round to note the effect of the story, 'you'd a larfed if you'd bin there. 'E was fairly flabbergasted! And wen I said that to 'im I seen 'is jaw drop! An' then 'e started apoligising and said as 'e 'adn't meant no offence, but I told 'im bloody straight not to come no more of it. "You bring the horder at a reasonable time," I ses – just like that – "and I'll attend to it," I ses, "but not otherwise," I ses.'

As he concluded this story, Crass drained his glass and gazed round upon the audience, who were full of admiration. They looked at each other and at Crass and nodded their heads approvingly. Yes, undoubtedly, that was the proper way to deal with such bounders as Nimrod; take up a strong attitude, an' let 'em see as you'll stand no nonsense!

'Yer don't blame me, do yer?' continued Crass. 'Why should we put up with a lot of old buck from the likes of 'im! We're not a lot of bloody Chinamen, are we?'

So far from blaming him, they all assured him that they would have acted in precisely the same way under similar circumstances.

'For my part, I'm a bloke like this,' said a tall man with a very loud voice – a chap who nearly fell down dead every time Rushton or Misery looked at him. 'I'm a bloke like this 'ere: I never stands no cheek from no gaffers! If a guv'nor ses two bloody words to me, I downs me tools and I ses to 'im, 'Wot! Don't I suit yer, guv'ner? Ain't I done enuff for yer? Werry good! Gimmie me bleedin' a'pence.' '

'Quite right too,' said everybody. That was the way to serve 'em. If only everyone would do the same as the tall man – who had just paid for another round of drinks – things would be a lot more comfortable than they was.

'Last summer I was workin' for ole Buncer,' said a little man with a cutaway coat several sizes too large for him. 'I was workin' for ole Buncer, over at Windley, an' you all knows as 'e don' arf lower it. Well, one day, wen I knowed 'e was on the drunk, I 'ad to first coat a room out – white; so thinks I to meself, If I buck up I shall be able to get this lot done by about four o'clock, an' then I can clear orf 'ome. 'Cos I reckoned as 'e'd be about flattened out by that time, an' you know 'e ain't got no foreman. So I tears into it an' gets this 'ere room done about a quarter past four, an' I'd just got me things put away for the night w'en 'oo should come fallin' up the bloody stairs but ole Buncer, drunk as a howl! An' no sooner 'e gits inter the room than 'e starts yappin' an' rampin'. "Is this 'ere hall you've done?" 'e shouts out. "Wotcher bin up to hall day?" 'e ses, an' 'e keeps on shouting' an' swearin' till at last I couldn't stand it no longer, 'cos you can guess I wasn't in a very good temper with 'im comin' along jist then w'en I thought I was goin' to get orf a bit early – so w'en 'e kept on shoutin' I never made no answer to 'im, but ups with me fist an' I gives 'im a slosh in the dial an' stopped 'is clock! Then I chucked the pot o' w'ite paint hover 'im, an' kicked 'im down the bloody stairs.'

'Serve 'im blooming well right, too,' said Crass as he took a fresh glass of beer from one of the others, who had just 'stood' another round.

'What did the b—r say to that?' enquired the tall man.

'Not a bloody word!' replied the little man, ' 'E picked 'isself up, and called a keb wot was passin' an' got inter it an' went 'ome; an' I never seen no more of 'im until about 'arf-past eleven the next day, w'en I was second-coatin' the room, an' 'e comes up with a noo suit o' clothes on, an' arsts me if I'd like to come hover to the pub an' 'ave a drink? So we goes hover, an' 'e calls for a w'iskey an' soda for isself an' arsts me wot I'd 'ave, so I 'ad the same. An' w'ile we was gettin' it down us, 'e ses to me, "Ah, Garge," 'e ses. "You losed your temper with me yesterday," 'e ses.'

'There you are, you see!' said the tall man. 'There's an example for yer! If you 'adn't served 'im as you did you'd most likely 'ave 'ad to put up with a lot more ole buck.'

They all agreed that the little man had done quite right: they all said that they didn't blame him in the least: they would all have done the same: in fact, this was the way they all conducted themselves whenever occasion demanded it. To hear them talk, one would imagine that such affairs as the recent exploit of Bill Bates and the Semi-drunk were constantly taking place, instead of only occurring about once in a blue moon.

Crass stood the final round of drinks, and as he evidently thought that circumstance deserved to be signalised in some special manner, he proposed the following toast, which was drunk with enthusiasm:

> 'To hell with the man,
> May he never grow fat,
> What carries two faces,
> Under one 'at.'

Rushton & Co. did a lot of work that summer. They did not have many big jobs, but there were a lot of little ones, and the boy Bert was kept busy running from one to the other. He spent most of his time dragging a handcart with loads of paint, or planks and steps, and seldom went out to work with the men, for when he was not taking things out to the various places where the philanthropists were working, he was in the paintshop at the yard, scraping out dirty paint-pots or helping Crass to mix up colours. Although scarcely anyone seemed to notice it, the boy presented a truly pitiable spectacle. He was very pale and thin. Dragging the handcart did not help him to put on flesh, for the weather was very hot and the work made him sweat.

His home was right away on the other side of Windley. It took him more than three-quarters of an hour to walk to the shop, and as he had to be at work at six, that meant that he had to leave home at a few minutes past five every morning, so that he always got up about half-past four.

He was wearing a man's coat – or rather jacket – which gave the upper part of his body a bulky appearance. The trousers were part of a suit of his own, and were somewhat narrowly cut, as is the rule with boy's cheap ready-made trousers. These thin legs appearing under the big jacket gave him a rather grotesque appearance, which was heightened by the fact that all his clothes, cap, coat, waistcoat, trousers and boots, were smothered with paint and distemper of various colours, and there were generally a few streaks of paint of some sort or other upon his face, and of course his hands – especially round the finger-nails – were grimed with it. But the worst of all were the dreadful hobnailed boots: the leather of the uppers of these was an eighth of an inch thick, and very stiff. Across the fore part of the boot this hard leather had warped into ridges and valleys, which chafed his feet and made them bleed. The soles were five-eighths of an inch thick, covered with hobnails, and were as hard and inflexible and almost as heavy as iron. These boots hurt his feet dreadfully and made him feel very tired and miserable, for he had such a lot of walking to do. He used to be jolly glad when dinner-time came, for then he used to get out of sight in some quiet spot and lie down for the whole hour. His favourite dining-place was up in the loft over the carpenter's shop, where they stored the mouldings and archi-traves. No one ever came there at that hour, and after he had eaten his dinner he used to lie down and think and rest.

He nearly always had an hour for dinner, but he did not always have it at the same time: sometimes he had it at twelve o'clock and sometimes not till two. It all depended upon what stuff had to be taken to the job.

Often it happened that some men at a distant job required some material to use immediately after dinner, and perhaps Crass was not able to get it ready till twelve o'clock, so that it was not possible to take it before dinner-time, and if Bert left it till after dinner the men would be wasting their time waiting for it: so in such cases he took it there first and had his dinner when he came back.

Sometimes he got back about half-past twelve, and it was necessary for him to take out another lot of material at one o'clock.

In such a case he 'charged' half an hour overtime on his time sheet – he used to get twopence an hour for overtime.

Sometimes Crass sent him with a handcart to one job to get a pair of steps or tressels, or a plank, or some material or other, and take them to another job, and on these occasions it was often very late before he was able to take his meals. Instead of getting his breakfast at eight, it was often nearly nine before he got back to the shop, and frequently he had to go without dinner until half-past one or two.

Sometimes he could scarcely manage to carry the pots of paint to the jobs; his feet were so hot and sore. When he had to push the cart it was worse still, and often when knocking-off time came he felt so tired that he could scarcely manage to walk home.

But the weather was not always hot or fine: sometimes it was quite cold, almost like winter, and there was a lot of rain that summer. At such times the boy frequently got wet through several times a day as he went from one job to another, and he had to work all the time in his wet clothes and boots, which were usually old and out of repair and let in the water.

One of the worst jobs that he had to do was when a new stock of white lead came in. This stuff came in wooden barrels containing two hundredweight, and he used to have to dig it out of these barrels with a trowel, and put it into a metal tank, where it was kept covered with water,[102] and the empty barrels were returned to the makers.

When he was doing this work he usually managed to get himself smeared all over with the white lead, and this circumstance, and the fact that he was always handling paint or some poisonous material or other was doubtless the cause of the terrible pains he often had in his stomach – pains that sometimes caused him to throw himself down and roll on the ground in agony.

*　　*　　*

One afternoon Crass sent him with a handcart to a job that Easton, Philpot, Harlow and Owen were just finishing. He got there about half-past four and helped the men to load up the things, and afterwards walked alongside the cart with them back to the shop.

On the way they all noticed and remarked to each other that the boy looked tired and pale and that he seemed to limp: but he did not say anything, although he guessed that they were talking about him. They arrived at the shop a little before knocking-off time – about ten minutes past five. Bert helped them to unload, and afterwards, while they were putting their things away and 'charging up' the unused materials they had brought back, he pushed the cart over to the shed where it was kept, on the other side of the yard. He did not return to the shop at once and a few minutes later when Harlow came out into the yard to get a bucket of water to wash their hands with, he saw the boy leaning on the side of the cart, crying, and holding one foot off the ground.

Harlow asked him what was the matter, and while he was speaking to him the others came out to see what was up: the boy said he had rheumatism or growing pains or something in his leg, 'just here near the knee'. But he didn't say much, he just cried miserably, and turned his head slowly from side to side, avoiding the looks of the men because he felt ashamed that they should see him cry.

When they saw how ill and miserable he looked, the men all put their hands in their pockets to get some coppers to give to him so that he could ride home on the tram. They gave him fivepence altogether, so he had more than enough to ride all the way; and Crass told him to go at once – there was no need to wait till half-past; but before he went Philpot got a small glass bottle out of his tool bag and filled it with oil and turps – two of turps and one of oil – which he gave to Bert to rub into his leg before going to bed: The turps – he explained – was to cure the pain and the oil was to prevent it from hurting the skin. He was to get his mother to rub it in for him if he were too tired to do it himself. Bert promised to observe these directions, and, drying his tears, took his dinner basket and limped off to catch the tram.

It was a few days after this that Hunter met with an accident. He was tearing off on his bicycle to one of the jobs about five minutes to twelve to see if he could catch anyone leaving off for dinner before the proper time, and while going down a rather steep hill the front brake broke – the rubbers of the rear one were worn out and failed to act – so Misery to save himself from being smashed against the railings of the houses at the bottom of the hill, threw himself off the machine, with the result that his head and face and hands were terribly cut and bruised. He was so badly knocked about that he had to remain at home for nearly three weeks, much to the delight of the men and the annoyance – one might even say the indignation – of Mr. Rushton, who did not know enough about the work to make out estimates without assistance. There were several large jobs to be tendered for just at that time, so Rushton sent the specifications round to Hunter's house for him to figure out the prices, and nearly all the time that Misery was at home he was sitting up in bed, swathed in bandages, trying to calculate the probable cost of these jobs. Rushton did not come to see him, but he sent Bert nearly every day, either with some specifications, or some accounts, or something of that sort, or with a note inquiring when Hunter thought he would be able to return to work.

All sorts of rumours became prevalent amongst the men concerning Hunter's condition. He had 'broken his spiral column', he had 'conjunction of the brain', or he had injured his 'innards' and would probably never be able to 'do no more slave-drivin' '. Crass – who had helped Mr. Rushton to 'price up' several small jobs – began to think it might not be altogether a bad thing for himself if something were to happen to Hunter, and he began to put on side and to assume airs of authority. He got one of the light-weights to assist him in his work of colourman and made him do all the hard work, while he spent part of his own time visiting the different jobs to see how the work progressed.

[Crass's appearance did him justice. He was wearing a pair of sporting trousers the pattern of which consisted of large] black and white squares. The previous owners of these trousers was taller and slighter than Crass, so although the legs were about a couple of inches too long, they fitted him rather tightly, so much so that it was fortunate that he had his present job of colourman, for if he had had to do any climbing up and down ladders or steps, the trousers would have burst. His jacket was also two or three sizes too small, and the sleeves were so short that the cuffs of his flannelette shirt were visible. This coat was made of serge, and its colour had presumably once been blue, but it was now a sort of heliotrope and violet: the greater part being of the former tint, and the parts under the sleeves of the latter. This jacket fitted very tightly across the shoulders and back and being much too short left his tightly clad posteriors exposed to view.

He however seemed quite unconscious of anything peculiar in his appearance and was so bumptious and offensive that most of the men were almost glad when Nimrod came back. They said that if Crass ever got the job he would be a dam' sight worse than Hunter. As for the latter, for a little while after his return to work it was said that his illness had improved his character: he had had time to think things over; and in short, he was ever so much better than before: but it was not long before this story began to be told the other way round. He was worse than ever! and a thing that happened about a fortnight after his return caused more ill feeling and resentment against him and Rushton than had ever existed previously. What led up to it was something that was done by Bundy's mate, Ted Dawson.

This poor wretch was scarcely ever seen without a load of some sort or other: carrying a sack of cement or plaster, a heavy ladder, a big bucket of mortar, or dragging a load of scaffolding on a cart. He must have been nearly as strong as a horse, because after working in this manner for Rushton & Co. from six in the morning till half-past five at night, he usually went to work in his garden for two or three hours after tea, and frequently went there for an hour or so in the morning before going to work. The poor devil needed the produce of his garden to supplement his wages, for he had a wife and three children to provide for and he earned only – or rather, to be correct, he was paid only – fourpence an hour.

There was an old house to which they were making some alterations and repairs, and there was a lot of old wood taken out of it: old, decayed floorboards and stuff of that kind, wood that was of no use whatever except to burn.

Bundy and his mate were working there, and one night Misery

came a few minutes before half-past five and caught Dawson in the act of tying up a small bundle of this wood. When Hunter asked him what he was going to do with it he made no attempt at prevarication or concealment: he said he was going to take it home for fire-wood, because it was of no other use. Misery kicked up a devil of a row and ordered him to leave the wood where it was: it had to be taken to the yard, and it was nothing to do with Dawson or anyone else whether it was any use or not! If he caught anyone taking wood away he would sack them on the spot. Hunter shouted very loud so that all the others might hear, and as they were all listening attentively in the next room, where they were taking their aprons off preparatory to going home, they got the full benefit of his remarks.

The following Saturday when the hands went to the office for their money they were each presented with a printed card bearing the following legend:

> Under no circumstances is any article or material, however trifling, to be taken away by workmen for their private use, whether waste material or not, from any workshop or place where work is being done. Foremen are hereby instructed to see that this order is obeyed and to report any such act coming to their knowledge. Any man breaking this rule will be either dismissed without notice or given into custody.
>
> Rushton & Co.

Most of the men took these cards with the envelopes containing their wages and walked away without making any comment – in fact, most of them were some distance away before they realised exactly what the card was about. Two or three of them stood a few steps away from the pay window in full view of Rushton and Misery and ostentatiously tore the thing into pieces and threw them into the street. One man remained at the pay window while he read the card and then flung it with an obscene curse into Rushton's face, and demanded his back day, which they gave him without any remark or delay, the other men who were not yet paid having to wait while he made out his time-sheet for that morning.

The story of this card spread all over the place in a very short time. It became the talk of every shop in the town. Whenever any of Rushton's men encountered the employees of another firm, the latter used to shout after them – 'However trifling!' – or 'Look out, chaps! 'Ere comes some of Rushton's pick-pockets.'

Amongst Rushton's men themselves it became a standing joke or form of greeting to say when one met another – 'Remember! However trifling!'

If one of their number was seen going home with an unusual amount of paint or whitewash on his hands or clothes, the others would threaten to report him for stealing the material. They used to say that however trifling the quantity, it was against orders to take it away.

Harlow drew up a list of rules which he said Mr. Rushton had instructed him to communicate to the men. One of these rules provided that everybody was to be weighed upon arrival at the job in the morning and again at leaving-off time: any man found to have increased in weight was to be discharged.

There was also much cursing and covert resentment about it; the men used to say that such a thing as that looked well coming from the likes of Rushton and Hunter, and they used to remind each other of the affair of the marble-topped console table, the barometer, the venetian blinds and all the other robberies.

None of them ever said anything to either Misery or Rushton about the cards, but one morning when the latter was reading his letters at the breakfast table, on opening one of them he found that it contained one of the notices, smeared with human excrement. He did not eat any more breakfast that morning.

It was not to be much wondered at that none of them had the courage to openly resent the conditions under which they had to work, for although it was summer, there were many men out of employment, and it was much easier to get the sack than it was to get another job.

None of the men were ever caught stealing anything, however trifling, but all the same during the course of the summer five or six of them were captured by the police and sent to jail – for not being able to pay their poor rates.

*   *   *

All through the summer Owen continued to make himself objectionable and to incur the ridicule of his fellow workmen by talking about the causes of poverty and of ways to abolish it.

Most of the men kept two shillings or half a crown of their wages back from their wives for pocket money, which they spent on beer and tobacco. There were a very few who spent a little more than this, and there were a still smaller number who spent so much in this way that their families had to suffer in consequence.

Most of those who kept back half a crown or three shillings from their wives did so on the understanding that they were to buy their clothing out of it. Some of them had to pay a shilling a week to a tally-man or credit clothier. These were the ones who indulged in shoddy new suits – at long intervals. Others bought – or got their wives to buy for them – their clothes at second-hand shops, 'paying off' about a shilling or so a week and not receiving the things till they were paid for.

There were a very large proportion of them who did not spend even a shilling a week for drink: and there were numerous others who, while not being formally total abstainers, yet often went for weeks together without either entering a public house or tasting intoxicating drink in any form.

Then there were others who, instead of drinking tea or coffee or cocoa with their dinners or suppers, drank beer. This did not cost more than the teetotal drinks, but all the same there are some persons who say that those who swell the 'Nation's Drink Bill'[103] by drinking beer with their dinners or suppers are a kind of criminal, and that they ought to be compelled to drink something else: that is, if they are working people. As for the idle classes, they of course are to be allowed to continue to make merry, 'drinking whisky, wine and sherry', to say nothing of having their beer in by the barrel and the dozen – or forty dozen – bottles. But of course that's a different matter, because these people make so much money out of the labour of the working classes that they can afford to indulge in this way without depriving their children of the necessaries of life.

There is no more cowardly, dastardly slander than is contained in the assertion that the majority or any considerable proportion of working men neglect their families through drink. It is a condemned lie. There are some who do, but they are not even a large minority. They are few and far between, and are regarded with contempt by their fellow workmen.

It will be said that their families had to suffer for want of even the little that most of them spent in that way: but the persons that use this argument should carry it to its logical conclusion. Tea is an unnecessary and harmful drink; it has been condemned by medical men so often that to enumerate its evil qualities here would be waste of time. The same can be said of nearly all the cheap temperance drinks; they are unnecessary and harmful and cost money, and, like beer, are drunk only for pleasure.

What right has anyone to say to working men that when their

work is done they should not find pleasure in drinking a glass or two of beer together in a tavern or anywhere else? Let those who would presume to condemn them carry their argument to its logical conclusion and condemn pleasure of every kind. Let them persuade the working classes to lead still simpler lives; to drink water instead of such unwholesome things as tea, coffee, beer, lemonade and all the other harmful and unnecessary stuff. They would then be able to live ever so much more cheaply, and as wages are always and everywhere regulated by the cost of living, they would be able to work for lower pay.

These people are fond of quoting the figures of the 'Nation's Drink Bill', as if all this money were spent by the working classes! But if the amount of money spent in drink by the 'aristocracy', the clergy and the middle classes were deducted from the 'Nation's Drink Bill', it would be seen that the amount spent per head by the working classes is not so alarming after all; and would probably not be much larger than the amount spent on drink by those who consume tea and coffee and all the other unwholesome and unnecessary 'temperance' drinks.

The fact that some of Rushton's men spent about two shillings a week on drink while they were in employment was not the cause of their poverty. If they had never spent a farthing for drink, and if their wretched wages had been increased fifty per cent., they would still have been in a condition of the most abject and miserable poverty, for nearly all the benefits and privileges of civilisation, nearly everything that makes life worth living, would still have been beyond their reach.

It is inevitable, so long as men have to live and work under such heartbreaking, uninteresting conditions as at present that a certain proportion of them will seek forgetfulness and momentary happiness in the tavern, and the only remedy for this evil is to remove the cause; and while that is in process, there is something else that can be done and that is, instead of allowing filthy drinking dens, presided over by persons whose interest it is to encourage men to drink more bad beer than is good for them or than they can afford, – to have civilised institutions run by the State or the municipalities for use and not merely for profit. Decent pleasure houses, where no drunkenness or filthiness would be tolerated – where one could buy real beer or coffee or tea or any other refreshments; where men could repair when their day's work was over and spend an hour or two in rational intercourse with their fellows or listen to music and singing. Taverns to which they could take their wives and children without fear of defilement, for a place that is not fit for the presence of a woman or a child is not fit to exist at all.

Owen, being a teetotaller, did not spend any of his money on drink; but he spent a lot on what he called 'The Cause'. Every week he bought some penny or twopenny pamphlets or some leaflets about Socialism, which he lent or gave to his mates; and in this way and by means of much talk he succeeded in converting a few to his party. Philpot, Harlow and a few others used to listen with interest, and some of them even paid for the pamphlets they obtained from Owen, and after reading them themselves, passed them on to others, and also occasionally 'got up' arguments on their own accounts. Others were simply indifferent, or treated the subject as a kind of joke, ridiculing the suggestion that it was possible to abolish poverty. They repeated that there had 'always been rich and poor in the world and there always would be, so there was an end of it'. But the majority were bitterly hostile; not to Owen, but to Socialism. For the man himself most of them had a certain amount of liking, especially the ordinary hands because it was known that he was not a 'master's man' and that he had declined to 'take charge' of jobs which Misery had offered to him. But to Socialism they were savagely and malignantly opposed. Some of those who had shown some symptoms of Socialism during the past winter when they were starving had now quite recovered and were stout defenders of the Present System.

Barrington was still working for the firm and continued to maintain his manner of reserve, seldom speaking unless addressed, but all the same, for several reasons, it began to be rumoured that he shared Owen's views. He always paid for the pamphlets that Owen gave him, and on one occasion, when Owen bought a thousand leaflets to give away, Barrington contributed a shilling towards the half-crown that Owen paid for them. But he never took any part in the arguments that sometimes raged during the dinner-hour or at breakfast-time.

It was a good thing for Owen that he had his enthusiasm for 'the cause' to occupy his mind. Socialism was to him what drink was to some of the others – the thing that enabled them to forget and tolerate the conditions under which they were forced to exist. Some of them were so muddled with beer, and others so besotted with admiration of their Liberal and Tory masters, that they were oblivious of the misery of their own lives, and in a similar way, Owen was so much occupied in trying to rouse them from their lethargy and so engrossed in trying to think out new arguments to convince them of the possibility of bringing about an improvement in their condition that he had no time to dwell upon his own poverty; the money that he spent on leaflets and pamphlets to give away might have been better spent on food and clothing for himself, because most of those to whom he gave them were by no means grateful; but he never thought of that; and after all, nearly everyone spends money on some hobby or other. Some people deny themselves the necessaries or comforts of life in order that they may be able to help to fatten a publican. Others deny themselves in order to enable a lazy parson to live in idleness and luxury; and others spend much time and money that they really need for themselves in buying Socialist literature to give away to people who don't want to know about Socialism.

One Sunday morning towards the end of July, a band of about twenty-five men and women on bicycles[104] invaded the town. Two of them – who rode a few yards in front of the others, had affixed to the handlebars of each of their machines a slender, upright standard from the top of one of which fluttered a small flag of crimson silk with 'International Brotherhood and Peace' in gold letters. The other standard was similar in size and colour, but with a different legend: 'One for all and All for one.'

As they rode along they gave leaflets to the people in the streets, and whenever they came to a place where there were many people they dismounted and walked about, giving their leaflets to whoever would accept of them. They made several long halts during their progress along the Grand Parade, where there was a considerable crowd, and then they rode over the hill to Windley, which they reached a little before opening time. There were little crowds waiting outside the several public houses and a number of people passing through the streets on their way home from Church and Chapel. The strangers distributed leaflets to all those who would take them, and they went through a lot of the side streets, putting leaflets under the doors and in the letter-boxes. When they had exhausted their stock they remounted and rode back the way they came.

Meantime the news of their arrival had spread, and as they returned through the town they were greeted with jeers and booing. Presently someone threw a stone, and as there happened to be plenty of stones just there several others followed suit and began running after the retreating cyclists, throwing stones, hooting and cursing.

The leaflet which had given rise to all this fury read as follows:

WHAT IS SOCIALISM?

At present the workers, with hand and brain produce continually food, clothing and all useful and beautiful things in great abundance.

BUT THEY LABOUR IN VAIN – for they are mostly poor and often in want. They find it a hard struggle to live. Their women and children suffer, and their old age is branded with pauperism.

Socialism is a plan by which poverty will be abolished, and everyone enabled to live in plenty and comfort, with leisure and opportunity for ampler life.

If you wish to hear more of this plan, come to the field at the Cross Roads on the hill at Windley, on Tuesday evening next at 8 p.m. and

LOOK OUT FOR THE SOCIALIST VAN[105]

The cyclists rode away amid showers of stones without sustaining much damage. One had his hand cut and another, who happened to look round, was struck on the forehead, but these were the only casualties.

On the following Tuesday evening, long before the appointed time, there was a large crowd assembled at the cross roads on the hill at Windley, waiting for the appearance of the van, and they were evidently prepared to give the Socialists a warm reception. There was only one policeman in uniform there but there were several in plain clothes amongst the crowd . . .

Crass, Dick Wantley, the Semi-drunk, Sawkins, Bill Bates and several other frequenters of the Cricketers were amongst the crowd, and there were also a sprinkling of tradespeople, including the Old Dear and Mr. Smallman, the grocer, and a few ladies and gentlemen – wealthy visitors – but the bulk of the crowd were working men, labourers, mechanics and boys.

As it was quite evident that the crowd meant mischief – many of them had their pockets filled with stones and were armed with sticks – several of the Socialists were in favour of going to meet the van to endeavour to persuade those in charge from coming, and with that object they withdrew from the crowd, which was already regarding them with menacing looks, and went down the road in the direction from which the van was expected to come. They had not gone very far, however, before the people, divining what they were going to do, began to follow them and while they were hesitating what course to pursue, the Socialist van, escorted by five or six men on bicycles, appeared round the corner at the bottom of the hill.

As soon as the crowd saw it, they gave an exultant cheer, or, rather, yell, and began running down the hill to meet it, and in a few minutes it was surrounded by a howling mob. The van was drawn by two horses; there was a door and a small platform at the back and over this was a sign with white letters on a red ground: 'Socialism, the only hope of the Workers.'

The driver pulled up, and another man on the platform at the rear attempted to address the crowd, but his voice was inaudible in the din of howls, catcalls, hooting, and obscene curses. After about an hour of this, as the crowd began pushing against the van and trying to overturn it, the terrified horses commenced to get restive and uncontrollable, and the man on the box attempted to drive up the hill. This seemed to still further infuriate the horde of savages who surrounded the van. Numbers of them clutched the wheels and turned them the reverse way, screaming that it must go back to where it came from; and several of them accordingly seized the horses' heads and, amid cheers, turned them round.

The man on the platform was still trying to make himself heard, but without success. The strangers who had come with the van and the little group of local Socialists, who had forced their way through the crowd and gathered together close to the platform in front of the would-be speaker, only increased the din by their shouts of appeal to the crowd to 'give the man a fair chance'. This little bodyguard closed round the van as it began to move slowly downhill, but they were not sufficiently numerous to protect it from the crowd, which, not being satisfied with the rate at which the van was proceeding, began to shout to each other to 'Run it away!' 'Take the brake off!' and several savage rushes were made with the intention of putting these suggestions into execution.

Some of the defenders were hampered with their bicycles, but they resisted as well as they were able, and succeeded in keeping the crowd off until the foot of the hill was reached, and then someone threw the first stone, which by a strange chance happened to strike one of the cyclists whose head was already bandaged – it was the same man who had been hit on the Sunday. This stone was soon followed by others, and the man on the platform was the next to be struck. He got it right on the mouth, and as he put up his handkerchief to staunch the blood another struck him on the forehead just above the temple, and he dropped forward on his face on to the platform as if he had been shot. As the speed of the vehicle increased, a regular hail of stones fell upon the roof and against the sides of the van and whizzed past the retreating cyclists, while the crowd followed close behind, cheering, shrieking out volleys of obscene curses, and howling like wolves.

'We'll give the b—rs Socialism!' shouted Crass, who was literally foaming at the mouth.

'We'll teach 'em to come 'ere trying to undermined our bloody morality,' howled Dick Wantley as he hurled a lump of granite that he had torn up from the macadamised road at one of the cyclists.

They ran on after the van until it was out of range, and then they bethought themselves of the local Socialists; but they were nowhere to be seen; they had prudently withdrawn as soon as the van had got fairly under way, and the victory being complete, the upholders of the present system returned to the piece of waste ground on the top of the hill, where a gentleman in a silk hat and frock-coat stood up on a little hillock and made a speech. He said nothing about the Distress Committee or the Soup Kitchen or the children who went to school without proper clothes or food, and made no reference to what was to be done next winter, when nearly everybody would be out of work. These were matters he and they were evidently not at all interested in. But he said a good deal about the Glorious Empire! and the Flag! and the Royal Family. The things he said were received with rapturous applause, and at the conclusion of his [[address, the crowd sang the National Anthem with great enthusiasm and dispersed, congratulating themselves that they had shown to the best of their ability what Mugsborough thought of Socialism]] and the general opinion of the crowd was that they would hear nothing more from the Socialist van.

But in this they were mistaken, for the very next Sunday evening a crowd of Socialists suddenly materialised at the Cross Roads. Some of them had come by train, others had walked from different places and some had cycled.

A crowd gathered and the Socialists held a meeting, two speeches being delivered before the crowd recovered from their surprise at the temerity of these other Britishers who apparently had not sense enough to understand that they had been finally defeated and obliterated last Tuesday evening: and when the cyclist with the bandaged head got up on the hillock some of the crowd actually joined in the hand-clapping with which the Socialists greeted him.

In the course of his speech he informed them that the man who had come with the van and who had been felled whilst attempting to speak from the platform was now in hospital. For some time it had been probable that he would not recover, but he was now out of danger, and as soon as he was well enough there was no doubt that he would come there again.

Upon this Crass shouted out that if ever the Vanner did return, they would finish what they had begun last Tuesday. He would not get off so easy next time. But when he said this, Crass – not being able to see into the future – did not know what the reader will learn in due time, that the man was to return to that place under different circumstances.

When they had finished their speech-making one of the strangers who was acting as chairman invited the audience to put questions, but as nobody wanted to ask any, he invited anyone who disagreed with what had been said to get up on the hillock and state his objections, so that the audience might have an opportunity of judging for themselves which side was right; but this invitation was also neglected. Then the chairman announced that they were coming there again next Sunday at the same time, when a comrade would speak on 'Unemployment and Poverty, the Causes and the Remedy', and then the strangers sang a song called 'England Arise', the first verse being:

> England Arise, the long, long night is over,
> Faint in the east, behold the Dawn appear
> Out of your evil dream of toil and sorrow
> Arise, O England! for the day is here!

During the progress of the meeting several of the strangers had been going about amongst the crowd giving away leaflets, which many of the people gloomily refused to accept, and selling penny pamphlets, of which they managed to dispose of about three dozen.

Before declaring the meeting closed, the chairman said that the speaker who was coming next week resided in London: he was not a millionaire, but a workman, the same as nearly all those who were there present. They were not going to pay him anything for coming, but they intended to pay his railway fare. Therefore next Sunday after the meeting there would be a collection, and anything over the amount of the fare would be used for the purchase of more leaflets such as those they were now giving away. He hoped that anyone who thought that any of the money went into the pockets of those who held the meeting would come and join: then they could have their share.

The meeting now terminated and the Socialists were suffered to depart in peace. Some of them, however, lingered amongst the crowd after the main body had departed, and for a long time after the meeting was over little groups remained on the field excitedly discussing the speeches or the leaflets.

The next Sunday evening when the Socialists came they found the field at the Cross Roads in the possession of a furious, hostile mob, who refused to allow them to speak, and finally they had to go away without having held a meeting. They came again the next Sunday, and on this occasion they had a speaker with a very loud – literally a stentorian – voice, and he succeeded in delivering an address, but as only those who were very close were able to hear him, and as they were all Socialists, it was not of much effect upon those for whom it was intended.

They came again the next Sunday and nearly every other Sunday during the summer: sometimes they were permitted to hold their meeting in comparative peace and at other times there was a row. They made several converts, and many persons declared themselves in favour of some of the things advocated, but they were never able to form a branch of their society there, because nearly all those who were convinced were afraid to publicly declare themselves lest they should lose their employment or customers.

CHAPTER 44

The Beano

Now and then a transient gleam of sunshine penetrated the gloom in which the lives of the philanthropists were passed. The cheerless monotony was sometimes enlivened with a little innocent merriment. Every now and then there was a funeral which took Misery and Crass away for the whole afternoon, and although they always tried to keep the dates secret, the men generally knew when they were gone.

Sometimes the people in whose houses they were working regaled them with tea, bread and butter, cake or other light refreshments, and occasionally even with beer – very different stuff from the petrifying liquid they bought at the Cricketers for twopence a pint. At other places, where the people of the house were not so generously disposed, the servants made up for it, and entertained them in a similar manner without the knowledge of their masters and mistresses. Even when the mistresses were too cunning to permit of this, they were seldom able to prevent the men from embracing the domestics, who for their part were quite often willing to be embraced; it was an agreeable episode that helped to vary the monotony of their lives, and there was no harm done.

It was rather hard lines on the philanthropists sometimes when they happened to be working in inhabited houses of the better sort. They always had to go in and out by the back way, generally through the kitchen, and the crackling and hissing of the poultry and the joints of meat roasting in the ovens, and the odours of fruit pies and tarts, and plum puddings and sage and onions, were simply maddening. In the back-yards of these houses there were usually huge stacks of empty beer, stout, and wine bottles, and others that had contained whiskey, brandy or champagne.

The smells of the delicious viands that were being prepared in the kitchen often penetrated into the dismantled rooms that the philan-thropists were renovating, sometimes just as they were eating their own wretched fare out of their dinner baskets, and washing it down with draughts of the cold tea or the petrifying liquid they sometimes brought with them in bottles.

Sometimes, as has been said, the people of the house used to send up some tea and bread and butter or cakes or other refreshments to the workmen, but whenever Hunter got to know of it being done he used to speak to the people about it and request that it be dis-continued, as it caused the men to waste their time.

But the event of the year was the Beano, which took place on the last Saturday in August, after they had been paying in for about four months. The cost of the outing was to be five shillings a head, so this was the amount each man had to pay in, but it was expected that the total cost – the hire of the brakes and the cost of the dinner – would come out at a trifle less than the amount stated, and in that case the surplus would be shared out after the dinner. The amount of the share-out would be greater or less according to other circumstances, for it generally happened that apart from the subscriptions of the men, the Beano fund was swelled by charitable donations from several quarters, as will be seen later on.

When the eventful day arrived, the hands, instead of working till one, were paid at twelve o'clock and rushed off home to have a wash and change.

The brakes were to start from the 'Cricketers' at one, but it was arranged, for the convenience of those who lived at Windley, that they were to be picked up at the Cross Roads at one-thirty.

There were four brakes altogether – three large ones for the men and one small one for the accommodation of Mr. Rushton and a few of his personal friends, Didlum, Grinder, Mr. Toonarf, an architect, and Mr. Lettum, a house and estate Agent. One of the drivers was accompanied by a friend who carried a long coachman's horn. This gentleman was not paid to come, but, being out of work, he thought that the men would be sure to stand him a few drinks and that they would probably make a collection for him in return for his services.

Most of the chaps were smoking twopenny cigars, and had one or two drinks with each other to try to cheer themselves up before they started, but all the same it was a melancholy procession that wended its way up the hill to Windley. To judge from the mournful expression on the long face of Misery, who sat on the box beside the driver of the first large brake, and the downcast appearance of the majority of the men, one might have thought that it was a funeral rather than a pleasure party, or that they were a contingent of lost souls being conducted to the banks of the Styx. The man who from time to time sounded the coachman's horn might have passed as the angel sounding the last trump, and the fumes of the cigars were typical of the smoke of their torment, which ascendeth up for ever and ever.[106]

A brief halt was made at the Cross Roads to pick up several of the men, including Philpot, Harlow, Easton, Ned Dawson, Sawkins, Bill Bates and the Semi-drunk. The two last-named were now working for Smeariton and Leavit, but as they had been paying in from the first, they had elected to go to the Beano rather than have their money back. The Semi-drunk and one or two other habitual boozers were very shabby and down at heel, but the majority of the men were decently dressed. Some had taken their Sunday clothes out of pawn especially for the occasion. Others were arrayed in new suits which they were going to pay for at the rate of a shilling a week. Some had bought themselves second-hand suits, one or two were wearing their working clothes brushed and cleaned up, and some were wearing Sunday clothes that had not been taken out of pawn for the simple reason that the pawnbrokers would not take them in. These garments were in what might be called a transition stage – old-fashioned and shiny with wear, but yet too good to take for working in, even if their owners had been in a position to buy some others to take their place for best. Crass, Slyme and one or two of the single men, however, were howling swells, sporting stand-up collars and bowler hats of the latest type, in contra-distinction to some of the others, who were wearing hats of antique patterns, and collars of various shapes with jagged edges. Harlow had on an old straw hat that his wife had cleaned up with oxalic acid, and Easton had carefully dyed the faded binding of his black bowler with ink. Their boots were the worst part of their attire: without counting Rushton and his friends, there were thirty-seven men altogether, including Nimrod, and there were not half a dozen pairs of really good boots amongst the whole crowd.

When all were seated a fresh start was made. The small brake, with Rushton, Didlum, Grinder and two or three other members of the Band, led the way. Next came the largest brake with Misery on the box. Beside the driver of the third brake was Payne, the foreman carpenter. Crass occupied a similar position of honour on the fourth brake, on the back step of which was perched the man with the coachman's horn.

Crass – who had engaged the brakes – had arranged with the drivers that the cortège should pass through the street where he and Easton lived, and as they went by Mrs. Crass was standing at the door with the two young men lodgers, who waved their handkerchiefs and shouted greetings. A little further on Mrs. Linden and Easton's wife were standing at their door to see them go by. In fact, the notes of the coachman's horn alarmed most of the inhabitants, who crowded to their windows and doors to gaze upon the dismal procession as it passed.

The mean streets of Windley were soon left far behind and they found themselves journeying along a sunlit, winding road, bordered with hedges of hawthorn, holly and briar, past rich, brown fields of standing corn, shimmering with gleams of gold, past apple-orchards where bending boughs were heavily loaded with mellow fruits exhaling fragrant odours, through the cool shades of lofty avenues of venerable oaks, whose overarched and interlacing branches formed a roof of green, gilt and illuminated with quivering spots and shafts of sunlight that filtered through the trembling leaves; over old mossy stone bridges, spanning limpid streams that duplicated the blue sky and the fleecy clouds; and then again, stretching away to the horizon on every side over more fields, some rich with harvest, others filled with drowsing cattle or with flocks of timid sheep that scampered away at the sound of the passing carriages. Several times they saw merry little companies of rabbits frisking gaily in and out the hedges or in the fields beside the sheep and cattle. At intervals, away in the distance, nestling in the hollows or amid sheltering trees, groups of farm buildings and stacks of hay; and further on, the square ivy-clad tower of an ancient church, or perhaps a solitary windmill with its revolving sails alternately flashing and darkening in the rays of the sun. Past thatched wayside cottages whose inhabitants came out to wave their hands in friendly greeting. Past groups of sunburnt, golden-haired children who climbed on fences and five-barred gates, and waved their hats and cheered, or ran behind the brakes for the pennies the men threw down to them.

From time to time the men in the brakes made half-hearted attempts at singing, but it never came to much, because most of them were too hungry and miserable. They had not had time to take any dinner and would not have taken any even if they had the time, for they wished to reserve their appetites for the banquet at the Queen Elizabeth, which they expected to reach about half-past three. However, they cheered up a little after the first halt – at the Blue Lion, where most of them got down and had a drink. Some of them, including the Semi-drunk, Ned Dawson, Bill Bates and Joe Philpot – had two or three drinks, and felt so much happier for them that, shortly after they started off again, sounds of melody were heard from the brake the three first named rode in – the one presided over by Crass – but it was not very successful, and even after the second halt – about five miles further on – at the Warrior's Head, they found it impossible to sing with any heartiness. Fitful bursts of song arose from time to time from each of the brakes in turn, only to die mournfully away. It is not easy to sing on an empty stomach even if one has got a little beer in it; and so it was with most of them. They were not in a mood to sing, or to properly appreciate the scenes through which they were passing. They wanted their dinners, and that was the reason why this long ride, instead of being a pleasure, became after a while, a weary journey that seemed as if it were never coming to an end.

The next stop was at the Bird in Hand, a wayside public house that stood all by itself in a lonely hollow. The landlord was a fat, jolly-looking man, and there were several customers in the bar – men who looked like farm-labourers, but there were no other houses to be seen anywhere. This extraordinary circumstance exercised the minds of our travellers and formed the principal topic of conversation until they arrived at the Dew Drop Inn, about half an hour afterwards. The first brake, containing Rushton and his friends, passed on without stopping here. The occupants of the second brake, which was only a little way behind the first, were divided in opinion whether to stop or go on. Some shouted out to the driver to pull up, others ordered him to proceed, and more were undecided which course to pursue – a state of mind that was not shared by the coachman, who, knowing that if they stopped somebody or other would be sure to stand him a drink, had no difficulty whatever in coming to a decision, but drew rein at the inn, an example that was followed by both the other carriages as they drove up.

It was a very brief halt, not more than half the men getting down at all, and those who remained in the brakes grumbled so much at the delay that the others drank their beer as quickly as possible and the journey was resumed once more, almost in silence. No attempts at singing, no noisy laughter; they scarcely spoke to each other, but sat gloomily gazing out over the surrounding country.

Instructions had been given to the drivers not to stop again till they reached the Queen Elizabeth, and they therefore drove past the World Turned Upside Down without stopping, much to the chagrin of the landlord of that house, who stood at the door with a sickly smile upon his face. Some of those who knew him shouted out that they would give him a call on their way back, and with this he had to be content.

They reached the long-desired Queen Elizabeth at twenty minutes to four, and were immediately ushered into a large room where a round table and two long ones were set for dinner – and they were set in a manner worthy of the reputation of the house.

The cloths that covered the tables and the serviettes, arranged fanwise in the drinking glasses, were literally as white as snow, and about a dozen knives and forks and spoons were laid for each person. Down the centre of the table glasses of delicious yellow custard and cut-glass dishes of glistening red and golden jelly alternated with vases of sweet-smelling flowers.

The floor of the dining-room was covered with oilcloth – red flowers on a pale yellow ground; the pattern was worn off in places, but it was all very clean and shining. Whether one looked at the walls with the old-fashioned varnished oak paper, or at the glossy piano standing across the corner near the white-curtained window, at the shining oak chairs or through the open casement doors that led into the shady garden beyond, the dominating impression one received was that everything was exquisitely clean.

The landlord announced that dinner would be served in ten

minutes, and while they were waiting some of them indulged in a drink at the bar – just as an appetiser – whilst the others strolled in the garden or, by the landlord's invitation, looked over the house. Amongst other places, they glanced into the kitchen, where the land-lady was superintending the preparation of the feast, and in this place, with its whitewashed walls and red-tiled floor, as in every other part of the house, the same absolute cleanliness reigned supreme.

'It's a bit differint from the Royal Caif, where we got the sack, ain't it?' remarked the Semidrunk to Bill Bates as they made their way to the dining-room in response to the announcement that dinner was ready.

'Not arf!' replied Bill.

Rushton, with Didlum and Grinder and his other friends, sat at the round table near the piano. Hunter took the head of the longer of the other two tables and Crass the foot, and on either side of Crass were Bundy and Slyme, who had acted with him as the Committee who had arranged the Beano. Payne, the foreman carpenter, occupied the head of the other table.

The dinner was all that could be desired; it was almost as good as the kind of dinner that is enjoyed every day by those persons who are too lazy to work but are cunning enough to make others work for them.

There was soup, several entrees, roast beef, boiled mutton, roast turkey, roast goose, ham, cabbage, peas, beans and sweets galore, plum pudding, custard, jelly, fruit tarts, bread and cheese and as much beer or lemonade as they liked to pay for, the drinks being an extra; and afterwards the waiters brought in cups of coffee for those who desired it. Everything was up to the knocker,[107] and although they were somewhat bewildered by the multitude of knives and forks, they all, with one or two exceptions, rose to the occasion and enjoyed themselves famously. The excellent decorum observed being marred only by one or two regrettable incidents. The first of these occurred almost as soon as they sat down, when Ned Dawson who, although a big strong fellow, was not able to stand much beer, not being used to it, was taken ill and had to be escorted from the room by his mate Bundy and another man. They left him somewhere outside and he came back again about ten minutes afterwards, much better but looking rather pale, and took his seat with the others.

The turkeys, the roast beef and the boiled mutton, the peas and beans and the cabbage, disappeared with astonishing rapidity, which was not to be wondered at, for they were all very hungry from the long drive, and nearly everyone made a point of having at least one helping of everything there was to be had. Some of them went in for two lots of soup. Then for the next course, boiled mutton and ham or turkey: then some roast beef and goose. Then a little more boiled mutton with a little roast beef. Each of the three boys devoured several times his own weight of everything, to say nothing of numerous bottles of lemonade and champagne ginger beer.

Crass frequently paused to mop the perspiration from his face and neck with his serviette. In fact everybody had a good time. There was enough and to spare of everything to eat, the beer was of the best, and all the time, amid the rattle of the crockery and the knives and forks, the proceedings were enlivened by many jests and flashes of wit that continuously kept the table in a roar.

'Chuck us over another dollop of that there white stuff, Bob,' shouted the Semi-drunk to Crass, indicating the blancmange.

Crass reached out his hand and took hold of the dish containing the 'white stuff', but instead of passing it to the Semi-drunk, he proceeded to demolish it himself, gobbling it up quickly directly from the dish with a spoon.

'Why, you're eating it all yerself, yer bleeder,' cried the Semi-drunk indignantly, as soon as he realised what was happening.

'That's all right, matey,' replied Crass affably as he deposited the empty dish on the table. 'It don't matter, there's plenty more where it come from. Tell the landlord to bring in another lot.'

Upon being applied to, the landlord, who was assisted by his daughter, two other young women and two young men, brought in several more lots and so the Semi-drunk was appeased.

As for the plum pudding – it was a fair knock-out; just like Christmas: but as Ned Dawson and Bill Bates had drunk all the sauce before the pudding was served, they all had to have their first helping without any. However, as the landlord brought in another lot shortly afterwards, that didn't matter either.

As soon as dinner was over, Crass rose to make his statement as secretary. Thirty-seven men had paid in five shillings each: that made nine pounds five shillings. The committee had decided that the three boys – the painters' boy, the carpenters' boy and the front shop boy – should be allowed to come half-price: that made it nine pounds twelve and six. In addition to paying the ordinary five-shilling subscription, Mr. Rushton had given one pound ten towards the expenses. (Loud cheers.) And several other gentlemen had also given something towards it. Mr. Sweater, of the Cave, one pound.

(Applause.) Mr. Grinder, ten shillings in addition to the five-shilling subscription. (Applause.) Mr. Lettum, ten shillings, as well as the five shillings subscription. (Applause.) Mr. Didlum, ten shillings in addition to the five shillings. (Cheers.) Mr. Toonarf, ten shillings as well as the five-shilling subscription. They had also written to some of the manufacturers who supplied the firm with materials, and asked them to give something: some of 'em had sent half a crown, some five shillings, some hadn't answered at all, and two of 'em had written back to say that as things is cut so fine nowadays, they didn't hardly get no profit on their stuff, so they couldn't afford to give nothing; but out of all the firms they wrote to they managed to get thirty-two and sixpence altogether, making a grand total of seventeen pounds.

As for the expenses, the dinner was two and six a head, and there was forty-five of them there, so that came to five pounds twelve and six. Then there was the hire of the brakes, also two and six a head, five pound twelve and six, which left a surplus of five pound fifteen to be shared out (applause), which came to three shillings each for the thirty-seven men, and one and fourpence for each of the boys. (Loud and prolonged cheers.)

Crass, Slyme and Bundy now walked round the tables distributing the share-out, which was very welcome to everybody, especially those who had spent nearly all their money during the journey from Mugsborough, and when this ceremony was completed, Philpot moved a hearty vote of thanks to the committee for the manner in which they had carried out their duties, which was agreed to with acclamation. Then they made a collection for the waiters, and the three waitresses, which amounted to eleven shillings, for which the host returned thanks on behalf of the recipients, who were all smiles.

Then Mr. Rushton requested the landlord to serve drinks and cigars all round. Some had cigarettes and the teetotallers had lemonade or ginger beer. Those who did not smoke themselves took the cigar all the same and gave it to someone else who did. When all were supplied there suddenly arose loud cries of 'Order!' and it was seen that Hunter was upon his feet.

As soon as silence was obtained, Misery said that he believed that everyone there present would agree with him, when he said that they should not let that occasion pass without drinking the 'ealth of their esteemed and respected employer, Mr. Rushton. (Hear, hear.) Some of them had worked for Mr. Rushton on and off for many years, and as far as *they* was concerned it was not necessary for him (Hunter) to say much in praise of Mr. Rushton. (Hear, hear.) They knew Mr. Rushton as well as he did himself and to know him was to esteem him. (Cheers.) As for the new hands, although they did not know Mr. Rushton as well as the old hands did, he felt sure that they would agree that as no one could wish for a better master. (Loud applause.) He had much pleasure in asking them to drink Mr. Rushton's health. Everyone rose.

'Musical honours, chaps,' shouted Crass, waving his glass and leading off the singing which was immediately joined in with great enthusiasm by most of the men, the Semi-drunk conducting the music with a table knife:

> For he's a jolly good fellow,
> For he's a jolly good fellow,
> For he's a jolly good fel-ell-O,
> And so say all of us,
> So 'ip, 'ip, 'ip, 'ooray!
> So 'ip, 'ip, 'ip 'ooray!
>
> For he's a jolly good fellow,
> For 'e's a jolly good fellow
> For 'e's a jolly good fel-ell-O,
> And so say all of us.'

'Now three cheers!' shouted Crass, leading off.

> Hip, hip, hip, hooray!
> Hip, hip, hip, hooray!
> Hip, hip, hip, hooray!

Everyone present drank Rushton's health, or at any rate went through the motions of doing so, but during the roar of cheering and singing that preceded it several of the men stood with expressions of contempt or uneasiness upon their faces, silently watching the enthusiasts or looking at the ceiling or on the floor.

'I will say this much,' remarked the Semi-drunk as they all resumed their seats – he had had several drinks during dinner, besides those he had taken on the journey – 'I will say this much, although I did have a little misunderstanding with Mr. Hunter when I was workin' at the Royal Caif, I must admit that this is the best firm that's ever worked under me.'

This statement caused a shout of laughter, which, however, died away as Mr. Rushton rose to acknowledge the toast to his health. He said that he had now been in business for nearly sixteen years and this was – he believed – the eleventh outing he had had the pleasure of attending. During all that time the business had steadily progressed and had increased in volume from year to year, and he hoped and believed that the progress made in the past would be continued in the future. (Hear, hear.) Of course, he realised that the success of the business depended very largely upon the men as well as upon himself; he did his best in trying to get work for them, and it was necessary – if the business was to go on and prosper – that they should also do their best to get the work done when he had secured it for them. (Hear, hear.) The masters could not do without the men, and the men could not live without the masters. (Hear, hear.) It was a matter of division of labour: the men worked with their hands and the masters worked with their brains, and one was no use without the other. He hoped the good feeling which had hitherto existed between himself and his workmen would always continue, and he thanked them for the way in which they had responded to the toast of his health.

Loud cheers greeted the conclusion of this speech, and then Crass stood up and said that he begged to propose the health of Mr. 'Unter. (Hear, hear.) He wasn't going to make a long speech as he wasn't much of a speaker. (Cries of 'You're all right,' 'Go on,' etc.) But he felt sure as they would all hagree with him when he said that – next to Mr. Rushton – there wasn't no one the men had more respect and liking for than Mr. 'Unter. (Cheers.) A few weeks ago when Mr. 'Unter was laid up, many of them began to be afraid as they was going to lose 'im. He was sure that all the 'ands was glad to 'ave this hoppertunity of congratulating him on his recovery (Hear, hear) and of wishing him the best of 'ealth in the future and hoping as he would be spared to come to a good many more Beanos.

Loud applause greeted the conclusion of Crass's remarks, and once more the meeting burst into song:

> For he's a jolly good fellow
> For he's a jolly good fellow,
> For he's a jolly good fellow,
> And so say all of us.
> So 'ip, 'ip, 'ip 'ooray!
> So 'ip, 'ip, 'ip 'ooray!

When they had done cheering, Nimrod rose. His voice trembled a little as he thanked them for their kindness, and said that he hoped he deserved their goodwill. He could only say that as he was sure as he always tried to be fair and considerate to everyone. (Cheers.) He would now request the landlord to replenish their glasses. (Hear, hear.)

As soon as the drinks were served, Nimrod again rose and said he wished to propose the healths of their visitors who had so kindly contributed to their expenses – Mr. Lettum, Mr. Didlum, Mr. Toonarf and Mr. Grinder. (Cheers.) They were very pleased and proud to see them there (Hear, hear), and he was sure the men would agree with him when he said that Messrs. Lettum, Didlum, Toonarf and Grinder were jolly good fellows.

To judge from the manner in which they sang the chorus and cheered, it was quite evident that most of the hands did agree. When they left off, Grinder rose to reply on behalf of those included in the toast. He said that it gave them much pleasure to be there and take part in such pleasant proceedings and they were glad to think that they had been able to help to bring it about. It was very gratifying to see the good feeling that existed between Mr. Rushton and his work-men, which was as it should be, because masters and men was really fellow workers – the masters did the brain work, the men the 'and work. They was both workers, and their interests was the same. He liked to see men doing their best for their master and knowing that their master was doing his best for them, that he was not only a master, but a friend. That was what he (Grinder) liked to see – master and men pulling together – doing their best, and realising that their interests was identical. (Cheers.) If only all masters and men would do this they would find that everything would go on all right, there would be more work and less poverty. Let the men do their best for their masters, and the masters do their best for their men, and they would find that that was the true solution of the social problem, and not the silly nonsense that was talked by people what went about with red flags. (Cheers and laughter.) Most of those fellows were chaps who was too lazy to work for their livin'. (Hear, hear.) They could take it from him that, if ever the Socialists got the upper hand there would just be a few of the hartful dodgers who would get all the cream, and there would be nothing left but 'ard work for the rest. (Hear, hear.) That's wot hall those hagitators was after: they wanted them (his hearers) to work and keep 'em in idleness. (Hear, hear.) On behalf of Mr. Didlum, Mr. Toonarf, Mr. Lettum and himself, he thanked them for their good wishes, and hoped to be with them on a sim'ler occasion in the future.

Loud cheers greeted the termination of his speech, but it was obvious from some of the men's faces that they resented Grinder's remarks. These men ridiculed Socialism and regularly voted for the continuance of capitalism, and yet they were disgusted and angry with Grinder! There was also a small number of Socialists – not more than half a dozen altogether – who did not join in the applause. These men were all sitting at the end of the long table presided over by Payne. None of them had joined in the applause that greeted the speeches, and so far neither had they made any protest. Some of them turned very red as they listened to the concluding sentences of Grinder's oration, and others laughed, but none of them said anything. They knew before they came that there was sure to be a lot of 'Jolly good fellow' business and speech-making, and they had agreed together beforehand to take no part one way or the other, and to refrain from openly dissenting from anything that might be said, but they had not anticipated anything quite so strong as this.

When Grinder sat down some of those who had applauded him began to jeer at the Socialists.

'What have you got to say to that?' they shouted. 'That's up against yer!'

'They ain't got nothing to say now.'

'Why don't some of you get up and make a speech?'

This last appeared to be a very good idea to those Liberals and Tories who had not liked Grinder's observations, so they all began to shout 'Owen!' 'Owen!' 'Come on' ere. Get up and make a speech!' 'Be a man!' and so on. Several of those who had been loudest in applauding Grinder also joined in the demand that Owen should make a speech, because they were certain that Grinder and the other gentlemen would be able to dispose of all his arguments; but Owen and the other Socialists made no response except to laugh, so presently Crass tied a white handkerchief on a cane walking-stick that belonged to Mr. Didlum, and stuck it in the vase of flowers that stood on the end of the table where the Socialist group were sitting.

[[When the noise had in some measure ceased, Grinder again rose.]] 'When I made the few remarks that I did, I didn't know as there was any Socialists 'ere: I could tell from the look of you that most of you had more sense. At the same time I'm rather glad I said what I did, because it just shows you what sort of chaps these Socialists are. They're pretty artful – they know when to talk and when to keep their mouths shut. What they like is to get hold of a few ignorant workin' men in a workshop or a public house, and then they can talk by the mile – reg'ler shop lawyers, you know wot I mean – I'm right and everybody else is wrong. (Laughter.) You know the sort of thing I mean. When they finds theirselves in the company of edicated people wot knows a little more than they does theirselves, and who isn't likely to be misled by a lot of claptrap, why then, mum's the word. So next time you hears any of these shop lawyers' arguments, you'll know how much it's worth.'

Most of the men were delighted with this speech, which was received with much laughing and knocking on the tables. They remarked to each other that Grinder was a smart man: he'd got the Socialists weighed up just about right – to an ounce.

Then, it was seen that Barrington was on his feet facing Grinder and a sudden, awe-filled silence fell.

'It may or may not be true,' began Barrington, 'that Socialists always know when to speak and when to keep silent, but the present occasion hardly seemed a suitable one to discuss such subjects.

'We are here today as friends and want to forget our differences and enjoy ourselves for a few hours. But after what Mr. Grinder has said I am quite ready to reply to him to the best of my ability.

'The fact that I am a Socialist and that I am here today as one of Mr. Rushton's employees should be an answer to the charge that Socialists are too lazy to work for their living. And as to taking advantage of the ignorance and simplicity of working men and trying to mislead them with nonsensical claptrap, it would have been more to the point if Mr. Grinder had taken some particular Socialist doctrine and had proved it to be untrue or misleading, instead of adopting the cowardly method of making vague general charges that he cannot substantiate. He would find it far more difficult to do that than it would be for a Socialist to show that most of what Mr. Grinder himself has been telling us is nonsensical claptrap of the most misleading kind. He tells us that the employers work with their brains and the men with their hands. If it is true that no brains are required to do manual labour, why put idiots into imbecile asylums? Why not let them do some of the hand work for which no brains are required? As they are idiots, they would probably be willing to work for even less than the ideal "living wage". If Mr. Grinder had ever tried, he would know that manual workers have to concentrate their minds and their attention on their work or they would not be able to do it at all. His talk about employers being not only the masters but the "friends" of their workmen is also mere claptrap because he knows as well as we do, that no matter how good or benevolent an employer may be, no matter how much he might desire to give his men good conditions, it is impossible for him to do so, because he has to compete against other employers who do not do that. It is the bad employer – the sweating, slave-driving employer – who sets the pace and the others have to adopt the same methods – very often against their inclinations – or they would not be able to compete with him. If any employer today were to resolve to pay his workmen not less wages than he would be able to live upon in comfort himself, that he would not require them to do more work in a day than he himself would like to perform every day of his own life, Mr. Grinder knows as well as we do that such an employer would be bankrupt in a month; because he would not be able to get any work except by taking it at the same price as the sweaters and the slave-drivers.

'He also tells us that the interests of masters and men are identical; but if an employer has a contract, it is to his interest to get the work done as soon as possible; the sooner it is done the more profit he will make; but the more quickly it is done, the sooner will the men be out of employment. How then can it be true that their interests are identical?

'Again, let us suppose that an employer is, say, thirty years of age when he commences business, and that he carries it on for twenty years. Let us assume that he employs forty men more or less regularly during that period and that the average age of these men is also thirty years at the time the employer commences business. [[At the end of the twenty years it usually happens that the employer has made enough money to enable him to live for the remainder of his life in ease and comfort. But what about the workmen? All through those twenty years they have earned but a bare living wage and have had to endure such privations that those who are not already dead are broken in health.]]

'In the case of the employer there had been twenty years of steady progress towards ease and leisure and independence. In the case of the majority of the men there were twenty years of deterioration, twenty years of steady, continuous and hopeless progress towards physical and mental inefficiency: towards the scrap-heap, the workhouse, and premature death. What is it but false, misleading, nonsensical claptrap to say that their interests were identical with those of their employer?

'Such talk as that is not likely to deceive any but children or fools.

We are not children, but it is very evident that Mr. Grinder thinks that we are fools.

'Occasionally it happens, through one or more of a hundred different circumstances over which he has no control, or through some error of judgement, that after many years of laborious mental work an employer is overtaken by misfortune, and finds himself no better and even worse off than when he started; but these are exceptional cases, and even if he becomes absolutely bankrupt he is no worse off than the majority of the workmen.

'At the same time it is quite true that the real interests of employers and workmen are the same, but not in the sense that Mr. Grinder would have us believe. Under the existing system of society but a very few people, no matter how well off they may be, can be certain that they or their children will not eventually come to want; and even those who think they are secure themselves, find their happiness diminished by the knowledge of the poverty and misery that surrounds them on every side.

'In that sense only is it true that the interests of masters and men are identical, for it is to the interest of all, both rich and poor, to help to destroy a system that inflicts suffering upon the many and allows true happiness to none. It is to the interest of all to try and find a better way.'

Here Crass jumped up and interrupted, shouting out that they hadn't come there to listen to a lot of speechmaking – a remark that was greeted with unbounded applause by most of those present. Loud cries of 'Hear, hear!' resounded through the room, and the Semi-drunk suggested that someone should sing a song.

The men who had clamoured for a speech from Owen said nothing, and Mr. Grinder, who had been feeling rather uncomfortable, was secretly very glad of the interruption.

The Semi-drunk's suggestion that someone should sing a song was received with unqualified approbation by everybody, including Barrington and the other Socialists, who desired nothing better than that the time should be passed in a manner suitable to the occasion. The landlord's daughter, a rosy girl of about twenty years of age, in a pink print dress, sat down at the piano, and the Semi-drunk, taking his place at the side of the instrument and facing the audience, sang the first song with appropriate gestures, the chorus being rendered enthusiastically by the full strength of the company, including Misery, who by this time was slightly drunk from drinking gin and ginger beer:

'Come, come, come an' 'ave a drink with me
Down by the ole Bull and Bush.
Come, come, come an' shake 'ands with me
Down by the ole Bull and Bush.
Wot cheer me little Germin band!
Fol the diddle di do!
Come an' take 'old of me 'and
Come, come, come an' 'ave a drink with me,
Down by the old Bull and Bush,
      Bush! Bush!'

Protracted knocking on the tables greeted the end of the song, but as the Semi-drunk knew no other except odd verses and choruses, he called upon Crass for the next, and that gentleman accordingly sang 'Work, Boys, Work' to the tune of 'Tramp, tramp, tramp, the boys are marching'. As this song is the Marseillaise of the Tariff Reform Party, voicing as it does the highest ideals of the Tory workmen of this country, it was an unqualified success, for most of them were Conservatives.

'Now I'm not a wealthy man,
But I lives upon a plan
    Wot will render me as 'appy as a King;
An' if you will allow, I'll sing it to you now,
    For time you know is always on the wing.

Work, boys, work and be contented
    So long as you've enough to buy a meal.
For if you will but try, you'll be wealthy – bye and bye –
    If you'll only put yer shoulder to the wheel.'

'Altogether, boys,' shouted Grinder, who was a strong Tariff Reformer, and was delighted to see that most of the men were of the same way of thinking; and the 'boys' roared out the chorus once more:

Work, boys, work and be contented
    So long as you've enough to buy a meal
For if you will but try, you'll be wealthy – bye and bye
    If you'll only put your shoulder to the wheel.

As they sang the words of this noble chorus the Tories seemed to become inspired with lofty enthusiasm. It is of course impossible to say for certain, but probably as they sang there arose before their exalted imaginations a vision of the Past, and, looking down the long vista of the years that were gone, they saw that from their childhood they had been years of poverty and joyless toil. They saw their fathers and mothers, wearied and broken with privation and excessive labour, sinking unhonoured into the welcome oblivion of the grave.

And then, as a change came over the spirit of their dream, they saw the Future, with their own children travelling along the same weary road to the same kind of goal.

It is possible that visions of this character were conjured up in their minds by the singing, for the words of the song gave expression to their ideal of what human life should be. That was all they wanted – to be allowed to work like brutes for the benefit of other people. They did not want to be civilised themselves and they intended to take good care that the children they had brought into the world should never enjoy the benefits of civilisation either. As they often said:

'Who and what are our children that they shouldn't be made to work for their betters? They're not Gentry's children, are they? The good things of life was never meant for the likes of them. Let 'em work! That's wot the likes of them was made for, and if we can only get Tariff Reform for 'em they will always be sure of plenty of it – not only Full Time, but Overtime! As for edication, travellin' in furrin' parts, an' enjoying life an' all sich things as that, they was never meant for the likes of our children – they're meant for Gentry's children! Our children is only like so much dirt compared with Gentry's children! That's wot the likes of us is made for – to Work for Gentry, so as they can 'ave plenty of time to enjoy theirselves; and the Gentry is made to 'ave a good time so as the likes of us can 'ave Plenty of Work.'

There were several more verses, and by the time they had sung them all, the Tories were in a state of wild enthusiasm. Even Ned Dawson, who had fallen asleep with his head pillowed on his arms on the table, roused himself up at the end of each verse, and after having joined in the chorus, went to sleep again.

At the end of the song they gave three cheers for Tariff Reform and Plenty of Work, and then Crass, who, as the singer of the last song, had the right to call upon the next man, nominated Philpot, who received an ovation when he stood up, for he was a general favourite. He never did no harm to nobody, and he was always willing to do anyone a good turn whenever he had the opportunity. Shouts of 'Good old Joe' resounded through the room as he crossed over to the piano, and in response to numerous requests for 'The old song' he began to sing 'The Flower Show':

> 'Whilst walkin' out the other night, not knowing where to go
> I saw a bill upon a wall about a Flower Show,
> So I thought the flowers I'd go and see to pass away the night,
> And when I got into that Show it was a curious sight.
> So with your kind intention and a little of your aid,
> Tonight some flowers I'll mention which I hope will never fade.'

> Omnes:
> 'Tonight some flowers I'll mention which I hope will never fade.'

There were several more verses, from which it appeared that the principal flowers in the Show were the Rose, the Thistle and the Shamrock.

When he had finished, the applause was so deafening and the demands for an encore so persistent that to satisfy them he sang another old favourite – 'Won't you buy my pretty flowers?'

> 'Ever coming, ever going,
>   Men and women hurry by,
> Heedless of the tear-drops gleaming,
>   In her sad and wistful eye
> How her little heart is sighing
>   Thro' the cold and dreary hours,
> Only listen to her crying,
>   "Won't you buy my pretty flowers?" '

When the last verse of this song had been sung five or six times, Philpot exercised his right of nominating the next singer, and called upon Dick Wantley, who with many suggestive gestures and grimaces sang 'Put me amongst the girls', and afterwards called upon Payne, the foreman carpenter, who gave 'I'm the Marquis of Camberwell Green'.

There was a lot of what music-hall artists call 'business' attached to this song, and as he proceeded, Payne, who was ghastly pale and very nervous, went through a lot of galvanic motions and gestures, bowing and scraping and sliding about and flourishing his hand-kerchief in imitation of the courtly graces of the Marquis. During this performance the audience maintained an appalling silence, which so embarrassed Payne that before he was halfway through the song he had to stop because he could not remember the rest. However, to make up for this failure he sang another called 'We all must die, like the fire in the grate'. This also was received in a very lukewarm manner by the crowd, some of whom laughed and others suggested that if he couldn't sing any better than that, the sooner *he* was dead the better.

This was followed by another Tory ballad, the chorus being as follows:

> 'His clothes may be ragged, his hands may be soiled
> But where's the disgrace if for bread he has toiled.
> His 'art is in the right place, deny it no one can
> The backbone of Old England is the honest workin' man.'

After a few more songs it was decided to adjourn to a field at the rear of the tavern to have a game of cricket. Sides were formed, Rushton, Didlum, Grinder, and the other gentlemen taking part just as if they were only common people, and while the game was in progress the rest played ring quoits or reclined on the grass watching the players, whilst the remainder amused themselves drinking beer and playing cards and shove-ha'penny in the bar parlour, or taking walks around the village sampling the beer at the other pubs, of which there were three.

The time passed in this manner until seven o'clock, the hour at which it had been arranged to start on the return journey; but about a quarter of an hour before they set out an unpleasant incident occurred.

During the time that they were playing cricket a party of glee singers, consisting of four young girls and five men, three of whom were young fellows, the other two being rather elderly, possibly the fathers of some of the younger members of the party, came into the field and sang several part songs for their entertainment. Towards the close of the game most of the men had assembled in this field, and during a pause in the singing the musicians sent one of their number, a shy girl about eighteen years of age – who seemed as if she would rather that someone else had the task – amongst the crowd to make a collection. The girl was very nervous and blushed as she murmured her request, and held out a straw hat that evidently belonged to one of the male members of the glee party. A few of the men gave pennies, some refused or pretended not to see either the girl or the hat, others offered to give her some money for a kiss, but what caused the trouble was that two or three of those who had been drinking more than was good for them dropped the still burning ends of their cigars, all wet with saliva as they were, into the hat and Dick Wantley spit into it.

The girl hastily returned to her companions, and as she went some of the men who had witnessed the behaviour of those who had insulted her, advised them to make themselves scarce, as they stood a good chance of getting a thrashing from the girl's friends. They said it would serve them dam' well right if they did get a hammering.

Partly sobered by fear, the three culprits sneaked off and hid themselves, pale and trembling with terror, under the box seats of the three brakes. They had scarcely left when the men of the glee party came running up, furiously demanding to see those who had insulted the girl. As they could get no satisfactory answer, one of their number ran back and presently returned, bringing the girl with him, the other young women following a little way behind.

She said she could not see the men they were looking for, so they went down to the public house to see if they could find them there, some of Rushton's men accompanying them and protesting their indignation.

*   *   *

[[The time passed quickly enough and by half-past seven the brakes were loaded up again and a start made for the return journey.]]

They called at all the taverns on the road, and by the time they reached the Blue Lion half of them were three sheets in the wind, and five or six were very drunk, including the driver of Crass's brake and the man with the bugle. The latter was so far gone that they had to let him lie down in the bottom of the carriage amongst their feet, where he fell fast asleep, while the others amused themselves by blowing weird shrieks out of the horn.

There was an automatic penny-in-the-slot piano at the Blue Lion and as that was the last house of the road they made a rather long stop there, playing hooks and rings, shove-ha'penny, drinking, singing, dancing and finally quarrelling.

Several of them seemed disposed to quarrel with Newman. All sorts of offensive remarks were made at him in his hearing. Once someone ostentatiously knocked his glass of lemonade over, and a little later someone else collided violently with him just as he was in the act of drinking, causing his lemonade to spill all over his clothes. The worst of it was that most of these rowdy ones were his fellow passengers in Crass's brake, and there was not much chance of getting a seat in either of the other carriages, for they were overcrowded already.

From the remarks he overheard from time to time, Newman guessed the reason of their hostility, and as their manner towards him grew more menacing, he became so nervous that he began to think of quietly sneaking off and walking the remainder of the way home by himself, unless he could get somebody in one of the other brakes to change seats with him.

Whilst these thoughts were agitating his mind, [[Dick Wantley suddenly shouted out that he was going to go for the dirty tyke who had offered to work under price last winter.

It was *his* fault that they were all working for sixpence half-penny and he was going to wipe the floor with him. Some of his friends eagerly offered to assist, but others interposed, and for a time it looked as if there was going to be a free fight, the aggressors struggling hard to get at their inoffensive victim.

Eventually, however, Newman found a seat in Misery's brake, squatting on the floor with his back to the horses, thankful enough to be out of reach of the drunken savages, who were now roaring out ribald songs and startling the countryside, as they drove along, with unearthly blasts on the coach horn.

Meantime, although none of them seemed to notice it, the brake was]] travelling at a furious rate, and swaying about from side to side in a very erratic manner. It should have been the last carriage, but things had got a bit mixed at the Blue Lion and, instead of bringing up the rear of the procession, it was now second, just behind the small vehicle containing Rushton and his friends.

Crass several times reminded them that the other carriage was so near that Rushton must be able to hear every word that was said, and these repeated admonitions at length enraged the Semi-drunk, who shouted out that they didn't care a b—r if he could hear. Who the bloody hell was he? To hell with him!

'Damn Rushton, and you too!' cried Bill Bates, addressing Crass. 'You're only a dirty toe-rag! That's all you are – a bloody rotter! That's the only reason you gets put in charge of jobs – 'cos you're a good nigger-driver! You're a bloody sight worse than Rushton or Misery either! Who was it started the one-man, one-room dodge, eh? Why, you, yer bleeder!'

'Knock 'im orf 'is bleedin' perch,' suggested Bundy.

Everybody seemed to think this was a very good idea, but when the Semi-drunk attempted to rise for the purpose of carrying it out, he was thrown down by a sudden lurch of the carriage on the top of the prostrate figure of the bugle man and by the time the others had assisted him back to his seat they had forgotten all about their plan of getting rid of Crass.

Meantime the speed of the vehicle had increased to a fearful rate.

Rushton and the other occupants of the little wagonette in front had been for some time shouting to them to moderate the pace of their horses, but as the driver of Crass's brake was too drunk to understand what they said he took no notice, and they had no alternative but to increase their own speed to avoid being run down. The drunken driver now began to imagine that they were trying to race him, and became fired with the determination to pass them. It was a very narrow road, but there was just about room to do it, and he had sufficient confidence in his own skill with the ribbons to believe that he could get past in safety.

The terrified gesticulations and the shouts of Rushton's party only served to infuriate him, because he imagined that they were jeering at him for not being able to overtake them. He stood up on the foot-board and lashed the horses till they almost flew over the ground, while the carriage swayed and skidded in a fearful manner.

In front, the horses of Rushton's conveyance were also galloping at top speed, the vehicle bounding and reeling from one side of the road to the other, whilst its terrified occupants, whose faces were blanched with apprehension, sat clinging to their seats and to each other, their eyes projecting from their sockets as they gazed back with terror at their pursuers, some of whom were encouraging the drunken driver with promises of quarts of beer, and urging on the horses with curses and yells.

Crass's fat face was pallid with fear as he clung trembling to his seat. Another man, very drunk and oblivious of everything, was leaning over the side of the brake, spewing into the road, while the remainder, taking no interest in the race, amused themselves by singing – conducted by the Semi-drunk – as loud as they could roar:

> 'Has anyone seen a Germin band,
>   Germin Band, Germin Band?
> I've been lookin' about.
>   Pom – Pom, Pom, Pom, Pom!

> 'I've searched every pub, both near and far,
>   Near and far, near and far,
> I want my Fritz,
> What plays tiddley bits
>   On the big trombone!'

The other two brakes had fallen far behind. The one presided over by Hunter contained a mournful crew. Nimrod himself, from the effects of numerous drinks of ginger beer with secret dashes of gin in it, had become at length crying drunk, and sat weeping in gloomy silence beside the driver, a picture of lachry-mose misery and but dimly conscious of his surroundings, and Slyme, who rode with Hunter because he was a fellow member of the Shining Light Chapel. Then there was another paper-hanger – an unhappy wretch who was afflicted with religious mania; he had brought a lot of tracts with him which he had distributed to the other men, to the villagers at Tubberton and to anybody else who would take them.

Most of the other men who rode in Nimrod's brake were of the 'religious' working man type. Ignorant, shallow-pated dolts, without as much intellectuality as an average cat. Attendants at various P.S.As. and 'Church Mission Halls' who went every Sunday afternoon to be lectured on their duty to their betters and to have their minds – save the mark! – addled and stultified by such persons as Rushton, Sweater, Didlum and Grinder, not to mention such mental specialists as the holy reverend Belchers and Boshers, and such persons as John Starr.

At these meetings none of the 'respectable' working men were allowed to ask any questions, or to object to, or find fault with anything that was said, or to argue, or discuss, or criticise. They had to sit there like a lot of children while they were lectured and preached at and patronised. Even as sheep before their shearers are dumb,[108] so they were not permitted to open their mouths. For that matter they did not wish to be allowed to ask any questions, or to discuss anything. They would not have been able to. They sat there and listened to what was said, but they had but a very hazy conception of what it was all about.

Most of them belonged to these P.S.As. merely for the sake of the loaves and fishes.[109] Every now and then they were awarded prizes – *Self-help* by Smiles,[110] and other books suitable for perusal by persons suffering from almost complete obliteration of the mental faculties. Besides other benefits there was usually a Christmas Club attached to the 'P.S.A.' or 'Mission' and the things were sold to the members slightly below cost as a reward for their servility.

They were for the most part tame, broken-spirited, poor wretches who contentedly resigned themselves to a life of miserable toil and poverty, and with callous indifference abandoned their offspring to the same fate. Compared with such as these, the savages of New Guinea or the Red Indians are immensely higher in the scale of manhood. They are free! They call no man master; and if they do not enjoy the benefits of science and civilisation, neither do they toil to create those things for the benefit of others. And as for their children – most of those savages would rather knock them on the head with a tomahawk than allow them to grow up to be half-starved drudges for other men.

But these were not free: their servile lives were spent in grovelling and cringing and toiling and running about like little dogs at the behest of their numerous masters. And as for the benefits of science and civilisation, their only share was to work and help to make them, and then to watch other men enjoy them. And all the time they were tame and quiet and content and said, 'The likes of us can't expect to 'ave nothing better, and as for our children wot's been good enough for us is good enough for the likes of them.'

But although they were so religious and respectable and so contented to be robbed on a large scale, yet in small matters, in the commonplace and petty affairs of their everyday existence, most of these men were acutely alive to what their enfeebled minds conceived to be their own selfish interests, and they possessed a large share of that singular cunning which characterises this form of dementia.

That was why they had chosen to ride in Nimrod's brake – because they wished to chum up with him as much as possible, in order to increase their chances of being kept on in preference to others who were not so respectable.

Some of these poor creatures had very large heads, but a close examination would have shown that the size was due to the extraordinary thickness of the bones. The cavity of the skull was not so large as the outward appearance of the head would have led a casual observer to suppose, and even in those instances where the brain was of a fair size, it was of inferior quality, being coarse in texture and to a great extent composed of fat.

Although most of them were regular attendants at some place of so-called worship, they were not all teetotallers, and some of them were now in different stages of intoxication, not because they had had a great deal to drink, but because – being usually abstemious – it did not take very much to make them drunk.

From time to time this miserable crew tried to enliven the journey by singing, but as most of them only knew odd choruses it did not come to much. As for the few who did happen to know all the words of a song, they either had no voices or were not inclined to sing. The most successful contribution was that of the religious maniac, who sang several hymns, the choruses being joined in by everybody, both drunk and sober.

The strains of these hymns, wafted back through the balmy air to the last coach, were the cause of much hilarity to its occupants who also sang the choruses. As they had all been brought up under 'Christian' influences and educated in 'Christian' schools, they all knew the words: 'Work, for the night is coming', 'Turn poor Sinner and escape Eternal Fire', 'Pull for the Shore' and 'Where is my Wandering Boy?'

The last reminded Harlow of a song he knew nearly all the words of, 'Take the news to Mother,' the singing of which was much appreciated by all present and when it was finished they sang it all over again, Philpot being so affected that he actually shed tears; and Easton confided to Owen that there was no getting away from the fact that a boy's best friend is his mother.

In this last carriage, as in the other two, there were several men who were more or less intoxicated and for the same reason – because not being used to taking much liquor, the few extra glasses they had drunk had got into their heads. They were as sober a lot of fellows as need be at ordinary times, and they had flocked together in this brake because they were all of about the same character – not tame, contented imbeciles like most of those in Misery's carriage, but men something like Harlow, who, although dissatisfied with their condition, doggedly continued the hopeless, weary struggle against their fate.

They were not teetotallers and they never went to either church or chapel, but they spent little in drink or on any form of enjoyment – an occasional glass of beer or a still rarer visit to a music-hall, and now and then an outing more or less similar to this being the sum total of their pleasures.

These four brakes might fitly be regarded as so many travelling lunatic asylums, the inmates of each exhibiting different degrees and forms of mental disorder.

The occupants of the first – Rushton, Didlum and Co. – might be classed as criminal lunatics who injured others as well as them-selves. In a properly constituted system of society such men as these would be regarded as a danger to the community, and would be placed under such restraint as would effectually prevent them from harming themselves or others. These wretches had abandoned every thought and thing that tends to the elevation of humanity.

They had given up everything that makes life good and beautiful, in order to carry on a mad struggle to acquire money which they would never be sufficiently cultured to properly enjoy. Deaf and blind to every other consideration, to this end they had degraded their intellects by concentrating them upon the minutest details of expense and profit, and for their reward they raked in their harvest of muck and lucre along with the hatred and curses of those they injured in the process. They knew that the money they accumulated was foul with the sweat of their brother men, and wet with the tears of little children, but they were deaf and blind and callous to the consequences of their greed. Devoid of every ennobling thought or aspiration, they grovelled on the filthy ground, tearing up the flowers to get at the worms.

In the coach presided over by Crass, Bill Bates, the Semi-drunk and the other two or three habitual boozers were all men who had been driven mad by their environment. At one time most of them had been fellows like Harlow, working early and late whenever they got the chance, only to see their earnings swallowed up in a few minutes every Saturday by the landlord and all the other host of harpies and profit-mongers, who were waiting to demand it as soon as it was earned. In the years that were gone, most of these men used to take all their money home religiously every Saturday and give it to the 'old girl' for the house, and then, lo and behold, in a moment, yea, even in the twinkling of an eye, it was all gone! Melted away like snow in the sun! and nothing to show for it except an insufficiency of the bare necessaries of life! But after a time they had become heartbroken and sick and tired of that sort of thing. They hankered after a little pleasure, a little excitement, a little fun, and they found that it was possible to buy something like those in quart pots at the pub. They knew they were not the genuine articles, but they were better than nothing at all, and so they gave up the practice of giving all their money to the old girl to give to the landlord and the other harpies, and bought beer with some of it instead; and after a time their minds became so disordered from drinking so much of this beer, that they cared nothing whether the rent were paid or not. They cared but little whether the old girl and the children had food or clothes. They said, 'To hell with everything and everyone,' and they cared for nothing so long as they could get plenty of beer.

The occupants of Nimrod's coach have already been described and most of them may correctly be classed as being similar to cretin idiots of the third degree – very cunning and selfish, and able to read and write, but with very little understanding of what they read except on the most common topics.

As for those who rode with Harlow in the last coach, most of them, as has been already intimated, were men of similar character to himself. The greater number of them fairly good workmen and – unlike the boozers in Crass's coach – not yet quite heartbroken, but still continuing the hopeless struggle against poverty. These differed from Nimrod's lot inasmuch as they were not content. They were always complaining of their wretched circumstances, and found a certain kind of pleasure in listening to the tirades of the Socialists against the existing social conditions, and professing their concurrence with many of the sentiments expressed, and a desire to bring about a better state of affairs.

Most of them appeared to be quite sane, being able to converse intelligently on any ordinary subject without discovering any symptoms of mental disorder, and it was not until the topic of Parliamentary elections was mentioned that evidence of their insanity was forthcoming. It then almost invariably appeared that they were subject to the most extraordinary hallucinations and extravagant delusions, the commonest being that the best thing that the working people could do to bring about an improvement in their condition, was to continue to elect their Liberal and Tory employers to make laws for and to rule over them! At such times, if anyone ventured to point out to them that that was what they had been doing all their lives, and referred them to the manifold evidences that met them wherever they turned their eyes of its folly and futility, they were generally immediately seized with a paroxysm of the most furious mania, and were with difficulty prevented from savagely assaulting those who differed from them.

They were usually found in a similar condition of maniacal excitement for some time preceding and during a Parliamentary election, but afterwards they usually manifested that modification of insanity which is called melancholia. In fact they alternated between these two forms of the disease. During elections, the highest state of exalted mania; and at ordinary times – presumably as a result of reading about the proceedings in Parliament of the persons whom they had elected – in a state of melancholic depression, in their case an instance of hope deferred making the heart sick.

This condition occasionally proved to be the stage of transition into yet another modification of the disease – that known as dipsomania, the phase exhibited by Bill Bates and the Semi-drunk.

Yet another form of insanity was that shown by the Socialists. Like most of their fellow passengers in the last coach, the majority of these individuals appeared to be of perfectly sound mind. Upon entering into conversation with them one found that they reasoned correctly and even brilliantly. They had divided their favourite subject into three parts. First; an exact definition of the condition known as Poverty. Secondly; a knowledge of the causes of Poverty; and thirdly, a rational plan for the cure of Poverty. Those who were opposed to them always failed to refute their arguments, and feared, and nearly always refused, to meet them in fair fight – in open debate – preferring to use the cowardly and despicable weapons of slander and misrepresentation. The fact that these Socialists never encountered their opponents except to defeat them, was a powerful testimony to the accuracy of their reasonings and the correctness of their conclusions – and yet they were undoubtedly mad. One might converse with them for an indefinite time on the three divisions of their subject without eliciting any proofs of insanity, but directly one enquired what means they proposed to employ in order to bring about the adoption of their plan, they replied *that they hoped to do so by reasoning with the others*!

Although they had sense enough to understand the real causes of poverty, and the only cure for poverty, they were nevertheless so foolish that they entertained the delusion that it is possible to reason with demented persons, whereas every sane person knows that to reason with a maniac is not only fruitless, but rather tends to fix more deeply the erroneous impressions of his disordered mind.

The waggonette containing Rushton and his friends continued to fly over the road, pursued by the one in which rode Crass, Bill Bates, and the Semi-drunk; but notwithstanding all the efforts of the drunken driver, they were unable to overtake or pass the smaller vehicle, and when they reached the foot of the hill that led up to Windley the distance between the two carriages rapidly increased, and the race was reluctantly abandoned.

When they reached the top of the hill Rushton and his friends did not wait for the others, but drove off towards Mugsborough as fast as they could.

Crass's brake was the next to arrive at the summit, and they halted there to wait for the other two conveyances and when they came up all those who lived nearby got out, and some of them sang 'God Save the King', and then with shouts of 'Good Night', and cries of

'Don't forget six o'clock Monday morning', they dispersed to their homes and the carriages moved off once more.

At intervals as they passed through Windley brief stoppages were made in order to enable others to get out, and by the time they reached the top of the long incline that led down into Mugsborough it was nearly twelve o'clock and the brakes were almost empty, the only passengers being Owen and four or five others who lived down town. By ones and twos these also departed, disappearing into the obscurity of the night, until there was none left, and the Beano was an event of the past.

CHAPTER 45

The Great Oration

The outlook for the approaching winter was – as usual – gloomy in the extreme. One of the leading daily newspapers published an article prophesying a period of severe industrial depression. 'As the warehouses were glutted with the things produced by the working classes, there was no need for them to do any more work – at present; and so they would now have to go and starve until such time as their masters had sold or consumed the things already produced.' Of course, the writer of the article did not put it exactly like that, but that was what it amounted to. This article was quoted by nearly all the other papers, both Liberal and Conservative. The Tory papers – ignoring the fact that all the Protectionist countries[111] were in exactly the same condition, published yards of misleading articles about Tariff Reform. The Liberal papers said Tariff Reform was no remedy. Look at America and Germany – worse than here! Still, the situation was undoubtedly very serious – continued the Liberal papers – and Something would have to be done. They did not say exactly what, because, of course, they did not know; but Something would have to be done – tomorrow. They talked vaguely about Re-afforestation, and Reclaiming of Foreshores, and Sea walls: but of course there was the question of Cost! that was a difficulty. But all the same Something would have to be done. Some Experiments must be tried! Great caution was necessary in dealing with such difficult problems! We must go slow, and if in the meantime a few thousand children die of starvation, or become 'rickety'[112] or consumptive through lack of proper nutrition it is, of course, very regrettable, but after all they are only working-class children, so it doesn't matter a great deal.

Most of the writers of these Liberal and Tory papers seemed to think that all that was necessary was to find 'Work' for the 'working' class! That was their conception of a civilised nation in the twentieth century! For the majority of the people to work like brutes in order to obtain a 'living wage' for themselves and to create luxuries for a small minority of persons who are too lazy to work at all! And although this was all they thought was necessary, they did not know what to do in order to bring even that much to pass! Winter was returning, bringing in its train the usual crop of horrors, and the Liberal and Tory monopolists of wisdom did not know what to do!

Rushton's had so little work in that nearly all the hands expected that they would be slaughtered the next Saturday after the 'Beano' and there was one man – Jim Smith he was called – who was not allowed to live even till then: he got the sack before breakfast on the Monday morning after the Beano.

This man was about forty-five years old, but very short for his age, being only a little over five feet in height. The other men used to say that Little Jim was not made right, for while his body was big enough for a six-footer, his legs were very short, and the fact that he was rather inclined to be fat added to the oddity of his appearance.

On the Monday morning after the Beano he was painting an upper room in a house where several other men were working, and it was customary for the coddy to shout 'Yo! Ho!' at meal-times, to let the hands know when it was time to leave off work. At about ten minutes to eight, Jim had squared the part of the work he had been doing – the window – so he decided not to start on the door or the skirting until after breakfast. Whilst he was waiting for the foreman to shout 'Yo! Ho!' his mind reverted to the Beano, and he began to hum the tunes of some of the songs that had been sung. He hummed the tune of 'He's a jolly good fellow', and he could not get the tune out of his mind: it kept buzzing in his head. He wondered what time it was? it could not be very far off eight now, to judge by the amount of work he had done since six o'clock. He had rubbed down and stopped all the woodwork and painted the window. A jolly good two hours' work! He was only getting sixpence-halfpenny an hour and if he hadn't earned a bob he hadn't earned nothing! Anyhow, whether he had done enough for 'em or not he wasn't goin' to do no more before breakfast.

The tune of 'He's a jolly good fellow' was still buzzing in his head; he thrust his hands deep down in his trouser pockets, and began to polka round the room, humming softly:

> 'I won't do no more before breakfast!
> I won't do no more before breakfast!
> I won't do no more before breakfast!
> So 'ip 'ip 'ip 'ooray!
> So 'ip 'ip 'ip 'ooray So 'ip 'ip 'ip 'ooray!
> I won't do no more before breakfast – etc.'

'No! and you won't do but very little after breakfast, here!' shouted Hunter, suddenly entering the room.

'I've bin a watchin' of you through the crack of the door for the last 'arf hour; and you've not done a dam' stroke all the time. You make out yer time sheet, and go to the office at nine o'clock and git yer money; we can't afford to pay you for playing the fool.'

Leaving the man dumbfounded and without waiting for a reply, Misery went downstairs and after kicking up a devil of a row with the foreman for the lack of discipline on the job, he instructed him that Smith was not to be permitted to resume work after breakfast. Then he rode away. He had come in so stealthily that no one had known anything of his arrival until they heard him bellowing at Smith.

The latter did not stay to take breakfast but went off at once, and when he was gone the other chaps said it served him bloody well right: he was always singing, he ought to have more sense. You can't do as you like nowadays you know!

Easton – who was working at another job with Crass as his foreman – knew that unless some more work came in he was likely to be one of those who would have to go. As far as he could see it was only a week or two at the most before everything would be finished up. But notwithstanding the prospect of being out of work so soon he was far happier than he had been for several months past, for he imagined he had discovered the cause of Ruth's strange manner.

This knowledge came to him on the night of the Beano. When he arrived home he found that Ruth had already gone to bed: she had not been well, and it was Mrs. Linden's explanation of her illness that led Easton to think that he had discovered the cause of the unhappiness of the last few months. Now that he knew – as he thought – he blamed himself for not having been more considerate and patient with her. At the same time he was at a loss to understand why she had not told him about it herself. The only explanation he could think of was the one suggested by Mrs. Linden – that at such times women often behaved strangely. However that might be, he was glad to think he knew the reason of it all, and he resolved that he would be more gentle and forbearing with her.

The place where he was working was practically finished. It was a large house called 'The Refuge', very similar to 'The Cave', and during the last week or two, it had become what they called a 'hospital'. That is, as the other jobs became finished the men were nearly all sent to this one, so that there was quite a large crowd of them there. The inside work was all finished – with the exception of the kitchen, which was used as a mess room, and the scullery, which was the paint-shop.

Everybody was working on the job. [[Poor old Joe Philpot, whose rheumatism had been very bad lately, was doing a very rough job – painting the gable from a long ladder.

But though there were plenty of younger men more suitable for this, Philpot did not care to complain for fear Crass or Misery should think he was not up to his work. At dinner time all the old hands assembled in the kitchen, including Crass, Easton, Harlow, Bundy and Dick Wantley, who still sat on a pail behind his usual moat.

Philpot and Harlow were absent and everybody wondered what had become of them.

Several times during the morning they had been seen whispering together and comparing scraps of paper, and various theories were put forward to account for their disappearance.]] [Most of the men thought they must have heard something] good about the probable winner of the Handicap and had gone to put something on. Some others thought that perhaps they had heard of another 'job' about to be started by some other firm and had gone to enquire about it.

'Looks to me as if they'll stand a very good chance of gettin' drowned if they're gone very far,' remarked Easton, referring to the weather. It had been threatening to rain all the morning, and during the last few minutes it had become so dark that Crass lit the gas, so that – as he expressed it – they should be able to see the way to their mouths. Outside, the wind grew more boisterous every moment; the darkness continued to increase, and presently there succeeded a torrential downfall of rain, which beat fiercely against the windows, and poured in torrents down the glass. The men glanced gloomily at each other. No more work could be done outside that day, and there was nothing left to do inside. As they were all paid by the hour, this would mean that they would have to lose half a day's pay.

'If it keeps on like this we won't be able to do no more work, and we won't be able to go home either,' remarked Easton.

'Well, we're all right 'ere, ain't we?' said the man behind the moat; 'there's a nice fire and plenty of heasy chairs. Wot the 'ell more do you want?'

'Yes,' remarked another philosopher. 'If we only had a shove-ha'penny table or a ring board, I reckon we should be able to enjoy ourselves all right.'

Philpot and Harlow were still absent, and the others again fell to wondering where they could be.

'I see old Joe up on 'is ladder only a few minutes before twelve,' remarked Wantley.

Everyone agreed that it was a mystery.

[[At this moment the two truants returned, looking very important. Philpot was armed with a hammer and carried a pair of steps, while Harlow bore a large piece of wall-paper which the two of them proceeded to tack on the wall, much to the amusement of the others, who read the announcement opposite written in charcoal.]]

Every day at meals since Barrington's unexpected outburst at the Beano dinner, the men had been trying their best to 'kid him on' to make another speech, but so far without success. If anything, he had been even more silent and reserved than before, as if he felt some regret that he had spoken as he had on that occasion. Crass and his disciples attributed Barrington's manner to fear that he was going to get the sack for his trouble and they agreed amongst themselves that it would serve him bloody well right if 'e did get the push.

When they had fixed the poster on the wall, Philpot stood the steps in the corner of the room, with the back part facing outwards, and then, everything being ready for the lecturer, the two sat down in their accustomed places and began to eat their dinners, Harlow remarking that they would have to buck up or they would be too late for the meeting; and the rest of the crowd began to discuss the poster.

'Wot the 'ell does P.L.O. mean?' demanded Bundy, with a puzzled expression.

'Plain Layer On,' answered Philpot modestly.

' 'Ave you ever 'eard the Professor preach before?' enquired the man on the pail, addressing Bundy.

Imperial Banquet Hall
'The Refuge'

on Thursday at 12.30 prompt

Professor Barrington
WILL DELIVER A
ORATION

ENTITLED
THE GREAT SECRET, OR
HOW TO LIVE WITHOUT WORK

The Rev. Joe Philpot P.L.O.
(Late absconding secretary of the light refreshment fund)

Will take the chair and anything else
he can lay his hands on.

At The End Of The Lecture
A MEETING WILL BE ARRANGED

And carried out according to the
Marquis of Queensbury's Rules.

*A Collection will be took up
in Aid of the cost of printing.*

'Only once, at the Beano,' replied that individual; 'an' that was once too often!'

'Finest speaker I ever 'eard,' said the man on the pail with enthusiasm. 'I wouldn't miss this lecture for anything: this is one of 'is best subjects. I got 'ere about two hours before the doors was opened, so as to be sure to get a seat.'

'Yes, it's a very good subject,' said Crass, with a sneer. 'I believe most of the Labour Members in Parliament is well up in it.'

'And wot about the other members?' demanded Philpot. 'Seems to me as if most of them knows something about it too.'

'The difference is,' said Owen, 'the working classes voluntarily pay to keep the Labour Members,[113] but whether they like it or not, they have to keep the others.'

'The Labour members is sent to the 'Ouse of Commons,' said Harlow, 'and paid their wages to do certain work for the benefit of the working classes, just the same as we're sent 'ere and paid our wages by the Bloke to paint this 'ouse.'

'Yes,' said Crass; 'but if we didn't do the work we're paid to do, we should bloody soon get the sack.'

'I can't see how we've got to keep the other members,' said Slyme; 'they're mostly rich men, and they live on their own money.'

'Of course,' said Crass. 'And I should like to know where we should be without 'em! Talk about us keepin' them! It seems to me more like it that they keeps us! The likes of us lives on rich people. Where should we be if it wasn't for all the money they spend and the work they 'as done? If the owner of this 'ouse 'adn't 'ad the money to spend to 'ave it done up, most of us would 'ave bin out of work this last six weeks, and starvin', the same as lots of others 'as been.'

'Oh yes, that's right enough,' agreed Bundy. 'Labour is no good without Capital. Before any work can be done there's one thing necessary, and that's money. It would be easy to find work for all the unemployed if the local authorities could only raise the money.'

'Yes; that's quite true,' said Owen. 'And that proves that money is the cause of poverty, because poverty consists in being short of the necessaries of life: the necessaries of life are all produced by labour applied to the raw materials: the raw materials exist in abundance and there are plenty of people able and willing to work; but, under present conditions no work can be done without money; and so we have the spectacle of a great army of people compelled to stand idle and starve by the side of the raw materials from which their labour could produce abundance of all the things they need – they are rendered helpless by the power of Money! Those who possess all the money say that the necessaries of life shall not be produced except for their profit.'

'Yes! and you can't alter it,' said Crass, triumphantly. 'It's always been like it, and it always will be like it.'

' 'Ear! 'Ear!' shouted the man behind the moat. 'There's always been rich and poor in the world, and there always will be.'

Several others expressed their enthusiastic agreement with Crass's opinion, and most of them appeared to be highly delighted to think that the existing state of affairs could never be altered.

'It hasn't always been like it, and it won't always be like it,' said Owen. 'The time will come, and it's not very far distant, when the necessaries of life will be produced for use and not for profit. The time is coming when it will no longer be possible for a few selfish people to condemn thousands of men and women and little children to live in misery and die of want.'

'Ah well, it won't be in your time, or mine either,' said Crass gleefully, and most of the others laughed with imbecile satisfaction.

'I've 'eard a 'ell of a lot about this 'ere Socialism,' remarked the man behind the moat, 'but up to now I've never met nobody wot could tell you plainly exactly wot it is.'

'Yes; that's what I should like to know too,' said Easton.

'Socialism means, 'What's yours is mine, and what's mine's me own,' ' observed Bundy, and during the laughter that greeted this definition Slyme was heard to say that Socialism meant Materialism, Atheism and Free Love, and if it were ever to come about it would degrade men and women to the level of brute beasts. Harlow said Socialism was a beautiful ideal, which he for one would be very glad to see realised, but he was afraid it was altogether too good to be practical, because human nature is too mean and selfish. Sawkins said that Socialism was a lot of bloody rot, and Crass expressed the opinion – which he had culled from the delectable columns of the *Obscurer* – that it meant robbing the industrious for the benefit of the idle and thriftless.

*   *   *

Philpot had by this time finished his bread and cheese, and, having taken a final draught of tea, he rose to his feet, and crossing over to the corner of the room, ascended the pulpit, being immediately greeted with a tremendous outburst of hooting, howling and booing, which he smilingly acknowledged by removing his cap from his bald head and bowing repeatedly. When the storm of shrieks, yells, groans and catcalls had in some degree subsided, and Philpot was able to make himself heard, he addressed the meeting as follows: –

'Gentlemen: First of all I beg to thank you very sincerely for the magnificent and cordial reception you have given me on this occasion, and I shall try to deserve your good opinion by opening the meeting as briefly as possible.

'Putting all jokes aside, I think we're all agreed about one thing, and that is, that there's plenty of room for improvement in things in general. (Hear, hear.) As our other lecturer, Professor Owen, pointed out in one of 'is lectures and as most of you 'ave read in the newspapers, although British trade was never so good before as it is now, there was never so much misery and poverty, and so many people out of work, and so many small shopkeepers goin' up the spout as there is at this partickiler time. Now, some people tells us as the way to put everything right is to 'ave Free Trade and plenty of cheap food. Well, we've got them all now, but the misery seems to go on all around us all the same. Then there's other people tells us as the "Friscal Policy" is the thing to put everything right. ("Hear, hear" from Crass and several others.) And then there's another lot that ses that Socialism is the only remedy. Well, we all know pretty well wot Free Trade and Protection means, but most of us don't know exactly what Socialism means; and I say as it's the dooty of every man to try and find out which is the right thing to vote for, and when 'e's found it out, to do wot 'e can to 'elp to bring it about. And that's the reason we've gorn to the enormous expense of engaging Professor Barrington to come 'ere this afternoon and tell us exactly what Socialism is.

'As I 'ope you're all just as anxious to 'ear it as I am myself, I will not stand between you and the lecturer no longer, but will now call upon 'im to address you.'

Philpot was loudly applauded as he descended from the pulpit, and in response to the clamorous demands of the crowd, Barrington, who in the meantime had yielded to Owen's entreaties that he would avail himself of this opportunity of proclaiming the glad tidings of the good time that is to be, got up on the steps in his turn.

Harlow, desiring that everything should be done decently and in order, had meantime arranged in front of the pulpit a carpenter's sawing stool, and an empty pail with a small piece of board laid across it, to serve as a seat and a table for the chairman. Over the table he draped a large red handkerchief. At the right he placed a plumber's large hammer; at the left, a battered and much-chipped jam-jar, full of tea. Philpot having taken his seat on the pail at this table and announced his intention of bashing out with the hammer the brains of any individual who ventured to disturb the meeting, Barrington commenced:

'Mr. Chairman and Gentlemen. For the sake of clearness, and in order to avoid confusing one subject with another, I have decided to divide the oration into two parts. First, I will try to explain as well as I am able what Socialism is. I will try to describe to you the plan or system upon which the Co-operative Commonwealth[114] of the future will be organised; and, secondly, I will try to tell you how it can be brought about. But before proceeding with the first part of the subject, I would like to refer very slightly to the widespread delusion that Socialism is impossible because it means a complete change from an order of things which has always existed. We constantly hear it said that because there have always been rich and poor in the world, there always must be. I want to point out to you first of all, that it is not true that even in its essential features, the present system has existed from all time; it is not true that there have always been rich and poor in the world, in the sense that we understand riches and poverty today.

'These statements are lies that have been invented for the purpose of creating in us a feeling of resignation to the evils of our condition. They are lies which have been fostered by those who imagine that it is to their interest that we should be content to see our children condemned to the same poverty and degradation that we have endured ourselves.

'I do not propose – because there is not time, although it is really part of my subject – to go back to the beginnings of history, and describe in detail the different systems of social organisation which evolved from and superseded each other at different periods, but it is necessary to remind you that the changes that have taken place in the past have been even greater than the change proposed by Socialists today. The change from savagery and cannibalism when men used to devour the captives they took in war – to the beginning of chattel slavery, when the tribes or clans into which mankind were divided – whose social organisation was a kind of Communism, all the individuals belonging to the tribe being practically social equals, members of one great family – found it more profitable to keep their captives as slaves than to eat them. The change from the primitive Communism of the tribes, into the more individualistic organisation of the nations, and the development of private ownership of the land and slaves and means of subsistence. The change from chattel slavery into Feudalism; and the change from Feudalism into the earlier form of Capitalism; and the equally great change from what might be called the individualistic capitalism which displaced Feudalism, to the system of Co-operative Capitalism and Wage Slavery of today.'

'I believe you must 'ave swollered a bloody dictionary,' exclaimed the man behind the moat.

'Keep horder!' shouted Philpot, fiercely, striking the table with the hammer, and there were loud shouts of 'Chair' and 'Chuck 'im out,' from several quarters.

When order was restored, the lecturer proceeded:

'So it is not true that practically the same state of affairs as we have today has always existed. It is not true that anything like the poverty that prevails at present existed at any previous period of the world's history. When the workers were the property of their masters, it was to their owners' interest to see that they were properly clothed and fed; they were not allowed to be idle, and they were not allowed to starve. Under Feudalism also, although there were certain intolerable circumstances, the position of the workers was, economically, infinitely better than it is today. The worker was in subjection to his Lord, but in return his lord had certain responsibilities and duties to perform, and there was a large measure of community of interest between them.

'I do not intend to dwell upon this point at length, but in support of what I have said I will quote as nearly as I can from memory the words of the historian Froude.[115]

' 'I do not believe,' says Mr. Froude, "that the condition of the people in Mediaeval Europe was as miserable as is pretended. I do not believe that the distribution of the necessaries of life was as unequal as it is at present. If the tenant lived hard, the lord had little luxury. Earls and countesses breakfasted at five in the morning, on salt beef and herring, a slice of bread and a draught of ale from a blackjack. Lords and servants dined in the same hall and shared the same meal."

'When we arrive at the system that displaced Feudalism, we find that the condition of the workers was better in every way than it is at present. The instruments of production – the primitive machinery and the tools necessary for the creation of wealth – belonged to the skilled workers who used them, and the things they produced were also the property of those who made them.

'In those days a master painter, a master shoemaker, a master saddler, or any other master tradesmen, was really a skilled artisan working on his own account. He usually had one or two apprentices, who were socially his equals, eating at the same table and associating with the other members of his family. It was quite a common occurrence for the apprentice – after he had attained proficiency in his work – to marry his master's daughter and succeed to his master's business. In those days to be a "master" tradesman meant to be master of the trade, not merely of some underpaid drudges in one's employment. The apprentices were there to master the trade, qualifying themselves to become master workers themselves; not mere sweaters and exploiters of the labour of others, but useful members of society. In those days, because there was no labour-saving machinery the community was dependent for its existence on the productions of hand labour. Consequently the majority of the people were employed in some kind of productive work, and the workers were honoured and respected citizens, living in comfort on the fruits of their labour. They were not rich as we understand wealth now, but they did not starve and they were not regarded with contempt, as are their successors of today.

'The next great change came with the introduction of steam machinery. That power came to the aid of mankind in their struggle for existence, enabling them to create easily and in abundance those things of which they had previously been able to produce only a bare sufficiency. A wonderful power – equalling and surpassing the marvels that were imagined by the writers of fairy tales and Eastern stories – a power so vast – so marvellous, that it is difficult to find words to convey anything like an adequate conception of it.

'We all remember the story, in *The Arabian Nights*, of Aladdin, who in his poverty became possessed of the Wonderful Lamp and – he was poor no longer. He merely had to rub the Lamp – the Genie appeared, and at Aladdin's command he produced an abundance of everything that the youth could ask or dream of. With the discovery of steam machinery, mankind became possessed of a similar power to that imagined by the Eastern writer. At the command of its masters the Wonderful Lamp of Machinery produces an enormous, overwhelming, stupendous abundance and superfluity of every material thing necessary for human existence and happiness. With less labour than was formerly required to cultivate acres, we can now cultivate miles of land. In response to human industry, aided by science and machinery, the fruitful earth teems with such lavish abundance as was never known or deemed possible before. If you go into the different factories and workshops you will see prodigious quantities of commodities of every kind pouring out of the wonderful machinery, literally like water from a tap.

'One would naturally and reasonably suppose that the discovery or invention of such an aid to human industry would result in increased happiness and comfort for every one; but as you all know, the reverse is the case; and the reason of that extraordinary result, is the reason of all the poverty and unhappiness that we see around us and endure today – It is simply because – the *machinery became the property of a comparatively few individuals and private companies, who use it not for the benefit of the community but to create profits for themselves.*

'As this labour-saving machinery became more extensively used, the prosperous class of skilled workers gradually disappeared. Some of the wealthier of them became distributers instead of producers of wealth; that is to say, they became shopkeepers, retailing the commodities that were produced for the most part by machinery. But the majority of them in course of time degenerated into a class of mere wage earners, having no property in the machines they used, and no property in the things they made.

'They sold their labour for so much per hour, and when they could not find any employer to buy it from them, they were reduced to destitution.

'Whilst the unemployed workers were starving and those in employment not much better off, the individuals and private companies who owned the machinery accumulated fortunes; but their profits were diminished and their working expenses increased by the fact that they were competing against each other; and this is what led to the latest great change in the organisation of the production of the necessaries of life – the formation of the Limited Companies and the Trusts; the decision of the private companies to combine and co-operate with each other in order to increase their profits and decrease their working expenses. The results of these combines have been – an increase in the quantities of the things produced: a decrease in the number of wage earners employed – and enormously increased profits for the shareholders.

'But it is not only the wage earning class that is being hurt; for while they are being annihilated by the machinery and the efficient organisation of industry by the trusts that control and are beginning to monopolise production, the shopkeeping classes are also being slowly but surely crushed out of existence by the huge companies that are able by the greater magnitude of their operations to buy and sell more cheaply than the small traders.

'The consequence of all this is that the majority of the people are in a condition of more or less abject poverty – living from hand to mouth. It is an admitted fact that about thirteen millions of our people are always on the verge of starvation. The significant results of this poverty face us on every side. The alarming and persistent increase of insanity. The large number of would-be recruits for the army who have to be rejected because they are physically unfit; and the shameful condition of the children of the poor. More than one-third of the children of the working classes in London have some sort of mental or physical defect; defects in development; defects of eyesight; abnormal nervousness; rickets, and mental dulness. The difference in height and weight and general condition of the children in poor schools and the children of the so-called better classes, constitutes a crime that calls aloud to Heaven for vengeance upon those who are responsible for it.

'It is childish to imagine that any measure of Tariff Reform or Political Reform such as a paltry tax on foreign-made goods or abolishing the House of Lords, or disestablishing the Church – or miserable Old Age Pensions,[116] or a contemptible tax on land, can deal with such a state of affairs as this. They have no House of Lords in America or France, and yet their condition is not materially different from ours. You may be deceived into thinking that such measures as those are great things. You may fight for them and vote for them, but after you have got them you will find that they will make no appreciable improvement in your condition. You will still have to slave and drudge to gain a bare sufficiency of the necessaries of life. You will still have to eat the same kind of food and wear the same kind of clothes and boots as now. Your masters will still have you in their power to insult and sweat and drive. Your general condition will be just the same as at present because such measures as those are not remedies but red herrings, intended by those who trail them to draw us away from the only remedy, which is to be found only in the Public Ownership of the Machinery, and the National Organisation of Industry for the production and distribution of the necessaries of life, not for the profit of a few but for the benefit of all!

'That is the next great change; not merely desirable, but imperatively necessary and inevitable! That is Socialism!

'It is not a wild dream of Superhuman Unselfishness. No one will be asked to sacrifice himself for the benefit of others or to love his neighbours better than himself as is the case under the present system, which demands that the majority shall unselfishly be content to labour and live in wretchedness for the benefit of a few. There is no such principle of Philanthropy in Socialism, which simply means that even as all industries are now owned by shareholders, and organised and directed by committees and officers elected by the shareholders, so shall they in future belong to the State, that is, the whole people – and they shall be organised and directed by committees and officers elected by the community.

'Under existing circumstances the community is exposed to the danger of being invaded and robbed and massacred by some foreign power. Therefore the community has organised and owns and controls an Army and Navy to protect it from that danger. Under existing circumstances the community is menaced by another equally great danger – the people are mentally and physically degenerating from lack of proper food and clothing. Socialists say that the community should undertake and organise the business of producing and distributing all these things; that the State should be the only employer of labour and should own all the factories, mills, mines, farms, railways, fishing fleets, sheep farms, poultry farms and cattle ranches.

'Under existing circumstances the community is degenerating mentally and physically because the majority cannot afford to have decent houses to live in. Socialists say that the community should take in hand the business of providing proper houses for all its members, that the State should be the only landlord, that all the land and all the houses should belong to the whole people . . .

['We must do this] if we are to keep our old place in the van of human progress. A nation of ignorant, unintelligent, half-starved, broken-spirited degenerates cannot hope to lead humanity in its never ceasing march onward to the conquest of the future.

> 'Vain, mightiest fleets of iron framed;
> Vain those all-shattering guns,
> Unless proud England keep, untamed,
> The stout hearts of her sons.

'All the evils that I have referred to are only symptoms of the one disease that is sapping the moral, mental and physical life of the nation, and all attempts to cure these symptoms are foredoomed to failure, simply because they are the symptoms and not the disease. All the talk of Temperance, and the attempts to compel temperance, are foredoomed to failure, because drunkenness is a symptom, and not the disease.

'India is a rich, productive country. Every year millions of pounds worth of wealth are produced by her people, only to be stolen from them by means of the Money Trick by the capitalist and official class. Her industrious sons and daughters, who are nearly all total abstainers live in abject poverty, and their misery is not caused by laziness or want of thrift, or by Intemperance. They are poor for the same reason that we are poor – Because we are Robbed.

'The hundreds of thousands of pounds that are yearly wasted in well meant but useless charity accomplish no lasting good, because while charity soothes the symptoms it ignores the disease, which is – the PRIVATE OWNERSHIP of the means of producing the necessaries of life, and the restriction of production, by a few selfish individuals for their own profit. And for that disease there is no other remedy than the one I have told you of – the PUBLIC OWNERSHIP and cultivation of the land, the PUBLIC OWNERSHIP of the mines, railways, canals, ships, factories and all other means of production, and the establishment of an Industrial Civil Service – a National Army of Industry – for the purpose of producing the necessaries, comforts and refinements of life in that abundance which has been made possible by science and machinery – for the use and benefit of the *whole of the people*.'

'Yes: and where's the money to come from for all this?' shouted Crass, fiercely.

'Hear, hear,' cried the man behind the moat.

'There's no money difficulty about it,' replied Barrington. 'We can easily find all the money we shall need.'

'Of course,' said Slyme, who had been reading the *Daily Ananias*, 'there's all the money in the Post Office Savings Bank. The Socialists could steal that for a start; and as for the mines and land and factories, they can all be took from the owners by force.'

'There will be no need for force and no need to steal anything from anybody.'

'And there's another thing I objects to,' said Crass. 'And that's all this 'ere talk about hignorance: wot about all the money wots spent every year for edication?'

'You should rather say – 'What about all the money that's wasted every year on education?' What can be more brutal and senseless than trying to "educate" a poor little, hungry, illclad child? Such so-called 'instruction' is like the seed in the parable of the Sower,[117] which fell on stony ground and withered away because it had no depth of earth; and even in those cases where it does take root and grow, it becomes like the seed that fell among thorns and the thorns grew up and choked it, and it bore no fruit.

'The majority of us forget in a year or two all that we learnt at school because the conditions of our lives are such as to destroy all inclination for culture or refinement. We must see that the children are properly clothed and fed and that they are not made to get up in the middle of the night to go to work for several hours before they go to school. We must make it illegal for any greedy, heartless profit-hunter to hire them and make them labour for several hours in the evening after school, or all day and till nearly midnight on Saturday. We must first see that our children are cared for, as well as the children of savage races, before we can expect a proper return for the money that we spend on education.'

'I don't mind admitting that this 'ere scheme of national ownership and industries is all right if it could only be done,' said Harlow, 'but at present, all the land, railways and factories, belongs to private capitalists; they can't be bought without money, and you say you ain't goin' to take 'em away by force, so I should like to know how the bloody 'ell you *are* goin' to get 'em?'

'We certainly don't propose to buy them with money, for the simple reason that there is not sufficient money in existence to pay for them.

'If all the gold and silver money in the World were gathered together into one heap, it would scarcely be sufficient to buy all the private property in England. The people who own all these things now never really paid for them with money – they obtained possession of them by means of the "Money Trick" which Owen explained to us some time ago.'

'They obtained possession of them by usin' their brains,' said Crass.

'Exactly,' replied the lecturer. 'They tell us themselves that that is how they got them away from us; they call their profits the "wages of intelligence". Whilst we have been working, they have been using their intelligence in order to obtain possession of the things we have created. The time has now arrived for us to use *our* intelligence in order to get back the things they have robbed us of, and to prevent them from robbing us any more. As for how it is to be done, we might copy the methods that they have found so successful.'

'Oh, then you *do* mean to rob them after all,' cried Slyme, triumphantly. 'If it's true that they robbed the workers, and if we're to adopt the same method then we'll be robbers too!'

'When a thief is caught having in his possession the property of others it is not robbery to take the things away from him and to restore them to their rightful owners,' retorted Barrington.

'I can't allow this 'ere disorder to go on no longer,' shouted Philpot, banging the table with the plumber's hammer as several men began talking at the same time.

'There will be plenty of tuneropperty for questions and opposition at the hend of the horation, when the pulpit will be throwed open to anyone as likes to debate the question. I now calls upon the professor to proceed with the second part of the horation: and anyone wot interrupts will get a lick under the ear-'ole with this' – waving the hammer – 'and the body will be chucked out of the bloody winder.'

Loud cheers greeted this announcement. It was still raining heavily, so they thought they might as well pass the time listening to Barrington as in any other way.

'A large part of the land may be got back in the same way as it was taken from us. The ancestors of the present holders obtained possession of it by simply passing Acts of Enclosure:[118] the nation should regain possession of those lands by passing *Acts of Resumption*. And with regard to the other land, the present holders should be allowed to retain possession of it during their lives and then it should revert to the State, to be used for the benefit of all. Britain should belong to the British people, not to a few selfish individuals. As for the railways, they have already been nationalised in some other countries, and what other countries can do we can do also. In New Zealand, Australia, South Africa, Germany, Belgium, Italy, Japan and some other countries some of the railways are already the property of the State. As for the method by which we can obtain possession of them, the difficulty is not to discover *a* method, but rather to decide which of many methods we shall adopt. One method would be to simply pass an Act declaring that as it was contrary to the public interest that they should be owned by private individuals, the railways would henceforth be the property of the nation. All railways servants, managers and officials would continue in their employment; the only difference being that they would now be in the employ of the State. As to the shareholders – '

'They could all be knocked on the 'ead, I suppose,' interrupted Crass.

'Or go to the workhouse,' said Slyme.

'Or to 'ell,' suggested the man behind the moat.

' – The State would continue to pay to the shareholders the same dividends they had received on an average for, say, the previous three years. These payments would be continued to the present shareholders for life, or the payments might be limited to a stated number of years and the shares would be made non-transferable, like the railway tickets of today. As for the factories, shops, and other means of production and distribution, the State must adopt the same methods of doing business as the present owners. I mean that even as the big Trusts and companies are crushing – by competition – the individual workers and small traders, so the State should crush the trusts by competition. It is surely justifiable for the State to do for the benefit of the whole people that which the capitalists are already doing for the profit of a few shareholders. The first step in this direction will be the establishment of Retail Stores for the purpose of supplying all national and municipal employees with the necessaries of life at the lowest possible prices. At first the Administration will purchase these things from the private manufacturers, in such large quantities that it will be able to obtain them at the very cheapest rate, and as there will be no heavy rents to pay for showy shops, and no advertising expenses, and as the object of the Administration will be not to make profit, but to supply its workmen and officials with goods at the lowest price, they will be able to sell them much cheaper than the profit making private stores.

'The National Service Retail Stores will be for the benefit of only those in the public service; and gold, silver or copper money will not be accepted in payment for the things sold. At first, all public servants will continue to be paid in metal money, but those who desire it will be paid all or part of their wages in paper money of the same nominal value, which will be accepted in payment for their purchases at the National Stores and at the National Hotels, Restaurants and other places which will be established for the convenience of those in the State service. The money will resemble bank-notes. It will be made of a special very strong paper, and will be of all value, from a penny to a pound.

'As the National Service Stores will sell practically everything that could be obtained elsewhere, and as twenty shillings in paper money will be able to purchase much more at the stores than twenty shillings of metal money would purchase anywhere else, it will not be long before nearly all public servants will prefer to be paid in paper money. As far as paying the salaries and wages of most of its officials and workmen is concerned, the Administration will not then have any need of metal money. But it will require metal money to pay the private manufacturers who supply the goods sold in the National Stores. But – all these things are made by labour; so in order to avoid having to pay metal money for them, the State will now commence to employ productive labour. All the public land suitable for the purpose will be put into cultivation and State factories will be established for manufacturing food, boots, clothing, furniture and all other necessaries and comforts of life. All those who are out of employment and willing to work, will be given employment on these farms and in these factories. In order that the men employed shall not have to work unpleasantly hard, and that their hours of labour may be as short as possible – at first, say, eight hours per day – and also to make sure that the greatest possible quantity of everything shall be produced, these factories and farms will be equipped with the most up to date and efficient labour saving machinery. The people employed in the farms and factories will be paid with paper money . . . The commodities they produce will go to replenish the stocks of the National Service Stores, where the workers will be able to purchase with their paper money everything they need.

'As we shall employ the greatest possible number of labour saving machines, and adopt the most scientific methods in our farms and factories, the quantities of goods we shall be able to produce will be so enormous that we shall be able to pay our workers very high wages – in paper money – and we shall be able to sell our produce so cheaply, that all public servants will be able to enjoy abundance of everything.

'When the workers who are being exploited and sweated by the private capitalists realise how much worse off they are than the workers in the employ of the State, they will come and ask to be allowed to work for the State, and also, for paper money. That will mean that the State Army of Productive Workers will be continually increasing in numbers. More State factories will be built, more land will be put into cultivation. Men will be given employment making bricks, woodwork, paints, glass, wallpapers and all kinds of building materials and others will be set to work building – on State land – beautiful houses, which will be let to those employed in the service of the State. The rent will be paid with paper money.

'State fishing fleets will be established and the quantities of commodities of all kinds produced will be so great that the State employees and officials will not be able to use it all. With their paper money they will be able to buy enough and more than enough to satisfy all their needs abundantly, but there will still be a great and continuously increasing surplus stock in the possession of the State.

'The Socialist Administration will now acquire or build fleets of steam trading vessels, which will of course be manned and officered by State employees – the same as the Royal Navy is now. These fleets of National trading vessels will carry the surplus stocks I have mentioned, to foreign countries, and will there sell or exchange them for some of the products of those countries, things that we do not produce ourselves. These things will be brought to England and sold at the National Service Stores, at the lowest possible price, for paper money, to those in the service of the State. This of course will only have the effect of introducing greater variety into the stocks – it will not diminish the surplus: and as there would be no sense in continuing to produce more of these things than necessary, it would then be the duty of the Administration to curtail or restrict production of the necessaries of life. This could be done by reducing the hours of the workers without reducing their wages so as to enable them to continue to purchase as much as before.

'Another way of preventing over production of mere necessaries and comforts will be to employ a larger number of workers producing the refinements and pleasures of life, more artistic houses, furniture, pictures, musical instruments and so forth.

'In the centre of every district a large Institute or pleasure house could be erected, containing a magnificently appointed and decorated theatre; Concert Hall, Lecture Hall, Gymnasium, Billiard Rooms, Reading Rooms, Refreshment Rooms, and so on. A detachment of the Industrial Army would be employed as actors, artistes, musicians, singers and entertainers. In fact everyone that could be spared from the most important work of all – that of producing the necessaries of life – would be employed in creating pleasure, culture, and education. All these people – like the other branches of the public service – would be paid with paper money, and with it all of them would be able to purchase abundance of all those things which constitute civilisation.

'Meanwhile, as a result of all this, the kind-hearted private employers and capitalists would find that no one would come and work for them to be driven and bullied and sweated for a miserable trifle of metal money that is scarcely enough to purchase sufficient of the necessaries of life to keep body and soul together.

'These kind-hearted capitalists will protest against what they will call the unfair competition of State industry, and some of them may threaten to leave the country and take their capital with them . . . As most of these persons are too lazy to work, and as we will not need their money, we shall be very glad to see them go. But with regard to their real capital – their factories, farms, mines or machinery – that will be a different matter . . . To allow these things to remain idle and unproductive would constitute an injury to the community. So a law will be passed, declaring that all land not cultivated by the owner, or any factory shut down for more than a specified time, will be taken possession of by the State and worked for the benefit of the community . . . Fair compensation will be paid in paper money to the former owners, who will be granted an income or pension of so much a year either for life or for a stated period according to circumstances and the ages of the persons concerned.

'As for the private traders, the wholesale and retail dealers in the things produced by labour, they will be forced by the State competition to close down their shops and warehouses – first, because they will not be able to replenish their stocks; and, secondly, because even if they were able to do so, they would not be able to sell them. This will throw out of work a great host of people who are at present engaged in useless occupations; the managers and assistants in the shops of which we now see half a dozen of the same sort in a single street; the thousands of men and women who are slaving away their lives producing advertisements, for, in most cases, a miserable pittance of metal money, with which many of them are unable to procure sufficient of the necessaries of life to secure them from starvation.

'The masons, carpenters, painters, glaziers, and all the others engaged in maintaining these unnecessary stores and shops will all be thrown out of employment, but all of them who are willing to work will be welcomed by the State and will be at once employed helping either to produce or distribute the necessaries and comforts of life. They will have to work fewer hours than before . . . They will not have to work so hard – for there will be no need to drive or bully, because there will be plenty of people to do the work, and most of it will be done by machinery – and with their paper money they will be able to buy abundance of the things they help to produce. The shops and stores where these people were formerly employed will be acquired by the State, which will pay the former owners fair compensation in the same manner as to the factory owners. Some of the buildings will be utilised by the State as National Service Stores, others transformed into factories and others will be pulled down to make room for dwellings, or public buildings . . . It will be the duty of the Government to build a sufficient number of houses to accommodate the families of all those in its employment, and as a consequence of this and because of the general disorganisation and decay of what is now called "business", all other house property of all kinds will rapidly depreciate in value . . . The slums and the wretched dwellings now occupied by the working classes – the miserable uncomfortable, jerry-built 'villas' occupied by the lower middle classes and by "business" people, will be left empty and valueless upon the hands of their rack renting landlords, who will very soon voluntarily offer to hand them and the ground they stand upon to the State on the same terms as those accorded to the other property owners, namely – in return for a pension. Some of these people will be content to live in idleness on the income allowed them for life as compensation by the State: others will devote themselves to art or science and some others will offer their services to the community as managers and superintendents, and the State will always be glad to employ all those who are willing to help in the Great Work of production and distribution.

'By this time the nation will be the sole employer of labour, and as no one will be able to procure the necessaries of life without paper money, and as the only way to obtain this will be by working, it will mean that every mentally and physically capable person in the community will be helping in the great work of PRODUCTION and DISTRIBUTION. We shall not need as at present, to maintain a police force to protect the property of the idle rich from the starving wretches whom they have robbed. There will be no unemployed and no overlapping of labour, which will be organised and concentrated for the accomplishment of the only rational object – the creation of the things we require . . . For every one labour saving machine in use today, we will, if necessary, employ a thousand machines! and consequently there will be produced such a stupendous enormous, prodigious, overwhelming abundance of everything that soon the community will be faced once more with the serious problem of OVER-PRODUCTION.

'To deal with this, it will be necessary to reduce the hours of our workers to four or five hours a day . . . All young people will be allowed to continue at public schools and universities and will not be required to take any part in the work of the nation until they are twenty-one years of age. At the age of forty-five, everyone will be allowed to retire from the State service on full pay . . . All these will be able to spend the rest of their days according to their own inclinations: some will settle down quietly at home, and amuse themselves in the same ways as people of wealth and leisure do at the present day – with some hobby, or by taking part in the organisation of social functions, such as balls, parties, entertainments, the organisation of Public Games and Athletic Tournaments, Races and all kinds of sports.

'Some will prefer to continue in the service of the State. Actors, artists, sculptors, musicians and others will go on working for their own pleasure and honour . . . Some will devote their leisure to science, art, or literature. Others will prefer to travel on the State steamships to different parts of the world to see for themselves all those things of which most of us have now but a dim and vague conception. The wonders of India and Egypt, the glories of Rome, the artistic treasures of the continent and the sublime scenery of other lands.

'Thus – for the first time in the history of humanity – the benefits and pleasures conferred upon mankind by science and civilisation will be enjoyed equally by all, upon the one condition, that they shall do their share of the work, that is necessary in order to make all these things possible.

'These are the principles upon which the CO-OPERATIVE COMMONWEALTH of the future will be organised. The State in which no one will be distinguished or honoured above his fellows except for Virtue or Talent. Where no man will find his profit in another's loss, and we shall no longer be masters and servants, but brothers, free men, and friends. Where there will be no weary, broken men and women passing their joyless lives in toil and want, and no little children crying because they are hungry or cold.

'A State wherein it will be possible to put into practice the teachings of Him whom so many now pretend to follow. A society which shall have justice and co-operation for its foundation, and International Brotherhood and love for its law.

> 'Such are the days that shall be! but
>   What are the deeds of today,
> In the days of the years we dwell in,
>   That wear our lives away?
> Why, then, and for what are we waiting?
>   There are but three words to speak

'We will it, and what is the foeman
  but the dream strong wakened and weak?
'Oh, why and for what are we waiting, while
  our brothers droop and die?
And on every wind of the heavens, a
  wasted life goes by.
'How long shall they reproach us, where
  crowd on crowd they dwell
Poor ghosts of the wicked city,
  gold crushed, hungry hell?
'Through squalid life they laboured in
  sordid grief they died
Those sons of a mighty mother, those
  props of England's pride.
They are gone, there is none can undo
  it, nor save our souls from the curse,
But many a million cometh, and shall
  they be better or worse?

'It is We must answer and hasten and open wide the door, For the rich man's hurrying terror, and the slow foot hope of the poor,
  Yea, the voiceless wrath of the wretched and their unlearned discontent,
  We must give it voice and wisdom, till the waiting tide be spent Come then since all things call us, the living and the dead, And o'er the weltering tangle a glimmering light is shed.'

       *   *   *

As Barrington descended from the Pulpit and walked back to his accustomed seat, a loud shout of applause burst from a few men in the crowd, who stood up and waved their caps and cheered again and again. When order was restored, Philpot rose and addressed the meeting:

'Is there any gentleman wot would like to ask the Speaker a question?'

[No one spoke and the Chairman again put the question] without obtaining any response, but at length one of the new hands who had been 'taken on' about a week previously to replace another painter who had been sacked for being too slow – stood up and said there was one point that he would like a little more information about. This man had two patches on the seat of his trousers, which were also very much frayed and ragged at the bottoms of the legs: the lining of his coat was all in rags, as were also the bottoms of the sleeves; his boots were old and had been many times mended and patched; the sole of one of them had begun to separate from the upper and he had sewn these parts together with a few stitches of copper wire. He had been out of employment for several weeks and it was evident from the pinched expression of his still haggard face that during that time he had not had sufficient to eat. This man was not a drunkard, neither was he one of those semi-mythical persons who are too lazy to work. He was married and had several children. One of them, a boy fourteen years old, earned five shillings a week as a light porter at a Grocer's.

Being a householder the man had a vote, but he had never hitherto taken much interest in what he called 'politics'. In his opinion, those matters were not for the likes of him. He believed in leaving such difficult subjects to be dealt with by his betters. In his present unhappy condition he was a walking testimonial to the wisdom and virtue and benevolence of those same 'betters' who have hitherto managed the affairs of the world with results so very satisfactory for themselves.

'I should like to ask the speaker,' he said, 'supposin' all this that 'e talks about is done – what's to become of the King, and the Royal Family, and all the Big Pots?'

' 'Ear, 'ear,' cried Crass, eagerly – and Ned Dawson and the man behind the moat both said that that was what they would like to know, too.

'I am much more concerned about what is to become of ourselves if these things are not done,' replied Barrington. 'I think we should try to cultivate a little more respect for our own families and to concern ourselves a little less about "Royal" Families. I fail to see any reason why we should worry ourselves about those people; they're all right – they have all they need, and as far as I am aware, nobody wishes to harm them and they are well able to look after themselves. They will fare the same as the other rich people.'

'I should like to ask,' said Harlow, 'wot's to become of all the gold and silver and copper money? Wouldn't it be of no use at all?'

'It would be of far more use under Socialism than it is at present. The State would of course become possessed of a large quantity of it in the early stages of the development of the Socialist system, because – at first – while the State would be paying all its officers and productive workers in paper, the rest of the community – those not in State employ – would be paying their taxes in gold as at present. All travellers on the State railways – other than State employees – would pay their fares in metal money, and gold and silver would pour into the State Treasury from many other sources. The State would receive gold and silver and – for the most part – pay out paper. By the time the system of State employment was fully established, gold and silver would only be of value as metal and the State would purchase it from whoever possessed and wished to sell it – at so much per pound as raw material: and instead of hiding it away in the vaults of banks, or locking it up in iron safes, we shall make use of it. Some of the gold will be manufactured into articles of jewellery, to be sold for paper money and worn by the sweethearts and wives and daughters of the workers; some of it will be beaten out into gold leaf to be used in the decoration of the houses of the citizens and of public buildings. As for the silver, it will be made into various articles of utility for domestic use. The workers will not then, as now, have to eat their food with poisonous lead or brass spoons and forks, we shall have these things of silver and if there is not enough silver we shall probably have a non-poisonous alloy of that metal.'

'As far as I can make out,' said Harlow, 'the paper money will be just as valuable as gold and silver is now. Well, wot's to prevent artful dodgers like old Misery and Rushton saving it up and buying and selling things with it, and so livin' without work?'

'Of course,' said Crass, scornfully. 'It would never do!'

'That's a very simple matter; any man who lives without doing any useful work is living on the labour of others, he is robbing others of part of the result of their labour. The object of Socialism is to stop this robbery, to make it impossible. So no one will be able to hoard up or accumulate the paper money because it will be dated, and will become worthless if it is not spent within a certain time after its issue. As for buying and selling for profit – from whom would they buy? And to whom would they sell?'

'Well, they might buy some of the things the workers didn't want, for less than the workers paid for them, and then they could sell 'em again.'

'They'd have to sell them for less than the price charged at the National Stores, and if you think about it a little you'll see that it would not be very profitable. It would be with the object of preventing any attempts at private trading that the Administration would refuse to pay compensation to private owners in a lump sum. All such compensations would be paid, as I said, in the form of a pension of so much per year.

'Another very effective way to prevent private trading would be to make it a criminal offence against the well-being of the community. At present many forms of business are illegal unless you take out a licence; under Socialism no one would be allowed to trade without a licence, and no licences would be issued.'

'Wouldn't a man be allowed to save up his money if he wanted to,' demanded Slyme with indignation.

'There will be nothing to prevent a man going without some of the things he might have if he is foolish enough to do so, but he would never be able to save up enough to avoid doing his share of useful service. Besides, what need would there be for anyone to save? One's old age would be provided for. No one could ever be out of employment. If one was ill the State hospitals and Medical Service would be free. As for one's children, they would attend the State Free Schools and Colleges and when of age they would enter the State Service, their futures provided for. Can you tell us why anyone would need or wish to save?'

Slyme couldn't.

'Are there any more questions?' demanded Philpot.

'Whilst we are speaking of money,' added Barrington, 'I should like to remind you that even under the present system there are many things which cost money to maintain, that we enjoy without having to pay for directly. The public roads and pavements cost money to make and maintain and light. So do the parks, museums and bridges. But they are free to all. Under a Socialist Administration this principle will be extended – in addition to the free services we enjoy now we shall then maintain the trams and railways for the use of the public, free. And as time goes on, this method of doing business will be adopted in many other directions.'

'I've read somewhere,' said Harlow, 'that whenever a Government in any country has started issuing paper money it has always led to bankruptcy. How do you know that the same thing would not happen under a Socialist Administration?'

' 'Ear, 'ear,' said Crass. 'I was just goin' to say the same thing.'

'If the Government of a country began to issue large amounts of paper money under the present system,' Barrington replied, 'it would inevitably lead to bankruptcy, for the simple reason that paper money under the present system – bank-notes, bank drafts, postal orders, cheques or any other form – is merely a printed promise to pay the amount – in gold or silver – on demand or at a certain date. Under the present system if a Government issues more paper money than it possesses gold and silver to redeem, it is of course bankrupt. But the paper money that will be issued under a Socialist Administration will not be a promise to pay in gold or silver on demand or at any time. It will be a promise to supply commodities to the amount specified on the note, and as there could be no dearth of those things there could be no possibility of bankruptcy.'

'I should like to know who's goin' to appoint the hofficers of this 'ere hindustrial harmy,' said the man on the pail. 'We don't want to be bullied and chivied and chased about by a lot of sergeants and corporals like a lot of soldiers, you know.'

' 'Ear, 'ear,' said Crass. 'You must 'ave some masters. Someone's got to be in charge of the work.'

'We don't have to put up with any bullying or chivying or chasing now, do we?' said Barrington. 'So of course we could not have anything of that sort under Socialism. We could not put up with it at all! Even if it were only for four or five hours a day. Under the present system we have no voice in appointing our masters and overseers and foremen – we have no choice as to what master we shall work under. If our masters do not treat us fairly we have no remedy against them. Under Socialism it will be different; the workers will be part of the community; the officers or managers and foremen will be the servants of the community, and if any one of these men were to abuse his position he could be promptly removed. As for the details of the organisation of the Industrial Army, the difficulty is, again, not so much to devise a way, but to decide which of many ways would be the best, and the perfect way will probably be developed only after experiment and experience. The one thing we have to hold fast to is the fundamental principle of State employment or National service. Production for use and not for profit. The national organisation of industry under democratic control. One way of arranging this business would be for the community to elect a Parliament in much the same way as is done at present. The only persons eligible for election to be veterans of the industrial Army, men and women who had put in their twenty-five years of service.

'This Administrative Body would have control of the different State Departments. There would be a Department of Agriculture, a Department of Railways and so on, each with its minister and staff.

'All these Members of Parliament would be the relatives – in some cases the mothers and fathers of those in the Industrial Service, and they would be relied upon to see that the conditions of that service were the best possible.

'As for the different branches of the State Service, they could be organised on somewhat the same lines as the different branches of the Public Service are now – like the Navy, the Post Office and as the State Railways in some other countries, or as are the different branches of the Military Army, with the difference that all promotions will be from the ranks, by examinations, and by merit only. As every recruit will have had the same class of education they will all have absolute equality of opportunity and the men who would attain to positions of authority would be the best men, and not as at present, the worst.'

'How do you make that out?' demanded Crass.

'Under the present system, the men who become masters and employers succeed because they are cunning and selfish, not because they understand or are capable of doing the work out of which they make their money. Most of the employers in the building trade for instance would be incapable of doing any skilled work. Very few of them would be worth their salt as journeymen. The only work they do is to scheme to reap the benefit of the labour of others.

'The men who now become managers and foremen are selected not because of their ability as craftsmen, but because they are good slave-drivers and useful producers of profit for their employers.'

'How are you goin' to prevent the selfish and cunnin', as you call 'em, from gettin' on top *then* as they do now?' said Harlow.

'The fact that all workers will receive the same pay, no matter what class of work they are engaged in, or what their position, will ensure our getting the very best man to do all the higher work and to organise our business.'

Crass laughed: 'What! Everybody to get the same wages?'

'Yes: there will be such an enormous quantity of everything produced, that their wages will enable everyone to purchase abundance of everything they require. Even if some were paid more than others they would not be able to spend it. There would be no need to save it, and as there will be no starving poor, there will be no one to give it away to. If it were possible to save and accumulate money it would bring into being an idle class, living on their fellows: it would lead to the downfall of our system, and a return to the same anarchy that exists at present. Besides, if higher wages were paid to those engaged in the higher work or occupying positions of authority it would prevent our getting the best men. Unfit persons would try for the positions because of the higher pay. That is what happens now. Under the present system men intrigue for and obtain or are pitch-forked into positions for which they have no natural ability at all; the only reason they desire these positions is because of the salaries attached to them. These fellows get the money and the work is done by underpaid subordinates whom the world never hears of. Under Socialism, this money incentive will be done away with, and con-sequently the only men who will try for these positions will be those who, being naturally fitted for the work, would like to do it. For instance a man who is a born organiser will not refuse to undertake such work because he will not be paid more for it. Such a man will desire to do it and will esteem it a privilege to be allowed to do it. He will revel in it. To think out all the details of some undertaking, to plan and scheme and organise, is not work for a man like that. It is a pleasure. But for a man who has sought and secured such a position, not because he liked the work, but because he liked the salary – such work as this would be unpleasant labour. Under Socialism the unfit man would not apply for that post but would strive after some other for which he was fit and which he would therefore desire and enjoy. There are some men who would rather have charge of and organise and be responsible for work than do it with their hands. There are others who would rather do delicate or difficult or artistic work, than plain work. A man who is a born artist would rather paint a frieze or a picture or carve a statue than he would do plain work, or take charge of and direct the labour of others. And there are another sort of men who would rather do ordinary plain work than take charge, or attempt higher branches for which they have neither liking or natural talent.

'But there is one thing – a most important point that you seem to entirely lose sight of, and that is, that all these different kinds and classes are equal in one respect – *they are all equally necessary*. Each is a necessary and indispensable part of the whole; therefore everyone who has done his full share of necessary work is justly entitled to a full share of the results. The men who put the slates on are just as indispensable as the men who lay the foundations. The work of the men who build the walls and make the doors is just as necessary as the work of the men who decorate the cornice. None of them would be of much use without the architect, and the plans of the architect would come to nothing, his building would be a mere castle in the air, if it were not for the other workers. Each part of the work is equally necessary, useful and indispensable if the building is to be perfected. Some of these men work harder with their brains than with their hands and some work harder with their hands than with their brains, *but each one does his full share of the work*. This truth will be recognised and acted upon by those who build up and maintain the fabric of our Co-operative Commonwealth. Every man who does his full share of the useful and necessary work according to his abilities shall have his full share of the total result. Herein will be its great difference from the present system, under which it is possible for the cunning and selfish ones to take advantage of the simplicity of others and rob them of part of the fruits of their labour. As for those who will be engaged in the higher branches, they will be sufficiently rewarded by being privileged to do the work they are fitted for and enjoy. The only men and women who are capable of good and great work of any kind are those who, being naturally fit for it, love the work for its own sake and not for the money it brings them. Under the present system, many men who have no need of money produce great works, not for gain but for pleasure: their wealth enables them to follow their natural inclinations. Under the present system many men and women capable of great works are prevented from giving expression to their powers by poverty and lack of opportunity: they live in sorrow and die heart-broken, and the community is the loser. These are the men and women who will be our artists, sculptors, architects, engineers and captains of industry.

'Under the present system there are men at the head of affairs whose only object is the accumulation of money. Some of them possess great abilities and the system has practically compelled them to employ those abilities for their own selfish ends to the hurt of the community. Some of them have built up great fortunes out of the sweat and blood and tears of men and women and little children. For those who delight in such work as this, there will be no place in our Co-operative Commonwealth.'

'Is there any more questions?' demanded Philpot.

'Yes,' said Harlow. 'If there won't be no extry pay and if anybody will have all they need for just doing their part of the work, what encouragement will there be for anyone to worry his brains out trying to invent some new machine, or make some new discovery?'

'Well,' said Barrington, 'I think that's covered by the last answer, but if it were found necessary – which is highly improbable – to offer some material reward in addition to the respect, esteem or honour that would be enjoyed by the author of an invention that was a boon to the community, it could be arranged by allowing him to retire before the expiration of his twenty-five years service. The boon he had conferred on the community by the invention, would be considered equivalent to so many years work. But a man like that would not desire to cease working; that sort go on working all their lives, for love. There's Edison for instance.[119] He is one of the very few inventors who have made money out of their work; he is a rich man, but the only use his wealth seems to be to him is to procure himself facilities for going on with his work; his life is a round of what some people would call painful labour: but it is not painful labour to him; it's just pleasure, he works for the love of it. Another way would be to absolve a man of that sort from the necessity of ordinary work, so as to give him a chance to get on with other inventions. It would be to the interests of the community to encourage him in every way and to place materials and facilities at his disposal.

'But you must remember that even under the present system, Honour and Praise are held to be greater than money. How many soldiers would prefer money to the honour of wearing the intrinsically valueless Victoria Cross?

'Even now men think less of money than they do of the respect, esteem or honour they are able to procure with it. Many men spend the greater part of their lives striving to accumulate money, and when they have succeeded, they proceed to spend it to obtain the respect of their fellow-men. Some of them spend thousands of pounds for the honour of being able to write "M.P." after their names. Others buy titles. Others pay huge sums to gain admission to exclusive circles of society. Others give the money away in charity, or found libraries or universities. The reason they do these things is that they desire to be applauded and honoured by their fellow-men.

'This desire is strongest in the most capable men – the men of genius. Therefore, under Socialism the principal incentive to great work will be the same as now – Honour and Praise. But, under the present system, Honour and Praise can be bought with money, and it does not matter much how the money was obtained.

'Under Socialism it will be different. The Cross of Honour and the Laurel Crown will not be bought and sold for filthy lucre. They will be the supreme rewards of Virtue and of Talent.'

'Anyone else like to be flattened out?' enquired Philpot.

'What would you do with them what spends all their money in drink?' asked Slyme.

'I might reasonably ask you, "What's done with them or what you propose to do with them now?" There are many men and women whose lives are so full of toil and sorrow and the misery caused by abject poverty, who are so shut out from all that makes life worth living, that the time they spend in the public house is the only ray of sunshine in their cheerless lives. Their mental and material poverty is so great that they are deprived of and incapable of understanding the intellectual and social pleasures of civilisation . . . Under Socialism there will be no such class as this. Everyone will be educated, and social life and rational pleasure will be within the reach of all. Therefore we do not believe that there will be such a class. Any individuals who abandoned themselves to such a course would be avoided by their fellows; but if they became very degraded, we should still remember that they were our brother men and women, and we should regard them as suffering from a disease inherited from their uncivilised forefathers and try to cure them by placing them under some restraint: in an institute for instance.'

'Another good way to deal with 'em,' said Harlow, 'would be to allow them double pay, so as they could drink themselves to death. We could do without the likes of them.'

'Call the next case,' said Philpot.

'This 'ere abundance that you're always talking about,' said Crass, 'you can't be sure that it would be possible to produce all that. You're only assoomin' that it could be done.'

Barrington pointed to the still visible outlines of the 'Hoblong' that Owen had drawn on the wall to illustrate a previous lecture.

'Even under the present silly system of restricted production, with the majority of the population engaged in useless, unproductive, unnecessary work, and large numbers never doing any work at all, there is enough produced to go all round after a fashion. More than enough, for in consequence of what they call "Over-Production", the markets are periodically glutted with commodities of all kinds, and then for a time the factories are closed and production ceases. And yet we can all manage to exist – after a fashion. This proves that if productive industry were organised on the lines advocated by Socialists there could be produced such a prodigious quantity of everything, that everyone could live in plenty and comfort. The problem of how to produce sufficient for all to enjoy abundance is already solved: the problem that then remains is – How to get rid of those whose greed and callous indifference to the sufferings of others, prevents it being done.'

'Yes! and you'll never be able to get rid of 'em, mate,' cried Crass, triumphantly – and the man with the copper wire stitches in his boot said that it couldn't be done.

'Well, we mean to have a good try, anyhow,' said Barrington.

Crass and most of the others tried hard to think of something to say in defence of the existing state of affairs, or against the proposals put forward by the lecturer; but finding nothing, they maintained a sullen and gloomy silence. The man with the copper wire stitches in his boot in particular appeared to be very much upset; perhaps he was afraid that if the things advocated by the speaker ever came to pass he would not have any boots at all. To assume that he had some such thought as this, is the only rational way to account for his hostility, for in his case no change could have been for the worse unless it reduced him to almost absolute nakedness and starvation.

To judge by their unwillingness to consider any proposals to alter the present system, one might have supposed that they were afraid of losing something, instead of having nothing to lose – except their poverty.

It was not till the chairman had made several urgent appeals for more questions that Crass brightened up: a glad smile slowly spread over and illuminated his greasy visage: he had at last thought of a most serious and insurmountable obstacle to the establishment of the Co-operative Commonwealth.

'What,' he demanded, in a loud voice, 'what are you goin' to do, in this 'ere Socialist Republic of yourn, with them wot WON'T WORK!!!'

As Crass flung this bombshell into the Socialist camp, the miserable, ragged-trousered crew around him could scarce for-bear a cheer; but the more intelligent part of the audience only laughed.

'We don't believe that there will be any such people as that,' said Barrington.

'There's plenty of 'em about now, anyway,' sneered Crass.

'You can't change 'uman nature, you know,' cried the man behind the moat, and the one who had the copper wire stitches in his boot laughed scornfully.

'Yes, I know there are plenty such now,' rejoined Barrington. 'It's only what is to be expected, considering that practically all workers live in poverty, and are regarded with contempt. The conditions under which most of the work is done at present are so unpleasant and degrading that everyone refuses to do any unless they are compelled; none of us here for instance, would continue to work for Rushton if it were not for the fact that we have either to do so or starve; and when we do work we only just earn enough to keep body and soul together. Under the present system everybody who can possibly manage to do so avoids doing any work, the only difference being that some people do their loafing better than others. The aristocracy are too lazy to work, but they seem to get on all right; they have their tenants to work for them. Rushton is too lazy to work, so he has arranged that we and Nimrod shall work instead, and he fares much better than any of us who do work. Then there is another kind of loafers who go about begging and occasionally starving rather than submit to such abominable conditions as are offered to them. These last are generally not much worse off than we are and they are often better off. At present, people have everything to gain and but little to lose by refusing to work. Under Socialism it would be just the reverse; the conditions of labour would be so pleasant, the hours of obligatory work so few, and the reward so great, that it is absurd to imagine that any one would be so foolish as to incur the contempt of his fellows and make himself a social outcast by refusing to do the small share of work demanded of him by the community of which he was a member.

'As for what we should do to such individuals if there did happen to be some, I can assure you that we would not treat them as you treat them now. We would not dress them up in silk and satin and broadcloth and fine linen: we would not embellish them, as you do, with jewels of gold and jewels of silver and with precious stones; neither should we allow them to fare sumptuously every day. Our method of dealing with them would be quite different from yours. In the Co-operative Commonwealth there will be no place for loafers; whether they call themselves aristocrats or tramps, those who are too lazy to work shall have no share in the things that are produced by the labour of others. Those who do nothing shall have nothing. If any man will not work, neither shall he eat.[120] Under the present system a man who is really too lazy to work may stop you in the street and tell you that he cannot get employment. For all you know, he may be telling the truth, and if you have any feeling and are able, you will help him. But in the Socialist State no one would have such an excuse, because everyone that was willing would be welcome to come and help in the work of producing wealth and happiness for all, and afterwards he would also be welcome to his full share of the results.'

'Any more complaints?' inquired the chairman, breaking the gloomy silence that followed.

'I don't want anyone to think that I am blaming any of these present-day loafers,' Barrington added. 'The wealthy ones cannot be expected voluntarily to come and work under existing conditions, and if they were to do so they would be doing more harm than good – they would be doing some poor wretches out of employment. They are not to be blamed; the people who are to blame are the working classes themselves, who demand and vote for the continuance of the present system. As for the other class of loafers – those at the bottom, the tramps and people of that sort, if they were to become sober and industrious tomorrow, they also would be doing more harm than good to the other workers; it would increase the competition for work. If all the loafers in Mugsborough could suddenly be transformed into decent house painters next week, Nimrod might be able to cut down the wages another penny an hour. I don't wish to speak disrespectfully of these tramps at all. Some of them are such simply because they would rather starve than submit to the degrading conditions that we submit to, they do not see the force of being bullied and chased, and driven about in order to gain semi-starvation and rags. They are able to get those without working; and I sometimes think that they are more worthy of respect and are altogether a nobler type of beings than a lot of broken spirited wretches like ourselves, who are always at the mercy of our masters, and always in dread of the sack.'

'Any more questions?' said the chairman.

'Do you mean to say as the time will ever come when the gentry will mix up on equal terms with the likes of us?' demanded the man behind the moat, scornfully.

'Oh, no,' replied the lecturer. 'When we get Socialism there won't be any people like us. Everybody will be civilised.'

The man behind the moat did not seem very satisfied with this answer, and told the others that he could not see anything to laugh at.

'Is there any more questions?' cried Philpot. 'Now is your chance to get some of your own back, but don't hall speak at once.'

'I should like to know who's goin' to do all the dirty work?' said Slyme. 'If everyone is to be allowed to choose 'is own trade, who'd be fool enough to choose to be a scavenger, a sweep, a dustman or a sewer man? nobody wouldn't want to do such jobs as them and everyone would be after the soft jobs.'

'Of course,' cried Crass, eagerly clutching at this last straw. 'The thing sounds all right till you comes to look into it, but it wouldn't never work!'

'It would be very easy to deal with any difficulty of that sort,' replied Barrington, 'if it were found that too many people were desirous of pursuing certain callings, it would be known that the conditions attached to those kinds of work were unfairly easy, as compared with other lines, so the conditions in those trades would be made more severe. A higher degree of skill would be required. If we found that too many persons wished to be doctors, architects, engineers and so forth, we would increase the severity of the examinations. This would scare away all but the most gifted and enthusiastic. We should thus at one stroke reduce the number of applicants, and secure the very best men for the work – we should have better doctors, better architects, better engineers than before.

'As regards those disagreeable tasks for which there was a difficulty in obtaining volunteers, we should adopt the opposite means. Suppose that six hours was the general thing; and we found that we could not get any sewer men; we should reduce the hours of labour in that department to four, or if necessary to two, in order to compensate for the disagreeable nature of the work.

'Another way out of such difficulties would be to have a separate division of the Industrial army to do all such work, and to make it obligatory for every man to put in his first year of State service as a member of this corps. There would be no hardship in that. Everyone gets the benefit of such work; there would be no injustice in requiring everyone to do his share. This would have the effect also of stimulating invention; it would be to everyone's interest to think out means of doing away with such kinds of work and there is no doubt that most of it will be done by machinery in some way or other. A few years ago the only way to light up the streets of a town was to go round to each separate gas lamp and light each jet, one at a time: now, we press a few buttons and light up the town with electricity. In the future we shall probably be able to press a button and flush the sewers.'

'What about religion?' said Slyme. 'I suppose there won't be no churches nor chapels; we shall all have to be atheists.'

'Everybody will be perfectly free to enjoy their own opinions and to practise any religion they like; but no religion or sect will be maintained by the State. If any congregation or body of people wish to have a building for their own exclusive use as a church or chapel or lecture hall it will be supplied to them by the State on the same terms as those upon which dwelling houses will be supplied; the State will construct the special kind of building and the congregation will have to pay the rent, the amount to be based on the cost of construction, in paper money of course. As far as the embellishment or decoration of such places is concerned, there will of course be nothing to prevent the members of the congregation if they wish from doing any such work as that themselves in their own spare time of which they will have plenty.'

'If everybody's got to do their share of work, where's the minister and clergymen to come from?'

'There are at least three ways out of that difficulty. First ministers of religion could be drawn from the ranks of the Veterans – men over forty-five years old who had completed their term of State service. You must remember that these will not be worn out wrecks, as too many of the working classes are at that age now. They will have had good food and clothing and good general conditions all their lives: and consequently they will be in the very prime of life. They will be younger than many of us now are at thirty; they will be the ideal men for the positions we are speaking of. All well educated in their youth, and all will have had plenty of leisure for self culture during the years of their State service and they will have the additional recommendation that their congregations will not be required to pay anything for their services.

'Another way: If a congregation wished to retain the fulltime services of a young man whom they thought specially gifted but who had not completed his term of State service, they could secure him by paying the State for his services; thus the young man would still remain in State employment, he would still continue to receive his pay from the National Treasury, and at the age of forty-five would be entitled to his pension like any other worker, and after that the congregation would not have to pay the State anything.

'A third – and as it seems to me, the most respectable way – would be for the individual in question to act as minister or pastor or lecturer or whatever it was, to the congregation without seeking to get out of doing his share of the State service. The hours of obligatory work would be so short and the work so light that he would have abundance of leisure to prepare his orations without sponging on his co-religionists.'

' 'Ear, 'ear!' cried Harlow.

'Of course,' added Barrington, 'it would not only be congregations of Christians who could adopt any of these methods. It is possible that a congregation of agnostics, for instance, might want a separate building or to maintain a lecturer.'

'What the 'ell's an agnostic?' demanded Bundy.

'An agnostic,' said the man behind the moat, 'is a bloke wot don't believe nothing unless 'e can see it with 'is own eyes.'

'All these details,' continued the speaker, 'of the organisation of affairs and the work of the Co-operative Commonwealth, are things which do not concern us at all. They have merely been suggested by different individuals as showing some ways in which these things could be arranged. The exact methods to be adopted will be decided upon by the opinion of the majority when the work is being done. Meantime, what we have to do is to insist upon the duty of the State to provide productive work for the unemployed, the State feeding of school children, the nationalisation or Socialisation of Railways; Land; the Trusts, and all public services that are still in the hands of private companies. If you wish to see these things done, you must cease from voting for Liberal and Tory sweaters, shareholders of companies, lawyers, aristocrats, and capitalists; and you must fill the House of Commons with Revolutionary Socialists. That is – with men who are in favour of completely changing the present system. And in the day that you do that, you will have solved the poverty "problem". No more tramping the streets begging for a job! No more hungry children at home. No more broken boots and ragged clothes. No more women and children killing themselves with painful labour whilst strong men stand idly by; but joyous work and joyous leisure for all.'

'Is there any more questions?' cried Philpot.

'Is it true,' said Easton, 'that Socialists intend to do away with the Army and Navy?'

'Yes; it is true. Socialists believe in International Brotherhood and peace. Nearly all wars are caused by profit-seeking capitalists, seeking new fields for commercial exploitation, and by aristocrats who make it the means of glorifying themselves in the eyes of the deluded common people. You must remember that Socialism is not only a national, but an international movement and when it is realised, there will be no possibility of war, and we shall no longer need to maintain an army and navy, or to waste a lot of labour building warships or manufacturing arms and ammunition. All those people who are now employed will then be at liberty to assist in the great work of producing the benefits of civilisation; creating wealth and knowledge and happiness for themselves and others – Socialism means Peace on earth and goodwill to all mankind. But in the meantime we know that the people of other nations are not yet all

Socialists; we do not forget that in foreign countries – just the same as in Britain – there are large numbers of profit seeking capitalists, who are so destitute of humanity, that if they thought it could be done successfully and with profit to themselves they would not scruple to come here to murder and to rob. We do not forget that in foreign countries – the same as here – there are plenty of so-called "Christian" bishops and priests always ready to give their benediction to any such murderous projects, and to blasphemously pray to the Supreme Being to help his children to slay each other like wild beasts. And knowing and remembering all this, we realise that until we have done away with capitalism, aristocracy and anti-Christian clericalism, it is our duty to be prepared to defend our homes and our native land. And therefore we are in favour of main-taining national defensive forces in the highest possible state of efficiency. But that does not mean that we are in favour of the present system of organising those forces. We do not believe in conscription, and we do not believe that the nation should continue to maintain a professional standing army to be used at home for the purpose of butchering men and women of the working classes in the interests of a handful of capitalists, as has been done at Feather-stone and Belfast; or to be used abroad to murder and rob the people of other nations. Socialists advocate the establishment of a National Citizen Army, for defensive purposes only. We believe that every able bodied man should be compelled to belong to this force and to undergo a course of military training, but without making him into a professional soldier, or taking him away from civil life, depriving him of the rights of citizenship or making him subject to military "law" which is only another name for tyranny and despotism. This Citizen Army could be organised on somewhat similar lines to the present Territorial Force, with certain differences. For instance, we do not believe – as our present rulers do – that wealth and aristocratic influence are the two most essential qualific-ations for an efficient officer; we believe that all ranks should be attainable by any man, no matter how poor, who is capable of passing the necessary examinations, and that there should be no expense attached to those positions which the Government grant, or the pay, is not sufficient to cover. The officers could be appointed in any one of several ways: They might be elected by the men they would have to command, the only qualification required being that they had passed their examinations, or they might be appointed according to merit – the candidate obtaining the highest number of marks at the examinations to have the first call on any vacant post, and so on in order of merit. We believe in the total abolition of courts martial, any offence against discipline should be punishable by the ordinary civil law – no member of the Citizen Army being deprived of the rights of a citizen.'

'What about the Navy?' cried several voices.

'Nobody wants to interfere with the Navy except to make its organisation more democratic – the same as that of the Citizen Army – and to protect its members from tyranny by entitling them to be tried in a civil court for any alleged offence.

'It has been proved that if the soil of this country were scientifically cultivated, it is capable of producing sufficient to maintain a population of a hundred millions of people. Our present population is only about forty millions, but so long as the land remains in the possession of persons who refuse to allow it to be cultivated we shall continue to be dependent on other countries for our food supply. So long as we are in that position, and so long as foreign countries are governed by Liberal and Tory capitalists, we shall need the Navy to protect our oversea commerce from them. If we had a Citizen Army such as I have mentioned, of nine or ten millions of men and if the land of this country was properly cultivated, we should be invincible at home. No foreign power would ever be mad enough to attempt to land their forces on our shores. But they would now be able to starve us all to death in a month if it were not for the Navy. It's a sensible and creditable position, isn't it?' concluded Barrington. 'Even in times of peace, thousands of people standing idle and tamely starving in their own fertile country, because a few land "Lords" forbid them to cultivate it.'

'Is there any more questions?' demanded Philpot, breaking a prolonged silence.

'Would any Liberal or Tory capitalist like to get up into the pulpit and oppose the speaker?' the chairman went on, finding that no one responded to his appeal for questions.

The silence continued.

'As there's no more questions and no one won't get up into the pulpit, it is now my painful duty to call upon someone to move a resolution.'

'Well, Mr. Chairman,' said Harlow, 'I may say that when I came on this firm I was a Liberal, but through listenin' to several lectures by Professor Owen and attendin' the meetings on the hill at Windley and reading the books and pamphlets I bought there and from Owen,

I came to the conclusion some time ago that it's a mug's game for us to vote for capitalists whether they calls theirselves Liberals or Tories. They're all alike when you're workin' for 'em; I defy any man to say what's the difference between a Liberal and a Tory employer. There is none – there can't be; they're both sweaters, and they've got to be, or they wouldn't be able to compete with each other. And since that's what they are, I say it's a mug's game for us to vote 'em into Parliament to rule over us and to make laws that we've got to abide by whether we like it or not. There's nothing to choose between 'em, and the proof of it is that it's never made much difference to us which party was in or which was out. It's quite true that in the past both of 'em have passed good laws, but they've only done it when public opinion was so strong in favour of it that they knew there was no getting out of it, and then it was a toss up which side did it.

'That's the way I've been lookin' at things lately, and I'd almost made up my mind never to vote no more, or to trouble myself about politics at all, because although I could see there was no sense in voting for Liberal or Tory capitalists, at the same time I must admit I couldn't make out how Socialism was going to help us. But the explanation of it which Professor Barrington has given us this afternoon has been a bit of an eye opener for me, and with your permission I should like to move as a resolution, "That it is the opinion of this meeting that Socialism is the only remedy for Unemployment and Poverty".'

The conclusion of Harlow's address was greeted with loud cheers from the Socialists, but most of the Liberal and Tory supporters of the present system maintained a sulky silence.

'I'll second that resolution,' said Easton.

[['And I'll lay a bob both ways,' remarked Bundy. The resolution was then put, and though the majority were against it, the Chairman declared it was carried unanimously.]]

By this time the violence of the storm had in a great measure abated, but as rain was still falling it was decided not to attempt to resume work that day. Beside, it would have been too late, even if the weather had cleared up.

'P'raps it's just as well it 'as rained,' remarked one man. 'If it 'adn't some of us might 'ave got the sack tonight. As it is, there'll be hardly enough for all of us to do tomorroer and Saturday mornin' even if it is fine.'

This was true: nearly all the outside was finished, and what remained to be done was ready for the final coat. Inside all there was to do was to colour wash the walls and to give the woodwork of the kitchen and scullery the last coat of paint.

It was inevitable – unless the firm had some other work for them to do somewhere else – that there would be a great slaughter on Saturday.

'Now,' said Philpot, assuming what he meant to be the manner of a school teacher addressing children, 'I wants you hall to make a speshall heffort and get 'ere very early in the mornin' – say about four o'clock – and them wot does the most work tomorrer, will get a prize on Saturday.'

'What'll it be, the sack?' inquired Harlow.

'Yes,' replied Philpot, 'and not honly will you get a prize for good conduck tomorrer, but if you all keep on workin' like we've bin doing lately till you're too hold and wore hout to do any more, you'll be allowed to go to a nice workhouse for the rest of your lives! and each one of you will be given a title – 'Pauper!' '

And they laughed!

Although the majority of them had mothers or fathers or other near relatives who had already succeeded to the title – they laughed!

As they were going home, Crass paused at the gate, and pointing up to the large gable at the end of the house, he said to Philpot:

'You'll want the longest ladder – the 65, for that, tomorrow.'

Philpot looked up at the gable.

It was very high.

CHAPTER 46

The 'Sixty-Five'

The next morning after breakfast Philpot, Sawkins, Harlow and Barrington went to the Yard to get the long ladder – the 65 – so called because it had sixty-five rungs. It was really what is known as a builder's scaffold ladder, and it had been strengthened by several iron bolts or rods which passed through just under some of the rungs. One side of the ladder had an iron band or ribbon twisted and nailed round it spirally. It was not at all suitable for painters' work, being altogether too heavy and cumbrous. However, as none of the others were long enough to reach the high gable at the Refuge, they managed, with a struggle, to get it down from the hooks and put it on one of the handcarts and soon passed through the streets of mean and dingy houses in the vicinity of the yard, and began the ascent of the long hill.

There had been a lot of rain during the night, and the sky was still overcast with dark grey clouds. The cart went heavily over the muddy road; Sawkins was at the helm, holding the end of the ladder and steering; the others walked a little further ahead, at the sides of the cart.

It was such hard work that by the time they were halfway up the hill they were so exhausted and out of breath that they had to stop for a rest.

'This is a bit of all right, ain't it?' remarked Harlow as he took off his cap and wiped the sweat from his forehead with his handkerchief.

While they rested they kept a good look out for Rushton or Hunter, who were likely to pass by at any moment.

At first, no one made any reply to Harlow's observation, for they were all out of breath and Philpot's lean fingers trembled violently as he wiped the perspiration from his face.

'Yes, mate,' he said despondently, after a while. 'It's one way of gettin' a livin' and there's plenty better ways.'

In addition to the fact that his rheumatism was exceptionally bad, he felt unusually low-spirited this morning; the gloomy weather and the prospect of a long day of ladder work probably had something to do with it.

'A "living" is right,' said Barrington bitterly. He also was exhausted with the struggle up the hill and enraged by the woebegone appearance of poor old Philpot, who was panting and quivering from the exertion.

They relapsed into silence. The unaccountable depression that possessed Philpot deprived him of all his usual jocularity and filled him with melancholy thoughts. He had travelled up and down this hill a great many times before under similar circumstances and he said to himself that if he had half a quid now for every time he had pushed a cart up this road, he wouldn't need to do anyone out of a job all the rest of his life.

The shop where he had been apprenticed used to be just down at the bottom; the place had been pulled down years ago, and the ground was now occupied by more pretentious buildings. Not quite so far down the road – on the other side – he could see the church where he used to attend Sunday School when he was a boy, and where he was married just thirty years ago. Presently – when they reached the top of the hill – he would be able to look across the valley and see the spire of the other church, the one in the graveyard, where all those who were dear to him had been one by one laid to rest. He felt that he would not be sorry when the time came to join them there. Possibly, in the next world – if there were such a place – they might all be together once more.

He was suddenly aroused from these thoughts by an exclamation from Harlow.

'Look out! Here comes Rushton.'

They immediately resumed their journey. Rushton was coming up the hill in his dog-cart with Grinder sitting by his side. They passed so closely that Philpot – who was on that side of the cart – was splashed with mud from the wheels of the trap.

'Them's some of your chaps, ain't they?' remarked Grinder.

'Yes,' replied Rushton. 'We're doing a job up this way.'

'I should 'ave thought it would pay you better to use a 'orse for sich work as that,' said Grinder.

'We do use the horses whenever it's necessary for very big loads, you know,' answered Rushton, and added with a laugh: 'But the donkeys are quite strong enough for such a job as that.'

The 'donkeys' struggled on up the hill for about another hundred yards and then they were forced to halt again.

'We mustn't stop long, you know,' said Harlow. 'Most likely he's gone to the job, and he'll wait to see how long it takes us to get there.'

Barrington felt inclined to say that in that case Rushton would have to wait, but he remained silent, for he remembered that although he personally did not care a brass button whether he got the sack or not, the others were not so fortunately circumstanced.

Whilst they were resting, another two-legged donkey passed by pushing another cart – or rather, holding it back, for he was coming slowly down the hill. Another Heir of all the ages – another Imperialist – a degraded, brutalised wretch, clad in filthy, stinking rags, his toes protruding from the rotten broken boots that were tied with bits of string upon his stockingless feet. The ramshackle cart was loaded with empty bottles and putrid rags, heaped loosely in the cart and packed into a large sack. Old coats and trousers, dresses, petticoats, and under-clothing, greasy, mildewed and mal-odorous. As he crept along with his eyes on the ground, the man gave utterance at intervals to uncouth, inarticulate sounds.

'That's another way of gettin' a livin',' said Sawkins with a laugh as the miserable creature slunk past.

Harlow also laughed, and Barrington regarded them curiously. He thought it strange that they did not seem to realise that they might some day become like this man themselves.

'I've often wondered what they does with all them dirty old rags,' said Philpot.

'Made into paper,' replied Harlow, briefly.

'Some of them are,' said Barrington, 'and some are manufactured into shoddy cloth and made into Sunday clothes for working men.'

'There's all sorts of different ways of gettin' a livin',' remarked Sawkins, after a pause. 'I read in a paper the other day about a bloke wot goes about lookin' for open trap doors and cellar flaps in front of shops. As soon as he spotted one open, he used to go and fall down in it; and then he'd be took to the 'orspital, and when he got better he used to go and threaten to bring a action against the shopkeeper and get damages, and most of 'em used to part up without goin' in front of the judge at all. But one day a slop was a watchin' of 'im, and seen 'im chuck 'isself down one, and when they picked 'im up they found he'd broke his leg. So they took 'im to the 'orspital and when he came out and went round to the shop and started talkin' about bringin' a action for damages, the slop collared 'im and they give 'im six months.'

'Yes, I read about that,' said Harlow, 'and there was another case of a chap who was run over by a motor, and they tried to make out as 'e put 'isself in the way on purpose; but 'e got some money out of the swell it belonged to; a 'underd pound I think it was.'

'I only wish as one of their motors would run inter *me*,' said Philpot, making a feeble attempt at a joke. 'I lay I'd get some o' me own back out of 'em.'

The others laughed, and Harlow was about to make some reply but at that moment a cyclist appeared coming down the hill from the direction of the job. It was Nimrod, so they resumed their journey once more and presently Hunter shot past on his machine without taking any notice of them . . .

When they arrived they found that Rushton had not been there at all, but Nimrod had. Crass said that he had kicked up no end of a row because they had not called at the yard at six o'clock that morning for the ladder, instead of going for it after breakfast – making two journeys instead of one, and he had also been ratty because the big gable had not been started the first thing that morning.

They carried the ladder into the garden and laid it on the ground along the side of the house where the gable was. A brick wall about eight feet high separated the grounds of 'The Refuge' from those of the premises next door. Between this wall and the side wall of the house was a space about six feet wide and this space formed a kind of alley or lane or passage along the side of the house. They laid the ladder on the ground along this passage, the 'foot' was placed about half-way through; just under the centre of the gable, and as it lay there, the other end of the ladder reached right out to the front railings.

Next, it was necessary that two men should go up into the attic – the window of which was just under the point of the gable – and drop the end of a long rope down to the others who would tie it to the top of the ladder. Then two men would stand on the bottom rung, so as to keep the 'foot' down, and three others would have to raise the ladder up, while the two men up in the attic hauled on the rope.

They called Bundy and his mate Ned Dawson to help, and it was arranged that Harlow and Crass should stand on the foot because they were the heaviest. Philpot, Bundy, and Barrington were to 'raise', and Dawson and Sawkins were to go up to the attic and haul on the rope.

'Where's the rope?' asked Crass.

The others looked blankly at him. None of them had thought of bringing one from the yard.

'Why, ain't there one 'ere?' said Philpot.

'One 'ere? Of course there ain't one 'ere!' snarled Crass. 'Do you mean to say as you ain't brought one, then?'

Philpot stammered out something about having thought there was one at the house already, and the others said they had not thought about it at all.

'Well, what the bloody hell are we to do now?' cried Crass, angrily.

'I'll go to the yard and get one,' suggested Barrington. 'I can do it in twenty minutes there and back.'

'Yes! and a bloody fine row there'd be if Hunter was to see you! 'Ere it's nearly ten o'clock and we ain't made a start on this gable wot we ought to 'ave started first thing this morning.'

'Couldn't we tie two or three of those short ropes together?' suggested Philpot. 'Those that the other two ladders was spliced with?'

As there was sure to be a row if they delayed long enough to send to the yard, it was decided to act on Philpot's suggestion.

Several of the short ropes were accordingly tied together but upon examination it was found that some parts were so weak that even Crass had to admit it would be dangerous to attempt to haul the heavy ladder up with them.

'Well, the only thing as I can see for it,' he said, 'is that the boy will 'ave to go down to the yard and get the long rope. It won't do for anyone else to go: there's been one row already about the waste of time because we didn't call at the yard for the ladder at six o'clock.'

Bert was down in the basement of the house limewashing a cellar. Crass called him up and gave him the necessary instructions, chief of which was to get back again as soon as ever he could. The boy ran off, and while they were waiting for him to come back the others went on with their several jobs. Philpot returned to the small gable he had been painting before breakfast, which he had not quite finished. As he worked a sudden and unaccountable terror took possession of him. He did not want to do that other gable; he felt too ill; and he almost resolved that he would ask Crass if he would mind letting him do something else. There were several younger men who would not object to doing it – it would be mere child's play to them, and Barrington had already – yesterday – offered to change jobs with him.

But then, when he thought of what the probable consequences would be, he hesitated to take that course, and tried to persuade himself that he would be able to get through with the work all right. He did not want Crass or Hunter to mark him as being too old for ladder work.

Bert came back in about half an hour flushed and sweating with the weight of the rope and with the speed he had made. He delivered it to Crass and then returned to his cellar and went on with the limewashing, while Crass passed the word for Philpot and the others to come and raise the ladder. He handed the rope to Ned Dawson, who took it up to the attic, accompanied by Sawkins; arrived there they lowered one end out of the window down to the others.

'If you ask me,' said Ned Dawson, who was critically examining the strands of the rope as he passed it out through the open window, 'If you ask me, I don't see as this is much better than the one we made up by tyin' the short pieces together. Look 'ere,' – he indicated a part of the rope that was very frayed and worn – 'and 'ere's another place just as bad.'

'Well, for Christ's sake don't say nothing about it now,' replied Dawson. 'There's been enough talk and waste of time over this job already.'

Ned made no answer and the end having by this time reached the ground, Bundy made it fast to the ladder, about six rungs from the top.

The ladder was lying on the ground, parallel to the side of the house. The task of raising it would have been much easier if they had been able to lay it at right angles to the house wall, but this was impossible because of the premises next door and the garden wall between the two houses. On account of its having to be raised in this manner the men at the top would not be able to get a straight pull on the rope; they would have to stand back in the room without being able to see the ladder, and the rope would have to be drawn round the corner of the window, rasping against the edge of the stone sill and the brick-work.

The end of the rope having been made fast to the top of the ladder, Crass and Harlow stood on the foot and the other three raised the top from the ground; as Barrington was the tallest, he took the middle position – underneath the ladder – grasping the rungs, Philpot being on his left and Bundy on his right, each holding one side of the ladder.

At a signal from Crass, Dawson and Sawkins began to haul on the rope, and the top of the ladder began to rise slowly into the air.

Philpot was not of much use at this work, which made it all the harder for the other two who were lifting, besides putting an extra strain on the rope. His lack of strength, and the efforts of Barrington and Bundy to make up for him caused the ladder to sway from side to side, as it would not have done if they had all been equally capable.

Meanwhile, upstairs, Dawson and Sawkins – although the ladder was as yet only a little more than half the way up – noticed, as they hauled and strained on the rope, that it had worn a groove for itself in the corner of the brickwork at the side of the window; and every now and then, although they pulled with all their strength, they were not able to draw in any part of the rope at all; and it seemed to them as if those others down below must have let go their hold altogether, or ceased lifting.

That was what actually happened. The three men found the weight so overpowering, that once or twice they were compelled to relax their efforts for a few seconds, and at those times the rope had to carry the whole weight of the ladder; and the part of the rope that had to bear the greatest strain was the part that chanced to be at the angle of the brickwork at the side of the window. And presently it happened that one of the frayed and worn places that Dawson had remarked about was just at the angle during one of those momentary pauses. On one end there hung the ponderous ladder, straining the frayed rope against the corner of the brickwork and the sharp edge of the stone sill, at the other end were Dawson and Sawkins pulling with all their strength, and in that instant the rope snapped like a piece of thread. One end remained in the hands of Sawkins and Dawson, who reeled backwards into the room, and the other end flew up into the air, writhing like the lash of a gigantic whip. For a moment the heavy ladder swayed from side to side: Barrington, standing underneath, with his hands raised above his head grasping one of the rungs, struggled desperately to hold it up. At his right stood Bundy, also with arms upraised holding the side; and on the left, between the ladder and the wall, was Philpot.

For a brief space they strove fiercely to support the over-powering weight, but Philpot had no strength, and the ladder, swaying over to the left, crashed down, crushing him upon the ground and against the wall of the house. He fell face downwards, with the ladder across his shoulders; the side that had the iron bands twisted round it fell across the back of his neck, forcing his face against the bricks at the base of the wall. He uttered no cry and was quite still, with blood streaming from the cuts on his face and trickling from his ears.

Barrington was also hurled to the ground with his head and arms under the ladder; his head and face were cut and bleeding and he was unconscious; none of the others was hurt, for they had all had time to jump clear when the ladder fell. Their shouts soon brought all the other men running to the spot, and the ladder was quickly lifted off the two motionless figures. At first it seemed that Philpot was dead, but [[Easton rushed off for a neighbouring doctor, who came in a few minutes.

He knelt down and carefully examined the crushed and motionless form of Philpot, while the other men stood by in terrified silence.]]

[Barrington, who fortunately was but momentarily stunned, was sitting against the wall and had suffered nothing more serious than minor cuts and bruises.]

[[The doctor's examination of Philpot was a very brief one, and when he rose from his knees, even before he spoke they knew from his manner]] that their worst fears were realised.

Philpot was dead.

CHAPTER 47

The Ghouls

Barrington did not do any more work that day, but before going home he went to the doctor's house and the latter dressed the cuts on his head and arms. Philpot's body was taken away on the ambulance to the mortuary.

Hunter arrived at the house shortly afterwards and at once began to shout and bully because the painting of the gable was not yet commenced. When he heard of the accident he blamed them for using the rope, and said they should have asked for a new one. Before he went away he had a long, private conversation with Crass, who told him that Philpot had no relatives and that his life was insured for ten pounds in a society[121] of which Crass was also a member. He knew that Philpot had arranged that in the event of his death the money was to be paid to the old woman with whom he lodged, who was a very close friend. The result of this confidential talk was that Crass and Hunter came to the conclusion that it was probable that she would be very glad to be relieved of the trouble of attending to the business of the funeral, and that Crass, as a close friend of the dead man, and a fellow member of the society, was the most suitable person to take charge of the business for her. He was already slightly acquainted with the old lady, so he would go to see her at once and get her authority to act on her behalf. Of course, they would not be able to do much until after the inquest, but they could get the coffin made – as Hunter knew the mortuary keeper there would be no difficulty about getting in for a minute to measure the corpse.

This matter having been arranged, Hunter departed to order a new rope, and shortly afterwards Crass – having made sure that everyone would have plenty to do while he was gone – quietly slipped away to go to see Philpot's landlady. He went off so secretly that the men did not know that he had been away at all until they saw him come back just before twelve o'clock.

The new rope was brought to the house about one o'clock and this time the ladder was raised without any mishap. Harlow was put on to paint the gable, and he felt so nervous that he was allowed to have Sawkins to stand by and hold the ladder all the time. Everyone felt nervous that afternoon, and they all went about their work in an unusually careful manner.

When Bert had finished limewashing the cellar, Crass set him to work outside, painting the gate of the side entrance. While the boy was thus occupied he was accosted by a solemn-looking man who asked him about the accident. The solemn stranger was very sympathetic and enquired what was the name of the man who had been killed, and whether he was married. Bert informed him that Philpot was a widower, and that he had no children.

'Ah, well, that's so much the better, isn't it?' said the stranger, shaking his head mournfully. 'It's a dreadful thing, you know, when there's children left unprovided for. You don't happen to know where he lived, do you?'

'Yes,' said Bert, mentioning the address and beginning to wonder what the solemn man wanted to know for, and why he appeared to be so sorry for Philpot, since it was quite evident that he had never known him.

'Thanks very much,' said the man, pulling out his pocket-book and making a note in it. 'Thanks very much indeed. Good afternoon,' and he hurried off.

'Good afternoon, sir,' said Bert and he turned to resume his work. Crass came along the garden path just as the mysterious stranger was disappearing round the corner.

'What did *he* want?' said Crass, who had seen the man talking to Bert.

'I don't know exactly; he was asking about the accident, and whether Joe left any children, and where he lived. He must be a very decent sort of chap, I should think. He seems quite sorry about it.'

'Oh, he does, does he?' said Crass, with a peculiar expression. 'Don't you know who he is?'

'No,' replied the boy; 'but I thought p'raps he was a reporter of some paper.'

' 'E ain't no reporter: that's old Snatchum the undertaker. 'E's smellin' round after a job; but 'e's out of it this time, smart as 'e thinks 'e is.'

Barrington came back the next morning to work, and at breakfast-time there was a lot of talk about the accident. They said that it was all very well for Hunter to talk like that about the rope, but he had known for a long time that it was nearly worn out. Newman said that only about three weeks previously when they were raising a ladder at another job he had shown the rope to him, and Misery had replied that there was nothing wrong with it. Several others besides Newman claimed to have mentioned the matter to Hunter, and each of them said he had received the same sort of reply. But when Barrington suggested that they should attend the inquest and give evidence to that effect, they all became suddenly silent and in a conversation Barrington afterwards had with Newman the latter pointed out that if he were to do so, it would do no good to Philpot. It would not bring him back but it would be sure to do himself a lot of harm. He would never get another job at Rushton's and probably many of the other employers would 'mark him' as well.

'So if *you* say anything about it,' concluded Newman, 'don't bring my name into it.'

Barrington was constrained to admit that all things considered it was right for Newman to mind his own business. He felt that it would not be fair to urge him or anyone else to do or say anything that would injure themselves.

Misery came to the house about eleven o'clock and informed several of the hands that as work was very slack they would get their back day at pay time. He said that the firm had tendered for one or two jobs, so they could call round about Wednesday and perhaps he might then be able to give some of them another start. Barrington was not one of those who were 'stood off', although he had expected to be on account of the speech he had made at the Beano, and everyone said that he would have got the push sure enough if it had not been for the accident.

Before he went away, Nimrod instructed Owen and Crass to go to the yard at once: they would there find Payne the carpenter, who was making Philpot's coffin, which would be ready for Crass to varnish by the time they got there.

Misery told Owen that he had left the coffin plate and the instructions with Payne and added that he was not to take too much time over the writing, because it was a very cheap job.

When they arrived at the yard, Payne was just finishing the coffin, which was of elm. All that remained to be done to it was the pitching of the joints inside and Payne was in the act of lifting the pot of boiling pitch off the fire to do this.

As it was such a cheap job, there was no time to polish it properly, so Crass proceeded to give it a couple of coats of spirit varnish, and while he was doing this Owen wrote the plate, which was made of very thin zinc lacquered over to make it look like brass:

JOSEPH PHILPOT
Died September 1st 19—
Aged 56 years.

*   *   *

The inquest was held on the following Monday morning, and as both Rushton and Hunter thought it possible that Barrington might attempt to impute some blame to them, they had worked the oracle and had contrived to have several friends of their own put on the jury. There was, however, no need for their alarm, because Barrington could not say that he had himself noticed, or called Hunter's attention to the state of the rope; and he did not wish to mention the names of the others without their permission. The evidence of Crass and the other men who were called was to the effect that it was a pure accident. None of them had noticed that the rope was unsound. Hunter also swore that he did not know of it – none of the men had ever called his attention to it; if they had done so he would have procured a new one immediately.

Philpot's landlady and Mr. Rushton were also called as witnesses, and the end was that the jury returned a verdict of accidental death, and added that they did not think any blame attached to anyone.

The coroner discharged the jury, and as they and the witnesses passed out of the room, Hunter followed Rushton outside, with the hope of being honoured by a little conversation with him on the satisfactory issue of the case; but Rushton went off without taking any notice of him, so Hunter returned to the room where the court had been held to get the coroner's certificate authorising the interment of the body. This document is usually handed to the friends of the deceased or to the undertaker acting for them. When Hunter got back to the room he found that during his absence the coroner had given it to Philpot's landlady, who had taken it with her. He accordingly hastened outside again to ask her for it, but the woman was nowhere to be seen.

Crass and the other men were also gone; they had hurried off to return to work, and after a moment's hesitation Hunter decided that it did not matter much about the certificate. Crass had arranged the business with the landlady and he could get the paper from her later on. Having come to this conclusion, he dismissed the subject from his mind: he had several prices to work out that afternoon – estimates for some jobs the firm was going to tender for.

That evening, after having been home to tea, Crass and Sawkins met by appointment at the carpenter's shop to take the coffin to the mortuary, where Misery had arranged to meet them at half-past eight o'clock. Hunter's plan was to have the funeral take place from the mortuary, which was only about a quarter of an hour's walk from the yard; so tonight they were just going to lift in the body and get the lid screwed down.

It was blowing hard and raining heavily when Crass and Sawkins set out, carrying the coffin – covered with a black cloth – on their shoulders. They also took a small pair of tressels, for the coffin to stand on. Crass carried one of these slung over his arm and Sawkins the other.

On their way they had to pass the 'Cricketers' and the place looked so inviting that they decided to stop and have a drink – just to keep the damp out, and as they could not very well take the coffin inside with them, they stood it up against the brick wall a little way from the side of the door: as Crass remarked with a laugh, there was not much danger of anyone pinching it. The Old Dear served them and just as they finished drinking the two half-pints there was a loud crash outside and Crass and Sawkins rushed out and found that the coffin had blown down and was lying bottom upwards across the pavement, while the black cloth that had been wrapped round it was out in the middle of the muddy road. Having recovered this, they shook as much of the dirt off as they could, and having wrapped it round the coffin again they resumed their journey to the mortuary, where they found Hunter waiting for them, engaged in earnest conversation with the keeper. The electric light was switched on, and as Crass and Sawkins came in they saw that the marble slab was empty.

The corpse was gone.

'Snatchum came this afternoon with a hand-truck and a corfin,' explained the keeper. 'I was out at the time, and the missis thought it was all right so she let him have the key.'

Hunter and Crass looked blankly at each other.

'Well, this takes the biskit!' said the latter as soon as he could speak.

'I thought you said you had settled everything all right with the old woman?' said Hunter.

'So I did,' replied Crass. 'I seen 'er on Friday, and I told 'er to leave it all to me to attend to, and she said she would. I told 'er that Philpot said to me that if ever anything 'appened to 'im I was to take charge of everything for 'er, because I was 'is best friend. And I told 'er we'd do it as cheap as possible.'

'Well, it seems to me as you've bungled it somehow,' said Nimrod, gloomily. 'I ought to have gone and seen 'er myself. I was afraid you'd make a mess of it,' he added in a wailing tone. 'It's always the same; everything that I don't attend to myself goes wrong.'

An uncomfortable silence fell. Cross thought that the principal piece of bungling in this affair was Hunter's failure to secure possession of the Coroner's certificate after the inquest, but he was afraid to say so.

Outside, the rain was still falling and drove in through the partly open door, causing the atmosphere of the mortuary to be even more than usually cold and damp. The empty coffin had been reared against one of the walls and the marble slab was still stained with blood, for the keeper had not had time to clean it since the body had been removed.

'I can see 'ow it's been worked,' said Cross at last. 'There's one of the members of the club who works for Snatchum, and 'e's took it on 'isself to give the order for the funeral; but 'e's got no right to do it.'

'Right or no right, 'e's done it,' replied Misery, 'so you'd better take the box back to the shop.'

Cross and Sawkins accordingly returned to the workshop, where they were presently joined by Nimrod.

'I've been thinking this business over as I came along,' he said, 'and I don't see being beat like this by Snatchum; so you two can just put the tressels and the box on a hand cart and we'll take it over to Philpot's house.'

Nimrod walked on the pavement while the other two pushed the cart, and it was about half-past nine when they arrived at the street in Windley where Philpot used to live. They halted in a dark part of the street a few yards away from the house and on the opposite side.

'I think the best thing we can do,' said Misery, 'is for me and Sawkins to wait 'ere while you go to the 'ouse and see 'ow the land lies. You've done all the business with 'er so far. It's no use takin' the box unless we know the corpse is there; for all we know, Snatchum may 'ave taken it 'ome with 'im.'

'Yes; I think that'll be the best way,' agreed Cross, after a moment's thought.

Nimrod and Sawkins accordingly took shelter in the doorway of an empty house, leaving the handcart at the kerb, while Cross went across the street and knocked at Philpot's door. They saw it opened by an elderly woman holding a lighted candle in her hand; then

Crass went inside and the door was shut. In about a quarter of an hour he reappeared and, leaving the door partly open behind him, he came out and crossed over to where the others were waiting. As he drew near they could see that he carried a piece of paper in his hand.

'It's all right,' he said in a hoarse whisper as he came up. 'I've got the stifficut.'

Misery took the paper eagerly and scanned it by the light of a match that Crass struck. It was the certificate right enough, and with a sigh of relief Hunter put it into his note-book and stowed it safely away in the inner pocket of his coat, while Crass explained the result of his errand.

It appeared that the other member of the Society, accompanied by Snatchum, had called upon the old woman and had bluffed her into giving them the order for the funeral. It was they who had put her up to getting the certificate from the Coroner – they had been careful to keep away from the inquest themselves so as not to arouse Hunter's or Crass's suspicions.

'When they brought the body 'ome this afternoon,' Crass went on, 'Snatchum tried to get the stifficut orf 'er, but she'd been thinkin' things over and she was a bit frightened 'cos she knowed she'd made arrangements with me, and she thought she'd better see me first; so she told 'im she'd give it to 'im on Thursday; that's the day as 'e was goin' to 'ave the funeral.'

'He'll find he's a day too late,' said Misery, with a ghastly grin. 'We'll get the job done on Wednesday.'

'She didn't want to give it to me, at first,' Crass concluded, 'but I told 'er we'd see 'er right if old Snatchum tried to make 'er pay for the other corfin.'

'I don't think he's likely to make much fuss about it,' said Hunter. 'He won't want everybody to know he was so anxious for the job.'

Crass and Sawkins pushed the handcart over to the other side of the road and then, lifting the coffin off, they carried it into the house, Nimrod going first.

The old woman was waiting for them with the candle at the end of the passage.

'I shall be very glad when it's all over,' she said, as she led the way up the narrow stairs, closely followed by Hunter, who carried the tressels, Crass and Sawkins bringing up in the rear with the coffin. 'I shall be very glad when it's all over, for I'm sick and tired of answerin' the door to undertakers. If there's been one 'ere since

Friday there's been a dozen, all after the job, not to mention all the cards what's been put under the door, besides the one's what I've had give to me by different people. I had a pair of boots bein' mended and the man took the trouble to bring 'em 'ome when they was finished – a thing 'e's never done before – just for an excuse to give me an undertaker's card.

'Then the milkman brought one, and so did the baker, and the greengrocer give me another when I went in there on Saturday to buy some vegetables for Sunday dinner.'

[[Arrived at the top landing the old woman opened a door and entered a small and wretchedly furnished room.

Across the lower sash of the window hung a tattered piece of lace curtain. The low ceiling was cracked and discoloured.

There was a rickety little wooden washstand, and along one side of the room a narrow bed covered with a ragged grey quilt, on which lay a bundle containing the clothes that the dead man was wearing at the time of the accident.]]

There was a little table in front of the window, with a small looking-glass upon it, and a cane-seated chair was placed by the bedside and the floor was covered with a faded piece of drab-coloured carpet of no perceptible pattern, worn into holes in several places.

In the middle of this dreary room, upon a pair of tressels, was the coffin containing Philpot's body. Seen by the dim and flickering light of the candle, the aspect of this coffin, covered over with a white sheet, was terrible in its silent, pathetic solitude.

Hunter placed the pair of tressels he had been carrying against the wall, and the other two put the empty coffin on the floor by the side of the bed. The old woman stood the candlestick on the mantelpiece, and withdrew, remarking that they would not need her assistance. The three men then removed their overcoats and laid them on the end of the bed, and from the pocket of his Crass took out two large screwdrivers, one of which he handed to Hunter. Sawkins held the candle while they unscrewed and took off the lid of the coffin they had brought with them: it was not quite empty, for they had brought a bag of tools inside it.

'I think we shall be able to work better if we takes the other one orf the trussels and puts it on the floor,' remarked Crass.

'Yes, I think so, too,' replied Hunter.

Crass took off the sheet and threw it on the bed, revealing the other coffin, which was very similar in appearance to the one they had brought with them, being of elm, with the usual imitation brass furniture. Hunter took hold of the head and Crass the foot and they lifted it off the tressels on to the floor.

' 'E's not very 'eavy; that's one good thing,' observed Hunter.

' 'E always was a very thin chap,' replied Crass.

The screws that held down the lid had been covered over with large-headed brass nails which had to be wrenched off before they could get at the screws, of which there were eight altogether. It was evident from the appearance of the heads of these screws that they were old ones that had been used for some purpose before: they were rusty and of different sizes, some being rather larger or smaller than they should have been. They were screwed in so firmly that by the time they had drawn half of them out the two men were streaming with perspiration. After a while Hunter took the candle from Sawkins and the latter had a try at the screws.

'Anyone would think the dam' things had been in there for a 'underd years,' remarked Hunter, savagely, as he wiped the sweat from his face and neck with his handkerchief.

Kneeling on the lid of the coffin and panting and grunting with the exertion, the other two continued to struggle with their task. Suddenly Crass uttered an obscene curse; he had broken off one side of the head of the screw he was trying to turn and almost at the same instant a similar misfortune happened to Sawkins.

After this, Hunter again took a screwdriver himself, and when they had got all the screws out with the exception of the two broken ones, Crass took a hammer and chisel out of the bag and proceeded to cut off what was left of the tops of the two that remained. But even after this was done the two screws still held the lid on the coffin, and so they had to hammer the end of the blade of the chisel underneath and lever the lid up so that they could get hold of it with their fingers. It split up one side as they tore it off, exposing the dead man to view.

Although the marks of the cuts and bruises were still visible on Philpot's face, they were softened down by the pallor of death, and a placid, peaceful expression pervaded his features. His hands were crossed upon his breast, and as he lay there in the snow white grave clothes, almost covered in by the white lace frill that bordered the sides of the coffin, he looked like one in a profound and tranquil sleep.

They laid the broken lid on the bed, and placed the two coffins side by side on the floor as close together as possible. Sawkins stood at one side holding the candle in his left hand and ready to render with his right any assistance that might unexpectedly prove to be necessary. Crass, standing at the foot, took hold of the body by the ankles, while Hunter at the other end seized it by the shoulders with his huge, claw-like hands, which resembled the talons of some obscene bird of prey, and they dragged it out and placed it in the other coffin.

Whilst Hunter – hovering ghoulishly over the corpse – arranged the grave clothes and the frilling, Crass laid the broken cover on the top of the other coffin and pushed it under the bed out of the way. Then he selected the necessary screws and nails from the bag, and Hunter having by this time finished, they proceeded to screw down the lid. Then they lifted the coffin on to the tressels, covering it over with the sheet, and the appearance it then presented was so exactly similar to what they had seen when they first entered the room, that it caused the same thought to occur to all of them: Suppose Snatchum took it into his head to come there and take the body out again? If he were to do so and take it up to the cemetery they might be compelled to give up the certificate to him and then all their trouble would be lost.

After a brief consultation, they resolved that it would be safer to take the corpse on the handcart to the yard and keep it in the carpenter's shop until the funeral, which could take place from there. Crass and Sawkins accordingly lifted the coffin off the tressels, and – while Hunter held the light – proceeded to carry it downstairs, a task of considerable difficulty, owing to the narrowness of the staircase and the landing. However, they got it down at last and, having put it on the handcart, covered it over with the black wrapper. It was still raining and the lamp in the cart was nearly out, so Sawkins trimmed the wick and relit it before they started.

Hunter wished them 'Good-night' at the corner of the street, because it was not necessary for him to accompany them to the yard – they would be able to manage all that remained to be done by themselves. He said he would make the arrangements for the funeral as soon as he possibly could the next morning, and he would come to the job and let them know, as soon as he knew himself, at what time they would have to be in attendance to act as bearers. He had gone a little distance on his way when he stopped and turned back to them.

'It's not necessary for either of you to make a song about this business, you know,' he said.

The two men said that they quite understood that: he could depend on their keeping their mouths shut.

When Hunter had gone, Crass drew out his watch. It was a quarter to eleven. A little way down the road the lights of a public house were gleaming through the mist.

'We shall be just in time to get a drink before closing time if we buck up,' he said. And with this object they hurried on as fast as they could.

When they reached the tavern they left the cart standing by the kerb, and went inside, where Crass ordered two pints of four-ale, which he permitted Sawkins to pay for.

'How are we going on about this job?' enquired the latter after they had each taken a long drink, for they were thirsty after their exertions. 'I reckon we ought to 'ave more than a bob for it, don't you? It's not like a ordinary "lift in".'

'Of course it ain't,' replied Crass. 'We ought to 'ave about, say' – reflecting – 'say arf a dollar each at the very least.'

'Little enough too,' said Sawkins. 'I was going to say arf a crown, myself.'

Crass agreed that even half a crown would not be too much.

' 'Ow are we goin' on about chargin' it on our time sheets?' asked Sawkins, after a pause. 'If we just put a "lift in", they might only pay us a bob as usual.'

As a rule when they had taken a coffin home, they wrote on their time sheets 'One lift in', for which they were usually paid one shilling, unless it happened to be a very high-class funeral, when they some-times got one and sixpence. They were never paid by the hour for these jobs.

Crass smoked reflectively.

'I think the best way will be to put it like this,' he said at length. ' 'Philpot's funeral. One lift out and one lift in. Also takin' corpse to carpenter's shop.' 'Ow would that do?'

Sawkins said that would be a very good way to put it, and they finished their beer just as the landlord intimated that it was closing time. The cart was standing where they left it, the black cloth saturated with the rain, which dripped mournfully from its sable folds.

When they reached the plot of waste ground over which they had to pass in order to reach the gates of the yard, they had to proceed very cautiously, for it was very dark, and the lantern did not give much light. A number of carts and lorries were standing there, and the path wound through pools of water and heaps of refuse. After much difficulty and jolting, they reached the gate, which Crass unlocked with the key he had obtained from the office earlier in the evening. They soon opened the door of the carpenter's shop and, after lighting the gas, they arranged the tressels and then brought in the coffin and placed it upon them. Then they locked the door and placed the key in its usual hiding-place, but the key of the outer gate they took with them and dropped into the letter-box at the office, which they had to pass on their way home.

As they turned away from the door they were suddenly confronted by a policeman who flashed his lantern in their faces and demanded to know why they had tried the lock . . .

The next morning was a very busy one for Hunter, who had to see several new jobs commenced. They were all small affairs. Most of them would only take two or three days from start to finish.

Attending to this work occupied most of his morning, but all the same he managed to do the necessary business connected with the funeral, which he arranged to take place at two o'clock on Wednesday afternoon from the mortuary, where the coffin had been removed during the day, Hunter deciding that it would not look well to have the funeral start from the workshop.

Although Hunter had kept it as quiet as possible, there was a small crowd, including several old workmates of Philpot's who happened to be out of work, waiting outside the mortuary to see the funeral start, and amongst them were Bill Bates and the Semi-drunk, who were both sober. Barrington and Owen were also there, having left off work for the day in order to go to the funeral. They were there too in a sense as the representatives of the other workmen, for Barrington carried a large wreath which had been subscribed for voluntarily by Rushton's men. They could not all afford to lose the time to attend the funeral, although most of them would have liked to pay that tribute of regard to their old mate, so they had done this as the next best thing. Attached to the wreath was a strip of white satin ribbon, upon which Owen had painted a suitable inscription.

Promptly at two o'clock the hearse and the mourning coach drove up with Hunter and the four bearers – Crass, Slyme, Payne and Sawkins, all dressed in black with frock coats and silk hats. Although they were nominally attired in the same way, there was a remarkable dissimilarity in their appearance. Crass's coat was of smooth, intensely black cloth, having been recently dyed, and his hat was rather low in the crown, being of that shape that curved outwards towards the top. Hunter's coat was a kind of serge with a rather rusty cast of colour and his hat was very tall and straight, slightly narrower at the crown than at the brim. As for the others, each of them had a hat of a different fashion and date, and their 'black' clothes ranged from rusty brown to dark blue.

These differences were due to the fact that most of the garments had been purchased at different times from different second-hand clothes shops, and never being used except on such occasions as the present, they lasted for an indefinite time.

When the coffin was brought out and placed in the hearse, Hunter laid upon it the wreath that Barrington gave him, together with another he had brought himself, which had a similar ribbon with the words: 'From Rushton & Co. with deep sympathy.'

Seeing that Barrington and Owen were the only occupants of the carriage, Bill Bates and the Semi-drunk came up to the door and asked if there was any objection to their coming and as neither Owen nor Barrington objected, they did not think it necessary to ask anyone else's permission, so they got in.

Meanwhile, Hunter had taken his position a few yards in front of the hearse and the bearers each his proper position, two on each side. As the procession turned into the main road, they saw Snatchum standing at the corner looking very gloomy. Hunter kept his eyes fixed straight ahead and affected not to see him, but Crass could not resist the temptation to indulge in a jeering smile, which so enraged Snatchum that he shouted out:

'It don't matter! I shan't lose much! I can use it for someone else!'

The distance to the cemetery was about three miles, so as soon as they got out of the busy streets of the town, Hunter called a halt, and got up on the hearse beside the driver, Crass sat on the other side, and two of the other bearers stood in the space behind the driver's seat, the fourth getting up beside the driver of the coach; and then they proceeded at a rapid pace.

As they drew near to the cemetery they slowed down, and finally stopped when about fifty yards from the gate. Then Hunter and the bearers resumed their former position, and they passed through the open gate and up to the door of the church, where they were received by the clerk – a man in a rusty black cassock, who stood by while they carried the coffin in and placed it on a kind of elevated table which revolved on a pivot. They brought it in foot first, and as soon as they had placed it upon the table, the clerk swung it round so as to bring the foot of the coffin towards the door ready to be carried out again.

There was a special pew set apart for the undertakers, and in this Hunter and the bearers took their seats to await the arrival of the clergyman. Barrington and the three others sat on the opposite side. There was no altar or pulpit in this church, but a kind of reading desk stood on a slightly raised platform at the other end of the aisle.

After a wait of about ten minutes, the clergyman entered and, at once proceeding to the desk, began to recite in a rapid and wholly unintelligible manner the usual office. If it had not been for the fact that each of his hearers had a copy of the words – for there was a little book in each pew – none of them would have been able to gather the sense of what the man was gabbling. Under any other circumstances, the spectacle of a human being mouthing in this absurd way would have compelled laughter, and so would the suggestion that this individual really believed that he was addressing the Supreme Being. His attitude and manner were contemptuously indifferent. While he recited, intoned, or gabbled, the words of the office, he was reading the certificate and some other paper the clerk had placed upon the desk, and when he had finished reading these, his gaze wandered abstractedly round the chapel, resting for a long time with an expression of curiosity upon Bill Bates and the Semi-drunk, who were doing their best to follow in their books the words he was repeating. He next turned his attention to his fingers, holding his hand away from him nearly at arm's length and critically examining the nails.

From time to time as this miserable mockery proceeded the clerk in the rusty black cassock mechanically droned out a sonorous 'Ah-men', and after the conclusion of the lesson the clergyman went out of the church, taking a short cut through the grave-stones and monuments, while the bearers again shouldered the coffin and followed the clerk to the grave. When they arrived within a few yards of their destination, they were rejoined by the clergyman, who was waiting for them at the corner of one of the paths. He put himself at the head of the procession with an open book in his hand, and as they walked slowly along, he resumed his reading or repetition of the words of the service.

He had on an old black cassock and a much soiled and slightly torn surplice. The unseemly appearance of this dirty garment was heightened by the circumstance that he had not taken the trouble to adjust it properly. It hung all lop-sided, showing about six inches more of the black cassock underneath one side than the other. However, perhaps it is not right to criticise this person's appearance so severely, because the poor fellow was paid only seven-and-six for each burial, and as this was only the fourth funeral he had officiated at that day, probably he could not afford to wear clean linen – at any rate, not for the funerals of the lower classes.

He continued his unintelligible jargon while they were lowering the coffin into the grave, and those who happened to know the words of the office by heart were, with some difficulty, able to understand what he was saying:

'Forasmuch as it hath pleased Almighty God of His great mercy to take unto Himself the soul of our Dear Brother here departed, we therefore commit his body to the ground; earth to earth; ashes to ashes, dust to dust – '

The earth fell from the clerk's hand and rattled on the lid of the coffin with a mournful sound, and when the clergyman had finished repeating the remainder of the service, he turned and walked away in the direction of the church. Hunter and the rest of the funeral party made their way back towards the gate of the cemetery where the hearse and the carriage were waiting.

On their way they saw another funeral procession coming towards them. It was a very plain-looking closed hearse with only one horse. There was no undertaker in front and no bearers walked by the sides.

It was a pauper's funeral.

Three men, evidently dressed in their Sunday clothes, followed behind the hearse. As they reached the church door, four old men who were dressed in ordinary everyday clothes, came forward and opening the hearse took out the coffin and carried it into the church, followed by the other three, who were evidently relatives of the deceased. The four old men were paupers – inmates of the work-house, who were paid sixpence each for acting as bearers.

They were just taking out the coffin from the hearse as Hunter's party was passing, and most of the latter paused for a moment and watched them carry it into the church. The roughly made coffin was of white deal, not painted or covered in any way, and devoid of any fittings or ornament with the exception of a square piece of zinc tacked on the lid. None of Rushton's party was near enough to recognise any of the mourners or to read what was written on the zinc, but if they had been they would have seen, roughly painted in black letters

J. L.

Aged 67

and some of them would have recognised the three mourners who were Jack Linden's sons.

As for the bearers, they were all retired working men who had come into their 'titles'. One of them was old Latham, the venetian blind maker.

CHAPTER 48

The Wise Men of the East

At the end of the following week there was a terrible slaughter at Rushton's. Barrington and all the casual hands were sacked, including Newman, Easton and Harlow, and there was so little work that it looked as if everyone else would have to stand off also. The summer was practically over, so those who were stood off had but a poor chance of getting a start anywhere else, because most other firms were discharging hands as well.

There was only one other shop in the town that was doing anything at all to speak of, and that was the firm of Dauber and Botchit. This firm had come very much to the front during the summer, and had captured several big jobs that Rushton & Co. had expected to get, besides taking away several of the latter's old customers.

This firm took work at almost half the price that Rushton's could do it for, and they had a foreman whose little finger was thicker than Nimrod's thigh.[122] Some of the men who had worked for both firms during the summer, said that after working for Dauber and Botchit, working for Rushton seemed like having a holiday.

'There's one bloke there,' said Newman, in conversation with Harlow and Easton. 'There's one bloke there wot puts up twenty-five rolls o' paper in a day an' trims and pastes for 'imself; and as for the painters, nearly everyone of 'em gets over as much work as us three put together, and if you're working there you've got to do the same or get the sack.'

However much truth or falsehood or exaggeration there may have been in the stories of the sweating and driving that prevailed at Dauber and Botchit's, it was an indisputable fact that the other builders found it very difficult to compete with them, and between the lot of them what work there was to do was all finished or messed up in about a quarter of the time that it would have taken to do it properly.

By the end of September there were great numbers of men out of employment, and the practical persons who controlled the town were already preparing to enact the usual farce of 'Dealing' with the distress that was certain to ensue. The Rev. Mr. Bosher talked of reopening the Labour Yard; the secretary of the O.B.S. appealed for more money and cast-off clothing and boots – the funds of the Society had been depleted by the payment of his quarter's salary. There were rumours that the Soup Kitchen would be reopened at an early date for the sale of 'nourishment', and charitable persons began to talk of Rummage Sales and soup tickets.

Now and then, whenever a 'job' 'came in', a few of Rushton's men were able to put in a few hours' work, but Barrington never went back. His manner of life was the subject of much speculation on the part of his former workmates, who were not a little puzzled by the fact that he was much better dressed than they had ever known him to be before, and that he was never without money. He generally had a tanner or a bob to lend, and was always ready to stand a drink, to say nothing of what it must have cost him for the quantities of Socialist pamphlets and leaflets that he gave away broadcast. He lodged over at Windley, but he used to take his meals at a little coffee tavern down town, where he used often to invite one or two of his old mates to take dinner with him. It sometimes happened that one of them would invite him home of an evening, to drink a cup of tea, or to see some curiosity that the other thought would interest him, and on these occasions – if there were any children in the house to which they were going – Barrington usually made a point of going into a shop on their way, and buying a bag of cakes or fruit for them.

All sorts of theories were put forward to account for his apparent affluence. Some said he was a toff in disguise; others that he had rich relations who were ashamed of him because he was a Socialist, and who allowed him so much a week so long as he kept away from them and did not use his real name. Some of the Liberals said that he was in the pay of the Tories, who were seeking by underhand methods to split up the Progressive Liberal Party. Just about that time several burglaries took place in the town, the thieves getting clear away with their plunder, and this circumstance led to a dark rumour that Barrington was the culprit, and that it was these ill-gotten gains that he was spending so freely.

About the middle of October an event happened that threw the town into a state of wild excitement, and such comparatively unimportant subjects as unemployment and starvation were almost forgotten.

Sir Graball D'Encloseland had been promoted to a yet higher post in the service of the country that he owned such a large part of; he was not only to have a higher and more honourable position, but also – as was nothing but right – a higher salary. His pay was to be increased to seven thousand five hundred a year or one hundred and fifty pounds per week, and in consequence of this promotion it was necessary for him to resign his seat and seek re-election . . .

[[The ragged-trousered Tory workmen as they loitered about the streets, their stomachs empty, said to each other that it was a great honour for Mugsborough that their Member should be promoted in this way. They boasted about it and assumed as much swagger in their gait as their broken boots permitted.

They stuck election cards bearing Sir Graball's photograph in their windows and tied bits of blue and yellow ribbon – Sir Graball's colours – on their underfed children.

The Liberals were furious. They said that an election had been sprung upon them – they had been taken a mean advantage of – they had no candidate ready.]]

They had no complaint to make about the salary, all they complained of was the short notice. It wasn't fair because while they – the leading Liberals – had been treating the electors with the contemptuous indifference that is customary, Sir Graball D'Encloseland had been most active amongst his constituents for months past, cunningly preparing for the contest. He had really been electioneering for the past six months! Last winter he had kicked off at quite a number of football matches besides doing all sorts of things for the local teams. He had joined the Buffalos and the Druids,[123] been elected President of the Skull and Cross-bones Boys' Society, and, although he was not himself an abstainer, he was so friendly to Temperance that he had on several occasions, taken the chair at teetotal meetings, to say nothing of the teas to the poor school children and things of that sort. In short, he had been quite an active politician, [[in the Tory sense of the word, for months past and the poor Liberals had not smelt a rat until the election was sprung upon them.

A hurried meeting of the Liberal Three Hundred was held, and a deputation sent to London to find a candidate but as there was only a week before polling day they were unsuccessful in their mission. Another meeting was held, presided over by Mr. Adam Sweater – Rushton and Didlum also being present.]]

Profound dejection was depicted on the countenances of those assembled slave-drivers as they listened to the delegates' report. The sombre silence that followed was broken at length by Mr. Rushton, who suddenly started up and said that he began to think they had made a mistake in going outside the constituency at all to look for a man. It was strange but true that a prophet never received honour in his own land.[124] They had been wasting the precious time running about all over the country, begging and praying for a candidate, and overlooking the fact that they had in their midst a gentleman – a fellow townsman, who, he believed, would have a better chance of success than any stranger. Surely they would all agree – if they could only prevail upon him to stand – that Adam Sweater would be an ideal Liberal Candidate!

While Mr. Rushton was speaking the drooping spirits of the Three Hundred were reviving, and at the name of Sweater they all began to clap their hands and stamp their feet. Loud shouts of enthusiastic approval burst forth, and cries of 'Good old Sweater' resounded through the room.

When Sweater rose to reply, the tumult died away as suddenly as it had commenced. He thanked them for the honour they were conferring upon him. There was no time to waste in words or idle compliments; rather than allow the Enemy to have a walk-over, he would accede to their request and contest the seat.

A roar of applause burst from the throats of the delighted Three Hundred.

Outside the hall in which the meeting was being held a large crowd of poverty stricken Liberal working men, many of them wearing broken boots and other men's cast off clothing, was waiting to hear the report of the slave-drivers deputation, and as soon as Sweater had consented to be nominated, Didlum rushed and opened the window overlooking the street and shouted the good news down to the crowd, which joined in the cheering. In response to their demands for a speech, Sweater brought his obese carcase to the window and addressed a few words to them, reminding them of the shortness of the time at their disposal, and intreating them to work hard in order that the Grand old Flag might be carried to victory.

At such times these people forgot all about unemployment and starvation, and became enthusiastic about 'Grand old Flags'. Their devotion to this flag was so great that so long as they were able to carry it to victory, they did not mind being poverty stricken and hungry and ragged; all that mattered was to score off their hated 'enemies' their fellow countrymen the Tories, and carry the grand old flag to victory. The fact that they had carried the flag to victory so often in the past without obtaining any of the spoils, did not seem to damp their ardour in the least. Being philanthropists, they were content – after winning the victory – that their masters should always do the looting.

At the conclusion of Sweater's remarks the philanthropists gave three frantic cheers and then someone in the crowd shouted 'What's the colour?' After a hasty consultation with Rushton, who being a 'master' decorator, was thought to be an authority on colours – green – grass green – was decided upon, and the information was shouted down to the crowd, who cheered again. Then a rush was made to Sweater's Emporium and several yards of cheap green ribbon were bought, and divided up into little pieces, which they tied into their buttonholes, and thus appropriately decorated, formed themselves into military order, four deep, and marched through all the principal streets, up and down the Grand Parade, round and round the Fountain, and finally over the hill to Windley, singing to the tune of 'Tramp, tramp, tramp, the Boys are marching':

> 'Vote, Vote, Vote for Adam Sweater!
> Hang old Closeland on a tree!
> Adam Sweater is our man,
> And we'll have him if we can,
> Then we'll always have the biggest loaf for tea.'

The spectacle presented by these men – some of them with grey heads and beards – as they marked time or tramped along singing this childish twaddle, would have been amusing if it had not been disgusting.

By way of variety they sang several other things, including:

> 'We'll hang ole Closeland
> On a sour apple tree,'

and

> 'Rally, Rally, men of Windley,
> For Sweater's sure to win.'

As they passed the big church in Quality Street, the clock began to strike. It was one of those that strike four chimes at each quarter of the hour. It was now ten o'clock so there were sixteen musical chimes:

Ding, dong! Ding Dong!
Ding dong! Ding dong!
Ding dong! Ding dong!
Ding dong! Ding dong! . . .

[They all chanted 'A-dam Sweat-er in time with the striking clock.
In the same way the Tories would chant:]

'Grab – all Close – land!
Grab – all Close – land!
Grab – all Close – land!
Grab – all Close – land!'

The Town was soon deluged with mendacious literature and
smothered with huge posters:

'Vote for Adam Sweater!
The Working-man's Friend!'
'Vote for Sweater and Temperance Reform.'
'Vote for Sweater – Free Trade and Cheap Food.'

or

'Vote for D'Encloseland: Tariff Reform and Plenty of Work!'

This beautiful ideal – 'Plenty of Work' – appealed strongly to
the Tory workmen. They seemed to regard themselves and their
children as a sort of machines or beasts of burden, created for the
purpose of working for the benefit of other people. They did not
think it right that they should Live, and enjoy the benefits of
civilisation. All they desired for themselves and their children was
'Plenty of Work'.

They marched about the streets singing their Marseillaise, 'Work,
Boys, Work and be contented', to the tune of 'Tramp, tramp, tramp
the Boys are marching', and at intervals as they tramped along, they
gave three cheers for Sir Graball, Tariff Reform, and – Plenty of
Work.

Both sides imported gangs of hired orators who held forth every
night at the corners of the principal streets, and on the open spaces
from portable platforms, and from motor cars and lorries. The
Tories said that the Liberal Party in the House of Commons was
composed principally of scoundrels and fools, [[the Liberals said
that the Tory Party were fools and scoundrels. A host of richly
dressed canvassers descended upon Windley in carriages and motor

cars, and begged for votes from the poverty-stricken working men who lived there.

One evening a Liberal demonstration was held at the Cross Roads on Windley Hill. Notwithstanding the cold weather, there was a great crowd of shabbily dressed people, many of whom had not had a really good meal for months. It was a clear night.]] The moon was at the full, and the scene was further illuminated by the fitful glare of several torches, stuck on the end of twelve-foot poles. The platform was a large lorry, and there were several speakers, including Adam Sweater himself and a real live Liberal Peer – Lord Ammenegg. This individual had made a considerable fortune in the grocery and provision line, and had been elevated to the Peerage by the last Liberal Government on account of his services to the Party, and in consideration of other considerations.

Both Sweater and Ammenegg were to speak at two other meetings that night and were not expected at Windley until about eight-thirty, so to keep the ball rolling till they arrived, several other gentlemen, including Rushton – who presided – and Didlum, and one of the five pounds a week orators, addressed the meeting. Mingled with the crowd were about twenty rough-looking men – strangers to the town – who wore huge green rosettes and loudly applauded the speakers. They also distributed Sweater literature and cards with lists of the different meetings that were to be held during the election. These men were bullies hired by Sweater's agent. They came from the neighbourhood of Seven Dials in London[125] and were paid ten shillings a day. One of their duties was to incite the crowd to bash anyone who disturbed the meetings or tried to put awkward questions to the speakers.

The hired orator was a tall, slight man with dark hair, beard and moustache, he might have been called well-looking if it had not been for an ugly scar upon his forehead, which gave him a rather sinister appearance. He was an effective speaker; the audience punctuated his speech with cheers, and when he wound up with an earnest appeal to them – as working men – to vote for Adam Sweater, their enthusiasm knew no bounds.

'I've seen him somewhere before,' remarked Barrington, who was standing in the crowd with Harlow, Owen and Easton.

'So have I,' said Owen, with a puzzled expression. 'But for the life of me, I can't remember where.'

Harlow and Easton also thought they had seen the man before, but their speculations were put an end to by the roar of cheering that heralded the arrival of the motor car, containing Adam Sweater and his friend, Lord Ammenegg. Unfortunately, those who had arranged the meeting had forgotten to provide a pair of steps, so Sweater found it a matter of considerable difficulty to mount the platform. However, while his friends were hoisting and pushing him up, the meeting beguiled the time by singing:

'Vote, vote, vote for Adam Sweater.'

After a terrible struggle they succeeded in getting him on to the cart, and while he was recovering his wind, Rushton made a few remarks to the crowd. Sweater then advanced to the front, but in consequence of the cheering and singing, he was unable to make himself heard for several minutes.

When at length he was able to proceed, he made a very clever speech – it had been specially written for him and had cost ten guineas. A large part of it consisted of warnings against the dangers of Socialism. Sweater had carefully rehearsed this speech and he delivered it very effectively. Some of those Socialists, he said, were well-meaning but mistaken people, who did not realise the harm that would result if their extraordinary ideas were ever put into practice. He lowered his voice to a blood-curdling stage whisper as he asked:

'What is this Socialism that we hear so much about, but which so few understand? What is it, and what does it mean?'

Then, raising his voice till it rang through the air and fell upon the ears of the assembled multitude like the clanging of a funeral bell, he continued:

'It is madness! Chaos! Anarchy! It means Ruin! Black Ruin for the rich, and consequently, of course, Blacker Ruin still for the poor!'

As Sweater paused, a thrill of horror ran through the meeting. Men wearing broken boots and with patches upon the seats and knees, and ragged fringes round the bottoms of the legs of their trousers, grew pale, and glanced apprehensively at each other. If ever Socialism did come to pass, they evidently thought it very probable that they would have to walk about in a sort of prehistoric highland costume, without any trousers or boots at all.

Toil-worn women, most of them dressed in other women's shabby cast off clothing – weary, tired-looking mothers who fed their children for the most part on adulterated tea, tinned skimmed milk and bread and margarine, grew furious as they thought of the wicked Socialists who were trying to bring Ruin upon them.

It never occurred to any of these poor people that they were in a condition of Ruin, Black Ruin, already. But if Sweater had suddenly found himself reduced to the same social condition as the majority of those he addressed, there is not much doubt that he would have thought that he was in a condition of Black Ruin.

The awful silence that had fallen on the panic-stricken crowd, was presently broken by a ragged-trousered Philanthropist, who shouted out:

'We knows wot they are, sir. Most of 'em is chaps wot's got tired of workin' for their livin', so they wants us to keep 'em.'

Encouraged by numerous expressions of approval from the other Philanthropists, the man continued:

'But we ain't such fools as they thinks, and so they'll find out next Monday. Most of 'em wants 'angin', and I wouldn't mind lendin' a 'and with the rope myself.'

Applause and laughter greeted these noble sentiments, and Sweater resumed his address, when another man – evidently a Socialist – for he was accompanied by three or four others who like himself wore red ties – interrupted and said that he would like to ask him a question. No notice was taken of this request either by Mr. Sweater or the chairman, but a few angry cries of 'Order!' came from the crowd. Sweater continued, but the man again interrupted and the cries of the crowd became more threatening. Rushton started up and said that he could not allow the speaker to be interrupted, but if the gentleman would wait till the end of the meeting, he would have an opportunity of asking his question then.

The man said he would wait as desired; Sweater resumed his oration, and presently the interrupter and his friends found themselves surrounded by the gang of hired bullies who wore the big rosettes and who glared menacingly at them.

Sweater concluded his speech with an appeal to the crowd to deal a 'Slashing Blow at the Enemy' next Monday, and then amid a storm of applause, Lord Ammenegg stepped to the front. He said that he did not intend to inflict a long speech upon them that evening, and as it was nomination day to-morrow he would not be able to have the honour of addressing them again during the election; but even if he had wished to make a long speech, it would be very difficult after the brilliant and eloquent address they had just listened to from Mr. Sweater, for it seemed to him (Ammenegg) that Adam Sweater had left nothing for anyone else to say. But he would like to tell them of a Thought that had occurred to him that evening. They read in the Bible that the Wise Men came from the East. Windley, as they all knew, was the East end of the town. They were the men of the East, and he was sure that next Monday they would prove that they were the Wise Men of the East, by voting for Adam Sweater and putting him at the top of the poll with a 'Thumping Majority'.

The Wise Men of the East greeted Ammenegg's remarks with prolonged, imbecile cheers, and amid the tumult his Lordship and Sweater got into the motor car and cleared off without giving the man with the red tie or anyone else who desired to ask questions any opportunity of doing so. Rushton and the other leaders got into another motor car, and followed the first to take part in another meeting down-town, which was to be addressed by the great Sir Featherstone Blood.

The crowd now resolved itself into military order, headed by the men with torches and a large white banner on which was written in huge black letters, 'Our man is Adam Sweater'.

They marched down the hill singing, and when they reached the Fountain on the Grand Parade they saw another crowd holding a meeting there. These were Tories and they became so infuriated at the sound of the Liberal songs and by the sight of the banner, that they abandoned their meeting and charged the processionists. A free fight ensued. Both sides fought like savages, but as the Liberals were outnumbered by about three to one, they were driven off the field with great slaughter; most of the torch poles were taken from them, and the banner was torn to ribbons. Then the Tories went back to the Fountain carrying the captured torches, and singing to the tune of 'Has anyone seen a German Band?':

> 'Has anyone seen a Lib'ral Flag,
> Lib'ral Flag, Lib'ral Flag?'

While the Tories resumed their meeting at the Fountain, the Liberals rallied in one of the back streets. Messengers were sent in various directions for reinforcements, and about half an hour afterwards they emerged from their retreat and swooped down upon the Tory meeting. They overturned the platform, recaptured their torches, tore the enemy's banner to tatters and drove them from their position. Then the Liberals in their turn paraded the streets singing 'Has anyone seen a Tory Flag?' and [proceeded to the hall where Sir Featherstone was speaking, arriving as the audience left.]

The crowd that came pouring out of the hall was worked up to a frenzy of enthusiasm, for the speech they had just listened to had been a sort of manifesto to the country.

In response to the cheering of the processionists – who, of course, had not heard the speech, but were cheering from force of habit – Sir Featherstone Blood stood up in the carriage and addressed the crowd, briefly outlining the great measures of Social Reform that his party proposed to enact to improve the condition of the working classes; and as they listened, the Wise Men grew delirious with enthusiasm. He referred to Land Taxes and Death Duties which would provide money to build battleships to protect the property of the rich, and provide Work for the poor. Another tax was to provide a nice, smooth road for the rich to ride upon in motor cars – and to provide Work for the poor. Another tax would be used for Development, which would also make Work for the poor. And so on. A great point was made of the fact that the rich were actually to be made to pay something towards the cost of their road themselves! But nothing was said about how they would get the money to do it. No reference was made to how the workers would be sweated and driven and starved to earn Dividends and Rent and Interest and Profits to put into the pockets of the rich before the latter would be able to pay for anything at all.

'These are the things, Gentlemen, that we propose to do for you, and, at the rate of progress which we propose to adopt, I say without fear of contradiction, that within the next Five Hundred years we shall so reform social conditions in this country, that the working classes will be able to enjoy some of the benefits of civilisation.

'The only question before you is: Are you willing to wait for Five Hundred Years?'

'Yes, Sir,' shouted the Wise Men with enthusiasm at the glorious [prospect].

'Yes, Sir: we'll wait a thousand years if you like, Sir!'

'I've been waiting all my life,' said one poor old veteran, who had assisted to 'carry the "Old Flag" to victory' times out of number in the past and who for his share of the spoils of those victories was now in a condition of abject, miserable poverty, with the portals of the workhouse yawning open to receive him; 'I've waited all my life, hoping and trusting for better conditions so a few more years won't make much difference to *me*.'

'Don't you trouble to 'urry yourself, Sir,' shouted another Solomon in the crowd. 'We don't mind waiting. Take your own time, Sir. You know better than the likes of us 'ow long it ought to take.'

In conclusion, the great man warned them against being led away by the Socialists, those foolish, unreasonable, impractical people who wanted to see an immediate improvement in their condition; and he reminded them that Rome was not built in a day.

The Wise Men applauded lustily. It did not appear to occur to any of them that the rate at which the ancient Romans conducted their building operations had nothing whatever to do with the case.

Sir Featherstone Blood sat down amid a wild storm of cheering, and then the procession reformed, and, reinforced by the audience from the hall, they proceeded to march about the dreary streets, singing, to the tune of the 'Men of Harlech':

> 'Vote for Sweater, Vote for Sweater!
> Vote for Sweater, VOTE FOR SWEATER!
>
> 'He's the Man, who has a plan,
> To liberate and reinstate the workers!
>
> 'Men of Mugs'bro', show your mettle,
> Let them see that you're in fettle!
> Once for all this question settle
> Sweater shall Prevail!'

The carriage containing Sir Featherstone, Adam Sweater, and Rushton and Didlum was in the middle of the procession. The banner and the torches were at the head, and the grandeur of the scene was heightened by four men who walked – two on each side of the carriage, burning green fire in frying pans. As they passed by the Slave Market, a poor, shabbily dressed wretch whose boots were so worn and rotten that they were almost falling off his feet, climbed up a lamp-post, and taking off his cap waved it in the air and shrieked out: 'Three Cheers for Sir Featherstone Blood, our future Prime Minister!'

The Philanthropists cheered themselves hoarse and finally took the horses out of the traces and harnessed themselves to the carriage instead.

' 'Ow much wages will Sir Featherstone get if 'e is made Prime Minister?' asked Harlow of another Philanthropist who was also pushing up behind the carriage.

'Five thousand a year,' replied the other, who by some strange chance happened to know. 'That comes to a 'underd pounds a week.'

'Little enough, too, for a man like 'im,' said Harlow.

'You're right, mate,' said the other, with deep sympathy in his voice. 'Last time 'e 'eld office 'e was only in for five years, so 'e only made twenty-five thousand pounds out of it. Of course 'e got a pension as well – two thousand a year for life, I think it is; but after all, what's that – for a man like 'im?'

'Nothing,' replied Harlow, in a tone of commiseration, and Newman, who was also there, helping to drag the carriage, said that it ought to be at least double that amount.

However, they found some consolation in knowing that Sir Featherstone would not have to wait till he was seventy before he obtained his pension; he would get it directly he came out of office.

*   *   *

The following evening Barrington, Owen and a few others of the same way of thinking, who had subscribed enough money between them to purchase a lot of Socialist leaflets, employed themselves distributing them to the crowds at the Liberal and Tory meetings, and whilst they were doing this they frequently became involved in arguments with the supporters of the capitalist system. In their attempts to persuade others to refrain from voting for either of the candidates, they were opposed even by some who professed to believe in Socialism, who said that as there was no better Socialist candidate the thing to do was to vote for the better of the two. This was the view of Harlow and Easton, whom they met. Harlow had a green ribbon in his buttonhole, but Easton wore D'Encloselarid's colours.

One man said that if he had his way, all those who had votes should be compelled to record them – whether they liked it or not – or be disenfranchised! Barrington asked him if he believed in Tariff Reform. The man said no.

'Why not?' demanded Barrington.

The other replied that he opposed Tariff Reform because he believed it would ruin the country. Barrington inquired if he were a supporter of Socialism. The man said he was not, and when further questioned he said that he believed if it were ever adopted it would bring black ruin upon the country – he believed this because Mr. Sweater had said so. When Barrington asked him – supposing there were only two candidates, one a Socialist and the other a Tariff Reformer – how would he like to be compelled to vote for one of them, he was at a loss for an answer . . .

During the next few days the contest continued. The hired orators continued to pour forth their streams of eloquence; and tons of literature flooded the town. The walls were covered with huge posters: 'Another Liberal Lie.' 'Another Tory Fraud.'

Unconsciously each of these two parties put in some splendid work for Socialism, in so much that each of them thoroughly exposed the hypocrisy of the other. If the people had only had the sense, they might have seen that the quarrel between the Liberal and Tory leaders was merely a quarrel between thieves over the spoil; but unfortunately most of the people had not the sense to perceive this. They were blinded by bigoted devotion to their parties, and – inflamed with maniacal enthusiasm – thought of nothing but 'carrying their flags to victory'.

At considerable danger to themselves, Barrington, Owen and the other Socialists continued to distribute their leaflets and to heckle the Liberal and Tory speakers. They asked the Tories to explain the prevalence of unemployment and poverty in protected countries, like Germany and America, and at Sweater's meetings they requested to be informed what was the Liberal remedy for unemployment. From both parties the Socialists obtained the same kinds of answer – threats of violence and requests 'not to disturb the meeting'.

These Socialists held quite a lot of informal meetings on their own. Every now and then when they were giving their leaflets away, some unwary supporter of the capitalist system would start an argument, and soon a crowd would gather round and listen.

Sometimes the Socialists succeeded in arguing their opponents to an absolute standstill, for the Liberals and Tories found it impossible to deny that machinery is the cause of the overcrowded state of the labour market; that the overcrowded labour market is the cause of unemployment; that the fact of there being always an army of unemployed waiting to take other men's jobs away from them destroys the independence of those who are in employment and keeps them in subjection to their masters. They found it impossible to deny that this machinery is being used, not for the benefit of all, but to make fortunes for a few. In short, they were unable to disprove that the monopoly of the land and machinery by a comparatively few persons, is the cause of the poverty of the majority. But when these arguments that they were unable to answer were put before them and when it was pointed out that the only possible remedy was the Public Owner-ship and Management of the Means of production,[126] they remained angrily silent, having no alternative plan to suggest.

At other times the meeting resolved itself into a number of quarrel-some disputes between the Liberals and Tories that formed the crowd, which split itself up into a lot of little groups and whatever the original subject might have been they soon drifted to a hundred other things, for most of the supporters of the present system seemed incapable of pursuing any one subject to its logical conclusion. A discussion would be started about something or other; presently an unimportant side issue would crop up, then the original subject would be left unfinished, and they would argue and shout about the side issue. In a little while another side issue would arise, and then the first side issue would be abandoned also unfinished, and an angry wrangle about the second issue would ensue, the original subject being altogether forgotten.

They did not seem to really desire to discover the truth or to find out the best way to bring about an improvement in their condition, their only object seemed to be to score off their opponents.

Usually after one of these arguments, Owen would wander off by himself, with his head throbbing and a feeling of unutterable depression and misery at his heart; weighed down by a growing conviction of the hopelessness of everything, of the folly of expecting that his fellow workmen would ever be willing to try to understand for themselves the causes that produced their sufferings. It was not that those causes were so obscure that it required exceptional intelligence to perceive them; the causes of all the misery were so apparent that a little child could easily be made to understand both the disease and the remedy; but it seemed to him that the majority of his fellow workmen had become so convinced of their own intellectual inferiority that they did not dare to rely on their own intelligence to guide them, preferring to resign the management of their affairs unreservedly into the hands of those who battened upon and robbed them. They did not know the causes of the poverty that perpetually held them and their children in its cruel grip, and – they did not want to know! And if one explained those causes to them in such language and in such a manner that they were almost compelled to understand, and afterwards pointed out to them the obvious remedy, they were neither glad nor responsive, but remained silent and were angry because they found themselves unable to answer and disprove.

They remained silent; afraid to trust their own intelligence, and the reason of this attitude was that they had to choose between the evidence of their own intelligence, and the stories told them by their masters and exploiters. And when it came to making this choice they deemed it safer to follow their old guides, than to rely on their own judgement, because from their very infancy they had had drilled into them the doctrine of their own mental and social inferiority, and their conviction of the truth of this doctrine was voiced in the degraded expression that fell so frequently from their lips, when speaking of themselves and each other – 'The Likes of Us!'

They did not know the causes of their poverty, they did not want to know, they did not want to hear.

All they desired was to be left alone so that they might continue to worship and follow those who took advantage of their simplicity, and robbed them of the fruits of their toil; their old leaders, the fools or scoundrels who fed them with words, who had led them into the desolation where they now seemed to be content to grind out treasure for their masters, and to starve when those masters did not find it profitable to employ them. It was as if a flock of foolish sheep placed themselves under the protection of a pack of ravening wolves.

Several times the small band of Socialists narrowly escaped being mobbed, but they succeeded in disposing of most of their leaflets without any serious trouble. Towards the latter part of one evening Barrington and Owen became separated from the others, and shortly afterwards these two lost each other in the crush.

About nine o'clock, Barrington was in a large Liberal crowd, listening to the same hired orator who had spoken a few evenings before on the hill – the man with the scar on his forehead. The crowd was applauding him loudly and Barrington again fell to wondering where he had seen this man before. As on the previous occasion, this speaker made no reference to Socialism, confining himself to other matters. Barrington examined him closely, trying to recall under what circumstances they had met previously, and presently he remembered that this was one of the Socialists who had come with the band of cyclists into the town that Sunday morning, away back at the beginning of the summer, the man who had come afterwards with the van, and who had been struck down by a stone while attempting to speak from the platform of the van, the man who had been nearly killed by the upholders of the capitalist system. It was the same man! The Socialist had been clean-shaven – this man wore beard and moustache – but Barrington was certain he was the same.

When the man had concluded his speech he got down and stood in the shade behind the platform, while someone else addressed the meeting, and Barrington went round to where he was standing, intending to speak to him.

All around them, pandemonium reigned supreme. They were in the vicinity of the Slave Market, near the Fountain, on the Grand

Parade, where several roads met; there was a meeting going on at every corner, and a number of others in different parts of the roadway and on the pavement of the Parade. Some of these meetings were being carried on by two or three men, who spoke in turn from small, portable platforms they carried with them, and placed wherever they thought there was a chance of getting an audience.

Every now and then some of these poor wretches – they were all paid speakers – were surrounded and savagely mauled and beaten by a hostile crowd. If they were Tariff Reformers the Liberals mobbed them, and vice versa. Lines of rowdies swaggered to and fro, arm in arm, singing, 'Vote, Vote, Vote, for good ole Closeland' or 'good ole Sweater', according as they were green or blue and yellow. Gangs of hooligans paraded up and down, armed with sticks, singing, howling, cursing and looking for someone to hit. Others stood in groups on the pavement with their hands thrust in their pockets, or leaned against walls or the shutters of the shops with expressions of ecstatic imbecility on their faces, chanting the mournful dirge to the tune of the church chimes,

> 'Good – ole – Sweate – er
> Good – ole – Sweat – er
> Good – ole – Sweat – er
> Good – ole – Sweat – er'.

Other groups – to the same tune – sang 'Good – ole – Close – land'; and every now and again they used to leave off singing and begin to beat each other. Fights used to take place, often between workmen, about the respective merits of Adam Sweater and Sir Graball D'Encloseland.

The walls were covered with huge Liberal and Tory posters, which showed in every line the contempt of those who published them for the intelligence of the working men to whom they were addressed. There was one Tory poster that represented the interior of a public house; in front of the bar, with a quart pot in his hand, a clay pipe in his mouth, and a load of tools on his back, stood a degraded-looking brute who represented the Tory ideal of what an Englishman should be; the letterpress on the poster said it was a man! This is the ideal of manhood that they hold up to the majority of their fellow countrymen, but privately – amongst themselves – the Tory aristocrats regard such 'men' with far less respect than they do the lower animals. Horses or dogs, for instance.

The Liberal posters were not quite so offensive. They were more cunning, more specious, more hypocritical and consequently more calculated to mislead and deceive the more intelligent of the voters.

When Barrington got round to the back of the platform, he found the man with the scarred face standing alone and gloomily silent in the shadow. Barrington gave him one of the Socialist leaflets, which he took, and after glancing at it, put it in his coat pocket without making any remark.

'I hope you'll excuse me for asking, but were you not formerly a Socialist?' said Barrington.

Even in the semi-darkness Barrington saw the other man flush deeply and then become very pale, and the unsightly scar upon his forehead showed with ghastly distinctiveness.

'I am still a Socialist: no man who has once been a Socialist can ever cease to be one.'

'You seem to have accomplished that impossibility, to judge by the work you are at present engaged in. You must have changed your opinions since you were here last.'

'No one who has been a Socialist can ever cease to be one. It is impossible for a man who has once acquired knowledge ever to relinquish it. A Socialist is one who understands the causes of the misery and degradation we see all around us; who knows the only remedy, and knows that that remedy – the state of society that will be called Socialism – must eventually be adopted; is the only alternative to the extermination of the majority of the working people; but it does not follow that everyone who has sense enough to acquire that amount of knowledge, must, in addition, be willing to sacrifice himself in order to help to bring that state of society into being. When I first acquired that knowledge,' he continued, bitterly, 'I was eager to tell the good news to others. I sacrificed my time, my money, and my health in order that I might teach others what I had learned myself. I did it willingly and happily, because I thought they would be glad to hear, and that they were worth the sacrifices I made for their sakes. But I know better now.'

'Even if you no longer believe in working for Socialism, there's no need to work *against* it. If you are not disposed to sacrifice yourself in order to do good to others, you might at least refrain from doing evil. If you don't want to help to bring about a better state of affairs, there's no reason why you should help to perpetuate the present system.'

The other man laughed bitterly. 'Oh yes, there is, and a very good reason too.'

'I don't think you could show me a reason,' said Barrington.

The man with the scar laughed again, the same unpleasant, mirthless laugh, and thrusting his hand into his trouser pocket drew it out again full of silver coins, amongst which one or two gold pieces glittered.

'That is my reason. When I devoted my life and what abilities I possess to the service of my fellow workmen; when I sought to teach them how to break their chains; when I tried to show them how they might save their children from poverty and shameful servitude, I did not want them to give me money. I did it for love. And they paid me with hatred and injury. But since I have been helping their masters to rob them, they have treated me with respect.'

Barrington made no reply and the other man, having returned the money to his pocket, indicated the crowd with a sweep of his hand.

'Look at them!' he continued with a contemptuous laugh. 'Look at them! the people you are trying to make idealists of! Look at them! Some of them howling and roaring like wild beasts, or laughing like idiots, others standing with dull and stupid faces devoid of any trace of intelligence or expression, listening to the speakers whose words convey no meaning to their stultified minds, and others with their eyes gleaming with savage hatred of their fellow men, watching eagerly for an opportunity to provoke a quarrel that they may gratify their brutal natures by striking someone – their eyes are hungry for the sight of blood! Can't you see that these people, whom you are trying to make understand your plan for the regeneration of the world, your doctrine of universal brotherhood and love are for the most part – intellectually – on a level with Hottentots? The only things they feel any real interest in are beer, football, betting and – of course – one other subject. Their highest ambition is to be allowed to Work. And they desire nothing better for their children!

'[They have never had an] independent thought in their lives. These are the people whom you hope to inspire with lofty ideals! You might just as well try to make a gold brooch out of a lump of dung! Try to reason with them, to uplift them, to teach them the way to higher things. Devote your whole life and intelligence to the work of trying to get better conditions for them, and you will find that they themselves are the enemy you will have to fight against. They'll hate you, and, if they get the chance, they'll tear you to pieces. But if you're a sensible man you'll use whatever talents and intelligence you possess for your own benefit. Don't think about Socialism or any other "ism". Concentrate your mind on getting money – it doesn't matter how you get it, but – get it. If you can't get it honestly, get it dishonestly, but get it! it is the only thing that counts. Do as I do – rob them! exploit them! and then they'll have some respect for you.'

'There's something in what you say,' replied Barrington, after a long pause, 'but it's not all. Circumstances make us what we are; and anyhow, the children are worth fighting for.'

'You may think so now,' said the other, 'but you'll come to see it my way some day. As for the children – if their parents are satisfied to let them grow up to be half-starved drudges for other people, I don't see why you or I need trouble about it. If you like to listen to reason,' he continued after a pause, 'I can put you on to something that will be worth more to you than all your Socialism.'

'What do you mean?'

'Look here: you're a Socialist; well, I'm a Socialist too: that is, I have sense enough to believe that Socialism is practical and inevitable and right; it will come when the majority of the people are sufficiently enlightened to demand it, but that enlightenment will never be brought about by reasoning or arguing with them, for these people are simply not intellectually capable of abstract reasoning – they can't grasp theories. You know what the late Lord Salisbury said about them when somebody proposed to give them some free libraries: He said: "They don't want libraries: give them a circus." You see these Liberals and Tories understand the sort of people they have to deal with; they know that although their bodies are the bodies of grown men, their minds are the minds of little children. That is why it has been possible to deceive and bluff and rob them for so long. But your party persists in regarding them as rational beings, and that's where you make a mistake – you're simply wasting your time.

'The only way in which it is possible to teach these people is by means of object lessons, and those are being placed before them in increasing numbers every day. The trustification of industry – the object lesson which demonstrates the possibility of collective owner-ship – will in time compel even these to understand, and by the time they have learnt that, they will also have learned by bitter experience and not from theoretical teaching, that they must either own the trusts or perish, and then, and not till then, they will achieve Socialism. But meanwhile we have this election. Do you think it will make any real difference – for good or evil – which of these two men is elected?'

'No.'

'Well, you can't keep them both out – you have no candidate of your own – why should you object to earning a few pounds by helping one of them to get in? There are plenty of voters who are doubtful what to do; as you and I know there is every excuse for them being unable to make up their minds which of these two candidates is the worse, a word from your party would decide them. Since you have no candidate of your own you will be doing no harm to Socialism and you will be doing yourself a bit of good. If you like to come along with me now, I'll introduce you to Sweater's agent – no one need know anything about it.'

He slipped his arm through Barrington's, but the latter released himself.

'Please yourself,' said the other with an affectation of indifference. 'You know your own business best. You may choose to be a Jesus Christ if you like, but for my part I'm finished. For the future I intend to look after myself. As for these people – they vote for what they want; they get – what they vote for; and by God, they deserve nothing better! They are being beaten with whips of their own choosing and if I had my way they should be chastised with scorpions![127] For them, the present system means joyless drudgery, semi-starvation, rags and premature death. They vote for it all and uphold it. Well, let them have what they vote for – let them drudge – let them starve!'

The man with the scarred face ceased speaking, and for some moments Barrington did not reply.

'I suppose there is some excuse for your feeling as you do,' he said slowly at last, 'but it seems to me that you do not make enough allowance for the circumstances. From their infancy most of them have been taught by priests and parents to regard themselves and their own class with contempt – a sort of lower animals – and to regard those who possess wealth with veneration, as superior beings. The idea that they are really human creatures, naturally absolutely the same as their so-called betters, naturally equal in every way, naturally different from them only in those ways in which their so-called superiors differ from each other, and inferior to them only because they have been deprived of education, culture and opportunity – you know as well as I do that they have all been taught to regard that idea as preposterous.

'The self styled "Christian" priests who say – with their tongues in their cheeks – that God is our Father and that all men are brethren, have succeeded in convincing the majority of the "brethren" that it is their duty to be content in their degradation, and to order themselves lowly and reverently towards their masters. Your resentment should be directed against the deceivers, not against the dupes.'

The other man laughed bitterly.

'Well, go and try to undeceive them,' he said, as he returned to the platform in response to a call from his associates. 'Go and try to teach them that the Supreme Being made the earth and all its fulness for the use and benefit of all His children. Go and try to explain to them that they are poor in body and mind and social condition, not because of any natural inferiority, but because they have been robbed of their inheritance. Go and try to show them how to secure that inheritance for themselves and their children – and see how grateful they'll be to you.'

For the next hour Barrington walked about the crowded streets in a dispirited fashion. His conversation with the renegade seemed to have taken all the heart out of him. He still had a number of the leaflets, but the task of distributing them had suddenly grown distasteful and after a while he discontinued it. All his enthusiasm was gone. Like one awakened from a dream he saw the people who surrounded him in a different light. For the first time he properly appreciated the offensiveness of most of those to whom he offered the handbills; some, without even troubling to ascertain what they were about, rudely refused to accept them; some took them and after glancing at the printing, crushed them in their hands and ostentatiously threw them away. Others, who recognised him as a Socialist, angrily or contemptuously declined them, often with curses or injurious words.

His attention was presently attracted to a crowd of about thirty or forty people, congregated near a gas lamp at the roadside. The sound of many angry voices rose from the centre of this group, and as he stood on the outskirts of the crowd, Barrington, being tall, was able to look into the centre, where he saw Owen. The light of the street lamp fell full upon the latter's pale face, as he stood silent in the midst of a ring of infuriated men, who were all howling at him at once, and whose malignant faces bore expressions of savage hatred, as they shouted out the foolish accusations and slanders they had read in the Liberal and Tory papers.

Socialists wished to do away with religion and morality! to establish free love and atheism! All the money that the working classes had saved up in the Post Office and the Friendly Societies, was to be

Robbed from them and divided up amongst a lot of drunken loafers who were too lazy to work. The King and all the Royal Family were to be Done Away with! and so on.

Owen made no attempt to reply, and the manner of the crowd became every moment more threatening. It was evident that several of them found it difficult to refrain from attacking him. It was a splendid opportunity of doing a little fighting without running any risks. This fellow was all by himself, and did not appear to be much of a man even at that. Those in the middle were encouraged by shouts from others in the crowd, who urged them to 'Go for him,' and at last – almost at the instant of Barrington's arrival – one of the heroes, unable to contain himself any longer, lifted a heavy stick and struck Owen savagely across the face. The sight of the blood maddened the others, and in an instant everyone who could get within striking distance joined furiously in the onslaught, reaching eagerly over each other's shoulders, showering blows upon him with sticks and fists, and before Barrington could reach his side, they had Owen down on the ground, and had begun to use their boots upon him.

Barrington felt like a wild beast himself, as he fiercely fought his way through the crowd, spurning them to right and left with fists and elbows. He reached the centre in time to seize the uplifted arm of the man who had led the attack, and wrenching the stick from his hand, he felled him to the ground with a single blow. The remainder shrank back, and meantime the crowd was augmented by others who came running up.

Some of these newcomers were Liberals and some Tories, and as these did not know what the row was about they attacked each other. The Liberals went for those who wore Tory colours and vice versa, and in a few seconds there was a general free fight, though most of the original crowd ran away, and in the confusion that ensued, Barrington and Owen got out of the crowd without further molestation.

Monday was the last day of the election – polling day – and in consequence of the number of motor cars that were flying about, the streets were hardly safe for ordinary traffic. The wealthy persons who owned these carriages . . .

The result of the poll was to be shown on an illuminated sign at the Town Hall, at eleven o'clock that night, and long before that hour a vast crowd gathered in the adjacent streets. About ten o'clock it began to rain, but the crowd stood its ground and increased in numbers as the time went by. At a quarter to eleven the rain increased to a terrible downpour, but the people remained waiting to know which hero had conquered. Eleven o'clock came and an intense silence fell upon the crowd, whose eyes were fixed eagerly upon the window where the sign was to be exhibited. To judge by the extraordinary interest displayed by these people, one might have thought that they expected to reap some great benefit or to sustain some great loss from the result, but of course that was not the case, for most of them knew perfectly well that the result of this election would make no more real difference to them than all the other elections that had gone before.

They wondered what the figures would be. There were ten thousand voters on the register. At a quarter past eleven the sign was illuminated, but the figures were not yet shown. Next, the names of the two candidates were slid into sight, the figures were still missing, but D'Encloseland's name was on top, and a hoarse roar of triumph came from the throats of his admirers. Then the two slides with the names were withdrawn, and the sign was again left blank. After a time the people began to murmur at all this delay and messing about, and presently some of them began to groan and hoot.

After a few minutes the names were again slid into view, this time with Sweater's name on top, and the figures appeared immediately afterwards:

Sweater	4,221
D'Encloseland	4,200

It was several seconds before the Liberals could believe their eyes; it was too good to be true. It is impossible to say what was the reason of the wild outburst of delighted enthusiasm that followed, but whatever the reason, whatever the benefit was that they expected to reap – there was the fact. They were all cheering and dancing and shaking hands with each other, and some of them were so overcome with inexplicable joy that they were scarcely able to speak. It was altogether extraordinary and unaccountable.

A few minutes after the declaration, Sweater appeared at the window and made a sort of a speech, but only fragments of it were audible to the cheering crowd who at intervals caught such phrases as 'Slashing Blow', 'Sweep the Country', 'Grand Old Liberal Flag', and so on. Next D'Encloseland appeared and he was seen to shake hands with Mr. Sweater, whom he referred to as 'My friend'.

When the two 'friends' disappeared from the window, the part of the Liberal crowd that was not engaged in hand-to-hand fights with their enemies – the Tories – made a rush to the front entrance of the Town Hall, where Sweater's carriage was waiting, and as soon as he had placed his plump rotundity inside, they took the horses out and amid frantic cheers harnessed themselves to it instead and dragged it through the mud and the pouring rain all the way to 'The Cave' – most of them were accustomed to acting as beasts of burden – where he again addressed a few words to them from the porch.

Afterwards as they walked home saturated with rain and covered from head to foot with mud, they said it was a great victory for the cause of progress!

Truly the wolves have an easy prey.

CHAPTER 49

The Undesired

That evening about seven o'clock, whilst Easton was down-town seeing the last of the election, Ruth's child was born.

After the doctor was gone, Mary Linden stayed with her during the hours that elapsed before Easton came home, and downstairs Elsie and Charley – who were allowed to stay up late to help their mother because Mrs. Easton was ill – crept about very quietly, and conversed in hushed tones as they washed up the tea things and swept the floor and tidied the kitchen.

Easton did not return until after midnight, and all through the intervening hours, Ruth, weak and tired, but unable to sleep, was lying in bed with the child by her side. Her wide-open eyes appeared unnaturally large and brilliant, in contrast with the almost deathlike paleness of her face, and there was a look of fear in them, as she waited and listened for the sound of Easton's footsteps.

Outside, the silence of the night was disturbed by many unusual noises: a far off roar, as of the breaking of waves on a seashore, arose from the direction of the town, where the last scenes of the election were being enacted. Every few minutes motor cars rushed past the house at a furious rate, and the air was full of the sounds of distant shouts and singing.

Ruth listened and started nervously at every passing footstep.

Those who can imagine the kind of expression there would be upon the face of a hunted thief, who, finding himself encompassed and brought to bay by his pursuers, looks wildly around in a vain search for some way of escape, may be able to form some conception of the terror-stricken way in which she listened to every sound that penetrated into the stillness of the dimly lighted room. And ever and again, when her wandering glance reverted to the frail atom of humanity nestling by her side, her brows contracted and her eyes filled with bitter tears, as she weakly reached out her trembling hand to adjust its coverings, faintly murmuring, with quivering lips and a bursting heart, some words of endearment and pity. And then – alarmed by the footsteps of some chance passerby, or by the closing of the door of a neighbouring house, and fearing that it was the sound she had been waiting for and dreading through all those weary hours, she would turn in terror to Mary Linden, sitting in the chair at the bedside, sewing by the light of the shaded lamp, and take hold of her arm as if seeking protection from some impending danger.

It was after twelve o'clock when Easton came home. Ruth recognised his footsteps before he reached the house, and her heart seemed to stop beating when she heard the clang of the gate, as it closed after he had passed through.

It had been Mary's intention to withdraw before he came into the room, but the sick woman clung to her in such evident fear, and intreated her so earnestly not to go away, that she remained.

It was with a feeling of keen disappointment that Easton noticed how Ruth shrank away from him, for he had expected and hoped, that after this, they would be good friends once more; but he tried to think that it was because she was ill, and when she would not let him touch the child lest he should awaken it, he agreed without question.

The next day, and for the greater part of the time during the next fortnight, Ruth was in a raging fever. There were intervals when, although weak and exhausted, she was in her right mind, but most of the time she was quite unconscious of her surroundings and often delirious. Mrs. Owen came every day to help to look after her, because Mary just then had a lot of needlework to do, and consequently could only give part of her time to Ruth, who, in her delirium, lived and told over and over again all the sorrow and suffering of the last few months. And so the two friends, watching by her bedside, learned her dreadful secret.

Sometimes – in her delirium – she seemed possessed of an intense, and terrible loathing for the poor little creature she had brought into the world, and was with difficulty prevented from doing it violence. Once she seized it cruelly and threw it fiercely from her to the foot of the bed, as if it had been some poisonous or loathsome thing. And so it often became necessary to take the child away out of the room, so that she could not see or hear it, but when her senses came back to her, her first thought was for the child, and there must have been in her mind some faint recollection of what she had said and done in her madness, for when she saw that the baby was not in its accustomed place her distress and alarm were painful to see, as she intreated them with tears to give it back to her. And then she would kiss and fondle it with all manner of endearing words, and cry bitterly.

Easton did not see or hear most of this; he only knew that she was very ill; for he went out every day on the almost hopeless quest for work. Rushton's had next to nothing to do, and most of the other shops were in a similar plight. Dauber and Botchit had one or two jobs going on, and Easton tried several times to get a start for them, but was always told they were full up. The sweating methods of this firm continued to form a favourite topic of conversation with the unemployed workmen, who railed at and cursed them horribly. It had leaked out that they were paying only sixpence an hour to most of the skilled workmen in their employment, and even then the conditions under which they worked were, if possible, worse than those obtaining at most other firms. The men were treated like so many convicts, and every job was a hell where driving and bullying reigned supreme, and obscene curses and blasphemy polluted the air from morning till night. The resentment of those who were out of work was directed, not only against the heads of the firm, but also against the miserable, half starved drudges in their employment. These poor wretches were denounced as 'scabs' and 'wastrels' by the unemployed workmen but all the same, whenever Dauber and Botchit wanted some extra hands they never had any difficulty in obtaining them, and it often happened that those who had been loudest and bitterest in their denunciations were amongst the first to rush off eagerly to apply there for a job whenever there was a chance of getting one.

Frequently the light was seen burning late at night in Rushton's office, where Nimrod and his master were figuring out prices and writing out estimates, cutting down the amounts to the lowest possible point in the hope of underbidding their rivals. Now and then they were successful but whether they secured the work or not, Nimrod always appeared equally miserable. If they got the 'job' it often showed such a small margin of profit that Rushton used to grumble at him and suggest mismanagement. If their estimates were too high and they lost the work, he used to demand of Nimrod why it was possible for Dauber and Botchit to do work so much more cheaply.

As the unemployed workmen stood in groups at the corners or walked aimlessly about the streets, they often saw Hunter pass by on his bicycle, looking worried and harassed. He was such a picture of misery, that it began to be rumoured amongst the men, that he had never been the same since the time he had that fall off the bike; and some of them declared, that they wouldn't mind betting that ole Misery would finish up by going off his bloody rocker.

At intervals – whenever a job came in – Owen, Crass, Slyme, Sawkins and one or two others, continued to be employed at Rushton's, but they seldom managed to make more than two or three days a week, even when there was anything to do.

CHAPTER 50

Sundered

During the next few weeks Ruth continued very ill. Although the delirium had left her and did not return, her manner was still very strange, and it was remarkable that she slept but little and at long intervals. Mrs. Owen came to look after her every day, not going back to her own home till the evening. Frankie used to call for her as he came out of school and then they used to go home together, taking little Freddie Easton with them also, for his own mother was not able to look after him and Mary Linden had so much other work to do.

One Wednesday evening, when the child was about five weeks old, as Mrs. Owen was wishing her good-night, Ruth took hold of her hand and after saying how grateful she was for all that she had done, she asked whether – supposing anything happened to herself – Nora would promise to take charge of Freddie for Easton. Owen's wife gave the required promise, at the same time affecting to regard the supposition as altogether unlikely, and assuring her that she would soon be better, but she secretly wondered why Ruth had not mentioned the other child as well.

Nora went away about five o'clock, leaving Ruth's bedroom door open so that Mrs. Linden could hear her call if she needed anything. About a quarter of an hour after Nora and the two children had gone, Mary Linden went upstairs to see Ruth, who appeared to have fallen fast asleep; so she returned to her needlework downstairs. The weather had been very cloudy all day, there had been rain at intervals and it was a dark evening, so dark that she had to light the lamp to see her work. Charley sat on the hearthrug in front of the fire repairing one of the wheels of a wooden cart that he had made with the assistance of another boy, and Elsie busied herself preparing the tea.

Easton was not yet home; Rushton & Co. had a few jobs to do and he had been at work since the previous Thursday. The place where he was working was some considerable distance away, so it was nearly half-past six when he came home. They heard him at the gate and at her mother's direction Elsie went quickly to the front door, which was ajar, to ask him to walk as quietly as possible so as not to wake Ruth.

Mary had prepared the table for his tea in the kitchen, where there was a bright fire with the kettle singing on the hob. He lit the lamp and after removing his hat and overcoat, put the kettle on the fire and while he was waiting for it to boil he went softly upstairs. There was no lamp burning in the bedroom and the place would have been in utter darkness but for the red glow of the fire, which did not dispel the prevailing obscurity sufficiently to enable him to discern the different objects in the room distinctly. The intense silence that reigned struck him with a sudden terror. He crossed swiftly over to the bed and a moment's examination sufficed to tell him that it was empty. He called her name, but there was no answer, and a hurried search only made it certain that she was nowhere in the house.

Mrs. Linden now remembered what Owen's wife had told her of the strange request that Ruth had made, and as she recounted it to Easton, his fears became intensified a thousand-fold. He was unable to form any opinion of the reason of her going or of where she had gone, as he rushed out to seek for her. Almost unconsciously he directed his steps to Owen's house, and afterwards the two men went to every place where they thought it possible she might have gone, but without finding any trace of her.

Her father lived a short distance outside the town, and this was one of the first places they went to, although Easton did not think it likely she would go there, for she had not been on friendly terms with her stepmother, and as he had anticipated, it was a fruitless journey.

They sought for her in every conceivable place, returning often to Easton's house to see if she had come home, but they found no trace of her, nor met anyone who had seen her, which was, perhaps, because the dreary, rain washed streets were deserted by all except those whose business compelled them to be out.

About eleven o'clock Nora was standing at the front door waiting for Owen and Easton, when she thought she could discern a woman's figure in the shadow of the piers of the gate opposite. It was an unoccupied house with a garden in front, and the outlines of the bushes it contained were so vague in the darkness that it was impossible to be certain; but the longer she looked the more convinced she became that there was someone there. At last she summoned sufficient courage to cross over the road, and as she nervously drew near the gate it became evident that she had not been mistaken. There was a woman standing there – a woman with a child in her arms, leaning against one of the pillars and holding the iron bars of the gate with her left hand. It was Ruth. Nora recognised her even in the semi-darkness. Her attitude was one of extreme exhaustion, and as Nora touched her, she perceived that she was wet through and trembling; but although she was almost fainting with fatigue she would not consent to go indoors until repeatedly assured that Easton was not there, and that Nora would not let him see her if he came. And when at length she yielded and went into the house she would not sit down or take off her hat or jacket until – crouching on the floor beside Nora's chair with her face hidden in the latter's lap – she had sobbed out her pitiful confession, the same things that she had unwittingly told to the same hearer so often before during the illness, the only fact that was new was the account of her wanderings that night.

She cried so bitterly and looked so forlorn and heartbroken and ashamed as she faltered out her woeful story; so consumed with self-condemnation, making no excuse for herself except to repeat over and over again that she had never meant to do wrong, that Nora could not refrain from weeping also as she listened.

It appeared that, unable to bear the reproach that Easton's presence seemed to imply, or to endure the burden of her secret any longer, and always haunted by the thought of the lake in the park, Ruth had formed the dreadful resolution of taking her own life and the child's. When she arrived at the park gates they were closed and locked for the night but she remembered that there was another means of entering – the place at the far end of the valley where the park was not fenced in, so she had gone there – nearly three miles – only to find that railings had recently been erected and therefore it was no longer possible to get into the park by that way. And then, when she found it impossible to put her resolve into practice, she had realised for the first time the folly and wickedness of the act she had meant to commit. But although she had abandoned her first intention, she said she could never go home again; she would take a room some-where and get some work to do, or perhaps she might be able to get a situation where they would allow her to have the child with her, or failing that she would work and pay someone to look after it; but she could never go home any more. If she only had somewhere to stay for a few days until she could get something to do, she was sure she would be able to earn her living, but she could not go back home; she felt that she would rather walk about the streets all night than go there again.

It was arranged that Ruth should have the small apartment which had been Frankie's playroom, the necessary furniture being obtained from a second-hand shop close by. Easton did not learn the real reason of her flight until three days afterwards. At first he attributed it to a recurrence of the mental disorder that she had suffered from after the birth of the child, and he had been glad to leave her at Owen's place in Nora's care, but on the evening of the third day when he returned home from work, he found a letter in Ruth's handwriting which told him all there was to tell.

When he recovered from the stupefaction into which he was thrown by the perusal of this letter, his first thought was to seek out Slyme, but he found upon enquiring that the latter had left the town the previous morning. Slyme's landlady said he had told her that he had been offered several months' work in London, which he had accepted. The truth was that Slyme had heard of Ruth's flight – nearly everyone knew about it as a result of the enquiries that had been made for her – and, guessing the cause, he had prudently cleared out.

Easton made no attempt to see Ruth, but he went to Owen's and took Freddie away, saying he would pay Mrs. Linden to look after the child whilst he was at work. His manner was that of a deeply injured man – the possibility that he was in any way to blame for what had happened did not seem to occur to his mind at all.

As for Ruth she made no resistance to his taking the child away from her, although she cried about it in secret. She got some work a few days afterwards – helping the servants at one of the large boarding-houses on the Grand Parade.

Nora looked after the baby for her while she was at work, an arrangement that pleased Frankie vastly; he said it was almost as good as having a baby of their very own.

For the first few weeks after Ruth went away Easton tried to persuade himself that he did not very much regret what had happened. Mrs. Linden looked after Freddie, and Easton tried to believe that he would really be better off now that he had only himself and the child to provide for.

At first, whenever he happened to meet Owen, they used to speak of Ruth, or to be more correct, Easton used to speak of her; but one day when the two men were working together Owen had expressed himself rather offensively. He seemed to think that Easton was more to blame than she was; and afterwards they avoided the subject, although Easton found it difficult to avoid the thoughts the other man's words suggested.

Now and then he heard of Ruth and learnt that she was still working at the same place; and once he met her suddenly and un-expectedly in the street. They passed each other hurriedly and he did not see the scarlet flush that for an instant dyed her face, nor the deathly pallor that succeeded it.

He never went to Owen's place or sent any communication to Ruth, nor did she ever send him any; but although Easton did not know it she frequently saw Freddie, for when Elsie Linden took the child out she often called to see Mrs. Owen.

As time went on and the resentment he had felt towards her lost its first bitterness, Easton began to think there was perhaps some little justification for what Owen had said, and gradually there grew within him an immense desire for reconciliation – to start afresh and to forget all that had happened; but the more he thought of this the more hopeless and impossible of realisation it seemed.

Although perhaps he was not conscious of it, this desire arose solely from selfish motives. The money he earned seemed to melt away almost as soon as he received it; to his surprise he found that he was not nearly so well off in regard to personal comfort as he had been formerly, and the house seemed to grow more dreary and desolate as the wintry days dragged slowly by. Sometimes – when he had the money – he sought forgetfulness in the society of Crass and the other frequenters of the Cricketers, but somehow or other he could not take the same pleasure in the conversation of these people as formerly, when he had found it – as he now sometimes wondered to remember – so entertaining as to almost make him forget Ruth's existence.

One evening about three weeks before Christmas, as he and Owen were walking homewards together from work, Easton reverted for the first time to their former conversation. He spoke with a superior air: his manner and tone indicating that he thought he was behaving with great generosity. He would be willing to forgive her and have her back, he said, if she would come: but he would never be able to tolerate the child. Of course it might be sent to an orphanage or some similar institution, but he was afraid Ruth would never consent to that, and he knew that her step-mother would not take it.

'If you can persuade her to return to you, we'll take the child,' said Owen.

'Do you think your wife would be willing?'

'She has already suggested doing so.'

'To Ruth?'

'No: to me. We thought it a possible way for you, and my wife would like to have the child.'

'But would you be able to afford it?' said Easton.

'We should manage all right.'

'Of course,' said Easton, 'if Slyme comes back he might agree to pay something for its keep.'

Owen flushed.

'I wouldn't take his money.'

After a long pause Easton continued: 'Would you mind asking Mrs. Owen to suggest it to Ruth?'

'If you like I'll get her to suggest it – as a message from you.'

'What I meant,' said Easton hesitatingly, 'was that your wife might just suggest it – casual like – and advise her that it would be the best way, and then you could let me know what Ruth said.'

'No,' replied Owen, unable any longer to control his resentment of the other's manner, 'as things stand now, if it were not for the other child, I should advise her to have nothing further to do with you. You seem to think that you are acting a very generous part in being "willing" to have her back, but she's better off now than she was with you. I see no reason – except for the other child – why she should go back to you. As far as I understand it, you had a good wife and you ill-treated her.'

'I never ill-treated her! I never raised my hand to her – at least only once, and then I didn't hurt her. Does she say I illtreated her.'

'Oh no: from what my wife tells me she only blames herself, but I'm drawing my own conclusions. You may not have struck her, but you did worse – you treated her with indifference and exposed her to temptation. What has happened is the natural result of your neglect and want of care for her. The responsibility for what has happened is mainly yours, but apparently you wish to pose now as being very generous and to "forgive her" – you're "willing" to take her back; but it seems to me that it would be more fitting that you should ask her to forgive you.'

Easton made no answer and after a long silence the other continued: 'I would not advise her to go back to you on such terms as you seem to think right, because if you became reconciled on such terms I don't think either of you could be happy. Your only chance of happiness is to realise that you have both done wrong; that each of you has something to forgive; to forgive and never speak of it again.'

Easton made no reply and a few minutes afterwards, their ways diverging, they wished each other 'Good-night'.

They were working for Rushton – painting the outside of a new conservatory at Mr. Sweater's house, 'The Cave'. This job was finished the next day and at four o'clock the boy brought the hand-cart, which they loaded with their ladders and other materials. They took these back to the yard and then, as it was Friday night they went up to the front shop and handed in their time sheets. After-wards, as they were about to separate, Easton again referred to the subject of their conversation of the previous evening. He had been very reserved and silent all day, scarcely uttering a word except when the work they had been engaged in made it necessary to do so, and there was now a sort of catch in his voice as he spoke.

'I've been thinking over what you said last night; it's quite true. I've been a great deal to blame. I wrote to Ruth last night and admitted it to her. I'll take it as a favour if you and your wife will say what you can to help me to get her back.'

Owen stretched out his hand and as the other took it, said: 'You may rely on us both to do our best.'

CHAPTER 51

The Widow's Son

The next morning when they went to the yard at half-past eight o'clock Hunter told them that there was nothing to do, but that they had better come on Monday in case some work came in. They accordingly went on the Monday, and Tuesday and Wednesday, but as nothing 'came in' of course they did not do any work. On Thursday morning the weather was dark and bitterly cold. The sky presented an unbroken expanse of dull grey and a keen north wind swept through the cheerless streets. Owen – who had caught cold whilst painting the outside of the conservatory at Sweater's house the previous week – did not get to the yard until ten o'clock. He felt so ill that he would not have gone at all if they had not needed the money he would be able to earn if there was anything to do. Strange though it may appear to the advocates of thrift, although he had been so fortunate as to be in employment when so many others were idle, they had not saved any money. On the contrary, during all the summer they had not been able to afford to have proper food or clothing. Every week most of the money went to pay arrears of rent or some other debts, so that even whilst he was at work they had often to go without some of the necessaries of life. They had broken boots, shabby, insufficient clothing, and barely enough to eat.

The weather had become so bitterly cold that, fearing he would be laid up if he went without it any longer, he took his overcoat out of pawn, and that week they had to almost starve. Not that it was much better other weeks, for lately he had only been making six and half hours a day – from eight-thirty in the morning till four o'clock in the evening, and on Saturday only four and half hours – from half-past eight till one. This made his wages – at sevenpence an hour – twenty-one shillings and sevenpence a week – that is, when there was work to do every day, which was not always. Sometimes they had to stand idle three days out of the six. The wages of those who got sixpence halfpenny came out at one pound and twopence – when they worked every day – and as for those who – like Sawkins – received only fivepence, their week's wages amounted to fifteen and sixpence.

When they were only employed for two or three days or perhaps only a few hours, their 'Saturday night' sometimes amounted to half a sovereign, seven and sixpence, five shillings or even less. Then most of them said that it was better than nothing at all.

Many of them were married men, so, in order to make existence possible, their wives went out charing or worked in laundries. They had children whom they had to bring up for the most part on 'skim' milk, bread, margarine, and adulterated tea. Many of these children – little mites of eight or nine years – went to work for two or three hours in the morning before going to school; the same in the evening after school, and all day on Saturday, carrying butchers' trays loaded with meat, baskets of groceries and vegetables, cans of paraffin oil, selling or delivering newspapers, and carrying milk. As soon as they were old enough they got Half Time certificates and directly they were fourteen they left school altogether and went to work all the day. When they were old enough some of them tried to join the Army or Navy, but were found physically unfit.

It is not much to be wondered at that when they became a little older they were so degenerate intellectually that they imagined that the surest way to obtain better conditions would be to elect gangs of Liberal and Tory land-grabbers, sweaters, swindlers and lawyers to rule over them.

[[When Owen arrived at the yard he found Bert White cleaning out the dirty pots in the paint-shop. The noise he made with the scraping knife prevented him from hearing Owen's approach and the latter stood watching him for some minutes without speaking. The stone floor of the paint shop was damp and shiny and the whole place was chilly as a tomb. The boy was trembling with cold and he looked pitifully undersized]] and frail as he bent over his work with an old apron girt about him. Because it was so cold he was wearing his jacket with the ends of the sleeves turned back to keep them clean, or to prevent them getting any dirtier, for they were already in the same condition as the rest of his attire, which was thickly encrusted with dried paint of many colours, and his hands and fingernails were grimed with it.

As he watched the poor boy bending over his task, Owen thought of Frankie, and with a feeling akin to terror wondered whether he would ever be in a similar plight.

When he saw Owen, the boy left off working and wished him good morning, remarking that it was very cold.

'Why don't you light a fire? There's lots of wood lying about the yard.'

'No,' said Bert shaking his head. 'That would never do! Misery wouldn't 'arf ramp if 'e caught me at it. I used to 'ave a fire 'ere last winter till Rushton found out, and 'e kicked up an orful row and told me to move meself and get some work done and then I wouldn't feel the cold.'

'Oh, he said that, did he?' said Owen, his pale face becoming suddenly suffused with blood. 'We'll see about that.'

He went out into the yard and crossing over to where – under a shed – there was a great heap of waste wood, stuff that had been taken out of places where Rushton & Co. had made alterations, he gathered an armful of it and was returning to the paintshop when Sawkins accosted him.

'You mustn't go burnin' any of that, you know! That's all got to be saved and took up to the bloke's house. Misery spoke about it only this mornin'.'

Owen did not answer him. He carried the wood into the shop and after throwing it into the fireplace he poured some old paint over it, and, applying a match, produced a roaring fire. Then he brought in several more armfuls of wood and piled them in a corner of the shop. Bert took no part in these proceedings, and at first rather disapproved of them because he was afraid there would be trouble when Misery came, but when the fire was an accomplished fact he warmed his hands and shifted his work to the other side of the bench so as to get the benefit of the heat.

Owen waited for about half an hour to see if Hunter would return, but as that disciple did not appear, he decided not to wait any longer. Before leaving he gave Bert some instructions:

'Keep up the fire with all the old paint that you can scrape off those things and any other old paint or rubbish that's here, and whenever it grows dull put more wood on. There's a lot of old stuff here that's of no use except to be thrown away or burnt. Burn it all. If Hunter says anything, tell him that I lit the fire, and that I told you to keep it burning. If you want more wood, go out and take it.

'All right,' replied Bert.

On his way out Owen spoke to Sawkins. His manner was so menacing, his face so pale, and there was such a strange glare in his eyes, that the latter thought of the talk there had often been about Owen being mad, and felt half afraid of him.

'I am going to the office to see Rushton; if Hunter comes here, you say I told you to tell him that if I find the boy in that shop again without a fire, I'll report it to the Society for the Prevention of

Cruelty to Children.[128] And as for you, if the boy comes out here to get more wood, don't you attempt to interfere with him.'

'I don't want to interfere with the bloody kid,' grunted Sawkins. 'It seems to me as if he's gorn orf 'is bloody crumpet,' he added as he watched Owen walking rapidly down the street. 'I can't understand why people can't mind their own bloody business: anyone would think the boy belonged to '*im*.'

That was just how the matter presented itself to Owen. The idea that it was his own child who was to be treated in this way possessed and infuriated him as he strode savagely along. In the vicinity of the Slave Market on the Grand Parade he passed – without seeing them – several groups of unemployed artisans whom he knew. Some of them were offended and remarked that he was getting stuck up, but others, observing how strange he looked, repeated the old prophecy that one of these days Owen would go out of his mind.

As he drew near to his destination large flakes of snow began to fall. He walked so rapidly and was in such a fury that by the time he reached the shop he was scarcely able to speak.

'Is – Hunter – or Rushton here?' he demanded of the shopman.

'Hunter isn't, but the guv'nor is. What was it you wanted?'

'He'll soon – know – that,' panted Owen as he strode up to the office door, and without troubling to knock, flung it violently open and entered.

The atmosphere of this place was very different from that of the damp cellar where Bert was working. A grate fitted with asbestos blocks and lit with gas communicated a genial warmth to the air.

Rushton was standing leaning over Miss Wade's chair with his left arm round her neck. Owen recollected afterwards that her dress was disarranged. She retired hastily to the far end of the room as Rushton jumped away from her, and stared in amazement and confusion at the intruder – he was too astonished and embarrassed to speak. Owen stood panting and quivering in the middle of the office and pointed a trembling finger at his employer:

'I've come – here – to tell – you – that – if I find young – Bert White – working – down in that shop – without – a fire – I'll have you – prosecuted. The place is not good enough for a stable – if you owned a valuable dog – you wouldn't keep it there – I give you fair warning – I know – enough – about you – to put you – where you deserve to be – if you don't treat him better – I'll have you punished – I'll show you up.'

Rushton continued to stare at him in mingled confusion, fear and perplexity; he did not yet comprehend exactly what it was all about; he was guiltily conscious of so many things which he might reasonably fear to be shown up or prosecuted for if they were known, and the fact of being caught under such circumstances with Miss Wade helped to reduce him to a condition approaching terror.

'If the boy has been there without a fire, I 'aven't known anything about it,' he stammered at last. 'Mr. 'Unter has charge of all those matters.'

'You – yourself – forbade him – to make a fire last winter – and anyhow – you know about it *now*. You obtained money from his mother under the pretence – that you were going – to teach him a trade – but for the last twelve months – you have been using him – as if he were – a beast of burden. I advise you to see to it – or I shall – find – means – to make you – wish you had done do.'

With this Owen turned and went out, leaving the door open, and Rushton in a state of mind compounded of fear, amazement and anger.

As he walked homewards through the snow-storm, Owen began to realise that the consequence of what he had done would be that Rushton would not give him any more work, and as he reflected on all that this would mean to those at home, for a moment he doubted whether he had done right. But when he told Nora what had happened she said there were plenty of other firms in the town who would employ him – when they had the work. He had done without Rushton before and could do so again; for her part – whatever the consequences might be – she was glad that he had acted as he did.

'We'll get through somehow, I suppose,' said Owen, wearily. 'There's not much chance of getting a job anywhere else just now, but I shall try to get some work on my own account. I shall do some samples of show-cards the same as I did last winter and try to get orders from some of the shops – they usually want something extra at this time, but I'm afraid it is rather too late: most of them already have all they want.'

'I shouldn't go out again today if I were you,' said Nora, noticing how ill he looked. 'You should stay at home and read, or write up those minutes.'

The minutes referred to were those of the last meeting of the local branch of the Painters' Society, of which Owen was the secretary, and as the snow continued to fall, he occupied himself after dinner in the manner his wife suggested, until four o'clock, when Frankie returned from school bringing with him a large snowball, and crying out as a piece of good news that the snow was still falling heavily, and that he *believed* it was freezing!

They went to bed very early that night, for it was necessary to economise the coal, and not only that, but – because the rooms were so near the roof – it was not possible to keep the place warm no matter how much coal was used. The fire seemed, if anything, to make the place colder, for it caused the outer air to pour in through the joints of the ill-fitting doors and windows.

Owen lay awake for the greater part of the night. The terror of the future made rest or sleep impossible. He got up very early the next morning – long before it was light – and after lighting the fire, set about preparing the samples he had mentioned to Nora, but found that it would not be possible to do much in this direction without buying more cardboard, for most of what he had was not in good condition.

They had bread and butter and tea for breakfast. Frankie had his in bed, and it was decided to keep him away from school until after dinner because the weather was so very cold and his only pair of boots were so saturated with moisture from having been out in the snow the previous day.

'I shall make a few enquiries to see if there's any other work to be had before I buy the cardboard,' said Owen, 'although I'm afraid it's not much use.'

Just as he was preparing to go out, the front door bell rang, and as he was going down to answer it he saw Bert White coming upstairs. The boy was carrying a flat, brown-paper parcel under his arm.

'A corfin plate,' he explained as he arrived at the door. 'Wanted at once – Misery ses you can do it at 'ome, an' I've got to wait for it.'

Owen and his wife looked at each other with intense relief. So he was not to be dismissed after all. It was almost too good to be true.

'There's a piece of paper inside the parcel with the name of the party what's dead,' continued Bert, 'and here's a little bottle of Brunswick black for you to do the inscription with.'

'Did he send any other message?'

'Yes: he told me to tell you there's a job to be started Monday morning – a couple of rooms to be done out somewhere. Got to be finished by Thursday; and there's another job 'e wants you to do this afternoon – after dinner – so you've got to come to the yard at one o'clock. 'E told me to tell you 'e meant to leave a message for you yesterday morning, but 'e forgot.'

'What did he say to you about the fire – anything?'

'Yes: they both of 'em came about an hour after you went away – Misery and the Bloke too – but they didn't kick up a row. I wasn't 'arf frightened, I can tell you, when I saw 'em both coming, but they was quite nice. The Bloke ses to me, "Ah, that's right, my boy," 'e ses. "Keep up a good fire. I'm going to send you some coke," 'e ses. And then they 'ad a look round and 'e told Sawkins to put some new panes of glass where the winder was broken, and – you know that great big packing-case what was under the truck shed?'

'Yes.'

'Well, 'e told Sawkins to saw it up and cover over the stone floor of the paint-shop with it. It ain't 'arf all right there now. I've cleared out all the muck from under the benches and we've got two sacks of coke sent from the gas-works, and the Bloke told me when that's all used up I've got to get a order orf Miss Wade for another lot.'

At one o'clock Owen was at the yard, where he saw Misery, who instructed him to go to the front shop and paint some numbers on the racks where the wallpapers were stored. Whilst he was doing this work Rushton came in and greeted him in a very friendly way.

'I'm very glad you let me know about the boy working in that paint-shop,' he observed after a few preliminary remarks. 'I can assure you as I don't want the lad to be uncomfortable, but you know I can't attend to everything myself. I'm much obliged to you for telling me about it; I think you did quite right; I should have done the same myself.'

[[Owen did not know what to reply, but Rushton walked off without waiting.]] . . .

CHAPTER 52

'It's a Far, Far Better Thing That I do, Than I have ever Done'[129]

Although Owen, Easton and Crass and a few others were so lucky as to have had a little work to do during the last few months, the majority of their fellow workmen had been altogether out of employment most of the time, and meanwhile the practical business-men, and the pretended disciples of Christ – the liars and hypocrites who professed to believe that all men are brothers and God their Father – had continued to enact the usual farce that they called 'Dealing' with the misery that surrounded them on every side. They continued to organise 'Rummage' and 'Jumble' sales and bazaars, and to distribute their rotten cast off clothes and boots and their broken victuals and soup to such of the Brethren as were sufficiently degraded to beg for them. The beautiful Distress Committee was also in full operation; over a thousand Brethren had registered themselves on its books. Of this number – after careful investigation – the committee had found that no fewer than six hundred and seventy-two were deserving of being allowed to work for their living. The Committee would probably have given these six hundred and seventy-two the necessary permission, but it was somewhat handicapped by the fact that the funds at its disposal were only sufficient to enable that number of Brethren to be employed for about three days. However, by adopting a policy of temporising, delay, and general artful dodging, the Committee managed to create the impression that they were Dealing with the Problem.

If it had not been for a cunning device invented by Brother Rushton, a much larger number of the Brethren would have succeeded in registering themselves as unemployed on the books of the Committee. In previous years it had been the practice to issue an application form called a 'Record Paper' to any Brother who asked for one, and the Brother returned it after filling it in himself. At a secret meeting of the Committee Rushton proposed – amid laughter and applause, it was such a good joke – a new and better way, calculated to keep down the number of applicants. The result of this innovation was that no more forms were issued, but the applicants for work were admitted into the office one at a time, and were there examined by a junior clerk, somewhat after the manner of a French Juge d'Instruction interrogating a criminal, the clerk filling in the form according to the replies of the culprit.

'What's your name?'

'Where do you live?'

'How long have you been living there?'

'Where did you live before you went there?'

'How long were you living at that place?'

'Why did you move?'

'Did you owe any rent when you left?'

'What was your previous address?'

'How old are you? When was your last birthday?'

'What is your Trade, Calling, Employment, or Occupation?'

'Are you Married or single or a Widower or what?'

'How many children have you? How many boys? How many girls? Do they go to work? What do they earn?'

'What kind of a house do you live in? How many rooms are there?'

'How much rent do you owe?'

'Who was your last employer? What was the foreman's name? How long did you work there? What kind of work did you do? Why did you leave?'

'What have you been doing for the last five years? What kind of work, how many hours a day? What wages did you get?'

'Give the full names and addresses of all the different employers you have worked for during the last five years, and the reasons why you left them?'

'Give the names of all the foremen you have worked under during the last five years?'

'Does your wife earn anything? How much?'

'Do you get any money from any Club or Society, or from any Charity, or from any other source?'

'Have you ever received Poor Relief?'

'Have you ever worked for a Distress Committee before?'

'Have you ever done any other kinds of work than those you have mentioned? Do you think you would be fit for any other kind?'

'Have you any references?' – and so on and so forth.

When the criminal had answered all the questions, and when his answers had all been duly written down, he was informed that a member of the Committee, or an Authorised Officer, or some Other Person, would in due course visit his home and make enquiries about him, after which the Authorised Officer or Other Person would make a report to the Committee, who would consider it at their next meeting.

As the interrogation of each criminal occupied about half an hour, to say nothing of the time he was kept waiting, it will be seen that as a means of keeping down the number of registered unemployed the idea worked splendidly.

When Rushton introduced this new rule it was carried unanimously, Dr. Weakling being the only dissentient, but of course he – as Brother Grinder remarked – was always opposed to any sensible proposal. There was one consolation, however, Grinder added, they was not likely to be pestered with 'im much longer; the fust of November was coming and if he – Grinder – knowed anything of working men they was sure to give Weakling the dirty kick out directly they got the chance.

A few days afterwards the result of the municipal election justified Brother Grinder's prognostications, for the working men voters of Dr. Weakling's ward did give him the dirty kick out: but Rushton, Didlum, Grinder and several other members of the band were triumphantly returned with increased majorities.

Mr. Dauber, of Dauber and Botchit, had already been elected a Guardian of the Poor.

During all this time Hunter, who looked more worried and miserable as the dreary weeks went by, was occupied every day in supervising what work was being done and in running about seeking for more. Nearly every night he remained at the office until a late hour, poring over specifications and making out estimates. The police had become so accustomed to seeing the light in the office that as a rule they took no notice of it, but one Thursday night – exactly one week after the scene between Owen and Rushton about the boy – the constable on the beat observed the light there much later than usual. At first he paid no particular attention to the fact, but when night merged into morning and the light still remained, his curiosity was aroused.

He knocked at the door, but no one came in answer, and no sound disturbed the deathlike stillness that reigned within. The door was locked, but he was not able to tell whether it had been closed from the inside or outside, because it had a spring latch. The office window was low down, but it was not possible to see in because the back of the glass had been painted.

The constable thought that the most probable explanation of the mystery was that whoever had been there earlier in the evening had forgotten to turn out the light when they went away; it was not likely that thieves or anyone who had no business to be there would advertise their presence by lighting the gas.

He made a note of the incident in his pocket-book and was about to resume his beat when he was joined by his inspector. The latter agreed that the conclusion arrived at by the constable was probably the right one and they were about to pass on when the inspector noticed a small speck of light shining through the lower part of the painted window, where a small piece of the paint had either been scratched or had shelled off the glass. He knelt down and found that it was possible to get a view of the interior of the office, and as he peered through he gave a low exclamation. When he made way for his subordinate to look in his turn, the constable was with some difficulty able to distinguish the figure of a man lying prone upon the floor.

It was an easy task for the burly policeman to force open the office door; a single push of his shoulder wrenched it from its fastenings and as it flew back the socket of the lock fell with a splash into a great pool of blood that had accumulated against the threshold, flowing from the place where Hunter was lying on his back, his arms extended and his head nearly severed from his body. On the floor, close to his right hand, was an open razor. An overturned chair lay on the floor by the side of the table where he usually worked, the table itself being littered with papers and drenched with blood.

Within the next few days Crass resumed the role he had played when Hunter was ill during the summer, taking charge of the work and generally doing his best to fill the dead man's place, although – as he confided to certain of his cronies in the bar of the Cricketers – he had no intention of allowing Rushton to do the same as Hunter had done. One of his first jobs – on the morning after the discovery of the body – was to go with Mr. Rushton to look over a house where some work was to be done for which an estimate had to be given. It was this estimate that Hunter had been trying to make out the previous evening in the office, for they found that the papers on his table were covered with figures and writing relating to this work. These papers justified the subsequent verdict of the Coroner's jury that Hunter committed suicide in a fit of temporary insanity, for they were covered with a lot of meaningless scribbling, the words wrongly spelt and having no intelligible connection with each other. There was one sum that he had evidently tried repeatedly to do correctly, but which came wrong in a different way every time. The fact that he had the razor in his possession seemed to point to his having premeditated the act, but this was accounted for at the inquest by the evidence of the last person who saw him alive, a hairdresser, who stated that Hunter had left the razor with him to be sharpened a few days previously and that he had called for it on the evening of the tragedy. He had ground this razor for Mr. Hunter several times before.

Crass took charge of all the arrangements for the funeral. He bought a new second-hand pair of black trousers at a cast-off clothing shop in honour of the occasion, and discarded his own low-crowned silk hat – which was getting rather shabby – in favour of Hunter's tall one, which he found in the office and annexed without hesitation or scruple. It was rather large for him, but he put some folded strips of paper inside the leather lining. Crass was a proud man as he walked in Hunter's place at the head of the procession, trying to look solemn, but with a half-smile on his fat, pasty face, destitute of colour except one spot on his chin near his underlip, where there was a small patch of inflammation about the size of a threepenny piece. This spot had been there for a very long time. At first – as well as he could remember – it was only a small pimple, but it had grown larger, with something the appearance of scurvy.[130] Crass attributed its continuation to the cold having 'got into it last winter'. It was rather strange, too, because he generally took care of himself when it was cold: he always wore the warm wrap that had formerly belonged to the old lady who died of cancer. However, Crass did not worry much about this little sore place; he just put a little zinc ointment on it occasionally and had no doubt that it would get well in time.

CHAPTER 53

Barrington Finds a Situation

The revulsion of feeling that Barrington experienced during the progress of the election was intensified by the final result. The blind, stupid, enthusiastic admiration displayed by the philanthropists for those who exploited and robbed them; their extraordinary apathy with regard to their own interests; the patient, broken-spirited way in which they endured their sufferings, tamely submitting to live in poverty in the midst of the wealth they had helped to create; their callous indifference to the fate of their children, and the savage hatred they exhibited towards anyone who dared to suggest the possibility of better things, forced upon him the thought that the hopes he cherished were impossible of realisation. The words of the renegade Socialist recurred constantly to his mind:

'You can be a Jesus Christ if you like, but for my part I'm finished. For the future I intend to look after myself. As for these people, they vote for what they want, they get what they vote for, and, by God! they deserve nothing better! They are being beaten with whips of their own choosing, and if I had my way they should be chastised with scorpions. For them, the present system means joyless drudgery, semi-starvation, rags and premature death; and they vote for it and uphold it. Let them have what they vote for! Let them drudge and let them starve!'

These words kept ringing in his ears as he walked through the crowded streets early one fine evening a few days before Christmas.

The shops were all brilliantly lighted for the display of their Christmas stores, and the pavements and even the carriage-ways were thronged with sightseers.

Barrington was specially interested in the groups of shabbily dressed men and women and children who gathered in the roadway in front of the poulterers' and butchers' shops, gazing at the meat and the serried rows of turkeys and geese decorated with coloured ribbons and rosettes. He knew that to come here and look at these things was the only share many of these poor people would have of them, and he marvelled greatly at their wonderful patience and abject resignation. But what struck him most of all was the appearance of many of the women, evidently working men's wives. Their faded, ill-fitting garments and the tired, sad expressions on their pale and careworn faces. Some of them were alone; others were accompanied by little children who trotted along trustfully clinging to their mothers' hands. The sight of these poor little ones, their utter helplessness and dependence, their patched, unsightly clothing and broken boots, and the wistful looks on their pitiful faces as they gazed into the windows of the toy-shops, sent a pang of actual physical pain to his heart and filled his eyes with tears. He knew that these children – naked of joy and all that makes life dear – were being tortured by the sight of the things that were placed so cruelly before their eyes, but which they were not permitted to touch or to share; and, like Joseph of old, his heart yearned over his younger brethren.[131]

He felt like a criminal because he was warmly clad and well fed in the midst of all this want and unhappiness, and he flushed with shame because he had momentarily faltered in his devotion to the noblest cause that any man could be privileged to fight for – the uplifting of the disconsolate and the oppressed.

He presently came to a large toy shop outside which several children were standing admiring the contents of the window. He recognised some of these children and paused to watch them and to listen to their talk. They did not notice him standing behind them as they ranged to and fro before the window, and as he looked at them, he was reminded of the way in which captive animals walk up and down behind the bars of their cages. These children wandered repeatedly, backwards and forwards from one end of the window to the other, with their little hands pressed against the impenetrable plate glass, choosing and pointing out to each other the particular toys that took their fancies.

'That's mine!' cried Charlie Linden, enthusiastically indicating a large strongly built waggon. 'If I had that I'd give Freddie rides in it and bring home lots of firewood, and we could play at fire engines as well.'

'I'd rather have this railway,' said Frankie Owen. 'There's a real tunnel and real coal in the tenders; then there's the station and the signals and a place to turn the engine round, and a red lantern to light when there's danger on the line.'

'Mine's this doll – not the biggest one, the one in pink with clothes that you can take off,' said Elsie; 'and this tea set; and this needlecase for Mother.'

Little Freddie had let go his hold of Elsie, to whom he usually clung tightly and was clapping his hands and chuckling with delight and desire. 'Gee-gee!' he cried eagerly. 'Gee-gee Pwetty Gee-gee! Fweddy want gee-gee!'

'But it's no use lookin' at them any longer,' continued Elsie, with a sigh, as she took hold of Freddie's hand to lead him away. 'It's no use lookin' at 'em any longer; the likes of us can't expect to have such good things as them.'

This remark served to recall Frankie and Charlie to the stern realities of life, and turning reluctantly away from the window they prepared to follow Elsie, but Freddie had not yet learnt the lesson – he had not lived long enough to understand that the good things of the world were not for the likes of him; so when Elsie attempted to draw him away he pursed up his underlip and began to cry, repeating that he wanted a gee-gee. The other children clustered round trying to coax and comfort him by telling him that no one was allowed to have anything out of the windows yet – until Christmas – and that Santa Claus would be sure to bring him a gee-gee then; but these arguments failed to make any impression on Freddie, who tearfully insisted upon being supplied at once.

Whilst they were thus occupied they caught sight of Barrington, whom they hailed with evident pleasure born of the recollection of certain gifts of pennies and cakes they had at different times received from him.

'Hello, Mr. Barrington,' said the two boys in a breath.

'Hello,' replied Barrington, as he patted the baby's cheek. 'What's the matter here? What's Freddie crying for?'

'He wants that there 'orse, mister, the one with the real 'air on,' said Charley, smiling indulgently like a grown-up person who realised the absurdity of the demand.

'Fweddie want gee-gee,' repeated the child, taking hold of Barrington's hand and returning to the window. 'Nice gee-gee.'

'Tell him that Santa Claus'll bring it to him on Christmas,' whispered Elsie. 'P'raps he'll believe *you* and that'll satisfy him, and he's sure to forget all about it in a little while.'

'Are you still out of work, Mr. Barrington?' enquired Frankie.

'No,' replied Barrington slowly. 'I've got something to do at last.'

'Well, that's a good job, ain't it?' remarked Charlie.

'Yes,' said Barrington. 'And whom do you think I'm working for?'

'Who?'

'Santa Claus.'

'Santa Claus!' echoed the children, opening their eyes to the fullest extent.

'Yes,' continued Barrington, solemnly. 'You know, he is a very old man now, so old that he can't do all his work himself. Last year he was so tired that he wasn't able to get round to all the children he wanted to give things to, and consequently a great many of them never got anything at all. So this year he's given me a job to help him. He's given me some money and a list of children's names, and against their names are written the toys they are to have. My work is to buy the things and give them to the boys and girls whose names are on the list.'

The children listened to this narrative with bated breath. Incredible as the story seemed, Barrington's manner was so earnest as to almost compel belief.

'Really and truly, or are you only having a game?' said Frankie at length, speaking almost in a whisper. Elsie and Charlie maintained an awestruck silence, while Freddie beat upon the glass with the palms of his hands.

'Really and truly,' replied Barrington unblushingly as he took out his pocket-book and turned over the leaves. 'I've got the list here; perhaps your names are down for something.'

The three children turned pale and their hearts beat violently as they listened wide-eyed for what was to follow.

'Let me see,' continued Barrington, scanning the pages of the book. 'Why, yes, here they are! Elsie Linden, one doll with clothes that can be taken off, one tea-set, one needlecase. Freddie Easton, one horse with real hair. Charlie Linden, one four-wheeled waggon full of groceries. Frankie Owen, one railway with tunnel, station, train with real coal for engine, signals, red lamp and place to turn the engines round.'

Barrington closed the book: 'So you may as well have your things now,' he continued, speaking in a matter-of-fact tone. 'We'll buy them here; it will save me a lot of work. I shall not have the trouble of taking them round to where you live. It's lucky I happened to meet you, isn't it?'

The children were breathless with emotion, but they just managed to gasp out that it was – very lucky.

As they followed him into the shop, Freddie was the only one of the four whose condition was anything like normal. All the others were in a half-dazed state. Frankie was afraid that he was not really awake at all. It couldn't be true; it must be a dream.

In addition to the hair, the horse was furnished with four wheels. They did not have it made into a parcel, but tied some string to it and handed it over to its new owner. The elder children were scarcely conscious of what took place inside the shop; they knew that Barrington was talking to the shopman, but they did not hear what was said – the sound seemed far away and unreal.

The shopman made the doll, the tea-set and the needlecase into one parcel and gave it to Elsie. The railway, in a stout cardboard box, was also wrapped up in brown paper, and Frankie's heart nearly burst when the man put the package into his arms.

When they came out of the toy shop they said 'Good-night' to Frankie, who went off carrying his parcel very carefully and feeling as if he were walking on air. The others went into a provision merchant's near by, where the groceries were purchased and packed into the waggon.

Then Barrington, upon referring to the list to make quite certain that he had not forgotten anything, found that Santa Claus had put down a pair of boots each for Elsie and Charlie, and when they went to buy these, it was seen that their stockings were all ragged and full of holes, so they went to a draper's and bought some stockings also. Barrington said that although they were not on the list, he was sure Santa Claus would not object – he had probably meant them to have them, but had forgotten to put them down.

CHAPTER 54

The End

The following evening Barrington called at Owen's place. He said he was going home for the holidays and had come to say goodbye for a time.

Owen had not been doing very well during these last few months, although he was one of the few lucky ones who had had some small share of work. Most of the money he earned went for rent, to pay which they often had to go short of food. Lately his chest had become so bad that the slightest exertion brought on fits of coughing and breathlessness, which made it almost impossible to work even when he had the opportunity; often it was only by an almost super-human effort of will that he was able to continue working at all. He contrived to keep up appearances to a certain extent before Rushton, who, although he knew that Owen was not so strong as the other men, was inclined to overlook it so long as he was able to do his share of work, for Owen was a very useful hand when things were busy. But lately some of the men with whom he worked began to manifest dissatisfaction at having him for a mate. When two men are working together, the master expects to see two men's work done, and if one of the two is not able to do his full share it makes it all the harder for the other.

He never had the money to go to a doctor to get advice, but earlier in the winter he had obtained from Rushton a ticket for the local hospital. Every Saturday throughout the year when the men were paid they were expected to put a penny or two-pence in the hospital box. Contributions were obtained in this way from every firm and workshop in the town. The masters periodically handed these boxes over to the hospital authorities and received in return some tickets which they gave to anyone who needed and asked for them. The employer had to fill in the ticket or application form with the name and address of the applicant, and to certify that in his opinion the individual was a deserving case, 'suitable to receive this charity'. In common with the majority of workmen, Owen had a sort of horror of going for advice to this hospital, but he was so ill that he stifled his pride and went. It happened that it turned out to be more expensive than going to a private doctor, for he had to be at the hospital at a certain hour on a particular morning. To do this he had to stay away from work. The medicine they prescribed and which he had to buy did him no good, for the truth was that it was not medicine that he – like thousands of others – needed, but proper conditions of life and proper food; things that had been for years past as much out of his reach as if he had been dying alone in the middle of a desert.

Occasionally Nora contrived – by going without some other necessary – to buy him a bottle of one of the many much-advertised medicines; but although some of these things were good she was not able to buy enough for him to derive any benefit from them.

Although he was often seized with a kind of terror of the future – of being unable to work – he fought against these feelings and tried to believe that when the weather became warmer he would be all right once more.

When Barrington came in Owen was sitting in a deck-chair by the fire in the sitting-room. He had been to work that day with Harlow, washing off the ceilings and stripping the old paper from the walls of two rooms in Rushton's home, and he looked very haggard and exhausted.

'I have never told you before,' said Barrington, after they had been talking for a while, 'but I suppose you have guessed that I did not work for Rushton because I needed to do so in order to live. I just wanted to see things for myself; to see life as it is lived by the majority. My father is a wealthy man. He doesn't approve of my opinions, but at the same time he does not interfere with me for holding them, and I have a fairly liberal allowance which I spend in my own way. I'm going to pass Christmas with my own people, but in the spring I intend to fit out a Socialist Van, and then I shall come back here. We'll have some of the best speakers in the movement; we'll hold meetings every night; we'll drench the town with literature, and we'll start a branch of the party.'

Owen's eye kindled and his pale face flushed.

'I shall be able to do something to advertise the meetings,' he said. 'For instance, I could paint some posters and placards.'

'And I can help to give away handbills,' chimed in Frankie, looking up from the floor, where he was seated working the railway. 'I know a lot of boys who'll come along with me to put 'em under the doors as well.'

They were in the sitting-room and the door was shut. Mrs. Owen was in the next room with Ruth. While the two men were talking the front-door bell was heard to ring and Frankie ran out to see who it was, closing the door after him. Barrington and Owen continued their conversation, and from time to time they could hear a low murmur of voices from the adjoining room. After a little while they heard some one go out by the front door, and almost immediately afterward Frankie – wild with excitement, burst into the room, crying out:

'Dad and Mr. Barrington! Three cheers!' And he began capering gleefully about the room, evidently transported with joy.

'What are the cheers to be for?' enquired Barrington, rather mystified by this extraordinary conduct.

'Mr. Easton came with Freddie to see Mrs. Easton, and she's gone home again with them,' replied Frankie, 'and – she's given the baby to us for a Christmas box!'

Barrington was already familiar with the fact of Easton's separation from his wife, and Owen now told him the story of their reconciliation.

Barrington took his leave shortly afterwards. His train left at eight; it was already nearly half-past seven, and he said he had a letter to write. Nora brought the baby in to show him before he went, and then she helped Frankie to put on his overcoat, for Barrington had requested that the boy might be permitted to go a little way with him.

There was a stationer's shop at the end of the street. He went in here and bought a sheet of notepaper and an envelope, and, having borrowed the pen and ink, wrote a letter which he enclosed in the envelope with the two other pieces of paper that he took out of his pocket-book. Having addressed the letter he came out of the shop; Frankie was waiting for him outside. He gave the letter to the boy.

'I want you to take this straight home and give it to your dad. I don't want you to stop to play or even to speak to anyone till you get home.'

'All right,' replied Frankie. 'I won't stop running all the way.'

Barrington hesitated and looked at his watch. 'I think I have time to go back with you as far as your front door,' he said. 'Then I shall be quite sure you haven't lost it.'

They accordingly retraced their steps and in a few minutes reached the entrance to the house. Barrington opened the door and stood for a moment in the hall watching Frankie ascend the stairs.

'Will your train cross over the bridge?' enquired the boy, pausing and looking over the banisters.

'Yes. Why?'

'Because we can see the bridge from our front-room window, and if you were to wave your handkerchief as your train goes over the bridge, we could wave back.'

'All right. I'll do so. Goodbye.'

'Goodbye.'

Barrington waited till he heard Frankie open and close the door of Owen's flat, and then he hurried away. When he gained the main road he heard the sound of singing and saw a crowd at the corner of one of the side-streets. As he drew near he saw that it was a religious meeting.

There was a lighted lamp on a standard in the centre of the crowd and on the glass of this lamp was painted: 'Be not deceived: God is not mocked.'

Mr. Rushton was preaching in the centre of the ring. He said that they had come hout there that evening to tell the Glad Tidings of Great Joy to hall those dear people that he saw standing around. The members of the Shining Light Chapel – to which he himself belonged – was the organisers of that meeting but it was not a sectarian meeting, for he was 'appy to say that several members of other denominations was there co-operating with them in the good work. As he continued his address, Rushton repeatedly referred to the individuals who composed the crowd as his 'Brothers and Sisters' and, strange to say, nobody laughed.

Barrington looked round upon the 'Brothers': Mr. Sweater, resplendent in a new silk hat of the latest fashion, and a furtrimmed overcoat. The Rev. Mr. Bosher, Vicar of the Church of the Whited Sepulchre, Mr. Grinder – one of the churchwardens at the same place of alleged worship – both dressed in broadcloth and fine linen and glossy silk hats, while their general appearance testified to the fact that they had fared sumptuously for many days. Mr. Didlum, Mrs. Starvem, Mr. Dauber, Mr. Botchit, Mr. Smeeriton, and Mr. Leavit.

And in the midst was the Rev. John Starr, doing the work for which he was paid.

As he stood there in the forefront of this company, there was nothing in his refined and comely exterior to indicate that his real function was to pander to and flatter them; to invest with an air of respectability and rectitude the abominably selfish lives of the gang of swindlers, slave-drivers and petty tyrants who formed the majority of the congregation of the Shining Light Chapel.

He was doing the work for which he was paid. By the mere fact of his presence there, condoning and justifying the crimes of these typical representatives of that despicable class whose greed and inhumanity have made the earth into a hell.

There was also a number of 'respectable', well-dressed people who looked as if they could do with a good meal, and a couple of shabbily dressed, poverty-stricken-looking individuals who seemed rather out of place in the glittering throng.

The remainder of the Brothers consisted of half-starved, pale-faced working men and women, most of them dressed in other people's cast-off clothing, and with broken, patched-up, leaky boots on their feet.

Rushton having concluded his address, Didlum stepped forward to give out the words of the hymn the former had quoted at the conclusion of his remarks:

> 'Oh, come and jine this 'oly band,
>   And hon to glory go.'

Strange and incredible as it may appear to the reader, although none of them ever did any of the things Jesus said, the people who were conducting this meeting had the effrontery to claim to be followers of Christ – Christians!

Jesus said: 'Lay not up for yourselves treasure upon earth', 'Love not the world nor the things of the world', 'Woe unto you that are rich – it is easier for a camel to go through the eye of a needle than for a rich man to enter the kingdom of heaven.'[132] Yet all these self-styled 'Followers' of Christ made the accumulation of money the principal business of their lives.

Jesus said: 'Be ye not called masters; for they bind heavy burdens and grievous to be borne, and lay them on men's shoulders, but they themselves will not touch them with one of their fingers. For one is your master, even Christ, and ye are all brethren.' But nearly all these alleged followers of the humble Workman of Nazareth claimed to be other people's masters or mistresses. And as for being all brethren, whilst most of these were arrayed in broadcloth and fine linen and fared sumptuously every day, they knew that all around them thousands of those they hypocritically called their 'brethren', men, women and little children, were slowly perishing of hunger and cold; and we have already seen how much brotherhood existed between Sweater and Rushton and the miserable, half-starved wretches in their employment.

Whenever they were asked why they did not practise the things Jesus preached, they replied that it is impossible to do so! They did not seem to realise that when they said this they were saying, in effect, that Jesus taught an impracticable religion; and they appeared to forget that Jesus said, 'Wherefore call ye me Lord, Lord, when ye do not the things I say? . . . ' 'Whosoever heareth these sayings of mine and doeth them not, shall be likened to a foolish man who built his house upon the sand.'[133]

But although none of these self-styled 'Followers' of Christ, ever did the things that Jesus said, they talked a great deal about them, and sang hymns, and for a pretence made long prayers, and came out here to exhort those who were still in darkness to forsake their evil ways. And they procured this lantern and wrote a text upon it: 'Be not deceived, God is not mocked.'

They stigmatised as 'infidels' all those who differed from them, forgetting that the only real infidels are those who are systematically false and unfaithful to the Master they pretend to love and serve.

Grinder, having a slight cold, had not spoken this evening, but several other infidels, including Sweater, Didlum, Bosher, and Starr, had addressed the meeting, making a special appeal to the working people, of whom the majority of the crowd was composed, to give up all the vain pleasures of the world in which they at present indulged, and, as Rushton had eloquently put it at the close of his remarks:

'Come and jine this 'Oly band and hon to glory go!'

As Didlum finished reading out the words, the lady at the harmonium struck up the tune of the hymn, and the disciples all joined in the singing:

'Oh, come and join this 'oly band and hon to glory go.'

During the singing certain of the disciples went about amongst the crowd distributing tracts. Presently one of them offered one to Barrington and as the latter looked at the man he saw that it was Slyme, who also recognised him at the same instant and greeted him by name. Barrington made no reply except to decline the tract:

'I don't want that – from you,' he said contemptuously.

Slyme turned red. 'Oh, I know what you're thinking of,' he said after a pause and speaking in an injured tone; 'but you shouldn't judge anyone too hard. It wasn't only my fault, and you don't know 'ow much I've suffered for it. If it 'adn't been for the Lord, I believe I should 'ave drownded myself.'

Barrington made no answer and Slyme slunk off, and when the hymn was finished Brother Sweater stood forth and gave all those present a hearty invitation to attend the services to be held during the ensuing week at the Chapel of the Shining Light. He invited them there specially, of course, because it was the place with which he was himself connected, but he entreated and begged of them even if they would not come there to go Somewhere; there were plenty of other places of worship in the town; in fact, there was one at the corner of nearly every street. Those who did not fancy the services at the Shining Light could go to the Church of the Whited Sepulchre, but he really did hope that all those dear people whom he saw standing round would go Somewhere.

A short prayer from Bosher closed the meeting, and now the reason for the presence of the two poverty stricken looking shabbily dressed disciples was made manifest, for while the better dressed and therefore more respectable Brothers were shaking hands with and grinning at each other or hovering round the two clergymen and Mr. Sweater, these two poor wretches carried away the harmonium and the lantern, together with the hymn books and what remained of the tracts.

As Barrington hurried off to catch the train one of the 'Followers' gave him a card which he read by the light of a street lamp –

COME AND JOIN THE BROTHERHOOD
at the Shining Light Chapel
P.S.A.
Every Sunday at 3 o'clock.
Let Brotherly Love Continue.
'Oh come and join this Holy Band
and on to Glory go.'

Barrington thought he would rather go to hell – if there were such a place – with some decent people, than share 'glory' with a crew like this.

*   *   *

Nora sat sewing by the fireside in the front room, with the baby asleep in her lap. Owen was reclining in the deck-chair opposite. They had both been rather silent and thoughtful since Barrington's departure. It was mainly by their efforts that the reconciliation between Easton and Ruth had been effected and they had been so desirous of accomplishing that result that they had not given much thought to their own position.

'I feel that I could not bear to part with her now,' said Nora at last breaking the long silence, 'and Frankie is so fond of her too. But all the same I can't feel happy about it when I think how ill you are.'

'Oh, I shall be all right when the weather gets a little warmer,' said Owen, affecting a cheerfulness he did not feel. 'We have always pulled through somehow or other; the poor little thing is not going to make much difference, and she'll be as well off with us as she would have been if Ruth had not gone back.'

As he spoke he leaned over and touched the hand of the sleeping child and the little fingers closed round one of his with a clutch that sent a thrill all through him. As he looked at this little helpless, dependent creature, he realised with a kind of thankfulness that he would never have the heart to carry out the dreadful project he had sometimes entertained in hours of despondency.

'We've always got through somehow or other,' he repeated, 'and we'll do so still.'

Presently they heard Frankie's footsteps ascending the stairs and a moment afterwards the boy entered the room.

'We have to look out of the window and wave to Mr. Barrington when his train goes over the bridge,' he cried breathlessly. 'And he's sent this letter. Open the window, quick, Dad, or it may be too late.'

'There's plenty of time yet,' replied Owen, smiling at the boy's impetuosity. 'Nearly twenty minutes. We don't want the window open all that time. It's only a quarter to eight by our clock now, and that's five minutes fast.'

However, so as to make quite certain that the train should not run past unnoticed, Frankie pulled up the blind and, rubbing the steam off the glass, took up his station at the window to watch for its coming, while Owen opened the letter:

'Dear Owen – Enclosed you will find two bank-notes, one for ten pounds and the other for five. The first I beg you will accept from me for yourself in the same spirit that I offer it, and as I would accept it from you if our positions were reversed. If I were in need, I know that you would willingly share with me whatever you had and I could not hurt you by refusing. The other note I want you to change tomorrow morning. Give three pounds of it to Mrs. Linden and the remainder to Bert White's mother.

"Wishing you all a happy Xmas and hoping to find you well and eager for the fray when I come back in the spring,

'Yours for the cause,

'George Barrington.'

Owen read it over two or three times before he could properly understand it and then, without a word of comment – for he could not have spoken at that moment to save his life – he passed it to Nora, who felt, as she read it in her turn, as if a great burden had been lifted from her heart. All the undefined terror of the future faded away as she thought of all this small piece of paper made possible.

Meanwhile, Frankie, at the window, was straining his eyes in the direction of the station.

'Don't you think we'd better have the window open now, Dad?' he said at last as the clock struck eight. 'The steam keeps coming on the glass as fast as I wipe it off and I can't see out properly. I'm sure it's nearly time now; p'raps our clock isn't as fast as you think it is.'

'All right, we'll have it open now, so as to be on the safe side,' said Owen as he stood up and raised the sash, and Nora, having wrapped the child up in a shawl, joined them at the window.

'It can't be much longer now, you know,' said Frankie. 'The line's clear. They turned the red light off the signal just before you opened the window.'

In a very few minutes they heard the whistle of the locomotive as it drew out of the station, then, an instant before the engine itself came into sight round the bend, the brightly polished rails were illuminated, shining like burnished gold in the glare of its headlight; a few seconds afterwards the train emerged into view, gathering speed as it came along the short stretch of straight way, and a moment later it thundered across the bridge. It was too far away to recognise his face, but they saw someone looking out of a carriage window waving a handkerchief, and they knew it was Barrington as they waved theirs in return. Soon there remained nothing visible of the train except the lights at the rear of the guard's van, and presently even these vanished into the surrounding darkness.

The lofty window at which they were standing overlooked several of the adjacent streets and a great part of the town. On the other side of the road were several empty houses, bristling with different house agents' advertisement boards and bills. About twenty yards away, the shop formerly tenanted by Mr. Smallman, the grocer, who had become bankrupt two or three months previously, was also plastered with similar decorations. A little further on, at the opposite corner, were the premises of the Monopole Provision Stores, where brilliant lights were just being extinguished, for they, like most of the other shops, were closing their premises for the night, and the streets took on a more cheerless air as one after another their lights disappeared.

It had been a fine day, and during the earlier part of the evening the moon, nearly at the full, had been shining in a clear and starry sky; but a strong north-east wind had sprung up within the last hour; the weather had become bitterly cold and the stars were rapidly being concealed from view by the dense banks of clouds that were slowly accumulating overhead.

As they remained at the window looking out over this scene for a few minutes after the train had passed out of sight, it seemed to Owen that the gathering darkness was as a curtain that concealed from view the Infamy existing beyond. In every country, myriads of armed men waiting for their masters to give them the signal to fall upon and rend each other like wild beasts. All around was a state of dreadful anarchy; abundant riches, luxury, vice, hypocrisy, poverty, starvation, and crime. Men literally fighting with each other for the privilege of working for their bread, and little children crying with hunger and cold and slowly perishing of want.

The gloomy shadows enshrouding the streets, concealing for the time their grey and mournful air of poverty and hidden suffering, and the black masses of cloud gathering so menacingly in the tempestuous sky, seemed typical of the Nemesis which was overtaking the Capitalist System. That atrocious system which, having attained to the fullest measure of detestable injustice and cruelty, was now fast crumbling into ruin, inevitably doomed to be overwhelmed because it was all so wicked and abominable, inevitably doomed to sink under the blight and curse of senseless and unprofitable selfishness out of existence for ever, its memory universally execrated and abhorred.

But from these ruins was surely growing the glorious fabric of the Co-operative Commonwealth. Mankind, awaking from the long night of bondage and mourning and arising from the dust wherein they had lain prone so long, were at last looking upward to the light that was riving asunder and dissolving the dark clouds which had so long concealed from them the face of heaven. The light that will shine upon the world wide Fatherland and illumine the gilded domes and glittering pinnacles of the beautiful cities of the future, where men shall dwell together in true brotherhood and goodwill and joy. The Golden Light that will be diffused throughout all the happy world from the rays of the risen sun of Socialism.

THE END

Mugsborough

Mugsborough was a town of about eighty thousand inhabitants, about two hundred miles from London. It was built in a verdant valley.

Looking west, north or east from the vicinity of the fountain on the Grand Parade in the centre of the town, one saw a succession of pine-clad hills. To the south, as far as the eye could see, stretched a vast, cultivated plain that extended to the south coast, one hundred miles away. The climate was supposed to be cool in summer and mild in winter.

The town proper nestled in the valley: to the west, the most beautiful and sheltered part was the suburb of Irene: here were the homes of the wealthy residents and prosperous tradespeople, and numerous boarding-houses for the accommodation of well-to-do visitors. East, the town extended up the slope to the top of the hill and down the other side to the suburb of Windley, where the majority of the working classes lived.

Years ago, when the facilities for foreign travel were fewer and more costly, Mugsborough was a favourite resort of the upper classes, but of late years most of these patriots have adopted the practice of going on the Continent to spend the money they obtain from the working people of England. However, Mugsborough still retained some semblance of prosperity. Summer or winter the place was usually fairly full of what were called good-class visitors, either holiday-makers or invalids. The Grand Parade was generally crowded with well-dressed people and carriages. The shops appeared to be well-patronised and at the time of our story an air of prosperity pervaded the town. But this fair outward appearance was deceitful. The town was really a vast whited sepulchre; for notwithstanding the natural advantages of the place the majority of the inhabitants existed in a state of perpetual poverty which in many cases bordered on destitution. One of the reasons for this was that a great part of the incomes of the tradespeople and boarding-house-keepers and about a third of the wages of the working classes were paid away as rent and rates.

For years the Corporation had been borrowing money for necessary public works and improvements, and as the indebtedness of the town increased the rates rose in proportion, because the only works and services undertaken by the Council were such as did not yield revenue. Every public service capable of returning direct profit was in the hands of private companies, and the shares of the private companies were in the hands of the members of the Corporation, and the members of the Corporation were in the hands of the four most able and intellectual of their number, Councillors Sweater, Rushton, Didlum and Grinder, each of whom was a director of one or more of the numerous companies which battened on the town.

The Tramway Company, the Water Works Company, the Public Baths Company, the Winter Gardens Company, the Grand Hotel Company and numerous others. There was, however, one Company in which Sweater, Rushton, Didlum and Grinder had no shares, and that was the Gas Company, the oldest and most flourishing of them all. This institution had grown with the place; most of the original promoters were dead, and the greater number of the present share-holders were non-residents; although they lived on the town, they did not live in it.

The profits made by this Company were so great that, being prevented by law from paying a larger dividend than ten per cent., they frequently found it a difficult matter to decide what to do with the money. They paid the Directors and principal officials – them-selves shareholders, of course – enormous salaries. They built and furnished costly and luxurious offices and gave the rest to the share-holders in the form of Bonuses.

There was one way in which the Company might have used some of the profits: it might have granted shorter hours and higher wages to the workmen whose health was destroyed and whose lives were shortened by the terrible labour of the retort-houses and the lime-sheds;[134] but of course none of the directors or shareholders ever thought of doing that. It was not the business of the Company to concern itself about *them*.

Years ago, when it might have been done for a comparatively small amount, some hare-brained Socialists suggested that the town should buy the Gas Works, but the project was wrecked by the inhabitants, upon whom the mere mention of the word Socialist had the same effect that the sight of a red rag is popularly supposed to have on a bull.

Of course, even now it was still possible to buy out the Company, but it was supposed that it would cost so much that it was generally considered to be impracticable.

Although they declined to buy the Gas Works, the people of Mugsborough had to buy the gas. The amount paid by the municipality to the Company for the public lighting of the town loomed large in the accounts of the Council. They managed to get some of their own back by imposing a duty of two shillings a ton upon coals imported into the Borough, but although it cost the Gas Works a lot of money for coal dues the Company in its turn got its own back by increasing the price of gas they sold to the inhabitants of the town . . .

NOTES

I am indebted to Professor Peter Miles's edition of *The Ragged Trousered Philanthropists* (2005, reissued 2008) in the Oxford World Classics series, for his expansive notes to the text.

1 (p. 36) *Tariff Reform Paradise*   Tariff Reform was a potent political issue of the day. The Tariff Reform League argued for the extension of tariff on imported goods as a counter measure to the policies of foreign governments, notably the United States and Germany, whose protectionist policies challenged Britain's global trade advantages accrued from the Industrial Revolution.

2 (p. 36) *bloater*   an ungutted smoked herring

3 (p. 38) *his complexion was ominously clear, and an unnatural colour flushed the thin cheeks*   a visible symptom of the onset of tuberculosis

4 (p. 40) *Sweater*   a common term for an employer who 'sweats' his workers and pays starvation wages

5 (p. 41) *fissical policy*   fiscal policy: the use of government spending and taxation to influence the economy, implicitly related here to the issue of tariff on imported goods

6 (p. 45) *the Ananias . . . the Daily Chloroform . . . the Hobscurer*   These symbolic names signify hypocrisy, anaesthesia and obfuscation; for the story of Ananias the hypocrite, see Acts 5:1–11.

7 (p. 45) *Board of Guardians*   The Poor Law Amendment Act of 1834 established locally elected Boards of Guardians to manage the implementation of poor relief.

8 (p. 46) *Free Trade for the last fifty years*   the practice of trading with other countries without the imposition of import or export duties, or other restrictive instruments

9 (p. 46) *Over-population*   In his *Essay on the Principle of Population* (1798), Thomas Malthus (1766–1834) argued that population grows faster than the food supply and that poverty was thus a condition with the force of a law of nature, anticipating Darwin's concept of the 'battle for life' in the natural world in his *On the Origin of Species* of 1859.

10 (p. 48) *most of us is walkin' about 'arf our time*   out of work and therefore walking around looking for employment

11 (p. 58) *strong soda water*   caustic soda or sodium hydroxide, a poisonous and corrosive alkali, hence Philpot's burnt and discoloured nails – *and the flesh round them cracked and bleeding*

12 (p. 60) *an enthusiastic jingo*   a patriot

13 (p. 70) *crewel*   thin worsted yarn used for tapestry and embroidery

14 (p. 70) *overcast*   in needlework, stitched over the edge to prevent unravelling

15 (p. 71) *oak paper*   wallpaper that has the appearance of oak grain

16 (p. 85) *graining*   a decorative effect in which the appearance of wood surfaces is replicated by a painter using tools known as graining-combs

17 (p. 91) *Satan often appears as an angel of light*   Before his fall from heaven, Satan's name was Lucifer, and he was said to be the brightest of the angels.

18 (p. 92) *The Lord is our shepherd. He careth for the widow and the father-less.*   See Psalm 23 and Malachi 3:5.

19 (p. 94) *Anathema Maran-atha.*   excommunicated. See 1 Corinthians 16:22: 'If any man love not the Lord Jesus Christ, let him be Anathema Maran-atha.'

20 (p. 96) *a tallyman's traveller*   A tallyman supplied goods on credit to be paid for in instalments, and the tallyman's traveller would collect payments due.

21 (p. 101) *save up a lot of money for themselves*   an allusion to Matthew 6:19

22 (p. 101) *Jesus also said that if anyone tried to do His disciples harm*   See the Sermon on the Mount, Matthew 5:38 and 39.

23 (p. 106) *the commissariat department*   food. In military terms, this was the department charged with providing food and other supplies for the army.

24 (p. 109) *close the register of the grate*   a metal plate for regulating the passage of air, heat or smoke in a chimney flue

25 (p. 109) *laudanum*   tincture of opium used as a painkiller

26 (p. 109) *vermillion . . . one of the most deadly poisons*   in decorating used as a bright red pigment

27 (p. 115) *white lead*   formerly used as an ingredient in paint, but now banned in most countries as a cause of lead poisoning

28 (p. 120) *to go in the union*   to enter the workhouse

29 (p. 125) *Moody and Sankey hymn*   Dwight Lyman Moody, an American evangelical preacher, and Ira D. Sankey, an American gospel-singer, collaborated on *Sacred Songs and Solos*, a book of Christian hymns which

became immensely popular in Britain, and is still commonly known as 'Moody and Sankey'.

30 (p. 127) *see-ise this 'ere tuneropperty* seize this opportunity

31 (p. 128) *stiver* a coin of low value

32 (p. 134) *to catch effets* a corruption of 'efts', meaning 'newts'

33 (p. 137) *taking off his blouse* a workman's protective upper body garment

34 (p. 138) *glazed with muranese obscured glass* from Murano, the Venetian island famous for its highly decorative glasswork

35 (p. 146) *Cholery morbus* cholera morbus, acute gastroenteritis

36 (p. 150) *a kind of jail* the workhouse

37 (p. 152) *Free Library* The Public Libraries Act was passed in 1850.

38 (p. 153) *a prize packet* a mixed bag of sweets

39 (p. 161) *my sins is all hunder the Blood* His sins are repented and therefore redeemed by Christ's sacrifice.

40 (p. 161) *As for the happiness that passes all understanding* See Philippians 4:7.

41 (p. 163) *the Great White Throne for judgement* the Day of Judgement. See Revelatiion 20:11–15.

42 (p. 163) *the moon turned inter Blood . . . wrath of the Lamb* See Revelation 6:12 and 15–16.

43 (p. 163) *I'm a Bush Baptist meself* a colonial term of uncertain meaning, defined in the Australian *Macquarie Dictionary* as meaning 'a person of doubtful religious persuasion'

44 (p. 166) *the Money System* In the context of Owen's argument here it means the capitalist economics of the day in which wealth accrues to a small portion of the population at the expense of the working classes.

45 (p. 170) *Ballcartridge Rent Day* an allusion to the history of the ways in which great wealth and landed estates were conferred on members of the nobility for military services to the country

46 (p. 174) *the Society* the National Amalgamated Society of Operative House and Ship Painters and Decorators, a trade union formed out of earlier societies and established under this name in 1904

47 (p. 181) *hiding his light under a bushel ... that house* 'Neither do men light a candle, and put it under a bushel, but on a candlestick; and it giveth light unto all that are in the house' – see Matthew 5:15.

48 (p. 181) *light-weights* those working for less than the normal rate of pay for the job

49 (p. 186) *Moses striking the Rock . . . the Golden Calf*   See Numbers 20:11 and Exodus 32.

50 (p. 190) *the widow's mite*   See Luke 21:1–4.

51 (p. 195) *the Labourer is worthy of his hire*   See Luke 10:7.

52 (p. 200) *A. Harpy*   In Greek mythology a harpy was a monster with a woman's face and a bird's wings and claws; the word has come to be used of a grasping, rapacious figure.

53 (p. 200) *jug and bottle department*   the off-licence section of a public house

54 (p. 200) *polyphone*   a precursor of the jukebox

55 (p. 201) *old French pennies*   coins in use on public shove-ha'penny boards to deter players pocketing legal-tender halfpenny coins

56 (p. 202) *porter*   a dark beer brewed from brown malt.

57 (p. 209) *brewer's dray*   a horse-drawn cart for heavy loads, especially as here for carrying beer-barrels

58 (p. 213) *Sheriff's sales*   auctions of goods seized from debtors by the sheriff and his bailiffs, on court instructions, in lieu of payment of debts

59 (p. 220) *The Reign of Terror*   the period of the French Revolution notorious for the execution of enemies of the state by the Committee of Public Safety.

60 (p. 231) *Slop*   slang for a policeman

61 (p. 233) *Featherstone and Belfast*   two notorious incidents involving the use of military force to put down striking workers. Industrial unrest in 1893 at Featherstone Colliery in Yorkshire led to the deaths of two men shot by troops sent to deal with the situation; a similar event took place in Belfast in 1907 when the Royal Irish Constabulary struck over pay, conditions and union rights; they were replaced by 7,000 troops from Dublin, and in August that year supporters of the Belfast police were confronted by troops and two people were shot dead.

62 (p. 239) *cross-cut*   in carpentry a term for a piece of wood cut against the grain: here with the implication of an ill-disposed young woman

63 (p. 241) *Resist not evil*   But I say unto you, That ye resist not evil – see Matthew 5:39.

64 (p. 241) *Lord, Lord*   Not everyone that saith unto me, Lord, Lord, shall enter into the kingdom of heaven, but that he doeth the will of my Father which is in heaven – see Matthew 7:21.

65 (p. 243) *the science of Phrenology*   the study of the shape of the human

head as an index to the inherent mental abilities of the individual studied – a pseudo-scientific theory of the late nineteenth century

66 (p. 243) *Monopole Stores* an invented name for a chain of privately owned shops as opposed to those run on the principles of co-operative stores.

67 (p. 250) *Be not deceived: God is not mocked* Galatians 6:7

68 (p. 251) *The wicked . . . shall be turned into hell* Psalms 9:17

69 (p. 253) *Where did Cain get 'is wife from?* a dispute with fundamentalist readings of the Christian creation narrative which implies that Cain's wife (who is not named) did not descend from Adam's seed, and that therefore not all human beings descend from the union of Adam and Eve

70 (p. 253) *'Im that bein' ofen reproved 'ardeneth 'is neck* See Proverbs 29:1.

71 (p. 270) *that corfin plate what Owen was writing* a reference to Owen's work as a sign-writer designing on paper the identifying nameplate for a coffin which would then be engraved in metal.

72 (p. 270) *a strange sort of death* death by spontaneous combustion. Tressell probably took this unscientific notion from Dickens's *Bleak House* (1853) in which the character called Krook is said to die this way.

73 (p. 271) *Jonydab Belcher* With due irony, Tressell takes Belcher's first name from Jehonadab, the son of Rechab, who founded an order against luxurious living, and made it a rule to abstain from wine and the cultivation of vineyards. Rechabites are total abstainers, unlike Belcher. See II Kings 10.

74 (p. 277) *the agent* estate agent

75 (p. 282) *them there Labour members of Parliament* Twenty-nine Labour MPs were returned at the 1906 election.

76 (p. 283) *Love their neighbours as themselves* See Matthew 22:39.

77 (p. 283) *Bearing one another's burdens* See Galatians 6:2.
Give to everyone who asks of me See Luke 6:30.
Give my cloak to the man See Matthew 5:40.

78 (p. 294) *block ornaments* meat on display on butchers' blocks or counters as advertisements, sold off cheaply at the end of the day

79 (p. 299) *It says in the Bible that the poor shall always be with us* See Mark 14:7.

80 (p. 307) *the Man of Sorrows* See Isaiah 53:3.
who had not where to lay His head See Luke 9:58.

81 (p. 311) *my Pandoramer* Bert's home-made panorama device for showing images

82 (p. 324) *small boys about twelve and thirteen years old bein' served out with their Labour Stifficats* The partial exemption system of 'half-time certificates' allowed schoolchildren at twelve years of age to go to work for part of the time.

83 (p. 326) *Band of Hope* a temperance organisation for children, founded in 1847

84 (p. 349) *the scullery copper* a vessel made of copper, particularly a large boiler for cooking or laundry purposes

85 (p. 350) *the story of Samson* See Judges 16: 4–21.

86 (p. 352) The first edition of this novel, published in 1914 by Grant Richards, ended with this chapter.

87 (p. 354) *the ticket system* paying benefits not in cash but in vouchers for specific goods and purposes defined by the giver

88 (p. 355) *a case of much cry and little wool* a proverbial expression for a lot of work for little profit

89 (p. 356) *Whited Sepulchre* Matthew 23:27: 'Woe unto you, scribes and Pharisees, hypocrites! for ye are like unto whited sepulchres, which indeed appear beautiful outward, but are within full of dead men's bones, and of all uncleanness.'

90 (p. 366–7) *And Jesus called a little child unto Him* See Matthew 18:2.
did it not to Me See Matthew 25: 41–5.
their hearts … their ears dull of hearing See Matthew 13:15.

91 (p. 368) *Distress Committee* An agency set up by the Local Government Board in Edwardian times by John Burns, President of the Board. Ensor takes the view that Burns was an able and compassionate man whose strategies for relief of the poor were persistently obstructed at regional and local levels by his civil servants – see Sir Robert Ensor, *England 1870–1914, The Oxford History of England*, Oxford University Press, 1936, pp. 516–17

92 (p. 375) *descended from monkeys* a reference to Darwin's *Origin of Species* and the vexed issue of an evolutionary link between apes and man

93 (p. 382) *the singing of the Doxology* the utterance of praise to God: in liturgical usage the Greater Doxology (the *Gloria in Excelsis*) and the Lesser Doxology (the *Gloria Patri*)

94 (p. 394) *distempers* oil-less paint for plaster

95 (p. 395) *the usual Beano* a beanfeast, a dinner for the workers paid for by the employer

96 (p. 396) *four brakes* horse-drawn wagons for carrying passengers

97 (p. 406) *Parrish's Food*   an iron tonic devised by the American doctor Edward Parrish.

98 (p. 409) *Morpheus*   the mythological god of sleep and dreams, from whom morphine, a narcotic painkiller made from opium, derives its name

99 (p. 413) *his back day*   a day's pay retained by the employer and only paid at the end of a period of employment. To ask for 'back day' was thus to resign.

100 (p. 416) *adventures of Claude Duval*   a French-born highwayman, executed at Tyburn in 1670

101 (p. 423) *As for me and my house, we will serve the Lord*   See Joshua 24:15.

102 (p. 439) *covered with water*   the way of storing white lead to limit the spread of toxic dust from it

103 (p. 444) *Nation's Drink Bill*   'Even in 1914, with the welfare state initiated and the demands of defence becoming daily more pressing, Britain was spending more on alcohol than on all the services of central government combined' – from 'The Economy' by Arthur J. Taylor, in *Edwardian England 1901–1914*, ed. Simon Nowell-Smith, p. 125.

104 (p. 447) *men and women on bicycles*   Robert Blatchford's 'Clarion Scouts' were founded in 1894 to foster recreation, fellowship and health, and to propagate Socialism.

105 (p. 448) *Look Out for the Socialist Van*   Horse-drawn caravans sent out to tour the towns and cities of England to spread the gospel of Socialism.

106 (p. 454) *which ascendeth up for ever and ever*   See Revelation 14:10–11.

107 (p. 458) *Everything was up to the knocker*   in the height of fashion

108 (p. 475) *Even as sheep before their shearers are dumb*   See Isaiah 53:7.

109 (p. 475) *for the sake of the loaves and fishes*   See the feeding of the five thousand in Mark 6:30–44.

110 (p. 475) *Self-help by Smiles*   Samuel Smiles's *Self Help* (1882) was a popular guide to self-improvement.

111 (p. 481) *all the Protectionist countries*   those countries such as France, the United States and Germany who turned from the principles of Free Trade and imposed protectionist measures on traded goods

112 (p. 481) *become 'rickety'*   develop rickets, a disease of children causing softening of the bones, a consequence of a deficiency of vitamin D

113 (p. 487) *pay to keep the Labour Members* MPs did not receive salaries until 1911 and the first Labour MPs were financially supported by trade unions.

114 (p. 490) *Co-operative Commonwealth* the title of a book of 1867 by the Danish socialist Laurence Gronlund, and a term that encapsulates the Socialist vision in the late nineteenth and early twentieth centuries

115 (p. 491) *the words of the historian Froude* James Anthony Froude (1818–94), author of the *History of England from the Fall of Wolsey to the Defeat of the Spanish Armada* (1856–70)

116 (p. 494) *or miserable Old Age Pensions* Payment of a means-tested old-age pension was introduced in Parliament by Lloyd George as Chancellor of the Exchequer in 1908, payable to those of seventy years of age or over with incomes of less than 12 shillings per week.

117 (p. 497) *the parable of the Sower* See Mark 4:3–20.

118 (p. 498) *Acts of Enclosure* the notorious legislation enacted between 1760 and 1820 by which common land was appropriated into private ownership. The effect on the rural peasantry was catastrophic, and led in due course to the system of day-labour and to industrial work in the cities.

119 (p. 513) *There's Edison for instance* Thomas Alva Edison (1847–1931), inventor of the light-bulb and the phonograph and many other electrical devices

120 (p. 516) *neither shall he eat* See II Thessalonians 3:10.

121 (p. 532) *a society* a Friendly Society or mutual insurance club

122 (p. 547) *thicker than Nimrod's thigh* See I Kings 12:10.

123 (p. 549) *the Buffalos and the Druids* The Royal Antediluvian Order of Buffaloes was a society established in the early nineteenth century to engage in charitable activities, and the Ancient Order of Druids was a Friendly Society established in 1781.

124 (p. 550) *honour in his own land* See *Matthew* 13:57.

125 (p. 553) *Seven Dials in London* a London area notorious for crime and violence

126 (p. 560) *Means of production* a key term in Marxist discourse

127 (p. 567) *chastised with scorpions* See II Chronicles 10:11.

128 (p. 584) *Society for the Prevention of Cruelty to Children* Founded in 1884, it eventually became the National Society for the Prevention of Cruelty to Children (NSPCC).

129 (p. 587) *It's a Far, Far, Better Thing That I do, Than I have ever Done*
       taken from the closing pages of Dickens's *A Tale of Two Cities* (1859)

130 (p. 592) *the appearance of scurvy*   a skin disease indicative of a general
       debility of the body, with tender gums, foul breath, subcutaneous
       eruptions on the skin and painful limbs. In this instance, the spot
       would now probably suggest a cancerous growth.

131 (p. 593) *like Joseph of old ... over his younger brethren*   a reference to the
       Genesis story of the boy Joseph, the favourite son of Jacob, who was
       sold into slavery in Egypt by his jealous brothers whom he later
       forgives

132 (p. 601) *Love not the world nor the things of the world*   See I John 2:15.
       Woe unto you that are rich . . . the kingdom of heaven   See Luke 6:24
       and 18:25.
       Be ye not called masters . . . ye are all brethren   See Matthew 23:4–10.

133 (p. 602) *Whosoever heareth these sayings ... upon the sand*   See Matthew
       7:26.

134 (p. 608) *retort-houses and the lime-sheds*   In gasworks, coal was heated
       in large vessels called 'retorts' to release coal-gas; in lime sheds, lime
       was mixed with iron oxide in a purifying process.